"Fiona Mountain is a major new talent in the field of historical fiction. This is history told with integrity, with an authentic feel for the period and vividly rounded characters, all the colors and textures of the seventeenth century are eloquently and evocatively realized here, in wonderful detail, and against this backdrop is set a haunting and tragic narrative."

—Alison Weir, author of *Captive Queen: A Novel of Eleanor of Aquitaine*

"It is a rare talent in an author to be able to mix rigorous historical research with the narrative energies and imagination of a true novelist. Fiona Mountain brings all of these skills to her entrancing *Lady of the Butterflies*. A vivid and fascinating novel about an extraordinary woman, I was gripped from beginning to end."

—Katie Hickman, author of *The Pindar Diamond*

"A fascinating story . . . Richly and brilliantly detailed and full of love and heartbreak." —Elizabeth Buchan, author of *Wives Behaving Badly*

"A lady lepidopterist may seem an unlikely real-life subject for historical romance, but Mountain makes it work in this first-person account of the life of Eleanor Glanville . . . A lush and confidently plotted historical."

—*Publishers Weekly*

"Mountain dives into her esoteric subject matter headfirst, telling Eleanor's moving story against a backdrop of rebellion and religious division and the scientific thinking of the time . . . Partly based on actual events, partly reliant on Mountain's rich imaginings, *Lady of the Butterflies* is a big, chunky, absorbing novel, passionately rendered. In a word: Sweeping." —*Townsville Bulletin* (Australia)

Lady
OF THE
Butterflies

FIONA MOUNTAIN

BERKLEY BOOKS

New York

THE BERKLEY PUBLISHING GROUP
Published by the Penguin Group
Penguin Group (USA) Inc.
375 Hudson Street, New York, New York 10014, USA
Penguin Group (Canada), 90 Eglinton Avenue East, Suite 700, Toronto, Ontario M4P 2Y3, Canada
(a division of Pearson Penguin Canada Inc.)
Penguin Books Ltd., 80 Strand, London WC2R 0RL, England
Penguin Group Ireland, 25 St. Stephen's Green, Dublin 2, Ireland (a division of Penguin Books Ltd.)
Penguin Group (Australia), 250 Camberwell Road, Camberwell, Victoria 3124, Australia
(a division of Pearson Australia Group Pty. Ltd.)
Penguin Books India Pvt. Ltd., 11 Community Centre, Panchsheel Park, New Delhi—110 017, India
Penguin Group (NZ), 67 Apollo Drive, Rosedale, Auckland 0632, New Zealand
(a division of Pearson New Zealand Ltd.)
Penguin Books (South Africa) (Pty.) Ltd., 24 Sturdee Avenue, Rosebank, Johannesburg 2196,
South Africa

Penguin Books Ltd., Registered Offices: 80 Strand, London WC2R 0RL, England

Copyright © 2009 by Fiona Mountain.
Published by arrangement with Preface Publishing, a division of The Random House Group Limited.
Cover illustration "Butterfly Cage" © by Susan Fox/Trevillion.
Cover illustration "Blonde Female" © by Tomasz Jankowski/Trevillion.
Cover design by Rita Frangie.

PRINTING HISTORY
Preface Publishing hardcover edition / July 2009
G. P. Putnam's Sons hardcover edition / July 2010
Berkley trade paperback edition / July 2011

Berkley trade paperback ISBN: 978-0-425-24117-2

The Library of Congress has catalogued the G. P. Putnam's Sons hardcover edition as follows:

Mountain, Fiona.
    Lady of the butterflies / Fiona Mountain.—1st American ed.
        p. cm.
    ISBN 978-0-399-15636-6
    1. Glanville, Eleanor, 1654–1709—Fiction. 2. Women entomologists—Great Britain—Fiction.
I. Title.
    PR6113.O935L33 2010   2010002283
    823'.92—dc22

PRINTED IN THE UNITED STATES OF AMERICA

10 9 8 7 6 5 4 3 2 1

For Tim, Daniel, James, Gabriel and Kezia

Also in memory of my mother,
Muriel Swinburn

You ask what is the use of butterflies? I reply to adorn the world and delight the eyes of men; to brighten the countryside like so many golden jewels. To contemplate their exquisite beauty and variety is to experience the truest pleasure. To gaze enquiringly at such elegance of color and form devised by the ingenuity of nature and painted by her artist's pencil, is to acknowledge and adore the imprint of the art of God.

John Ray, *History of Insects* (1704)

If a man will begin with certainties, he shall end in doubts; but if he will be content to begin with doubts, he shall end in certainties.

Sir Francis Bacon, author, courtier and philosopher (1561–1626)

Lady

OF THE

Butterflies

November

1695

They say I am mad and perhaps it's true.

Look. Can't you see? There are butterflies, bright orange butterflies, even though it's night, even though it's November. The black sky is filled with them. They are reflected in the dark floodwaters that lie over the wetlands. But no, I realize in an instant that I am mistaken, of course. It is nothing but the glowing ashes of the Gunpowder Treason Night bonfire, flitting upward in the smoke and the mist.

I hug my arms around myself inside my cloak. I try not to scream.

At the very time when I need all my wits about me, it is frightening to think I can't even depend upon myself, that my own mind, my own eyes, might betray me, even for a moment. This turbulent century that is nearly at an end has seen brother turn against brother and fathers take up arms against their own sons, but for my little family the treachery goes on.

I walk toward the end of the cobbled causeway that stretches straight and unhindered across the floodwater, all the way to Nailsea. The ground is sodden. The mud sucks at me and the sodden hem of my gown grabs and slaps at my ankles. My feet are so cold and wet I can hardly feel them. But there are far worse troubles than cold toes.

At first no one dares to meet my eyes. They regard me with superstitious fear, as if I were a will-o'-the-wisp. Tenant farmers, eelers, fishermen, wildfowlers and sedge-cutters, they are all gathered here with their kin at the edge of the flooded fields, their faces ghoulish in the flickering flames. No one misses this annual festival of hatred, but in Tickenham this year, it feels as if much of the hatred is turned upon me. My heart is beating too fast and my legs feel weak as reeds. But I keep my head held high. I keep on walking. Though I may only be slight, I am much stronger than people always assume. None shall see that I am afraid.

Fingers reach out to clutch at my cloak; others claw at my arm, at a windblown wisp of my hair. Alice Walker, once my little cookmaid, is the first to throw a rotten apple. It hits my shoulder and splatters. Surprisingly hard they are, apples, when turned into missiles. There is a dull pain and the sudden cloying smell of decay. Someone else spits and the disgusting gob lands on my cheek. I wipe it away with the palm of my hand and pretend not to care. These people were once my neighbors, servants and friends, my family, but now, instead of warm greetings, I hear only their insults, their whispered accusations:

"Papist!"

"Whore!"

"Witch!"

"Lunatic!"

I am none of those things, am I? How could a passion for small, bright-winged creatures have led to this? Just as it led me to James Petiver, the dearest friend any person could hope to have.

But it was another man who set passion burning within me more fiercely than all the fires that flame across England this night, who consumed me until I am nothing but a husk blowing on the wind. It is Richard Glanville, beautiful as a girl with his black curls and blue eyes, who brought me light in the darkness and warmth in the cold in a way that no winter bonfire ever can. In my memory his caress is like the brush of a butterfly's wing upon my skin, upon my breasts and the secret places beneath my shift, but all memories have turned to dust in the glare of what I have discovered.

What have you done, Richard? What have you done? Is it the flames of Hellfire that you conjured? My own Judas, did you betray me with a kiss?

Why?

I began keeping a journal to record my work. Though I don't presume it amounts to much, is of any great significance to the world of natural philosophy, James told me it was the best way to record my observations and to learn. I'm glad now that I've done it, for reasons I'd never have considered.

The time is coming when my voice may be silenced for good. God in Heaven, how has it come to this? It is well known that lust brings madness and desperation and ruin. But upon my oath, I never meant any harm.

All I ever wanted was to be happy, to love and to be loved in return, and for my life to count for something.

That is not madness, is it?

Part One

Winter

1662

 was woken in darkness by the joyful pealing of church bells. The church stood not a hundred yards from my chamber window, just across the Barton wall, so the room was filled with the merry and insistent clamor. My head was filled with it, and my heart. It was the loveliest sound. I stuck out my hand to part the heavy crewel drapes that were drawn around the great bed-frame to keep out the icy winter drafts, but it was bright silvery moonlight that shone through the chink in the curtains at the window. Why ever were the bells ringing with such jubilation in the middle of the night? Then I remembered. It was Christmas morning. The bells were calling everyone to the predawn Christmas service, everyone except my father and me. Christmas was to be celebrated across the whole of England again this year, in practically every household, except for a few of the staunchest Puritan ones, such as ours, where it was still forbidden, as it had been under Oliver Cromwell.

I dropped back against the pillows, fighting tears. I was nine years old, not a baby anymore. I was too old to cry just because I could not have what I wanted. I knew that in any case crying was a waste of time, would make no difference at all. With a little sigh I pulled the blankets up to my chin, wriggled down beneath them seeking non-existent warmth, and stared up at the dark outline of the bed canopy. I should be counting my blessings rather than feeling sorry for myself. I was very privileged, after all. I lived in the manor house of Tickenham Court, with its medieval solar wing and dairy, its ancient cider orchards and teeming fishponds. My father owned all the land for miles around, over a thousand acres of furze and heath and fen meadow, or moors as they were called in Tickenham. I was far more fortunate than the village children, wasn't I? The children who at this very moment were clutching excitedly at their mothers' hands as they left their holly-bedecked cottages to make their way in their little boats over the flooded fields to church, with the prospect of a day of feasting on plum pottage and mince pies and music and games before them.

I laid my hand on my flat belly as it rumbled its own protest. In rejection of what my father saw as the evil gluttony of Christmas, I was to be made to fast all day. All day, and already I was hungry. If I were really lucky, there'd be a dish of eel stew tomorrow, bland and unspiced, according to Puritan preferences.

The bells chimed on, ringing out their tumult in the darkness, the high tinkling of the treble bell and the low boom of the tenor, and round again in a circle. It was as if they were summoning me, had an urgent message to impart. Oh, I did so want to go. We had a merry king on the throne of England now, a king who had thrown open the doors of the theaters again and restored the maypoles, much to my father's disgust. But I did so want to know what it was to be merry, to dance and sing and laugh and wear bright, pretty gowns and ribbons. Even just to see the candlelit church would be something. What harm could it do just to look? If God had gifted me with my irrepressible curiosity, surely he would forgive me for giving in to it now. Wouldn't he?

I pushed back the blankets, exhaling mist, bracing myself for the rush of icy air through my linen shift. But it was not the cold that made my fingers shake as I crouched by the stone fireplace to light a candle from the dying embers. I was afraid of going out in the dark on my own, wary too of the reception I would receive from the villagers. The serving girl had warned me that, since we shunned all their celebrations, my appearance at one might well be regarded with animosity, mistrust. But inquisitiveness eclipsed all else, as it always did for me. I was too impatient to put on my woolen dress, and I left my hair in its long, thick golden night-plait. In bare feet I crept down the narrow spiral stone stairs that led from the solar to the great hall. I put on my mud-stained shoes and my hooded riding cloak. It was made of the thick red West Country cloth that was so traditional in Somersetshire that even my father did not balk at its bright color.

My heart hammering fit to burst with a mixture of excitement and terror, I slipped out of the door and through the gate in the Barton wall that led into the misty moonlit churchyard, stole silent as a ghost through the silvery lichen-encrusted tombstones, past the graves of my little sister and my mother, both dead over a year now. I breathed deep of the cool air and listened to the honking and trilling of the swans and marsh birds feeding out on the floodplains, the beating of hundreds upon hundreds of wings. An owl hooted and the air was redolent with the familiar tang of marsh and peat and mist. Out on the vast, dark water there was a straggling line of bobbing lanterns from the rowing boats carrying the worshippers to the service. They seemed to me like small stars traveling through the night to join with the great illumination that emanated from the wide-open door of the church of St. Quiricus and St. Juliet, a holy golden light that blazed a welcome.

I peered tentatively round the great oak doorway, not quite daring to let my feet cross the threshold, and I gasped wide-eyed at the beauty and color of it. There must have been a hundred candles or more, all around the altar and the pulpit and lining the nave and pews. There were garlands of rosemary and holly and fresh-scented rushes strewn on the floor and wicker baskets of marchpane sweets and sugarplums set out for the children. The fiddlers and drummers were waiting to begin the music and the players were already assembled at the front of the church, the kings with beautiful velvet cloaks trimmed with real ermine, the shepherds accompanied by real sheep. Two cows had been brought in too, and a placid-looking donkey.

I felt a light tap on my shoulder and nearly jumped out of my skin. It was Thomas Knight, the dark-haired, dark-eyed son of a sedge-cutter. He was over a foot taller than I and three years older, twelve years to my nine, and for some reason I'd not been able to fathom, he hated me. I wanted Thomas to like me, as all children want people to like them, I think, and I had made a consistent effort to be friendly and polite to him, even when sometimes what I really wanted to do was stick out my tongue at him. But it seemed to make no difference what I did. Except that now, there was the definite curve of a smile softening his long, swarthy face. I returned it gladly, but warily. "Hello, Thomas," I said.

"Merry Christmas, Miss Eleanor," he said, with what I took, delightedly, to be complicity, acceptance.

"Merry Christmas to you too," I replied. The forbidden greeting felt peculiar on my lips, beneficent as a charm, not like a sin at all.

"D'you think it so very evil then?" He nodded toward the gilded interior of the church.

"Oh, Thomas. I've never seen anything so lovely."

"Here. I've got something for you." People were walking toward the porch now and Thomas grabbed hold of my arm and pulled me round the side into the dark. I was not frightened, only surprised and very interested to see what it was that he had. He uncurled the palm of his big hand to reveal a little marchpane sweet, delicate as a rosebud, incongruous against his chapped and cold-reddened skin. My mouth watered, but even if it hadn't looked so delicious and appealing, I'd have wanted to take it, just because Thomas had been so kind and generous as to think to offer it to me. I hated to think how I might hurt his feelings if I rejected his gift.

He thrust the sweet impatiently toward my face. "Well, go on, then," he said gruffly. "What are you waiting for?"

Still I hesitated, then gave a small shake of my head. "I thank you, Thomas. But I had better not."

His expression suddenly changed. His deep-set dark eyes narrowed and there was a glint of challenge, of a slow-burning resentment. "Not good enough for you, taking food from the hand of a sedge-cutter's son, is that it?"

I was mortified. "Oh, Thomas, please don't think that. Please don't be offended. I am grateful, really I am." With a child's fear of being seen to be different, I was almost ashamed to admit the real reason, yet it was preferable to having him think me haughty. "It's just that I'm not supposed to eat anything at all today."

"Who's going to know?" He said it in such a conniving, nasty way that all of a sudden I was no longer so concerned about upsetting him. I didn't like the feeling that I was being forced to do something against my will. I didn't want the sweet at all now anyway. "Leave me be, Thomas," I said quietly.

Susan Hort, one of the tenants' daughters, stepped out from behind a gravestone where she'd obviously been hiding and watching.

"Told you," she scoffed. "Told you you'd not get her to touch it. She's stubborn as a little ox, that one."

Thomas shoved the sweet right up under my nose. "Just one bite," he said. "You know you want to." He glowered at me threateningly so that I felt a twinge of panic, but I would not give him the satisfaction of seeing it. "Let me alone, Thomas," I said with as much confidence as I could summon. "I said I don't want it."

I took a step back, but out of the corner of my eye I saw Susan Hort move behind me as if to trap me. Thomas thrust out his arm and forced the sweet against my mouth as though he were going to ram it through my closed lips. With a rush of rage and humiliation I batted his hand away so that the sweet went flying. Almost before I knew what was happening, Susan had grabbed my plaited hair and jerked me back, had me by the waist, trapping my arms at my sides. She was a sturdy country girl and easily tall enough to lift my feet off the ground. I twisted and squirmed, but she held me all the tighter, so I struck back with my boots at her shins.

"You vicious little rat!" She threw me to the ground, where I fell, sprawled on the soggy grass. I saw the marchpane lying by a clump of sedges right beside my hand. Thomas saw it too and snatched it, and before I could get up he had sat himself down on top of my chest, turning me over and pinning me flat on my back on the damp, chill earth, the crushing weight of him making it hard for me to breathe. He gripped my jaw tightly between his roughened forefinger and thumb and squeezed.

"Get up. Right now. Leave that child alone." It was Mary Burges, the new rector's wife, and at the sound of her firm command Thomas reluctantly released me and scrambled to his feet as Susan fell back.

Mary was not much past twenty, but she had had five younger brothers and sisters, so she knew very well how to manage scrapping. She was bustling and plump and maternal, with a soft, round face and eyes as sweet as honey. I was always glad to see her, though never so much as now.

She offered her hand to help me up. "Are you hurt, Eleanor?" she asked, concerned, bending to draw my cloak around me.

I shook my head, blushing. Bar a few scratches, it was only my pride that was wounded. I stood up straight and tried to be dignified, though there was mud on my shift and I could feel a wet smear of it on my cheek. Tendrils of my hair had sprung free and were falling down around my face. I smoothed them away, rubbed at my dirty cheek. I felt very foolish and embarrassed to be the cause of such a scuffle and over something as trifling as a sweetmeat.

"What do you think you were doing, the pair of you?" Mary said sternly to Thomas and Susan. "And on our Lord's birthday, a time of goodwill and peace."

Thomas turned his sullen eyes on her and did not answer.

I licked at my lips and tasted the faintest trace of almond sweetness. "It was nothing, Mistress Burges," I said, wanting it over and done with now. "Just a silly game."

Mary glanced at me appreciatively. "It seems little Eleanor here has enough goodwill for all three of you." She fixed Thomas with a reproachful look, as if she knew him to be the main culprit. "It didn't look like a game to me, but if you both apologize and run and take your seat in the pews, we'll say no more of it."

Thomas glowered menacingly at me while he and Susan mumbled an apology of sorts and slunk away. I watched them scurry together into the bright church, where the fiddlers and drummers were starting to play. Only now did I realize that I was trembling.

"We'd better get you back to the house," Mary said kindly. "Before your father finds you're missing. Look at you, child. You're not even properly dressed."

Someone came to close the church door and the emission of lovely, gilded light was abruptly shut off, leaving only the darkness and the cold moonlight. "Why does Thomas hate me?" I asked. "Is it just because we are Puritans?"

"That is no doubt part of it." Mary put her hands on my small shoulders and looked down into my face. "But I expect it is not only that."

"What then?"

She smiled. "Well, it does not help that you are such an unusual child. When people see you down on the moor climbing trees for birds' eggs, pond dipping and hunting under rocks for beetles and whatnot, they do not understand why a little girl should take such an interest in such things—a little girl who will one day be their lady of the manor at that. Most people are very fond of you, for all your strange ways, on account of your sweet nature and kind heart. But that does not mean that gossip does not get passed around and exaggerated. One of the first things the kitchen boy told me when we first came here was that you have a collection of animal skulls and bones in a little casket in your chamber."

"Oh, but I do," I said honestly, my disappointment suddenly forgotten in a rush of enthusiasm. "It is amazing what you find in owl pellets. I think the bones must belong to water voles or mice, since they are the right size and owls hunt them. I have a dead grass snake and damselfly too, and all kinds of shells and feathers and fossils."

"I am sure they would look very well in a curio cabinet," Mary said. "But in a little girl's bedchamber?"

"If I was a boy nobody would think it so strange, would they?"

She did not deny that. "The trouble is that people fear what they do not understand, and all too often that kind of fear makes them hostile."

My eyes widened. "Thomas Knight and Susan are afraid of me?"

"A little, perhaps."

It seemed extraordinary, unlikely, but not altogether unpleasing. I had never considered that I could be capable of frightening anyone. Then I remembered the flinty resentment in Thomas's eyes and I shuddered. "No," I said. "There is more to it than that, some other reason he does not like me. I'm sure of it."

"Well, it's not a problem you'll have with many lads in a few years' time," Mary said, smiling down at me. "No boy with eyes in his head will be able to do anything but fall in love with you, since you are so uncommonly pretty." She stroked my cheek with the back of her finger. "Even with dirt on your face."

"Thank you," I said politely as we started walking together, but I was sure she was only trying to cheer me. My father's wish to protect me from the depravity of the world had not stopped me glimpsing the tall and curvaceous Digby girls from Clevedon Court and the Smythe sisters from Ashton Court. I saw them riding out to suppers at their fathers' mansions and to Bristol, in their ringlets and ribbons and gowns of satin and brocade. Though I did not possess a single looking glass, I'd seen my reflection in the water and in windowpanes plenty of times. I knew that my hair was thick and fair and my eyes were large and wide-set and blue as cornflowers, but my skin was not marble white like those other girls', it was honey-colored from being so much outside, and rather than a long, straight nose to look down, mine was small and turned up very slightly at the end, like an infant's nose. And there was something else. "I am so small," I said to Mary despondently.

"You are indeed," she agreed. "You are as delicately delightful as a pixie."

I pulled a face, not at all sure of the appeal of that.

Mary laughed. "You are a dear child and I am glad you are so humble." She fell silent, then went on in a less happy tone. "Your father strives after humility above all else, and so far it has served him well. He commands respect and affection, despite being such a zealot. But I do fear for him, for you, if ever he gives in to the pressure he is under to drain these wetlands. If the people are hostile to you now, a move like that will stir up no end of trouble."

"Oh, he'll not do it," I said confidently. "Tickenham Court was my mother's. He'd want it to stay just the way she left it."

"I'd not be so sure about that."

ONE THING I was entirely sure of was that I would not escape the severest punishment if my father found out where I'd been. I had intended to be back long before he woke for morning prayers and so drew back into Mary's shadow when I saw him waiting for me in the gloom by the cavernous stone fireplace in the great hall, beneath the impressive display of armory. I trembled a little as he came to loom over me in the flickering torchlight, taking in my muddy cloak and state of undress in one scornful glance. His frugal suppers of a single egg and draft of small beer had always kept him lean, but now grief for my mother and my sister, coupled with long bouts of penitence and fasting for the punishment of their deaths, had made him gaunt. His craggy face, with its long, aquiline nose and strong jaw, had lost nothing of its power and authority, though. In his black coat with starched square white collar worn over it, he was as imposing as ever. He was every inch Major William Goodricke of the Parliamentarian army, Cromwell's formidable warrior.

But he was all I had in the world now and I loved him above anything. I was truly sorry for displeasing him, knew that what I had done was wrong. It was just that it had not felt so wrong, and in my heart I could not regret it. Life could be so confusing sometimes.

"You should be ashamed of yourself, Eleanor," he said.

I hung my head only half in repentance, but also so that he would not see the lack of contrition in my eyes.

Mary Burges tightened her arm protectively around my shoulders and drew me into her skirts. "On the contrary, you should be very proud of your little daughter, sir. She showed great courage and strength of will this day."

I stole a glance at my father and relaxed a bit as I caught his look of faint relief and pleasure.

"I am glad to hear it," he said, as if he would have expected no less from me.

"Some of the village children had dared each other to make her eat marchpane," Mary explained. "But Eleanor refused to so much as touch it, even when they had her pinioned on the ground. There's not many a child would not give in to such taunting and temptation."

My father harrumphed as he addressed me. "Who was it?"

"Thomas and Susan, Papa. But they said they were sorry," I added quickly. "They didn't mean anything by it."

I desperately didn't want my father to cause more trouble with their families. Puritans could be as harsh and unforgiving as their God sometimes, and after what I had seen, and what Mary had told me, I wasn't at all sure we could afford to be.

The Somersetshire nobility, along with most of the people hereabouts, had been Royalist during the civil war and now Anglicanism was increasingly the religion of the gentry, so for one reason or another our own class had largely disowned us. And every member of our household, every one of our neighbors and servants who were made to attend the secret Puritan prayer meetings in our great hall, saw their lord's empty pew during church services, knew that my father's deliberate absence from church branded him a recusant, still a capital crime. It would take only one person to denounce

him to the court or the bishop to render him liable for fines and penalties, to send him to gaol, or worse. So far his fairness and the
esteem in which he was held locally had secured his safety, my safety,
and enabled him to continue to stay true to his conscience and practice his beliefs in private. I did not want him to demand Thomas
Knight be punished. We had already set ourselves far enough apart
from the rest of this little community. There seemed nothing to
be gained from drawing more attention to the fact that we were
different.

My father reached out and took me by the arm. "I thank you for
bringing her back," he said brusquely, dismissively.

Mary gave me an encouraging smile as she turned to leave.

"I only went to watch, Papa," I said when we were alone. "I just
wanted to see what it was like."

"And did you like what you saw?"

I hesitated, not wanting to appear defiant but feeling too passionate to lie, even if it might spare me much trouble. "I liked it
very much," I said. "Oh, Papa, it was so lovely, and so holy. Not sinful at all. If you would only go and see for yourself then I know
you'd . . ."

"I am going nowhere, child," he said stonily. "And neither are you
for a good while. It is not those village children who need to be
taught a lesson, I think, but you."

He took me by the arm and led me back up the narrow stone stairs
to my chamber. Fear tightened my throat when he put his hand in
his pocket and produced a large key. I'd have preferred to have my
hands or backside whipped, really I would. Anything was better than
being locked up. I hated being inside for any length of time. I needed
open air and space and the sky above me and freedom to roam. Even
in the winter, when I had to go everywhere by boat and there were

weeks and weeks of rain and mist and ice, I loved to be outside, lived to be outside. I had a strange terror of doors and walls and of locks and keys. Of being confined.

"You'll stay in this room until this day is done," my father said. "And if you have any sense you will spend much of that time on your knees praying for forgiveness for your disobedience." He turned to go, his hand on the door latch.

"Why is it so wrong to celebrate the birth of Jesus?" I asked quickly.

My father turned back to me, as I had known he would. "You should not need me to tell you, child," he said, exasperated but patient, always ready to answer my questions and explain. "The Bible does not tell us to observe Christ's birthday. Christmas is just an excuse for debauchery, a commemoration of the Catholic idol of the mass." He took a deep breath and I saw the dangerous glint of fanaticism in his eyes. "We must be on ever more constant guard now that the King has placed a Catholic queen on the throne of England. The danger from Rome is present now more than ever. The hand of the Jesuit is still too much amongst us."

The questions were pushing against my lips and I had no choice but to ask them. "Most Puritan ministers call themselves Protestants now," I persisted, my mouth drying at my own audacity. "Why can't we be Protestants? Why must we always be different, always excluded?" I gulped a breath. "What's the harm in lighting up midwinter with a church full of candles?"

I braced myself for my father's rage, but instead he regarded me with deep sorrow, as if I was the greatest disappointment to him. More than that even, as if he feared that all the time he had spent answering my questions and explaining his doctrines had been wasted. He looked at me as if he feared for my immortal soul. I was appalled to see there were tears in his eyes. I had never seen my father cry, not even when my mother and my sister died.

I ran to him and threw my arms around his legs. "Oh, Papa, I'm sorry. Please don't be upset. I'll try to be good from now on, I promise."

He uncoiled my arms and held me gently away from him. "Little one," he said with great weariness. "Will you never learn? The only light we need is the light of the Lord."

With that he turned away, picked up the candle and left me, closing the low, studded door behind him. I heard the key turn with a grating click in the rusty lock. My chest tightened. I felt as if I couldn't breathe, as if all the air were being pressed out of my lungs, and I was sure that I was going to faint. I forced myself to resist the urge to rush at the door and hammer on it until my fists were bruised and bleeding. I knew it would do no good, only make matters worse. I was expected to accept my punishment meekly and with penitence, no matter how frightening it was, no matter how unjust I believed it to be. What was the use in trying to be virtuous? I might as well have eaten that marchpane, since I was being punished anyway.

I went to sit quietly on the edge of the high bed, picked up my poppet doll and hugged it. I took deep breaths, tried to think calm thoughts, to imagine myself somewhere else. It was a trick I had practiced ever since my mother's death, to take myself back in time to another place, a happier, better place. If I concentrated hard I could see her kind and radiant smile quite clearly, as if she were still with me. Almost.

Dawn had only just broken but it would be a short day, would be pitch-dark again in just a few hours, and I had no candle. I had always been petrified of the dark, no matter how much I tried to rationalize the terror away. Eleanor Goodricke, I told myself very sternly now, how can you ever hope to be a natural philosopher if you are prey to such superstitious fears? But I did not dare turn my head toward the far corners of the chamber where strange-shaped shadows already lurked. If only I had a candle. But I knew there was no use calling for that either.

The only light we need is the light of the Lord.

I bit my lips against blasphemy but still my heart cried out: It is not enough for me.

January

1664

Thomas Knight's sister, Bess, was my new maid, and despite her brother's dislike of me, Bess and I had become fast friends.

"Hold still now," she commanded, giving me an apple-cheeked smile that revealed the wide gap between her two top front teeth. "Or the gentleman visitors will take you for a little vagabond."

I was so excited by the prospect of visitors that I didn't mind having to stand still for an age while Bess brushed and brushed at the hem of my plain dark dress to rid it of the worst of the ever-present rim of mud stains. Made of wool, it could never be washed or it would shrink. I didn't mind either that Bess combed and combed at my long fair hair until it crackled with life and sparkled like spun gold, only for the great mass of it to be pinned and braided and tightly fastened away beneath a lace cap that was starched as crisp and white as my square collar.

I went to kneel upon the seat in the oriel window, my nose practically pressed against the uneven panes of leaded glass, keeping a lookout over the ghostly waterland patterned with droves and causeways that rose above the submerged world. I was determined to be the first to see our guests, though the drifting mist had rendered even the nearby stables indistinct. It had been raining all night, was raining still, and the floodwaters were lapping at the Barton wall now. We were half marooned, accessible from the south only by the main causeway or by boat.

As my father chose to shield me from the world and all that was worldly, he allowed me to mix with only the most restricted society. I seldom saw a new face, seldom saw anyone but the servants who made up our wider family. I had hardly ever traveled beyond the confines of the estate, beyond the isolated village of Tickenham, had never even been to Bristol.

I didn't mind much, because I didn't know any different, but also because I loved Tickenham, so that I could not in all honesty imagine myself away from it. Tickenham was a part of me, was who I was. I was Eleanor Goodricke of Tickenham Court. Since the day I was born I had imbibed the water from the springs and the cider from the apples in the orchard along with my mother's milk. What little flesh there was on my small limbs was nourished by the fish from the rivers and the wildfowl from the wetlands. And Tickenham's moods, its spirit, reflected my own. The isolation and secrecy caused by the winter floods and mist echoed my own unusual need for seclusion, for time to myself, whilst the profusion and lushness of summer on the moor satisfied my deep and unquenchable yearning for color and sunshine. Tickenham for me was the world and I did not want to be anywhere else. Though that did not mean I did not relish the chance to meet outsiders.

William Merrick, a Bristol merchant, had visited several times recently to talk to my father, about financial matters mostly, but never before had he brought anyone else with him. Eventually I saw them riding along the causeway. Mr. Merrick was a barrel-chested and bulbous-nosed man who took great pains to hide his lack of refinement beneath immaculate clothes. He was a Puritan, supposedly, yet he could not help displaying his considerable wealth in a flash of silk brocade waistcoat, in subtle but obviously expensive rings, in the finest silk stockings. He sat, square-shouldered and square-jawed, on his dun mare as it trotted up the miry path past the rectory. Even the way he rode was brash. But it was the other rider on the roan gelding who interested me, the tall, straight-backed gentleman from Suffolk.

I ran round to the cobbled stable yard, then held back, suddenly struck by shyness as I watched them dismount amidst a scattering of chickens. They were both wearing long black cloaks and tall hats which shadowed their faces. I could see rain dripping from the brims by the time they'd walked the short distance to the door beneath the oriel.

With a look of distaste on his florid features, Mr. Merrick wiped his highly polished beribboned shoes with a clump of straw. He lived in a smart new street in Bristol, by the docks, where the marshland had been nicely tamed, so he had little patience with mud and damp, or with anything with even the slightest tendency to disorderliness, such as me.

He wasted no time in introducing Edmund Ashfield, who shook my father's hand. It was an odd greeting, only used by true Parliamentarians. Then he turned to me and bowed, removing his hat. As he came up again, he smiled at me and my eyes widened in wonder. It was as if the mist had cleared to reveal a burst of sun, or else his entrance had been announced with a fanfare of trumpets. His short-cut hair was thick and wavy, and of the brightest copper I'd ever seen. When he straightened, I took in just how very tall and how broadshouldered he was. He had clear gray eyes, an open, ready smile, and his nose and cheeks were sprinkled with pale gold freckles. He was as different from the rustic Tickenham boys as it was possible to be. He shone. He lit up the austere gray stone-walled hall like a sunbeam, and seemed to me like a knight in gleaming armor who had stepped straight from the pages of a romance.

Still beaming warmly at my father and me, he clutched his hat in front of him in both hands and turned it round like a spinning top. "I beg your pardon for our late arrival. We had a slight skirmish with an uprooted tree on the high road, and we didn't dare venture round it onto the flooded fields, lest we be washed away or sink up to our waists in the bog. It's mightily hostile out there, I tell you. But this is a delightful place in which to wait out the siege."

I wasn't in the least disheartened to hear that his manner of speech was not as unusual as his appearance. Overuse of military language was common amongst my father's few visitors, an inevitable consequence of the years when the chief topics of conversation had been civil war and armory and battle strategy. Just like me, Mr. Ashfield must have a father who had fought for Cromwell.

"Didn't I tell you Major Goodricke had a pretty little daughter?" Mr. Merrick interposed. He had never, ever paid me even the scantest compliment before, and it did not sound very sincere now. But I barely wondered at it. I barely noticed his cold and calculating smile, and for once did not pause to consider what he, ever the merchant, might be looking to trade this time. I did not think of him at all.

"I've been looking forward very much to coming here," Edmund Ashfield said with sincerity enough for both of them.

I silently cursed myself for being so tongue-tied. For what must have been the first time in my life, I could think of absolutely nothing to say.

"Are you staying in Bristol for the winter, Mr. Ashfield?" my father inquired.

"Oh, no, sir. I'm on my way home from the Twelfth Night celebrations in London."

My eyes flew anxiously to my father and I saw his bushy gray brows knit in a tight, disapproving scowl. My need to cover his displeasure and make Mr. Ashfield feel entirely comfortable was so great that it helped me to find my voice at last. "Have you been to London before, sir?" I asked.

He turned to me and gave me his full attention. "I have, miss. Several times."

I felt myself flush in the full warmth of his glorious smile, now miraculously directed solely at me. "And is it very foul and wicked and full of thieves and cutthroats?" I asked.

"And many more things besides. Not all bad." His eyes shone with such amusement that I could not help but smile back. I thought how I had never seen a face so full of laughter. He looked like a person who was always happy, would never have a care in the world. A person who could never look dour or severe or puritanical. He seemed made for Twelfth Night festivities, for capering and merrymaking, and, for me, the knowledge that he had come direct from such forbidden entertainments, from the great and wicked capital city, only served to add to his appeal.

"Have you seen the lions in the Tower?" I asked. "What do they feed them?"

"Nosy little girls, I shouldn't wonder," Mr. Merrick sniffed.

Mr. Ashfield ignored that remark completely. "I am afraid I have not been there at feeding time," he answered, finding my question worthy of a considered reply. "I shall make an effort to do so and report back, since it interests you."

"Thank you, sir."

"You are most welcome."

I wondered who had been lucky enough to enjoy the Twelfth Night festivities in his company. "Do you have family in London, Mr. Ashfield?"

"Do hush, Eleanor," my father chided. "You mustn't interrogate our guest before he has even taken some refreshment." He apologized on my behalf. "My daughter is renowned for her curiosity."

"I was there with a very good friend of mine," Mr. Ashfield said to me, and my heart melted, because again he'd taken the trouble to answer me. "Another lad from Suffolk. Name of Richard Glanville."

I saw my father tense.

"Ah, that young blade again," Mr. Merrick snorted obsequiously. "You mustn't judge a man by his friends," he added hastily, with a glance at my father that was, astonishingly, almost nervous. "Edmund's a very respectable fellow, aren't you? For all that you choose to mix with Cavaliers."

My mouth fell open. I gaped at Edmund Ashfield, whose allure had suddenly multiplied beyond all imagining with this new revelation. He actually knew a Cavalier! Was friends with a Cavalier! He might as well have admitted to supping with the King himself, or rather with the Devil. Which, in my father's eyes, amounted to exactly the same thing.

"Richard has never been anywhere near Whitehall Palace and he was born during the Commonwealth," Edmund said very amiably. "After the war was over."

"Makes no difference," Mr. Merrick said, with another fawning glance at my father. "He's the son of defiantly Royalist parents who mixed with the court in exile, which makes him as Cavalier as Rupert of the Rhine."

"I'm surprised that an upstanding gentleman such as yourself would choose to fraternize with men of pleasure," my father said critically.

"They are not half as debauched as we've been led to believe, you know." Mr. Ashfield smiled, his cordiality still totally unruffled.

"Come now," my father said. "You'll not tell me that the news of lewdness and perversion that reached us from Europe was all fabrication? The depravity of the public and private morals of Charles Stu-art and his band was the scandal of the country—still is, now that they've brought their vile wickedness to Whitehall. It was well re-ported how they abandoned themselves to their lusts, and drank and gambled, fornicated and committed adultery. How they committed these blackest of sins and saw none of it as any sin at all. These are men in contempt of all decency and religious observation. Or would you deny that they are a crowd of short-tempered quarrelers, violent heavy drinkers and murderous ruffians who would brawl and duel to the death over so little as a game of tennis?"

Carried away by his fervor, my father seemed to have entirely for-gotten that I was standing there in wide-eyed enthrallment, listening raptly to every word. Oh, I was used to hearing him rail against Cav-aliers. In many ways they stirred up his moral indignation even more than did Catholics. But never before had he been so specific, and I was caught between utter fascination and an acute embarrassment that made me half wish I could fall into a hole and hide. I felt so dreadfully sorry for poor Mr. Ashfield, though he did not appear at all affronted.

"I can't speak for all Royalists," he said good-naturedly. "But I as-sure you that Richard Glanville is possessed of great wit and courage and is one of the most cultured and charming young men I have ever had the pleasure to socialize with."

"Cultured?" my father snorted. "It is a culture of monstrous indul-gence, drunken gaiety and sensual excess that our monarch and his circle cultivate and would wish to impose on this country. The sooner they all rot and decay in their own filth, the better. God forbid it bring us all to moral ruin first."

There was an excruciating silence. "I heard young Richard swims as though he were a fish, not a boy," Mr. Merrick interjected rather desperately. "He'll have his pick of the new drainage channels and widened rivers next time he visits Ashfield land, eh?"

Fen drainage was Mr. Merrick's favorite topic of conversation, one he unfailingly managed to bring up at every visit. It might have made me uneasy, after my conversation with Mary Burges, but I didn't much mind what the three of them talked about so long as they were not insulting poor Mr. Ashfield and his friend. So long as I could listen to him and watch him and stay near him.

But it was not to be. "I suggest we move into the parlor for some coffee," my father said brusquely, remembering his manners at last. "Eleanor," he said to me. "Find Bess, would you, and ask her to send a pot through to us."

I wished I knew why Mr. Merrick was honored with the great luxury of coffee every time he visited, but I was very glad Mr. Ashfield was to be given the best that we had, would not begrudge him anything at all.

He went with the others toward the oak-paneled parlor, and when I took a step to follow, my father halted me with one of his sharp looks. I actually shivered, as if, deprived of the nearness of Edmund Ashfield's bright hair and sunny smile, I was being cast back out into shadows and darkness. I lingered like a little phantom beneath the vaulted roof in the empty hall as he took the seat of honor in a carved oak chair that was drawn up beside the fire as the wind boomed outside like distant cannon fire and the rain peppered the windowpanes like tiny arrows. The flames behind him were pale in comparison, only served to make him appear all the more burnished and gleaming. He had all the glorious grandeur of autumn, a blaze of red and gold that defied the closeness of winter.

He was talking of windmills that were used in his home county to drive back the water. "There's clearly a great advantage to be gained

from combating the floods and claiming the territory for lush meadows in their stead," he said mildly.

"You tell him, Edmund, my boy," William Merrick said. "For he'll
not listen to me."

"On the contrary, William," my father replied. "I listen to you very
carefully."

"Yet you do not heed my advice. Even when it seems you have
little choice."

"There is always a choice," my father added gravely. "If we trust in
God to provide."

"And what if His way of provision is by way of reclaiming land
from water?"

My father hesitated, as if to consider, and I held my breath as I
waited for his reply. "You know I have the gravest reservations about
that, William," he said. "Your gentlemen adventurers are playing God,
tampering with His creation, and not only is that wrong, it is also
highly dangerous."

THE MIST AND RAIN had cleared when I stood with my father
and watched our visitors ride on to Bristol beneath a glorious winter
sunset that shimmered on the sheets of water. In the dusky light I
could see, both inside and out, the translucence of my face reflected
in the panes of gray-green leaded glass, and beyond, the lapwings and
redshanks and curlews wading in the shallows and the great herds of
swans and wild geese out on the lake, gliding between the rows of
half-submerged pollarded willows that were always an eerie sight, no
matter how familiar.

Had Mary Burges been telling the truth when she said I was pretty,
I wondered? Never had it seemed to matter so much before. But I
wanted to be pretty enough to make a man like Edmund Ashfield fall

in love with me when I grew up. Bess constantly complimented my gold hair and blue eyes, but it was their liveliness and brightness she said she liked, and I was not sure that gentlemen would like that at all. Ladies were supposed to be demure and docile and saintly, and I was none of those things.

"Will Mr. Ashfield come here again?" I asked, making a great effort not to sound as forlorn as I felt.

"He'd not be unwelcome," my father said, surprising me. "An extremely likable young fellow. I shall pray for him, that he is not ruined by his objectionable associations."

"Do you even know Richard Glanville, Papa?" I asked, feeling a strange need to defend this man whom I had never met.

"I know of his family." My father scowled. "I know his type."

"Men of pleasure." I whispered it like a creed. At the age of eleven, my naive notion of pleasure extended not much beyond music and dancing and feasting, all that was forbidden to me and therefore infinitely fascinating and desirable. Was Edmund Ashfield a man of pleasure, despite being a Parliamentarian? He must be, a little, to have such a friend.

"Young Edmund was probably not as persuasive as William Merrick had hoped he would be," my father added. "So maybe he'll be brought back again for another try, since it seems Merrick will use any ploy to try to convince me that we are sitting on a fortune and that our drained fields could become the richest pastureland in all of England."

I loved it when my father talked to me as if I was an adult rather than a child, as he had taken to doing more and more, recently. But I remembered Mr. Merrick's opportunistic smile, predatory as a vulture, and even the small surge of joy I'd experienced at the prospect of seeing Edmund Ashfield again was marred by the notion of its being for Mr. Merrick's benefit.

He had even turned being a Puritan dissenter to his own advantage. Barred from the professions, he'd made a great fortune as a merchant trading in tobacco and sugar. My father saw it as a sign of God's supreme approval that Mr. Merrick's business ventures had flourished and as a result generally relied wholeheartedly on his financial acumen and shrewdness. Seemingly not in this one instance, though.

"You disagree with him totally about drainage, then, Papa?"

"If I had a shilling for all the failed schemes to drain Somersetshire, I'd have not needed to take out a mortgage with him, or even consider letting him act as my agent to embark on some risky scheme here. But I can't deny that it's tempting . . . even making a small fortune would be useful to us now." He stroked my hair. "Don't look so alarmed, my little one. We're not facing ruin just yet."

I was about to ask him what a mortgage was but I didn't get the chance.

"It's the war, of course," he ran on. "We're still suffering for maintaining a troop of horse rather than our land, and we've still not recouped the revenue that was forfeit to the new king for his pardon. But we will, given time, and at least our house is not a burned-out shell like so many others. At least our fields do not lie abandoned and overgrown with weeds, even if they are underwater for half the year."

"If we drained them, would we become very rich, then?"

Rich to me meant satin and silk and ribbons aplenty. It meant diamonds and rubies. Although not for rich Puritans, of course.

"If only it was as easy as that," my father sighed. "What William Merrick conveniently omits to mention is the disorder and violence that erupted when attempts were made to drain the Fens, the mobs and riots led by Fenlanders who feared the destruction of their way of life. I would think long and hard before stirring up that kind of strife here. I have lived through enough years of war and discord to value being at peace with our neighbors."

I knew better than to remind him that some of them, Bess's brother Thomas for one, were not so peaceful toward us even now; he still looked at me with disdain and contempt whenever I met him on the moor.

My father smoothed an escaped little lock of hair off my brow, rested his big hand on the top of my head, and I looked up at his craggy, kindly face, dearer to me than any other. "Running this estate is the gravest responsibility," he said. "It is your birthright, precious to us as the crown jewels to a royal heir. Tickenham Court has been in your mother's family for generations. I want to do what is right in her memory, to safeguard it for you and for your children. I am only a custodian here, after all. This house is your future, your children's future."

My mother gave birth to my sister and me late in her life, so I had grown up knowing that there would be no sons to follow, and that one day the manor of Tickenham Court would be mine. I used to dream of being a grand and gracious lady of a grand and gracious mansion. But now I fully understood that what had to happen for me to attain this position was the last thing I wanted. I moved closer to my father and slipped my hand into his as if to hold on to him. "Don't speak of it, Papa," I said quietly. "I don't want you to die."

He gave my hand a little squeeze. "I'm afraid there's no avoiding that, Eleanor. We may live in an age when physicians are constantly making new discoveries about the workings of the body, but not even they can shy away from the one inevitability of life: death. You must be mindful of that, living your life in such a way as to prepare yourself for entry into the Kingdom of Heaven."

God help me and my rebellious heart, but I felt a sudden surge of defiance that was like anger, like desperation. I did not want to listen to him anymore, did not want to be dragged down into melancholy with him. I did not want to be mindful of death. I was eleven years old and I did not want to prepare myself for Heaven.

My sister died of ague not a month after my mother, and to think of her now gave me such a dreadful sense of my own mortality, of death's nearness and its inevitability. I thought of all the delights of this life that little Margaret would never have the chance to experience, some of which I was not even sure my mother had ever experienced. Music and dancing. Singing and pretty clothes. Beauty and color. Christmas and feasting. Love. I could not, would not die until I had had a taste of those things. I had such a powerful yearning to taste them, such a yearning to be happy, that it made me feel like a chick trapped inside an egg. I knew that all that separated me from light and from life was the thinnest shell, if only I could shore up enough strength to break through, to find my way out. Well, one day I would. Oh, I would. I felt the strength growing inside me all the time, a tough, unshakable determination. For my sister's sake as well as my own, I was not going to die until I had truly lived.

warm spring had turned into the most swelter-
ing summer anyone could remember, and today
was yet another day of achingly bright blue skies.
Knowing how I preferred to be outside, my father suggested that rather than have morning
lessons in the parlor, we should have them out on the moors. "We
shall see what wonders of nature we can find to study," he said, tucking my hand into the crook of his arm.

The moors always had a profound tranquillity in summer, but
in the uncommon heat the pace of life seemed to have grown even
more restful. The air was heavy with the scent of meadowsweet and
the meadows were a riot of color, with orchids and yellow iris lining
the ditches and silvery water-filled rhynes, as our drainage ditches are
called, and the knapweed like exploding bright pink fireworks. Lazy
shorthorn cattle nibbled at the river's edge where mallards bobbed
their heads beneath the surface. Even the Yeo flowed more sluggishly,
dotted with water violets, parts of it growing stagnant with weeds.

We watched pond skaters and mayflies and water boatmen. I
caught a stickleback and found the conical shell of a limpet to add to

my collection. When my father, usually so hale and fit, had to pause to catch his breath, I assumed it was on account of the cloying humidity. "Shall we go to the woods now and look for fungi, Papa?" I suggested. "It will be cooler."

"That is thoughtful of you, Eleanor. But I am not suffering from the heat," he said. "Not at all."

We were by a bend in the riverbank, just upstream of where Susan Hort's father, John, was inspecting his wicker eel traps. I kicked off my shoes and went to dip my toes in the gurgling Yeo. A heron stood with a fish in its beak and I smiled to see an otter slip out of the reed bed and go for a swim. "The river won't dry up completely, will it, Papa?" I asked.

He smacked his cheek where the gnats were biting again and I saw that his wrist was ringed with raised and angry sores. "Even if it does there's always the spring water."

Springs gushed up through the peat all across the land and it was thanks to them that instead of an island in the midst of a lake, our little manor and its estate were now a lush haven in a desert. The pastures were red-brown in places, not from dust and drought like elsewhere in the country, but from sorrel and herbs.

"We can count on the springs to water our beasts and crops," my father added. "We'll have eggs and fowl, beef, cheese and vegetables. Nobody will starve. We must thank the Lord that even if it does not rain for months yet, we will be spared here."

"You said the same thing when we heard there was plague in London, sir," John Hort grunted over his shoulder, then turned to face us with a slippery eel writhing in his huge hands. "Those first two cases in St. Giles . . . are you still so sure we're safe? They say it's spreading toward the city. What stops it from spreading west?"

My father clutched his leather jerkin tighter around his shoulders and I realized with a stab of alarm that he'd been wearing it all morning, despite the sweltering heat, despite it being the hottest month anyone could remember. I noticed also that his hand shook slightly, and it sent tremors reverberating through my own body.

It was my turn now to fend off the mosquitoes. I slapped them away as if I could slap away the threat of disease. There was nothing at all to fear, was there? London was miles and miles away. As we walked back toward the garden, scores of butterflies crisscrossing our path, it might have been another world. I turned a cartwheel in the grass, skipped off determinedly through the long sedges, the activity and the prettiness of the bright wings helping me to forget the trembling of my father's hand. My hands brushed the top of the long grass stems, and a little multicolored cloud of butterflies swirled around my dark skirts and my head like living flowers broken free of their stems.

In the walled garden, I stopped to watch two sulfur yellows playing together over the flower beds, fresh and rich as new-churned butter. Butter-flies indeed.

I felt my father's eyes move approvingly to my upturned face. "It is the duty of everyone, women as well as men, to admire our creator in all the works of His creation," he said. "Butterflies are an overlooked though beautiful part of that creation, and surely the most wondrous of all. Wait here. I'll show you something."

He strode off toward the kitchen garden, and I watched, delighted and astonished, as he crouched down and started rummaging about examining the underside of the cabbage leaves, his jerkin trailing in the peaty soil. I was filled with warmth and love for him. I was so fortunate to have him for a father, someone scholarly, who was always looking to inspire and stimulate, who delighted in teaching me and wanted to share his knowledge with me. Daily lessons had followed morning prayers ever since I was old enough to hold a quill, and they weren't confined to a girl's usual lot, but extended instead to the fascinating subjects generally reserved for boys: botany, geography, astronomy.

"Hold out your hand," my father instructed when he eventually came back, for all the world as if he was going to cane me out there in the garden. There was a fervent sparkle in his brown eyes that I had only ever seen before when he was at his devotions.

I did as he bade, and he placed a little worm on my palm. It was the same color as a cabbage, green with a hint of blue. It wriggled and arched its segmented back, straightened, arched again, crawled toward my thumb. I giggled. "It tickles me."

"Consider now, Eleanor," my father said. "Just as raindrops yield frogs and rotten meat births worms, so this little creature has been spontaneously generated from the leaves of those cabbages over there. And it will eat those leaves that birthed it until it grows rather fatter than it is now. Then it will weave a tiny silken coffin around itself and inside that coffin a transformation will take place that is truly miraculous. The coffin will open and the humble worm will have turned into a beautiful butterfly."

I gazed at the squirming maggot. The idea of a grub springing forth from a leaf and then growing bright wings was too fantastical. We were supposed to be living in an age that was throwing aside all belief in magic. But I had not quite lost my childish belief that my father was as omniscient as God, that there was nothing he did not know, and so how could I not believe it? "Where do they build their coffins? How do they do it? Can I see one of them now?"

"I've never even seen one myself." He patted my head. "I know you always want to see proof of a thing with your own eyes, my little one, but the only way to acquire great knowledge is to read and build on the knowledge of those who have gone before."

By which he meant dusty, ancient texts, the pens of Pliny and

Aristotle and others who were long dead, could not be called to account.

"Why do you think God made butterflies?" he asked.

I thought for a moment, wanting to give the right answer, or a considered one at least. "To make the world beautiful?"

"In part, no doubt. But as far back as the ancient Greeks, it has been believed that butterflies represent the souls of the dead. They are a token, Eleanor, a promise. A caterpillar begins as a greedy worm, which surely represents the baseness of our life on earth. Then they are entombed, just as we are entombed in the grave. They emerge on glorious wings, just as the bodies of the dead will rise at the sound of the last trumpet on the final Judgment Day. God put butterflies on this earth to remind us of paradise, of His promise of eternal life. To give us hope."

I looked from the caterpillar to the bright yellow butterflies, dancing so joyfully in the bright sunshine over the bright flowers, and I was filled with hope. God must love beauty and color to create such beautiful and colorful things. It was not wrong to want to be happy, to want all the things I so badly wanted.

I DECIDED THAT if I could not see a butterfly coffin, I could at least try to observe spontaneous generation. So next morning I went off to the scullery, where Jack Jennings, the kitchen boy, was peeling a mound of carrots. When I thought he wasn't looking I sneaked past him to the coolness of the larder, where hung a row of dead, plucked ducks. Bunching my skirt out of the way, I clambered onto a cupboard and hooked down the one that looked the freshest. Its skin wasn't particularly nice to touch, all pimply and cold, like you'd imagine the skin of a grass snake might feel, though actually they don't feel like that at all. Snakeskin is quite nice to touch. But I'd never been remotely squeamish and I didn't even grimace at the dead duck. I hid it behind my back, dangling it by its scraggy neck, peeked out into the kitchen and, when Jack and Mistress Keene, the cook, were busy at last with the various pots simmering over the great hearth, I stepped across the drainage channel and was out the door.

Since I didn't want the numerous household dogs or cats to maul the duck, the only safe place to take it was my chamber. The chambermaid had done her tidying for the day and it wouldn't be immediately obvious, since I'd have to cover it up to prove the maggots didn't get at it from the air. I set it down by the window, reasoning that as not much was born in winter, warmth and sun were likely contributing factors to birth. There was something quite disturbing about the bird's lifeless beady eyes, so I wrapped it quickly in a thick blanket. Content as it always made me to be caught up in the thrill of discovery and experiment, I ran off gaily to learn of far-flung lands: New Spain, Surinam, and the rest of the Americas.

I'd never have imagined one dead duck could cause such a rumpus. It took Mistress Keene until the following morning to discover that it was missing from the larder. But as soon as she did she came in a fluster to the parlor, where my father was hearing me recite a passage in Latin. Mistress Keene was as round as she was tall and she had a permanently red face and bright beady eyes like a blackbird. "I beg your pardon for interrupting, sir," she said with a glance at me, as I stood demurely with the leather-bound book open in my hands. "But I'm afraid I have to report that we've been robbed of a duck. Fresh-caught and plucked just the other day."

My father bade her wait until I had finished my recitation, which I achieved, somehow, with only the faintest faltering in my voice.

"Well done, Eleanor," my father said, indicating I might close the tome. "That was a pleasure to listen to." He condemned the reciting of Latin in church and advocated the Bible being written in English for all to understand, but he accepted that Latin was still the gateway to science, the language in which all the most interesting books were written, and he was very keen for me to be fluent. "Nobody who heard you as I do could go along with the common belief that one tongue is enough for any woman."

Pride leapt inside me like a hare in springtime. But one glance at Mistress Keene and I feared my happiness was going to be very short-lived. I didn't want my father to be angry with me, to let him down. Nor did I want to be locked in my chamber again, especially on such a lovely sunny day. But I did not see how it was to be avoided.

My father had returned his attention to Mistress Keene. "Now, just one duck, you say? Nothing else? None of the cheeses or butter or cider?"

"Not that I am aware of, sir. But a duck is a duck."

"Indeed," my father agreed.

"I know how insistent you are on honesty, sir," Mistress Keene simpered, wiping her hands on her apron. "I'd hate you to blame me or little Jack."

I sneaked my hands behind my back guiltily, as if I could hide what I'd done. I'd concealed the duck under my bed away from Bess and the other maids, but now that they had finished upstairs, it was back by the window again, plain as day.

"I am not blaming anybody," my father was saying patiently. "Now, did you see anything suspicious? Anyone lurking about in the kitchen the other day who shouldn't have been there?"

"Well, sir." Another glance at me that was enough to tell me she suspected exactly where the duck might be. "I don't like to say."

"Out with it, Mistress Keene."

She didn't get a chance to come out with anything, for just then Jack Jennings came bursting in through the parlor door, holding the duck up by its neck so its body swung back and forth.

"It is found," he proclaimed, triumphant as if it was a cache of silver that had been recovered. He threw an odd look at me, his eyes wide. "You'll never guess where."

"I don't have time for puzzles, Jack," my father said.

Mistress Keene had gone over to Jack to relieve him of the dead bird. "Poof!" she said rather melodramatically, grasping her nose with one hand while holding the bird at arm's length with the other. "It reeks to high Heaven. It surely can't be the same bird you plucked just the other day, to have gone bad so quick."

"It was laid beside the window in Miss Eleanor's chamber." Jack announced it with a mixture of scandalmonger's glee and horrified awe. "Swaddled tight in a good blanket it was, lying in the sunshine, just like a small babe that needed to be kept warm and snug."

All eyes were on me now, sickened and appalled. My heart had started hammering and I gripped my own hands very tight.

"Surely you knew it was dead, miss?" Mistress Keene asked me patronizingly, as if I was two years old or a simpleton. "Surely you've lived on this moor long enough to know a dead duck when you see one and to not let it upset you?"

"Of course I knew it was dead," I said quietly. "I wasn't upset. I wasn't trying to keep it warm."

"Then what were you doing, wrapping it up and keeping it in your chamber, child?"

"Seeing if maggots would grow in it."

My father made a noise in his throat, a mixture of a suppressed laugh and a groan. Mistress Keene gave a sharp intake of breath and her hand flew to her throat. Jack Jennings flinched away. The two of them looked at me as if, instead of a slight young girl with fair hair and blue eyes, wearing a long, plain black wool gown, they saw a freak, a grotesque hunchback, or a child with two heads. They looked at me as if the Devil himself had come to sit upon my shoulder. Tears pricked my eyes, and my belly fluttered with fear. Why did they look at me like that? I remembered what Mary Burges said about people being afraid and aggressive toward what they did not understand, and I had a sense then that I might make life very difficult for myself if I did not curb this passion I had for discovery and observation. And yet I did not want to curb it, did not think it was even possible. Nor, in truth, did I see why I should.

"I thank you, Mistress Keene. Jack," my father said quickly, "that will be all. You may go back to your work."

Mistress Keene gathered herself as if she was about to faint away with terror and revulsion. "What would you have me do with the bird, sir?"

My father waved his hand impatiently, then went to take it from her. "Best to leave it with me." I was alarmed to see that his hand was shaking again, more noticeably than it had done on the moor.

He turned to me with the duck aloft as the servants scurried out of the room, casting furtive backward glances at me. By the look on my father's face I guessed that whatever amusement he had felt when I first mentioned maggots was long gone. It was at such times that I understood how, with a powerful combination of praise and chastisement, he had won the fierce loyalty of all the soldiers who served under him in the Roundhead army. Why every man there had willingly followed him into the most bloody of battles, would have laid down their lives for him, why every man loved him and feared him in equal measure.

Above all else I wanted him to love me, to be proud of me and pleased with me.

He tossed the stinking bird on the floor and pinched the bridge of his nose. "In pity's name, Eleanor, but what were you thinking of?"

"Spontaneous generation, sir."

His eyes softened. He coughed into his hand, rubbed his chin. "And what do you suppose the servants will make of that?"

A tendril of my hair had come free from the braids and pins again, had drifted down over my cheek. I smoothed it away, gave a small shrug, shifted my feet. "Probably that I am a little odder than they already thought?"

"It would have been a good deal better if you had let them go on thinking that you had grown overly sentimental, had formed an attachment to a dead duck and wanted to coddle it like a poppet."

"That's macabre!"

"Indeed it is." His mouth was twitching with a smile, which made mine do the same. "But not quite so macabre as keeping dead meat in your room just to see if you can breed maggots from its rotting flesh. It is all well and good to be curious," he said. "You are a persistent little thing, and also, it appears, somewhat ingenious and I would not have you any other way. Nor would I have you conform simply in order to placate narrow minds. I blame myself for encouraging your curiosity." He sighed. "But have a care. Folk are used to seeing you with jars of water beetles and shrimps. They doubtless think it odd but let it pass as a harmless enough activity for a child, but this tale of maggots and rotting flesh will inspire nothing but fear. Jack and Cook will add the grisly story to the pot, and who knows what will come out of it? What they will all think of you? They are still burning witches in Somersetshire," he said, deadly serious now. "Have a care, Eleanor."

"I will, Papa." I took a breath. "May I have my duck back, please?"

He looked at me as if he couldn't believe he had heard me correctly. "No, child. You may not have your duck back. Have you listened to one single word I have said?"

"I just want to see if there are any maggots yet."

"Fortunately, there are not. Otherwise the poor little kitchen boy might never recover from the shock."

"I'm sorry, Papa. I didn't mean any harm."

"I know that, little one."

"Please don't send me to my chamber."

"Now, why ever would I do that? Surely you know I'd never punish you for this kind of inquisitiveness, it is different altogether from running off to the church on Christmas morning." He held out his hand to me and I tried so hard to ignore how terribly cold it was, and how pale was his face, but my skill for forcing out unwanted thoughts completely failed me for a moment. His hand felt just as my mother's had done a few days before she died. It felt just like my little sister's before she started to shiver uncontrollably.

My father said I was to come with him over to the far corner of the parlor, where he kept his ever-expanding case of books behind a dusty brocade curtain. "I'll show you something very special, arrived not more than a week ago from London," he said. "I think you'll find it of great interest."

I HADN'T NOTICED the book box on top of the settle. As my father moved it in order to sit, I came to sit next to him. He lifted out a large folio and rested it on his lap, running his fingers over the embossed lettering on the glossy tooled calf binding, which read: *Robert Hooke, Micrographia.*

I nestled closer to him, inhaling the comforting leathery, smoky scent of my father as he moved the book so it lay companionably between us. I rested my hand on his arm as he lifted the front cover and turned a few of the thick creamy leaves, past pages of lavish illustrations, then folded out one of the plates. It was breathtakingly strange and beautiful, even more astounding when I realized what I was looking at.

"A louse!" I exclaimed. "But Papa, it can't be."

We both had a sudden urge to scratch our heads, which made me giggle. Lice had always seemed mightily troublesome for something no larger than the head of a pin, but this one was bigger than my foot, and it had eyes not unlike my own, and hairs on its legs. He turned another page and there was part of the leaf of a stinging nettle, such as I had never seen a stinging nettle before, with barbs as big as claws.

"He's a brilliant man, isn't he?" my father commented, clearly both delighted and surprised by the intensity of my interest. "He uses a microscope, an instrument such as is used to study the heavens. But instead of looking upward it's used to look down, at all manner of nature's miniature marvels, and see them as if they were a hundred times their real size. It's the latest fashionable device, so I'm told, though very expensive."

If only I could make some such discoveries one day, see something that nobody else had ever really seen before, see it in a way it had never before been seen. Imagine seeing a dragonfly wing through a microscope, or a leaf of watercress. "Papa, could we . . . ?" I wanted a microscope so badly but I knew there was no point in asking. It was more out of reach than the stars.

"Educating a girl on books is one thing." My father tweaked my nose. "If people found you with your big blue eyes pressed up against a microscope, dabbling in the male domain of experimentation, they'd think I'd been infecting you with the wrong ideas for sure."

"There's a far worse contamination to fear from that book, sir."

Shocked, we looked up to see Mary's husband, Reverend John Burges, framed in the doorway. A sandy-bearded, neat-featured and surprisingly hesitant and unassuming young man, given his calling.

I'd never heard him speak with the gravity he had just now, even when delivering a sermon.

My father was just as bewildered. "Reverend, whatever do you mean?"

"The plague has reached the city of London. It is far worse than the usual summer outbreaks. Nearly a thousand died there last week."

At the mention of that dreaded word, the heavy book slid from my father's fingers and crashed to the floor. I didn't need him or John Burges to explain the reference to contamination. The book over which we'd been poring, so newly arrived from London, could have carried the seeds of plague with it.

The reverend was wringing his hands, seemed even more anxious and uncertain than he usually did. "Poor Mary is beside herself with worry," he said, coming toward us. I remembered then that her entire family, her mother and father and brothers and sisters, all worked in the textile trade and lived in Southwark. "I confess I don't know what to do."

Reverend Burges never looked sure enough of anything, not even of his own fitness to be God's voice on earth. But that was probably at least partly because he was so awkward in my father's presence, could never feel entirely welcome.

He and Mary had come to Tickenham four years ago, after the Act of Uniformity had come down like a brutal sword of retribution against Puritans for beheading a king, forcing my father's closest friend, the previous Puritan minister, out of the Anglican Church and out of Tickenham. Reverend Burges's arrival was an insult to everything my father had striven and fought for. Ordained by a bishop, rejecting the solemnly sworn covenant, Reverend Burges accepted Prayer Book rubrics, including the wearing of Popish surplices and the idolatrous kneeling to receive the sacrament. He had even brought with him a pair of silver candlesticks for the altar.

But Reverend Burges had much sympathy for my father and for all dissenters. He allied himself with the Latitudinarians, who thought the act too harsh and wanted to see it relaxed. He overlooked the heresy of our absence from his church services, was even willing to act as chaplain and lead our morning prayer meetings. Toleration was not enough for my father, though. He was convinced that Puritans belonged to the English Church, were indeed the body of it, and could not come to terms with schism. For him, being a dissenter was akin to being cast into the wilderness like the Children of Israel. It was a very uneasy situation, but one we all had no choice but to accept, since our house, our minister's house and God's house stood in such close proximity, in one another's shadow, isolated together from the rest of the straggling village, on a little mound of higher ground.

I knew that my father was concerned that Reverend Burges's willingness to quote from Puritan tracts and to stress the weekly cycle of the Lord's day in the privacy of our parlor, whilst he could also abide by the new decrees of the Church for the benefit of his parishioners and in order to retain his living, signified a dangerous lack of conviction.

"We must trust in God to keep us all safe," my father said now, with enough conviction for ten men.

"Amen to that," John Burges said.

"Amen," I whispered fervently.

"Mary's sister says there is panic throughout the whole of London," John Burges said. "Her letter is filled with unimaginable horror. She writes of bodies and coffins piled high in the churchyards and of death carts rumbling through the streets at night with cries to bring out the dead. They are slaughtering dogs and cats to try to stop the contagion. The whole city stinks of rotting flesh. The King has moved to Hampton Court Palace, the nobility have all fled for their country estates, followed by the merchants and lawyers and anyone else who is able. Even the physicians have abandoned the sick." He dragged on his beard. "I don't know what to do for the best. If they were to come here to us, do we risk the plague coming with them? I'm afraid it may already be too late. There's talk of the Lord Mayor closing the gates to anyone who hasn't a certificate of health."

"Then we can be sure the forgers will be the only ones who stand to benefit," my father said.

I waited for him to say more, since he'd long predicted a terrible calamity would befall London to punish its people for their wickedness and depravity. The plight of Mary's relatives would not normally cause him to miss such an ideal opportunity to illustrate the mortal danger of sin. But he remained gravely silent and I knew it was because he feared the plague may already have come to our godly house in the pages of a lovely book.

He laid the book in the grate and sent for the tinder book to set it alight. A shiver ran through me too when I looked at his rugged, pale face as he suggested Reverend Burges should lead us in a short prayer to call upon God to show mercy to the people of England's great capital.

John Burges bowed his head and as usual he talked to God not as a mighty unseen being on high, but as if he was his dearest and most trusted friend. I clasped my hands as tight as I could and squeezed my eyes shut, as if that might make my prayer stronger, all the more likely to be heard and answered. As John spoke of suffering on earth for a far greater reward in Heaven, my stomach clenched too, clenched with dread, and I prayed for those whom I loved. For Bess and for Mary and John. For myself and my father. But even as I prayed I imagined the plague wind blowing and the deadly miasma drifting inexorably westward like smoke, so noxious that no amount of sweet-scented flowers could ward it off.

"How does slaughtering dogs and cats stop the plague spreading?"
I asked when the prayer was done.

John Burges shook his head in despair. "It is believed the animals
are the plague carriers."

"How do they carry it?"

"This is no time for questions, Eleanor," my father admonished
gently.

I kept my mouth shut, but it seemed to me that it was very much
the time. I thought of the giant flea in the beautiful book that must
now be burned and it seemed that we knew so little still about nature
and the world we lived in, so little about disease. Except, as my father
constantly warned, that death has a thousand ways to guide us to the
grave.

NEXT MORNING MY FATHER was late for prayers. John and
Mary Burges arrived before first light as usual and I joined the rest of
the household who'd fallen to their knees on the hard stone floor in
the great hall in readiness for the candlelit routine with which we all
began each day. It was unknown for my father not to be the first there
and cold fear gripped my heart. I tried to hide it, as I knew my father
would expect me to hide it, but I knew by the way that Bess looked
at me that I had failed.

Please God, I prayed silently, do not let there be plague in this
house, do not let my father be ill. Don't let him have survived the
Royalist muskets and cannons and bayonets to be struck down now.
Don't let him die. Oh, I know he must, one day. But do not let it be
for a very long time. You already have Mama and Margaret. Please
let me keep my papa for a little while longer.

I told myself how my father was robust and straight as a pikestaff from his regular exercise on horseback. He was much stronger than my mother and my sister. Wasn't he?

There was much tittering while we all waited. Fear was in the air and would ignite like kindling at the slightest spark. Even those who couldn't read the newssheets had heard of how disease was laying waste to London, had decimated whole streets, whole districts, claiming thousands. Everyone was afraid that it might spread west. Bess told me that her mother had made her wear three spiders in her shoes for protection. Everyone was ill at ease.

It made little difference when Papa sent the chambermaid down with word that he was suffering from a chill and had decided to remain in bed. I knew it would take more than a chill to keep him from prayers. I knew that, in any case, chills and fevers were cause for greatest concern, that the first sign of one could come in the morning and could herald death by night. "I'll see if he needs anything," I said, rising to my feet on legs as unsteady as my voice.

"I'll go, Eleanor," John Burges said, swiftly. "He'll want a blessing."

More waiting. People were standing now, rubbing their sore, cramped knees. I did not want them to act as if my father might not be coming to join us any minute, that the day would not go on as normal. And then at last I heard John Burges come back down the stairs from the solar. "How is he, sir?" I asked.

"I am no surgeon, Eleanor," he said carefully. "But Ned will fetch one."

"It's not . . . ?"

"I doubt it very much but we will know soon enough, child. We will know soon enough."

"Is he shivering?" I persisted quietly. "Does he have a headache? Has he vomited?"

A single nod.

Mary Burges instantly enfolded me into her arms, pressed my head against her chest. She must have seen my terror, everyone must have seen it. But they would not have known its cause. I didn't either, not for sure. I didn't know which I feared the most: the plague, that most dreaded disease, or ague, which had already killed the rest of my family.

Shivering, aching muscles, nausea. The same symptoms for both diseases.

Plague.

Ague.

They both sounded the same to me.

They both sounded like death.

I WASN'T ALLOWED NEAR my father until Dr. Duckett had made his diagnosis.

I should have been relieved to see the Tickenham surgeon and yet I wasn't, not at all. He was a tall, thin man, not unlike a heron in his gaunt, gray watchfulness, and I could not help but shiver at the mere sight of him. In my mind his presence on our land, in our lives, was so closely connected to sickness and loss that I could only view him as a prophet of doom. I so wanted to put my trust in him, to believe he had the power to heal the sick, but so far, in my experience, he had always failed. Even with all the hope in Heaven, I could not summon any confidence in him at all.

We didn't have to wait long for him to deliver his verdict. Soon, too soon, we heard his ponderous footsteps descending the stone stairs to the great hall, where Mary was waiting with me, her arm around me as I clutched the worn poppet doll I had discarded as a babyish plaything years ago but had resurrected, finding I had a sudden need of it again.

Dr. Duckett spoke. "I am pleased to be able to tell you that there are no signs of swellings under the arm or in the groin, no marks upon the skin. Which means . . ."

"He doesn't have the plague."

Dr. Duckett looked both very startled and intensely annoyed at my interruption. "That is my considered opinion," he admitted tersely.

"So it is ague that sickens him." My voice was a cracked whisper.

His look of grudging surprise widened, so I knew my deduction was correct. "I believe so," he said through pursed lips.

I was small for my age, had a small child's wide eyes, and I was wearing a little lace cap and clutching a poppet, so I could not blame him for taking me for several years younger than I was, but did he not remember that I had been here before? Twice? Did he think me a fool not to remember the symptoms that had preceded the deaths of Margaret and our mother as if they were yesterday?

"I have made a thorough examination of Major Goodricke's urine," he said. "It is of good color and taste, but his body is filled with noxious matter which must be released. I have lanced his leg and the cut must be kept open with a seton. If that doesn't work, I will try a cantharide and pierce the blisters to let more matter out."

I remembered the agony my mother had suffered from the cantharides and the blisters they had caused, needless agony, since they had not saved her.

"I have consulted the stars," Dr. Duckett added. "Jupiter is in the ascendant, which is not at all good. Its qualities are hot and moist, which leads me to predict fever and sweats."

"Forgive me, sir, but if my father has tertian ague, you don't need the charts to predict fever and sweats," I said evenly. "There is always a cycle of shaking and heat and sweats."

"Eleanor," Mary chided gently. "Dr. Duckett is only trying to help."

I had not meant to be rude, it was just that I was not used to being treated as a child, or a fool, and I did not take very kindly to it. I was going to lose my father. My father was going to die, and there was nobody to help him.

"I wonder that you sent for me at all," the surgeon said snidely. "When you have such a knowledgeable young physician already in situ. Perhaps the little lady would like to prescribe an appropriate treatment?"

Mary laid a restraining hand on my arm, as if she was worried I might actually put forward a suggestion. If I had done, it would only be to say that I would be sure not to give my father anything that would cause him more distress. "Please tell us what we must give Major Goodricke to help speed his recovery," Mary said.

"The patient is to have feverfew and sage mixed with half a pennyworth of pepper, one little spoonful of chimney soot and the white of an egg, all laid together on the wrist."

"And if that doesn't do any good?" I whispered, trying not to despair.

"I have every confidence . . ."

"It didn't help my mother or my sister."

"You can also try a spider bruised in a cloth, spread upon linen and applied to the patient's forehead. Or dead pigeons placed at his feet to draw down the fever." He glanced round the great hall with distaste as he left us. "It's living for so long in this place that's the problem. It is not healthy to live in such proximity to bogs and marshes and unhealthy damp vapors. You only have to meet a few inhabitants to see how it twists the body and subdues the spirit."

So why was it that ague struck most often in the heat of summer? The physicians said it was bad air that caused ague, and who was I, a mere child—a girl child at that—to question them? And yet question them I did. The fact remained: My sister and mother had both fallen ill and died, not in the dankness of winter, but on beautiful sunny days both. And now my father was dying in the hottest summer for decades.

MY POOR FATHER'S BODY was subjected first to convulsive shivering and then to raging fever, followed by another punishing bout of quaking and shuddering two days after the onset of the first. Propped up on pillows, he no longer looked like a man who'd commended himself at the Battle of Langport, the battle that had heralded the beginning of the end for the Royalists in this county. He had not been defeated then, but even I had to admit that he looked defeated now, or rather as if he had willingly surrendered, as if there was no fight left to be won. The seton on his leg had turned smelly and nasty and his skin had become a waxy yellow, but I recoiled at the prospect of calling Dr. Duckett back for more of his purges.

"Can we not send for the London physician?" I beseeched Mary as she met me, coming out of the chamber with an untouched dish of toast soaked in small beer.

It was Ned Tucker, when he took pike and eels to market, who'd heard that Thomas Sydenham, the West Country gentleman said to be the most eminent physician in all of England, had fled his practice in Pall Mall to escape the plague and had come with his wife and sons to stay with relations near Bristol.

"Some kind of physician he must be," Mary said, a judgmental tone to her voice that I'd never heard from her before. "If he can abandon the dying to save his own skin, I guarantee he won't set foot outside his front door for less than five guineas either."

"I don't care what it costs," I said. "We will pay him whatever he wants."

She cupped my face in her hands and looked down into my eyes that were shadowed with worry and the exhaustion of caring for my father. Mary and Bess had both offered to sit up with him through the night, but I had insisted upon doing the bulk of it, needed to do it.

"Send for the physician, by all means," she said with a smile. "So long as I don't have to be civil to him."

I smiled back ruefully. "Shall you be as uncivil to him as I was to Dr. Duckett?"

She laughed, stroked my hair. "Maybe not quite."

We sent to Mr. Merrick, begging him to use his connections to find the physician, and later that day he escorted him to us on horseback, and for once looked shabby and insignificant in comparison. Dr. Sydenham was dressed in a dark gray cloth riding suit with a wide collar trimmed with lace. He wore no wig and his own light brown hair, parted at the center, fell gently to his shoulders with threads of silver at his temples. He rode his enormous bay hunter as if he and the beast were one. Gait prancing, muscles rippling, his powerful steed was docile as a lamb under the reins. Dr. Sydenham was the kind of man whom even diseases would obey, I decided, still hoping.

Ned had been sweeping the stable yard and Bess had been fetching water from the pump, but as the physician dismounted a hush descended upon everyone. He was like a king riding into our cobbled yard, yet he didn't seem in the least perturbed to find himself amidst manure and warm straw, still steaming with horse piss.

"I thank you for coming so quickly, sir," I said shyly, as he gave a low bow.

He held up his hand to stem my words of gratitude. "Please take me to your father, child."

I glanced at him as I led him up to the bedchamber, taking long and quick strides to keep abreast with him. Despite his eminence there was something about him that put me instantly at ease. "Have you treated many patients with ague before, sir? Forgive me for asking, but I wondered if Londoners suffered from it as much as we do in Tickenham."

"I've seen enough cases of the disease to call myself something of a specialist," he replied conversationally. "I am presently writing a classification of the fevers which I hope to publish next year. But your comment about marsh-dwellers being most at risk is very pertinent. I've observed for myself how particular dispositions of the atmosphere do cause a particular fever to predominate. And around marshland and stagnant rivers, for whatever reason, it is intermittent fever that prevails. An effervescence of the blood."

"My mother died of ague. And my sister."

"I am most sorry to hear that."

I ushered him into the stiflingly hot chamber that was dimly lit with candles, all the drapes closed and a fire banked high in the hearth despite the hot day. As the physician approached my father's bedside I made to leave.

"Please stay, Miss Goodricke. I shall need to ask you some questions."

My father had stirred at the sound of a strange voice.

"Ah, remember me, do you, Goodricke, my good fellow?"

"Sydenham," Papa murmured with surprise. "Cromwell's Captain of Cavalry."

I was in even greater awe of him than before and I took great heart from the fact that he was a staunch Parliamentarian, that he and my father had fought battles together before, and won.

"I'm a physician now, not a soldier," Dr. Sydenham said. "I'd rather try to cure than kill."

He began his examination by asking me for a full history of my father's illness. He took out a small notebook and lead pencil in which he wrote down any physical signs and symptoms, paying great attention to everything I said, as if I were an esteemed colleague, not just a young girl.

I watched, impressed and inspired by his attention to detail and patient analysis. He must have seen hundreds of fevers before, and yet he approached my father's case as if it were the first and most intriguing instance he had ever come across, as if he could learn more at this bedside than he could in books and were privileged to have been asked to attend. He took my father's pulse and listened to his breathing.

I asked him if he wanted to examine my father's water and he dismissed it as "piss-pot science for quacks," which made me giggle for the first time in days.

"Ah, that is better." He smiled. "See, Goodricke, I have wrought one important cure already. Your lovely daughter here had the most tragic, woebegone little face when I arrived, and such enormous wistful eyes as would break any man's heart. Now she is smiling, and such a vivacious and dimpled smile at that, it gladdens me to see it."

My father gave a weak smile before his eyes slid closed again.

The physician gently took hold of my elbow and drew me away from the bed to speak to me. "His humors are putrefied and need rebalancing," he said confidentially, and I listened intently, feeling very proud to think he trusted me to carry out his instructions. "It must not be achieved by any interventionist methods. The most important thing to do is to do nothing to hinder the removal of froth through the pores of the skin."

"You mean let him sweat, sir?"

"Just so. Just so. But don't force it, try to cool him rather than let him overheat. Put that fire out, open windows, cover him with light bedclothes and make sure he has plenty of rest. Let nature do its work."

"Yes. I will. Oh, I will." I clasped his hand. I wanted to throw my arms around him and kiss him. "I don't know how to thank you, Doctor."

He looked at me as if my exuberant appreciation pained him. "No thanks are due, child," he said with a sorrowful tone. "I can't promise that any of what I tell you will do any good. I guarantee it won't do any harm, but it may not be enough."

"Dr. Sydenham, is my father going to get well again?" I saw there was a practiced reply already waiting on his lips. "Please tell me the truth, sir. I want to know. Is he going to die?"

He looked at me almost in wonder. "That is a very courageous question to ask, child. In all my years as a physician I have hardly ever been asked it so directly. But I am afraid that in this instance, I honestly do not know the answer."

"I don't want my father to die, sir."

"I don't want him to die either, Miss Goodricke. I would save him for you if it was in my power to do so. But I am not God. Unlike some in my profession, I don't pretend to hold dominion over life and death."

"There must be something more you can do."

He stood back as if to make a proper study of me. "What a singular child you are. Tell me, are you always so determined?"

I smiled faintly. "I am told that I am."

He was thoughtful for a moment, gave my arm a quick tap. "As a matter of fact, there is something." He was a wonderfully kind and caring man, I decided, even if he had deserted the plague victims. I was sure he must have had a perfectly valid reason for it. He glanced toward the bed, then stepped even further away from it, motioned me to come with him and lowered his voice to the faintest whisper. I leaned in slightly toward him, tilted my head, amused by such clandestine behavior, which seemed entirely unnecessary but rather fun.

It was almost as if we were playing a game. "There's a new remedy for ague," he murmured, "heralded as a miracle cure. But I did not suggest it before because I guarantee your father will not want to touch it."

"Why not, sir?" I whispered, turning to look at the still figure in the bed. "What is it?"

"Powdered tree bark, brought from Peru to Spain and just this year made readily available in this country." He dropped his voice still lower. "It is commonly known as Jesuits' Powder, on account of the fact it was discovered by Jesuit missionaries." He saw that I understood instantly. This was no longer a game. Anything connected to the most despised order was highly suspect. "He will know that Oliver Cromwell himself allegedly refused the powder," Dr. Sydenham explained quietly. "And died as a result, I believe. He will also know that it was given to an important London alderman during the last major outbreak of ague in the city seven years ago. The alderman died, and Protestants all across England, no doubt your father amongst them, scented a Jesuit plot. They believed the bark to be an insidious poison which the Jesuits had brought to Europe for the express purpose of exterminating all those who have thrown off their allegiance to Rome."

I blinked, fixed my eyes on him. "But you do not believe that, sir?"

"I do not. However, I've not had the opportunity to conduct proper trials of the powder, though I hope to soon, but I've heard from numerous other sources that it is very effective." He looked across at my father, his expression a great deal less impartial now. "If we could only get him to take it, I believe it would be worth a try."

"What is?" my father mumbled, his eyes still closed. "What's all this whispering?" When neither of us answered, my father's eyes snapped open. Somehow he guessed what we had been discussing and I swear his yellow skin turned white. "I'll tell you now, I'll not touch that newfangled potion peddled by Jesuit priests. I'll not be Jesuited to death."

"Please, Father." I tried not to sound desperate.

"It has been used in Peru and Italy with remarkable results," Dr. Sydenham persuaded.

"Bah." My father exploded in a coughing fit that turned his face puce. "The work of the Devil. How could you, Sydenham? You who matriculated at the very center of Oxford Puritanism?"

"You'll not die for Puritan intolerance, I trust, Goodricke?"

My father had marched into war beneath a banner proclaiming, "Down with the Papists." He'd risked fines and imprisonment and the plundering of his property rather than renounce his principles and his faith. He was a zealot.

Of course he would die for Puritan intolerance. And there was nothing I or anyone else could do about it.

MR. MERRICK HAD BEEN CLOSETED with my father, the chamber door firmly shut, since after dinner. Whatever it was they were discussing at such length, I only hoped it was not tiring Papa too much.

I wandered out into the garden but there was no escaping the somber tolling of the church bell that announced the coming death and called everyone to the bedside to pay their last respects. I wanted to run from it, to put my hands over my ears to try to block it out, but it would have been a pathetically childish thing to do and I knew, already, that I was leaving childhood behind me forever. I went down onto the moor, watched the dragonflies and damselflies flashing azure wings, listened to the willow warblers, the booming of a fat little bittern in the reed beds, the joyous call of lapwings and the low, soft whistle of a wigeon. Life was going on all around, heartlessly, even whilst my father's life was ending.

When finally Mr. Merrick emerged he looked like a cat with a dish of cream. He said that my father was asking for me so that he could give me his special blessing. I walked into the darkened chamber feeling much older than twelve. During the fever I had done as Dr. Sydenham suggested and opened the drapes and the windows, but now that my father was close to death, he had wanted them all closed again. If I was dying, I thought, I'd demand to be taken outside, into the brightest sunshine.

"You must not grieve too hard, child," my father said quietly, seeing my stricken face. "You must not grudge Him for taking me when it is my time. I just pray that I can make a good death."

How could there be such a thing?

I knelt on the plaiting of matted rushes by the bed and took his hand and felt him place his other hand upon my lace cap. "My little Eleanor, may your father in Heaven bless you and keep you. May He watch over you when I can do it no longer."

I was so determined not to disappoint him now, to appear brave and composed and accepting as he would want me to be, but the effort of holding back tears was making my head hurt terribly. Like a seawall holding back a great weight of water, the pressure was building up behind it. There was a pain in my throat as if I had tried to swallow a rock.

I sat on a low stool, holding his large hand in both of mine. It was neither cold nor hot now, but somehow desiccated. "I wish I could make up for all the times I've ever displeased you, Papa," I choked, lifting his hand to my lips and kissing it, holding it to my cheek. "I am sorry . . . so sorry."

"You are a good girl," he said, then gave me a wan smile. "For the most part. Just try to live the rest of your life as you know I would want you to live it." His once commanding voice was now so feeble that I had to lean in closer to hear him. "John Burges has given me his word that he will tutor you as best he can, but he will not have as much time to devote to it as I have done, nor the inclination to teach the things I did. You must continue those studies in private. Promise me that you will?"

"I promise," I said waveringly, fighting for control. "I promise."

"Don't be sad for me, little one. None should fear death, for it sets us free. It is better than birth, for we are born mortal, but we die immortal. Remember the butterflies. Remember how they rise from their coffins on shining wings."

"Papa, do you swear to me that is true?"

"As God is my witness, it is my firmest belief that it is."

"I keep thinking . . . I'm worried . . ."

"What are you worried about, my little darling?"

"All the thousands of people dying of plague and all the millions of people who have ever lived and died. How can there be room in Heaven for them all?"

"I am a great advocate of scientific exploration, but Heaven forbid it takes such precedence that nobody believes in anything unless they can fully explain or understand it." He pointed to his cup and I held his head, tilted the cup to his lips and helped him drink some water, guessing he was girding himself for a final sermon. How bitterly I regretted the times I had inwardly groaned as he had begun one before. Now I was determined to listen closely to every precious word he spoke. It was the last guidance I was to have from him and I must take good note so it could sustain me for the rest of my life. Oh, but there was so much I wanted to ask him, would never have the chance now to ask.

"The whole purpose of studying nature is to bring us closer to God through a better understanding of His creation," he said, with a heartrending echo of his previous fervor. "It is not to cast doubt over His works and throw His very existence into question." He grimaced, continued, his voice weakening again. "Science must not lead us to a godless world. We may strive to learn but we must never take a bite from the tree of knowledge." He laid his head back on the pillow, exhausted from his short speech.

I knew I should urge him to rest but did not want to, wanted to prolong this last conversation I was ever to have with him as much as I could. There was so much still to be said.

"If only you had been a boy," he sighed.

I straightened my spine on hearing that, assuming that now the time had come for the most important conversation of any land-owner's life, he regretted not being able to have it with a son, regret-ted not having a boy to carry on his name and to whom he could bequeath Tickenham Court. Which hurt me sorely. "I can care for this estate as well as any man," I said spiritedly.

"Oh, I do not doubt that for a moment." He gasped a breath. "How I would have welcomed men with your courage and fortitude to march beside me against the Cavaliers. But you are not a man, Eleanor. One day you will marry, and the man who seeks to win your hand in marriage will first and foremost seek to gain land and a fortune—to win Tickenham Court. You have a loving nature, a trust-ing nature, and no guardian or trustee will watch over your interests the way a father would. To make matters worse, you are growing to be a little beauty. There is a radiance about you that will attract men like bees to nectar, the worst kind of men, the type I fear you will find all too appealing." He was struggling now to talk and breathe at the same time, which only lent extra weight to his words, since it cost him such effort to voice each one. "On every count you will be sus-ceptible to all manner of philanderers and ne'er-do-wells. May the

Lord help you, but you will be prey to every unscrupulous Cavalier who happens by."

"Do not worry, Papa," I said reassuringly, adamantly. "When the time comes I will choose a husband wisely."

"Ah, my child, the heart is seldom wise."

"I swear to you, Papa, I will ensure the man I marry will be a good lord for Tickenham Court." Like Edmund Ashfield, I thought. My father had liked Edmund.

"You can speak dispassionately now," Papa said. "But you are just a child still. When you do marry you will be a woman, with a woman's baser nature, a woman's low passions and greater temptations." I was shocked at his sudden severity, especially when the woman he had known most intimately had been my mother, who I considered to be as unblemished as the Virgin Mary. He took a labored breath. "Never forget, Eleanor, that you carry the stain of Eve's sin upon your soul. Never forget that Eden was lost to her because of that sin."

Those were the very last words he ever spoke, to me or to anyone else.

We gathered round his bed and we watched life slowly leaving him. He grew gradually whiter and colder but the end, when it came, was quiet, very gentle. A breath and then no breath. A heartbeat and then no heartbeat. A little trail of spittle had dribbled from the corner of his mouth and when I wiped it away he looked as if he was only sleeping still. His hand around mine was still warm and I did not ever want to let it go. I wanted to hear his voice again, for him to say something else to me. Anything. I laid my head on his arm, where I used to nestle when I was tired of walking and he carried me home from the moor. It felt so familiar and safe, even now. I twisted my face round to look up at his. One of his eyelids had slightly opened and I saw there was no life at all behind his eyes.

I let go of him and bolted, his last words ringing inside my head, louder and more ominous even than the death knell.

I fled down the stairs and out through the garden, running until there was a pain in my side as if I had been stabbed. Only when I reached the moor did I stop.

It was dusk and a little cooler now, the air fragrant with the heady scents of summer, but all the colors of the wildflowers in the meadows were muted, fading to gray.

Mary found me in my favorite place, down by the humpbacked bridge. She put her arm around my shoulder. "Let me tell you something," she said, as we watched bats flit over the fields and listened to the strange triple call of the whimbrel. "When John and I first came here, what immediately impressed me was how, in a land as flat as this, the sky is such an overwhelming presence. I told John that it was a good place for us to be, a place where it's as if the border between earth and Heaven has been blurred and weakened. Nobody who crosses it is ever very far away when you view it from here."

"At least Papa will be with my mother now," I whispered. "He has missed her so much." I realized with dismay that I could no longer picture her face. My father's insistence on modesty meant that I didn't even have so much as a rough charcoal sketch to remind me. "I can't remember what she looked like," I cried to Mary in distress. "I can't even see my mama's face anymore."

Mary took me into her arms and rocked me like a baby against her soft breasts, stroking my hair as tears poured down my face and soaked the front of her dress. "Yes you can," she said. "Think hard enough and you can."

I felt her own breath turn ragged and I looked up to see that she was crying too, and I forced my own anguish aside. "Mary, you have news from London?"

"A letter, from my cousin," she said quietly. "She went to call at my family's house and found fires burning outside the door and a fearful red cross daubed upon it. The doors and windows were all nailed shut until the contagion passes or all inside have succumbed to it. She saw the children's little faces at the locked window. Now I see them too. I cannot get them from my mind."

BESS AND MARY WASHED my father's body, wrapped him in the white linen winding-sheet and laid him on the long oak table in the great hall.

In all other aspects William Merrick assumed control the minute my father was gone and nobody questioned him. I'd been judged too young to take a turn watching over my mother's body, but when I asked, Mr. Merrick said I might do it this time. Or rather, he said that I could do whatsoever I pleased. Nobody had ever said that to me before, but dismayingly, it gave me little pleasure. Even if I could do anything, there was nothing I particularly wanted to do. It was beyond me even to decide if I wanted a cup of small beer or not. Perversely, without my father there to rebel against, I could see little joy to be had from being free to wear ribbons or eat a whole plate full of marchpane. There was no point in anything. No pleasure in being good and clever either, if there was no one to praise and be proud of me. But that felt dangerously close to self-pity, and I would not give in to self-pity.

My situation was not uncommon, I reminded myself. Mine was by no means the only family to suffer such a loss. Almost every child my age had some close experience of death, had lost a parent, a sibling. People died all the time, every day, every hour, every minute. Remember Mary's family. Remember them, and the thousands of others dying of plague. The graveyard across the Barton wall and the crypt beneath the church were filled with the dead. Death was perfectly normal and natural. Yet it didn't feel normal or natural to me at all.

"Won't you be very afraid?" Bess whispered, her almond-shaped brown eyes clouded with alarm as she glanced at my father's shrouded corpse, her normally rosy cheeks pale and pinched. Her hands pecked worriedly at her homespun apron. "What if his soul's not quite detached, is still hovering nearby? It can happen, you know."

Her simple but powerful country-girl superstitions did not touch me. Despite my small stature I felt as if I looked down at her from a great height, or as if a great distance separated her from me, this girl who would soon go home to her brother and both her parents. I stared down at my father's face, the skin already waxen and sinking against the bones to reveal the shape of his skull. I had no mother and no father anymore. The two people who'd given me life were dead. I was no longer anybody's little girl.

I hardly noticed Bess quietly leave the hall, eager for escape. But there were no ghosts here. It was only Mr. Merrick who hovered like a specter by the oriel. He came silently across the floor and moved a lighted taper off the table to the court cupboard in the corner of the room. "There must be no candles near the body, no question of Popish practices," he muttered, taking up another candle and standing in the flickering light with the stick in his hand. "Your father entrusted me with his last wishes, as he entrusted me with so much else." I felt his eyes resting on me, wished he would just go. "Now is perhaps not the time, but you may as well know. He has appointed me as your guardian."

I stared at my father's beloved face in consternation. Too late now to ask him why.

I knew anyway. Wardships were bought and sold just as anything else, and since part of the estate of Tickenham Court was mortgaged to Mr. Merrick, my father would have had little choice but to sell the rest of the guardianship to him. He cared for me but it was more important that the estate was left in safe hands. Tickenham Court, my family's past and its future. I was just a passing encumbrance, part of the package.

🦋 "WHY MUST it be done in the dark?" I asked Mary, as the wooden bier, draped with black mortuary cloth, was brought from the church after dusk.

She stroked my hair. "It was your father's wish that the burial be conducted at night, in the latest Puritan fashion, to help keep the vulgar at bay."

There were to be no rings or gloves for the visitors, no feasting or distribution of alms and dole of bread. Biscuits and burned wine were to suffice. With her customary frankness, Bess had told me how peeved everyone was to be denied a spectacle, though they'd expected nothing more.

I wore a black taffeta cloak and hood and Mr. Merrick and the other men had black silk weepers falling from their hats down their backs, but true to my father's last wishes, neither the house nor the church was hung with mourning drapery. Mr. Merrick headed the pallbearers, who carried the lead-lined oak coffin the short distance to the churchyard. The bells gave one short peal, and the procession, lit by links and flaming torches, moved with silent dignity through the dark. Reverend Burges met us at the church stile, and the coffin was taken into the church and set to rest on two trestles near the pulpit, where just a few candles burned, flickering wildly in the drafts and casting an eerie sepulchral glow.

My father had naturally wished to forgo all ceremony but at the final hour Reverend Burges lost the courage entirely to abandon standardized church practice. He began with a touching eulogy praising

my father's virtues, followed by a sermon designed to draw attention
to our own mortality.

The coffin was taken to a prominent position beside my mother
on the south side of the graveyard. Reverend Burges read from the
Order of the Burial of the Dead. *"Ashes to ashes, dust to dust, in sure and
certain hope of the resurrection."*

My father had surely been certain of it. Was I? I did not know.

I stared down into the dark pit of the grave. It was supposed to
be six feet deep but was not nearly that much because of the water
and the soft black peat, which flowed back to fill any hole or ditch as
quickly as it was dug. Even in the worst drought the country had
known, our land was still waterlogged at its very heart. Water had disappeared from the surface but was still there, had merely retreated to
its subterranean depths. It was glimmering now, in the torchlight, as
at the bottom of a well.

The coffin was lowered and I heard a faint plashing as the wood
slapped against the water, like a little boat being put to sea.

"Ironic, isn't it?" Mr. Merrick was standing at my shoulder and
spoke in a hushed voice, for my ears alone. "Duckett and Thomas
Sydenham were both of the opinion that it was living in such close
proximity to marsh and floodwater that killed him, and now in death
the water is receiving him into its depths."

"He need not have died." Tears stung my eyes, blurred my vision,
so I was only vaguely aware of everyone staring at me. "He could have
been cured."

I had a sudden disturbing realization that my father was not infal-
lible; he was not incapable of making a mistake, of being foolish and
stubborn. He was just a man, a normal man, with weaknesses and fail-
ings just like everyone else.

I was standing suddenly on sand, with the waves sucking it away
beneath my feet. Everything I believed in, everything my father had

told and taught me, the very foundations of my life were all stripped away from beneath me, cast into doubt. I did not know if butterflies rose up from tiny coffins as he had said they did. I did not know if death was the beginning or the end. I knew only one thing for sure. It was not bad air that had taken my father from me, nor ague. It was Puritan fanaticism and prejudice that had killed him.

I turned and ran through the churchyard, crashed through the gate in the Barton wall, all the way into the darkened hall of the house. I climbed onto a bench and reached up to the sword that hung on the wall. It was heavy, nearly as tall as I, but I had good, strong muscles from climbing trees and wielded it like an avenging angel. I was already halfway up the winding stone stairs before I saw torches coming through the dark garden.

I flung the sword on the bed and ripped off my black dress. Holding it at arm's length, standing like a ghost in the darkness in just my shift, I slashed at the black material with the sword, slashed and slashed with all my might, until my dress was torn to shreds, a mass of black ribbons. Black for mourning. Black for Puritanism. Black for despair.

I threw it on the floor and dragged my other identical dress from the chest. I hacked at that too, stuck in the sword and twisted to gouge great holes. When I was satisfied at the damage I'd caused, I cast the ruined garment onto the pile of rags and stamped on it, the tears streaming down my face now. Then I stood there in my shift in the silence, the ripped dresses an unidentifiable black mass, like a crouching shadow at my feet.

But it wasn't totally silent. Something was tapping lightly on the glass, like ghostly fingers. I stood perfectly still and listened, my heart pounding, a sudden flood of guilt convincing me that my father had come back from the dead to punish me for what I had just done.

I made myself creep over to the window. I lifted my hand and tentatively moved the drapes aside. I gasped at what I saw. A white butterfly, luminous in the dark, trapped behind the heavy crewelwork, was trying to escape. I remembered what my father had said about butterflies symbolizing the souls of the dead and a shiver ran down my spine. I flung open the window to set the little creature free. It fluttered out instantly and as I watched it disappear into the warm, dark sky, my heart soared with it.

My father's hand had been so dry after the fever, but I tried to see his entry into the watery grave not as sinking but as a baptism. I tried to picture the water seeping into him, replenishing his body, making it whole so that one day it would rise again, just as he had described, as if on white shimmering wings.

Find a way to believe in that, Eleanor, find a way to believe in it.

Spring

1673

EIGHT YEARS LATER

Crisp March sunlight streamed in at the window of the smart Bristol tailor's shop where I stood amidst bright bolts of satin and silk. I turned around slowly, making the sky-blue silk skirt of my lovely new gown swish and sway around my ankles. The gown was full-sleeved, with a low, broad neckline and tightly boned, pointed bodice with a full overskirt drawn back to reveal a petticoat heavily decorated with silvery braid and cascades of frothy white Italian lace.

"It's been smuggled into the country," the fashionably dressed young tailor informed me proudly. "Much finer than regulation English lace."

"It's beautiful," I murmured, rubbing it gently between my thumb and forefinger. "Like a cobweb."

He raised a brow. "You're the first girl I've ever met who's referred to a cobweb as a thing of beauty. Most ladies find them rather ghastly."

"Oh, but they are beautiful, sir," I exclaimed, looking up at him with an avid smile. "Every bit as beautiful and intricate as this lace.

With the frost or the dew sparkling on them first thing in the morning, they are more lovely even than a necklace of diamonds. There is nothing in the world more lovely. Spiders are amazing creatures, don't you think, to be able to create such things?"

"You're a quaint one, all right."

"You must have seen silkworms at work?" I asked. "Since you work with the material all the time."

He laughed at that. "I've no interest whatsoever in the worms themselves or how they do what they do. Just so long as they keep on doing it, that's all I ask."

"Did you know, a single silkworm cocoon is made of one unbroken thread of raw silk over three thousand feet long?"

"Is it, now?"

"Don't you think that's astonishing?"

"I suppose it is."

I stroked the material of my beautiful new gown. Well, I at least was very grateful to the little worms that had spent so much time and energy spinning it for me to wear.

"D'you like it, then, miss?"

"Oh, yes. Very much. Thank you."

He smiled at my unrestrained gratitude. "A beautiful girl like you was born to wear a gown like this." His words sounded genuine, for all that they were probably a practiced trick of his trade.

Under his appraising eyes I felt myself flush and glanced away, surreptitiously, to the tall mirror on the far wall. I was still so unaccustomed to seeing my own image so clearly that it utterly fascinated me, but I cast a critical glance over the stranger I saw reflected back at me, a girl in a shimmering blue silk gown, with eyes of the same color framed by long, sooty lashes. They were still as wide as a child's, those eyes, but they were a woman's eyes now, and they were far too direct, too animated and vivid, not at all docile and modest as all definitions of feminine beauty dictated. Even after a long winter, this girl's skin was creamy rather than alabaster, the impression of vitality enhanced by the brightness of her curls. She was like the water meadows in springtime, bursting forth with an abundance of life, too much life to be contained in such a slight little body. Was she really me? And was she beautiful? I was not at all sure many respectable gentlemen would think so.

There was only one gentleman whose opinion mattered to me, though, and I would know soon enough what it was.

"Hold still, now," the tailor said, "while I adjust the hem." He removed a pin from where it was stowed between his teeth and stuck it into the fabric. "I'll need to take up another inch. How old did you say you are?"

"Almost twenty." I smiled proudly, as if it was a very great age indeed.

He looked at me as if he didn't quite believe me. But it was true. I was under five feet tall, a good three or four inches shorter than most girls my age, but I didn't have any more growing to do.

"For a special occasion, is it, the gown?" the tailor asked. "Sweetheart paying you a visit, is he?"

My blush deepened. "Oh, I don't have a sweetheart."

He glanced up at my pink cheeks, winked. "Ah, but there is someone you like, I think?"

I had not seen Edmund Ashfield since I was eleven. Nine whole years had passed since then. I knew for a fact that my guardian had long favored a match between us and he had surely invited Edmund to visit to determine if he too was in favor of it. Why else was I to have a lovely new gown for the occasion? Edmund was arriving from Suffolk on Friday, and for so many reasons I was half in dread of seeing him again. What if he had changed? It was surely impossible for him to be as wondrous as I remembered him. As I had grown from

child to woman, all my fantasies of falling in love had centered on
him. And how could any man possibly live up to them, live up to my
most cherished memory of a gleaming knight striding in out of the
rain and lighting up my life?

What if he did not want me?

To help pass the time until Edmund's arrival, I went to tend
the bulbs beneath my mother's walnut tree. It stood on the stretch of
grass bordered by the cow barn and the rectory. She had planted it
herself but never lived to see its first blossom. Soon it would be a mass
of white petals and fresh green leaves and, despite its smallness, it
already hinted at the majesty it would one day possess.

I was kneeling down on a jute sack, pulling weeds from the black
peaty earth, when Mr. Merrick came strutting across the soggy
ground with his stiff lacquered cane and—never seen before this—a
book in his hands. I wrenched out a particularly tenacious dandelion
by its roots, showering my skirt with particles of soil in the process,
then stood, as was expected of me in my guardian's presence, not that
I was favored with it very often. He was too busy attending to his
business interests in Bristol. My aged great-aunt Elizabeth from
Ribston had been installed in the house to watch over me. Supposedly. She was kind, but she had had apoplexy a year ago and barely
moved from her chamber now.

I wiped my dirty hands hastily on the jute and then smoothed
away a lock of hair that had broken free from its fastenings as usual
and had tumbled down over my brow.

"Why must you be forever fussing with that blessed shrub?" Mr.
Merrick snapped.

I judged that question unworthy of a reply, saw that the dignity
and splendor of the little tree didn't touch him at all. Though doubt-

less he'd be quick to calculate how much its wood would be worth in a few years to the cabinetmakers and gunsmiths.

"I was wondering when the walnuts will come, since they're such a delicacy," he said. "No doubt you can tell me precisely, given that you have an answer for everything."

I shaped my mouth to say October, but he didn't wait to hear. "I had a most interesting conversation with the tailor when I went to settle the bill for your gown," he said acidly. "You made quite an impression on him."

"Did I, sir?"

"He's not accustomed to having conversations with ladies about insects while he's doing his measuring."

"Isn't he?"

"You know damned well he's not, girl." His small, nondescript eyes had all but vanished they were so narrowed in his reddened face, and he puffed up his pigeon chest and glowered at me. "I blame John Burges for this entirely," he exploded. "I left him and his wife in charge of your welfare and only now do I find that they have been utterly negligent."

"That's not true," I said, indignantly. "John and Mary have cared for me very well."

"Evidently," he spat. "They have taught you that it is acceptable for a young lady to quarrel with and contradict her guardian. And instead of ensuring you are proficient at embroidery, drawing and dancing, as well as balancing budgets and managing a household, you have been learning about worms."

I could have told Mr. Merrick that if he had taken any interest in me whatsoever over the past years, he would have discovered long ago that though I had no liking for embroidery I loved to dance, had a whole sketchbook filled with studies of butterflies and orchids and water snails and had paid great attention to the lessons I had been given on how to balance budgets, since I wanted to manage the estate competently as I had promised my father I would do. Admittedly I had given just as much attention and care to the books in the library and to my own natural observations. If Mr. Merrick had ever bothered about my welfare before now, he would have known that those books had become my constant companions, that I loved them so well I had practically memorized every page. I had taught Reverend Burges as much about God's natural creation, about the behavior of grass snakes and damselflies, as ever he had taught me about algebra and Latin and geography. "John made a pledge to my father that he would make sure I continued my studies," I said quietly. "I made a pledge to him too."

"Well, then, you will have to break it." Mr. Merrick rounded on me spitefully. "You will continue these absurd studies no more. From now on you will receive instruction *only* in dancing and music and drawing and housewifery, like a proper young lady. You have had your final lesson with the reverend, or he will find he has preached his final sermon in this parish. Do I make myself clear?"

For John and Mary's sake, I nodded submissively, even as I clenched my hands into fists behind the folds of my skirt.

"I have already removed all of your father's books from the house."

"No! Please, sir, anything but . . ."

"They will be returned to you when you come into your inheritance and are no longer my concern. Your father made the gravest mistake teaching you to take an interest in masculine concerns," he added superciliously. "The weaker sex may have fruitful wombs but they've barren brains. Learning makes them impertinent and vain and cunning as foxes. I fear I shall never get you off my hands, even if you do come with a fine manor and a good income. I caution you to mind your tongue when you meet Mr. Ashfield again." He smirked nastily, as if he knew very well how what he was about to say would cut me to the quick. "No gentleman wants to marry an educated girl."

"I understand your wife is very competent in business, sir," I said, voicing what I had always taken as an assurance that women had an accepted place beyond homemaking. "She is your trusted partner in most of your ventures, I gather."

"She is a city wife."

He did not need to elaborate. City merchants were happy to have wives who were helpmeets, whereas gentry marriages were bound by an entirely different set of rules. What gentry husbands looked for were meek and dutiful wives. What a man like Edmund Ashfield would be looking for was a meek and dutiful wife, not a know-it-all.

Not me.

"Your father chose me as your guardian because he knew I would make a good guardian for Tickenham Court," Mr. Merrick continued. "You have me and the trustees to thank for the fact that you shall have an income of six hundred pounds a year." He touched the bedraggled edge of my dress with the toe of his highly polished buckled shoe. "Enough to keep you in pretty gowns, no matter how many you'll undoubtedly ruin by wandering around like a Romany. But pretty gowns do not come cheap and I'd like to see a return on my investment. I'd like to see you betrothed and off my hands as soon as possible." He glanced at the book he had been holding, drummed his stubby beringed fingers on the cover. "This is the only book you will be reading from now on, and since you are so keen on study, I urge you to study this particularly well."

He held it out to me and I took it reluctantly, glanced at the cover.

"It's a conduct book, in case you are wondering. For most gentry girls it is as important as the Bible. It instructs you on how to behave.

The skills you will need in order to secure a husband and then fulfill your wifely duties."

Stubbornly, I knelt back down on the ground. I laid the conduct book to one side on the grass and attacked another dandelion. But as soon as Mr. Merrick had gone, I picked up the book and flicked through the pages.

EDMUND ASHFIELD ARRIVED at Tickenham Court in the early evening while Bess was dressing me in my new gown. He and Mr. Merrick immediately shut themselves away in the parlor, so I did not get to see him until supper, when my guardian seated himself beside our guest at the polished oak refectory table.

I took the place directly opposite Edmund and tried not to gaze at him and act the mute ninny I had been before. It was not easy. For he was just as I had remembered him after all, and more. He had filled out in the intervening years, lost any trace of boyish lankiness, so that he seemed even taller and broader-shouldered and more imposing than ever. But his gray eyes were just as merry, and in the light from the candles in the wall sconces his wavy copper hair rippled and shone luxuriantly. If I touched it, I wondered, would it be soft as kitten fur or prickly as a bulrush?

As he helped himself to a slice of cold beef off the pewter platter, I stared at the flurry of pale freckles and red-gold hairs scattered across the back of his hand. I reached out for a slice and my fingers brushed his and made every fiber of my body start to tingle. Solicitously, he moved the platter nearer to me, but I found that I was not in the least hungry, despite the fact that I had been too excited to eat all day. I did not think I could manage one bite. There was no room in my belly anyway. With my corset laced up tight, there was hardly room to take air into my lungs, not that I was complaining. With my hair piled on my head and ringlets coiling down to my shoulders, I had never felt so grown-up or so elegant.

I watched Edmund cut his meat as if I had never seen a person use a knife before. Then he stopped cutting and his hands were quite still. I looked up and our eyes met. He gave me one of his gloriously sun-lit smiles and my heart skipped.

"Eat up, girl," Mr. Merrick scolded. "What's the matter with you today?"

"Yes, do eat, Miss Goodricke," Edmund said, and the little apple in his neck bobbed up and down as he swallowed. "I have never tasted beef this good."

"We've killed the fatted calf for you, my boy," Mr. Merrick said heartily. "Mind you, if this land were to be drained and reclaimed like your father's, we'd have no end of fatted cows. These pastures would breed the fattest, most succulent calves in all of England, isn't that so?"

So that was why Mr. Merrick was so keen on marrying me off to Edmund, I realized with sickening dismay. I should have guessed. I should have known. If I tried to eat the beef now, I thought, I might very well choke on it.

Edmund must have been looking at me closely enough to notice the color drain from my face. "Reclaimed land may breed fat cattle, but wetlands draw and breed good, fat wild geese," he said support-ively. Astonishingly he must have even noticed the faintest flicker of disagreement in my eyes, for he added quietly: "Or don't you think so, Miss Goodricke?"

I parted my lips to speak, hesitated.

"Please, do go on," he said, encouragingly. "You had something to say, I think."

"The girl always has something to say," Mr. Merrick said through gritted teeth, his eyes like daggers intended to pierce my tongue and hold it still.

I gave a small shake of my head, my eyes downcast. "It was nothing."

"But I should like to hear it all the same," Edmund persisted gently.

I set down my knife and fork as if throwing down armor and relinquishing weapons. I looked up defiantly. It was absurd to try to pretend to be what I was not, especially since every thought I had seemed to show on my face. If Edmund Ashfield did not like the fact that I was educated, that I took an interest in the natural world and so-called masculine concerns, then so be it. I might as well know sooner rather than later. I had always been proud of my learning, too proud maybe, but I could not, would not, consider it a shameful thing that must be concealed. I had not read the conduct book Mr. Merrick had given to me, nor had any intention of ever doing so, but I had glanced at sufficient pages to know that I could never be the kind of modest and maidenly girl it set out to create. I would never be content with a life of needlework and gossip. If Edmund wanted such a girl, then I would never be happy with him, did not want him at all, no matter how handsome he was, no matter how his smile made me feel all warm inside and aware of my body in a way I never had been before.

I gulped down my wine, swallowed, handed the glass to Jack Jennings to be refilled. Edmund was still looking at me expectantly.

"It is just that . . . well, the wild geese never breed here," I said.

Mr. Merrick snorted derisively. "Miss Goodricke is a proper little know-it-all, I am afraid," he said grimly. "Though I imagine much of what she says is nonsense. How can anyone possibly know a thing like that?"

I flushed hot with embarrassment and anger. "All the wild geese have flown away by spring," I countered with quiet confidence. "Long before the mallard ducklings and the heron chicks are born. I have watched them." Overcome suddenly with a need to make mischief, I turned my head slightly, flicked my eyes sideways at Edmund as I had seen Bess do to Ned, the stable boy, whom she had married a year ago. "I've never once seen wild geese climbing on each other's backs like the cock does to the hens."

Mr. Merrick spluttered as if the succulent beef was poisoned. This was followed by a deathly hush. I hardly dared even glance at Edmund Ashfield. But when I did I saw with enormous relief that he was grinning from ear to ear as if I had said the most amusing and delightful thing he had ever heard. I could not help but grin back at him. I had not meant to test him, not really, and yet it had been a kind of a test and my heart sang at how completely he had passed it.

"This is not a conversation for the supper table," Mr. Merrick said when he had recovered. "Indeed it is hardly fit conversation for any young lady in any situation."

"My father taught me that it is a godly duty to take a keen interest in the world," I said with a pert smile.

"You take rather too keen an interest in worldly things," Mr. Merrick grunted. "I ask you! How the deuce do you even know that the behavior you so eagerly describe results in the begetting of offspring?"

"Oh, I've thought about it a lot," I said, so happy and so emboldened by how much Edmund Ashfield seemed to be enjoying the conversation that I felt almost invincible. "You couldn't live amongst livestock for long and not work it out."

"It's true, Merrick," Edmund said supportively. "You merchants and town-dwellers are shielded from the basic facts of life in a way that those of us who work the land and live in proximity to beasts and birds can never be. I'd say there was nothing at all amiss with having an earthy approach to life."

"You may be nineteen years old, Eleanor," Mr. Merrick said. "But I've a mind to send you to your chamber at once, supper or no. You are too forward by half."

I hated my guardian then. I hated him for making me appear like a child when I was trying so very hard not to be one. But again Edmund Ashfield leapt to my rescue.

"Oh, don't send her away, William," he said in his affable tone. "I beg of you. She's such delightful company and we would be so dull without her. And I have to say, I don't think she's too forward at all."

Actually, until that day, I'd considered myself rather backward when it came to the intriguing subject of mating. Though when I thought of Edmund when I was out riding it made me shift restlessly in the saddle, I'd been quite disturbed at the idea of men and women doing together what I had watched the bull doing to the cows. But now I did not think I should mind it so very much at all, so long as it could be Edmund Ashfield who was doing it to me.

"Are you on your way back from London," I asked him, "as you were when last you came to Tickenham?"

"Fancy you remembering that after all this time," he said.

I blushed, feeling I had given away the secrets of my heart too freely and he would know now that I had been half in love with him since I had been a little girl. That might perhaps be a grave mistake. But then I saw the way he was looking at me, almost wonderingly, and I knew I need not be concerned. He would never use such knowledge against me, never do anything to hurt me. He seemed very straightforward, not the kind of person to appreciate dissembling at all. I did not care if I had inadvertently declared my feelings. In fact, I was glad that I had.

He looked at me as if he could hardly believe I had been that little girl in the drab dress he had first met all those years ago. "I am on my way to rather than from London this time," he replied.

"And are you going to meet your friend again?" I asked.

"Richard Glanville, yes."

"I wonder, does young Glanville ever spend any time at Elmsett?" Mr. Merrick asked disparagingly.

"He doesn't like to," Edmund said with a glance down the table at the other man. For just a moment the merriment dimmed in his eyes. "You can surely sympathize with him on that score, sir."

"Or is it just that he prefers the attractions of London?" Mr. Merrick blundered on. "The theaters and coffeehouses?"

"The taverns more like." Edmund smiled with such fondness and familiarity that I was almost jealous of his friend, for the fact that Edmund clearly had such affection for him. "Though he loves horses and weapons every bit as much as he does canary wine and tobacco. He is an extraordinary young horseman and swordsman."

"And does he still like to swim?" Mr. Merrick asked.

"Oh, aye. He's set on teaching me, did his utmost to get me into the Thames with him."

"Would it be safe for you to learn to swim in the Thames, sir?" I was dismayed by the depth of fear I felt for him, the fact that already he meant so much to me the idea of him coming to harm was intolerable. That too must have been written all over my face, but I saw that it delighted Edmund to know that I was so concerned for him.

"I promise you, I will take good care of myself," he said.

WHEN IT WAS TIME for the gentlemen to go to the parlor to drink their port and smoke their clay pipes, I went to my chamber, where the candles and the fire had been lit, and waited impatiently for Bess to come to get me ready for bed. I rushed at her and grabbed her hands as soon as she came into the room. "Bess, tell me honestly, do you not think Edmund Ashfield very pleasing?"

"Passable," she said wryly, taking the candle from the stand and holding it up to examine my excited face by its light. Her almond eyes missed nothing. She sighed and smiled, revealing the large gap between her two front teeth. "Oh my, here we go. It is my guess that you still find Mr. Ashfield as pleasing as you did when you were a child. And I know what you're like when you fix on a thing. You can never do anything by half measures, can you? So I suppose that's all I'm going to hear from now on. Edmund. Edmund. Edmund. But then it makes a change from butterflies and caterpillars, I suppose. Or—what was it before? Tadpoles?"

"Bess, he's the finest gentleman I've ever met."

"Not that that is saying much. I can count the number of gentlemen you've had contact with on the fingers of my one hand. Or is it just the one finger? It's no wonder you're in such a stew, poor lamb."

"I feel as if I'm floating."

"Well, how about you float into your nightshift?" I lifted my arms obediently and she slipped the cool linen over my head, fastened the ties under my chin, then pressed me onto a stool beside the fire. "Now, sit and I'll brush your hair."

Bess took out the pins, let my hair tumble down my back and started work with the ivory comb, long, luxuriant strokes that normally made me feel pleasantly drowsy, but not this time. "I shall never be able to sleep," I sighed. "I couldn't eat my supper."

"Well, that'll not do you much good. There's nothing of you as it is, and if you don't eat you'll disappear entirely and he'll not even notice you."

"He noticed me tonight, I think."

"Oh, he most certainly did." When I swiveled round to face her, nearly jerking the comb from her hand, she gave me a knowing look. "I happened to hear him."

Bess was as inquisitive about people as I was about the natural world, and her friendliness and fondness for chatter meant that she received the confidences of all the servants. There was not much she didn't happen to hear, either through their ears or her own. "What did he say?" I asked, not entirely sure I wanted to know.

"He was talking about you when I went to knock on the parlor door to take in the Bristol milk. I felt obliged to wait until he'd done before entering."

"But what did he *say*, Bess?"

She shrugged nonchalantly. "Oh, just some nonsensical prattle about you not being nearly so bold as Mr. Merrick suggested, but how there was a refreshing sweetness and honesty about you that brightened his day."

"Did he really say I brightened his day?"

"I'd be hardly likely to invent such silly mooning, now, would I?"

"I can't believe he'd talk like that about me to Mr. Merrick, of all people."

"Oh, your guardian seemed more than pleased to encourage the praise."

I turned away. "I do not doubt it," I said with a stab of unease that I did my best to ignore.

"So what was it that you liked so much about *him* anyway?" Bess asked cheerfully.

"Oh, every part of him." I closed my eyes and tilted my head back as the strokes of the comb sent delicious tingles down my spine. "His hair," I began. "And his smile. His hands, his lips."

"His lips!"

"I wanted them to kiss me."

"Just what do you know about kissing?"

"I know what it is to feel desire now."

"Desire! You're practically a child still."

"I am not. I've been having my courses every month for six years," I reminded her.

"Seems like only last week that I warned you about them." Bess chuckled to herself. "You were that shocked!"

"Is it any wonder? How can it not come as a shock, to suddenly hear that you're going to bleed, once a month, from between your legs?"

"You scolded me for lying to you, as I do recall."

"I was sure you must be. Until you told me that when it happened it meant I had become a woman, that my body was readying itself to make and to carry a child."

"You've always loved to talk about babies," Bess said softly, no doubt thinking of her little Sam who had been born almost a year ago, after she had allowed Ned Tucker to take her to the hayloft for a fondle. I had been allowed to keep Bess on as my maid after her hasty marriage because I could not bear to part with her, and Sam was cared for by his doting grandmother. "You always wanted to know all about them," Bess said. "About making them and tending them and everything."

"I remember I asked you if it hurt, the bleeding I mean, if it was like when you cut your finger? You told me it was just an ache inside. Oh, Bess, I have such an ache inside me now," I said plaintively. I looked down at my hands as they rested lightly clasped in my lap, my hair falling over my shoulders in a cascade of glossy new-combed gold curls. "He's leaving in the morning and I don't know when he'll come back."

"But you know that he will. If Mr. Merrick wants to see you wed to him, then wedded you will be."

"I suppose so." Again that confusing prickle of disquiet. Because I knew why Mr. Merrick wanted me wed to Edmund. And though I wanted very much to be wedded to him, I did not want what must come with it. Perhaps I was wrong. Perhaps I could talk to Edmund and explain. Perhaps there was a way around the problem.

"When you do have a baby," Bess said, "I suppose you've got it into your head that it must be Edmund Ashfield's baby?"

"I'd like to bear him a little son to carry on his name." I smiled dreamily. "And a little girl too, with hair as red as his."

Bess tutted. "I'm tired of him already. I think I prefer your fixation for butterflies after all."

"A little boy with freckles over his nose," I ran on, "and a smile as sunny as his father's. Oh, just imagine, Bess! A son of Edmund's would be so placid. He would never cry and I would love him so much. Edmund would teach him to ride and I would make sure he learned all about the world and we would all be so happy. . . ."

"You'll doubtless make some gentleman ecstatically happy one day," Bess said salaciously. "There's not a man I know who doesn't want a hot and passionate lover. Every gentleman wants the joy of a whore in his bed even as he is expected to have a docile little miss on his arm in the parlor." Then more seriously: "All men want to be adored and I don't think you're capable of doing any less than throwing your whole heart into a thing, and it is a big heart you have, for such a small person. Only be warned—there's many folk think it unnatural to see such passion in a lady as they have always seen in you."

I DID NOT SLEEP AT ALL. I did not even feel tired and I longed to be outside, to clear my head with fresh air and exercise. Heedless of drafts, I opened the hangings a little way at one side of the bed so that I could see out of the window and watch for the first blue tinge of dawn to creep into the sky. As soon as it did, I dressed myself in my gray wool gown, my boots and cloak. It seemed odd to be clothed for the day and have my hair all plaited still for bed, so I undid it and left it free. It was much more comfortable like this than in the pins and tight braids that pulled and scraped my scalp and always made my head ache by the end of the day. I liked to feel the weight and sway of it, tumbling over the hood of my cloak and down to my hips like a thick gold mantle. What did it matter that it was improper? Who was going to see me at this hour?

I wandered down toward the edge of the flooded moor, my feet squelching through the mud, the cold water lapping against my ankles, enjoying the special magic of dawn breaking over the wetlands. I breathed in the clean, cool air and listened to the piping of the waders and the somber beating of swans' wings. There was no wind and the water was mirror calm. Ethereal wraiths of mist turned the flooded meadows into a land of great mystery, wreathing the pollarded willows so that only the tops of the trees were visible. The lone mound of Cadbury Camp floated above the grayness like a galleon, the only easily distinguishable natural feature for miles.

I untethered the flat-bottomed boat that was moored by the humpbacked bridge and set the lantern down in the bottom, away from the bilge. I clambered aboard and took up the oars.

The water could flood up to six feet deep in places in the winter, quite enough to drown a girl as small as me. The thought of it always made me afraid and exhilarated at the same time. It was the closest I ever came to an adventure.

I tried to imagine what kind of person could swim like a fish, as Edmund's friend could apparently do. What an advantage it would be in a waterland such as this, to be able to slip away beneath the surface of the lake, to a world that none but the fishes ever saw.

Richard Glanville. The Cavalier. The fine horseman and swordsman.

His name had always held a fascination for me but I tried to push him out of my mind. He was just a phantasm. It was Edmund Ash-field to whom my heart belonged. Yet I was intrigued by his friend Richard. He must be very fearless, very strong, very strange. We were not made to swim any more than we were made to fly, or surely God would have given us gills and fins. I looked down at the dark water and almost imagined I saw a lithe body moving through it, a face looking back at me, ghostly through the ripples, a cloud of long, black Cavalier curls.

So powerful was the vision that I was almost afraid to turn around in case he had climbed soundlessly aboard my boat and was sitting right behind me. He could grab hold of me with cold hands and drag me over the side, take me down with him, into the depths of the lake where the drowned grass of summer still grew but was no longer green. I would not be able to breathe down there, but he would put his mouth to mine and breathe air and life into my lungs.

I took a deep breath to clear my head of such fanciful, romantic nonsense.

But when I looked up I saw a solitary light moving ahead in the mist, where the water gave way to bog and marsh, and I froze in real fear. There was no doubting this was real, even as unearthly as it ap-peared, a wandering marsh light, a will-o'-the-wisp, a creature of the Devil. Well, it served me right. I'd always yearned for color and brightness, silk and ribbons and Christmas candles, and here I finally had my wish, in the form of an evil apparition come to seek me out. It was growing brighter still and there was a long shadow moving beside it, gaining in substance as it came closer, the disembodied head and shoulders of a cloaked figure, drifting above the mist.

My grip tightened on the oars but as I kept on watching I saw that there was nothing unearthly about the light at all. It came from an ordinary lantern, carried by Edmund Ashfield. I rowed back to the bridge, my heart beating far faster than ever it had done from fear.

"You worry about me swimming in the Thames and yet you come out here all by yourself?" There was a touch of admiration and respect in Edmund's voice.

"I know what I am doing, sir."

"I can see that you do. May I join you nonetheless?"

"Gladly."

He climbed into the boat, sending it rocking wildly and dipping lower in the water. I moved to the facing bench so he could take the oars. There was not very much room for the two of us and we had no choice but to sit with our knees pressed up tightly together. Not that I minded that at all.

I watched his large hands, tilling expertly back and forth, his big, powerful shoulders flexing in a smooth, easy rhythm. I was about to warn him to steer away from a clump of rushes poking just above the water, indicating where we would run aground, but he had judged for himself, was already resting the right oar in the oarlock and we were turning. He took a deep, appreciative breath. "As a boy I spent all my free hours in a boat just like this," he explained. "Now that our land is drained, we never have cause to use one."

I was instantly on my guard. "Mr. Merrick sent you to talk to me, didn't he?"

He glanced away awkwardly so that I knew I was right. "I would have come anyway," he said quietly. "I wanted to see you."

"I am well aware that Mr. Merrick was always trying to influence my father to drain Tickenham," I said. "As heir to this estate, it is I who must now be influenced and I am afraid, sir, that he means to use you to do it. I may as well tell you now that I am against it."

He laughed. "And I do pity any poor soul who hopes to urge you against your wishes." His eyes sparkled with kindly and disarming humor. "I give you my word," he said earnestly. "I would never try to convince you to do something I did not consider to be in your best interests. Do you believe that?"

I considered him. "I do," I answered quite truthfully.

"So do you think you could trust me, even a little?"

"Yes," I said without hesitation. I was sure that I could trust him more than a little, could trust him completely.

"You are very young to be worrying about land management," he commented after a while. "It is a great weight to carry on such small shoulders."

I gave those shoulders a quick shrug. "There has been nobody else to do it."

"I have never met anyone like you before," he said. "You are not at all like other girls."

"Is that a good thing or bad?" I asked lightly, but with trepidation.

"Most girls do not run around at dawn with their hair trailing down their back. They do not know about the behavior of wild geese and chickens."

"Don't they?" I noted that he had neatly sidestepped my question.

"They can be very tiresome," he added. "With their polished manners and their practiced coquetry and their perfectly painted faces." He gave his easy laugh. "I confess I am terrified of most of them. I have no sisters, you see, so the ways of young women are a mystery to me. But you, I think, are as plainspoken and courageous as a boy. I like that. I feel I know where I am with you. You must call me Edmund, by the way."

I had called him by that name in my head for so long that I was itching to speak it out loud to him, even though for a moment I could think of nothing else to say. "Edmund," I said simply.

He smiled expansively. "Eleanor."

If we were married, we should both have the same initials. Edmund Ashfield. Eleanor Ashfield. When I had sat at my little writing desk aged about fourteen, allegedly transcribing a passage in Greek, I had played at writing the name that I would have if I became Edmund's wife, and it had seemed an impossible and lovely dream. It still did, and yet he was here with me now, wasn't he? When I was fourteen that would have seemed just as unlikely. Which was probably why I expected to wake up any minute and find that I had been dreaming, that I had never come down to the lake, but was still alone in my great bed.

"What is it like, having William Merrick for a guardian?" Edmund asked affably. "Don't worry, he's no particular friend of mine. And I promise not to repeat one word of what you say."

"Oh, I hardly ever see him," I said, determined to be gracious. I glanced at Edmund's open face and instantly lost my resolve. "To be honest, that is a most blessed relief."

"I can imagine," he said, making me giggle.

"He's always in Bristol. Except when he leaves his wife to mind his interests so he can come here for a day or two, but even then he is usually too busy with the estate to pay any attention at all to me, except for when he wants something. Have you ever met his wife?"

"Once."

"What's she like?"

"Not nearly so friendly or forthright as you." He smiled. "For all her city sociability she's like William in many ways, shrewd and shrewish. She likes everything immaculate and gleaming, new as their wealth. Their mansion is not so luxurious as to be unbefitting for a Puritan mind, but I swear not one item is more than a decade old. I can't imagine she'd feel much inclination to care for a little orphan." He looked at me with sudden pity. "You must have been lonely."

"I don't know what it is to be lonely," I said frankly. "I am used to being on my own. I like it, in fact. Though sometimes"—I smiled at him a little shyly—"it is good to have company. Depending on who the company is, of course."

Nevertheless I could not help thinking how lovely it would be to be part of a real family again, to make a new family of my own, here on this land that I loved, with a husband I loved and who loved me.

"So who said your prayers with you at night?" he asked as if it genuinely concerned him. "Who was it who comforted you when you were hurt?"

"Our minister John Burges and his wife, Mary, have cared for me very well," I said gratefully. "John made sure I said my prayers. He used to play skittles with me, too, and he rides with me as far as Clevedon when he has time. I had Mary to put salves on my knees when I grazed them, and she always came to kiss me good night. And my maid Bess was always ready to play leapfrog with me and fly kites." I did not add that all that had been missing, all I had needed, and increasingly so, was somebody to love. One person on whom I could lavish all the love that seemed to be filling my heart until it was almost ready to burst. "So you see, all Mr. Merrick had to do was manage the estate," I finished.

"Even so, I for one will be forever grateful to him," Edmund said quietly.

"Why is that?"

His cheeks had turned a soft pink beneath the pale freckles. "For introducing me to you." His smile was bashful, as if he was not accustomed to having such conversations, and it made me like him even more than I already did, if that was possible.

"I am thankful for that too," I said quietly. And then: "Why are you blushing?"

He smiled with mild surprise, as if nobody had ever asked him such a personal question before, then raised his hand and touched his head. "It is the hair," he said diffidently. "All redheads blush annoyingly easily."

"Oh." I grinned. "I can see that must be a great nuisance."

"It is." He drew in the oars and took hold of my hands, held them inside both of his as we drifted. His hands were very warm from all the rowing and his eyes were just as warm as he gazed into mine, making my heart race. "May I come and see you again, Eleanor?"

"Isn't it my guardian's permission you should be seeking?"

"I am conscious that your guardian would arrange a match between us, but I shall not court you unless you are happy for me to do so."

"I am happy." I smiled.

He smiled with relief. "May I come again soon, then?"

"Soon."

"And may I kiss you?" he asked with aching politeness.

I did not think gentlemen asked ladies if they could kiss them. I thought they just did it. "You may," I said, my heart pounding.

He leaned forward in the boat and made it rock. I closed my eyes and waited. I felt his lips lightly brush my own.

"I should like to help you carry the burden of running this estate, and all others you may have," he said soberly. "If you would let me."

I STOOD at the great oriel window and watched Edmund ride away along the causeway, the surface of the water that lay all around him ruffled in a brisk breeze. I did not know how to feel, was caught halfway between misery and joy. He was leaving, but he had kissed me and told me he wanted to come back.

In such a flat land, when the mist had lifted, it took a long time for people to disappear completely from view. They just grew smaller and smaller until they were no more than a speck on the wide horizon. But I stayed at the window until Edmund and his horse had vanished beyond it. I did not know what else to do with myself. I would find no solace on the moor as I usually did, for I was sure the little boat would seem utterly desolate now without him in it.

"Why look so melancholy?" Mr. Merrick said, with an unusually genial tone that would have made me very wary had I not been so preoccupied. He had come to stand by my side but I did not even acknowledge him. "Extraordinary as it may seem, Edmund Ashfield appears to be bewitched enough by your pretty little face and blue eyes to overlook completely the initial peculiarities he cannot have failed to notice in your character. I expect he is charmed by your quaintness, views you as something of a curiosity." He paused. "He wishes to enter into a courtship with you. He knows of course that his own family would approve fully of such an advantageous match. As the second son it is most desirable for him to form an alliance with an heiress of some means."

Something in his self-satisfied gloating alerted me, and my mouth dried. "An advantageous match?" I repeated slowly, turning to him. "Advantageous to whom, sir?"

"To all concerned."

"The alliance would benefit you too, wouldn't it? My father's will forbade you to use your custodianship of me and this estate to advance a drainage scheme, but if I marry Edmund, you are counting on him doing it for you, aren't you?"

Smugly, he dusted an invisible fleck of dust off the shiny brass buttons of his embroidered saffron silk waistcoat, neither agreed nor disagreed.

"I know all about coverture," I said.

"I do not doubt it."

"I know that a husband and wife become one person when they

marry, and that legally that one person is the husband. I know that as a wife I must relinquish all my rights, my identity, my belongings. Upon our marriage Tickenham Court would belong solely to Edmund, every acre of it, his to do with as he saw fit. And if he, like you, saw fit to drain it, there is nothing I could do to stop it."

The prospect of marriage had seemed so distant that I had not fully considered what it would mean until now. And it dragged at my heart to realize that in order for Edmund Ashfield to be mine, Tickenham Court would no longer be. And yet at that precise moment I'd have given anything just to see him again.

Mr. Merrick gave a swift tug on his waistcoat, his grin sly. "Hard as it is for you, you must accept that coverture is an unavoidable consequence of marriage."

"But I do not have to accept Edmund's hand in marriage. He only wants me if I want him. He told me so. He will not allow you to force me into marriage with him against my will."

"Ah, but you want to be his wife, do you not?"

I was being trapped. Gain Edmund. Lose Tickenham Court to drainage. It was a trade, a bargain. Mr. Merrick bargained with everyone and everything. Why should he not bargain with my heart?

"You also have to accept that drainage will happen sooner or later," he said. "If not in your generation, then in the next. This land is in a deplorable condition and eventually it must be reclaimed, like the rest of the wetlands in the Fens and at King's Sedgemoor."

I said nothing. Instinctively, with every ounce of my being, I resisted the very idea of this land that I loved being dug up and dredged and destroyed. For what? For profit primarily, as I saw it. It seemed a heresy, a sacrilege. I loved bright satin and ribbons and Christmas celebrations, but there seemed something very treacherous in rejecting this ardent belief of my father's, one he had so cared about he had it written into his will, one not born from bigotry but surely from common sense. So steeped was I in my respect for God's creation that to even consider tampering with it, to countenance the idea that we could attempt to control the elements, seemed an arrogant and hazardous thing to do.

"I urge you not to waste too much time deliberating," Mr. Merrick said. "Edmund's father is pressing him to make a match before his third of a century, which is not long off. Are you prepared to see him promised to someone else?" I failed to hide my misery at this prospect and he smirked. "No. I thought not."

I WAS IN THE HABIT of taking a slice of apple pie and custard and a glass of Bristol milk up to my great-aunt Elizabeth in the afternoon, of sitting with her and keeping her company while she ate. She liked to hear of the servants and doings in the village, of how I was progressing with my dancing and music lessons.

I was her only real contact with the outside world. Since the mild attack of apoplexy had left her left side slightly weakened, she was permanently ensconced in the small lime-washed guest chamber, where she spent most of the day in a high-backed oak chair drawn up to the window, her violet-veined hands still stiffly busy with a needle. She seemed ancient to me, but she did not seem to feel the cold and kept the small leaded casement window open no matter how thick the fog that curled up off the river. She still had the noble bearing of the girl who had been presented at King James's court as the daughter of a baronet, and a complexion as pale as the ornate square lace collar she always wore over her black gown. She had wispy silver hair like moonlit mist and she was most profoundly deaf. But her kindly gray-blue eyes more than compensated for it. With their aid she missed not a thing.

She set down her crewelwork as soon as she saw me. "You come and tell me what's troubling you, my dear," she said in her clipped, aristocratic voice. "And don't say it's nothing, because I won't believe it. You've had such a wistful look in those lovely great eyes of yours these past days. Now I've had quite enough of seeing you moping about, all lost and lovelorn."

I brought round a small tapestry-draped table, removed the covering and put down the plate and glass, finding that I wanted nothing more than to tell my aunt exactly what had been troubling me.

I sat at her feet, took hold of her hands and looked up into her handsome, wise face so she could read the words on my lips even if she could not hear them. As soon as I started I wanted to pour it all out, but I made myself speak carefully and calmly so that she could catch every word. I told her everything, how I was in love with Edmund and was sure he had feelings for me, but that if I married him it seemed inevitable that he would push for Tickenham land to be drained. "My father did not want that to happen," I said. "And yet he did approve of Edmund, I know it. He said he was very likable."

"And since people always want most what they cannot easily have—you especially, I think—I am quite sure that he seems a lot more than likable to you now."

"I love him," I said mournfully.

"Are you quite sure about that, my dear?"

"Oh, what does it matter?" I sighed, my shoulders drooping.

My great-aunt laughed. "You have your father's Yorkshire cussedness combined with a wetlander's tenacity—what a combination! You'd not even consider drainage on principle, would you? Just because William Merrick wishes it. Not even if you knew it to be for the best."

"Do you think it is for the best, Aunt Elizabeth?"

"There's plenty that do."

"My father was not one of them," I said grimly. But this land had belonged to someone else before it belonged to him, hadn't it? "You knew my mother," I pleaded. "What would she have had me do?"

"Well now." She sat back a little in her chair. "Your Uncle Henry, my son, the Baronet of Ribston, was very fond of both your parents and they of him. He spent a lot of time here after they were first married. Somersetshire is as different from Yorkshire as it is possible to be, as low and flat as Yorkshire is high and hilly, yet your mother taught him to love Tickenham as she did, precisely for these differences. My Henry told me how she loved this land, but most of all she loved its people. She was the first person the village women called on if they went into labor and the midwife was busy. There's dozens of your neighbors and servants who were brought into the world by her."

"I never knew."

"Well, now you do. She would be very proud of you. You want to do what is right, and you are prepared to sacrifice your own happiness in order to do so. There could be nothing nobler than that. The question is, what is the right thing? Your mother's overriding concern was the good of the people of Tickenham, so if you want to know what she would have done, what she would think was right, it would be whatever is best for them. I cannot tell you what that is. But if anyone can work it out for themselves, it is you."

I kissed the old lady's parchment hand. "Thank you, Aunt," I said.

"I've not done anything, child."

"Oh, you have," I said. "You've given me hope."

"Hope?" She smiled. "You usually have a way of finding a little of that for yourself, I think. May you always." She took my face in her hands, lifted it to hers.

"Perhaps it is your hopefulness that makes your eyes and your smile so bright. You are such a pretty girl. You know, once in a while, in the middle of an ordinary life, love gives us a tale straight from the pages of a romance. And if ever there was a girl made for such a tale it is you. But I fear you want it so badly you're at risk of running headlong in the wrong direction."

"What do you mean?"

She allowed a silence. "I hope Edmund Ashfield is the great love of your life, child. Not everyone has a great love, but you, I think, must have one, or it will be the most dreadful waste."

I THOUGHT ABOUT WHAT my great-aunt had said about my mother as I accompanied Mary on her rounds of the poor thatched cottages straggling along the line of the road that ran parallel to the track of the River Yeo. They were not high enough to escape the winter floods, which forced their inhabitants to cook and sleep in a single room upstairs for months, and I began to think that surely anything was better than that. Even when the floodwaters finally diminished, leaving the rivers gurgling and hidden pools of bright water in the ditches all across the moor, they left the lower earthen floors of the cottages thick with viscous mud, which no amount of rushes could properly soak up.

When Bess told me her father had a persistent and hacking cough, I helped mix up salad oil and aqua vitae and took it to the Knights' little hovel myself. Bess's mother was crippled with rheumatism, hobbling about around the table where they'd just finished eating their pottage. Bess's little boy, Sam, toddled after her with mud smeared up to his knobbly knees. There was a smoky fire burning in the grate but it had made little impression on the damp wattle walls, and yet the dark little room felt surprisingly warm and homely, a well-loved and cared-for place. There was a bunch of marsh marigolds in a jug in the middle of the scrubbed table, and a battered but polished copper pot still simmering over the fire.

"If you're stopping you'd better sit down," Mistress Knight said in a friendly way when I made no move to leave. She had a deeply wrinkled face, a gruff almost manly voice, but her eyes were kind. She plonked a wooden spoon and a bowl of curds and whey on the table together with a pot of small beer. "There. You eat up now."

"Thank you." I smiled, taking a rickety stool beside Mr. Knight and only cursorily tucking up my skirts to stop them trailing in the sludge, not really caring if they did. Mr. Knight looked at me with genuine pleasure and surprise, as if he had not expected me to want to sit and stay, but was glad I did. He had spent so many years on the moor cutting sedges that he was almost as much a feature of the landscape as the birches and willows. He seemed at one with the sky and the water, and yet he did not look out of place in this small, smoky room, but quite comfortable and content. He was tall and lean as a withy, with short and thinning brown hair and eyes as dark brown as coffee beans. I wondered how the two of them had fathered a son as disagreeable as Thomas, who was thankfully nowhere to be seen.

I handed over the cough mixture. "I hope it helps, Mr. Knight."

He was a typical marsh man. To foreigners we are strange people living in a strange land. Isolation and dependence on soggy marshes, which only those born here know how to survive, breed a spirit that is taciturn, obstinate and determined. Yet as Mr. Knight took the remedy he seemed to wish he could shrug off his habitual uncommunicativeness and say much more to me than thank you. "You could have sent it with Bess, you know," he said. "You needn't have come all this way."

"It is no trouble. I wanted to come."

"You're a good girl, miss, despite what some folk say about you."

I laughed. "Thank you, I think. My aunt Elizabeth told me how well my mother cared for the people of Tickenham," I added.

"Oh, aye, she cared for us all right." Mistress Knight gave an ironic laugh, shuffled over to give the fire a sharp, stabbing poke. "Some of us at least." Her husband cast her an equally sharp glance as if to silence her. I was left feeling that I had inadvertently made a terrible blunder, but since I did not know how, or why, I was at a loss as to how to even begin to make amends.

Sam presented me with a crudely carved little horse. "Thank you, Sam." I smiled, gratefully, lifting him into my lap, heedless of his little muddy feet.

Mr. Knight sipped his pot of ale awkwardly. I noticed that his nails were broken and dirty, the skin around them cracked and sore from constant exposure to cold and wet. They were outdoor hands, but the fingers were as long and slender as the fronds of sedges he spent his life cutting, though the knuckles on his right hand looked so stiff and sore it was a wonder he could do his job at all. "I'll bring a rub for your joints next time," I told him.

"We'll have no need of rubs soon," Mistress Knight retorted. "His joints won't trouble him, nor mine me, soon as we get some warm, dry days."

It was not the best moment to ask, but ask I did. "Mr. Knight, don't you sometimes wish you could live somewhere that was dry all year round?"

The affection was suddenly gone from his eyes, to be replaced by an expression of extreme truculence. "I'm a sedge-cutter," he said almost aggressively. "I've cut sedges all my life. I've reared my son to be a sedge-cutter. As you know full well, Mistress Goodricke, sedges don't grow where it's dry. They only grow in marshland."

I STOOD BEFORE my guardian's desk, my feet together and my hands lightly laced in front of me as he pored over his great ledger, his fleshy features pursed in concentration. I drew a deep steadying breath. "Please invite Edmund Ashfield to come and visit again," I told him.

Mr. Merrick set aside his quill pen and looked up with a victorious smile that did not quite reach his small eyes. "I am glad to hear that you've come to your senses. By God, it has taken long enough."

I had rehearsed what I was going to say a dozen times. Why had I not accounted for him leaping to such a conclusion? I let my hands fall to my sides, flexed my fingers, knowing that what I was about to say now would anger him beyond all reason, but there was nothing for it but to plow on. "I have not yet reached a decision on whether I will consent to having him court my hand, sir. I need to ask him some questions first, about drainage, in order that I might do so."

Mr. Merrick slammed his fist against the desk, making the quills and the silver inkpot bounce. "You and your damned questions. Out with them. I'll answer them myself and be done with it."

I felt a bead of sweat trickle down my back but I was not going to be intimidated. "With respect, sir, you do not understand drainage as Mr. Ashfield understands it. As you said yourself, he has firsthand experience. I have none, and I cannot be expected to make such an important decision in ignorance. I want to ask him what it will be like, what it will entail, what it will mean for everyone living here."

"What kind of fool do you take me for?" roared my guardian.

But I was my father's daughter. I knew how to stand my ground. "Mr. Ashfield is in favor of drainage, is he not? So talking to him about it can only persuade me that it is a good thing, surely?"

There was no rejoinder to that. Mr. Merrick banged the ledger shut with a puff of dust and an ire that made me flinch. But inside I was smiling, for I knew that I had won. This first battle at least.

"Very well," he growled. "I will send for Ashfield."

. . .

I RAN AS FAST as I could through the tangle of reeds and sedges, for no other reason than the sheer joy of feeling the sun on my face. I stretched out my arms at either side like wings. If only I could run just a little faster I really might take off. On days like this we lived in a cloudland; the ground was insignificant, there was only the wide dome of the sky, and I wanted to be as much a part of it as were the birds.

The faint sound of pipes and drums reached me from across the fen meadows.

Spring had arrived early this year and already it felt like summer. The moor was teeming with life, ablaze with color. Frogs croaked and otters slipped in between the bulrushes, while above me skylarks sang as they climbed higher and higher in the heavenly blue sky. Against the emerald of the rushes blazed purple loosestrife and yellow rattle, while the ditches and riverbanks were flushed pink with orchids. In my long, plain black cloth dress I was the only point of darkness in the wide, flat wasteland. It was hardly the thing to wear to the May Day celebrations, but Mr. Merrick had been left strict instructions by my father not to condone my attendance at pagan celebrations, and had confiscated my blue silk gown. But today I did not care. Edmund Ashfield was coming to visit again. Winter was over. And at least the gold of my hair could not be dulled, Bess had said as she'd combed it earlier, braiding it tightly upon my head, whispering naughtily about how she'd be wearing hers loose with flowers in it for the festivities.

It didn't look too far to the edge of Horse Ground Meadow, where the revels were taking place, but the moor was deceptive. It took a long time to cross the shortest distance because of the continuous obstruction of rivers that were too wide to jump, stretches of open water and ponds and bog. I crossed the Boundary Rhyne by Causeway Bridge, and beyond it was a little grove of alder, willow and birch that formed a natural screen. The silver-blue pointed leaves of the willows seemed to be swaying and quivering to the music that was much louder now. I saw flashes of color and frantic movement beyond the trees.

The May king and his queen presided over everything in their flower-decked arbor, the dancers were merry in their red and white girdles and embroidered jackets, bells jingling and handkerchiefs swinging. The Devil's Dance, my father had called it. And maybe it was, for it took tight hold of me. There was nothing in the world I could do then to stop my hips from swaying, my cold, wet toes from tapping along to the rhythm.

"Very bawdy and lewd, is it not?" Bess's voice in my ear made me leap an inch in the air. She gave a voluptuous trill of laughter, cupped her hand round her mouth and bent her chestnut head to whisper to me again. "Not half as bawdy and lewd as the way I've been dancing with my Ned, mind."

I pulled her back into the trees. "Did you love Ned on your first sight of him, Bess?"

"What? Up to his elbows in horse dung? Can't remember exactly when I realized I loved him, or a time when I didn't." There was a saucy gleam in her eyes. "But I have a mind to take him into the bushes and let him love me back right now." She tilted her head alluringly. Her round cheeks were flushed and she had a crown of foliage askew on her head. "D'you think he'll be able to resist?"

"Oh, definitely not." I looked at her seriously. "Am I irresistible, do you think?"

For a moment I thought she would tease me, but instead she gave me a quick, tight hug. "Of course you are, little lamb."

"You're not to flatter me, Bess. I need to know. Am I pretty? Tell me, honestly?"

"You are sweet as a sugarplum."

"I was up at dawn this morning collecting May dew," I told her. "So my skin will be beautiful when I see Edmund again. He won't have changed his mind, will he? He will still like me?"

"How could he not? But there's plenty more gentlemen in the world besides Edmund Ashfield, you know."

"But he's the only one I want."

"He's the only one you've met, you mean." She peered at me. "Never mind about May dew. Your skin is soft as a rose petal. A cowslip wash on your nose would not go amiss, mind. I do believe you've got the beginnings of sunspots already. If you're not careful they'll turn into freckles."

"I don't mind if they do. I have changed my mind about freckles entirely. I think they are very attractive and desirable. I don't mind at all if I grow a whole speckling of them."

Bess rolled her eyes. "Is he really all you can think about?"

"Weren't you the same with Ned? Didn't you think about him all the time?"

"Not likely." She gave me a hug, kissed my cheek. "But then, I'm not you. You're like those blue birds diving for fish. When your mind's set on a thing, that's all you see."

She linked her arm through mine and took me back through the trees. "Stop pining now. Look at that."

The throng parted and I had a proper view of the slender tower of the maypole, covered with herbs and garlands of hawthorn and pinks, with streamers and flags flying.

"The hated heathen idol." Bess quoted the Puritans with a ribald smile. "Encouragement to wantonness and lust. Not that some people need much encouragement."

As if to prove her point, Ned Tucker came up behind her and

seized Bess round her shapely waist. "I was beginning to think you'd gone and left me for good, bonny Bessie."

"Would I ever?" She twisted round in his arms and he trickled a few drops of ale from his tankard down the top of her dress, then tried to lick them off. She writhed and screeched and slapped him away until he fumbled her for a kiss.

Ned was a hefty sandy-haired lad with a pleasant, round ruddy face and I watched, giggling at them, thinking that I very much wanted to be kissed myself.

"Stop it, Ned." Bess laughed. "Miss Eleanor will have me for a common strumpet."

Ned winked at me and then flung Bess away toward the dancing, swiping a pie from a long table as he passed by. With no contribution from the lord of the manor, the spread today was simple fare, but no less mouthwatering for that: rye breads and curds, custards and cakes, hogsheads of ale and cider. Our dining table in the great hall never looked half so laden and my belly felt empty as usual.

I stepped toward the table, about to help myself to a jam tart, when I saw someone who made me lose my appetite in an instant. Thomas Knight was standing sullenly at the edge of the trees, his hands stuffed in the pockets of his breeches.

He turned and stared right at me with his insolent black eyes and I shrank back into the trees. I looked for Bess but I could not see her.

I retreated back into the trees, almost wishing I had never come. It was cool and damp in the wood, almost primeval, the floor blanketed with huge ferns and moss and fungi. A nightingale was singing, and there was the hollow rap-tap of a woodpecker at work. A shimmer of brightness flashed past my nose. A crimson and gold butterfly. My eyes darted after it but at first I couldn't see where it had gone. There it was again. It fluttered its gilded wings, dipped, drew a little wave in the air, a gliding aerial dance of more beauty and color than any I'd just watched. A tiny, bright-winged creature, it reminded me of the fairies Bess swore lived in these trees.

But it was gone again. Where? I was struck with disappointment, as if I'd been handed a precious gift only to have it snatched away.

A glittering, fleeting little presence. There it was! I ran forward. It was playing a game with me, leading me on, flickering over the low vegetation. It stopped on a thistle. I stopped. It flittered off. I followed. It finally settled on a water dock. It folded its wings coyly, revealing an underside of orange and white and blue.

I crept as near as I could.

The wings suddenly flipped open, magnificent golden-red wings with snowy fringes and inky black spots. I thought it prettier even than the maypole. I cupped my hands, lifted them slowly, trapped the butterfly in a single downward swoop.

In that instant I felt a sharp pain in the small of my back, heard feet smashing through the sedges right behind. I spun round.

"Well, if it isn't the little lady of the manor, little Miss Eleanor Goodricke." Thomas Knight's voice was thick and slurred with drink. "What were you up to, then? Chasing after fairies, were you?" He sniggered. "I knew you were soft in the head. Not got your full wits about you."

He was red-faced and dazed, his shirtsleeves rolled up, showing brown and brawny arms. He had a nasty smirk on his thick lips and another jagged stone in his hand, much larger than the one that had already hit me. He rubbed his bleary black eyes, flexed his arm. I squared my small shoulders and lifted my chin, told myself that he must not see I was afraid. I tightened my cupped hands and felt the butterfly's wings frantically beating against the cage of my palms, so strong for such a small, fragile-looking thing, a peculiar echo of the feelings inside my belly.

"So much for quality folk having better brains than us," Thomas sneered. "You're obviously missing half yours. Your father educated you like a son, so maybe that's what's turned you softheaded, eh? Maybe that's what makes you think you're better than the rest of us, that you know what's best for us all, that you've got the right to steal what's ours. As if you've not stolen enough from me already."

I frowned. "I don't understand, Thomas. What are you talking about? What have I stolen from you?"

He lowered his spiteful eyes to my breasts, lurched forward. "Maybe I'll take something from you, to make it even. Maybe I'll teach you a few things myself."

I pressed my hands against my chest, my arms shielding my body. The butterfly had quieted, as if it was waiting, its wings trembling against my skin. "Don't you dare touch me," I threatened. "Don't you dare come any closer."

"Or what? Tell Merrick, will you?" He stepped up to me. "Bet he doesn't know you're here. Bet nobody knows it, do they? Mary Burges will not be coming to rescue you this time, will she?" He looked me up and down with his leering eyes. I could smell the acrid sweat from his armpits; it reminded me that he was a grown man now and this was no childish scrap. We were no longer children. He was a man and I was a woman and this time it would be much more than a marchpane sweet that he was trying to force inside me.

"I'll scream. I swear I will."

"Nobody can hear you scream out here," he jeered. "Even if they do, they'll just think you're enjoying yourself."

He took a step nearer. "Tiny and light as a little fairy yourself, aren't you?" he smirked. "Let's see if you have a little pair of wings hidden away somewhere." He lunged at me and thrust his hand down my bodice.

I ducked away, jerking free of his grasp, and ran as fast as I could.

Drink may have made him too unsteady on his feet to pursue me but it hadn't damaged his aim much. I felt the stone graze the side of my head. Bright lights shot in front of my eyes and a hot drop of liquid trickled down my brow. I kept running. I ran all the way back across the moor, up the winding stone stairs to my bedchamber. I kicked the door shut and rested my back against it, my chest heaving and my head throbbing.

I carefully uncurled my fingers. The butterfly lay at an angle against my palm, wings firmly closed and crumpled at the top. I gave the little creature a prod. It didn't move. I touched its small brown furry body. Nothing.

The poor little thing was dead. It must have been the shock, or else I'd held it too tight, squeezed the life out of it. I felt sad for a moment but then realized that at least I could keep it now, could look at it whenever I wanted. It was bright and beautiful and it was mine. Gently, I picked it up by its folded wings, its threadlike legs dangling, its feet briefly sticking to my skin. Gently, I prized open the wings.

I lifted my great King James Bible from beneath my pillow and carefully smoothed the butterfly between the pages of the Gospel of Saint John, beside the meadow flowers I'd collected with my mother.

I closed the book, turned my hand palm up and saw that it was stained with the finest sparkling of golden powder, which looked for all the world like fairy dust, as if marking me out as someone under an enchantment, someone chosen, someone to whom special things might happen.

IN THE AFTERNOON I was in the parlor with my father's pair of globes, one of the earth and one of the heavens. I rested my finger on the earth and spun, waited to see where it would come to land. The Atlantic Ocean. I spun again. The continents whizzed past dizzyingly.

But it wasn't only that which was making me dizzy. There was a scab as well as a bruise on my temple and it hurt when I moved my eyes. I shut them for just a moment, opened them to see Mr. Merrick scrutinizing me with thunder in his eyes.

"What's wrong with you, girl?"

"Nothing, sir. I've a headache, that's all."

"That is not what I meant and you know it. Tell me, how did you enjoy the Maying?"

Any number of tenants could have told him they had seen me there, but I didn't understand why he was so angry about it. I knew for a fact, from what Bess had overheard, that he was holding a supper for his merchant friends tonight in Bristol. Though not exactly a traditional May celebration, it happened to be taking place on the very same day.

"It was . . . interesting," I said, picking the right word carefully. "I can't see what's so wrong with letting the villagers dance and enjoy themselves."

"According to your father, it is what it invariably leads to that's so wrong. Can you tell me there wasn't all manner of wanton and ungodly behavior?"

That I could not. My cheeks flared as I remembered the encounter with Thomas Knight.

"What happened?"

"Nothing."

He repeated: "Name of God, what happened?"

"Thomas teased me for chasing after a butterfly."

Mr. Merrick's arms were hanging down at his sides and I saw him clench and unclench his fists. "What exactly did he say to you?"

"That I must be soft in the head."

A mirthless laugh of agreement. "Is that all he did?"

I was too ashamed to tell him, did not want to tell a blatant lie either, so I said nothing.

He seized me by my shoulders, and as he did, a carefully placed lock of my hair fell back, revealing the bruise and crusted scab.

"He threw a stone at me," I said quickly.

The corded veins thickened in his broad neck. I did not see why his anger was directed at me rather than at Thomas Knight, as if it were I who had done the greater wrong.

"You are a little fool," he hissed, thrusting me from him, "who deserves to have stones thrown at you. You are a little fool to think you can ask the likes of the Knights to pass comment on the fate of this land. Now every damned commoner and tenant knows what is afoot. I've already had a half-dozen of them marching up here demanding to know what is going on."

"Why shouldn't they know what you are considering? Why should they not have their say? They are accustomed to using the common. Why shouldn't they have an opinion on what is to happen to it?"

"Why? Why? Why? Why don't you realize there are some questions you just do not ask?"

"Why not?"

"Because"—spittle showered from his mouth as he shouted and he flexed his knuckles and punched his clenched fist against his own palm, as if it was me he really wanted to hit, and hard—"because the Levellers and Diggers were crushed before you were born, and their foolish radical ideals with them. All men are not freeborn. They do not have natural rights. Commoners have no right to an opinion. They do not have a natural God-given right to the land. That is the way of it. And that is the way it will always be, whether you like it or not. Do you understand?"

I did not. But I knew better than to say so.

. . .

I COULD NOT BEAR to wait around inside for Edmund's arrival, so I asked the kitchen to make me up a parcel of white manchet bread and cheese and apple chutney, and went down to the moor to watch for him. Irises and purple orchids were in flower along the riverbank and the radiance of their petals matched my mood of optimism. Once he was here, once I could talk to him, all would be well.

When at long last I saw him, wearing no hat, his cropped copper hair bright in the sun and ruffled by the soft breeze as his horse cantered along the causeway, I abandoned all pretense of modesty. My blue silk dress had been returned to me for his visit, but neither the whalebone corset clamping my lungs nor my full petticoat with its tiers of lace stopped me picking up my skirts and running to him as fast as my legs would go, tresses of hair tumbling about my cheeks. He saw me, and his face relaxed into one of his wide, open smiles. If I wasn't completely in love with him before, I thought, I was then.

He reined in and dismounted. We stood looking at each other as I caught my breath.

"I waited and waited for an invitation, until I was sure I must have offended you in some way. Please tell me I did not?"

"You didn't. Of course you didn't."

"Well, I am here now. That is all that counts," he said with his unwavering and infectious good humor.

"So you did want to see me again?" I asked, shyly flirtatious.

"You need not ask that, surely? Surely you know I wanted it more than anything else."

He took my hand in his, leading his horse by the reins, and we started to walk back to where I had left the food beneath a willow. He shouted a cheery good day to the fishermen nearby. "Fortunate

fellows," he commented to me. "Having such a delightful place as this
to wait for their catch."

"Will it be as delightful after drainage?"

"Ah, William warned me that you had questions to ask me." He
grinned. "It wasn't just a ruse to bring me here?"

"Partly. Edmund, the tenants and commoners, everyone who lives
here . . . they all seem totally opposed to the very idea of draining the
land."

"Of course they are," he said mildly.

"They seem entirely content with the state of the moors, are willing to tolerate them being inundated for half the year and waterlogged for a good time longer. They would rather that than have their
way of life changed."

"Of course they would. Life on the wetlands is all they have ever
known."

"It is all I have ever known."

"But they do not have your intelligence and imagination. They are
simple people and lack the foresight to appreciate the benefits that
drainage will bring. But benefits aplenty there are. Fertile pastures all
year round to grow crops and graze livestock. Dry cottages to live in."

"But what about the people whose livelihoods depend on eeling
and fishing and fowling? It would seem like robbery to them. I am
not so sure it is not."

"They will still have the rivers after drainage," he said kindly.
"Wider ones, deeper ones, and a whole network of drainage ditches
too. There will still be fish and eels to catch. I grant the sedges will
be lost with the loss of the marsh, but fertile agricultural land yields
other crops. There'll be hemp, flax, woad and mustard, and opportu-
nities for new, more wholesome labor than wading up to your knees
in a bog all day."

"But they will lose the common for grazing their cattle, won't they?"

"The majority will be apportioned other land. An acre-per-beast lease, which should satisfy."

"You make it all sound so straightforward."

"Then I mislead you, which I hope you know I would never wish to do. Make no mistake, what we are contemplating here is a process fraught with difficulty and opposition, not straightforward at all, but when it is all complete the problems will be quickly forgotten and few would want to go back to the way it was before."

"You have absolutely no doubts that it is for the best?"

"No, I have no doubts whatsoever."

"My father was wrong, then?" I asked thoughtfully.

"No," Edmund said. "He was a man of a different time, that is all. In recent years practically every lowland area has seen some attempt at reclamation now." He halted while his horse bent its head to a pool of water to drink. He squeezed my hand, lifted it to his mouth in a very courtly gesture, kissed it. "Dear Eleanor, let us talk no more of it now. Drainage or no, Tickenham is the most delightful place to me because you are here. There is nowhere I'd rather be, and no one I'd rather be with."

I leaned in closer to him and laid my cheek against his arm. "That is the loveliest thing anyone has ever said to me."

"Is it? Well, it's fortunate for me that you've seen so little of the world, or you would realize that I am really very poor at this kind of thing."

"I have seen enough of the world to know that, for me, you are the center of it," I said with girlish impetuosity.

He looked touched if a little overwhelmed by my declaration. "I could not hope for more than that."

Just then a large copper-gold butterfly came flying swiftly at us, the sunlight glinting on its magnificent shiny wings. It swooped and glided right in front of my eyes, as if it was taunting me. I itched to catch it to stow in my Bible along with the other one, as if I really had fallen under an enchantment. When it danced away I held on to Edmund's hand just a little tighter, to stop myself from hitching my skirts up to my knees there and then and chasing after it.

Edmund looped his horse's reins round a branch and spread out his riding cloak for us to sit on while we ate the food that I had brought. But I did not sit. I waited and watched to see what plant the butterfly chose to land on. A water dock, I noted with interest.

When I did sit down and broke off a piece of the crusty bread, my mind was still elsewhere.

Edmund tickled me under my chin with a grass stalk. "What are you thinking about now?"

I smiled at him. "Oh, nothing really." Determined as I was that he should love me for myself, I feared he might think me completely crack-brained if I said I was wondering what it was about water docks that made them appealing to copper-colored butterflies.

Did it really matter so much anyway? Perhaps, for Edmund, I would not mind so much becoming like every other good wife. Perhaps if I was his wife I would be perfectly content with embroidering my sampler with great bumbling caterpillars and brilliant giant butterflies. It would not really matter that they could never be as beautiful as the real thing, no matter how many minute seed pearls I painstakingly stitched onto their wings.

"You like butterflies," Edmund observed idly, relaxing back on his elbow.

"What girl could not? They are very pretty."

"Not half as pretty as you."

I turned to look at his handsome face beneath his cap of copper hair, and all thoughts of the Large Copper butterfly flew from my head.

Edmund sucked the reed between his teeth. "D'you like them

too?" he asked, with a nod toward the dragonflies and damselflies which were busy about the tall reeds, their diaphanous wings all a-whir.

I considered this for a moment. "Not so much," I said. "They are all too frenzied, too agitated. They lack the playful joy of butterflies."

"You have clearly given it much thought," he said, amusedly.

I broke off a piece of bread, threw it to one of the mallards that had come waddling out of the river, and was instantly surrounded by two dozen of its greedy, quacking, flapping companions, all threatening to peck the rest of the bread from my hands and take my fingers with it. I jumped to my feet and Edmund followed suit, laughing to see me ambushed by the sudden commotion of ducks. He threw a piece of his own bread overarm so it traveled some distance, luring the whole flock away to search for it in the long grass. Then he looked at me as if he had just realized something.

I cocked my head to the side. "What?"

"I think, dear Eleanor, that you are playful and joyful as a butterfly yourself. For such a staid fellow, I do seem drawn to people who like to enjoy themselves."

"You are not staid at all," I said passionately.

"Richard says I am. He thinks me far too settled in my habits."

"He is not, then?" I said, bending down to pick a little white mallow.

Edmund laughed. "Oh, no."

I twirled the flower between my fingers. "He does not have a sweetheart?"

"He's had a good many. But they do not tend to last very long."

"Why not?"

"Hard to say. Except that he's entirely driven by emotion, which makes him rather impulsive. That is part of his appeal, I suppose, but it also makes him a difficult person to be with for too long. Though most ladies like to try. When you see him you'll understand immediately why he leaves a string of broken hearts behind him. He's damnably attractive, curse him, if you like pretty boys."

I added that to my list. Cavalier. Swimmer. Fine horseman and swordsman. Breaker of hearts.

"You are very fond of him, aren't you?"

"It is impossible not to be. Richard can charm the birds right out of the sky. I am sure he will charm you too." He took the little mallow from my hand, leaned toward me and tucked it in my hair, behind my ear. "But not too much, I trust."

I smiled into his handsome, sunny face. "I have already been charmed," I said.

He looked lovingly into my eyes. "I promise you this, dearest Eleanor. Your heart is quite safe with me. I shall never break it."

Summer

1675

 ess poured warm water into the small bowl on the three-legged table and I washed my face with Castile soap, put salt on my fingers to scrub my teeth, stripped off my shift so that I could rub my body, under my arms and between my legs, with a linen cloth wrung in water perfumed with herbs and essences.

"I must say, I can't see why you insist on going through all this rigmarole every time Mr. Ashfield is due a visit," Bess grumbled. "He's been coming to see you every fortnight for two years and the pair of you do no more than hold hands and coo at one another. What's the point of having your privates smelling sweet as roses if he's not going to have a sniff of 'em?"

"Bess!" I exclaimed with laughter. "You are disgraceful."

"I do know what it is to want a man and to want to make him wild for you," she retaliated, as she started removing the curl papers from my hair. "I just can't say I'd ever be prepared to go to half as much trouble as you gentry ladies do."

"It's hardly a great chore to be clean and to have to wear ringlets and ribbons and lace," I said, smiling.

"I meant the dancing lessons and the drawing," she sniffed.

"That's not for Edmund. Well, not just for him. I have always wanted to dance, and it would be wonderful to be a competent enough artist to be able to capture the colors of a butterfly's wing or the clouds at sunset, not that I have any talent for drawing at all. But my dancing master says dancing comes as naturally to me as breathing," I added proudly. "He said only yesterday that he's never seen a girl who is so light on her feet."

"That you are, lamb," Bess agreed, unraveling another curl. "But you should try dancing barefoot round a bonfire. Or with a fiddler in the fields at harvesttime. I daresay you'd find it more to your liking than balancing precariously on your toes and bobbing back and forth as stiff as a bobbin on a loom."

"Gliding to a rhythm of eight, you mean?" I looked at her out of the corners of my eyes. "D'you think Edmund would like to see me dancing round a fire?"

Bess grinned with satisfaction as she took up my new lemon-colored gown from where it was spread out on the bed. "That's my girl."

I giggled. "You really shouldn't talk to me like that, you know," I teased, my nose held in the air. "You must be more respectful or I shall have to consider hiring a French maid."

Bess was too busy now to rise to my teasing. She had been shown how to help me dress by a very affected French maid loaned to us by one of Mr. Merrick's Bristol neighbors, but it was a complicated business that still required her utmost concentration.

"If I was really doing all I could to convince Edmund I'd make a good wife for him, I'd make sure I was fluent in French rather than Latin," I said thoughtfully as I leaned forward against the bedpost while Bess wrestled with the laces of my corset. "And I'd make sure I was as practiced in the art of carving at table as I am at naming all the continents and constellations."

"I'd have thought any man might consider himself very fortunate to be loved by a lady who spoke the language of goddesses and could find her way amongst the stars."

I could tell from the sound of her voice that Bess wasn't fooling anymore, was entirely sincere, and I twisted round to look at her, as surprised by her vehemence as by her eloquence and very touched by both. "I thank you, Bess," I said, heartfelt. "That was very nicely put."

"You're welcome. And to think, all my Ned expects of me is that I know how to please him in bed, an' he's happy enough to teach me that himself!"

I laughed, pressing my hand against my corseted waist.

"Stop it, or I'll never manage it," Bess chided, trying to straighten her own face as she pulled the laces tighter round my small ribs. "Suck your breath in harder."

Much as I'd longed to wear fine clothes, I did not like the feeling that I might die for lack of air. With the great piece of whalebone thrust down the middle of my stomacher, I could barely breathe or eat, let alone laugh. I certainly couldn't skip about on the moor and play leapfrog and turn cartwheels on the grass anymore. I did sometimes wonder, just for a moment, why I had been so keen to wear such silly garments. It seemed to me they must have been invented by men, to hamper women and keep us in our place.

When Bess had done trussing me she finished dressing my hair in a knot on top of my head, from which cascaded a mass of long, shiny golden ringlets fastened with gold ribbon.

Finally she stood in front of me to admire her work. "Don't let him find you in amongst the trees or he'll take you for a nymph."

"I feel like one." When I moved the lemon silk swished and sounded like a breeze rustling through leaves.

I fastened on some delicate topaz drop earrings and the matching necklace, which Edmund had given to me last Valentine's Day.

"Pity you don't have any rouge to put some color in your cheeks." Bess reached out and gave both of them a pinch with her fingers. "Try that just before he sees you." She tutted. "I do believe you have a touch of the green sickness. You are in the most dire need of bedding."

"Oh, I am." I giggled. "I am."

"Bite your lips too, like this." She demonstrated. "It'll make them look so red with lust he'll have to push his tongue between them, even if he can't get his cock between your legs."

"Bess!" I gaped at her, then burst out laughing. "Here." I grabbed the damp cloth and threw it at her, showering us both with droplets of water. "You are far more in need of a wash than me. I've never heard such filthy talk! As you well know, Mr. Ashfield's tongue has never been near my mouth. Nor even his lips, for more than one fleeting moment, more's the pity." Amidst a great billow of skirts, I sighed and threw myself backward onto the high bed, where, earlier, I'd been examining my collection of love tokens for the hundredth time. "Maybe he's read that conduct book Mr. Merrick thrust upon me. It is very clear that mutual liking and respect is all that is called for between a man and a woman who vow before God to share their lives. Amorous love is a contemptible disease. But I want to be loved," I breathed, staring up at the faded crewelwork canopy. "I want Edmund to love me." I snatched up a pair of salmon pink gloves he'd sent to me and clutched them to my heart. "Liking will never be enough for me."

"I do wonder if Mr. Ashfield will ever be enough for you," Bess said, coming to perch beside me and clucking. "Or rather that you will be altogether too much for him." Her dancing, almond-shaped eyes grew uncommonly serious then, their expression almost protective, and as I sat up beside her on the edge of the bed she kissed my cheek. "I just hope he is capable of loving you even half as much as you love him."

I unfolded the letter from him that had arrived days ago.

"You've read it so often it's in tatters already." Bess smiled. "Shame he hasn't written you a few more."

"I don't mind," I said, quick to defend him. "He told me not to be offended or think badly of him for not writing more often. He doesn't have an easy way with written words."

"Let's see, then." She scrambled up behind me and tucked her chin onto my shoulder. "'My best beloved'"—she knew that bit by heart—"'O-u-r-p-a-r-l-e-y-i-s-n-e-a-r-i-n-g . . .'" She broke off.

With the help of a little bone tablet I was trying to teach her to read, but she never concentrated for long enough and we were having great trouble progressing past isolated letter sounds.

"Oh, it's too hard," she huffed. "You do it."

I shuffled back further onto the bed and read aloud: "'Our parley is nearing an end. Now that I have stormed the cherry bulwarks of your sweet mouth, I am convinced I may gain your surrender. But if I must lay siege to your heart to secure my final victory, then I shall do so willingly.' He goes on to describe another week he's spent in London with Richard Glanville. They've visited the playhouse a dozen times and marveled at the novelty of seeing females onstage, but Edmund says none of the actresses were as enchanting as me."

"How does he end it?"

"'I shall be making advances in your direction again very soon. I beg of you, Eleanor, remove all fortifications against me, or I am crushed.'"

Bess chortled. "You have to admit he uses some very peculiar words to woo a girl. I just hope he can do better than that when he gets you between the sheets or his weaponry might prove woefully inadequate!"

"Oh, stop it." I giggled, giving her a gentle shove that toppled her. "I think his letter is very charming. And he doesn't talk the way he

writes, or at least he only does when he is unsure of himself. Besides,"
I sighed, "it's entirely appropriate. After all, gentry love is very like
the waging of war. Allies are sought to make approaches, concessions
are bargained over. The reason I'm certain Edmund is about to propose now is because I know very well he's been in negotiation with
Mr. Merrick for weeks and they've finally reached an agreement."

All Bess did was raise her brow. As well she might.

EDMUND TUCKED MY HAND into the crook of his arm and we
went to walk in the garden, where the light was so thick and golden
that it gilded everything it touched.

"I feel as if I have drunk a barrel full of this sunshine." I smiled.
"Or else I cannot imagine how it is that I feel so happy and warm
inside."

"You're sure it's not Somersetshire cider you've been drinking?"
Edmund quipped. "It tends to have that effect on me." He grinned
down at me again. "As does the sweetness of your face."

"Oh, Edmund. I do like it when you talk to me like that. Say
something else."

"I am not sure that I can pay compliments on command." His
brow creased as he tried to think of another all the same.

I did not have to try at all. "I can't decide if it is the sunshine or
having you here that has made the colors of all the flowers seem so
much brighter," I said, quite truthfully.

"Oh, it is me, most definitely." Edmund looked down at me and I
looked up at him and neither of us took another step, so that for one
wild and wonderful moment I thought he was going to kiss me properly, finally, amidst the beds of pink hollyhocks.

Instead he let his arm drop to his side, took hold of my hand and carried on walking. He talked about his journey and how his horse had lost a shoe. "I've saved it for you so you can hang it on your door to bring you good luck."

I did not tell him that we were living in an age that was supposed to be casting aside such talismans, to be moving from the dark age of superstition into an enlightened age of science, because I would be glad to have a horseshoe on my door if it had belonged to Edmund's horse and he had given it to me. Besides, I was too busy trying to think of a way I could contrive to get him to take me in his arms and kiss me.

"Let's play Barley Break," I said suddenly.

"Barley Break?"

"Yes. Oh, you must have played it. It's very simple. I run away and you have to chase me."

"I'm not sure I like the sound of that at all," he said with a grin. "I don't think I want to have to catch you. I like having you right here, by my side at all times."

"Oh, but this is far more exciting." I let go of his arm and slipped away from him across the scythed lawn, my gold curls bouncing and my yellow silk skirt swishing out behind me. Even my laughter sounded gilded and bell-like in the still afternoon. I had forgotten that I could not run very fast in a corset and petticoats, but it did not matter since the only point in running was to be caught and as soon as possible. I glanced over my shoulder, saw Edmund coming after me but not very fast, as if he didn't want to spoil the game for me. Just as he turned the corner by the stone bench I hid behind a rosebush, hoping he'd spied the edge of my skirt as I disappeared. I peeped round the bush to watch him, then scampered off when he was almost upon me, giggling deliciously at the prospect of my imminent capture.

I let him catch me by the arbor entwined with honeysuckle. He grabbed my hand and I pretended to take a little stumble so that he had to grasp me properly around my tightly laced waist. I twisted round in his arms and he held me close to him for a moment as we both caught our breath. I felt a hardness between his legs, pushing against my stomacher, secret and surprising. He bent his head and placed a swift kiss on my lips, but it was over in an instant, leaving me yearning for more.

He plucked a blossoming honeysuckle off its stem and held it under my nose for me to smell its sweet fragrance, and I didn't know whether to laugh or cry with frustration when I remembered what Bess had said about the fact that I smelled of roses but that Edmund would never get close enough to me to find out.

Why did he have to be so maddeningly respectful? It would all change when he was my husband and was permitted by law and by God to love me, wouldn't it? But I did not know how I was going to wait that long. I touched his flame-red hair and imagined him inflamed with desire, running his tongue all over my skin as Bess said Ned did to her. I was sure that when the time came Edmund would be a very passionate husband.

"EDMUND, THERE IS SOMETHING I have to ask you."

We had gone inside for glasses of cider in the parlor, and Edmund was sitting facing me in the window embrasure.

"Ask and I shall grant it," he said, setting his glass down on the side table.

"Will you take me to the Fens? So that I may see for myself what has been done there?"

"It would be my pleasure." He took a deep breath and looked very

somber all of a sudden. "It would be the perfect opportunity to introduce you to my father and brother. They are longing to meet you."
He paused. "Actually, there is something I have to ask you too." He
took my hands in his, looking more earnest than ever, so that I
thought I knew exactly what he was about to ask me. Even though I
was expecting it, my heart started fluttering frantically.

"It's such a beautiful day," I said impetuously, jumping to my feet
without letting go of his hand. "Let us go back into the garden and
you can ask me there." I would treasure the memory of my betrothal
forever, and it would be so much more memorable if it was done under
a blue sky, surrounded by flowers and butterflies and serenaded by
birdsong, instead of in this somber oak-paneled room. He stood too
and I tried to lead him but he stayed as rooted to the spot as a tree.
Apparently he needed formal surroundings for such a formal event.
It was so like him to want to do everything just right.

I sat down again. He sat down. He cleared his throat. "Difficult
maneuver," he said, his face turning a little pink. "I'm not sure where
to begin. I don't suppose Mr. Merrick has said anything to you?"

"About what?" I asked, all innocence.

"About my . . . my intentions. No. Of course. Not up to him. Not
the occasion to mount a joint ambush."

I waited, smiling encouragingly, wondering how I might help him
along. It was touching that he was so nervous, though I did not know
why he should be.

"We'd do well against the world, you and I, if we joined forces,
don't you think?"

"I do."

"So you'll be my wife?"

This was it, then, the most important decision I'd ever make. I was
about to enter a binding contract to change my life, that would de-

termine my entire future, and now that it came to it, I hesitated. As Edmund himself had jested, I had seen so little of the world, so very little of men. In accordance with my father's last and very strict wishes, I'd still been to only a few sedate local gatherings at Ashton Court. No dances or dinners. I had not mixed in society like most girls of my age. All I really had to measure Edmund against were heroes from romances and ballads. He was kind and infinitely patient and very fine-looking, and from the moment I first saw him, I'd believed we were meant to be together, but how could I be certain he was the man to whom I wanted to be yoked forever? At the very back of my mind was a very troubling doubt, a notion that somewhere out there, someone else was waiting for me.

"Do you love me, Edmund?" I asked him, very quietly, realizing he had never actually said that he did.

He blushed. "I hope to have the chance to grow to love you more each day."

"And would you love me if I was not the heiress of Tickenham Court?"

"Dear Eleanor," he said, looking flustered. "What questions you do ask." I thought he was going to say that of course he would love me whatever my circumstances. But that was not what he said at all. "You look at me with those great searching eyes of yours that demand an answer, demand the truth, but how can I answer such a thing truthfully without hurting you? For you *are* the heiress of Tickenham Court. And if you were not, you would not be as you are."

"Oh," I said despondently, but I saw that what he said was entirely true. And I knew I should consider myself very fortunate even so, since so many courtships between gentry couples were conducted for financial reasons alone. I realized also that Edmund had answered my question bravely, for it would have been much easier for him to reassure with false platitudes.

"Be frank with *me* now," he said gently. "Would you have allowed yourself to fall in love with me if I was a chandler or an innkeeper, for instance, if I were not the son of a landed family, born to a life of squiring an estate like Tickenham Court?" He quickly put his finger across my lip. "No need to answer," he said with a dazzling smile. "I ask only so that you do not think less of me for the answer I gave you."

I experienced such a rush of love for him then, coupled with a powerful sense of romantic sacrifice, that suddenly the prospect of losing my home mattered to me not at all. I would give it up, gladly. In fact, I loved Edmund so very much that I was pleased I had something so valuable to offer to him.

Perhaps out of dismay that it was taking me such a long time to answer his proposal, Edmund sank down on one knee at my feet. "Say you will marry me, Eleanor, please?"

I was presented with a view of the top of his head. The sun had appeared from behind a cloud and a long golden ray slanted in through the window, lighting the spot where he knelt, waiting for me to say yes to him. It lit up his copper hair, surrounding him in a dazzling golden corona. I couldn't have been sent a more potent sign. It was my beacon, guiding me forward to a bright new future. I reached down to stroke the copper waves, almost expecting them to be flame hot or for something like lightning to crackle up through my fingers.

"Oh, Edmund my love, I will marry you. Gladly."

He scrambled to his feet and hugged me with relief. He couldn't really have doubted me. I couldn't really have doubted myself.

Mr. Merrick suddenly burst through the door, so I knew he had been listening outside.

"Blessings to you both," he said as he kissed me and shook Edmund's hand.

Edmund dug his hand in his pocket and brought out a twenty-shilling piece, put it between his teeth and bit the thin coin in two, handed me half. "Proof of our promise."

I reached out and closed my fingers over it, the sliver of broken metal that sealed my fate. The ceremony in church would just be a formality now that our contract was legally witnessed.

"When will we do it?" I asked. "When shall we be married?"

"Next spring, I thought," Edmund said.

"Oh yes," I said delightedly. A May wedding, with music and dancing and a feast in the meadow. I could hardly wait. I should be a May queen after all.

"I'll purchase an ecclesiastical license so that we can marry quietly and privately," Edmund said. "Without the banns being read and our affairs declared to the whole world."

The sun seemed to disappear behind the clouds again. "But I want the whole world to know . . ."

"Surely you don't want all the neighbors gawking and hundreds of noisy, drunken guests?"

Oh, but I do, I do.

"Practically all gentry marriages are by license now," he asserted. "It's quite the custom to marry without any fanfare on a weekday morning, with just two witnesses and the minister and sexton in attendance. I'd like our marriage to begin as it should go on, in quietness and tranquillity. In such troubled times as we were born into, that's all I've ever hankered after."

"But Edmund, I've always dreamed of a merry wedding."

"A license means we can marry in a parish away from home," he said with a puzzled but patient smile. "I know how much you want to see London. I thought we would marry there."

"London?" I felt a stir of excitement, even if it was hard to adjust to the idea of not marrying in Tickenham.

"I shall have to go to London just as soon as I've been to Suffolk to give the news to my father and brother," Edmund said happily. "I can't break it to Richard in a letter that I am betrothed. Oho, he will be so vexed to learn that I have found a bride before him!"

WILLIAM MERRICK WAS so gleeful that I half expected him to break into a jig. "Come the next floods, a survey will be conducted to ascertain exactly what extra channels are required to draw off the water," he explained with unbridled enthusiasm. "We also need to know what quantities of wood and stone will be needed."

"Then what happens?" I asked.

"We draw up the documents to petition the court of sewers and state our case."

"And how long does that take?"

"Impossible to say," Edmund said.

I knew very well that at Congresbury it had taken years, with the local commissioners delaying making any decision to task the area with drainage because they were not sure of their power to order new channels. Eventually the petitioners had had to obtain an act of Parliament, which had taken another age to obtain. The process here might be equally protracted.

"You can leave it all to me and my partners," William Merrick said to Edmund. "We will act as your agents, arrange all the financial and legal matters, instruct the surveyors and then the engineers. The court of sewers will supervise all the works and future maintenance. You yourself will have to do nothing."

"Except grant you a significant acreage of the drained land," I said wryly.

"A fair price for our labors," Mr. Merrick intoned. "We will be investing considerable sums in this project ourselves and that is the only reasonable way we can be recompensed. As we discussed, to keep all the newly drained land for yourself and the commoners and reward us with payment out of the rent is too slow a process to commend itself to any prospective investor."

"Rest assured, William," Edmund said mildly. "You will have your land."

Autumn

1675

I had hoped Edmund would take me back with him to Suffolk, but though Mr. Merrick had initially been in complete agreement with my wish to see the reclaimed Fens, he inexplicably changed his mind, forcing me to remain behind.

Edmund ended up staying in Suffolk for more than three months to tend his father, who was suffering so severely from gout in both feet that he could barely walk. I missed him very much, the more so because, though I sat at my little desk and composed long, impassioned letters to him almost daily, the sporadic ones he sent in reply continued to be stilted and a little awkward. I almost began to fear he did not miss me at all, until he wrote promising to return to Tickenham before traveling on to London, said he could not go so long without seeing me.

Even so, he did not come back until the swans started flying in for the winter, until the rivers had burst, and the three men from Bristol had already been to conduct their surveys. On the day of Edmund's return, after we had spent not an hour alone over a dinner of roast duck, Mr. Merrick arrived with the charts of the proposed drainage works.

He rolled out the parchment on the long refectory table in the parlor, and the three of us gathered round. I looked down at a carefully drawn map of the moor, the place I knew so intimately and loved best in the world. There were the existing pastures, Cut Bush and Church Moor and Court Leaze, the little humpbacked bridge where the boat was moored in winter. There were the boundary rhynes and tributaries that flowed from Cadbury Camp and on into the Yeo and Middle Yeo, toward the clay belt and out to sea.

"The course of the river will need to be widened and straightened, here and here." Mr. Merrick pointed a finger with a clean, perfectly trimmed nail to the beautiful natural curve in the Middle Yeo that would be bypassed. "The end of the old course may need to be dammed with stones. The banks will need to be strengthened, a new bridge built, and droves for the cattle. The earth thrown up for the cuts will be used to make embankments. The old drainage channels will be deepened and reoriented, and new ones will be dug that will link up to the existing drains. Here, here and here." He pointed again, at the places where the moor would be carved up by a network of new ditches. "We will need to explore the possibility of erecting a tidal sluice, strengthening the seawalls at Clevedon."

"It's a very ambitious plan," I said quietly.

"Well, what did you expect? There's no point going to all this effort just to turn common grazing pastures into meadows that produce an occasional hay crop. We might as well drain so thoroughly it can be properly cultivated. It could be worth fifteen shillings per acre, eight at least."

I hadn't noticed Bess come into the room with coffee. She set the tray down on the table without a word, with only a glance at the parchment. But I knew her well enough to know she would have overheard and seen everything and I felt like a conspirator, a traitor.

"Thank you, Bess." I touched the sleeve of her dress as she busied herself by my side arranging the cups. She paused and looked at my hand on her arm as if a pigeon had dropped its excrement on her. I removed it and she didn't so much as acknowledge me as she turned to go.

"This may be about how many shillings we can make per acre for you, sir," I said to Mr. Merrick when I was sure Bess was safely up the stairs. "For me it is more about improving local living conditions." I straightened to my full, if still insufficient, height. "You propose destroying the thickets that families have been using for generations, for wood to build their houses and to burn on their fires."

He shrugged. "Unavoidable, I am afraid."

"They have always been able to gather brushwood and firewood by the boatload. What right have we to take even that from them?"

He gave an indifferent wave of his hand. "That is for the courts to decide."

Edmund tried to mollify. "Eleanor, it is the surveyor's opinion that the moors of Tickenham, Nailsea and Kenn are in a lamentable condition compared with the rest of the county . . . the rest of this country, for that matter. They are the areas most badly affected by flooding but where the least has been done. Half measures are no good here. What they are proposing is no more than was begun at the monastery at Glastonbury before the Dissolution. We are only trying to ensure these moors are neglected no longer."

"There must be some reason they've been neglected?" I asked pointedly. "Why have speculators avoided Tickenham until now?"

"Peat lands are the hardest to drain," William Merrick explained nonchalantly. "Dig wet peat and it flows back to fill the pits. Build anything on it, sluices or walls, and come wet weather the foundations are rendered unstable. But with modern engineering methods these difficulties can be overcome."

"Just like that?"

"They are not insurmountable problems," Edmund said, placating.

I looked at him with dread weighing heavy in my chest. "Perhaps those difficulties can be solved, but they may be the least of our concerns." I ran my fingers across the plans. "Once all this gets under way, I am not so confident that the problem of the commoners and freeholders can be so easily overcome."

And if we could not overcome them . . . I heard an echo of my father again. I did not want to forfeit the goodwill of my neighbors. I did not want to stir up discord and live amongst people I had turned into my enemies.

I WENT TO FIND Bess in my chamber, where she was brushing the dried mud off the hems of one of my gowns, a relentless task, given that we lived in a world of mud.

"Bess, please stop what you're doing for a moment. I need to talk to you."

She set the brush down, obediently but not willingly, and waited with belligerent eyes for me to speak. I took a deep breath. "You know this has to happen sooner or later?" I realized I was echoing Mr. Merrick's argument and hated myself for it.

"I never thought I'd see it. I never thought you'd do it."

Edmund's argument then: "Everyone stands to gain."

"That's a lie, and you know it! We'll be left with a paltry share of land, and the meanest, wettest share at that. My father keeps four cows and if we no longer have the common he will not be able to keep so much as a goose, and you ask me what we *lose* by it?"

"Bess, can't you see what Edmund is trying to do? Can't you see how drainage will transform Tickenham, how our land will become dry and warm and solid and full of fruit, with well-fed oxen and the fattest sheep? It will be like summer all year long." I picked up the teasel she'd been using and waved it at her temptingly. "No more mud?"

"Nothing wrong with mud."

She held out her hand for the tool. I gave it to her with a sigh and she went back to her work. I had always told her everything, we had always shared our innermost thoughts. She was as dear to me as a sister. And yet she believed I had betrayed her.

Winter

1675

pears of icicles still hung outside the window, frost flowers clung to the leaded panes. The floodwaters had turned to ice that extended all the way to Yatton.

I had been sitting by the window for days, for an eternity it seemed, my face white as the snow with fear. I had watched the ice whiten and thicken, blessedly changing from the thinner, deadly kind that was strong enough to hinder the passage of boats and yet not able to bear the weight of a man. Bess had brought a brazier of hot coals from the kitchen but I felt as frozen as the earth and the water. Still I vowed to keep my vigil until Edmund appeared.

Today icicles were dripping, the frost flowers fading. The deadly ice would return. He should have been here by now; he should have been back from London days ago. He was no doubt waiting out the big freeze in some wayside inn, but I knew how perilous rutted tracks could be when they flooded and iced over. Horses frequently sank right up to their bellies in them. I was terrified in case he was lying frozen in an icy ditch somewhere, with his leg broken or his neck. I was terrified in case death should snatch him from me before my wedding day. I had worn the colors of mourning all my childhood. I did not want to feel like a widow before I had the chance to be a bride.

But now, at last, there were two dark shapes moving closer along the silver ribbon of causeway. Not one horse and rider but two. Just like the first time he had come to Tickenham.

Almost weeping with relief, I flung on my red riding cloak and raced outside as they came cantering into the yard, with their swords glinting like icicles at their sides.

Riding beside Edmund on an ebony Spanish stallion was a slim, black-haired boy, about twenty years of age. He was dressed in a long, elaborate coat and breeches of jade silk, with flounces of elegant white lace at collar and cuffs. He wore knee-high riding boots and a shallow, wide-brimmed hat that danced with exotic green ostrich plumes. In the sparkling white winter world, he looked like a prince. His hair was glossy-black as the King's, loosely curly and worn long enough to reach his shoulders. Framed by those black curls was the most exquisitely beautiful face: the face of an angel. His mouth was soft and sensitive with the slightest pout to his upper lip and little indents at the corners, like dimples. His eyes were heavy-lidded, long-lashed, and of a sparkling blue, deeper and brighter than my own.

Seated on his impressive mount, his slender fingers lightly resting on the tooled saddle, he affected an elegant, heroic pose that distinguished the Cavaliers I'd been brought up to so scorn and to fear, but who had therefore always held for me a glamorous allure. Everything about him marked him out as just the type of boy my father had warned me against. It almost felt that simply by admitting him onto this land I was doing something dangerous and forbidden, something that could only end in trouble.

Except that he was smiling at me, a smile of gentle charm, the loveliest smile I had ever seen.

I had the strangest feeling that I was falling. I had completely forgotten my anxiety of moments before. I had completely forgotten who I was, a girl betrothed to be married. I could barely tear my eyes away from this beautiful stranger who seemed no stranger to me at all, but like someone whose image I had carried forever in my heart, held in my imagination like a promise of something more, something better, of escape, of the essence of life itself. The very idea of him spoke of color and richness, of gaiety and beauty, in a life that had felt so drained of those things. And now at last he was here, he had come, and nothing could ever be the same for me again.

Edmund dismounted, bowed courteously and kissed my cheeks.

"I'm so glad you are safe, Edmund," I said. "I have been so worried."

"We would not have been here now if I'd had my way," he said. "We almost turned back. But Richard was adamant we keep going."

"Richard?" My lips shaped his name and I turned to him again as he removed his hat and swept it low. He bowed, his horse did a little prance, and he pulled back smoothly on the reins.

"I'm pleased to meet you, sir," I said. "Edmund did not say that you were to come with him. What brings you to Somersetshire?"

He gazed searchingly into my face for a moment, said in an unusually softly spoken voice: "You do."

The odd thing was that I was not at all surprised to hear him say it.

"As soon as I told Richard we were to be married, he insisted on coming to see you for himself," Edmund explained cheerily.

His friend swung down from his saddle, his silver, star-shaped spurs jangling in the crisp air. He was tall, though not as tall as Edmund, his shoulders and chest not as broad, tapering to narrow hips and long legs.

"I congratulate you on an excellent choice, Edmund, my friend," he said warmly, his eyes never leaving my face. "But even your glowing description did not do her justice. She is a dainty little maid for sure. I do fear, great ginger bear of a man that you are, you will crush her."

Edmund smiled, not seeming at all put out by such an overt reference to bedsport, and any embarrassment I might have felt at this sally was outweighed by a mild sense of indignation. "I assure you, sir," I said. "I am much stronger than I look."

Richard laughed, but kindly. "We shall soon see."

He turned back to his horse and unstrapped from the saddle a small portmanteau, inside which was a wooden box elegantly wrapped in silver tissue and ribbons. He presented it to me, his blue eyes twinkling. "A Twelfth Night gift for the bride-to-be, but since I am returning to London for the festivities, you may open it early."

"Thank you," I said, suddenly shy. "That was very thoughtful of you."

"Oh, you will find Richard a master of the grand gesture," Edmund quipped.

I could not think what the box might contain. Too large and heavy by far to be the jewelry or gloves that Edmund always gave to me. Books perhaps.

Edmund came forward and pecked my cheek. "I'll leave you in my friend's good care. The fire beckons and my toes need to thaw."

I was nonplussed. "We may as well all go inside."

"You need to open your present out here," Richard said. "Don't worry, Edmund," he added, turning his head slowly toward his friend but letting his eyes linger on mine. "I shall not let anything happen to her. I promise to take very good care of her."

"That is just what gives me cause for worry," Edmund joked in parting. "But even though I know what's in that box, I guarantee Eleanor will not fall at your feet like the rest of them. She's very different from other ladies."

"I can see that," Richard said quietly.

I untied the ribbon around the box and lifted off the lid. In the bottom lay two strips of metal attached to leather straps.

"You fasten them to your shoes," Richard explained. "They're for skating on the ice. They are all the fashion in the Fens since the Dutch brought the idea over. I had them forged specially," he added quietly. "I trust they're the right size. Edmund told me you had tiny feet."

"They look a perfect fit. Thank you," I said again, touched that he would have gone to so much trouble for a person he had never even met. I found that I could not look him in the face.

"Don't be shy with me," he said very gently. "I want to be your friend, if you will let me."

I raised my eyes, a strange feeling in my belly that was like excitement, but much nicer.

"Shall we be friends, do you think?" he asked, as if it mattered to him very much.

"Surely," I said briskly, trying to hide my mounting confusion.

I moved quickly over to rest against the mounting block, trying to work out how to put the skates on. It would never have occurred to me to ask for directions. But my fingers were numb with cold, which didn't help.

"Ouch! Damn." I dropped one of the skates onto the frozen yard and it rang out like the echo of the blacksmith's hammer that had beat it into shape. A bead of dark red blood had sprung up on the pad of my thumb.

"Be careful, they're very sharp."

"You could have told me that before."

"I didn't know you'd be so impatient."

I glanced up, prepared to glare at him, but he was smiling at me again, a tender smile, with neat white teeth softly biting his lower lip and his dark eyebrows drawn up together in a little quizzical peak.

"Do you think you could help me?" I asked him.

"With the greatest pleasure."

He sauntered over and took hold of my wrist with slender fingers that were partially covered by intricately patterned lace. "You are hurt," he said. "Let me see."

The ruby bead of blood had grown into a large droplet that was threatening to brim over and snake down my arm. Without preamble he lifted my hand and pushed my thumb into his beautiful mouth, and almost before I knew what was happening I felt his lips close around it, felt the hard, moist heat of his tongue slide round and over. He withdrew my thumb, looking with some amusement at my stunned expression: "All better now, I think."

My gaze shifted sideways in search of Edmund, not in an appeal for help, but for guidance as to how I should manage this friend of his, with whom I now felt entirely out of my depth. But Edmund had gone, which oddly helped put me at ease. He knew what his friend was like; had no doubt seen him behave this way countless times. He would have known that such flirtation meant nothing at all. I reminded myself that Richard Glanville came from another world, a morally corrupt and licentious world that my father despised, a world that was entirely different from and far more sophisticated and complex than my own. This was evidently how people behaved in that world. The very last thing I wanted was to appear gauche or prudish, so I should just have to do my best to play along.

Richard had gone on one knee at my feet to help me with the skates, but it did look for all the world as if he was going to ask me to be his wife.

"I am afraid you are too late, sir," I said teasingly. "I am already taken."

He carried on adjusting a strap on the skate and, without fully lifting his head, smiled again, flicked up his sapphire eyes to look at me through his lashes, lowered them again to check what he was doing, raised them once more so swiftly that they sparkled. It was an extraordinary coquettish gesture that left my bones feeling as if they had been turned to water. "Maybe Edmund and I shall fight a duel over you," he said. "Would you like that?"

What was it my father had said about Cavaliers being murderous ruffians who would duel over a game of tennis? "I should not like either of you to be wounded, or worse, for my sake."

He lifted my right foot and placed it on his thigh. "Already you care for me so much you don't want me to be hurt?"

"Not before you have taught me how to skate, at least. I should like to learn to swim too. You are very good at it, I hear."

"You'd have to undress for me to teach you that." He half raised the hem of my skirt. "May I?"

It took me half a moment to realize he only needed to see what he was doing with the skate, was not seeking permission to strip me naked there and then. He was just a boy, but he seemed so cocksure, so well versed in the ways of men that it was I, a betrothed woman, who was made to feel young and naive. I smiled down at this angel-faced, dark-haired boy who would seduce me away from his friend and said, "Please do."

He tucked my skirt out of the way, cupped his hand around my heel. One of his fingers slipped over the top of my shoe and caressed my silk stocking. I wanted to snatch my foot away and yet I did not, could not. I clutched at the mounting block for support, sure that my legs would give way beneath me as shivers of sensation shot all the way up the insides of my thighs and carried on deep inside me until it felt as if the ice was cracking and splintering all around me and I was melting from the inside out.

He deftly secured the straps across first one foot and then the other. "Have you never worn pattens?"

"No."

"You don't know what they are, do you?"

"Please don't mock me, sir."

"I would never mock you," he said seriously. "Ladies in London strap pattens under their shoes," he explained. "So that they don't get spoiled in the filth."

I laughed out loud at the very idea. "London filth could never be so bad as living on a marsh! Here we just grow used to having dirty, wet feet."

He stood, dusted down his green breeches. "You deserve much better. Desire it too, I think."

"Do you now?" I stood up and immediately wobbled over.

"Whoa! Steady." He caught both my hands in his, held them for a moment longer than was necessary, blue eyes locked with mine, a strange expression in them now that was almost like sadness. He rested me back against the mounting block again. "Wait for me."

There was a small voice speaking inside my head. I refused to listen to it but it whispered: I have been waiting for you all of my life.

Richard had quickly strapped skates to his own boots. "Ready?"

I nodded, not trusting myself to speak, and then, gripping his arm for support, I hobbled with him across to the edge of the ice.

He let go of me and strode gracefully out onto it with complete mastery and control. "One step at a time," he cautioned, spinning round to face me with a hiss of blades cutting ice. "I suspect it is completely against your nature, but you need to go slowly at first."

It couldn't be as hard as all that, could it? I stepped out determinedly and immediately felt my foot slip away alarmingly beneath me. I tightened my muscles and froze.

"Not as easy as you thought?" Richard's eyes sparkled as bright as sunlight on water. He offered me his hand and I took it. I was glad of the tightness of his grip as he slid forward, pulling me with him. I wobbled once but didn't fall.

He slipped his hand beneath my cloak and around my waist, and I felt the hard strength of his young body against mine as he held me steady at his side.

"Right, left, march," he commanded. I had just enough time to think how, spoken in his softly melodious voice, military language was powerful and compelling, rather than friendly but formal as it had sounded to me on Edmund's lips. "Hold tight on to me."

We shot forward with dizzying speed. I was gliding beside him, not daring to take my eyes off my feet, appearing and disappearing beneath my skirt, following his lead. It was more like dancing than marching, a mysterious, forceful kind of dance, and I could feel the muscles of Richard's strong legs working as they pressed against mine, feel his arm encircling me tight, our skates slicing parallel lines with a swishing sound, like a sword being drawn, or the noise a comet or a falling star might make if only you could hear it.

And then I looked up and realized how fast we were going, a dizzying, magnificent speed such as I had never thought possible. Faster than a galloping stallion, faster than the wind.

He glanced at me, smiling with pleasure at my obvious delight.

"Let me go," I said. "I can do it now."

"Are you sure?"

"Yes."

Suddenly I was on my own, racing forward. I pushed my legs into the glide, harder and harder, until I picked up even more speed. I screamed with glee but the wind snatched away my voice, my very breath. I cut an arc toward the causeway, the sunken trees whizzing past, the clouds wheeling overhead.

I lifted my arms to each side of me like wings, as I liked to do when I was running. This time I was really soaring. My cloak flew out behind me. At last I really did have wings like the swans and the butterflies. I was no longer earthbound. For the first time in my life I felt utterly free. I was flying.

I skated right into Richard Glanville's arms. He caught me as I skidded to an abrupt halt and I was thrown against the hardness of his chest, windblown, laughing, my face aglow. "You never told me how to stop."

"I never expected you to go so fast."

I was motionless but the world had carried on spinning around me faster than ever, the trees and clouds whipped up like a storm. I clung to him as if he was the still center of my orbit. I couldn't let go of him or I was sure I would fall. He had taught me how to fly. Like an eagle, he had seized me and carried me up with him into the infinite sky, and if he released me I should come crashing down again and be shattered.

"That was extraordinary."

"It is you who are extraordinary, Eleanor Goodricke." There was not a hint of flirtation in his voice anymore. He had slipped his hands inside my cloak again, on either side of my small corseted waist, and though I was perfectly balanced now, he had not let go of me. "You are utterly fearless," he said. "A little force of nature." Wisps of hair had blown free across my face. He brushed them away with the tip of his finger. "A little Viking. Golden flames without signifying golden flames within, I wonder?"

I slipped backward away from him, like a boat casting off from the shore. "That is for my husband to find out."

He held on to my extended arms until only our fingertips were touching.

As Edmund had once been a beacon of light in the dark hall, so now was this boy, in rich green velvet, a single point of color in a white wilderness, as glamorous and gleaming and as rare and precious as an emerald.

He must not be. Could never be. I loved Edmund. I had always loved Edmund. I must not let myself be attracted to this man. He was no more than a boy in any case, a dangerous, raffish boy, and I was promised to another. I was promised to his friend.

I twirled round as if I was in the tailor's shop once more, trying on my first gown. With a swirl of my crimson cloak I skated off in a wide sweep, into the sparkling white world.

"You learn very quickly," Richard called.

I shouted back to him over my shoulder, "You'll never keep up with me now."

His voice came to me on an icy wind. "I shall enjoy trying."

THE NEXT DAY WAS one of unremittingly bright sunshine of surprising warmth and strength for the time of year, and it raised the temperature well above freezing. By mid-morning it was slowly but surely thawing the ice, laying upon it a shimmering sheen of treacherous water, ruining any hopes I'd had of being able to go skating again and practically confining all three of us to the house, since the conditions were not fit for riding either.

"How about a game of dicing," Edmund suggested when he had finished his small beer and cheese. "Or cards perhaps?"

"I'd rather chess," Richard said amiably.

"I'm sure you would." Edmund grinned. "But at least I have half a chance of beating you if some luck is involved." He glanced at me considerately. "Besides, only two can play chess."

"Oh, please don't worry on my account," I said, reaching for Edmund's hand and giving it a quick pat. "I'll read."

"Maybe Eleanor should play against you, Richard," Edmund suggested. "She beats me more often than not."

"No," I said quickly, picking up a travel journal that had just arrived from the bookseller's. "You two play."

Bess brought a tray of hot, spiced cider, and I made myself comfortable in the chair by the fireside as Richard and Edmund drew up chairs to the little table by the window and perused the chessboard.

I read a little, sipped the cider, watched as Richard reached across to pick up a black marble knight, the trailing lace at his cuff almost upending Edmund's castle. I went back to the story of a sailing ship battling the storms of Cape Horn and had read a dozen or so pages, become quite lost in the adventure, when, with that strange sixth sense that tells us we are being observed, I looked up to find Richard's eyes resting on me. Edmund was deciding on his next move, totally absorbed in his pawns and knights, and I wondered how long his friend had been studying me. As our eyes met he gave me a lovely, enigmatic smile. There was a fragility about it, as if despite the physical strength that made him such a good rider, swimmer and skater, there was within him a part that was not strong, could easily be damaged, had perhaps been damaged already, and it stirred in me an unexpected protectiveness. He seemed so different today from the boy I had skated with, not nearly so self-assured, and I was intrigued by the change in him. Had something shaken his confidence, or was that confidence just a disguise, a mask that easily slipped?

I smiled back at him and his blue eyes seemed to light up, illuminating his whole face. I was struck afresh by his beauty, the almost feminine prettiness which contrasted so starkly with his long, lean legs, stretched out in front of him, booted ankles crossed, in a way that was utterly, powerfully male.

Edmund made his move and Richard languidly picked up his cider, drank, turned back to the chess pieces. He moved his black queen without appearing to give it any thought at all.

"Hah." Edmund gave his castle a triumphant nudge. "Checkmate."

Richard lounged back in the chair. "So it is," he said with an air of indifference.

"Well, well," Edmund chortled. "When was the last time I won against you at chess?"

"I can't remember, it was so long ago." Richard smiled very charmingly.

"You've not been concentrating, lad," Edmund replied. "You've not had your mind on the game at all."

THE EVENING WAS MARKED by the most magnificent winter sunset. Badly needing to escape the house, I walked down to the bridge the better to enjoy it. The vast sky was streaked with crimson and bright orange, soft pink and mauve, and it was reflected in the wide sheets of icy water. It was as though I hung suspended in a shimmering world of radiant color.

As if from nowhere the sky was filled with swarms of chattering starlings, a black mass against the inflamed sky, swirling and spilling down in unbroken ribbons to fill the branches of the bare trees, then swirling up again as if blown by unseen winds, the whole throng plunging, turning in on itself, sucked upward in a spiraling current and then sweeping out again horizontally. How did they do it? How did they all know which way to go? It was an awesome sight, and I was struck with an almost desperate desire to preserve the magic and the wildness of this place for my children, and for theirs. It suddenly seemed the greatest tragedy and folly that it would be lost.

Or maybe it would not be, I thought, ever hopeful.

What made William Merrick and his partners so sure they would succeed where more grandiose schemes had failed, where even the agents of the crown had failed? King James himself had been thwarted in his repeated efforts to drain the peat lands of King's Sedgemoor. Cornelius Vermuyden, the greatest drainage engineer there was, under a commission from Cromwell, as Lord Protector, had his bill rejected because the tenants and freeholders did not consent. His skill as a drainage engineer, his ownership of a third of the land and his position of influence could not prevail against the opposition of the commoners.

And there was similar opposition in Tickenham. I sensed it now whenever I went up to the village with Mary, in my daily dealings with the servants. Talks with local families were under way, to settle and untangle the complicated claims for common rights, to establish the validity of the claims and allot land in proportion, but resentment seethed not far beneath the surface. It expressed itself in surliness, small acts of defiance that became increasingly annoying and disturbing. Ink spilled on one of my father's books and nobody admitting fault, general refusal to pay rents on time, my little mare lamed by a rusted iron nail that had mysteriously been driven into her hoof. It could have been an accident, but I suspected it was not.

It was not just the commoners who were implicated, but uplands farmers and freeholders and tenants who had enjoyed unlimited grazing rights here and had taken cattle in for fattening from other areas for a fee.

I didn't like to think what would happen if these near and far-flung neighbors of mine were to rise up and act together to try to put a stop to what we had determined to do. It had happened in the Fens: mobs and gangs destroying the work of the engineers, ripping out the sluices, filling in the drains as quickly as they were dug. I could imagine all too easily how such violence could rip apart this little community—after all, it had happened in the civil wars.

I felt the lightest touch on the small of my back, turned to see that it was Richard, not Edmund, who had come to find me. My heart gave an odd little flutter.

"There will still be sunsets even when the water is gone, you know," he said, perceptively.

"But they won't look like that."

He raised his eyes skyward, making them seem bigger and bluer and more beautiful than ever. "No," he admitted softly, lowering them slowly once again to look out over the lake, and then at me. "They won't."

The colors were changing, deepening to shades of luminous rose-pink. Like this, with the sky lit with the most wondrous shades and the swans and wild geese like dark silhouettes sailing on a bright sea, it was impossible to see it as a dark or unwholesome place. It was surely the loveliest place on earth. Even when the color faded and the mist swirled in, it brought with it a mysterious sense of peace, a special haunting beauty that I realized now I would miss dreadfully. I listened to the wild bugle call of the swans, the sepulchral clap of their great white wings, and I felt such a sense of loss it was almost overwhelming.

"You feel bound to this place," Richard said, not a question but a statement of fact. "And it to you. For as long as you live. You do not want it to change, to be lost. It will be like losing a part of yourself that you can never get back."

I turned to him, startled. "Yes." I might have said more, but he looked almost grief-stricken and I was afraid of treading too close to the source of whatever was causing him such hurt.

"Edmund is so keen for it to happen," I said.

"But what about you? What do you want?"

"Oh, nobody really stopped to ask me."

"I am asking you now."

"Edmund is so certain that what we are doing is for the good of all," I said after a moment. "I wish I shared that certainty."

"Better that you do not."

"Is it?"

"It means you care," he said. "You care about what it will mean to the people who live here."

I should have been astounded that this man who rode Spanish stallions and was dressed now in a velvet cloak and the finest lace should spare even a thought for commoners and tenants. And yet I was not at all.

"It is not only their land and their rights they are losing," he said with fierce empathy. "It is their independence, their ability to provide the basic necessities of life for their families that is at stake. And pride. There is pride in being able to put bread into your children's mouths, in seeing them grow strong on milk from your own cow and eggs from your own hens. Edmund has no comprehension—how could he be expected to have? How could you? And yet you do, don't you? You think about such things."

I smiled. "Sometimes too much, perhaps." I paused, glanced at him. "You too, I think."

"Since time began, men have been prepared to fight and die to defend their land," he said. "It makes no difference if that land is a miserable strip, good for nothing but a few vegetables, or a thousand acres of fields and meadows." It was as if he had ceased talking about the commoners now, nameless people he did not know, but was speaking from some direct personal experience, and I was sure then that his must have been one of the Royalist families who had suffered from the sequestration of their estate under Cromwell—except that he was surely too young to remember it, to feel it so deeply. So deeply that I felt entirely prevented from asking him about it.

I shivered and, seeing that I was cold, he wordlessly took off his cloak, draped it around my shoulders. Heat drawn from his body still clung to the fabric of it and I pulled it closer about me than I needed to for warmth alone. The collar felt very soft against my cheek.

He cupped his hands round his mouth, blew on his fingers.

"Now I am warm and you are cold." I smiled. "We should go back."

"Not yet," he said. "It is so lovely here, and I shall be leaving for London in the morning."

"You are very welcome to stay," I said, the words coming unbidden. "For as long as you like."

"That is kind of you," he said, his tone strangely tight. "But I cannot."

As we walked back to the house I wondered at what he had meant, wondered at the sadness behind his beautiful eyes, but as we were approaching the yard something broke through my thoughts. My nostrils twitched and I inhaled, like a wild creature alert to the first sign of danger. A smell of smoke. The air over the stables was thick with a gray pall that was not mist. I almost heard the crackle of the flames before I saw them, bright and luminous as the sunset had been. I heard the panicked whinnying and snorting of the horses, the frantic thud of their hooves against the stable door. The whole of the building was ablaze.

I ran, shouting for someone to come, for someone to help.

Ned was already running from the kitchen garden.

"The horses," I yelled. "Help me get them out."

"I'll go," Richard said to me. "You stay here."

But I was already inside the burning stable. The smoke was so thick and billowing that I couldn't see where I was going, couldn't breathe. I choked and covered my mouth with the edge of my cloak. My eyes stung as if scorched and the heat was a solid barrier in front of me, pressing me back, tongues of fire leaping and writhing. I bent my arm up over my face, pushed forward through flames that were licking through straw and bedding, were leaping from the roof and the hayloft and from the bubbling, cracking walls. I smelt the bitter stench of singed horsehair.

The horses were bucking, their eyes rolling in terror. With my hand on the halter and using the most soothing words I could marshal, I dragged out Edmund's hunter, let him bolt for safety in the direction of the churchyard, where Richard's stallion was already heading. I dived back in for my little gray mare and her foal, not able to find my way to their stall. The walls of the stable were sheets of fire now, the roaring sound like an angry mob. A length of timber crashed to the ground in front of me in an eruption of crimson sparks which stung like demonic gnats from Hell. I couldn't see where I was, which way I had come and which was the way out. Then I felt a hand grasp mine, pull me back just in time as another beam came smashing down on the place where I had been standing a second before.

"This way!" Richard shouted.

I could barely see him. He was just a hand to hold on to in the fiery darkness and I gripped it tight, let him lead me to safety.

"They're all out, miss," Ned shouted, leading a cob in one hand and the carthorse in the other.

I bent double and coughed, rubbed my sore, stinging eyes.

"Here, drink this." From somewhere Richard had produced a cup of water and I tipped it gratefully down my dry throat. "Are you all right?" he asked.

"Yes. Thank you. Are you?"

He nodded, raised his arm and turned his head into it to wipe the smuts and sweat off his brow.

Bess and Mistress Keene and Jane the cookmaid were all running back and forth across the yard with water buckets, doing their best to douse the flames. I ran to Jane and took the other side of the handle, helping her carry a heavy bucket, to lift it up and throw the contents over the fire. I was about to run and fetch some more when someone stopped me.

"It's no use, Eleanor." It was Edmund who held me back as the flames leapt toward the sky. "It's no use."

I pulled away from him in a fury. The flames were licking round the whole of the building, fanned by the breeze that was blowing off the moor, toward the cow barn . . . toward the house. "We can't just give up, damn it! We must at least try to contain it, make sure it doesn't spread. Please, God," I heard myself say. "Don't let it spread to the house."

"It won't," Richard said.

I stopped fighting against Edmund for a moment and looked to his friend, his face still smeared with soot just as mine must be and his eyes full of compassion, as if he felt my anxiety in his very core and wanted only to ease it. "It is raining," he said, with an upward glance at the darkening sky. "The rain will put the fire out."

Rain was by no means a rare occurrence in Somersetshire in September, but this felt like a miracle. It was just a fine drizzle, so fine that I had not felt it, but in minutes it turned into a typical autumn deluge of heavy, fat raindrops which poured down from the darkening sky and did for us the work of a hundred men and buckets.

I let it lash me, soak me, saw it washing the soot in black streaks from my skin. I turned my face to the rain as I usually would to the sun, letting it pour down upon me, over me, cleanse and cool me. I had never been so glad of rain in all my life. I opened my lips and drank it in, letting it rid me of the foul, choking taste of soot. The taste of the water on my tongue was sweet as wine.

In hardly any time the stable had been reduced to a smoking ruin, a blackened skeleton. It was hissing angrily like a snake, would smolder for a long time yet.

"What could have started it?" Edmund asked.

"I don't know."

There was straw and hay aplenty in the stable, and when Ned had slept there, before he married Bess, there would have been tallow candles with naked flames. But Ned had not slept above the horses for years. Nobody did now.

Richard bent down, picked up something that had been discarded or dropped in haste on the ground. He held it out in his hand and looked at me. It was an empty liquor flask, and no words were necessary. *Since time began, men have been prepared to fight and die to defend their land.* The fire was no accident. It was no coincidence that, as the day when the drainage project would start grew ever closer, a fire had been started. Discontent had ignited something dangerous and sinister.

I WAS KNEELING on the rush-strewn church floor by the altar, helping Mary arrange branches of greenery to decorate it for Christmas. The whole place was filled with the warm, spicy scent of the rosemary and bay that adorned the pews. We'd lit a dozen candles and the light of them gleamed on the gilded candlesticks and dark oak.

We were keeping the front of the aisle clear for the musicians and theater troupe to perform the nativity play. Afterward there would be fiddlers and drummers and a wassail procession, dancing and feasting and blindman's buff. If I was to be denied a grand wedding celebration, I would at least enjoy the Christmas festivities to the full. I was determined to find the charm in the cake and be Queen for a Day.

"It will be wonderful to be married in London, even quietly," Mary said, knowing where my thoughts often strayed these days.

I handed her another bough of holly. "You must come with us. Please say you will?"

She was expertly twisting ivy around the holly and didn't take her eyes off her task. "We shall already be there."

I assumed she meant she'd be visiting her mother and little brother, the only members of her family who had survived the plague and who still lived in Southwark.

She stopped what she was doing and glanced at me. "I've been meaning to tell you, Eleanor. John and I are leaving Tickenham. We're returning to live in London."

I felt as if I had suddenly lost my way in a dark wood. "Leaving?"

"I promised your father that I would take care of you, but you are grown now and about to be a wife. It's my mother and my brother Johnnie who need looking after now."

She came to put her arms around me, as if I were still the orphaned little girl I often felt myself to be, the little girl who disguised herself in the colorful gowns of a lady and hid behind a pretense of self-possession and poise. "Come now. It's not so bad. You can visit whenever you like."

I thought I might cry. "But I shall miss you so much."

"I shall miss you too." She was past thirty but she still looked young, her waist and breasts only slightly more plump. "You have been my blessing, Eleanor. Each time another month passed and still I bled, I thanked God for the little girl he had already given to me. That though the cradle was empty, my arms were always full."

"Oh, Mary."

"It is you who showed me my vocation, with your love of learning and constant quest for knowledge. You were our first little pupil, always the most special. John and I are going to run a boarding school."

I grasped both of her hands. "You will be excellent tutors, both of you. There could be none better. Oh, I wish I could come, Mary. I wish I could come with you and help you with your school."

Her smile hid a hint of concern. "Your life now is with your new husband, with Edmund." She peered into my face. "Eleanor, you do still want to marry him?"

I glanced away. "Of course."

I could not tell her that my most precious possessions were now the little skates that Richard Glanville had given to me, could not tell her of the strange, secret vice I did not seem able to give up. Every night before I went to sleep I took the skates out of their box and stroked them, ran my finger along the blade, dangerously close to the sharp edge, risking a cut, almost wanting a cut, wanting to feel that sharp sting of pain so I could better remember the warmth of his mouth as he had sucked my pain away.

I was no wiser about the source of his own pain, was afraid that if I tried to talk to Edmund about him, if I so much as allowed Richard's name to touch my lips, I would give myself away.

"You've been so good to me, Mary," I said.

"It is kind of you to say so, but I'm not so sure your father would agree. I fear he'd be of the opinion I'd led you a long way off the path of righteousness."

"No, he wouldn't."

She looked at me, considering her words before she spoke. "Do you remember the prayers we used to say, Eleanor? How we came when the church was empty, like it is now, and we lit candles for all those we loved who were no longer with us: your sister and mother and father, and my father and brothers and sisters, who had all perished in the plague year? Do you remember that we asked that they be safe and happy in Heaven?"

I nodded.

"Eleanor, you do know it's only Catholics who say prayers for the souls of the dead?"

There had seemed nothing wrong in it at the time. It had seemed a fitting thing to do.

"In my heart, I converted to Catholicism a long time ago," Mary continued, keeping her voice as quiet as if the ancient stones of the church might be listening.

I stared at her in utter disbelief. "You are Catholic."

"I would never have practiced while I had you to mind. It would have felt like the most dreadful betrayal of your father. Now our work here is done and we are leaving, I am free to follow my conscience."

I had been so steeped in anti-Catholicism that I couldn't help but look at her with a mixture of dismay and horror. I turned away, toward the simple altar. Once so carefully divested of crucifixes, gilded cloths or other obvious Catholic trappings, it looked almost Papist now, festooned with greenery and ablaze with candles.

"And John is a Catholic too? But how can he be? When he delivered his sermon on Gunpowder Treason Night he thanked God for delivering England from the hellish plots of the Papists."

Mary smiled. "John is a follower, not a leader. As you are well aware, he is easily influenced. He can see all sides and goes wherever the wind blows him, so long as he believes it to be God's wind. He would like nothing more than for England to be a haven of religious pluralism. He was a Puritan while ever Puritans were shouting the loudest, until the new laws meant he would have lost his pulpit if he clung to such ideology. He was happy to be called a Protestant then, though your father could still bring out the Puritan in him. Now I am to become a Catholic, he'll convert with me. I can help him see the reason in it."

I was suddenly consumed with terror for her and gripped her arm. "But Mary, it's so dangerous. If only you could hear the things Mr. Merrick and his Bristol friends discuss over their claret. The Duke of York's declaration of his conversion to Rome, and the Test Act that has expelled Catholics from public office . . . they have made fear of Popery greater than ever. It is worse for Catholics even than it was when everyone blamed the Great Fire on the treachery and malice of a Papist plot. There have been Pope burnings all across London and here in Somersetshire, in Bridgewater."

"It's almost as if the civil war has never ended," Mary agreed quietly. "There's no safe side to be on. One moment our enemy is the Papists, the next the Dutch, then it's the French, or even our own neighbors. Intolerance and suspicion are as rife as they ever were when the Roundheads and Cavaliers were slaughtering each other in their beds. Effigies of the Pope are burned on bonfires. I'd not even be surprised to see Thomas Knight cry witchcraft when he sees you chasing after butterflies. It's not safe to be different, but different you are. And so am I. And what is the good of living if we must live a lie, if we cannot be true to ourselves?"

I stared at the candlelit altar, lovely and glittering and, to be quite honest, far more appealing to me now than it ever was under my father's direction. Just as the maypole had once looked lovely to me too, even though I knew it to be evil and Popish. But was it truly? I was beside my father's grave again, in my black taffeta funeral cape, and the ground was falling away beneath my feet. Was nothing at all I had grown up believing actually true?

I looked at Mary, the first Catholic I had ever known. There were so many questions buzzing in my head, I did not know where to begin. "I was taught to despise Catholics. I was taught that they are Hell spawn, the Antichrist."

"Except that you do not despise me, do you?"

"Never."

She smiled. "Do I appear any different to you now at all? Do I look evil to you?"

I looked deep into her soft brown eyes and slowly shook my head. "Of course you do not."

I realized I was no better than the commoners who had always been prejudiced against me, for being a Puritan and a girl with an interest in science.

"You are not your father," Mary said gently. "You do not have to hate Catholics because he did. Your mind is your own."

"What if I do not always know my mind?"

"That means it is an open one like John's, a good one."

Was it? I thought of Richard, the most beautiful, intriguing boy, a boy my father would have reviled.

I realized I had not even asked Mary the reason for her conversion. "Why, Mary?"

"My namesake, for one," she replied simply. "Far better for womanhood to have saintly, motherly Mary as their guide than to be left with only wicked Grandmother Eve. Don't you think?"

I could not disagree with her.

"The Catholics have women for saints, too." She let me ponder that for a moment. "I believe, in time, women will accomplish much in this world as well, by example from the next."

THE WEEK AFTER CHRISTMAS, Edmund received a letter from his brother, telling of a severe flood in the Fens that had caused much damage: washed away whole cottages, uprooted ancient trees, torn down bridges, ripped up gravestones, made ancient droves and trackways vanish as if they had never been.

"But I thought there could be no more floods now that the land had been reclaimed?" It felt as though my heart had come up into my throat and I swallowed hard, as if to force it down.

"So did I. So did we all." Edmund stared at the letter in disbelief, then concentrated on folding it very slowly, as if it was important to follow the original creases exactly. "It seems the dried-out peat is shrinking. And as the surface of the land dries, crumbs of soil are picked up and carried away by the fen winds. The rivers are now running higher than the fields around them."

I was horrified by the image of such an upside-down, unnatural world. It seemed the stuff of nightmares. My father's nightmares. "That's why Mr. Merrick didn't want me to go to Suffolk with you, isn't it? He didn't want me to see what was happening."

"My brother says the fear is that serious floods will become commonplace."

"So Papa was right about that after all," I said tremulously. "We are fools to think we can tamper with God's creation."

"No," Edmund said firmly. "We learn by making mistakes. What the engineers are trying to accomplish is a monumental feat. There will inevitably be setbacks."

"But we must call a halt to the plans for Tickenham," I said resolutely. "Edmund, you do see that? We cannot proceed until we know how to avoid these same problems here."

"I doubt even William Merrick and his associates would argue with the prudence of that."

So, a reprieve.

Spring

1676

The next time Richard Glanville came to Tickenham Court, he came riding up the lane past the rectory in sharp spring sunshine and apple-blossom-scented air, with an invitation from our most illustrious neighbor, George Digby no less, to attend a banquet and dancing at Clevedon Court that very same evening. I had been gathering marsh orchids to take to Bess's mother, whose rheumatism was troubling her so much she wasn't able to venture far to pick any for herself.

"We're all three of us invited," Richard said, leaning forward, his arms lightly crossed and resting on the pommel as he smiled very gallantly down at me from the elegantly tooled saddle of a powerful Barbary bay. His dark curls were tumbling to his shoulders—in a way my father would have considered a sure sign of a debauched and decadent character, I swiftly reminded myself. He was more modestly dressed than before, though the riding suit of smooth brown wool that he was wearing did not detract from the beauty of his face, but rather threw it into relief, like a lovely and perfect pearl set upon a bed of homespun. "Digby's welcome extends to me, to you and to Edmund," he said, then glanced toward the house. "I take it he's here?"

"He is." It was Edmund's last visit to Tickenham before he became my husband and Tickenham his permanent home. Before Tickenham became his.

Richard swung down from the horse, stood before me with a cursory examination of the bouquet of purple and white flowers in my hand. "You look as delighted by my news as a little maid who's never been dancing before," he said, with gentle amusement. "Or is it that you are just pleased to see me?"

He had the most expressive brows, I noticed, silky, dark and high-arched. The way they had of drawing up together at a slightly oblique slant when he smiled was very endearing and highlighted the humor in his eyes.

"As a matter of fact, I haven't ever been to a dance before," I said, a little defensively. "But I do know all the steps."

"Then, since it is I who brought your first invitation, I hope you will reward me by allowing me to have the first dance with you?"

There was invitation to much more than a dance in those lovely twinkling blue eyes of his, but I was wise to his flirtation now and met them boldly. "I would be honored to dance with you," I said. "So long as Edmund does not mind."

He looked so discouraged and unhappy that it made me feel as if I had been unnecessarily cruel, and I was struck again by a strangely compelling need to reassure him in some way.

"How ever did you manage it?" I asked brightly. "I've lived but four miles away from Clevedon Court all my life and not once have I been past the gatehouse."

He gave a nonchalant shrug. "I met one of the Digby girls and her father out riding just now and I introduced myself."

I laughed. "You just rode up and introduced yourself to the Earl of Bristol?"

His confidence was apparently entirely restored, I was glad to see, and he smiled at me as if to say, What of it?

George Digby, the Earl of Bristol, was one of the most striking figures of our time, a great orator in the House of Commons and a remarkably handsome person of irrepressible good spirits. He had assumed a great mystique for me because of the staunch disapproval he had earned from my father for his role as advisor to the first King Charles. The Digby family had suffered dispossession at the hands of Oliver Cromwell's army, and only recently had Clevedon Court been restored to them.

Richard turned his head and flashed a smile at Edmund, who was hurrying over, face lit with pleasure at the sight of his friend. He trapped him in a rough hug that Richard returned with as much affection.

"I cannot wait for a banquet before I eat," Edmund said, after they had discussed the invitation. "I'm ravenous."

"When are you not?" Richard said laughingly. "Shall we go and catch something fresh for an early supper, then?"

He and Edmund rode off over the moor with their fishing rods, and I went inside to fetch a book. My father's library had been returned to me in its entirety after my betrothal, and I chose a volume, going to sit on the sunny grass by the walnut tree to read. I found I could not settle but kept reading the same line over and over again without taking it in. All I saw before me was Richard Glanville's face, his smile, as if it had been burned onto my brain.

The shadows were lengthening when Edmund came back with a brace of gleaming pike.

"Well done," I said as I stood and he kissed my cheek, handing over his catch with pride. "We shall have them baked with almonds. Where's Richard?"

"Oh, he wanted to stay at the river a while longer."

Richard rode up not long after, his own catch slung over his shoulder. He had taken off his coat and his frilled white linen shirt was undone, revealing a scattering of fine, dark chest hairs. I clasped my hands together, as if I did not trust myself not to slip my fingers inside his shirt to stroke them.

"We'd go hungry if it was left to Edmund here," he said to me sweetly, producing not a brace but a half-dozen larger fish, their translucent tails almost as wide as the span of his hand. He stuck his tongue into the side of his cheek. "The rivers here are very bountiful, if only you know what you are about."

Edmund was shaking his head in affectionate disbelief. "How the devil did you manage to land all those?" He chuckled softly. "I should have known you'd not be outdone, especially when there is a pretty lady to impress. Eleanor, you must look suitably amazed by this plenitude or the effort will have all been in vain."

"It is an excellent catch," I said offhandedly, keeping my eyes very firmly fixed on the fish rather than the person who had caught them.

I WAS THANKFUL THAT I had a new gown to wear to Clevedon Court. It was made of sea-green silk with a beaded stomacher and a long, tight, off-the-shoulder bodice. Bess arranged my hair so that long elaborate curls framed my face, and decorated it with tiny pearls. I wore an emerald necklace and eardrops that Edmund had given me.

Richard had been waiting in the great hall, and as I descended the stairs from the solar, he turned and fastened his eyes on me.

"You look beautiful," he said, almost bleakly.

"Thank you."

Standing alone in the gloomy, cavernous hall, he looked very young, troubled, a little lost. He wore a heavy pewter ring on the middle finger of his left hand, was twisting it back and forth in a way that must have chafed at his skin. I wanted to put my hand over his and hold his fingers still. Wanted at least to ask him if he was all right.

But Edmund came up behind me then and wrapped me in a dark green velvet cloak that had once belonged to my great-aunt Elizabeth, who had passed quietly and peacefully from this world the winter before Edmund and I were betrothed. "Time to go," Edmund said.

It was a clear night, almost a full moon, and the wide, wild, featureless landscape was flooded with a milk-white light. Edmund wore a topaz brocade vest and coat, and Richard was very elegant in a coat of burgundy silk, so that as we rode out three abreast at dusk, I felt like a princess with her handsome young courtiers trotting on either side, swords at their hips.

As we made our way up the Tickenham Road to Clevedon, we were joined by a stream of fine coaches. More coaches were already drawn up outside the house, where flaming torches had been lit. Clevedon Court was a medieval manor on a much grander scale than Tickenham, with a massive thirteenth-century tower and a great hall twice the size and several hundred years older than Tickenham Court's.

Tonight it was lit up even brighter than a church at Christmastime. Candlelight gleamed on the oak-paneled walls and long polished tables laid with silver platters and engraved glasses. Musicians were playing: lute, viola, cello, oboe and bassoon.

We were introduced to George Digby, the Earl of Bristol, resplendent in crimson and gold, but I was so overawed just to be in his presence in such magnificent surroundings that I barely noticed what he said, except that it was something about how he hoped I could set aside my father's prejudices, so that we might be strangers no longer. We ate a feast of roast gull and lark, stuffed swan and carbonado, drank claret and sack, then had sweetmeats in the parlor while we waited for the tables to be cleared away.

"Are you enjoying yourself?" Richard asked me.

"Never more." I smiled. "I hope you are too."

"You would not look at me when I came back from the river this afternoon," he said quietly. "Why? What did I do?"

I was stunned. "You didn't do anything," I said, wondering what in the world had happened to him to make him so sensitive. "I'm so sorry if I offended you."

Everyone was moving back into the hall.

"Dance with me," he urged, and before I had a chance to ask for Edmund's blessing, he had led me away into a courante. At first I was so busy concentrating on counting the vigorous beats that I did not even notice the feel of his hand pressing warmly against my boned waist, as it had done when we skated.

Then his soft black curls tickled my face as he leaned in toward me, his cheek against mine, to whisper something in my ear. "Look at me," he murmured. "Not at your feet."

I turned my eyes up to his, his face still so close to mine that I could feel the warmth of his breath. The irises of his eyes were intricate and delicate as flower petals.

"I'll not let you make a mistake," he said, as if he referred to far more than dance steps, but I had no time to consider his meaning because I was so determined not to put a foot wrong.

One, two, three. Pause, hop, glide, turn. I quickly found, though, that I did not need him to guide me at all. As my dancing master had said, dancing came to me as easily as walking. I stopped concentrating and let my body move as it had always yearned to do. I let myself be swept up in the glorious swish and rustle of silk clothes, the tap and drag of leather-soled shoes.

"I knew you would dance as gracefully as you skate," Richard said to me.

"So do you," I replied, wishing to God that he would stop looking at me like that, as if he wanted to eat me.

The music changed to the saraband, a slow and halting Spanish dance. I had never been held so close by a man before. It was an extraordinary sensation to feel the heat of his body close to mine, to feel the muscles in his chest and arms and legs, the sway of his slim hips as we moved to the alien rhythm. I knew that, for the rest of my life, whenever I heard the saraband I would be back in this room, with Richard. It was like a wonderful dream, the sounds and sights so piercingly bright and colorful that I was spellbound.

"So if you have never been to a ball, Edmund has never danced with you?"

I shook my head.

Richard seemed inordinately pleased by that news. "Shame on him. He does not know what he is missing."

Except that, seemingly, he did. On the edge of my vision I glimpsed Edmund coming toward us as the music faded and I felt a stab of shame for having abandoned him for so long. I smiled across at him and immediately went to extricate myself from Richard. But he held on to my hand as tightly as if he was trying to stop me from slipping over the side of a boat into a floodtide, or as if he himself was slipping.

I tried surreptitiously to tug myself free, but when it was clearly no use and as Edmund came closer, I pulled our still interlocked hands behind me in a vain attempt to hide them in the folds of my skirts.

"My turn now, I think," Edmund said amiably. "You'll have to let her go, I'm afraid, my friend. She's to be my bride, after all."

Richard slipped his fingers through mine, weaving us together, and he drew me imperceptibly but firmly closer to him, away from Edmund. "One more dance," he bargained. His tone was mischievous and yet it was underlaid with a challenge that was entirely serious, so I was caught between feeling touched, amused, embarrassed and annoyed.

Edmund was merely annoyed. "Damn it, lad," he hissed under his breath, the first time I had ever seen him riled. "You go too far. Unhand her." The trumpets sounded for Lord Monk's March and Edmund stepped between us. "Now."

Richard's eyes darkened to indigo, and anger flared in them, as sudden and as bright as quicksilver. But he had no alternative but to release me or else cause a spectacle. He relaxed his hold on my hand and I took it from his, feeling suddenly deprived. He stood for a moment where he was as we moved away; then he turned and made for the side of the dance floor.

"I'm sorry," I said to Edmund a little breathlessly, not quite sure exactly what I was apologizing for, not really quite sure even what had just happened.

"Oh, you're not to blame, my dear," he said with a tone now of fond amusement. He planted a kiss on my cheek and smiled as we started marching together. "It is just that he finds it insufferable to see me with the most beautiful girl in the hall."

I glanced back quickly to where Richard was leaning against the dark, carved wainscoting, beneath a flaming wall sconce. He was surrounded by people, yet seemed totally alone. "Were you jealous of him dancing with me?"

Edmund looked at me as if he did not know the meaning of the word. "Jealous? No. I trust him and I trust you," he said simply. "Because you are to be my wife and he is my friend. It's a sorry affair if we cannot trust our friends and our spouses."

He clearly did not possess one jealous bone in his body. Unless it was just that he did not love me enough to be jealous.

"You are very tolerant of him. I wonder that you are such good friends."

"I swear I have no idea what goes on in the lad's head half the time," Edmund said. "Except that everything is a competition to him. He can't help himself. And since he has no brother to compete against, I am his natural opponent."

"You don't mind?" But I saw that, on the contrary, Edmund enjoyed the challenge. "You were right when you said he is not an easy person. He seems rather"—I searched for a word—"erratic."

"He is inclined to brood. Has a great deal to brood upon." The dance formation parted us, so for a moment Edmund could say no more. As soon as we were marching side by side again, he quietly explained. "He never speaks of it, or at least not to me, would far rather suffer in silence. But I do know, from what I have gleaned from those who knew him as a child, that he has endured the most dreadful hardship, deprivation and unhappiness in his young life."

I felt a pain somewhere beneath my ribs. "Has he?"

We parted, came together again. The music switched to the longways country dance.

"He was born into exile, spent his entire childhood as a fugitive, shifting from place to place, in constant and severe want of both friends and funds. As I understand it, he came close to perishing for lack of bread and clothing. His brother did not survive the ordeal. Nor his mother. She was of Irish descent, had relations who were massacred by Cromwell's New Model Army at Drogheda and others who were amongst the Royalists who were deported to Barbados. The death of one son proved too much for her. Richard was left in a state of abject destitution with his embittered father, who treated him rather harshly, from what I can gather."

I turned my eyes back to the side of the hall to where Richard had been standing. I needed to look upon him in the light of this new knowledge I had of him. But he was gone. I scanned the room, suddenly desperate to seek him out amidst the blur of silk and smiling candlelit faces. And then he was there again, by my side, as the music faded. It started up again with the gavotte and Richard cupped his hand beneath my elbow, his eyes locked on mine. "Please, Edmund," he said in a low voice. "You have had your turn. Do not keep her all to yourself."

"Time enough together when we are wed, I suppose," Edmund said, graciously stepping aside.

We danced the whole of the gavotte in silence. Then the music slowed into a piece that required partners to kiss twice on the turn and I felt such a longing and need in Richard's brief kiss on my cheek, in the way that he held me, it made tears start to my eyes.

"What's the matter?" he asked anxiously. "Why are you crying?"

"I'm not crying." I blinked, and a single tear spilled down my cheek and rolled to the corner of my mouth.

"It is my fault for . . ."

"No." I shook my head. "No."

There were two little vertical furrows between his brows, just above his nose. They gave him an expression that was softly pained, and I had the most powerful urge to put my fingers to them and smooth them away.

When he stepped up to kiss me again, he turned his head slightly and instead of kissing my cheek he aimed for the tear, his lips brushing gently against the corner of mine, kissing it away. It was a surprising and tender thing to do, and yet he managed to imbue it with a delicate eroticism.

As the lines of dancers parted I stared at him over the divide.

I held out my hands to him as the other dancers held out their hands for their partners. Richard took hold of my fingers with the lightest touch, a tingling, magnetic touch, and I was drawn back to him as the needle of a compass is drawn to its true north.

But I had no compass to guide me through this strange and alien territory I had stumbled blindly into, a dangerous and dark place where I could seemingly care for two different men at the same time. I did not know which way to turn, whom to run to and whom to run from. I was utterly lost.

AS SOON AS the ball was over, Richard made his farewells to the Earl, as was polite, but did not seem able to get away fast enough. Outside in the crisp moonlit night, he thrust his boot into the groom's cupped hands and threw himself up into the saddle, spurring the flanks of his horse as if he were riding into battle.

Edmund and I caught up with him on the open Tickenham Road.

"A race, Edmund?" Richard suggested with fevered enthusiasm. "Across the moors?"

I turned to Edmund and to my amazement saw that rather than dismiss it for the extraordinarily foolhardy idea it so obviously was, he nodded almost as eagerly.

I looked quickly from one of them to the other, then back again. "Are you quite mad, the pair of you?"

The horses seemed to sense their riders' excitement and were already tossing their heads, prancing and snorting and champing at their bits, as the coaches clattered past.

"It is folly," I argued. "It is past midnight. The moor is covered in marsh and bog. You'll not even see the river."

"We'll jump the damned river," Richard said.

"And break your necks."

"The moonlight is bright enough to see by," Edmund placated me. "And we'll stop before the mill. Agreed, Richard?"

He gave an agitated nod, but the dangerous glint of recklessness in his eyes made me lean over and grab the rein of Edmund's horse. "Edmund please, I beg you, use your sense. I know these moors, every inch of them, and would not do what you are about to do. I know how dangerous they can be. Don't do this."

He glanced across at Richard. "I don't have much choice," he said grimly. "I've not seen him quite like this before, but when this sort of mood is on him he needs some release. Believe me, a midnight gallop is far safer than a clash of swords, or much else he might try." He leaned across, grabbed my hand and delivered a firm, swift kiss to it. I could see that what he had said was just an excuse. He was itching for the thrill of the race every bit as much as his friend was.

Richard was the first to dig his spurs into his horse's flanks. With a whoop and a clatter of hooves they were both off.

This is my doing, I thought despairingly. If anything happens to either of them, I will be to blame. Except that I did not know quite what I had done wrong or what I could have done differently that might have prevented it.

I watched the two riders streak away across the moonlit moor, expecting at any moment to see a foreleg buckle, snap like wicker, for horse and rider to go down. But it did not happen. Their cloaks billowed out behind them like black sails as they splashed headlong through an area of marsh, the spray flashing in the moonlight as silvery bright as their swords. I could not bear just to trot along on my own far behind them, so I urged my own little mare into an easy gallop that soon had me splattered with clods of mud and droplets of icy water. I felt my hair tear free from its pins and whip away behind my back. I yelped with the thrill of it, understanding exactly why Richard had suggested this wild, starlit chase. Not recklessness at all but high spirits and a zest for life, and there was nothing wrong with that, nothing wrong with it at all.

Edmund had been out in front at first by a head, but now it seemed that Richard had edged closer and taken the lead. Both riders had leaned lower over their horses' straining necks, but Edmund looked to be gaining ground again. They were careering toward the mill house now and just beyond that was the Yeo. Neither horse showed any sign of slowing. Richard was ahead and I knew with a sickening certainty that he, at least, was going to try to jump the river. I knew also that it was too wide to jump and that he would fail to clear the bank. If Edmund tried to follow him, they might both be dead or fatally wounded or drowned, in a matter of minutes.

"Stop!" I called at the top of my voice, galloping full pelt at them now. "Edmund! Richard! For the love of God, stop."

Edmund reined in at the moment that Richard's stallion sat back on its hocks and launched itself over the river. For a moment both horse and rider seemed suspended over the water, then both crashed down just short of the far bank. With an almighty splash, the horse landed awkwardly with its hind legs in the river and its forelegs floundering and thrashing halfway out. Propelled by momentum, Richard was thrown headfirst over the horse's neck onto the bank, one of his legs for a moment tangled messily in the stirrup.

As I galloped on toward them Edmund had already abandoned his mount and was wading chest deep through the fast-flowing river. Richard could swim, Edmund could not, but I thanked God that he was tall and strong, that the sluice would be down and there had been no heavy rainfall to speed the flow of the millrace.

Richard, I could see, was lying very still on his back on the ground. As the horse flailed to try to gain a footing, he was seriously in danger of being crushed or trampled to death. If he was not dead already.

Edmund had reached the far bank now and, at no small risk to himself from the thrashing hooves, was grappling with the stallion's reins to try to haul it to its feet and lead it safely away.

One glance at the surging river and I knew I would stand no chance in it. I hauled on the reins, spun my horse around, blinded for a moment as the wind whipped hair across my face, then tossed my head to shake it free. I galloped along the bank to the bridge that crossed by Church Lane. It seemed to take forever to reach it. I made a promise to myself that night that if Richard survived, I would damn well make him teach me how to swim.

Edmund had tethered Richard's horse to a tree and was now crouched beside his friend, speaking to him, urgently trying to elicit a response. "Richard! Can you hear me?"

He gave no sign that he could. His eyes were closed. Against the black of his hair and lashes his skin seemed bloodless, white as chalk in the moonlight.

"Move back, Edmund," I ordered, surprised at how authoritative I sounded when inside I was sick with dread. Edmund did move, immediately, seemingly relieved to have someone take charge, someone who appeared to know what to do: not that I did at all, but I did at least have the common sense to crouch down by Richard and lay my ear against his chest. I felt it rise and fall, heard his heart beating, fast and uneven, but strong. I had never heard such a welcome sound. "He's alive, at any rate."

I wanted to shake him, make him wake up, clasp him to me. Idiot man, what had he thought he was doing?

"There's no blood," Edmund said. "I can't see any blood."

"It doesn't mean he's not bleeding somewhere inside." I quickly unfastened my cloak and laid it over his prostrate body. "Stay with him," I said to Edmund, getting to my feet. "I'll fetch Ned, and the cart."

Just then Richard groaned and opened his eyes. Groggily, he looked at Edmund and then to me.

"Thank God." I knelt back down beside him and took hold of his hand in both of mine. "Richard, do you have any pain?" I asked him gently.

He looked at me pathetically, gave a small shake of his head.

"Can you move your legs, do you think?" I looked down the length of them and saw his boots twitch.

He was wet from the waist down, shivering now, and there was a cold wind that I felt keenly through the thin silk of my dress. All I wanted to do was to gather him into my arms and wrap him up warm and hold him. "I'm going to fetch the cart. I'll be back soon," I explained to him softly, but as I moved away he clutched at my arm with surprising strength and almost pulled me down on top of him. "Don't leave me," he said. "Let Edmund go." An afterthought: "He'll be faster."

I looked over at Edmund, who nodded at the logic of that and quickly went to mount my horse.

"Take Richard's," I said.

He shook his head. "Too skittish. Yours will carry me. It's not far."

He rode off at a gallop, and then there was just the profound and soothing peace of the moonlit moor. An owl hooted, hunting low over the reed beds, and the slight breeze rushing through the reeds was like a deep sigh.

Richard's eyes were open and he was looking up at me, his lips slightly parted.

"Are you still cold?" I asked him.

He nodded.

I moved closer to him, positioned myself with my legs out in front of me. "Here." I gently lifted his head and cradled it in my lap, tucking my cloak around him more snugly. "Is that better?"

"Much."

I held him tighter and my hair fell down around us both like a pale shroud. "You're still trembling," I said anxiously. "It is the shock."

He lifted his hand and stroked a tendril of hair back off my face. "I do not think it is that."

"Do you always take such risks, Richard?"

He did not reply, but looked at me almost as if he did not understand the question.

"You do remember what happened?" I asked fearfully.

"I am forever doing and saying things I later live to regret. I cannot seem to help it. But I could never regret this. Even if I had broken both my legs, it would have been entirely worth it."

I sucked in a breath. "You don't mean . . . ?"

He gave a brief grin. "I am far too good a horseman to have misjudged that jump so badly. Though I had intended a softer landing in the water."

I was incredulous. "You could have been killed."

"I do not think so."

He looked up at me with eyes that were fathomless in the silvery darkness. There was a graze on his temple and I wanted so much to put my lips to it.

"We only have one life," he said. "And to love and be loved, that is all there is."

"Hush." I could not resist stroking his black curls, glossy with river water. "You must not say such things to me. You must not. You know I am promised to Edmund. You know we are to be married within a sennight."

"I know it. And it makes me wish I had broken my neck just now."

"Never say that. Don't even think it."

"I can't help it."

"Richard, you hardly know me."

"I know you well enough to know that Edmund is not the man for you."

I smiled. "If you had not just fallen from your horse, I would scold you for being so presumptuous."

"It is not presumption. You forget how well I know him. And I know him to be the most solid, steadfast, even-tempered man I have ever met."

"Most women would think themselves fortunate indeed to find a steadfast and even-tempered husband."

"But you are not most women, Eleanor. You have a heart that is all on fire."

I felt it hammering so hard now it was like a throbbing pain in my chest, and I was sure he must feel it, must see the tremors of it.

"You have an energy and a passion for life," he said softly. "A capacity for love that a man like Edmund could never understand. That he can never match."

"Oh, and you could, I suppose?"

"Yes," he said levelly. "I could."

"You judge Edmund unfairly. He is a good man."

"Meaning that I am not?"

I said, half smiling, "I don't think you can be. If you were a good man, you would not be having this conversation with your friend's betrothed, especially after that friend has just saved your life."

"It takes two to make a conversation," he said softly. "I was not aware that I had been talking to myself. You like talking to me, I think."

"You are being presumptuous again." Except that I understood the reticence in his smile now, understood that the confidence and swagger he so often displayed were just a shield. His glamour and vulnerability were two sides of the same coin and, to me at least, made him utterly irresistible. "I do like talking to you," I admitted gently. "Very much. Of course I do. And I hope we shall still talk to one another after I am married to Edmund."

"I love you, Eleanor," he said desperately. "I think about you all the time. I cannot sleep for wanting you. I don't know what to do."

And I did not know what to say, but my soul was singing with the irresistible joy of being so needed and loved.

"I think I loved you before I even met you," he said. "When Edmund told me how he had found you in a little rowing boat, in the mist, at dawn. I pictured you like a water sprite, with your gold hair trailing down your back and only the swans for company. When I met you, when I saw you skating, I saw that wildness in you and I was captivated. I knew you were the only person I should ever love. That you had ruined me for anyone else."

"Don't."

"You love me too, don't you? I can see that you do."

I gave a small shake of my head. "No." I did not mean that I did not love him, only that I could not. "I love Edmund."

He suddenly heaved onto his side, winced and clutched his arm around his ribs, pain evident on his face as it had not been before, almost as if it was what I had said that had wounded him. I took hold of him to make him be still. "Don't try to get up. Wait for the cart."

"I cannot wait." He pressed determinedly down with his hand on my legs and struggled to sit, grimacing with pain.

"Where does it hurt?"

He touched his hand to his right side.

"Let me see."

I knelt by him, undid his coat with shaky fingers, pulled his shirt free from his breeches and pushed it up. Even by the light of the moon, the red-purple welt that ran along his rib cage was clearly visible. I touched the edge of it with my fingertips and he jerked away from me. "For the love of God, stop!" He dragged down his shirt, as if the touch of my fingers on his bare skin was too much for him to bear.

"I'm sorry."

He drew up his knees, then supporting himself with his hand on my shoulder, struggled to his feet. I stood with him, let him lean on me for a moment. He staggered and I tried to take hold of his arm. He gave a grunt of pain.

"Your arm is hurt too?"

"My shoulder," he said carelessly. "I expect it will mend." He shook me off and walked unsteadily to where his horse was waiting peacefully now, tethered to a willow.

"Where are you going?"

He unhooked the reins and turned to me. "I shall go back to your house, unless you have any objection to that. I do not think I am fit enough to ride back to London tonight."

"Of course, I didn't mean . . ."

"I know you didn't." He put his boot in the stirrup and with a grunt, clutching his arm around his ribs, managed to heave himself into the saddle. "I would offer to let you ride back with me," he said, taking up the reins. "But I don't think it would be wise. If I had you close to me for one more minute, I am not sure that I could answer for my actions." He walked the horse up to where I stood, and looked down at my upturned face. "I'll try not to cause you further embarrassment. I shall leave at first light. Please don't come to bid me farewell. I do not think that I could bear it."

I did not think that I could bear it either. But I must. What other choice did I have?

EDMUND AND I LEFT for London three days later in a smart blue post coach which Edmund had hired, and as it rocked over the uneven road that linked the straggled cottages of Tickenham, I had leaned my beribboned, ringleted head out past the canvas screens for one last glimpse of my home while it was still mine. My last glimpse of home as an unwedded and unbedded girl.

Everything was golden, a burst of shining yellow. In the water meadows celandines and dandelions gleamed like small suns, whilst the rivers were edged with yellow flag irises. For a moment I thought I saw one of the first yellow butterflies of the spring, dancing in the churchyard, but it was just the bright bloom of a kingcup.

As we passed onto the Fosse Way, which would take us east, our guide told us it would take three days to reach London. I couldn't imagine being on the road so long. Near Winchester we were stuck in the mire for six hours without food or water. We arrived at the inn by torchlight when it was too late for supper and next morning were woken to get back into the coach before dawn to make up time. We were jolted and shaken and before we reached Guildford, we'd crashed headlong into a great pothole that caused the leather straps to break, sending the coach careering off its wheels and entailing another long wait for it to be mended. I felt battered and bruised and weary. It was by no means a smooth and painless journey to the altar for me, but today was the end of that journey and the start of another one, from which there was no turning back. Today was my wedding day.

I rested my head against the velvet seat of the swaying carriage and thought of my father's fantastical story of transformation, tiny caterpillars weaving their mythical little coffins. Today it was I who was to be transformed, about to enter holy wedlock, to pass from one state to another. Dressed in my gown of cherry silk with scarlet and silver brocade and gold lace, I was as bright as any butterfly and this carriage might as well be my coffin. I would emerge from it to take my nuptial vows, after which I would not be as I was before. I would have a different name. I would be expected to adhere to a higher standard of virtue. My good name, and that of my husband, would depend upon my housewifely accomplishment and modesty.

I had no mother to tell me how to be a good wife, but I was thankful that at least I had had Bess, married for years now and twice as experienced as me in the art of love. She had instructed me on how to fulfill my marriage duties and make my husband happy on his wedding night. I smiled to myself as I remembered the advice she'd given me the previous night when we'd lain awake in bed together, talking beneath the sloping roof of the inn.

"Every man knows that we women have much stronger carnal appetites than them," Bess said. "Since they can only reach a peak of pleasure once at a time but we can do it over and over again. So he'll expect you to look as if you're enjoying yourself. You will, eventually, but you might not the first time because it'll hurt. Just pretend it hurts much more than it actually does. Moan and sigh as though you are in the most dreadful agony and he will think you are in an ecstasy of pleasure. Before you know it, he will be moaning and groaning too."

It seemed very comical, not to mention complicated, but I'd do my best. I slid my eyes across for a peek at Edmund. The sprig of willow I'd tucked into the scarlet ribbon of his hat was nodding and jigging to the movement of the carriage.

Bess was sitting opposite me in the carriage, beside Mr. Merrick. She and my guardian, together with Mary and John Burges and Edmund's brother, were to be our only guests, unless Richard came too, which I very much doubted. He had been invited. Of course he had been invited, and he had not sent word that he would not attend, but somehow I knew that he would not be there and I was doing my very best not to think how I felt about that, to not think about him at all.

Edmund's father still suffered badly from gout and was unable to travel any distance, so it would be a quiet wedding, but I didn't mind so much now. I was on an adventure, the farthest I had ever traveled in my life.

"Are we nearly there now?" I asked Edmund, for what must have been the tenth time.

"Your nose will tell you," Mr. Merrick instructed me. "You smell London long before you see it."

"There'll be nothing but fresh countryside smells in Marylebone," Edmund reassured. "Though it's on the outskirts of London, it's in truth a small rural village, entirely distinct and separate, divided from the metropolis by acres of green fields."

I was crestfallen. "You mean we shan't even see the river and the Palace of Whitehall and the lions in the Tower?"

He patted my arm as if I was a small child, and I suppose I was behaving rather like one. "We can take a drive to see the sights tomorrow, if you'd like."

I sighed and stared out at the woods and rivers and fields. The countryside was not as flat as Somersetshire, but somehow less interesting for it, and I felt suddenly very homesick. I slid up closer to Edmund and whispered in his ear. "Let me see my ring?"

"Certainly not."

"At least tell me what it's like. Does it sparkle?"

"It does."

"You mean it has diamonds?"

"Wait and see."

"Do you know where diamonds come from? Do you know how they are made?"

He smiled his broad, jovial smile. "Can't say I've ever thought about it."

I retreated back into my corner as if I was traveling in a stagecoach with only strangers for companions. While the potholes grew more numerous the nearer we got to London, and the coach jolted on, the questions started up inside my head again, clamoring to be heard. What was the point of living if it was not to learn? There were things I wanted to know, that I couldn't live without knowing, couldn't die not knowing, or at least without trying to find out. I did not think that, as my husband, Edmund would try to stop me, but nor did I think he would encourage it. And I would have liked to have been able to have discussions with him.

We were passing a great park at the edge of which was a gabled brick mansion as sumptuous as a royal palace, but which Edmund told me was the Manor House of Marylebone. It made the little manor of Tickenham look no more than a cottage. We carried on past it and I waited to see how similarly grand would be the church where I was to be married.

Presently I saw a humble chapel, built of stone and flint, standing entirely alone in a field, except for the crooked gravestones that surrounded it. It looked as if it was hundreds of years old, had been there since before the Reformation. It had small arched windows and a little pinnacled tower on top of which was a weathercock. We were approaching it up an ancient, narrow, winding track and had to stop twice to let a horse and cart pass, and then a farmer driving a herd of cattle. As we came nearer I saw that it stood on the banks of a little burbling brook that ran down from the slopes of undulating hills to the north.

Surely that could not be it.

"St. Marylebone," Edmund announced.

It was a somewhat unpromising start to what I'd hoped would be my bright and colorful future.

THERE WAS NO SIGN of Richard, and I told myself I was relieved rather than disappointed. Edmund acted as if he were totally unsurprised. "He is the son of a Cavalier, after all," he said flippantly, as though that should be explanation enough. "We all know there's only one thing upon which you can utterly rely in a Cavalier—and that is that he will be utterly unreliable. He'll probably turn up half-way through the service, or more likely sometime next week. I did write to him twice to give him the details but he has no notion of time, no concern at all for instructions, or for duty and responsibility for that matter, especially if he can wash it all away with a bottle or two of sack."

That seemed a little harsh, so that I knew Edmund was more disappointed than he was admitting, but I was very glad to learn that Richard could be unreliable. Even if he did not give that impression, or at least not to me, it was exactly what I needed to hear. For what would life be like married to such a man? Even the most adorable, fascinating man. I had promised my father I would choose a husband well. And what kind of lord would Richard Glanville have made for Tickenham?

I hoped for Edmund's sake that Richard's absence did not mar his enjoyment of the day, but all my own disappointment in the unprepossessing church vanished as soon as I saw Mary and John Burges, waiting round the side with a gentleman who, despite his much paler ginger hair, could be none other than Edmund's elder brother.

"You look so beautiful," Mary said admiringly, as she kissed me and pressed into my hands a little aromatic posy of rosemary and myrtle and daisies. "Do you know the great Sir Francis Bacon was married here?" she chatted on, linking her arm through mine. "In an extravagant purple suit, and his bride in a gown of cloth of silver that cost half her dowry."

"Dear Mary, how is it you always know exactly what to say to cheer me?" I felt wholly better now. It seemed an extraordinary coincidence. My father had always commented on my inability to accept anything without evidence, and now here I was, about to be married in the very same church as Sir Francis Bacon, my hero, remembered as the inventor of the "Scientific Method" of testing a theory by controlled experiment. "If this church is good enough for Sir Francis, it must surely be good enough for me," I said to Mary.

Edmund must surely be good enough for me. Until I had met Richard Glanville, I had wanted nothing more than him.

"Are you happy?" Mary asked.

"Yes," I said, glancing at Edmund, who did look very grand and handsome as he strode ahead with his brother. "I am." If I had never met Richard, I would have been blissfully happy this day. But I had managed to find happiness in far less favorable circumstances, had resisted unhappiness all my life.

Mary was looking as radiant as a new bride herself. "City air's obviously good for you," I told her.

"Hackney's far from the city. But it's home to me now."

I thought with a pang of Tickenham, which I had left behind for the first time, and which in a matter of minutes would be mine no longer. "Have you any pupils for your boarding school yet?"

"Two keen girls."

I stopped walking, looked at her. "Girls!"

"Of course," she said, pulling me on. "What do I know about boys? We're not the first. There's two Quaker establishments and a fine girls' school in Chelsea that's already quite famous."

"Am I too old to go?"

She laughed. "In a few minutes you'll be a wife."

"And wives, of course, can never pursue their education, Heaven forfend." I do not know if I sounded resentful, did not mean to, but it did feel for a tiny moment as if my life, in a way, was ending instead of beginning.

Mary relinquished me to Mr. Merrick, who took my arm as we all walked into the chapel. The heavy doors swung closed behind us with a resounding clang. The interior smelled musty and damp and was very dim after the brightness of the spring sunshine, so that for a few seconds, until my eyes adjusted, I couldn't see where on earth I was going. I walked slowly past the boxes of locked pews toward the altar as one who is blind, my footsteps ringing down the stone nave.

Eventually I could see enough to make out that the little church was in a very poor state of repair. The banners and escutcheons were dusty and faded. The monumental slabs we walked upon were crumbling. The Apostles' Creed was marked with damp and there was a dusty spider's web over the poor box. Not a particularly auspicious start to my marriage at all. I saw also that the stone commandments upon the wall were riven with a great diagonal crack, and it made me shudder in premonition.

The plain little altar had at least been adorned with bays, but I yearned again for Tickenham. I thought of the golden morning on which we had left it and I wished with all my heart that we were marrying in the familiar surroundings of the church of St. Quiricus and St. Juliet, sharing this day with our neighbors and household family, with Mistress Keene from the kitchen, with Bess's parents. I even found myself thinking quite fondly of Thomas Knight and Susan Hort. I should like to have had Reverend Burges officiating, or even the new young curate, John Foskett, and blessings and psalms of rejoicing and a procession of pipers to lead the way and make the occasion feel festive and joyous, instead of rather furtive and solemn, as it did now.

The minister was waiting with his service book already open, two worn hassocks placed at his feet in readiness for us. He looked extraordinarily old and as worn as his church, his hair wispy and white and his eyes almost lost in the deep wrinkles and furrows of his face. He spoke in a hushed voice more suited to a funeral than a wedding.

But the marriage service is a grave and somber affair, though beautiful and dignified nonetheless, for all that it comes from the notorious Book of Common Prayer.

"Not to be entered into unadvisedly, lightly or wantonly . . . those whom God hath joined together let no man put asunder."

With a monumental effort I pushed away the thought that it should be someone else standing by my side at this altar.

The minister read the part about "accustomed duty" and Edmund dutifully fished in his pocket for a five-shilling piece, which he placed on the minister's service book to pay him for marrying us. Then came the ring, and Edmund found it in another pocket and placed that, too, upon the pages of the open book, a band of gold, set with many jewels. Considerate of my background, he'd asked me if I would find the ritual of the ring offensive, as did scores of Puritans who saw its part in the marriage ceremony as a relic of Papistry.

He could not have been more wrong. I had secretly dreamed of the day when the man I loved would place the ring upon my finger, from which it was said a certain vessel ran directly to the heart.

I looked at it, gleaming with jewels in the dim light. The symbol of my transformation, its placing upon my hand as powerful as the placing of a crown upon the head of a new queen. The ring. Token and symbol of constancy, of a love that has no end but death, a heart that is sealed from even the thought of another man.

But as I held out my hand for Edmund to slip the ring onto my finger, I suddenly remembered how it felt when Richard Glanville encircled my thumb with his lips. I remembered the caress of his tongue upon my skin as he tasted my blood. How ever was I to vanquish such thoughts?

As I made my vows, I turned my head from the ominous tablet of stone upon which were engraved God's Ten Commandments. I did not want to see how the sacred edict had been broken, split asunder as if by a wrathful bolt of lightning.

. . .

WE WENT DIRECTLY from the church to the Rose of Normandy public house on Marylebone Lane, the oldest building in the
parish, or so we were told by the landlord, set inside a brick-walled
garden with fruit trees and broad walks and a square center bowling
green, edged with quickset hedges.

Our small wedding party was served a good dinner of rabbit fric-
assee, and we started to work our way merrily through several flagons
of claret and ale.

I sat on the bench beside my new husband in the pale, smoky
rushlight and we held hands beneath the table. Though I convinced
myself I had to be happy, I seemed bent on self-destruction, oblivion,
on blotting out all thought. I must have drunk more wine in that
night than I usually drank in a month. As the evening wore on, I felt
my cheeks grow very pink, and when the room started to spin around
me, I tilted my head against Edmund's broad shoulder.

"You make a pretty sight." Mary smiled. "It puts me in mind of my
own wedding night."

"Oh, do tell." I giggled and then hiccupped behind my hand.
Which made me giggle all the more.

"Perhaps it is time to show a little restraint, Eleanor," Mr. Merrick
suggested reproachfully.

I giggled again. Hiccupped again more loudly and didn't even try
to be polite and conceal it. "I'm afraid I don't know the meaning of
the word, sir."

"Neither do I," Bess said, taking it literally. "You should though,
miss. You read enough books." Her hand flew to her mouth. "Beg
pardon. Is that supposed to be a secret now?"

"Restraint means moderation and self-control, my dear," Mr. Merrick answered patronizingly.

"How dull," I replied. Hooking my foot around Edmund's ankle, I let my satin brocade slipper slide off and wiggled my toes against his silk stockings. He gave a little jerk of surprise and then smiled at me, rather drowsy-eyed. "I do not believe in moderation," I whispered to him. "Or self-control. Especially not on my wedding night." I clapped the palm of my hand against the table. "Now, all of you be quiet and let Mary tell us about hers."

The look Mary gave John was so loving and devoted that it pierced through my fuzzy brain. "I was very gauche and green," she remembered softly, her eyes lowered. "I was marrying a man of the cloth, so I assumed we'd be very chaste and only be able to kiss and touch in the dark. You can imagine my surprise when I went to sit beside my husband in an inn much like this and he pulled me down into his lap and fondled me all evening."

"Dearest John," I said gushingly. "God bless you. I do believe you are blushing as pink as does Edmund."

I was overcome with a rush of affection and wanted to fling my arms around both John and Mary and hug them. But I saw that they only had eyes for each other. So I sprang onto my rather wobbly feet and promptly flopped in a puff of petticoats into Edmund's lap, much to his surprise and everyone's amusement.

"That's it, Eleanor." Bess clapped. "You lead the way. I was starting to worry the pair of you were just going to hold hands all night long."

"That's all you and Ned did after your nuptials, I'm sure?"

"He wanted me to hold a lot more of him than just his hand, I can tell you." She winked at me and burped very loudly. "I was more than happy to oblige."

Uninhibited with wine, I lunged across the bench, nearly upsetting a glass, and smacked a kiss on her cheek. "Bess, you are so perfectly coarse and shocking." I gave another loud hiccup. "Have I ever told you how much I love you for it?"

"You love everyone tonight, I think, Ma'am. But you best save some of it for your new husband." She smiled at me warmly as I twined my arms around Edmund's neck. "Mind, you do have more of it to give out than most people I know. I hope Mr. Ashfield appreciates that."

Drunk as I was, I was concerned for a moment that he would disapprove of a maid speaking so out of turn, but I should not have worried at all. As I felt his arms go around my waist he looked at Bess and a playful look came into his clear gray eyes. "Tell me, Bess. Is my wife wearing a garter?"

"Certainly, sir. I helped her put it on myself." She grinned at me, then at him. "Now I'd say it's high time it came off, wouldn't you agree?" She made a grab at my skirts. "Come on, Mistress Burges, lend me a hand. It's about time we brought these two to bed, don't you think?"

I giggled and squirmed and kicked on Edmund's lap and he did not help me at all, but only laughed delightedly as they started pulling at my laces and ribbons and the silk sashes tied below my knees.

Bess started singing a bawdy song and Edmund's brother joined in. Then they all grabbed my hands and Edmund's hands and dragged us both, still giggling and protesting, to our small sloping room at the top of the inn.

Mary and Bess had conspired to make our own Hymen's revels to compensate for my wedding being so quiet. They had bedecked our half-tester bed with ribbons, scented it with essence of jasmine and strewn it with violets. Mary had even gone so far as to ask the landlady to make up a sack posset for us to drink and I swigged it down, barely savoring the delicious combination of wine and cinnamon and egg.

Bess took charge of flinging the garter and John helped Edmund undo his buttons and stumble out of his breeches.

"Time to leave you in peace now," Mary said, kissing my forehead.

"I hope neither of you have any peace at all." Bess tittered, with another wink. "Go to it, the pair of you. Heaven knows, you've waited long enough."

Edmund's brother slapped him between the shoulder blades. "Time to let your little wife see your goods." He guffawed.

Then they were gone. And there we were, with a single candle and clothes scattered around the floor and the smell of jasmine entirely vanished, replaced by the acrid stink from the tallow candle. Edmund was still in his knee-length drawers and I in my voluminous shift.

We lay on our backs, side by side, like the marble statues of a knight and his lady upon their tomb. The room seemed to be rocking slightly, as if we were in a boat. But apart from that I felt exactly the same, as if being married made no difference at all. I flicked my eyes sideways to see what Edmund was doing. I wished he would make some move, make of our two bodies one flesh, make us truly man and wife.

The sheets smelt faintly of damp and tobacco and of unwashed bodies. There was a draft coming from a gap in the ill-fitting window. I missed my own bed, my home, and I wished Edmund would at least hold me. He had his eyes closed and I feared he'd drunk so much he might soon fall asleep. It was my wedding night and I totally refused to feel miserable and homesick. I reached out and touched Edmund's freckled cheek, which was prickly with a fresh crop of coppery whiskers. He gave a mock drowsy smile, so I knew he'd been teasing me by pretending to have dozed off.

I bounced up onto my knees, gold curls tumbling down around my face. "Don't you dare, Edmund."

He reached out his arms and pulled me into them, then rolled me onto my back and heaved himself on top of me, smiling down into my face. "How do you do, Mistress Ashfield?"

I giggled. "How do you do, Mr. Ashfield?"

"Very well indeed. Pistol's loaded and ready for its first husbandly foray."

"Oh! Ouch!"

He was a big man, in every way, I was alarmed to discover. He was squashing me and I could feel his cock, hard and hot, pressing into my pubic bone. I'd hardly taken a proper breath before he was fumbling with my shift, dragging it up. I closed my eyes as he rubbed himself up and down against me and poked and prodded about as if he was tending a fire, rather than inflamed with passion.

Then suddenly he stopped.

I opened my eyes.

"I'm afraid of hurting you. You will say if I am?"

I wrapped my arms around his broad back and pulled him closer. "Oh, Edmund, I think you must hurt me. Bess said it would hurt the first time. I shan't mind."

He looked at me doubtfully and I wriggled underneath him.

Alarmingly, he reared up as if he had been stabbed in the back, let out a groan and impaled me with one single thrust. The hot, piercing pain made me think how very aptly pricks are named, for my insides were most definitely being jabbed, his cock indeed a burning poker. He thrust again and I banged my head on the bedpost. He flopped down on me, heavy and leaden as a bag of grain.

"Sorry," he mumbled against my shoulder.

"It's all right."

We lay there for a minute or two.

"Edmund?"

He moaned contentedly and didn't reply, so I knew, this time, he really was asleep.

I put my hands against his shoulders and, with some effort, managed to push him off.

He lay stretched out beside me, his red-gold head on my shoulder.

I lifted up the sheets. There was a spot of blood, token of my lost maidenhead. I tried so hard not to think of what else I had lost. Most of all I tried not to think how it had felt when Richard Glanville's tongue had licked away a drop of my blood. But vexingly, the very act of trying not to think brought him more swiftly and powerfully to my mind.

An hour later Edmund stirred, stroked me a little and entered me again, very gently this time. It did not hurt so much, and it might have been all I could ever have imagined wanting, if only I did not have something else with which to compare it. I might have been quite happy and satisfied, had I not been secretly hoping to experience again what I had felt when Richard had touched the tips of my fingers as we danced. Edmund gazed down at my face lovingly, but not even on our wedding night did he look at me as intensely as Richard did every time he saw me.

I lay on my back and hot tears slid out of the corners of my eyes and trickled into my hair.

I glanced across at my now softly snoring husband and stroked his head, thought sadly of how all was not gold that glistened. I was terribly, bleakly afraid that I had married the wrong man, and I knew also, bewilderingly, that I did love Edmund and that he deserved much, much better. I vowed there and then that I would never hurt him. I could not control how I felt, but I could control what I did about it. I would make the very best of my marriage, would honor my wedding vows. Somehow I would find a way to banish Richard Glanville forever from my head and from my heart.

BANISHING HIM from my head was going to be much the easier of the two, I decided. I should start with that. And I thought I knew just the way to do it. Fill it up with something else.

I waited for dawn to lighten the sky before I crept out of bed. My head throbbed, my mouth was dry, and there was a hollow, nauseated feeling in my belly, but I draped a green morning gown and cloak over my arm, found a lead pencil and scribbled a brief note, telling Edmund that I had woken early and didn't want to disturb him, so had gone for a drive into London.

I dropped a kiss on his brow, tucked the sheet back around him and left the letter beside him on the pillow. I softly opened the door and tiptoed down the dark corridor to the first door on the right.

Bess was snoring soundly, huddled down beneath the sheets on her little truckle bed. I gave her a firm shake, putting my hand over her mouth to stop her squealing. "Help me get dressed, Bess, quick as you can."

She sat bolt upright. "You're not running away, are you? It wasn't that bad, surely?"

"Of course I am not running away, silly."

She put her hand to her head. "Ugh, I don't feel very well."

"Nor do I."

"Then why are you sneaking about in my room? Why aren't you enjoying your new husband and your marriage bed?"

"Hurry." I pushed her shoes at her. "I don't want Edmund to hear us and decide to come along too."

"So you have had enough of him? Poor fellow."

"There is no need to feel sorry for him, Bess," I said tetchily. "Really."

"How was it, then?" she asked, circumspect, as she slipped her shoes on, fastened my gown for me.

"I'll tell you later." Impatient, I turned to go.

She caught my arm. "I'm not going anywhere unless you tell me all, right now."

"It is private."

"That is so unfair," she wailed. "I tell you everything. We promised to always tell each other everything."

It was true. But I did not want to be disloyal to Edmund. Nor could I lie to Bess. She would see straight through it anyway. "You said that I might still be left wanting more," I said. "So I am sure it was perfectly normal." I reached for the door latch.

She held on tighter. "Normal? That's hardly the word to describe your wedding night."

I looked at her. "We women are ruled by insatiable lust. We are driven by stronger sexual desires and much lower passions than are men, is that not so?"

"So the preachers are always telling us, yes."

"Men are allegedly governed instead by reason and intellect."

She smirked. "Now that, I'm not so sure of."

I laughed. "Well, I think it must be just so. And I think I have married an extremely reasonable and intelligent man."

Bess gave me a skeptical frown.

"Now, please, can we go!"

"As you wish, miss, I mean, Ma'am."

DOWNSTAIRS THE MAID WAS already about, sweeping grates and fetching pails of water. The door to the yard was already unlocked.

It was a dull, gray morning, very different from yesterday. Bess shouted up to our coachman, who was sleeping in a loft above the stable, and told him to make the coach ready.

"Where to, Ma'am?" he asked.

"Pall Mall."

Bess looked at me. "I thought you wanted to see the river and the lions?"

"But first I want to find Dr. Sydenham, the physician who came to treat my father. There's something very important I have to ask him."

As we came to the fashionable squares and myriad streets of Soho, London assailed my senses. Bess was all for putting up the canvas screens, but I didn't want to miss a thing, not even the stench. It wasn't the countryside stink of dung but a much less wholesome combination of what I could see all around: decaying refuse that littered dirty cobbled streets and alleys running with filthy open sewers. I clasped my scented handkerchief to my nose but almost retched at the reek of rotten eggs which came from the sulfurous smoke belching out of the mass of crooked chimneys and darkening the air into a yellow choking smog as thick as any mist that descended over the Tickenham moors. But this fog was not accompanied by an unearthly peace as it was in Somersetshire.

On the contrary, horses neighed and the deafening clatter of iron-bound carriage wheels competed with the shouts of drivers of drays and wagons and the apprentices who bellowed from open shops. I had never seen so many vehicles and animals and people all crammed together. Sailors and mountebanks rubbed shoulders with women carrying baskets of fruit on their heads; grandees rode in velvet-lined coaches and sedan chairs, escorted by liveried servants and black slave boys.

The mess and chaos of London diverted me for a while from the mess and chaos I had seemingly already managed to make of my young life, just married to one man and already hopelessly in love with another. But Bess wasn't enjoying the experience at all. "This question you have to ask Dr. Sydenham, it had better be important, worth going to all this trouble for," she muttered.

I let the screen drop over the window and leaned back, clasping my hands in my lap. "It's as important as can be. It's a matter of life and death."

Bess stared at me white-faced.

I laughed to see her look of panic. "Oh Bess, I'm so sorry." I grabbed her hand. "I'm not ill. Unless, of course, Galen was right to treat love as a disease. It's just that I'm afraid I might die of longing for something I can never, ever have."

She looked bemused. "Dr. Sydenham has a cure for longing?"

"I believe he might. I pray he might. If only we can find him."

I knew Bess was waiting for me to tell her what it was that I longed for, but I did not want to. For once, this was something I did not want to share. I did not want to have these powerful, delicate, confusing emotions held up to her scrutiny, picked over and belittled. I wanted to keep them close and safe, a secret, even as I sought to dispel them. Whatever Bess saw in my face then, it was enough to stop her from inquiring any further.

Onto Pall Mall, a fine, paved thoroughfare, lined with a row of shady elm trees behind which were grand mansions. I leaned my head and shoulders rather precariously out of the window, and searched up and down the street. We were passing a redbrick mansion with wings, pediments and porticos, which looked far too impressive even for an eminent physician.

"Be sure you have the right place or you could find yourself calling on the King's mistresses," Bess said. "Mary told me Lady Castlemaine has a residence here, and Nell Gwynn."

I remembered dimly something else Mary had told me, from the time of the plague, when London was a place of death. I had listened as always to any details about it with a morbid fascination. I shouted for the carriage to stop outside the sign of the feathers, the only place where you could buy the Countess of Kent's Powder Virtues, allegedly believed by all the physicians of Christendom to guard against malignant distempers.

I walked into the dark little shop, where a wizened old man in a long apron was busy behind the counter, dusting bottles of potions. He told me that Dr. Sydenham lived over near the pheasantry.

I set off toward a small grove of chestnut trees and did my best not to gape at two ladies who were walking down the wide pavement carrying vizards which they held up to their faces on short sticks, beneath which it was possible to glimpse the tiny black leather patches in moon and star shapes that they wore stuck to their cheeks. Even in my fine silk morning gown I looked like a country girl who didn't belong here, much as I might wish I did.

I tried to appear serene and sophisticated, glanced up at the house I was passing.

And there I saw him, a face I recognized, despite the luxuriant periwig he wore upon his head, despite the passage of over ten years. He was sitting by the open sash window, deep in thought as he smoked a clay pipe, with a silver tankard set before him on the table.

My step faltered. I almost carried on walking. All at once I felt extremely foolish. What in the world did I think I was doing? What was I going to say? Well, it was too late now to turn back. I would be very annoyed with myself later if I did not go through with it, now that I had come so far.

I told Bess to wait on the pavement and made myself climb the stone steps to the door. He saw me and came to open it himself, giving me a bow.

"Dr. Sydenham, sir. I am sorry to trouble you, but we met when I was just a child, in Somersetshire."

"Ah, of course. I remember you very well. Miss Goodricke, isn't it?"

I was astonished. "I'm Mistress Ashfield now."

He held open the door. "Won't you come inside, Mistress Ashfield?"

I stepped into a regular and well-proportioned hall, from which tall white-painted double doors led into an equally sumptuous room, the light flooding in through enormous sash windows. The high ceilings were adorned with elaborate swags of plaster, the walls covered in flocked paper decorated with curlicues of flowers.

There was a huge gilded mirror on the opposite wall that completely diverted me from my purpose. It was so strange to see myself reflected within something so ornate and extravagant, and the gold frame reminded me of the gold dust that had once stained my palm, like a mark of destiny.

I turned my head. "I'm surprised you remember me, sir," I said. "It was such a long time ago."

"You made a great impression on me," Dr. Sydenham said genially. "Such a brave little girl. I never felt my limitations as a man of medicine more strongly than I did then, not even when I ran from the plague because I knew I was powerless against it. I was very sorry I was no help to you either."

"I need your help now, sir. You are the most learned gentleman I know, the only learned gentleman I know in fact, so there is nobody else I can ask. I wonder, do you know how I might learn more about the study of butterflies?"

He looked at me for a moment as if I'd dumbfounded him. Then the skin around his eyes creased and he bellowed with laughter. "Forgive me, Mistress Ashfield," he said when he recovered himself and saw my puzzled smile. "I don't mean to offend. It's just that I have all manner of callers at my door making all manner of strange requests. But I do believe that is the most original inquiry that has ever been put to me. You were the most enchanting and unusual child and I am delighted to see you have grown into a most enchanting and unusual young lady. You will join me in drinking some coffee?"

"I wish I could, sir. But I was married only yesterday and I left my husband asleep at an inn in Marylebone. I mustn't abandon him for too long."

His eyes widened with renewed amusement. "I'd have thought any man would gladly wait a lifetime for such a remarkable person," he replied. "Even if she did flit off immediately he had ensnared her."

"Oh, I don't know about that, sir."

"Spare me the time to tell me this at least—why butterflies?"

I couldn't very well tell him that I had come for the sake of my marriage. That I needed a distraction to stop me from lusting after another man, who happened to be my husband's closest friend. Maybe I should have asked him for a cure for lovesickness too. But I doubted that the standard remedies would work nearly so well for me as the study of butterflies.

"I want very much to learn more about them," I told him. "I find them . . . irresistible. And I'm sure I'm not as original as you suggest, sir. Surely there are others who are as interested in them as I?"

"Indeed there are whole hosts of dusty natural philosophers who devote hours to the careful study of insects and sit around in coffee-house societies discussing their finds. But I'm afraid they'd not admit a woman, not even one of your intelligence, and in any case I'd hesitate to introduce you to them, in case their earnestness caused you to lose your spark."

"Can you at least tell me how I might contact them, perhaps obtain their scientific papers?"

He reflected for a moment. "There's an apothecary who lives on this street, a smart young man by the name of Thomas Malthus, from a very intelligent family who are good friends of mine. Young Thomas is a member of the Society of Apothecaries, naturally, and has mentioned an associate of his, James Petiver, who sounds like just the type of eccentric and enthusiastic young person you'd get along with very well."

I smiled. "How might I find James Petiver?"

"Easily. I hear he all but lives at the apothecaries' new physic garden in Chelsea, supposedly herbalizing and botanizing, but not in fact studying the plants at all, only the butterflies that are attracted to them. The best way to get there is by the river."

I took a small step toward the door. "Thank you, sir. You've given me exactly what I wanted."

"I'm glad to see you still know what you want and pursue it so single-mindedly, Mistress Ashfield."

I thought of Edmund and how I had dreamed for more than a decade of marrying him. "I'm very afraid that I do, sir, and it will probably be my undoing."

BESS WAS HUNGRY, so we bought game pies from a cookshop and made our way toward the Thames. Our first sight of the bridge with its tall houses and archways of elaborate shops was marred by the shock of seeing the stakes impaled with the rotting heads of traitors, blackened gargoyles with rictus grins and holes where their eyes and noses once were.

I shuddered and looked down at the torrent of water surging with terrifying force beneath the stone piers. The tide was at low ebb. We made our way over stinking mud to the slippery pier to hire a tilt boat to take us upstream.

The Yeo in full gushing winter flood was nothing to the sheer expanse of London's river. Bess cowered behind the narrow skiff's canopy as we rocked alarmingly from side to side. I held on tight to the shallow sides and I was sure the swell and suck and power of the currents would capsize us or drag us under.

We negotiated a throng of pleasure boats and sailing ships, their masts as thick as a forest, and presently the air cleared and the river quieted and widened into a fine reach. Our oarsman said it was called Hyde Park on the Thames on account of the fact that it was a fashionable rendezvous, where even the King himself came to bathe in the calm, clean water.

So His Majesty King Charles, like Richard Glanville, also knew how to swim. With his rich velvet suit and sword at his side, Richard could easily be a royal courtier, my own sweet, dark prince. Except that he was not mine, and never would be. Somehow I must find a way to school myself not to think of him as anything other than my husband's friend.

The busy wharves had given way to open fields and a large mulberry garden and then a country village with a terrace of redbrick houses that faced out over the water. Upstream from the riverside Swan Tavern was a small bay with steps leading up to a landing pier that our oarsman was steering us toward. "This is the place, madam."

I could see now that the land that lay behind the pier, open to the river, had been transformed into a garden. It was laid out in regular beds with neat hedges of box, straight rows of plants and narrow avenues created between them. But it smelled like no ordinary garden. It smelled like Christmas, like Maytime, it smelled like the wedding day of my dreams. The air was filled with the scent of bay, rosemary, lavender and thyme.

In the center, where all the avenues converged, was a sundial. In the bed nearest to it a man bent low over one of the shrubs, plucking leaves and placing them in a widemouthed glass jar. Two bewigged gentlemen were standing about smoking pipes by an ornate boathouse. I drew myself up to my full height, such as it was, and walked toward them. I asked where I might find James Petiver, the young apothecary who studied butterflies.

One of the gentlemen nodded toward a secluded area of the garden behind some fruit trees. "Expect that's who you mean."

I told Bess to wait on a nearby stone bench and went on alone.

The first thing I saw was a little cloud of yellow butterflies, a whole throng of them. Then I saw that they were massing around the head and shoulders of a boy. He had a pleasant, clever face and corn-fair hair, two shades darker than my own. He was perhaps four or more years younger than I. His shirtsleeves were rolled up to his elbows and he was dressed in the blue apron of an apprentice. As many as a dozen butterflies were fussing and flitting around him, brushing him with their wings. He had one of them poised on the tip of his finger and, miraculously, it stayed there, perfectly still, as he lifted his finger until it was on a level with his nose, at which point it obligingly unfolded its wings as if for his sole admiration.

I stood and stared until he noticed me watching him. He crouched down and placed his finger next to a white flower. The yellow butterfly dutifully hopped off.

"How do you make them do that?" I said in wonder.

He stood. "*Vin rose.* You sprinkle it on your hands and they come and drink it."

"Could I try?"

"If you like." His smile was friendly but doubtful, as if he couldn't quite believe I was interested, couldn't quite believe I was even real.

I walked closer and offered him my hand and he sprinkled some pinkish liquid from a glass vial onto my skin. The butterflies started swirling around me. I stood very still. One settled on my shoulder, another in my hair and one on my hand. They were tame as kittens. I felt a curled antenna probe my skin, quick and fleeting as a grass snake.

"See, they think you're a flower."

I laughed. "I wonder what kind."

"Something rare and pretty," he said, matter-of-factly.

I raised my eyes but I could hardly see the sky. All I could see were butterflies. "I'm Eleanor. Eleanor Goodri . . . I mean Ashfield."

He didn't seem perturbed by the fact I appeared not to even know who I was.

"James Petiver." He gave a quick bow, like a country boy from Tickenham would do, and I found it enormously refreshing in the midst of London polish and sophistication. I felt as if I had come home.

"I understand you're interested in butterflies," I said. "Well, I can see very well that you are." Now both of us had them in our hair. "So am I and I want very much to learn more about them. I hoped that perhaps you could help me."

He looked at me keenly, through the fluttering wings. "What is it that you want to know?"

"Oh, everything."

"That'll take a long time." He smiled but not in a derisive way. "But if everyone learns as much as they can and shares that knowledge, then we shall make a good start. I'll gladly help you."

"You will?"

"Of course. Butterflies are such a neglected though beautiful part of God's creation, but I hope in time that will change."

I noticed some intricate drawings carelessly scattered on the ground at his feet and bent down to pick one up. It depicted a red and black butterfly, and beside it a thistle. "Did you do these?"

"Yes."

"They're beautiful."

"Thank you. They're not as accurate as I'd like, but I do my best."

"I'm not very good at drawing at all."

"No matter. You can make accurate descriptions instead."

"I caught one of these," I said, leafing through more drawings and recognizing the red and orange markings and the orange tips on the antennae.

"You have a Large Copper?" James Petiver's eyes had opened wide. "They are most prized amongst butterfly collectors."

I could hardly see why, when they were so abundant on the moor. "Do you collect butterflies too?"

"You can't study a creature from a sketch."

"Mine are pressed between the pages of a book, but they're damaged so easily."

"That's not such a bad way. Adam Buddle and Leonard Plukenet preserve their specimens like flowers too. But butterflies have mealy wings so the colors get rubbed off. I place mine between sheets of mica, or sometimes in frames, like lantern slides. I'll send you some mica, if you like."

"Thank you."

His enthusiasm and directness were a little overwhelming. Already my head was spinning with all this new information, but I was hungry for more. "And is there a way of catching them without damaging them?"

"Ah, what you need is one of these." He produced a strange contraption that had been lying on a bench behind him. "It's a clap net, or butterfly trap." It was a strip of muslin held between two poles. He held them out to demonstrate. "You clap them together to trap the butterfly, see? The poles are of hazel."

I imagined willow withies would do just as well. "Now, why didn't I think of that?"

"It's not my idea either. It's the only useful piece of information I learned at school. One of the masters collected butterflies for his curio cabinet."

"Didn't you care for school?" I'd known him only a few minutes yet we were talking as if we'd known each other for years. I felt I could ask James anything.

"I was born in Warwickshire. My father was a haberdasher. My grandfather had high ambitions for me and wanted me to have an education. He paid for me to go to Rugby but I've learned a lot more since I left."

"We're the same, then." I grinned. "I don't much like being told what to do, or what to believe."

We were alike in so many ways. For a start, it was unusual for me to be able to have a conversation with a person eye-to-eye, rather than have to look up. His eyes, I noticed, were impossible to describe. They were hazel, flecked with green and gold and blue, as if they had absorbed something of the grass and the trees and the sunshine and the sky, and there was an extraordinary warmth and intelligence in them that was reflected in his smile. The butterflies still encircled and flickered around us, as if drawing us together, and I felt a bond between us, something strong and simple, not at all like my girlish infatuation with my husband, nothing like my disturbing desire for his friend. I thought of the dangerous rush of the Thames and of how this would be better than being able to swim, would be something to hold on to if my new life turned out to have such undercurrents. I knew I had found a friend, and had a strange sense that we were meant to find each other.

James was just a boy. He was the same height as I, lean as a withy, and his shoulders beneath his white shirt were bony still. He looked as if he had plenty of growing left to do but would never be particularly sturdy.

"How old are you?" I inquired.

I smiled to see him do what I so often did and straighten to make himself appear taller. "I became bound apprentice to St. Bart's three years ago," he said, with all the touching pride of a boy trying to be a man. I thought how frightening it must be to leave home and come down alone from the country to live in a strange city. "I'm supposed to be here studying plants, but everyone is doing that. I want to show that insects are equally worthy of effort, for the ultimate benefit of mankind."

"How?"

"There are two reasons to collect and cultivate plants: taxonomy and nomenclature." When he saw that I didn't understand he added quickly: "So we can classify and name them according to their shared characteristics, as well as keep a record of their medical and commercial uses."

"You think butterflies could be similarly useful?"

"I'm sure of it. They can teach us much about the processes that have generated the diversity of life on earth. Their transformation seems to hold the key to the origins of life itself."

"My father told me it held the key to life after death."

"He is far from alone in that belief. Metamorphosis is the source of much speculation, particularly in the Netherlands. A painter there claims to have kept caterpillars in jars and observed the entire cycle. In his book he compares it to resurrection, the rebirth of the soul after death."

I was elated. "There are others, in the Netherlands, who have seen this happen?"

"Jan Swammerdam has written a *Natural History of Insects*, which categorizes them by type of metamorphosis. He is certain worms come from eggs rather than being born from dew or cabbages, though I don't believe he has seen an egg or even a pupa. And he also says that Adam and Eve contained all the humans that came after them, which seems a rather wild notion."

Now I was confused.

"It's just a matter of time," he said brightly, as if he understood my bemusement. "There is still much to be discovered, about metamorphosis and everything else. But all is possible from the observation of nature. If we study birds and butterflies, I believe even people will be able to take to the skies one day."

Human flight seemed an impossible but splendid fantasy. I'd thought it had been mine alone. "Do you, honestly?"

He shrugged. "Why not?"

"Your grandfather must be very proud of you."

"He was, I think. He died in January."

"I'm sorry for that. Both my parents are dead."

"I'm sorry too." He looked at me speculatively, then put his hand in his pocket and offered me a hard-boiled egg. I thanked him, peeled it, took a bite, and then he handed me a hip flask. I took a long swig and molten fire ran down my throat. My eyes watered and I screwed up my face, laughing. "What in devil's name is that?"

"Whiskey." Grinning, he took the flask back, swallowed a nip himself and secured the top. "I want to help to encourage a free exchange of specimens and opinions," he said. "To build a community of scholars, with everyone contributing. If nobody communicates properly, progress will be very slow and fragmented, with nobody knowing what anyone else is doing or has discovered. To avoid duplication of effort, and in the broader interest of science, I believe very strongly that correspondence with like-minded people in other countries is as important as private study and experiment."

" 'Many shall pass to and fro, and knowledge will increase,' " I said, quoting Francis Bacon, feeling almost as if the father of science was watching over me, guiding me.

"Exactly," James said. "Ship's surgeons constantly visit apothecaries to provision their chests of medicines before a voyage. It is my plan to enlist their help. If I can send them off with instructions for collecting, they will spread an interest in insects across the seas at the same time as they bring specimens back. There are butterflies in the

New World that nobody here has ever seen, that we will never see in England, but this way we have access to them all."

I could hardly believe my luck in finding this boy. He was a genius, a visionary. He made everything seem possible. My own ambitions at once seemed very limited, yet I had never felt so inspired.

"I could write to you?" he offered.

"I'd like that."

"And will you write to me?"

"I will." I agreed with all the wholehearted solemnity and sweet joy of a wedding vow.

WE WERE HOME. It was pitch-dark with no moon, and it was raining, a fine, windswept spring rain that brushed my face like cobwebs as Edmund handed me down from the carriage and I breathed in the familiar peaty tang of the marshes. I was tired and I was hungry and it was so good to be home.

I knew this house, with its long-standing absence of mirrors, far better than I knew my own face. It called to me, spoke to me in a way that nowhere else ever could. I knew the sound of the great hinges and the bolts of the studded oak door as well as I knew the sound of my own voice. The cracks in the flagstones were as familiar to me as the lines in the palms of my own hands. My feet directed me without the need to think. I knew how many worn stairs to climb up to my bedchamber, how many paces took me from the parlor to the great hall. I had been on a long journey, but here I was again, back where I belonged. Though Tickenham Court was now entirely Edmund's, had passed from my father to him as if I did not count, I did not feel disoriented or displaced by that, as I had expected to. I had an unaccountable feeling that I had not really lost it at all.

Edmund looked very comfortable at the head of the long table, in the great carved chair with arms that had been polished by the repeated touch of my father's hands. I was in the smaller carved chair, my mother's chair, and had a very strong sense of the generations of ladies of the manor who had sat before me in this very hall. Edmund and I would eat our supper here, more a late dinner, really, since it was hot, and then we would go up the stone stairs to the bedchamber which generations of Tickenham Court ladies had shared with their lords. We would sleep together in the sturdy oaken matrimonial bed, the very same bed in which my mother and father had spent their first nights as newlyweds. There was a reassuring continuity in it all, though I felt and understood, as if for the first time, the weight of responsibility my father had always spoken of.

Edmund smiled benignly at me down the table, then went back to enjoying his meal, chewing with relish, as if he had not a care in the world, as if nothing troubled him or indeed ever would.

There was one small thing that marred my pleasure in being home. I set my fork down on the pewter plate, pushed it away, leaned back against the unyielding carved wood of the chair and folded my arms. "Do you know, I hate eel pie. I have always hated eel pie."

Edmund glanced up at me, his mouth full. "Can't think why. It's delicious."

I smiled. "Not when you've had to eat it at least three times a week for your entire life, it's not. I hate eels in whatever way they are served. Salted, cured, smoked, stewed."

"So tell the cook what you'd like prepared instead," Edmund said, forking another generous helping. "You have governance of the kitchen now, of the entire household. This is like our own little commonwealth."

"Didn't you know? The days of commonwealths are over. Thanks be to God. Just because you are sitting in my father's chair, there is no need to start talking like him."

He grinned back at me. "You sit in your mother's chair, yet I see you do not intend to emulate her at all. Pity. I have heard exceptional reports of her from William Merrick. It is my understanding that she was chaste and loyal as well as meek and modest. The best things a wife can be."

I was sure he must be teasing, but still I stiffened.

Edmund did not appear to notice, or else chose not to. "My own father always advised of the benefits of marrying a young girl," he added. "One not yet spotted or sullied, one I could shape and mold into the wife I wanted her to be. There's no need to look at me like that." He smiled. "I mention it only because I should like you to know that I am very content with your shape, just as it is."

The tension left my shoulders.

He stood and walked the length of the long table, taking my hands in his and raising me to my feet, kissing my fingers with his soft lips. "We have never had a falling-out, have we?" he said. "And I do not ever want us to have one."

That seemed a rather daunting aim, though maybe not for someone as mild-mannered as my husband. "We are bound to have misunderstandings I think, aren't we? At least at first," I ventured. "There is so much we still do not know about each other."

"We have plenty of time to learn. We have our whole lives ahead of us. Our whole lives to spend together."

"Dearest Edmund." I looked at his open handsome face and much of the emotional turmoil of the past few days drained away like the winter floods in spring. I just needed a little time to adjust to my new situation, that was all.

"We shall be happy here," he said. "This is a beautiful house." He kissed the tip of my nose, then my forehead. "It is our house now. Our home."

I looked around the gloomy hall and an idea glinted at the back of my mind, like a solitary jewel swept beneath the floorboards. I could make Tickenham Court truly ours. I could make it beautiful, transform its Puritan austerity with brightness and comfort.

"We can hang printed calico or striped muslin at the windows," I whispered, tentative at first and then growing bolder as fresh plans rushed at me. "We can replace all the dark oak with rosewood and walnut. We can light the rooms with great candelabra. And we can have mirrors, and padded armchairs upholstered in striped silk, and replace the rush matting with Oriental carpets. And we can buy pepper and ginger and cinnamon too, so we can eat food that doesn't taste of marsh and peat." I was grinning now, thinking that I could and would do it. I would work very hard to make a success of this marriage. Edmund was good and kind and I did love him. What I felt for Richard was surely just desire and lust, not love at all. And I didn't need desire and lust to make me happy, did I? I would make Edmund happy too. "The very first thing we shall have," I said, "is a silk quilt for our bed, stitched with all the colors of the rainbow."

Edmund was looking concerned. "I doubt we can afford quite all that," he said.

"But of course we can, we're wealthy landowners. Mr. Merrick has always said so."

"We've lived through enough dire and changeable times to learn that we can never know what's waiting round the corner," he said judiciously. "The King might make a levy on us tomorrow, for horses or arms for another war with the Dutch."

"Then we may as well spend it first."

"We should invest and save. We mustn't be reckless."

The rain had turned heavier, beating at the windows, and it was blowing a gale. It would only take a high spring tide to pile up the waters in the estuary and block the outflow of the already swollen rivers. They would burst their banks, inundate the fields and drown all the fresh grass and the bright spring flowers in their first bloom. Suddenly, I knew just how that felt. "Surely buying a few new furnishings for our marital home is not reckless?" I rested my palms against his chest and felt how steady his heart still was. I picked at a thread in his waistcoat, tweaking the stitched cloth gently between my fingers. "Besides, I'd like to be reckless, just a little. I'd like to know what it feels like. For a short while, at least."

"I know how much you liked the trinkets I sent you before we were betrothed," Edmund said. "I realized then you had a rather worrisome liking for material possessions. But we don't need such folderols. We have each other. We have this lovely house and a comfortable income. We already have everything we could possibly need." He smiled at me softly, a little shyly. "And if, with God's grace, we were to have a child, I should have everything I could ever want."

I slipped my arms around his back and rested my cheek against the bumpy brocade of his waistcoat. "Oh, Edmund, so would I. I want a baby too. I want your baby. Lots of your babies."

He dropped a kiss on the top of my head. "The household accounts are in your charge now," he encouraged me brightly, as if he was presenting me with the key to a castle. "The monthly housekeeping is yours to spend as you see fit. I daresay there's enough to buy some spices at least."

NEXT MORNING, I struggled with the practicalities of adjusting to my new position and duties. Mary and John were gone. Mr. Merrick had handed over all the great ledgers and account books and receipts and bills of fare, which were my responsibility now. I sat at my mother's small writing desk, in her tiny green-paneled closet, as if I might feel her guiding presence. I felt nothing but claustrophobia, and mounting frustration and inadequacy. The ledger had been open at the same page for what seemed hours. I rubbed the tips of my fingers against the closed lids of my eyes. When I opened them again the neat rows and columns of figures swam before me worse than before.

Bess bustled past the open door with an armful of linen. "Still there, miss? I mean, Ma'am?"

"Bess, I am not a nincompoop, am I?"

"You're the cleverest person I've ever met," she said, coming to stand in the doorway.

I smiled appreciatively at her loyalty. "Bless you for that, Bess. Oh, I should be able to do this easily," I said determinedly. "There is nothing especially difficult about it. A simple case of balancing profits from rents and the fisheries against outgoings on wages and expenses."

"That all sounds quite difficult to me."

I propped my chin in my hand and frowned at the ledger. I knew what to do in principle, but the practice was rather different. The real trouble was that I wasn't overly interested, never had been, never would be, I suspected. But it was my life now. "It looks as if it does balance. We do have a small fortune, but it seems to cost as much to run this estate. And it's up to me now to see that the larder and pantry are amply stocked with provisions, to make arrangements for meals, to make sure you and the other maids are paid."

"Keeping house can't be as hard as learning to read a whole book in Latin," she said helpfully.

"It can, Bess. It is bewildering."

"Your mother was good at it, by all accounts."

"I know it. You don't need to tell me again." The servants and villagers had told me a hundred times how her gentleness had hidden formidable organizational skills. "I know she ordered the kitchen garden and the dairy and the fishery with patience and grace. I know she was always willing to roll up her sleeves and lend a skilled hand with the cookery and fruit preserving."

"You are gentle and graceful, Ma'am, and willing and hardworking. And I am sure you can learn to be ordered."

I laughed. "Well, right now I can't even calculate if we can afford a new carpet."

"Your father taught you arithmetic, didn't he?"

"He did, but he did not rear me to be a housekeeper."

And yet he entrusted this house into my keeping. He taught me that it was my first and foremost obligation to be a good custodian of my birthright, of my children's inheritance, but at the same time had encouraged my interests in a world beyond mere accounts-keeping.

"You could ask Mr. Merrick to help you," Bess suggested, tentatively.

"I could, yes. If I could put up with the I-told-you-so look on his face. I don't need him to remind me that much good geography has done me, when what I really needed to be paying attention to was how many loaves of bread are needed to feed a houseful of servants."

"I'd best leave you to work on it, then," Bess quipped. "Unless I want to go hungry."

She left me gazing longingly out of the tiny closet window, absently brushing the quill feather against my cheek. The rain of the previous night had passed, and with the typically capricious nature of spring, the sun was shining enticingly. A buzzard wheeled higher and higher in the milky blue sky. For my father this house represented my security. To me just then, much as I loved it, it felt more like a kind of imprisonment, the one thing that frightened me above all else. I groaned and laid my head down on the table, folding my arms up around me as if I feared the roof of this grand and ancient manor might fall down and crush me.

"It can't be that bleak," Edmund said breezily, as well he might when he'd been out riding all morning. "Mr. Merrick assured me all was in good order."

I sat up, saw him and stared, aghast. "Good God!" Then I laughed.

"Don't you like it?" he asked chirpily. "It's very fashionable."

He was wearing the most vile brown periwig.

"It just arrived with the carrier from Bristol. I ordered it last time I was there. Thought, now I am a husband, I'd better have one, so I look more distinguished."

"Take it off," I pleaded. "Edmund, I mean it. Take it off right now, please."

"Why?"

I stood up and swiped the horrid thing off his head myself. My hands flew to my mouth. "Edmund! What have you done?"

To accommodate the wig, he had shaved off every lock of his own lovely copper hair.

I sank back into the chair. Ridiculously, I looked from Edmund's shaved head to the ledger in front of me and a tear slid down my cheek. It splashed onto the page, instantly blurring the neat inked figures. I made to wipe it away but Edmund whipped the book from under my fingers.

"You'll only smudge it and make it worse," he said, with no hint of reproof, handing me a neatly laundered cloth as he sat the ghastly wig back on his bald head. "I'll grow my hair back if it really means so much to you. Please don't cry about it. For Heaven's sake, it is nothing to cry about."

"I know it's not," I said, hurriedly wiping the tears away. "I'm sorry. I don't know what's the matter with me."

Edmund handed the accounts back to me.

"I don't know what to do with them," I admitted.

"You'll soon learn," he said. "You'll be a prudent and frugal house-

keeper before you know it. Here's something to cheer you anyway."
He produced a flat, square parcel from behind his back.

"Oh, Edmund! A present!"

"It's not from me. The carrier brought it as well. From the bookseller, I assume."

I hadn't ordered any books, and if it was a book, it was a decidedly
thin one. But it was definitely addressed to me: Eleanor Ashfield,
Tickenham Court, Somersetshire. The writing was small and crabbed.
It was the first time I had seen my new name in writing and it gave
me a strange feeling, made me feel like a small tributary that flows
down from Cadbury Camp and loses itself in the Yeo, as it is swept
onward toward the sea.

Edmund had walked away, not at all curious to see what was inside
the parcel.

I slipped my finger beneath the brown paper wrapping. It was not
a book at all, but a sheaf of papers bound in vellum. I caught my breath
as I carefully turned over the leaves. It was a collection of original
colored drawings of butterflies, rich with yellows, oranges, reds, blues.
Beside each illustration were notes on the location of sightings, on
flight patterns and preferred food plants. It was like looking through
a rich illuminated manuscript, like the one John Burges had shown
me once.

There was an inscription on the covering page, in the same untidy,
almost childish hand as had penned the address.

*There are no books in existence that are solely devoted to butterflies, so
I have made one for you. Your friend, James Petiver.*

There were tears in my eyes again but for a totally different reason.
I dashed them away before they had time to fall and spoil the lovely
paintings. I was stunned by such thoughtfulness and generosity. It
must have taken him hours, days, to copy out all his drawings and

notes for me. I might know nothing of the cost of a bottle of claret, or of running a household, but I knew that what I had here was worth more than money could buy. This gift was more precious than any silk or silverware, more precious than any trinkets or lace. I knew, somehow, that this gift, this friendship, would be my salvation.

Summer

1676

I held my breath. Some distance away but unmistakable, flying powerfully over the sedges, was the magnificent lemon and black butterfly with scalloped, sickle-shaped wings, like the Gothic arches in a church or a swallow's tail. It was larger than any other butterfly and so stunning it seemed almost unreal. It was my most burning ambition to see one up close. I'd learned their favorite haunts, knew they seemed to like milk parsley, but they were proving extraordinarily elusive.

I walked forward slowly, at the ready, remembering how kittens learned to wait for the right moment to pounce. I whispered a quick prayer that this specimen would drift within my reach. Miraculously, it alighted on a thistle and I crept as close as I dared, then sprang forward, my hands cupped. I tripped and landed flat on my face, while the butterfly danced off, gaily evading capture, much to Edmund's amusement and the other fishermen's undisguised and total mystification.

"It seems rather cruel, anyway," Edmund said, having set down his fishing rod on the riverbank to watch me. "How can you like butterflies and also quite happily kill them?"

"This from the person who likes nothing better than a plate of eels fried alive for his dinner? James says it is the only way to study them properly."

Edmund was no more jealous of my correspondence with James Petiver than he had been of Richard's attentions to me. "I can't see any point whatsoever in catching what you cannot eat," he added indulgently. "But if it makes you happy, then so be it."

It did make me happy, and I was sure that I could remain so, could be quite content with this life, if only Richard did not come to visit, as he soon must, to upset my equilibrium again.

I turned my mind determinedly to the problem of the elusive specimen. I needed a net like James Petiver's.

I had written to James to thank him for the drawings and enclosed one of the copper-colored butterflies he so valued. In little more than a week, in almost no time at all, I had had a reply to my letter.

I did not open it at once, did not want household distractions to ruin my concentration or enjoyment, so I waited until I could take it down to the moor. Then, leaning against a willow trunk by the Yeo's curved bank, I broke the seal.

It was a long letter, scrawled in his untidy, hurried, boyish writing that was rather a struggle to read, but which pleased me because it suggested that the author had far more important matters with which to concern himself than the forming of neat curves and hooks. Just the sight of his handwriting made me feel unaccountably, uncomplicatedly happy and I smiled to myself as I read, imagining him bent over a little desk, scribbling away with ink-stained fingers, all the things he wanted to tell me coming into his head faster than he could write them down.

Besides asking me how I did, the letter contained directions on how to study, preserve and log butterflies. He emphasized the importance of keeping an observation book, to note down exactly where and when I had found each specimen, to record colors in case they faded. He had drawn a little diagram of a clap net, in case I'd forgotten how it looked, and explained how I might make one for myself.

Over the next days I set about hacking off withies and cut up two perfectly fine muslin kerchiefs. With a notebook and lead pen, I spent hours amidst the lilac haze of lady's-smock and cuckooflowers on the moor. I wrote to tell James the net was a miraculous invention that let me swipe butterflies from the air, of how amazed I was each time I trapped one, saw its fine legs poking through the tiny holes.

I found that cataloguing and preserving butterflies in the mica James had sent to me seemed to give me extra enthusiasm for other tasks. With Edmund's patient help, I mastered the accounts, and though I'd never find my vocation as a bookkeeper, butterfly collecting brought out a methodical side to my nature which, when applied to the household finances, made them start to make sense. It gave me great satisfaction to see neat rows of figures in my own sloping hand and to realize that I could make a success of running this house. If I felt Edmund was shaping me slowly and very subtly into a good housewife, for all that he had said he would not want to, then, I told myself, it was not such a bad thing and I did not really mind so much after all.

I did not even mind overseeing the beating of the bed hangings or the ordering of the linen cupboard because, surprisingly, there were other aspects of housewifery that I found interesting, and which even offered me opportunity for experiment and observation. From Bess I learned that pewter was best burnished with mare's tail, brass cleaned with charcoal, and silver with salt and vinegar. Ned Tucker's sister, Lizzie, who worked in the cider house and stillroom, taught me all about the process of fermentation. I pored over the book of herbal remedies, used by my mother and Mary Burges, and made up poultices and ointments, as and when they were needed.

"You like being lady of the manor, I think?" Edmund said to me one evening, as we shared a supper of cold beef and talked about our day, in the manner that had quickly become routine for us. Usually, the conversation centered on impersonal matters: boundary disputes between the tenants, the hiring of laborers to tend the orchard for the harvest, the incompetence of the dairymaid who had let the milk sour. It was rare for him to express an interest in my likes and dislikes, in what I wanted from life, and I welcomed the opportunity to talk to him about what was close to my heart.

I reached for the fruit bowl and took a bite from a juicy purple plum. "I like walking up to the cottages and drinking dishes of cold cream and sympathizing over toothaches and boils and fractious babies," I said. "I like feeling needed and appreciated."

"I shall always need you and appreciate you." Edmund smiled fondly at me. "But the villagers certainly seem to have taken you to their hearts."

It pleased me perhaps more than anything that the people of Tickenham seemed to have accepted me as mistress of the manor so readily. I had brought them a new lord who was far more lenient than their previous one, and was proving to be a good wife to him, in their eyes. And, as they saw it, I had called a halt to the drainage plans. True, Thomas Knight and Susan Hort did whisper aside together when they saw me with my strange butterfly trap, but I did not let that trouble me.

"I like rocking the babies best of all," I said. "I could do that for hours."

Edmund's eyes softened. "You will be an expert mother."

"I hope I can be one very soon. If only so I don't have to pretend not to see the women's knowing glances at my belly and answer their constant inquiries after my own health." I chuckled. "When I tell them I am well, they are so disappointed. They'd rejoice if I said I was nauseous and exhausted. As would I."

"I too," Edmund agreed.

"I do pray every night and every morning that God will let me be fruitful."

"My dear, I am certain He will. If only you were more patient and at ease about it."

"That is easier said than done."

"Aye, for you, most certainly."

"It is only that I cannot think of a punishment much worse than barrenness."

"My wife, why ever should you be punished? What have you ever done that is so wrong?"

There was a moment of silence which I hurried to fill. "I was raised a strict Puritan, remember? I live in constant fear of punishment."

"It is of course a Puritan's duty to multiply," he said with levity. "Your bounden duty as a wife."

I licked the plum juice from my fingers. "My bounden duty and my most passionate wish," I said seductively, but he looked almost alarmed as I took his hand and led him toward the stone stairs leading to our bedchamber.

Autumn

1676

Five months later, still in my nightshift, I drew my knees up on the oriel window seat and hugged them as I waited for Bess to come and help me dress. I turned my head and rested my cheek against my folded legs and gazed out of the window. The sky was colorless, an even blanket of thick cloud, and a low ground-mist hung over the rivers and flat fields.

"What's the matter?" Bess asked.

"My courses have started again," I said to Bess, twisting my head round to her. "Bess, why aren't I with child yet?"

She put her arm around me and sat herself down beside me in the embrasure. "Have you been doing it with your husband regularly?" she asked, coming straight to the heart of it as usual.

I stared at my bare toes, twiddled them. "Is every other night regular enough?"

"Not every night? Not several times a night?"

"He's very considerate," I said quickly, not wanting her to think less of Edmund.

She gave me a look that was almost pitying. "Does he not like it if you try to lead him, lamb?"

I tucked a loose lock of hair behind my ear, shook my head.

Bess tutted. "Does the man not accept you have needs of your own?"

I smiled. "Oh, I think he'd be most disconcerted by the very idea of that."

"Doesn't sound very considerate to me, then." She sniffed. "Does he at least take longer over it than he did at first?"

"Does that make a difference?"

"Well, it most certainly would to me."

I could not help but laugh. "I mean, surely it doesn't make any difference to whether you can make a baby or not? So long as his seed is inside me, surely that's all that counts?"

"Pumping seed is probably all it takes to make a baby, but if you ask me, it's most definitely not all it takes to make a husband."

I laughed again, even as I drew my knees tighter as if to banish and deny the dull ache in my abdomen. "Is it true that a woman has to experience real pleasure in bed for the seed to take root?"

"Absolutely vital. I thought everyone knew that. So has he found your little mound of pleasure yet? Do you still have to pretend?"

I didn't answer immediately. We had always talked like this, Bess and I, and there had seemed nothing wrong in it until now. I knew Edmund would be so hurt if he knew I had discussed the most intimate details of our lovemaking and found him wanting. And yet I needed somebody to talk to, to confide in.

"Maybe I'll never have a baby, then," was all I said.

Winter

1677

had woken up hungry in the middle of the night and was in the pantry helping myself, by the light of a single candle, to cheese and rye bread. My breath was misty and I shivered in my nightshift. It was not much warmer when I took my little feast through to the kitchen, where the glowing embers of yesterday's great cooking fire had been covered over with a brass dome, waiting for the bellows to breathe life back into them come the morning.

I set the round of crumbly cheddar on the long scrubbed table and cut off a chunk. I had just put it in my mouth when I heard a soft tap at the door in the great hall. It was still completely dark outside and I was sure I'd misheard. But there it came again. Firmer this time, more urgent, a definite rap against the thick studded oak. I hesitated, uncertain what to do. There were no servants about yet, nobody else to answer it except me, and I was hardly dressed to receive a visitor. Yet I couldn't ignore it. Nobody would call at this hour unless it was an emergency.

I took up my candlestick, shielded its guttering flame with my hand as I made my way through the drafty cross passage and across the great hall, bracing myself to find a distressed commoner who'd not been able to rouse the midwife, or had news, God forbid, of a breach in the seawall. I drew back the bolts and swung open the door. Froze.

"Richard!"

"Eleanor," he echoed, with almost as much surprise. "Not a butler or a serving girl, but the little lady herself. How very fortunate." He slid one leg forward, swept his feathered hat off his black hair, bowed low and came up again gracefully, the white lace ruffles of his shirt luminous in the dark.

"Is something the matter?" I asked him. "What are you doing here at this hour?"

His eyes twinkled with mischief. "I might have hoped for a warmer welcome. When I've ridden all through the night, and a bitterly cold night at that, just to be sure I was the first person to see you this Saint Valentine's Day morning, just to be sure I was in time to take you as my own Valentine."

"In time to . . . as your . . . what?"

"Your Valentine," he repeated with a smile, his teeth biting softly on his bottom lip and his eyebrows slanting rakishly. "Or had you forgotten it's February the fourteenth? The feast of Saint Valentine? The one day in the calendar when even a wedded girl is free to kiss whosoever claims her first."

There was not a trace now of the vulnerability he had revealed when he had lain wounded with his head in my lap. I did not know which of these different sides of his personality was the more devastating. One moment he had all the sweetness of an angel, the next all the charm of a Devil. The very way he swung between the two left me breathless and strangely exhilarated.

"Aren't you going to let me in?" he asked. "Before I catch my death of cold."

I moved aside and he stepped through the door, pushing it closed with his foot.

I was acutely aware of the contours of my body, silhouetted inside my fine linen shift, my breasts and nipples hardened by the cold and by a desire that descended on me like the mist over the moor, occluding my senses, blocking out all else save his beautiful face, his black curls, the swirling folds of his riding cloak and the soft, velvety richness of his voice. "Since I've explained why I'm here," he said, "why don't you tell me what you're doing, wandering around a dark house at night all alone?"

"I was hungry."

"I can see hunger in those pretty eyes of yours well enough. But I doubt very much that it's the kind of hunger that anything in your larder can satisfy."

"Richard, stop it. Please."

He removed the candleholder from my hand, set it on a little table. He moved closer to me and I took a step back. He followed, as if we were conducting some strange, silent dance. Then he reached out one finger and traced the line of my cheek, making me quiver with a pleasure so intense it was almost like pain. "Please," I said again. "You have to leave."

"Not before I have claimed my Valentine's kiss."

My eyes moved to his mouth, the lips slightly parted. It was the most fascinating mouth, as beautiful as the rest of him. Small and neat and with a slight pout, it had an almost childish sweetness. His upper lip curved like a bow. It was a mouth made to kiss and to be kissed.

I swallowed. "You aren't the first to see me this morning at all," I argued lamely. "Edmund and I share a bed, naturally. So he was the first person I saw when I woke. I am not for the claiming."

"I assume Edmund was sleeping. He didn't see you. It does not count."

"I've never heard that before." I half smiled. "You can't just make up your own rules, you know."

"If I can't make them, I'm quite prepared to discard them if they stand in my way."

"What would you have done if I had not been awake, had not heard you at the door?"

"I'd have broken in and woken you with a kiss."

"And what if one of the servants had been about to open the door to you?"

"I'd have told them I had a most urgent and private message to give to you and I'd have sent them to fetch you to me."

"You had an elaborate plan."

"But I didn't need it. You were here yourself, waiting for me, as if you knew I was coming. As if this was meant to be."

"It is not meant to be, Richard," I said slowly. "You know that."

He cupped my face in his hand, his expression suddenly desolate. "Little Nell, I know nothing anymore."

I struggled for something to say, anything that might anchor me in some normality. "Nobody has ever called me Nell."

He stroked his thumb firmly along my cheekbone. "D'you like it?"

"Yes," I said, laying my hand over the back of his, as if to remove it, though instead I just held it closer, tilted my head into his touch. "Yes."

"Nell," he said again, making it sound like the sweetest endearment. "You must let nobody but me ever call you by that name."

"I don't really think you can take such possession of another man's wife."

He let his hand slip away, fall to his side, leaving my cheek feeling suddenly cold and exposed. "I am sorry that I missed your wedding."

"Edmund did say you are dependably undependable."

He did not return my brief smile. "You know the reason I did not come."

"It was very quiet anyway. We had only a few guests."

"If you were my bride I should want to celebrate it before everyone, with a feast that went on for twelve days."

"I never can be your bride, Richard."

He did not answer. There was for an instant an awareness for both of us that what I had said was not wholly true, but that there was only one eventuality that would leave me free to marry again. For one wild beat of my heart I was afraid of what he was capable of and of what he might do. I looked into those capricious, quicksilver eyes of his and for one chilling, insane half-beat of time, it wasn't so very hard to see him as amoral and corrupt, like the worst picture my father had ever painted of Cavaliers, a murderous dueler, the kind of man who'd stop at nothing to have what he wanted.

"I love my husband," I said firmly. "I love Edmund."

"I love Edmund too," he echoed savagely. "I've known him all my life. His father and my father knew each other all their lives. Do not think I am not tortured by guilt for this, for how I feel about you. But I cannot help myself. I cannot help it that for these past months I have tossed and turned in my bed every night for longing for Edmund's little wife. Nell, I have never wanted a woman as I want you."

When I said nothing he slid his hand around my waist, drew me closer to him. Then his hand moved around my back as he held me. "You know what it is like to be driven by an obsession, I think," he whispered. "You know what it is to want something and to strive after it, and to desire it all the more the harder it is to catch, the more unattainable it is." He fixed me with a melting blue gaze. "I saw Edmund when he was last in Suffolk. He told me how you have a favorite butterfly that is yellow and black but you can never catch one of them. He made me look for them with him, but he wouldn't look as you look, as if your life itself depended on finding one, as if your whole being was caught up in pursuit of it, in possessing it and having it to keep with you forever. Edmund doesn't know the power of such an obsession. He is not passionate. He does not know the force of a desire that overrules all reason, a hunger that can never be satisfied yet demands to be satisfied."

I had forgotten how to breathe. "That sounds like madness." Except that I understood exactly what he was talking about, saw that he understood me, as if he had seen into my soul.

"If it is madness, little Nell, then it is you who have driven me mad," he said. "And I must have my kiss, or I cannot account for what I might do."

"Very well," I said quietly, feeling my lips already softening to receive him. "A Valentine kiss. That is all it is."

Almost before I knew what was happening he bent his head and pressed his mouth against mine, so softly at first, slow and tender, and then harder, deeper, more insistent. Sensation rippled down through my body, through every limb, to the ends of my fingers and the tips of my toes, to an agonizingly sweet peak of sensation between my legs. I felt the firm, warm moistness of his tongue as it slipped inside my mouth and sought my own, tasting and exploring. I raised my hand in a halfhearted attempt to push him off, but he caught my wrist and held it, poised in midair, as if time itself had stopped, as if the night would never end and the sun would never rise. For once I didn't mind, didn't long for morning, for light, only for this, only for him.

He clasped me to him, his fingers splayed against the small of my back, pressing me urgently against his groin. I could feel the shaft of his arousal through my shift, against my belly. I did not move away but found myself pressing back. With his other hand he was caressing my breast, stroking and kneading. Entirely of their own accord, as if driven by instinct alone, my own hands had slipped up inside his shirt, were traveling up the warm nakedness of his back to his smooth shoulders, round again onto his taut belly, brushing against the fastenings of his breeches. He trembled at my touch, his eyes closed, long lashes shadowing his cheek. He moaned softly. I tipped my head back as his tongue traveled from my lips and down my throat. He held me tighter, pushed his leg between mine.

"No!" I broke free and shoved at him with both palms against his chest. "No. I cannot."

His eyes opened and they were full of hurt, of rejection, shadowed now by the agony of frustrated desire that matched my own.

"Go!" I said hoarsely, feeling faint, wanting to weep with desire for him. "You've had your kiss. You've got what you came for. Please, just go!"

"I have had what I came for, but I find it wasn't nearly enough," he said. "It can never be enough."

I COULD NOT SLEEP. I felt ill. So ill that I thought love must indeed be a sickness. I was lovesick. I must have been suffering what the physicians called erotic melancholy, the dangerous, infectious malady that was caused by excessive passion and unfulfilled desire. A physical disease that inflamed the body, boiled the blood, took possession of the mind, caused the humors to combust and consumed the liver. A rage of love that could, it was said, actually burn the sufferer's heart so that, upon examination after death, the organ resembled a charred timber.

I did manage to doze, eventually, but when I woke later in the morning I gagged the instant I sat up. I reached for the ewer and was violently sick, sicker than I had ever been since I was a child and my mother stroked my brow and murmured to me that she was there.

Now it was good, kind Edmund who sat with me on the edge of the bed and stroked the hair off my face and I was swamped by intolerable, crippling guilt. I thought how I had never felt so wretched, but fully deserved to feel much worse. Wanted to feel much worse. I spewed into the basin again and when I had done, Edmund handed me his own cup of warm ale, holding it for me while I sipped.

"Eleanor, my love, can it be . . . ?"

My lips still felt bruised by Richard's kiss, my cheeks still scratched by his stubble. I could still taste him, could feel his body imprinted against my own. I could not bear to look at Edmund's trusting, expectant face. I hardly dared to hope myself. It was preferable to lovesickness, at any rate. It could be true. I was hungry in the night, sick in the morning. Was I with child? "Maybe," I said hesitantly.

Edmund kissed my hand, in that formal, chivalrous gesture of his, but his kindly, freckled face was radiant with such pure joy that it made him look saintly, and beside him I felt like the very blackest and most wicked of sinners.

"Oh, Eleanor, that's wonderful news, the best news." He kissed the side of my head. "And I almost forgot. It is Saint Valentine's Day."

I HAD BEEN TAUGHT to be observant of signs and portents, but did not wholly believe in them and for that I was very glad. For if I saw this pregnancy as a sign that my marriage had been blessed, that the sin I had committed would go unpunished, there soon followed more ominous signs that the blessing might be taken away.

The sickness worsened around the forty-fifth day, the time when it is said that a baby's soul is born. I felt nauseous as soon as I sat upright and I could barely keep down a morsel of food. The constant retching left me limp as a wet leaf, but I believed I deserved no less, welcomed it, bore it like a penance.

Edmund was as thoughtful as he had sworn always to be. He touched me cautiously as if I was made of porcelain and refused to lie with me at all for risk of dislodging the baby. He took over the household management, so I wouldn't tire too much, and he took me on outings to Bath, where the waters were said to be beneficial for women who were with child. His concern and his love for me and for our baby were almost unbearable. The kinder he was to me, the more wretched I felt.

When he came to find me one morning, I was sitting on the chamber floor in my cambric chemise, my hair lank and loose, my back against the wall and my legs outspread before me like a rag doll as I cradled a basin in my lap.

"What is it about being with child that causes a woman to vomit?" I wondered apathetically, trying to be objective in the hope it might help a little. "Maybe it's the growing womb pressing on my insides, but surely that would be worse at the end of term rather than at the start?"

Edmund, not at all interested, took the basin off me and helped me to my feet. "Darling, this cannot go on."

"I'm sure it will ease soon."

"You've been saying that for weeks."

I grabbed the basin off him again, tossed my hair over my shoulder, doubled over and heaved, until it felt like my guts were being torn from within me. The retching was dry. There was nothing left inside my belly but a baby, and I was increasingly afraid that if this went on much longer, the baby must be ripped from me too.

And if it was not . . . It is well known that the womb is absorbent, that womb children are in danger from corruption, and I had exposed this little soul to so much wickedness. Richard had caressed my body wherein, unbeknownst to me, there had been planted my husband's seed. My body had been shaken to its core with a sinful passion for a man who was not the father of the child it carried. I was sure there could be no greater carnal sin. If my baby was not shaken from me, I feared it would be marked with the most baleful influences for the rest of its life.

Edmund must have seen fear in my face. "That's it," he decided. "I'm sending for Dr. Duckett."

"No."

"Eleanor, be sensible. We must."

"I will not see that charlatan, no matter how ill I am."

"He could bring you some physic," Edmund reasoned. "He could make you well."

"I have never seen Dr. Duckett make anyone well. All he has ever brought to this house is suffering and death."

Edmund looked at me, uncomprehending. "You are being absurd," he said helplessly.

I saw myself for a moment as he must see me, long fair hair in tangles, eyes enormous in a face that was drawn and pale with sickness, and I almost agreed to do as he wanted, just to make him happy, even if it did me no good at all. But I could not. "I have so longed for this baby," I said as I rested my hand on my still-flat belly. "Already I love him so much."

"Him?" Edmund smiled questioningly.

"I am sure we shall have a boy," I said. "I feel it. I cannot bear to think that anything will go wrong."

I let Edmund take me into his arms. "Eleanor, it is so unlike you to be so gloomy," he said, stroking my back. "Be of good cheer. Have faith."

I could not tell him that it was faith that made me gloomy. I had thought I had thrown off much of the indoctrination of my Puritan upbringing, but in the empty void of guilt it had rushed back with a vengeance. How could I forget the Puritan God who was always watching, waiting to reward good deeds and punish the bad? How could I ever forget the Puritan code which deemed that ill fortune followed wrongdoing just as night followed day? How could I ever forget years of teaching about how carnal lust was the way only to madness and ruin? Puritan law had once made adultery a capital crime, but it made no difference that it was no longer enforced, made no difference that Richard and I had not actually lain together. By God's law, I had committed adultery almost nightly ever since the day I learned to skate. I had no need of Dr. Duckett and his purges. It felt as if my body was trying to purge itself of my longed-for little child. The worst punishment I could imagine.

"Lie still and rest, at least," Edmund said.

But I knew that what I needed was not rest but reparation.

Alone in my chamber, I went down on my knees, clasped my hands and begged God for forgiveness, for allowing myself to be led into sin and temptation. I read the Bible and I murmured the catechism I had learned as a child. "My duty toward my neighbor is to do to all men as I would they should do unto me . . . to bear no malice nor hatred in my heart . . . to do my duty unto God, to keep my body in soberness and chastity."

I had learned to repeat those words before I even knew their meaning. I could say them backward, in my sleep. I did want to live by and be all those things. I did want to be sober and chaste. But oh, it was so much easier to say than to do.

Autumn

1677

The nausea did abate, to be replaced by ravenous hunger. My stomach gnawed as if there was a hole growing there, not an infant, but I delighted in piling my plate with odd combinations of cheese and fruit, pastries and meats, thinking how my baby had a fine appetite, must be growing strong and healthy after all. I had been forgiven, even if I could not forgive myself.

When I wrote to tell James I was expecting a child and that Edmund would not risk having me go chasing after butterflies, James sent me one small wing, iridescent purple-blue, from a butterfly he'd caught on an expedition to the fields that lay around King Henry VIII's great Hampton Court Palace. I wondered what had happened to the other half of the butterfly. It was an odd thing to send me, when we were usually so concerned with pristine specimens, but it was very pretty nonetheless, like a little petal or a fragment of sky, and I stored it away in the back of my Bible.

The bigger and less mobile I grew, the more I looked forward to receiving James's letters and the more I enjoyed replying to them. He said he and his friends had been butterfly hunting in Greenwich too, beside the new observatory, and on Primrose Hill, in the Mitcham lavender fields and in Fulham Palace Gardens. I would have been envious of this like-minded group of men, for whom a passion for butterflies was a social pursuit, who could visit such romantic-sounding places and share their discoveries, but for once I was glad to be a woman, for only a woman could know the joy of feeling a child move inside her own body.

James told me to drink sage ale to strengthen my womb, said that lilies and roses, cyclamen, or sowbread and columbine would nourish my unborn child and procure an easy and speedy delivery for me. I was very touched by his concern and told him what a skilled apothecary he was going to become.

He wrote, too, of the debate raging amongst his naturalist friends, one faction questioning spontaneous generation as a relic of ancient times, while another arguing that if a caterpillar could become a butterfly inside a pupa, why could a leaf not transmute into a caterpillar? All sides were calling for more investigation.

Preoccupied as I was by the changes in my own body, I tried to describe to him how the subject of metamorphosis had a strange resonance for me at this time. My swelling womb was just like a tightly wrapped pupa, ripening with the promise of new life. A new life that kicked and squirmed inside me, with tiny limbs forming and fluttering beneath my taut skin, just like wings. As I wrote the words, it occurred to me that I had never tried to describe the experience to Edmund, because he had never shown any real interest, considered it women's work. It was to James that I told of my eagerness to meet my baby. To James I explained how the promise of holding the little thing in my arms even helped ease my utter dread of banishment to a darkened lying-in chamber for weeks on end.

"Is that really all you are afraid of?" Bess said in disbelief, as I sat on a stool and let her rub my aching back. "Do you really fear the banishment more than the pain and peril of childbirth itself?"

"I was doing my best not to think of that." I grinned. "Until you kindly brought it up."

"Ned lived for the whole nine months in terror of my being taken from him for good, and I was petrified myself, I won't pretend otherwise. Any more than I can pretend that your danger is not great and the pains will not be grievous."

I laughed. "I thank you for your honesty, Bess. I can always rely on you to tell it to me as it is."

I wondered. Was Edmund afraid like Ned had been? If he was, he had not shared it with me at all. But then, when he came into the chamber as I lay half asleep, I felt the mattress dip to his weight as he sat down beside me. He laid his hand very gently upon my head, and I heard his whispered private prayer. "Lord, look upon my dear wife as she is great with child, give her strength and a gracious delivery from these perils."

It sounded very much like the prayers Puritans still said on Gunpowder Treason Night, to thank God for delivering us from the deadly plot of the Papists.

I AWOKE to a dull pain in my lower back, which sent out aching tentacles all the way round to my belly. It eased. I listened to the rain pit-pattering on the window. Then came another twinge, which also passed. The next one was more severe but it, too, subsided. So it went on for hours, with the spasms growing sharper as the downpour became more and more torrential, windswept and battering the glass, so that when I finally cried out for Edmund, for Bess, sleeping nearby, I was not sure they would hear me above the clatter.

For weeks I had been confined to this room. The bed had been drawn with hangings and drawn close to the fire, the windows and doors kept closed and covered, and I had a sudden need just to open the curtains and see daybreak, even if it was only a dank and murky one. I rolled clumsily to the edge of the mattress, pushed open the bed curtains. Bess woke and ran to the bed just as I stood up, and a huge gush of water poured out of me, dousing my feet and the floor, as if I had lived on the wetlands so long even my body had been flooded.

"Get back in bed," Bess ordered, almost pushing me back under the blankets as Edmund rushed in, still in his nightshirt, tousle-haired and blurry-eyed and carrying a candle.

I drew up my knees against another wave of pain. "It's started, Edmund," I grunted. "The baby is coming."

He was by my side in an instant. "Are you sure?" he asked, his voice ringing with panic.

"Don't sound so shocked. It is not as if we have not been expecting it to happen these past nine months."

"I'll send for the midwife, and the gossips."

"The midwife first," I urged.

"Yes, yes. Of course. The midwife." He was rushing to the door fast as a scalded cat but I called him back.

"Would you open the curtains for me before you go, Edmund?"

He hesitated. "But the manuals are very strict."

"I do not want this baby to be born into darkness," I said firmly. "Please, do as I ask."

Reluctantly, he went to the window while I screwed a ball of blanket in my hand as another wave of pain reached its peak.

Edmund came back to my side and watched my face twist with pain. "I would be so much happier if you were attended by a surgeon."

"If the parish midwife is good enough for the yeomen's wives, she is good enough for me," I said when the spasm abated. "Mother Wall may not even be able to write her own name, but her knowledge is the best there can be. It comes from the experience of her own eyes and ears and hands, and from the scores of babies she has safely delivered before."

He nodded. "I will fetch her for you." He left the room, hurtled back to give me a kiss, rushed off again. As Bess went to fetch the linen and I listened to a horse galloping off from the stables, I looked over at the canopied oak rocking cradle that had been moved over from the corner of the room to the side of my bed. "Please, God," I whispered, "let me rock my baby in his crib. Have compassion for me through the torture that's coming. Preserve my life and the life of my little child."

I felt much safer when Mother Wall arrived, with her stool and her knife, followed by more than a dozen gossips: Ann Smythe from Ashton Court; Bess and her mother; Mistress Keene, the cook; Jane Jennings, the former kitchenmaid, with her baby daughter in her arms; Mistress Bennett, wife of a wildfowler; Mistress Walker from the mill; and lastly Mistress Hort.

Between eating pasties and caraway comfits from the kitchen, they drew up stools around the bed and kept up a constant flow of chatter about their own labors and childbeds, their numerous children and their households. I was not expected to join in and it was comforting to listen to them, enjoying being all together, and to have their support, companionship and recollected experience as the crushing pains grew stronger and closer together, until I gripped Bess's fingers hard enough to break them and screamed that I couldn't bear it any longer. "Something must be wrong!" I yelled through gritted teeth. My shift clung to my body, soaked in perspiration, and my hair hung below my waist in sweaty rats' tails. "This cannot . . . cannot be normal."

"It is normal, child," Mistress Bennett soothed. "More's the pity. Now you stop worrying about it and let nature do its work."

"Why is it never like this for cows in calf?"

"We have grandmother Eve to thank for that," Mistress Keene said.

"Thank her!" I grunted. "I'd like to strangle her."

Bess chuckled.

The pain subsided once more and I took consolation from watching Mother Wall issuing confident instructions for the fire to be got ready, the candles kept lit. She could have been forty or she could have been a hundred. Her hair was silvery, her back stooped, but her fingers, with their neatly trimmed nails, were soft and remarkably supple for a marsh dweller. She anointed my womb and her own hands with oil of lilies, rubbed soothing salves and liniments into my skin, and gave me cups of caudles and herbal infusions. I did not ask her what was in them; for once I was content just to obey without question.

She probed me gently to see how the birth progressed and how the baby lay, and all the while she talked to me in her soothing country burr, telling me to move about and not lie still on the bed, to stand and lean against the bedposts, as the great waves of pain rose ever higher, so that I was sure they would rip me apart.

She patted my hand as I bore down and pushed with all my might. "You are doing very well, Ma'am," she said. "You screech all you want. We are nearly there now."

"You'll meet your little one soon enough," Mistress Knight soothed, and the thought of that made it more bearable, reminded me what lay at the end of my labor.

"How much longer?" I gasped.

"The babe will come in its own good time," Mother Wall said.

That turned out to be just before midnight. I squatted over a pile of rushes, with Bess supporting me under my arm on one side and her mother on the other, while Mother Wall knelt below me and peered up between my legs. "Its head is crowned," she said, as if he were a little prince.

And then, in one fiery eruption of ripping, gushing, hot, wet agony, my baby boy came slithering out like a fish between my knees, into the waiting arms of Mother Wall, who caught him like a boy catches a football. She flipped him over and slapped him on the back and he howled in protest, his little balled fists punching the air, his face red and contorted with anger.

I sat where I was on the floor, and tears of joy and relief spilled down my hot cheeks. I had a child. A healthy, living child, and I had survived to see him born. He was so perfect. I held out my arms. "Let me hold him," I said. "I want to hold my baby."

I did not need anyone to tell me to use my hand to support his fragile little skull. Holding him was for me as natural and instinctive as his first breath. I held him in my left arm, close to my heart, and with my right hand I carefully wiped the blood and stickiness off his tiny head with the edge of my shift. I noted that he had the blackest hair. Where Edmund was redheaded and I was fair, our son had hair as black as peat, and for a while, at least, he also had soft blue eyes. I kissed him and rocked him, stroked him and crooned over him, could not take my eyes off him. I was filled with love, a protective and pure love that was so powerful it was overwhelming.

"Thanks be to God," Bess's mother said. "You are delivered of your firstborn son."

Everyone crowded round with blessings for us both, examined him and pronounced him very well made. I was struck by an enormous sense of affection and kinship with these women who had been with me through my travail. They were my sisters now and it was a joy to be a woman, to be in the exclusive company of women. I felt exalted. With God's help, and with some help from my husband, admittedly, I had created life inside me. I had brought life forth. And I had survived to see a miracle. If death had seemed an everyday tragedy, so birth was an everyday wonder.

The midwife took my son back into her expert hands and I watched as she took her knife to cut the navel string. She dressed it with frankincense; then, as I was put to bed, she took the baby to the basin of warm water and sweet butter to bathe him.

"So, I have a son."

I tore my eyes away from the perfect little bundle and saw that Edmund had come into the birthing room. Poor Edmund. He looked so exhausted and so happy and so alarmed amidst the carnage, that all at once my heart went out to him.

I held out my hand and he came and took it and bent down to kiss my damp forehead. "Eleanor darling, I heard your screams and I was sure you were dying."

"You were not the only one." I smiled across at our baby as he was being swaddled by the midwife. "But it was worth the pain. I've almost forgotten it already."

He kissed me again. "I'm so proud of you. You were so brave."

The midwife handed our son to Edmund, who took him tenderly but awkwardly. "Father, see, there is your child. God give you much joy with him."

Much joy indeed. I felt a sweet elation that I had never felt before. I didn't even feel tired. Edmund placed the baby back in my arms and I kissed the top of his downy head, his sticky ebony hair.

"I feel as if it is I who have been born," I said. "Born again this day as a mother."

. . .

WE CALLED HIM FOREST. It was my choice and I was adamant that he must have his own name. He was to be Forest Edmund
but would be known as Forest. He was a child born to inherit this
land and I wanted him to have a name taken from nature.

Edmund acquiesced, no doubt thinking the name rather whimsi-
cal, but despite agreeing to that, for all he said he never wanted us to
have fallings-out, we did have an almighty disagreement about Forest's baptism.

Edmund was determined it should be just like our wedding, quietly and privately done, removed from public view, with only a select
gathering present. He wanted it to take place in the evening, in the
chamber where Forest was born. He wanted to present his son himself, with witnesses rather than sponsors, without the font or the sign
of the cross.

"The Roundhead kind of christening, you mean," I said disapprovingly, leaning back wearily against the angled pillows. "The kind of
christening my father gave me and my sister."

"Surely you would prefer it to be done in your presence?" Edmund
reasoned. "Rather than have him taken away from you? Surely you'd
prefer to be there to see our little one become a Christian soul?" He
looked down at our baby as he slept peacefully in the crib at the side
of the bed. "You have not been parted from him since he was born. I
can't believe you'd consider letting him go to the church without you.
I'd have thought that nothing would induce you to send him away."

I shifted to a more comfortable position, wriggled my feet under
the blankets to get some feeling in them. I was sure I'd have forgotten
how to use them once I was allowed out of this room again. "Of course
I would rather be with him. But since I am not permitted to leave my
chamber so soon after I have given birth, it is not possible."

"Then have it done here, in the chamber. It is more comfortable and more convenient, after all, and healthier too, to have the minister come to us rather than risk infection by taking someone so tiny out in the cold and the wet."

"The church is hardly very far." But I knew everything Edmund said was right, and did not blame him for thinking me very contrary. My fingers idly pleated the woven blanket. "Of course I would like to be at my son's baptism, but it is more important to me that it be a joyous celebration. What matters to me more than anything is that Forest should have the most joyous start to his life."

I may have submitted to the prescribed three days in the dark to give me time to recover from the birth, with the help of restorative drinks and dressings and doses of burned wine. But I would not allow them to move my baby's cradle into a dark and shadowy corner, no matter that the manuals said not to let the beams of the sun or moon dart upon him as he slept. I didn't care what the manuals said, any more than I cared if mothers were supposed to play no part in the arranging of a baptism. I could not let Edmund do it his way.

"I want it to be a grand celebration," I said. "I know if it's done in church it means I can't come, but so be it. You can tell me all about it afterward. I shall be content just to imagine the benches adorned with arras and cloth of gold and the font framed by heraldic banners, and our little boy, mantled in silk lawn and wool, carried proudly at the front of the procession in the arms of Mother Wall."

Edmund harrumphed. "Your father will turn in his grave."

It was undoubtedly true. For him the font was an enchanted holy relic, or an abomination left over from Popery, and the sign of the cross was akin to Devil worship, the mark of the beast. It was no wonder we were arguing about it. After all, friction over fonts had helped spark the civil war. Baptism was an issue that had split families, communities and congregations.

"My father made his choices and I'm making mine," I said. "I cannot agree that our baby might just as well be baptized in a pail. When I was born, the font was being used as a trough for the cattle to drink from, but John Burges saw to it that it was gilded again and reinstalled. It is fit for use now and I want us to use it. I want our baby baptized in it."

"John Burges can no more call himself a Puritan than can you," Edmund said, rather pompously.

"I don't call myself Puritan."

"Except in one respect." Forest had started wailing again and I had reached over and lifted him gently to my breast to give him suck. "And for that, I can forgive you much," Edmund said gently, watching us.

I settled the baby and gazed down as he guzzled contentedly, kneading my breast with his little dimpled hand. "Yes, I suppose I am Puritan in this, at least. How could I not agree with the Puritan ministers who claim nursing is a godly responsibility? Even if it is so exhausting and unrelenting."

Forest was uncommonly greedy, seemed to be constantly hungry, impossible to satisfy. He fed at all hours, all through the day and all through the night. But such was my infatuation with him that I couldn't bear to leave him to cry even for five minutes. I wanted to hold him and touch him and gaze at him all the time. My nipples were sore and cracked, so that when he latched on to them with his surprisingly sharp little gums, the pain sometimes made my toes curl. But I wouldn't have missed even that. "I could no more give him to a wet nurse than I could cut off my own hand."

Edmund handed me a cup of small beer, anticipating the raging thirst that hit me as soon as I started feeding. I drank, and then Forest let go of me and drew up his legs and started to squawk again. I lifted him onto my shoulder and patted his back. "There, there, my little man. Do you have a pain? I'll soon make it go away." I bent my head to him and kissed the crown of his head.

"How many times a day do you kiss him and tell him he is handsome and how much you cherish him?" Edmund asked me softly.

I kissed Forest again and smiled. "Not nearly often enough."

"We will do as you wish," Edmund said, bending to drop a kiss on my own head.

I caught hold of his fingers as he moved away. "Thank you, Edmund."

He turned to me at the door. "I shall ask Richard to be Forest's sponsor."

"Richard?" His name shattered the peace of the chamber like a clap of thunder on a sultry summer day.

"Richard," Edmund repeated, with what passed for harshness in his mild-mannered nature. "Or do you have objections to that too? Since it's your wish that our baby have a grand baptism, with cloth of gold and holy water and sponsors and whatnot, at least allow me to have my say over who those sponsors should be."

Because we had already had such a lengthy disagreement, I had to agree to this, wrong and twisted as it felt.

"I shall write to Richard now and ask him to come as soon as he can. I am sure he will accept. He is very fond of you, you know."

How could he be so trusting, so oblivious?

THEY'D ALL GONE to the church, and as I waited alone, the chamber desolate without Forest in it, I tried very hard to concentrate on imagining my little son being anointed, John Foskett, the curate, saying the words of the baptism over him. How we were born in sin, entered this wicked world bathed in blood, and were born again, through water. I prayed that the Holy Ghost would descend upon my boy and live within him, would give him grace and goodness, such as it seemed I did not have. For I had heard Richard Glanville's soft-spoken voice in the garden as the party returned to begin the evening of festive drinking, and my heart had tuned to its cadence as my ears strained only to hear him again.

I listened to the noisy merriment downstairs and for once I didn't long to join in. I clung to the seclusion and safety of my chamber like a startled rabbit will hide in the woodpile when a fox is about.

Now they'd all raised a glass or three of canary wine and enjoyed the christening supper in the hall. They'd had their fill of oysters and anchovies and wafers and caraways and christening cake, and the other guests had all been brought to my bedside to congratulate me and see the gifts of silver spoons and gilt bowls on formal display in the chamber.

"God bless your little one and grant you as much comfort as every mother had of a child," said Mary Burges, the other sponsor.

Edmund had given the midwife her ten shillings, the nurse her five, and every gossip had her sweetmeats to carry away in her handkerchief.

Still I had not seen Richard. And I would not let his name touch my lips to ask after him, told myself that it would be for the best if he did not come to see me.

Surely he must come.

The Smythe girls, Florence and Arabella from Ashton Court, crowded round Forest adoringly, kissed me and him and wished me much joy in my new little Christian. One of the boys from Clevedon Court poked his head between the beribboned heads of the sisters and looked at them cheekily in turn out of the corner of his eyes. "There's just as much joy to be had in begetting a babe as there is in cooing over one," he said, setting the girls to blushing and giggling.

"At this rate, this one christening will beget a hundred," Mr. Merrick complained to me as he kissed my hand. "You look well. Mother-hood suits you."

"It certainly does." The voice had come from the other side of the room.

I looked up to see Richard framed in the doorway, standing at the entrance to my bedchamber with an anxious look in his beautiful blue eyes, as if he was not certain he would be welcome.

I smiled at him, and as soon as I did he smiled back, strode confidently toward the high bed as if there was nobody in the room but the two of us, as if he would throw aside the blankets and climb in beside me, would gather me into his arms, with the drapes drawn to shut out the rest of the world.

"Motherhood does suit her indeed," he whispered tenderly, as if in response to the earlier comment, but speaking to me alone. "She has never looked more lovely."

"I thank you, sir," I said, as if there had been nothing more to it than a regular compliment. Only the hammering of my heart and a slight trembling of his hands told otherwise.

"It must be sweet torture for her husband," he added with feeling. "He must be in torment, knowing the joy of her, but being barred from her bed, not being able to touch her. When she lies there half dressed like a goddess of fertility, with her rosy cheeks and golden hair and her ripe breasts."

I was sure that everyone must hear the torment in his voice, must see the need in his eyes. But not even one eyebrow was raised at this lewd exchange. Of course not. It was, after all, entirely in order at baptisms to spice the talk with plenty of bawdiness. Only I guessed it was spoken with a real emotion. And I did not know how to man-age it. I heard little Forest stir and I called for them to bring him to me, even though he hadn't yet worked himself up to a proper cry. I clutched him before me as a knight might hold up a shield.

Richard seemed quite unable to stop his eyes wandering from my face to the fullness of my breasts, so that I hesitated before opening my shift in front of him. But Forest could smell the milk and began to nuzzle and root with his open mouth for my nipple, then to wail with impatience.

Richard looked down at him with a sudden sweet smile. "I never thought Edmund had it in him to father such a lusty child."

I thought with utter dismay how I was as lusty and greedy as my son. Richard had kissed me, and even if he had made love to me, I knew it would never sate my longing for him, not at all, but would only make me want him all the more. I had prayed for forgiveness and believed my prayers had been granted, but oh, how terrifyingly easy it would be to fall again. Was it always to be like this, every time I saw him? Was there to be no peace at all for either of us?

I bent my head low over my baby, my cheeks burning with a mixture of shame and longing and utter panic. "Our marriage has been blessed," I whispered.

"Edmund is a fortunate man. I would think myself the most fortunate man alive had I found such a pretty little mother for my son." The others had moved tactfully away from the bed to allow Forest's sponsor to get a better look at him. Richard leaned closer and with one slender finger pushed back the blanket as if to better study my baby's face. The lace cuff of his shirt brushed against the inside of my wrist like a caress. "What would a son of ours be like, I wonder?" he whispered, so quietly that nobody but me could hear, his eyes seeking mine. "Would his hair be black as night like this one, or golden as the sun, like yours?"

"We shall never know."

"Is that a note of regret I detect in your voice, Nell?"

I should have come back instantly with a retort to let him know he was in danger of overstepping the limit of permissible baptism banter, but I could not do it to him. There was a quiet desperation about him, as if he was barely holding himself together. One small push and he would fall to pieces. It seemed to make him revel in the risk he was taking, in talking to me this way in a crowded room, and I felt the safest thing for me to do was to play along. Or at least that is what I pretended to myself I was doing. "You can never get a son on me, but you can at least kiss me," I murmured lightly. "That is what is done at these occasions, after all. Everyone here has kissed me and so far you are the only one who has not. It would be entirely in order."

"Forgive me," he said a little harshly, as if he did not want to be flirted with. "This is a new experience for me. I have not attended many baptisms. Indeed I have seldom been with a lady in her bed-chamber without covering her skin with kisses."

I felt my own skin tingle, as if it had been sprinkled all over with icy water. It was with a stab of my own torment now that I imagined those other ladies who had lain naked with him, who had tasted what I could never taste.

"I'm curious," he said abruptly. "How long must you remain abed?"

"One month. Until I am churched."

He smiled, bit his lip. "Until then, you are still impure?"

"I am not a Jewess, Richard. I don't need cleansing. Only to give thanks."

As he moved closer to me still, as his lips brushed against my hair, I breathed in the scent that emanated from his clothes and his black curls, a faint mix of masculine sweat and horses, overlaid with sweet cologne. I felt his breath on the nape of my neck, on the soft lobe of my ear. If there was ever a girl in need of cleansing, it was me.

I tilted my head closer, toward his mouth.

He drew back.

I had to bite my own lips to stop a little moan escaping from my throat.

"I shall not kiss you again," he said quietly, and it felt as if the world had suddenly gone very dark, so dark that if it had not been for my little son, I might as well have closed my eyes and never opened them again.

MY MONTH OF PRIVILEGE after bearing my child was at an end. But when it came to the matter of how it should end, to whether or not I should be churched, Edmund had me all wrong yet again.

"I see that, now you are mistress of this house, you choose to reject every principle and value upon which you were reared. Surely a progressive little spirit like you wouldn't want anything to do with such a ritual? Surely you can't go along with the view of childbed taint, that there's something loathsome in the natural birthing of a child? My father was not the radical yours was, but even he saw churching as heretical Popish foolery that mocked God."

"Oh, Edmund." I groaned in exasperation, pulled a pillow round to the front of me, clasped it as I threw myself back against the rest. Then I glanced at him out of the corner of my eye as he stood beside the bed with his mug of small ale. I did not want to argue again. "D'you know, for someone so seemingly even-tempered and set on harmony, you can be mighty quarrelsome and opinionated?"

"You'd like a husband you could lead like a bull by the nose, a man with no mind of his own?"

"No. Not at all." I cuffed him playfully with the pillow. "I like a good debate very much. I am progressive, as you say. Which is why I want a churching."

He reached down and took the pillow off me, carefully set it aside. "You're all for discarding the old and embracing the new. But there's nothing new about churching, you know. It was restored to the churches with the King's restoration to the throne. Restored, not invented, mark."

"Resistance to it was one of the surest signs of Puritan feeling before Cromwell, before the war," I added. "I know all that very well. I don't need a lesson in history, thank you very much. But I am too young to have known the time before the war, as are you. It may not be new and different to the world, but it's new and different for me. I'm ready to walk out into our bright new age, but all the time I'm held back in the shadows. First by my father and now by you."

"I am sorry you feel that way."

"I just want to be like everyone else, for once."

He laughed. "You have a damnably odd way of showing it."

"In some things, at least." I demurred. "It's the current law and custom to be churched and for once I want to go along with that. That's all." I took Edmund's hand, drew him down to sit on the bed beside me. "I don't see it as a blasphemous ritual but a joyous occasion, a time for thanksgiving." I held his hand against my heart. "We have so much to give thanks for, Edmund," I said. "I was so very afraid, so very sure that I would never get to hold our son in my arms, that he would be taken from us." I said it as an affirmation, to remind myself. "I want to celebrate Forest's life." I glanced across at his crib. "I want to celebrate being alive, being a mother. Being your wife."

"You are my wife, but why is it we want such different things?" Edmund said, wearily. "I had hoped we would pull together, that we were yoked as close as two oxen at the plow, but so often these days you pull one way and I pull t'other."

I lowered my eyes so that he would not see that, though it saddened me, I knew it to be true. But it need not be, it must not be. I looked back at him suggestively. "Once the churching is over, you need no longer be excluded from my bed," I said.

"Won't it sour your milk if I lie with you?"

"Oh, I don't believe that nonsense. And I don't believe Forest would care too much anyway. He's far too greedy to be so particular." I let my eyes linger on Edmund's kind face. "I shall be as a virgin again, your bride again. It will be like our wedding night."

"You mean, when you ran away from me while I was sleeping, as if you couldn't bear to face me in the cold light of day?"

"Dear Edmund, that is not how it was and it's not how it will be this time."

He waved his hand in a resigned gesture of capitulation. "I lack the will to stand against you. It's far too tiring. Your victory again."

"There's no battle between us, Edmund."

He stood, kissed my nose end. "Aye, only because I always surrender."

I smiled. "That's how you used to talk before we were married, remember? When you were shy with me, I think." I quoted from the letter he once sent me. "Now that I have stormed the cherry bulwarks of your sweet mouth, I am convinced I may gain your surrender."

"You ridicule me?"

"No! No, not at all, you silly goose. It's just that I read your letter so often, I learned every word of it by heart. I treasured it and I've still not forgotten it."

"You are not so very different from your father, you know," he said thoughtfully. "You are a little fighter. You fight for what you believe in until the very end, don't you?"

"Is nothing worth the fight to you?"

"I would fight for my family," he said with all the touchingly protective pride of a new father. "I would do anything for my son, and for you."

I cocked my head. "Anything?"

He gave me a wry smile. "If it is what you really want, I'll send for Mother Wall right away."

I caught his hand as he stood. "Edmund, tell me you don't really mind if we do this?"

He beamed at me. "I don't really mind." He kissed my hand. "You are a rebel, Eleanor Ashfield. I am not, and so I do admire you for it."

AS MY MIDWIFE, Mother Wall organized my churching, and when the day came, it was she who escorted me to the church. I wore a new gown of creamy silk with a stomacher decorated with seed pearls, and we were followed by a gaggle of wives and mothers, all wearing their most fashionable outfits. We walked arm in arm and giggled and chatted and were truly as bawdy as wives at a gossiping.

In view of the whole congregation, I was led by my attendants through to the main body of the church, to the most prominent benches covered with the kersey churching cloth. As I knelt at the altar, to be sprinkled with holy water, and as I let the droplets of water fall upon me, I bowed my head and closed my hands in prayer. I prayed silently that the blessed water from Tickenham's springs would cleanse me, not from the stain of childbirth but from all shameful desires and impure thoughts. I prayed with all my heart that I could be a good mother to Forest and a good wife to his father.

The minister recited the psalms and spoke of my deliverance from the peril of childbirth.

Oh, it was so lovely to be out of seclusion at last, to return to normal life, and it was nice to be the center of attention with all eyes upon me. I felt special, that this was a very special day. As my wedding day should have been. It was a new beginning, this baby our pledge of love.

I looked across at my husband, who rocked our son in his arms, shushing to quieten him when he wriggled and whimpered and started to look for yet more food and root around against Edmund's brown brocade waistcoat, little head bobbing and mouth opened like a baby chick. Edmund stuck his little finger into it just as I had shown him how to, and Forest started to suck. They made a pretty picture and it occurred to me that Richard might not have made such a devoted father to my children. I vowed before God to try very hard to be as good to Edmund as he was to me. We had all been spared and I would strive harder to show my gratitude.

When we'd all gone back to the house and eaten our venison pasties, I left the women's room and went to seek out the gentlemen in theirs. Bawdiness was as much in order at churchings as it was at baptisms and this time I would turn that practice to good use. In my heart I was as brazen as an orange girl waiting for custom outside the doors of the theater, but with my eyes lowered to the ground and my quiet step, I sought to appear chaste as an angel, come to steal a soul in its sleep.

Inhaling an intoxicating fug of pipe smoke and brandy fumes, I walked straight through the men without once looking at any of them. I ignored their ribald comments as I went up to Edmund and took hold of his hand. "Excuse me, gentlemen," I said, looking only at Edmund. "But I have missed my husband. I have more need of him this night than do you."

Edmund appeared shocked, a little embarrassed, but I could tell he was also aroused by my boldness. I drew him gently toward me, and then I turned and, still holding him by the hand, led him back through the lewd laughter and cheering of his friends.

Mr. Merrick clapped him on the back. "I do believe you're blushing, dear fellow."

I imagined that was true, since Edmund still blushed remarkably easily, but I didn't look back to see. I didn't look at him until I had him in the chamber, with his back against the limed wall.

"My wife, what has come over you?" he whispered thickly. "You are so thankful for being a mother that you want me to make another child on you tonight?"

I stood up on my tiptoes as I always had to do if I wanted to kiss him, and he bent his head so that we met halfway. I slid my hand up under his shirt and walked my fingers up his smooth chest, let my palm rest flat against his hot, damp skin. For once his heart was racing much faster than mine. "If you do," I said, "I promise that this time I will still be close beside you when you wake."

Summer

1678

The sunlight was sweet and golden as the best cider, and it was the time of year when every lovely day was a bonus that could not be wasted. The air already smelled of wood fires and of distant rain. Humming a happy tune to myself and to Forest, I carried him down onto the moor straddled across my hip, butterfly net over my shoulder. My black lead pen and notebook were tucked inside my corset, along with a little book of psalms. I didn't have enough hands to bring a cushion of pins and a pine collecting box, so I had reverted to my original method of pressing specimens between the pages of a book. Since my Bible was also too big and too heavy, the psalms would have to do.

At nine months, Forest was growing heavier by the day, but I'd always had strong arms and legs and lungs from rowing and walking and riding, and it was no great effort to carry him, even on such a warm day. Edmund had gone on a visit to his father and brother in Suffolk and I had stayed behind, hoping to have some time to please myself. I hadn't quite accepted that now I had a baby there was no such thing unless I entrusted him to someone else's care, which I could not bear to do, not even for a little while.

On the far side of the moor was a little group of roe deer, half concealed in the long grass, and I stood and watched them grazing, glad to be given a glimpse into their private and secret lives.

Forest wriggled and I set him down amidst the buttercups and sat beside him. There was no point going all the way to the river. All summer I had been trying to show him the otters, but he was never quiet or still for two seconds and they understandably kept well out of our way.

I laid him on his back so he could look up at the kestrels and sparrow hawks soaring above him, but he was instantly squirming to roll over onto his belly, and before I knew it, he'd be trying to chew the grass, no matter how much I told him babies weren't supposed to eat grass. Though maybe it would be a good thing if this one did. Maybe it would help to satisfy him, since nothing else seemed to.

I sat cross-legged and scooped him up onto my lap, dandled him up and down, making him gurgle with delight. I dropped a kiss on his fat little cheek, rubbed our noses together and he suddenly grabbed at my hair and pulled very hard.

"Ouch, little whelp. That hurts."

He blew bubbles at me with his mouth and pulled all the harder, so that I had to prize open his grasping fist and unwind my hair from it.

"I'll always love you, no matter how you hurt me," I said.

With eyes that were turning from blue now to a brown so dark it was almost black, he regarded me as if he understood every word I spoke. Then his whole body suddenly went rigid and he arched his back to free himself and be off again, so I put him back down on the grass.

I slid my arms out behind me and turned my face up to the sun. The movement of grass snakes sounded like the rustle of dead leaves and already there was the scent of autumn in the air. Where had the summer gone? I hadn't caught a single butterfly since Forest was born. I'd not even made one entry in my observation book. Though James still wrote to me it was with less regularity, his letters growing shorter. I'd only managed a few brief replies.

Now Forest was tearing at a buttercup. Pity any butterfly that came near while I had this tiny destroyer with me. Why had I even bothered to bring my net along?

"We might as well pay a visit to Mistress Knight," I sighed. "She'd love to see how you've grown into such a pudding."

We were nearly at the Knights' cottage when I saw it, not too far away, in an open area of sedge and reeds where the milk parsley grew. It was flying, slowly and powerfully, a spectacular sweep of yellow and red and blue. I gently deposited Forest in a soft patch of grass. "I'll be right back, poppet," I whispered.

I bunched up my petticoats, kicked off my slippers and ran, slowing as the butterfly came drifting down toward me. It hovered, not quite settling, its wings aflutter, as it sucked the juice from the milk parsley. It was a fine example, the colors still luminously vivid in the bright sunshine, wings perfectly unragged. Almost before I knew what had happened it was there, unbelievably, imprisoned like a rare jewel beneath the veil of my muslin trap.

I pinched its black and yellow abdomen carefully and swiftly between my finger and thumb, just below its head. Wings and antennae quivered a moment, then were still, outspread and undamaged, not a single pearly scale missing. A yellow stain appeared on my palm. I suffered an instant of remorse at the loss of its little life, that it would no longer flutter innocently in the sunshine. But it was outweighed by the satisfaction of having a pristine Swallowtail specimen to add to my collection, at last. I stared in wonder at the glorious Gothic, sculptured wings, the magnificent markings, and I thought only of how I would describe in a letter the thick dusting of lemon meal that gave it its predominant color. I thought only of how I couldn't wait to tell James about my find.

I laid it carefully inside the psalms and closed the little book, reverential as a Puritan girl should be, tying a ribbon round it to keep it shut tight.

"What kind of unnatural, unfeeling mother are you?" Mistress Knight, Bess's mother, was standing right behind me, clutching Forest to her in her gnarled old hands as if she had snatched him out of the jaws of death itself. "Tom heard your child wailing from yards away, even if you did not. You are not fit to care for a babe if you leave it crying in a marsh, amidst a herd of cattle, to go gadding after butterflies."

It made no difference to Mistress Knight that I was lady of the manor now. She had known me as a little girl, a little girl she had felt quite entitled to chastise if need be. That Forest had been wailing I doubted very much. He looked perfectly content. And since I heard his every snuffle from the depth of sleep, I would not have failed to hear him crying. There were indeed a great number of cattle on the moor, not just those of the commoners, but the beasts of others they grazed for a fee, but they were all so far off as to be almost invisible. Not so Thomas Knight. He was loitering by the bend in the river, hands stuffed in his pockets and a pile of cut sedges at his feet.

Annoyed, but doing my utmost not to show it, I quickly pushed the psalms back inside my gown, took Forest into my arms, cradled his head in the crook of my neck. "I was only gone a moment, Mistress Knight."

"A moment is all it takes for a cow to trample him, or for him to roll into the bog or ditch, or eat a poison plant that will make him vomit for a week, or worse," she said gruffly. "The wild swans and geese tend their chicks better than you tend yours."

I knew Mistress Knight cared very much for my little son, whose birth she had witnessed. She had supported me as he was being born, and walked behind me and laughed with me at my churching. "I thank you for your concern," I said evenly. "But Forest was perfectly safe, I assure you. I know very well which are the poison plants and there were none near him. He was nowhere near any bogs or ditches either."

"This is no place for a child."

"I came down here every day when I was one."

"Aye, and look how you've turned out."

"I will ignore that comment. We were on our way to see you," I said shortly. "But I think we had better go back to the house instead."

"And I think you had better stay there, out of harm's way, until your husband is returned." She cast a strange, longing glance at Forest, as if she wanted to run off with him and rear him herself. "Your father should have shown you a stiffer hand. He should have known you'd grow to be as wild and wayward as your mother."

I was astounded. "What do you mean?"

"I mean nothing," she said, flustered. "Now be off with you, before I say more than is wise."

"I think you had better say it, Mistress Knight."

"I think I had better not." She flicked her rheumy eyes toward Thomas.

He was still standing there, watching us. For some reason that I was no closer to understanding, he hated me still. He was my enemy, and an increasingly dangerous, insidious and underhanded one, who would use whatever weapons he could muster against me. He would make sure that this was round the village like wildfire, spread by scandalmongers and gossips, exaggerated and distorted. Everyone would hear of it. Edmund would hear of it.

"I once clouted my boy for calling you whimsy-headed, for putting it about that you must be cracked to go chasing after fairies," Mistress Knight went on. "But now I think he was maybe not so wrong."

"You've been a good friend to me and to my family, Mistress Knight," I said carefully. "But I'll ask you to mind your tongue. I would never put my baby in any danger."

"So you say." She turned and hobbled off on arthritic legs toward her son.

I held my own son very close, in the middle of the milk parsley, and stroked his broad little back. "You weren't upset at all, were you, my little cherub? You know I'll always look after you."

I couldn't face going inside yet, so I took him into the orchard and sat with him under an apple tree. "If she could see us, she'd likely criticize me for endangering your life from falling apples," I jested.

Forest was sleepy after so much sun and fresh air, so I rested him against my shoulder and rocked him gently. Instead of singing to him, I told him about a letter I had written to him before he was born.

"I wrote it in case I died giving birth to you," I whispered into his pink shell of an ear. "I wrote down all my hopes for you, in case I wasn't there to bring you up and tell you them myself. It's very important, even though I am still here, so please listen very carefully.

"I want you to grow to be a good man, like your father and your grandfather. Above all else, I hope that you are just and wise and honest in all that you do. I pray you take an interest in the world around you and find some worthy occupation that pleases you and is of some service to God and to mankind. For then you will be sure to be happy and fulfilled." I paused and slipped my hand between my waist and his dangling legs. "Find yourself a pretty and kind girl and be good to her, and be good to any little brothers and sisters you may have. Take care of them, protect them, and be someone they look to for counsel and guidance. I always wished I'd had an older brother. Be the brother I would have wanted. Be a son to make me proud." I nuzzled his warm neck, kissed it. "Oh, and most important of all, always be good to your mother."

He'd grown even heavier, so I knew that he was asleep, a puzzling phenomenon I could not even begin to comprehend, since surely a sleeping child did not in actual fact gain extra pounds, to be lost again the moment he woke. So why did it feel as if that was exactly what happened? I tilted him over to cradle him and look down into his peaceful sleeping face. He had pushed his thumb in his mouth, and now and then his little lips puckered with sucking movements that seemed to comfort him as once only my breast or finger had done. Something about this tiny show of independence tore at my heart. He was already growing away from me. Day by day, he needed me less.

I opened my book of psalms. The beautiful Swallowtail, the first I had ever caught, was broken in two. No matter. I would give one of the wings to James. He would like that. In his most recent letter to me he had enclosed another of his strange little broken gifts, the single brilliant emerald and black wing of a large tropical butterfly that had been sent back to him from a ship's surgeon who had sailed to Brazil. James was sticking to his plan, his life's task of building a worldwide community of natural scientists.

Maybe that was why my walk on the moor today hadn't been the balm to me it usually was. The wide wetland horizon just drew attention to how vast the world was and how little of it I would ever see, how far I would never travel.

I had been a small part of something important which had mattered to me more than anything else. Now I had my baby, and he mattered more than life itself. So I was torn, for it felt as if all time borrowed from my child was misspent, but also that when I was not studying butterflies, I was somehow missing out on what I was supposed to do.

I closed the psalms. If I wanted to be a good mother, I could not be a good scientist. If I wanted to be a good scientist, I could not be a good mother.

I wanted so very much to be able to be both, to be good at being both.

Autumn

1678

The autumn rains returned before Edmund did, steady, incessant rain. Accustomed to it as I was, it was still alarming to watch a deluge of water pouring down from the sky as more water rose up the riverbanks and the rhynes, came gushing up through the very earth to meet it, quickly turning the moors into a desolate, wild morass of bog and marsh and wide lagoons.

I sat on the window seat in the parlor and traced the raindrops with my finger as they raced haphazardly down the small panes, like animated versions of the tiny air bubbles trapped within the glass. I was Persephone of the Greek myths, abducted by Hades, the King of the Underworld. I was a child of Somersetshire: land of the summer people, fated to live out half of each year in darkness.

Though it was London, now, that was gripped by a great ague epidemic. The latest gazette lay on the table, filled with news of how the King himself had contracted the disease and had demanded the services of an Essex man, Robert Talbor, a self-styled feverologist who the college of physicians had dubbed a quack. No one knew his secret and he refused to reveal it, but he had seemingly cured the King and was to be knighted for his services.

Jesuits' Powder? I wondered. Was that his secret cure? It would certainly explain why he'd be so desperate to hide the truth now, at the very time Jesuits were being accused of plotting to assassinate the King and put his Catholic brother on the throne. The gazette reported that all of London was hysterical with terror at a clergyman's claim that thousands of Jesuits were crouching in cellars, ready at the signal to leap out and slaughter all Protestants in England. They were, apparently, conspiring to poison the whole world by means of the so-called medicine commonly known as the Jesuits' Powder.

I was expecting Edmund to be home today before dark, in plenty of time for supper, and I couldn't sit here any longer. Forest was sleeping, with luck would sleep for another hour, and Bess would listen out for him. I snatched my red, hooded riding cloak and set out for the causeway.

The rain had eased, but the cobbles were slick and slippery and I walked carefully to avoid twisting my ankle. There was a stiff southwesterly wind and I clutched my cloak tight, pulling up the hood.

The heavy sky was the color of pewter and the willows were delicately penciled in the mist. The water meadows were shimmering with pools of silver, while flocks of little dunlins skimmed the air, their flight rapid and direct, all abruptly changing direction at once, like a wave breaking in the air as they flashed their dark backs and then white undersides.

I'd gone about half a mile before I heard the faintest sound of a horse's hooves above the wild and lonely call of the curlews. Like a beast from the legends of King Arthur, Edmund's chestnut gelding came splashing across the causeway, with only the head and shoulders of his rider visible above the mists, a rider with copper hair which shone warm as the welcoming light of a distant inn to a lone traveler.

He reined in beside me. "Eleanor, what are you doing out here? What's wrong? Little Forest . . . ?"

"Is fast asleep in his crib. Nothing's wrong." I held on to the horse's bridle as the animal snorted and tossed its head, the bit jangling, and smiled up at my husband, my hood falling back from my face. "I've been lonely without you. That's all."

"Have you? Have you really?" He beamed down at me, like he did the first time I ever saw him, the first time he'd come to Tickenham, on a day not unlike today.

"You're going to tell me I'm foolish," I said. "That you've not been gone very long."

He reached out his hand to pull me up into the saddle in front of him, settled his arms around me. I rested my hands on the reins between his as he gave them a jerk.

"As a matter of fact, I've been lonely without you too," he said. "I'm very glad to be home."

"Do you still think of your father's house as home, too?"

"My father barely recognizes it himself. Drainage doesn't just alter the landscape, it creates a whole new society, a whole new economy. But tell me, how does my little boy? Is he talking yet? Has he missed me too, do you think?"

"He is greedier than ever," I said fondly. "He's probably doubled in size since last you saw him." I paused, and then my confession came tumbling out of my mouth, like the river over a weir.

As I told him about the Swallowtail and Mistress Knight's accusations, Edmund's hold on the reins remained light and his arms around me didn't tense or recoil.

"I wanted you to hear it from me, rather than through village scandalmongers," I finished. "I know Forest was perfectly safe and yet I

am annoyed with myself. He is still waking twice in the night and I'm
so tired that, it's true, I probably wasn't as alert as I should be. But I
would never neglect him. Never."

"I know you wouldn't. You are a wonderful mother. And he's thriv-
ing, as you said yourself. That's all that matters." Edmund kissed the
top of my head and then tucked it under his chin. "What's done is
done, and there's no use worrying about what might or might not
have been."

How much easier life would be if I was as unruffled as Edmund,
if I could skim along as he did and not look too closely or delve too
far beneath the surface of things, if I didn't have to question from
every angle and worry about what might never be. It was good that I
had him to act as my counterbalance. And maybe, once I'd been married to him for a few more years, I'd become a little more like him.

"So, did you catch your prize?"

"I did."

"I'm glad. I know how much you wanted one."

That surprised me. But I remembered then how Richard had said
Edmund had once made him look for one.

"Do you find them all over the country? Does your butterfly friend
in London see them there?" He sounded genuinely interested.

"No. He's seen dead ones others have collected, but he has never
seen one on the wing." I nestled up closer to Edmund's shoulder and
almost drew back a little on the reins. The steady clop and gait of the
horse was as pleasant and easy as our conversation. I didn't even feel
the cold and the rain, was warm and cozy as if we were curled up
together beneath the blankets in bed, with a fire glowing in the brazier. "Since when were you so interested in butterflies, anyway?"

"Since I saw that they interested you."

"Oh."

"Whatever matters to you matters to me too."

I put my small hands over Edmund's much larger ones, slipped my fingers down so they were meshed with his. I knew, clearer than I could see the summit of Cadbury Camp on a sunny day, that though he had been prompted at least in part to marry me because I was the heiress of Tickenham Court, and though he may not have loved me as I wanted to be loved, he loved me with all that he had. And I valued that love more than ever.

"William is keen to press on with the drainage again here now," he said presently.

I felt my muscles tauten. "Must we?"

"There's a fresh move across the whole of the country for agricultural improvement. William has watched a hundred acres being successfully recovered at Wick St. Lawrence, not so very far away, and it's renewed his enthusiasm for land reclamation here. But we are under no obligation now, since that first scheme was abandoned. It is not William's decision."

I didn't want to ruin the closeness between us with another disagreement, so I chose my words carefully. "You don't sound as if you share his enthusiasm so much anymore."

"It's not that I can't still see the benefits. But for all that, I would rather leave well alone for as long as is possible."

"You would? Why?"

"I am growing soft and sentimental in my old age, that's why." I heard the humor in his voice. "I can't say for sure. All I *can* say is this. If we drained the moor, you'd have seen the last of your Swallowtails here. When I was a boy, they were as abundant in the Fens as they are in Tickenham. But now the water has gone, the Swallowtails have gone with it."

"They can't have!"

"They have."

"Are you certain?" Dry meadows should mean more butterflies, not less, surely?

"Believe me, Eleanor, I looked. I looked last summer and I looked again this time. Knowing how much you love them, I looked hard. But I didn't see a single one."

I was still coming to terms with the fact that he even knew what a Swallowtail was.

"It's the same with the red and orange ones you once told me are so prized amongst collectors. They were plentiful too, as they are here, but now, in the Fens, they have totally vanished."

I would have felt a jolt of dismay at this discovery, except that I was so delighted it was Edmund who had made it, that he had made it because of me. "I can't believe you noticed."

"You notice. So I notice."

I twisted my head sideways against his shoulder, felt his bristly copper whiskers snag my hair. We carried on in silence but my mind was not at all quiet, was whirring busily as ideas crystallized inside me. "It must mean they can live only on marshes, that there is something about marshland necessary for their life."

"That seems a fair conclusion."

"So if all the wetlands in England are to be drained, will Swallowtails and Large Coppers disappear completely? The specimens in the collections of butterfly hunters might be all that is left to prove they ever existed." There was something portentous in that. "If drainage causes a little creature at the bottom of the great chain of being to die out, then could it have some effect upon those further up—on people? Could land unable to sustain a tiny butterfly ever sustain us?"

"I am afraid you are losing me." Edmund laughed.

It seemed too dramatic and too abstract a theory to dwell upon now. What mattered far more right at this moment was that I was having a proper conversation with my husband at last. I had thought that I might grow more like Edmund. Instead it seemed he was growing more like me. That was probably not a wholly good thing, but I liked the idea all the same. I liked being able to talk to him about things I cared about. I liked this new feeling of closeness very much.

We had reached the stable. Edmund released the reins to dismount, but something prompted me to hold on to his hands. Maybe it was because of the ominous disappearance of the butterflies, but I didn't want him to let go of me. I had the alarming sense that, though he was here with me now, I was losing him, just as he had jokingly said I was during our conversation. But to what, I did not know.

He swung to the ground, turned around to help me down.

I slid into his arms and held him tight, standing on tiptoe to kiss him, as always.

The mist seemed to close in around us.

BESS TOLD ME THAT Forest was awake and had just that moment started to bawl for food, or attention, or both. I told her I would go to him. He was lying on his back, kicking his sturdy little legs, and I lifted him out, surprised afresh by how solid and strong he was growing. "Come here, little fellow. Your papa's home and wants to see you." I swung him, still kicking, onto my hip, and he quieted as we made our way down the stairs to the parlor, where I handed him over to Edmund, who promptly tossed him in the air and caught him, much to Forest's delight.

"Do you think he's changed while you've been away?" I asked.

"You make it sound like I've been gone months."

Forest was playing with the brass buttons on Edmund's waistcoat.

"He's changing all the time, can't you see it? His legs are a fraction longer, his eyes darker. His cheeks just a bit more plump."

Edmund looked bemused. "All to the good, surely. Why look so sad about it?"

"Oh, I don't know. I'm being foolish. But I do wish I were a better artist. I'd draw him every day so I could hold on to each moment. I want to see him walk and hear him speak proper words to me, yet I hate the thought of him even being old enough to be breeched. I want him to stay a baby forever."

"Ah, but then he'd not grow to be a fine young lord for Tickenham Court. That is what I want to see, above all else. I do realize, of course, that he cannot actually take the seat until I have vacated it," he added jocularly, "but I shall enjoy rearing him to sit in it well."

Forest promptly stuffed the lace-trimmed edge of Edmund's square white collar into his little gummy mouth.

"So you have a taste for finery, do you, my little lad?" Edmund said. "Just like your godfather. Richard sends you his love, by the way, Eleanor, promises to come and visit very soon."

"You have seen him?" I asked, as casually as I could.

"Aye, rather ironically he asked if he could come to the Fens to escape the ague outbreak, not to mention the outbreak of mass hysteria at this Popish Plot."

"They are still claiming that we are all to be poisoned?"

"Would you believe, a facsimile of Jesuits' Powder has been paraded through the city streets, with great signs warning of exactly that."

"But what if Jesuits' Powder really does hold the cure for ague? Thousands who fear it might die needlessly, just like my father." It seemed to me that the world had gone totally mad.

"That man who cured the King swears he does not use it, that he has seen most dangerous effects follow the taking of it."

"But he has to say that, Edmund, doesn't he?"

Bess had been in to light the candles in the wall sconces but I felt a sudden, powerful need to light some more. I went and stuck a candle into the fire and went round lighting all the others in the candelabra on the table and the buffet, one by one, until the shadows retreated and the room was shimmering with light.

"You are an extravagant little wench." Edmund smiled.

But still it did not seem enough to hold the darkness at bay.

Winter

1679

I studied Richard's pensive profile as he leaned against the parlor doorway, watching Edmund capering with Forest and a puppy in front of the fire. It was well past the time that Forest should have been in his cot, but Edmund, so bent on routine in all other matters, constantly chose to forgo this one, in order to enjoy a few extra minutes of play with our little boy.

The sound of sleet slapping the windows made the room seem cozy and warm, and the supper we had all just eaten, finished off with frumenty and baked apple tart, had left me feeling pleasantly drowsy as I took up a botany book and sat in the chair beside my little family.

But the feeling of content vanished when I happened to glance up from my reading and saw Richard lingering by the threshold, as if he felt unable or unwilling to intrude on our little scene of happy domesticity. As Edmund held the pup for Forest to fondle its floppy brown ears, there was envy and jealousy plain to see in Richard's eyes. What I could not tell was whom he most envied, of what he was most jealous. Edmund, for having a son and a wife? Or Forest, for robbing him almost totally of Edmund's attention, for enjoying a privileged childhood and having a happy and hearty young father, when, according to Edmund, Richard had seen his own father embittered and demoralized in exile. Either way, I could not bear to watch any longer.

I put down my book, went to my husband and quietly held out my hands for him to give Forest to me. "Time for sleep," I said.

"Since when has your mother ever been governed by time?" Edmund smiled, picking Forest up and handing him over to me, thereby eliciting a squeal of protest. "I think the puppy needs its bed too," he said firmly. Doting as Edmund was, he never gave in to Forest's tantrums. Forest knew it and the squawks soon turned to mewling.

"Why don't you ride into Bristol tonight with Richard?" I suggested to Edmund.

He stood, stroked Forest's sleek little head. "What for?"

"I don't know." I shrugged. "Go to a tavern or the coffeehouse," I suggested rather exasperatedly. "Whatever the pair of you used to do together in London."

Edmund looked as abashed as a mischievous lad caught under a table, trying to sneak a look up ladies' skirts. "That'd not do at all." He blushed. "Not now that I have a wife."

Edmund had never spoken of women he had known before me, but I had the impression there had not been a great many. I did know that now he was wed, there would be no more. I trusted him in this, as in all things, trusted him absolutely, and so I let the comment pass. "Go to Bath, then." I sought to persuade him. "There's time if you leave now. Give Richard a taste of the waters to refresh him, before he goes back to the city."

"Why are you so keen to be rid of me all of a sudden?" my husband asked.

"Oh, you know it's not that. I think it would do you good. You used to enjoy gallivanting together, did you not?"

"That was before," Edmund said affectionately. "Before I had a wife and a family. Now I've no wish to seek entertainment elsewhere. Now everything I need and want is right here in this house. And here," he added gently, laying his palm against the small curve of my three-months-pregnant belly.

I gave him a grateful smile, glanced at Richard and saw his disappointment as he turned and absently picked up my lute. He slouched down into a chair, one long booted leg hooked over the carved arm, and started idly plucking a remarkably pretty and competent melody. For a moment I watched his fingers on the lute strings, the wistful expressions that crossed his face as he played, but I tore my gaze back to Edmund, leaned in closer to him over our son's little head. "I think Richard would like you to go to Bristol with him."

"Aye, he's restless as a tomcat." Edmund smirked. "The lad needs to find himself a wife."

"Yes," I said quietly. "But for now he does not have one. And you are his friend."

Edmund deposited a kiss on my forehead. "You would be friend and mother to all waifs and strays. And I do treasure you for that."

I squeezed his arm affectionately. "Good. Then listen to what I am saying, why don't you?"

"All right, but I'll settle Forest in the nursery first."

Forest went very willingly back into his father's arms and Edmund hoisted him up onto his shoulders and away.

I drew up a chair opposite Richard. He tilted his head slightly, looked back at me out of the corners of his eyes as he continued to play.

"It is very pretty," I said. "What's it called?"

"L'Amour Médecin," he replied, perfectly accented.

I laughed. *"The Love Doctor?"* I was glad that my French studies had proven useful at last.

"It is a comedy by Molière."

"What's it about?" I thought, even as I spoke, that I might well regret asking.

Richard kept his head lowered over the lute, raised his eyes to look at me in a way that made them seem darker, smoldering. I'd always thought blue was either a cold color, of ice and of water, or at most only as gently warm as a summer sky. I'd never have imagined that blue eyes could burn with the slow, gentle heat that his did now. Yet his voice was strangely flat. "Lucinde is depressed," he related tonelessly. "Desperate to cheer her, Sganarelle offers her whatever she wishes. When she declares that she wants to be married to Clitandre, Sganarelle becomes angry, refuses to grant her desire." The music stopped. His fingers were still. "He admits that his reason for refusing her request is that he cannot stand the thought of her with another man."

I was out of the chair in an instant, on my way straight out of that room.

He cast the lute aside with a discordant clang, swung his legs to the floor and sprang to his feet. He caught my hand, the momentum of my flight swinging me back round so I was flung against him.

"That was unfair of me," he said.

Our bodies were touching down the entire length of them. "Yes," I breathed, standing back from him. "It was."

He let go of me with obvious reluctance, held on to me only with the intensity of his gaze, a hold more powerful than ever his hand had been on my arm. "You did ask." He smiled at me then.

I smiled back. "I did, and I knew it to be a bad idea." I picked up the lute, handed it back to him. "Would you play some more?"

I sat again, as did he, but he looked at the instrument for a moment as if he had forgotten what to do with it, or as if it had entirely lost its appeal for him. Then he turned his eyes to me meditatively. "Being with you is like listening to a Lully ballet," he said. "It is music that is filled with vitality and stirs the deepest sentiment. That is how you make me feel, Nell, how you have always made me feel. I have tried and tried to understand what it is about you. But look at you. With your golden hair and honey skin, you are a Rubens painting come alive, that's what you are. All exuberance and emotion and depth of color and sensuality. And, as if you really were a painting, I must content myself with just looking at you."

Nobody had ever talked to me the way he did. But I could have listened to his voice forever, no matter what he spoke of.

"I cannot disagree with you," I said, "since I have never seen a Rubens painting or heard a Lully ballet." I imagined that even in poverty he must have been exposed to all kinds of new experiences during his years of exile in Europe and I felt again that restless desire to see more of the world myself, to make of my life more than it was. "It must be wonderful to compose a piece of music, or paint a picture that will last for all time," I said. "So that your name is forever linked to something beautiful."

"Is that what you want to do?" he asked me gently. "To be like Rubens or Lully?"

I smiled. "I have no particular talent for art or music, but since I was a child I have wanted to discover something, to do something of lasting significance. I should like to be remembered." I realized I had never confided that to anyone before, not even to James Petiver. "That doesn't sound very humble, does it?"

"I think it is a fine ambition." He gave me a little meaningful smile. "I too should like to have my name linked to something beautiful."

I would have loved to ask him about Rubens and Lully, about art and ballet, but Edmund came back into the room and so they went off to Bristol, and whatever they found to do there kept them occupied until the early hours of the next morning.

. . .

I WAS TENDING to Forest when I heard them crash and stumble through the door, spurs and swords jangling. Edmund, in particular, was talking and laughing loud enough to rouse the dead.

I settled Forest in his crib and went back to bed. Later, I heard one set of footsteps mount the stairs, the quiet tap of expensive leather-soled boots in the passage. They paused outside my door. And then there was a light touch on the wood.

No, Eleanor. Do not go to him. If you know what's good for you, ignore it, pretend you are sleeping. If you open that door to him, you are undone.

I threw on a loose gown, padded in bare feet across the cold oak boards.

"I hope that I did not wake you," Richard said softly.

I shook my head, clutched the neck of my gown and held on to the door, fooling myself that I was entirely capable of closing it at any moment in his beautiful face.

He was still wearing his long cloak but had removed his hat and unbuckled his sword. His eyes were sparkling like a moonlit sea and I could detect the warm scent of brandy on his breath, although he seemed entirely sober.

"I wondered where I might find some spare blankets," he said.

"Blankets?" I felt mildly annoyed, was in no mood now to bandy innuendo with him. "You were not warm enough last night?"

He gave me a wry smile. "Nell, if that was so, I would have spoken to your maid about it earlier. I would not trouble you with my discomfort in bed, whatever its cause."

I felt my cheeks flush, not sure if it was from my blunder or the intimate inference.

"I'm afraid poor Edmund can't hold his drink the way he used to," Richard explained. "He's sound asleep in the chair in the parlor, and

I'll never manage to get him up all these stairs to bed. We are in for snow tonight, I think. I don't want him to catch cold."

"There are plenty of rugs in the linen cupboard. I'll fetch some for you."

He gestured with his hand. "I'll get them," he said quietly. "Go back to bed. I am sorry for disturbing you."

I could have told him that his very presence in this house disturbed me constantly. But I didn't want him to go now, wanted to keep him with me for as long as I could, just to talk to him again. "Did you have a good evening?"

"We did. Thank you. It was thoughtful of you to suggest it. Edmund will probably not thank either of us for it in the morning, mind."

I smiled at him, found my eyes were irresistibly drawn to the loose black curl that shaped itself around his ear and lay so softly coiled against his neck, brushing his left shoulder. I wanted to touch it, was ridiculously envious of it. I wanted to rest my head on his shoulder the way it did, wanted to nuzzle into his neck, to put my lips against that tender skin where a little pulse was beating.

I pulled my plait of hair over my shoulder, toyed with the end of it. "Were you very wild, the pair of you, when you were in London?" I asked him.

"Come now, Nell." He smiled. "You can hardly expect me to answer that."

"No. I suppose not." For just a second I had forgotten that his companion in these exploits had been my own husband.

"Well, good night, then."

"Good night."

He paused, half turned to go, turned back. "London is a bed of vice and sin," he said, "as I am sure your father warned you. Bristol is not so different, if you know where to look. It would be very easy for me to sow a seed of doubt that would despoil your contented marriage. For me to tell you that your husband is not nearly so upstanding as you think him. I could easily tell you how you do wrong to trust Edmund so implicitly, as you so clearly do trust him. I could tell you how, under the influence of drink and bad company, he did not deserve your trust, did not behave honorably toward you this night." His look was reflective. "But none of it would be true. Oh, I don't deny that Edmund has enjoyed a dalliance from time to time, with society beauties and strumpets alike, as have we all, but not once has he ever behaved with less honor than you would expect of him. And tonight, amidst the myriad temptations of Bristol, all he did was talk and talk about your son and the new baby. And about you. Not that I need him to tell me how wonderful you are and how very fortunate he is to have you. There is not one day goes by that I do not brood upon it."

He sounded so terribly sad and lonely, I wished I could think of something to say to make it better. Felt also an intense irritation with Edmund for his lack of sensitivity and tact, for bragging about his own happiness when anyone with half a heart could surely see that Richard was unhappy.

"Nell, do you ever wish that you were married to me instead of Edmund?" He shot his hand out to hold the door as if he expected me to slam it shut on him. "Please," he said quickly. "I think it would help me to know."

When I did not answer, his eyes flicked over my face, reading it, as seemingly he could do all too easily. He let his arm slide down the door, sighed disconsolately. I do not know what he had seen. Indecision? Alarm? Denial? Whatever it was, it plainly did not help him at all, and I so wanted it to.

I reached down, touched the back of his hand with my fingertips, said very quietly: "I wish."

His answering smile was very sweet and uncertain. It made little crescent-shaped dimples appear at either side of his mouth. I almost laughed out loud at myself. I could write a whole book on this man's features and expressions, so carefully did I note each one, so carefully did I store them all up in my heart, like so many treasures.

"What is so amusing?" he asked me.

I wanted to tell him. I wanted just to say to him: You are so very beloved to me that I could describe your face well enough for an artist to paint a perfect portrait, without ever once having seen you.

If I had not known it before, I knew it then. It was not lust I felt for him, not just desire, but love. And how could such a love be a sin? It did not feel like a sin at all, but something pure and special, something to be cherished. I had kissed him once, just once, and there could never be more between us than that. I could never have him, but nothing would ever stop me loving him. I loved him, would always, always love him even if I could not be with him, even if I never saw him again. There it was, and there was no use in denying it or fighting it anymore. Nor could I regret it. How could I ever have regretted that kiss? How could I regret having known, even just once, for such a short time, the feel of his sweet, beautiful mouth upon mine? If I had a heart that was all on fire, as he had told me I had, it was love for him that had set it blazing. Until then, it had been more like a little barrel of gunpowder, waiting for the spark that would make it explode into life. And if he had not lit it, I would have spent my whole existence not knowing what it felt like to have a furnace inside my soul, would never have known that such a dark, wild, sweet passion could exist. Rather experience that passion, even if it brought more grief than joy, than die not knowing it was even possible.

"What happened to you?" I asked him very quietly, suddenly needing to know more than I had ever needed to know anything else. "In the war. Can you tell me?"

Instantly I cursed myself and my confounded curiosity. Never had I seen those little indentations above his nose appear so defined. He looked to be in actual bodily pain, a pain that I felt as if it were my own.

I laid my hand on his wrist. "Forgive me. I should not be so inquisitive."

"It is all right," he said very softly. "I want to tell you."

I wished we could go somewhere else to talk, wished I could pour a glass of wine for him, and for myself, but it was so late and I could not invite him into my chamber, did not want to go downstairs to where Edmund was sleeping, and so I leaned against the door and he did the same.

"When the Parliamentarians drove away all my family's cattle and pillaged just about everything else, Edmund's family saw to it that mine did not starve," he began, almost shyly. "But when victory came for Cromwell and for the Ashfields, our estate was confiscated and that, together with punitive fines, deprived my family of any means of existence. Not that my father's pride would ever have permitted him to sign engagements of loyalty to the Commonwealth, to submit to the authority of those he always called rebels and regicides. And so he fled from this country as from a place infected with plague." He took a breath, fixed his eyes on my face, as if he needed something to hold on to. "My brother went with him, and my mother, sick and big with a child who turned out to be me. They were accompanied by two servants but had nothing else but the poor riding suits they stood up in. They took ship for Bruges but I was born in Antwerp, after they had endured months of grinding hardship. I do not know exactly how my brother perished, but apparently he had never been strong, and the rough sea passage and harsh conditions proved too much for him. And for my mother, who died in a miserable charity hospital. They said she had an ulcer in the gut, but I think it must have been terrible homesickness and unhappiness that did for her. She was half

Irish and had lost so many people she had loved and cared for. So many."

His eyes had grown distant as the horizon, as if he had withdrawn into himself, into this painful past. I wanted to reach for him and bring him back but I was almost afraid to, sensed that it would be more damaging to stop him talking, now that at last he had begun. The kindest thing I could do was just to let him talk and listen to him.

"My earliest memories are of traveling," he said. "Always traveling. Calais, Boulogne, Rotterdam, Normandy, Brussels, Amsterdam. But wherever we were, it was always the same, always huddling in miserable lodgings and hiding from creditors. We were entirely dependent on the willingness of innkeepers and tradesmen and the keepers of lodgings to extend indefinite credit, and were doomed to wander from place to place, in search of ever-cheaper rooms and more generous hosts. We lived destitute of friends, begging our daily bread of God and fearing every meal would be our last. I seemed always to be hungry and cold for want of clothes and fuel for a fire. I still have dreams where I am cold, so cold I can never get warm. My father felt his powerlessness to relieve our distress acutely. He refused to admit that the royal cause had been defeated, but he kept away from the bitter feuding and factions, the quarreling and dueling, the endless failed conspiracies that made his unrealistic hopes swing to the deepest depths of despair. It was loss of pride and respect that upset him as much as anything, I think. He admitted to me once that for three months he had had not a crown, that he owed for all the meat and bread we had eaten the past weeks to a poor woman who was no longer able to trust him. It was that lack of trust he found insufferable." He broke off as if something had jolted him back to the present. He reached out to my face and wiped away the tears from my cheek with his hand. "Oh, Nell, don't cry for me. Please don't cry. I didn't mean to make you cry."

"I thought I had it so hard." I sobbed with self-loathing. "I used to feel so sorry for myself. Because my father forbade Christmas and would not let me wear ribbons in my hair. And you . . . you . . ."

"There is nothing wrong with wanting ribbons and Christmas," he said very tenderly. "To my mind it is cruelty to deprive a little girl of such things, especially one as pretty as you. But then I have ever been of the opinion that Parliament men were rather cruel. When I came to England at last, it was to a once beautiful moated manor house that had been sacked and plundered and was little more than a burned-out ruin. Parliament men seemed to me more hateful than Hell, fully deserving of the Royalist vow to seek revenge by cutting a passage to the throne through their traitorous blood."

I was not at all shocked by the apparent malice of his words since there was none whatsoever in his voice, nothing but a weary irony that was almost indifference.

He gave me the ghost of a smile. "And yet here I am, having spent a very pleasant evening with my good friend, the son of a staunch Parliamentarian, about to sleep under the roof of a house that belonged to a Roundhead major, tarrying late at night with his lovely daughter."

I sniffed, then smiled. "Something convinced you that Cromwell's supporters were not to be so despised?"

He ran his fingers through his black curls. "One day, when I was about ten years old, I saw an older boy flying a kite on a water meadow, very like your water meadows here. I did not see the son of my father's onetime friend. Nor did I see the son of a Parliamentarian. All I saw was a friendly, laughing face, and bright copper-gold hair, and a kite made of red silk that soared in the wind. The boy offered to let me have a turn, without even knowing my name, let alone my father's allegiances, and then he offered to share his bread and cheese, just as later he offered to share his fishing pole, even his new dappled pony.

For years, Edmund Ashfield had everything and I had nothing." He broke off and his eyes met mine, held them. "And still, it is just the same."

I saw that if I could find solace in knowing that I loved him, even if I could not have him, it was intolerable for him when he had been deprived of so much. "It is not true that you have nothing now," I said. "You have . . ."

"Oh, yes, thanks to a small grant paid to my father by our grateful new King, I have enough to indulge in the best clothes, the best horses and the best wine. But still, Edmund has the only thing that really matters, the only thing I really want."

I forced myself to say it, even if I could not bear to think of it, self-ish as that was. "You will find someone else, Richard."

"I shall need to take a wife, but I shall not love her. Which will make me no different from many a husband, of course. Except that I shall not be able to find ease in the arms of a mistress as such hus-bands are wont to do, unless I close my eyes and do not look upon her face."

I held his eyes, as if somehow I could tell him without words that it was the same for me, just the same. But I wanted to give him so much more. I could not help the cold, hungry and friendless little boy he had been, but I wanted to comfort the man he had become, find a way to mend the wounds that had gone so deep within that little boy that they had never stopped hurting. When I was miserable after the death of my mother and sister, I retreated into happier memories, but he had no such consolation, he had nowhere to go, and I wished only to give him somewhere now, a safe, warm place, that he need never leave.

"You would look well in Europe, Nell," he said to me. "The build-ings are as elaborate and theatrical as the paintings and music we were talking about earlier. There are churches filled with columns and curves, with painted rays of golden light and angels streaming to the clouds of Heaven. You would like it, I think."

But only if I could see it all with you. Only if you were there to show it to me. And that can never be.

"Do not misjudge me," he said. "Just because Edmund shared everything with me when we were boys, I did not expect him to share his wife. Doubtless you think me the most abominable cur for trying to seduce you, but I swear I cannot help it. I despise myself for it. I am tortured by guilt for it. Yet I cannot even promise I will never attempt it again."

"I could never think of you as a cur."

"I am trying to be good." He gave me the most gentle, heartbreaking, contrite smile. "But it is not easy."

"No," I said. "It is not."

For a moment neither of us spoke. Then he said: "I shall at least take that blanket to my friend before he gets cold, and I promise you I will not try to take advantage of the fact that his pretty wife is left all alone in her bed. For tonight at least, you are quite safe."

God help me, but I did not want to be safe from him. As he turned to go, I almost grabbed his hand. I almost begged him to kiss me again, to take me, to make me his. No matter my good intentions of a few minutes ago, I did not think I could go on living without knowing what it was to be loved by him. But I let him go. I did what was right, not what my heart and my body demanded. I went alone to bed, let him go to his own down the passageway. I wrapped my arms around the bolster, wanting to go to him, aching to go to him. I buried my face in the hard pillow, so that none but me should know that I had cried myself to sleep with love and longing for him.

And when I went downstairs in the morning, Edmund was still fast asleep in the parlor chair, just as Richard had left him. The blankets were tucked around him as carefully and caringly as I would have wrapped little Forest.

So I could not understand how Edmund seemed still to have caught a chill, which kept him huddled by the brazier all day as the snow fell softly and silently all around.

THE NIGHT BEFORE RICHARD was due to leave, I dreamed of the first time I had carried a child inside me and had been kissed by him in the dark kitchen. I woke in the eerie blue light of fresh-fallen snow and my body was damp with sweat, on flame with desire, or so I thought when I kicked off the blankets and felt the shock of the icy air on my burning skin. I thought it was the lustfulness of my dreams that had caused me to overheat, until I realized that the sweat on my body was not my sweat, that the heat I felt was not heat from my own body. I was so hot because Edmund had curled himself around me and, though he was trembling still, his body was as fiery as a black-smith's furnace. The chill had passed, and it had been replaced by a raging fever. I touched his scorching brow and recoiled in horror, as if my fingers were scalded.

"Edmund!" I shook him, gripped by a blind panic. "Edmund, wake up!"

He looked dazedly at me through his delirium, as if he didn't even know who I was. His lids slipped shut again as a low moan escaped his parched lips.

I backed away from the bed, the drapes falling closed between us like a final curtain, as one word clanged its death knell inside my head.

Ague. Ague. Ague.

Why now? Why again? It hardly ever struck in winter. I would not let it claim Edmund too. I would save him. I would not let him die. I would not.

I turned and fled from the room and down the corridor, to the room where Richard was sleeping. I burst through the door without seeking permission to enter and ran to his bed, threw back the hangings. He was sprawled on his stomach atop the blankets, still half dressed in shirt and breeches, with his head turned to the side, one arm flung up over his head and one knee crooked. I put my hands on his shoulders and shook him harder than I had shaken Edmund. "Richard, help me! Edmund is sick."

He sat up, regarded me with sleepy eyes for a moment, as if I was a visiting seraph.

"You have to ride to London right away," I said frantically. "As fast as you can." I grabbed his cloak off the trunk and thrust it at him, followed by my pocketbook. "Take this. You will probably need it."

"What for?"

"It is very expensive."

"What is?" He looked at me now as if I was a jabbering loon. He took firm hold of my shoulders and held me still, looked into my eyes. "Nell, you are not making any sense at all. What's wrong with Edmund?"

"A fever," I said. "He has a fever. I am sure it is ague."

"Tell me exactly what it is that you want me to do."

"Find Robert Talbor," I said more calmly. "The man who cured the King of it."

"How do I find him?"

"Go to Dr. Sydenham on Pall Mall. He is sure to know."

He nodded, released me to push his arms through the sleeves of his coat and his feet in his boots. He stood and threw his cloak over his shoulders, handed me back my pocketbook from where it lay on the bed. "I have money, Nell."

"You may not have enough."

"I am sure that I do."

A dusting of snow lay on the ground and still came down in flurries, but I followed him out to the stables in just my shift and with no shoes on my feet, and barely felt the bite of the wind or the coldness between my bare toes. As Ned hurriedly bridled and saddled Richard's horse, he glanced askance at me, as if to say that even in the direst distress he'd have expected me to make some pretense at respectability.

Richard put his right boot in Ned's cupped hands and vaulted into the saddle.

"Ride as fast as you can," I pleaded.

"You can be sure of it," he said. "Do not worry, Nell." He dropped his feathered hat onto his head with gravitas, as if a part of him relished the chance to do me this service, had been waiting for a reason to ride to my aid. "I will be back within four days, I promise you."

I was so grateful to him I could have wept. I clutched at his hand for a last moment. "Godspeed, Richard. Go safely."

I watched him gallop away through the snow toward the church, with all my hopes and prayers resting on him, and felt quite reassured.

This was not like before. Edmund might have sat in my father's chair and taken his position as the head of Tickenham Court, but he was not my father. He would not refuse the Jesuits' Powder, if that was what Robert Talbor used. Richard would fetch the miracle remedy and Edmund would take it and be cured. My father had been past his prime when he'd died, weary and disillusioned from the wars, crushed by grieving. Edmund was different. Edmund was young and strong. He had a small son and another baby expected. He had a wife who loved him. Who did truly love him. He'd said it himself: He had everything he could ever want. He had everything to live for. He had to live.

. . .

🦅 I WILLED MY HUSBAND TO LIVE. I held on to his palsied hand as if I could stop him slipping away from me, but the feel of it sent my own hand shaking in fear. It was so icily cold it hardly felt like a hand at all, it felt as if he had died already, and his teeth rattled so hard in his head that he could not speak to me.

I slept in a wooden chair by his bed, if I slept at all. I watched over him constantly, trying to understand his incoherent ramblings and mumbles and anticipate his every need, so he would not have to exert himself. When he was shivering with cold I kept him warm, brought rugs and blankets and made sure the fire was kept banked high. As soon as the chill passed and the heat started again, I soaked cloths and sponged his scarlet face. When his parched tongue licked at the moisture, I reached for the cider cup and trickled some into his mouth, glad just for the opportunity to have something to do. His hand, when I held it, was burning now. The sweat poured off him in waves and I brought dry sheets when the ones beneath him became quickly drenched.

"Edmund, I cannot bear to see you suffer," I said, turning the damp compress over to the cool side and placing it back on his scarlet brow.

Even ravaged and weakened by disease, he had lost none of his placid acceptance. Even in his misery he did his best to smile through it. "I don't feel so bad now, really I don't."

"I know that is not true. I wish you would complain. You are allowed to, you know. I know I would in your place."

He squeezed my hand as his smile remained. "No, you would not. You would be magnificently strong and brave. Just as you always are. As you are now."

"But you have to fight this," I pleaded. "You once told me you would fight for me and for our son. You need to fight for us now. You have to hold on, do you hear me?" I stroked his damp hair, which had turned the color of wet rust. "Just hold on. Richard will be here soon."

"Oh, aye, so long as he's not waylaid by some pretty harlot with a fair face and fairer bosom. Or else by a not-so-fair bottle of wine that will make him forget entirely where he is going, or what he is going there for."

"He won't," I said firmly. "You'll see. He knows how important it is that you have the powder. He promised to be back in four days."

"I'm sure he did. Well intentioned he may be, diligent he is not."

Judged against Edmund's steadfastness, all would be found wanting, me included. "Richard will be diligent if it matters enough," I said. "He will."

"So how long has it been now?"

"Nearly five days."

"So already he has broken his promise." My husband smiled wanly. "To think, my life now depends on a most undependable person."

BUT NEXT MORNING, just after daybreak, I heard the blessed sound of hooves clattering on the slushy cobbles and I rushed to the window. "He is here!" I shouted. "Edmund, Richard is back."

Edmund was dozing fitfully, his face still flushed with fever, and he did not appear to hear me.

I ran down the stairs and outside to see Richard's black Spanish stallion steaming in the glittering white light of sun reflected on snow. Flecks of froth were dripping from the bit.

"How is he?" Richard asked.

"Weakening," I said, more harshly than I intended. "What took you so long?"

He slid slowly from the saddle with a wince of pain.

"Are you all right?"

He nodded grimly, as he handed the reins to Ned. "Besides a few saddle sores, I've never been better."

I took in the dark stubble that covered his cheeks and noted the signs of hard riding: his ragged curls, dry lips, the dust that coated his clothes and the shadows of exhaustion beneath his eyes. "Forgive me," I said.

"I've ridden without stopping, except to change horses, for two days and two nights," he said. "I'd have got back in half the time, if you'd not sent me on some damned wild-goose chase."

"You did find Robert Talbor?"

"I found his shop all right, but he was not there. His butler told me he was called to France to tend the Dauphin and the King. He sent me to Mr. Lords, a barber in St. Swithins Lane, but I didn't trust the look of him at all. So I went back to Pall Mall, to Dr. Sydenham, had to wait around all day for him until he came back from his visits. He swore that Talbor's secret cure is Jesuits' Powder and gave me directions to an apothecary who receives the bark directly from the Jesuit college of Saint Omer in Belgium, guaranteeing the highest quality . . ."

I was barely listening. "You do have it?"

"I said I would get it for you, Nell, and I have."

Considering what he had told me, it was a wonder he had managed to be back so quickly. With hands that trembled with fatigue, he took the precious little brown-paper package out of his pocket and held it out to me.

"Thank you, Richard."

"You do not need to thank me."

I turned to go back to the house, but when he started to walk with me I saw that he was almost bow-legged from so many hours on horseback. He was all but stumbling in his tiredness and looked to be in considerable pain from the saddle sores. He took a flask of brandy out of his pocket and swigged from it.

"I'll tell Bess to fill you a bath and have the kitchen make you something to eat," I said gently. "It's food and rest you need, not brandy."

"I needed it to keep me awake, and now I shall need it to help me sleep."

"You've done all you can," I said gratefully, resting my hand on his arm as we came to the bottom of the solar stairs. "Pray this will do the rest." I looked down at the package. "How much do I give to him?"

Richard tipped back his head as he took another hefty swig of brandy, held it in his mouth, swallowed. "As much as he needs." He wiped his mouth with the back of his hand as I waited for further instructions. "Two spoonfuls," he said.

"How often?"

He fastened the top of the flask. "Give it to him morning, noon and night. In between times too, if there's no improvement."

The dried, powdered bark was a deep red-brown color, like cinnamon. I tasted a few grains, spat it out in disgust. It was extraordinarily bitter. I spooned a dose into a glass of claret, sat on the bed beside Edmund and put my arm around his shoulders to lift his head and hold the cup to his mouth.

The fever did not break, so I woke him after dinner to give him another dose, and again before supper. He said his stomach and his head were hurting a little, but he seemed restful enough, so that I curled up beside him and went to sleep myself, comforted by the thought that the curative was inside him now, doing its work.

When he woke just after midnight and I asked him how he was, he complained that there was a ringing sound in his ears and he rubbed at his eyes, said everything appeared blurred.

By midday he lay with his legs drawn up to his abdomen and was moaning that his muscles felt as taut as if he was on the rack, that he badly wanted to be sick. It was as if it was some quack remedy I had fed to him. Jesuits' poison, just as the Protestants had claimed.

When Edmund vomited, I sent for Richard, who had been sleeping since he arrived, over twenty-four hours ago. "Did Dr. Sydenham say it was an emetic?" I asked him.

He stood at the side of the bed in his rumpled shirt and stared down at Edmund's contorted face. He seemed unable to speak.

"Richard!"

He turned on me defensively, almost violently, his face white and sweat breaking out on his brow. He put his hands to the side of his head, raked his fingers through his hair, clutched at it. "He said nothing. Damn it, nothing! Why would he? He was not prescribing it, only giving me what I asked for."

"If only Dr. Talbor had been there," I said. "Maybe his remedy does not contain the powder after all." I sat by Edmund and put my arms around him as he writhed in pain. Sweat trickled down his brow and his heart was racing. "I do not understand. I did not take Thomas Sydenham for a mountebank and I am sure as I can be that he is no Papist conspirator." I glanced at Richard. "You are certain that it was Jesuits' Powder you were given? Peruvian bark?"

"Yes, and Thomas Sydenham swore his supplier was entirely reputable," Richard said tersely. "That he'd not be one to adulterate the powder with worthless substitutes."

"But surely he would have warned you if there was even a danger of this?"

"Maybe it means it is working." Richard's voice was oddly constricted. "Perhaps you should give him another dose."

"In all conscience, I cannot." I laid the back of my hand on Edmund's pain-furrowed brow and made a swift decision. "Fetch Dr. Duckett. Edmund set more store by him than I ever have—he would want to see him. And after all, he can do no more harm than we have done, can he?"

When the surgeon pulled back the bedclothes, drew up the sleeve of Edmund's nightshirt to bleed him, we both saw that Edmund's skin was covered in a livid purple-copper rash. Dr. Duckett lifted the hem of the shirt and I gasped to see that the same rash was all over his body.

The surgeon made no comment, pressed the blade of his knife against the mottled flesh of Edmund's forearm, and I watched the dark red rivulet of blood snake into a cup until it was brimful, filling the chamber with its ferrous tang. I saw Edmund grow limp, but peaceful at last.

I was alone at his bedside when he awoke later, opened his eyes and cried out in great fear and distress, as if he had seen the reaper himself over my shoulder. I immediately felt his cheek, fearing a return of the fever and delirium. But he was cold to the touch, not hot. "What's wrong, Edmund?"

"It is so dark. Why is there no candle?"

"Of course there is a candle, darling." I spoke calmly, quietly, as if to a child. "Bess lit it an hour ago. Can you not see it, over there on the washstand?"

He had turned his head at the sound of my voice, groped for my hand. "I can't see you. Help me, Eleanor. I can't see anything."

I stared into his eyes and saw that they were blank, flickering wildly from side to side, the pupils so dilated that the gray iris was all but gone, leaving his eyes almost totally black. He clutched at me in panic, cried pitifully for me not to leave him.

I called for Richard, but he came no further than the doorway, a half-empty brandy bottle in one hand and a candlestick in the other.

"Hand me your candle," I said, without taking my eyes off Edmund.

Richard seemed too afraid to come near the bed. I all but snatched the pewter stick off him and held the wildly flickering flame up to Edmund's face. "Do you see it, Edmund? The light? Do you see it?"

"No." He stared in the vague direction of the flame, as if into an abyss. "I see nothing. Eleanor, what is happening to me?"

"I don't know. I don't know." I looked deep into his sightless eyes, saw the wavering candle flame reflected in the large black centers, but nothing else. I was holding his hand, he was right there before me, but it seemed as if he were already a very long way away.

I did not know what to do anymore, and the only person I could think of who could help Edmund now was John Foskett, the curate, a pimply-faced youth still, who nevertheless was devout and good.

I left him alone to pray with Edmund. When he came out of the chamber to say that my husband had asked for his friend, the color drained from Richard's face and he looked as though he had been asked to step through the gates of Hell.

"For God's sake, go to him," I said. "He wants to see you."

It was not that I was unsympathetic. I knew that seeing Edmund suffer must awaken for Richard memories of the loss of other loved ones, but it was not as if I had no memories like that of my own, such searing, similar memories.

Had my father been right all along? I wondered in amazement. Right to refuse Jesuits' Powder, right to fear it?

Richard was not with Edmund long, and then it was my turn. An hour later, Edmund died in my arms. As if lured by the peace and silence into thinking there had been an improvement to Edmund's condition, Richard came quietly into the room. When he saw, instead, the inert body laid out on the bed, I thought he was going to collapse. He clutched at the bedpost and stared at Edmund in horror and disbelief. I saw that there were tears standing in his eyes.

I should have taken him into my arms and comforted him then.

We should have been a comfort to each other. But with all that had passed between us I could not bring myself even to touch him now. Those two words. *I wish*. They stood between us like crossed swords. And he seemed to know it and to feel the same way.

I brushed past his rigid shoulder as I walked slowly out of the room, walking as if in a daze down the stairs to the kitchen, to fetch a carving knife. Then I walked back to the chamber with it held down at my side in the folds of my silk skirts, like a murderess.

Richard's eyes widened almost in fear and he stepped away from me. "What the devil are you doing?"

Lifting my cumbersome skirts, I clambered up on the bed beside Edmund. With silent tears spilling down my face, I cradled his head in my silk-draped lap and took a lock of his copper hair between my fingers. Tenderly, with utmost care, I sliced right through it with the knife. I coiled it around my finger, dragged a silver ribbon from my own head to tie around it. "I always loved his hair," I said. "It was the very first thing about him that I loved. Its brightness. I don't ever want to forget. I don't ever want it to fade."

Richard left the room, and Bess told me later that he had left Tickenham without even saying good-bye to me.

I BARELY NOTICED when it grew dark again. I was worn-out from caring for Edmund and yet I didn't want to sleep now that I could. I didn't want to wake to a new day that Edmund would never see, to know that already, so soon, I had left him behind. I sat at my writing desk with a candle, at dead of night, and wrote out a list of tasks for the arranging of a funeral. But it was to be a very different funeral from the last one I had attended. On no account was Edmund to be buried at night. He was to be laid to rest in the morning, inside rather than outside the church, where it was always dry.

When Mary and John Burges traveled back to Tickenham after hearing the news of his death, I told Mary how much it would amuse Edmund that even in the matter of his funeral I stood contrary to Puritan preferences. "I know he will not mind me doing it as I want it done."

"It will be hard for you to be barred from being there," Mary said, her arm about my shoulder, as we sat on the Tudor settle by a flickering fire.

I placed my hand protectively on the mound of my belly. "I would not risk harmful spirits reaching this baby," I said. The precious last baby Edmund would ever give me. "But even if I am not there, it must not be as before."

I did not even want to think of another dark pit in that wet and misty graveyard, another coffin descending into the watery ground. Even to think of it was to feel myself sinking too, to feel darkness closing around me, finally and forever.

Mary drew me into her embrace.

"I can't believe he is gone," I said, weeping against her plump shoulder.

I should have been used to it by then, the terrible finality of death. But I couldn't accept it. Even if butterflies rise from coffins and we are like them and will rise again into everlasting life, even if Edmund and I were to meet again one day in Heaven, I could not bear to think I would never, ever see him again in this world. His boots were still where he had left them by the door, still shaped to the contours of his feet. I couldn't believe he would never wear them again. His fishing pole and net were still propped in the corner. How could it be that he had used them for the very last time? He'd never again sit with them by the humpbacked bridge in the sunshine, or ride his horse, or eat his supper with me, or play with his son and see him grow.

"I just want him back," I said. "I want him back."

. . .

🦋 I COULD NOT QUITE conform to the ideal of a courageously constant and modest widow, any more than I had been able to conform to the ideal of a modest wife. On the day of Edmund's funeral, I stood alone in my chamber at the latticed casement. As I looked down at the funeral procession, weaving between the brackish pools of floodwater, I found that my eyes were involuntarily seeking a man who was still very much alive. Despite myself, despite everything, I was looking for Richard. It was not with any desire that I sought him, just to know that he was near. That was all I wanted, for him to be close.

Then I reeled with self-disgust at what I threatened to become: that most feared and despised of all women, the lascivious widow. A temptation and provocation to morally upstanding gentlemen, a threat to the natural order, a girl who had sampled the pleasures of the flesh and craved them still from the confines of her desolate widow's bed.

I ran down to the great hall and I stood in the middle of the empty room, beneath the vaulted roof, as far away from any window as could be. I turned my head from the view of the Tickenham floodplains to the far wall, where hung a faded tapestry depicting the Great Flood, the flood sent by God to cleanse the world of sinners. I wished it would take me. I wished that I could die for my sin. It did not seem right that I lived, when good, kind Edmund lay moldering in a coffin.

I had begged forgiveness, but still I had not been true to my husband in my heart and it was for this that I was being punished now. Or maybe there was no one who could punish or forgive me or hear my prayers. Maybe ague was a random executioner and there was no almighty power to intervene on our behalf. God had not saved my sister, or my mother, or my father, or my husband, and I totally failed to see any divine purpose in the loss of them. It was previously impossible for me even to consider the idea that God did not exist, but I found myself considering it now, dabbling with atheism, disregarding finally everything that I had ever believed in.

I rested my forehead against the stitched image of Noah's Ark and pummeled it with my fists. "Why? Why?" Never had that question screamed at me so loudly. "Why?"

Even as I cried out, the answer insinuated itself in my head. It was my fault. It was Richard's fault. I needed someone to blame and I blamed him the most. I was dissolute and wanton, but it was he who had made me so, he who had unleashed that wantonness within me. My father was right to condemn long Cavalier curls as a dangerous incitement to lust. Edmund had died because I had acted like a whore, because I had not loved him enough, because I had broken God's sacred commandment. I had broken my wedding vows. Edmund's death was punishment. Because I had not loved him and no other as I had forsworn to do.

With both hands clawed, I gripped the tapestry and tore it from its hangings, let it crumple in a great plume of dust on the stone floor. I hauled it over to the great fireplace and rolled it and kicked it onto the flames. But rather than catch light, the heavy wool snuffed out the fire in an instant. The room turned colder and darker. If He did exist, then God had forsaken me.

I raised my face to the vaulted roof and cried out into the emptiness: "Where are you?"

"I am right here, Nell." It was a softly spoken and achingly familiar voice that had answered me.

I spun round to the door. "What are you doing?"

"I have come to pay my respects to Edmund," Richard said with a small, stiff bow.

He was dressed in a velvet suit as black as his hair, with high boots and a black feather on his hat. There were dark shadows beneath his eyes. Even lightly tanned as he always was, he looked very pale.

I had ripped holes in my black Puritan dresses after my father's funeral. Now I felt as if it was my heart that had been ripped to shreds. But I hardened it. "Have you no shame?" I asked him.

He hesitated. "I can never be ashamed of loving you."

"You have no right to love me," I said, my voice very cold. "You had no right to love another man's wife."

"Nell, please listen to me." He took a few echoing steps and they brought him closer to me, too close. "Edmund asked me to take care of you and Forest for him."

"Oh, God! Don't tell me that. Don't say that to me."

"He asked me. That is all he asked of me."

"And all I ask is that I never see you again. Not ever. Do you understand?"

His eyes raked my face. "You do not mean that?"

"I do."

"I came to see if there was anything I could do for you," he said. "Is there?"

"The only thing you can do for me is to stay away from me."

"Edmund Ashfield was my friend," he said slowly. "I grieve for him just as you do, Nell. I would like very much to be a friend to you." He glanced at the tapestry smoldering on the fire. "You look to be in dire need of one."

As did he. But how could I be a friend to him, when I had once wanted to be so much more? "Do you not hear me? The last person in the world that I need is you."

He was before me in a stride, had gripped my shoulders very tight as if he would shake me, but instead pulled me roughly toward him. He held me against him for a moment and then abruptly released me.

I did not want him to. I wanted him to take me in his arms again.

I wanted to beat at his chest with my balled fists and for him to hold me tighter still. I wanted to bury my face in his neck, to lay my head against the soft velvet of his coat and sob out my grief. I wanted him to kiss my tears away and later, much later, I wanted to know that he would stroke me with warm, soft, healing hands and love me with such passion that I forgot all else.

"Stay away from me," I rasped. "Do not ever touch me again."

"Sacrificing our own happiness will not bring Edmund back," he said, bereft. "He would not want this."

"How can you speak of what he wanted?" I hissed, clenching my hands and digging the nails into my flesh until I drew blood. "Don't you see? You were a false friend to him and I a faithless wife. We are to blame. We ill-wished him. Something catastrophic is conjured between us when we are together. When I said I could never be your bride, you knew there was one way. You asked me once if I wished I was married to you instead, and I said that I did wish it. We as good as welcomed the possibility of Edmund's death. You must see that we can never, ever take advantage of his death or allow ourselves one moment of pleasure because of it. We can never be together now."

There were tears in his eyes and in mine. I let them stream unchecked down my cheeks, hot against my ice-cold face. I made myself say it. "I will never see you again."

Summer

1680

Mary Burges stayed in Tickenham with me awhile, and then she insisted Forest and I go back with her to Hackney, with Bess in attendance, so that I could have my baby there. She had made all the necessary arrangements, secured a written certificate of my widowhood so no suspicion would befall me when I was brought to bed in childbirth away from home. I hadn't had time to ponder my new circumstances for it even to occur to me that, without this paperwork, I was likely to be treated as barely better than a harlot, my little children as bastards.

"Bring your butterflies," Mary suggested gently, as she and Bess helped me pack a small trunk of my own and Forest's clothes.

She might have spoken to me in an unknown language. "Butterflies?"

"There's plenty of room for them. We can invite your friend James to visit. He still writes to you, doesn't he?"

"Yes, he still writes." I'd not replied to his last two letters.

"I'm sure he'd like to see your collection."

I had let Mary wrap my gowns and petticoats around the leather-bound book and pine boxes in which I'd pasted the butterflies. Not that I could ever imagine showing them to James, nor ever myself looking at them or finding joy in them again. The only reason I carried on breathing was for Edmund's children, for little Forest and the baby inside me who would never meet its father, whom Edmund would never see. I tortured myself that I was to blame. I should never have given him the Jesuits' Powder. His death felt like the greatest cross that I could ever bear. I was sure that I would weep myself as blind as he had been at the end.

Huddled inside a cloak, despite the warm weather, I took in nothing of the journey, or of Hackney itself, beyond that it was a rural, grassy little place, more like a village than an outlying parish of a great city, for all it was becoming a center of genteel education.

I knew it no better when I'd been there several weeks.

I sat shelling peas on a stool by the open door in Mary's little white-walled kitchen, with its shining brass pans and pots of aromatic flowers, now and again pausing to throw a wooden ball at the skittles for Forest, before he exploded in one of the increasingly regular and incandescent tantrums that only his father's calm firmness had been able to control. After dinner I fetched sand from the barrel that stood in the corner of the kitchen and started to help Mary to clean. But she insisted I rest and drink up my fortified wine and cordial.

"Why don't you write to James Petiver and tell him you are in Hackney?" she suggested, but I shook my head. I didn't want to see him. I didn't want to see anyone.

Before I knew it, it was time for my confinement, and I retreated to the small, dark birthing room beneath the eaves almost with relief. Mary and Bess were the only companions I wanted. One day Mary brought me a gift, a curious little stone within a stone on a neck chain.

"It's an eaglestone," she told me as I took it from her. "From Africa."

"How did you get it?"

"They're readily enough to be had in London. Here, let me put it on for you." She leaned toward me and slipped it over my head, kissing my forehead as she did it. "You're supposed to wear it touching your skin when you're with child, to keep you both safe. I thought it was a pretty notion. See." She held the little pendant in the palm of her hand. "The two stones, one nested within the other, are like a child in the womb."

I took it into my own hand and I wanted to weep. "Thank you, Mary. Thank you for wanting to keep me safe."

I hated the thought that I was a burden to her, when she had enough worries of her own. She was in far more danger than was I. The Popish Plot and the subsequent wild allegations against Catholics had seen thirty-five put to death and the Catholic Duke of York exiled abroad for the alleged plot to murder the King. Anti-Papist feeling still ran dangerously high. Which is why I had not told her the precise nature of Edmund's death, could never tell her, did not even want to explore my confused, suppressed fear that it was Catholic poison which had killed him.

"I know you don't believe in amulets," Mary said.

"I believe in them as much as I can believe in anything now." I wrapped my fingers around the little charm and slipped it inside my cambric chemise. "I might as well put my faith in this as in anything else. Maybe good luck or bad luck is all there is. Maybe a talisman is all I need."

I WAS IN BED, with barely the strength to lift my head, when Mary brought a tiny baby girl to me, all clean and pink and wrapped up in soft swaddling cloths.

"There, little one," Mary crooned, as she placed this tranquil little stranger carefully in my arms. "She's been waiting so very patiently to meet her mother." Mary sat down on the edge of the bed. "We thought you'd taken leave of us, Eleanor. Do you have any recollection at all?"

I tried, shook my head. "I remember the pains starting. Then nothing."

"It is probably just as well," she said. "The birth wasn't an easy one. You've been grievously sick."

I gazed down into my baby's sweet face, as she made a little O with her mouth. All rosy and content, she was so utterly different from my first sight of Forest, bloody and naked and blue, still attached to me by the slippery, pulsating cord.

"What happened?"

Mary hesitated.

"I want to know, Mary. Everything."

"The baby came wrong," Mary began, gently. "She was stuck so long the midwife had to drag her out of you by her legs." Her kind, calm voice removed only some of the horror of her words. "You fainted from an overflow of blood just after it was over. You regained some sensible pulse and color, but after a few days fell faint again from noxious impurities that nature should have cleaned out of you. It is a miracle you're still with us. That both of you are still with us." She paused, looked down at the baby with adoration. "She's the most docile, easy little thing. Hardly ever cries or complains. It's almost as if, after the violence of her delivery and the fight she had to come into the world, she wants only calmness and peace."

"Her father wanted that too."

"Pray he has peace now."

"I cannot pray for anything anymore. I wish I could."

I stroked my baby's silken little cheek, shifted her slightly and felt my own flattened belly. "She is a new life," I whispered. "Just like a little butterfly bursting forth from a pupa. If I could only believe in that. I owe it to her grandfather's memory to believe it."

If I had taken more heed of his warnings, perhaps this little girl would have known a father's love as I had known it, even though I had rejected all that my father stood for. Had he been right all along? Had I been so very wrong to doubt him?

"If only I could be sure that Edmund is not merely rotting in the ground but that his soul has been reborn," I said quietly. "If only I could be sure that he will meet his little daughter one day."

"I pray that you find your faith again," Mary said. "I will always pray for you, Eleanor, and your dear girl. And for Forest."

I had a pang of yearning to see my son. "Where is Forest?"

"Busy learning to chop wood with John. Would you have me fetch him?"

"No. Leave him be," I said. "I'll not drag him from a boy's pleasure into a nursery. He will have precious little opportunity to do manly things, since he is adrift in a little family of women now." The baby mewed like a kitten then, so I put her to my breast. Her gums didn't hurt me as Forest's had done, her suckling no more than a gentle tug and tickle.

"Your milk will come again soon," Mary said, standing. "I'll tell the wet nurse we have no more need of her."

"Thank you for caring for her so well for me."

"I've cherished her as if she was my own."

"She shall be named after you."

"I'd like that."

"Hello, my Mary," I said when we were alone. The baby blinked her mild blue eyes, then looked around as if in wonder at a world still so new to her. She wrinkled her nose and it was the most delightful thing. She yawned and it was like a miracle. She fascinated me. She was my cherub, my fairy, my little princess, my companion. I was overcome with a love as profound and consuming as the love I had felt when I first saw Forest, entirely different this time, though, because Mary was of my sex. We would understand each other, would share similar experiences, similar hopes and fears. She was like me, made anew.

I loosened the swaddling cloths and gave her freedom to wave her arms about. Her tiny fingers jumped open like a little frog, a starfish, like the leaves of a marsh pimpernel. They curled around my thumb and clung to me. Then the swaddling fell back from her head and I saw that she was not like me at all. She was like Edmund. She had a fluffy fuzz of the brightest copper hair. And it undid me.

I stared at the downy auburn tufts and tears streamed down my face. Edmund's daughter gazed back at me with unfocused eyes and looked completely calm and accepting, just like her father. I held her to my face and kissed her, wetting her cheeks with my tears. I clutched her to me and rocked her, rocked myself, and told her how her father would have loved her so.

MARY LET ME BE until a few days after I was churched; then she laid out my blue gown on the bed and sent Bess in, armed with curling tongs for my hair.

"There's someone coming to see you later," she said as Bess stuck the tongs in the fire to heat them.

I was lounging back on the pillows feeding the baby, but was instantly alert. "Who?"

"James Petiver."

"Oh." I tried not to sound disappointed that it was not someone else, tried not even to feel it.

"I asked him to come. I hope you don't mind." Mary seemed well pleased with herself. "He's just what you need. He has been such a good friend to you, keeping up his correspondence all this time. He's also an apothecary. One of those qualifications, or the combination of them, surely mean he will be able to help you where the rest of us have failed." She took the baby off me and pulled me out of bed and onto a stool. Then she picked up an ivory comb to start on my hair herself.

"I can't think what I'll find to say to him," I said, as Bess took over and coiled a silken lock of my fresh-combed hair round the tongs. "I fear I shall be very dull company."

Mary watched as the rich yellow curls bounced up around my shoulders. "Sweet girl, I doubt any man could ever find you dull. But we shall let James be the judge."

John had taken Forest to market with him and Mary had the baby with her in the schoolroom, so I was sitting alone by the fire when the maid brought James in.

He had changed so much since the first and only time I'd met him face-to-face in the Apothecaries' Garden, and yet I would have known him anywhere. After so many letters had passed between us, I felt I knew him as well as I knew myself. He could have been my brother. We even looked alike, both of us fair and slight.

He was dressed in a well-cut suit of blue serge with brass buttons and a square white collar edged with lace. He had let his corn-blond hair grow longer and had tied it back with a dark blue ribbon—a practicality, I imagined, but it suited him well. In physical stature he was still only head and shoulders above me, but I could see instantly that in other respects he had grown from a boy to a man. He had an air of assurance he'd not had before, but was still as unaffected as ever. He took both my cold hands in his warm ones, didn't raise them to his lips and kiss them, or do anything at all gallant, but kept them pressed inside his and held them there as we sat down, me on the little settle and him on a stool beside me.

"It is so good to see you," he said. This was no platitude, was not spoken out of politeness but as if he meant it from the bottom of his heart. "I am so very sorry for your loss."

He moved toward me slightly and then away again, and I caught a scent of the herbs and lavender and the other aromatic plants he worked with and turned into medicines. It was the scent of the meadows and the gardens he frequented for his trade, and it reminded me of what I'd been missing: this essence of nature, of fresh air, which emanated from his hands, his clothes, from his very being. It was somehow reflected in his indefinable eyes, flecked with hazel and green and gold, which had in them all the warmth and brightness of a sunny glade. They radiated enthusiasm, intelligence and affection.

"It is good of you to come, James."

"I'd have come much sooner if I'd been invited." He studied me as a botanist might study a flower, to appreciate its complexities but also to comprehend what it needed in order to blossom. "I can't believe you've been but a few hours' walk away all these weeks."

"I've lost all grasp of time. So much has happened to me. I've become a wife and widow and a mother, twice over, all in the space of four years." Silently, I added adulteress to that list. "James, have you . . . have you ever used Jesuits' Powder?"

"I have too much regard for my career even to stock it at present. Why do you ask?"

I shook my head, found I did not want to speak of Edmund's death. Having it confirmed that Jesuits' Powder was a deadly poison could change nothing. For once in my life, it seemed better not to ask, better not to know the answer.

"I should love to meet your little son and daughter," James said. "They must be a great comfort to you."

There seemed no point at all in pretending, or even trying to make idle chat with him. "They are my joy and my torment," I said. "I see

Edmund in them, but the very thought of them makes my heart shrink because I remember his great pleasure in them. And I am so terrified of some illness or accident befalling them, of losing them too, that I am never at peace."

James considered me. "You are grieving," he said gently. "But you are also suffering from fits of the mother, I think. It's very common after giving birth to succumb to a kind of melancholy, especially when you've experienced trauma in your life. It passes, after a while. There's a physic I can give you to help." He was still holding my hands, chafing them gently as we talked, and I felt the blood flowing in my veins again, like the sap rising in spring. "You're in very good company as well, you know. All the great intellectuals of our time are tormented by morbid dispositions . . . Hooke, Locke, Newton." He kept the warmth of his eyes focused on me so that I felt as if I really was a flower, opening to the warmth of the sun. "Mistress Burges told me you'd brought your collection with you. I'd like to see it, if you would show it to me."

I went to fetch an armful of books and cases, handed them to him with some reluctance, sat back in my seat and watched in an agony of suspense as he turned over a page, paused to examine a specimen, then turned another, on and on, in complete silence.

He spent the longest time looking at his beloved copper-colored butterflies, and then, mercifully, he reached the end. At last he looked up. "The quality and variety of your collection puts the rest of us to shame."

It was so simply said, and yet it meant so very much to me.

"Thank you, James."

"No need to thank me when I speak only the truth."

I hadn't realized how much I had wanted his approval—almost more than I used to want my father's. And I smiled. For the first time since Edmund died, I felt a flush of joy. And with it came hope, without which I think life is unbearable. I had collected my butterflies devotedly but I hadn't thought they amounted to much. Now I wondered if I might find some meaning to life after all, might even make some lasting contribution.

James had turned back to the middle of the book. "This insect here," he said, pointing to a checkered red and black. "I've only ever seen one before, or one very like it. Captured in Cambridgeshire."

"Conditions in the Fens were once very similar to those where I live. I see those butterflies almost every day." I told him then about the Swallowtails and Large Coppers and how they seemed to have deserted the Fens when they were drained.

"That's a remarkable discovery." James looked back at the red and black specimen. "It would be interesting to know if it's the same with these. They're the ones you once described to me as having markings like a chessboard?"

"That's right."

"I've a checkered dice box that looks just the same. Fritillary."

"It should be called a Marsh Fritillary, then."

"A good name. I'll propose it at our next coffeehouse meeting."

"You can give names to butterflies, just like that?"

"A proper system of nomenclature is vital to bring order out of the chaos of the natural world. If a butterfly doesn't already have a Latin name or a common name, we should give it one. You already speak of Swallowtails and Large Coppers. Let's do some more, shall we?" He spun the book back toward me, as if we were to play a board game, pointed to a butterfly with bands of bright red across its brown velvety wings.

"It reminds me of one of the flags you see on naval ships."

"The Red Admiral?" he said.

"Red Admiral. I like it. We should call it that."

"And this?" He pointed to one with jagged orange-brown wings, marked with black and blue. "What would be a good name for this one, do you suppose?"

Puzzled, I leaned forward with my elbows on my knees, chin resting in my hands to think. "Hmmm. Not so easy."

James reached out toward me and produced a little comb, like a conjuror at a fair might produce a coin from the sleeve of his coat. It took me a moment to realize he'd taken it from my hair. "It looks rather like this pattern, don't you think?"

A curl flopped across my eyes. I pushed it away with my hand. "Tortoiseshell."

"Tortoiseshell it shall be."

"How do you know for sure you've found a different species, that it's not just a variation?"

"There's always much debate about species divisions. That's why we all need to keep collecting and share our findings."

"Will other people use those names we've chosen?"

"They could still be in use hundreds of years from now."

The notion of that amazed and cheered me, the idea that there might just be butterflies called Red Admirals and Tortoiseshells flying around when we were long gone.

"Did I ever tell you," I said, "a boy once accused me of being soft in the head for chasing butterflies."

"That doesn't surprise me in the least. You should see the strange looks I attract when folk see me out walking with a net over my shoulder, a pincushion round my neck, and butterflies fastened round the brim of my hat."

I giggled. "You pin them round the brim of your hat? What a perfect place."

"You see, only you'd appreciate that. To the rest of the world I look an oddity indeed."

He stayed for hours and, when he came back the next week, he arrived with a posy of flowers he'd picked from Chelsea, and a draft of physic he'd prepared for me himself.

"What is in it?" I asked.

He smiled to see a glimmer of my natural curiosity returning. "Water pimpernel and marsh marigold, mainly."

"Both those plants grow on Tickenham Moor," I pondered. "I never knew they had medicinal properties. Something else that might be lost, then, if the land were converted from marsh into permanent arable land?"

"Well, for now they are plentiful enough." He spooned out a measure of the physic for me before we had glasses of wine and slices of Mary's almond tart. Then he talked to me about his work with the paupers at St. Bartholomew's Hospital and about how he wanted to open his own apothecary shop. He talked animatedly about his group of friends who'd started meeting every Friday evening at the Temple Bar coffeehouse off Fleet Street, to talk about botany and insects. "It's the only society in the country devoted to the study of the natural world," he said, excitedly. "We've gathered together some of the greatest minds of our day and intend to formalize our club and make it a focus for promoting botanical knowledge."

"James, you have such an illustrious circle of friends and such a full and interesting life, I can't imagine why you'd choose to spend your precious days off with me, eating tarts in a little boarding school in Hackney."

"Can't you?" he asked, suddenly serious.

But as the time drew nearer for his third visit, I became convinced that he'd send a message to say he couldn't come after all. I wasn't sure how I'd manage a whole week without a few hours of his company, though. The physic he gave me helped heal my body, but his presence soothed my soul. He was like a window opening out onto the world.

Through his bright hazel eyes I saw, for the first time in weeks, beyond Mary's little kitchen and school, beyond my loss and my guilt and sorrow.

But he did come, and he suggested that next time we go on a butterfly-hunting expedition together. "We'll take provisions. Make a day of it."

"Wouldn't you have a much better time with your friends?"

"I thought you were my friend."

I couldn't have felt happier if I'd been the staunchest Royalist given an invitation to the royal court on the King's own birthday.

"So. Where shall it be? Where would you like to go?"

I remembered the pretty names of all the places he'd mentioned in his letters. Fulham Palace Gardens. Hampton Court. Primrose Hill. The lavender fields of Mitcham. "Oh, I don't know. I can't decide."

He looked at me, considering. "Let's go to Fulham Palace, then," he said. "It's like a scene from a romance. I think you'd like it the best of anywhere."

"WHAT IS THAT you are reading so avidly?" Mary asked me, looking up from the table where she was crushing almonds for marchpane.

I showed her the cover of *Philosophical Transactions*. "It's the journal of the Royal Society. James brought it for me. He said he thought I'd find it helpful."

"Helpful in what way?"

"I'll show you," I said excitedly, feeling the familiar thrill of experiment and discovery stir in me again. I put the journal down, scooped up little Mary and carried her over to the sunny leaded window. I held up my left hand toward the light, the hand upon which I still wore the bejeweled band that Edmund had slipped onto my finger on our wedding day. I turned the back of my hand toward the glass and tilted it slowly, this way and that, keeping my eyes trained intently on the far wall. "Watch very carefully," I whispered to Edmund's little daughter.

"Whatever are you doing now?" Bess had been wiping the dishes. She put down the cloth.

"We are contemplating Isaac Newton's theory of light and color," I told her and Mary with a grin.

"You are an addlebrain for sure," Bess muttered.

But at that moment I got the angle just right and a myriad of dancing colors, red, orange, yellow, green, blue, indigo and violet, were splashed across the white walls of the little lime-washed kitchen.

"Isaac Newton has proved that we are surrounded by color all the time," I said. "Light itself is made up of a spectrum of colors." With my thumb I stroked the band of my ring with its diamonds that were doing the job of a prism. "So you see, my little Mary, your father can still bring some brightness to our lives, even though he is gone from them."

"It seems to me that it is James Petiver who has done that for you," Mary said gently.

"Maybe. But do you see," I said animatedly. "Mr. Newton has shown how rainbows are made."

"Pity John didn't know that when he was preaching." Mary looked from one tiny rainbow to another. "How lovely to think God not only created light to banish the dark, but made it so beautiful, just like a true artist."

"If experiment can reveal the components of light," I posed tentatively, "maybe it really can illuminate the rest of God's work. If I could only see how a butterfly is born, I could perhaps be sure that Edmund is in Heaven with my parents and my sister. I could still believe I will see them all again."

. . .

🦋 "IT'S NOT MUCH FURTHER NOW," James said. "Those are the gardens over there."

We were walking along a raised path called Bishop's Walk that ran along the bank of the Thames. To the other side of us was a wide channel of still water, uncannily like one of the rhynes on Tickenham Moor. But the land behind it was nothing like the moor. It was crowded with trees, not wispy willows, but great stately trunks, with roots that spidered the ground like the veins on an old man's hand, beneath a canopy of enormous arching branches. "The entrance is only about a quarter of a mile away," James said.

I slid my hand into the crook of his arm and gave him a quick squeeze. "Stop fretting about me, James. I'm not in the least tired."

I hardly knew which way to turn my head. On one side of us was the forested garden and on the other was the river, busy with barges and tilt boats and fleets of collier ships, the skyline punctuated with Wren's graceful spires that had arisen from the ashes of the Great Fire.

We entered the Palace Gardens under an avenue of limes, and I saw then that the wide ditch was in fact a great moat which encircled the entire acreage of the grounds. It was like a scene from a myth. In front of us was a drawbridge and beyond it was the house, or palace, very old and ruinous, with battlemented towers.

"What is this place? Who lives here?"

"It's been the summer residence of the bishops of London for centuries. The gardens are of great antiquity, have been famous for their beauty and scientific value since the reign of Queen Elizabeth. That's a tamarisk tree." James pointed. "From Switzerland. Over there is a cork tree."

With my hand still resting in the crook of his arm, he led me deeper into the strange and beautiful forest.

"The trees grew even more thickly once," he said. "Until one of the bishops thinned them. Legend has it that Sir Francis Bacon visited just afterward and said that, having cut down such a cloud of trees, he must be a good man to throw light on dark places."

"I should like to throw light on dark places."

"Eleanor, you could do nothing but."

I gave his arm another squeeze. "Did I ever tell you? I was married in the same church as Francis Bacon?"

"How grand."

"Actually, it was far from it."

"Really?"

"'Truth requires evidence from the real world,' Sir Francis said. That is such a good creed. My father had his writings in his library but never could agree that there must be evidence for everything before we can believe in it . . . even before we can believe in God."

"Do you think we can ever see evidence of God?"

"I used to think it was all around us, in the splendor of his creation. I used to think that was the very reason we must study it, to bring us closer to Him. Or that's what my father taught me. I no longer know which of the things he taught me are true, but I have a hope that it is more than I have come to suspect." I stopped and turned to him. "James, do you believe absolutely in metamorphosis?"

He pursed his lips. "I am as uncertain as the next man about oft-repeated claims. Experts contradict each other. The only truly reliable approach to the study of the natural world is through one's own observations. I can't entirely believe it without the evidence of my own eyes."

That was not what I wanted to hear at all. "Have any of your friends at the coffeehouse even seen it?"

"They are more interested in collecting and marking one species off from another than in seeing how they are born. Though it has not yet been studied properly, metamorphosis is recognized as a fact, so . . ."

"So what? It was recognized as fact, since the time of Aristotle, that the earth was at the center of the universe. But now we are told that the earth in fact moves round the sun. It seems to me that the only truth we have is that we live in a chaos of superstition and experiment. How can we know where we are while natural philosophy is still vying with the old world of magic and traditional lore?

"Few now believe in unicorns as they once did, but if horned beasts are to be relegated to legend, where does that leave the poor old rhinoceros? We cannot believe Aristotle now, so does that mean we should also question the authority of the Bible? If the earth is not the center of the universe, then where does that leave God and His creation of it? If there is a chance that a piece of rotten fruit, or a cabbage leaf, or a pile of dung can create life, where does that leave God as the ultimate creator? Where does that leave the promise of eternal life?" I ran out of breath and smiled to see James both stunned and speechless.

"Well," he said at last, "you appear to have rediscovered your curiosity. Along with your voice."

I laughed. "So I do."

"What a truly remarkable person you are, and what a pity it is that you can't join our club. You've a quicker and more interesting mind than many virtuosi."

"Why can't I join your club? Why can't I go to the coffeehouse with you?" I waved my hand. "Oh. Don't even bother to tell me. I already know the answer. It's only open to gentlemen."

"I'd welcome you right away," James said as we walked on. "But I'm afraid we'd be a club of only two."

"Nobody else would stay if I was there?"

"They'd be afraid a woman would hinder and corrupt their flow of ideas, cast a malign influence over their experiments."

I rolled my eyes in exasperation. "You do know that is ridiculous?"

He grinned. "I certainly have no evidence of it."

"The Duchess of Newcastle was permitted to attend the Royal Society meeting," I ventured.

"Just once. And she, poor lady, is considered a freak of nature, an embarrassment to her sex and her family, for her interest in science." He tucked my hand back under his arm. "There's something I want to show you. The conditions are perfect, so I'm sure they'll be there."

"What will be there?"

"Wait and see. It is a surprise."

We came to a copse of magnificent oaks with a small clearing in the middle.

"There," James said, and looked up.

I followed his gaze into the shelter of green leaves and filtered rays of gold light.

Flickers of violet. A dozen indigo wings. Purple-black butterflies, like the drawings from the pages of the book James had made for me after first I met him.

I ran ahead a few steps, into the glade. The butterflies flitted just a little higher, riding the currents of the air. I stood with face up-turned to the arching branches and the sky beyond. Something about their twirling flight made it impossible to stand still. I turned round slowly, watching them. I held out my arms like a swaying tree, danc-ing in the breeze, my silk skirt swishing. The butterflies flitted higher and higher toward the tops of the trees and I was suddenly giddy.

James caught me as I almost lost my balance. As he set me back on my feet and looked into my smiling face, the light seemed to dim in his own eyes, as if he had transferred all his strength and happiness to me and had nothing left for himself. "James, you look so sad."

"Not at all. And neither are you anymore, I think."

I shook my head. "I don't know how you do it."

"Do what?"

"Make me feel again how I felt as a little girl. That everything is there to be discovered. Everything is possible. That life can be good."

"It is the study of butterflies that makes you feel that way, and having a passion, and never, ever letting go of it."

"Thank you," I said. "For not allowing me to let go. For bringing me here."

He appeared about to say something more, then changed his mind. "Those purple butterflies are so shy, you've no chance of netting one unless you come prepared."

"Which, of course, you have."

He produced from his pocket not a flower but a small lump of meat wrapped in paper. He set it at some distance from us on the grass.

We watched. We waited. Soon enough a flicker of purple descended from above, came drifting down and settled on the carrion, to be followed by another. They fluttered their wings once or twice, then folded them up, revealing an underside of shimmering purple, like shot silk.

James didn't pounce, as I was about to do. He seemed content to watch, to stand back respectfully and admire from a distance, to let them just be.

"Now, what name would you give to them?" he whispered.

I was entranced, as in the presence of a king all cloaked in royal purple. One was smaller than the other, and one brighter. Was one a female and one a male, one a princess and one an emperor, and if so which way around was it? Purple Emperor. Purple Princess. I'd never considered there could be butterflies that fed on meat, like human beings. They seemed to be relishing the little feast we'd brought for them.

"Do they have teeth?" I asked quietly.

"Ah, now, you'd only find that out by observing up close. Would you like to have one of them, for your collection?"

"You have one already?"

"A perfect pair."

"Did you catch them here?"

"Last spring."

"So they're likely to be of the exact same species?"

We could study James's specimens, learn from them; we didn't have to take anymore. But that didn't stop me craving one of these exquisite beauties for myself. And James knew it. He knew me too well. Without a word from me, he was already creeping toward the spot where the butterflies had alighted. He moved very slowly, as if in a dream; then at the last moment was quick as a cat with a mouse. He clapped his net around the two of them, pinched one, then the other, between his fingers, impaled them on a pin upon the brim of his hat and placed his hat back on his head, while I was still marveling at the deftness of his fingers.

Standing in the middle of the sunny clearing, wearing a pincushion on a ribbon like a medallion, his hat adorned with purple butterflies, he looked like a very young and clever magician. He conjured two boiled eggs from his pocket and handed me one. We peeled the eggs and ate them; then he handed me his flask of whiskey. "Not a very grand picnic, I am afraid."

I took a nip and wiped my mouth with the back of my hand. "It is the very best kind."

As we walked back through the oaks toward the moat, I glanced at my butterflies on his hat.

"They'll be perfectly safe," he assured me. "I told you, a hat's the finest receptacle there is."

"I can see it. I'm just thinking what a shame it is that I don't have that kind of a hat."

He stopped, took it off and placed it firmly on my head. It slid down over my eyes, so he adjusted it, tilted it slightly at a jaunty angle. "Very becoming."

"I've often thought I'd be best suited as a boy."

"Well, I'm sincerely glad you're not one." He gave a little cough, as if to cover what he'd just said. "If you were a boy, I'd have no female acquaintances at all," he finished.

"I don't believe that for one instant."

"Well, it is quite true."

Surely there were plenty of girls, one girl at least, who'd like to see his bright, clever eyes light up even more brightly with love for her, for her alone? "You must have a sweetheart," I questioned curiously. "Surely there is some pretty girl whom you've restored to health with your magic potions and who has lost her heart to you?"

"I wish that was so," he said. "But I'm afraid it has not happened."

For a moment I thought I could almost be that girl. For James had cured me, undoubtedly he had. But my heart? It was most certainly lost, but long before this day. When Edmund ambled into the hall of Tickenham Court out of the rain. When I first saw Richard Glanville smiling down at me from the saddle of his black Barbary stallion, like a winter prince. In such different ways, I loved them both. I mourned Edmund still, with a grief sharpened by remorse. And I missed Richard. I missed him so much. I still met him in my dreams— sweet, tortured, passionate dreams that made me wake restlessly in the morning, with the pain of parting from him as fresh as if it had been only yesterday that I had told him never to touch me or come near me again.

I was a typical lusty widow after all, wasn't I? I saw something in

James's eyes that made me think I must tread very carefully with him. It would not be fair, even for one moment, to let him think he could love me, even if he had a mind to. He was my dearest friend and I could not imagine him as anything else. I would not risk hurting him, ruining our friendship, when I needed a good friend far more than I needed another lover. My heart had been split in two. And a thing cannot be split without being broken.

I took James's hat off my head and put it firmly back on his, for all the world as if I was handing him back his heart. "There. You look after my butterflies for me." I lifted the pincushion that hung round his neck, let it rest in the palm of my hand. "Why so many different-sized pins?"

"If you stick a small fly with a large pin its joints will break and it will fall to pieces."

I looked up at him and spluttered. "Well, if I ever marry again, then, I'd best make sure my husband's yard is not too big, since I am so very small."

He froze, mouth agape. The years fell away and he was the unworldly boy he'd been the first time we'd met. I collapsed in laughter. He started laughing too. We both laughed until we were bent double like a pair of crones, clenching our sides with pain, tears rolling down our cheeks.

Autumn

1680

James was coming for dinner and there was something of great importance that I had to ask him.

"Mary, would you take the children for me awhile?"

"You know I'm glad to have them anytime." She glanced at me quickly, as she carried on with her brocading. "But we shall be going to mass later. They'll have to come with us."

I gazed down at my little daughter, asleep in my arms, and I almost said no straightaway. "I'm not sure."

"Since you no longer care for any religion, what does it matter if they attend an Anglican ceremony or a Papist one?"

Because Jesuit poison killed their father. "I do not know. But it does. Force of habit, I suppose."

"A father's influence runs so deep you can never be entirely free of it, especially when that father was as commanding and powerful as yours." Mary stuck the needle into the brocade, set it to one side and gave me her full attention. "But you know, not all your ancestors were so set against Catholics, or Cavaliers for that matter. Your uncle, who lives in Ribston Hall in Yorkshire, is a baronet. Your mother's father,

Rice Davies, is still remembered in Tickenham for being as noble as they come. It takes ambition and desire for grandeur to build a great house such as Ribston or Tickenham Court, to be granted acres of land. It takes favors from the King. Your family has the blood of brave knights running through its veins. Who knows? Maybe even royal blood."

Mary smiled as she saw my eyes open wide at the daring, almost traitorous thought that I, the daughter of one of Cromwell's men, could have royal blood. I almost felt it stirring dangerously inside me, rousing me.

"And it's not just royal blood you may have," she said with gravity. "When you go back to Tickenham, you look very carefully at the wainscoting around the chimney breast in the great hall."

I smiled. "Is this a riddle?"

"There's a tiny chamber, a cell, built into the side of the chimney," she said. "There used to be a tunnel from it that led to the church, but I understand it is now blocked. It's a priest's hole," she added with great significance. "Where they hid Catholic priests during the Reformation. Your Catholic lineage, your children's Catholic lineage, is strong."

"Maybe that explains my hankering for satin and gold."

"Maybe it does." She paused. "So, the little ones can come to mass, then?"

"I suppose they can."

JAMES ARRIVED just after Mary and John and the children had left. He brought part of his collection, in pine boxes of yellow and white and blue, because later he was going on to join his club at the Temple Bar coffeehouse. And I was determined that he was going to take me with him. They might not talk so freely in front of me and I would surely never be allowed to come back. But like Margaret Cavendish, the Duchess of Newcastle, I was going to risk all and go just the same, just once.

"Will you show these to your friends?"

James looked at me over a little square box of blues, neatly arranged in pairs, a female beside a usually larger and more brightly colored male. Quick as a flash, I thought of Edmund's red hair, and of Richard Glanville in green silk, and me in drab Puritan black, fluttering toward them both. Was I a butterfly or was I a moth, fluttering irresistibly toward a bright flame that would burn me alive?

I looked at James, with his hair the color of ripened corn and his extraordinary multicolored eyes. Now, why could I not have fallen in love with someone like him?

"Leonard Plukenet and Adam Buddle will be there tonight," he said. "They like to see my latest acquisitions, are as passionate about butterflies as you and I."

"You could discuss the differences between the sexes?" I said leadingly.

"Maybe."

"A one-sided debate, given the single sex of your club."

He smiled, feigning innocence. "We're a botany society. We'll talk about male and female butterflies, or ants, or the reproduction of flowers, not about men and women. But still."

"Still, what?"

He frowned, his finger over his lips, making a show of giving something the greatest consideration.

I giggled. "What, James?"

"There are greater differences between men and women than between male and female butterflies, for sure. But the differences are not so great if the woman is, how can I say it . . . not as voluptuous as the fashions of our age usually dictate."

"Well, there's no need to be rude."

"Not at all. I have no time for fashion, as is surely evident." He lifted one of his feet, encased in outdated flat-heeled shoes. "I think it is far more appealing for a lady to have the delicate prettiness of a butterfly."

"Well redeemed."

But he was still studying me, as if reflecting on a possibility. "What differences there are could perhaps be concealed, with a little ingenuity," he said.

I had an inkling then of where this was leading, but I didn't dare hope. Didn't dare hope that, once again, James knew me so well that he knew what I wanted or needed, almost before I knew it myself.

"There is perhaps one insurmountable difference," he deliberated. "The small matter of courage. It's generally accepted that a man is far braver than a woman. A man would take risks that a woman would not. A man would keep his head where a woman would lose hers at the first sign of trouble. In which case it could never be achieved." His playful tone had turned more earnest. "I would lose the trust and respect of my friends, all I've worked for. If they found out I'd be a laughingstock. Would never be taken seriously again. No. It's no use. It cannot be done."

I held my breath and leaned forward, arms pressing on my knees, and peered into his face. "What cannot be done, James?"

He expelled a long breath. "It's no good telling you now. It'll only spoil your evening."

"It is already spoiled," I admitted. "Because you are going off to your club and leaving me behind. You were thinking you could take me with you, weren't you?"

He grinned. "Now, whatever gave you that idea?"

I grabbed his hands. "Take me with you, James. I *am* brave, as brave as any boy. My father told me he wished he had men of my courage

marching with him for Cromwell. I will not be intimidated by anyone, I promise you. I won't fail you."

He wavered, or pretended to waver, then sized me up. "When we
first met we were almost exactly the same size, wouldn't you say?"

I knew what he was going to suggest before he said it.

"My scheme, extraordinary as it may seem, was to take you along
in disguise, dressed as a boy."

I clapped my hands. "James, that is the most harebrained, madcap
idea!"

"One you might have thought of yourself, I think?"

"Only far better. It's perfect. But who would I be?"

"I thought to introduce you as my assistant, my butterfly boy."

"And what would be my name? I'd have to have a name."

"Isaac, I thought, in homage to the great Mr. Newton himself,
founder of the most exclusive scientific society in Britain and the in-
vestigator of light."

"Isaac . . . I can be Isaac. Oh, let me be Isaac. Let me do it. I will
not disappoint you, I swear it."

HE HAD BROUGHT a parcel of clothes, and I laughed to think
how our thoughts ran in such extraordinary parallel. All the time I'd
been plotting how to find a way to go with him to the coffeehouse,
he'd been plotting how to enable me to do it, packing up his own
shirts and breeches and waistcoat and boots to disguise me in.

He handed the parcel to me, but I hesitated. I realized there was
one problem and did not know how to broach it, without risking
having him take it the wrong way.

"You need assistance with unfastening your gown?" he asked, very
pragmatically.

I nodded. "Bess and Mary's maid have the afternoon off. There is nobody else here, and I can't do it on my own."

We went up to my little sloping-roofed chamber above the schoolroom and locked the door. Discreetly, James went to look out of the little dormer window, hands lightly clasped behind him, his flaxen pigtail falling down the middle of his back.

I took the parcel then and laid all the items out on the bed, ran my fingers lightly across them. There was something rather poignant about them. They were the clothes James had worn as a boy, when he'd been about the age he was when I first met him, and been the same size as me. The shirt had been freshly laundered and carried a faint scent of lavender, but I could see where the cuffs had frayed slightly around his hands, and the cloth breeches still bore the faint creases which had formed as he had worn them, as he had walked and sat and knelt down to examine herbs and flowers and butterflies. Too small for him now. He had grown and I had not.

"I'm ready," I said.

He made a great show of breathing deeply and gathering himself, as if he was about to do some onerous but unavoidable task. I turned my back to him so he could get at the tiny buttons and laces that held my costume together.

I expected to feel fumbling, nervous fingers, for him to take a long time over it, but instead I felt him working the tiny row of pearl buttons with the deftness with which he pinned a tiny butterfly. The realization hit me and surprised me: He knows exactly what he is doing. He had done this before. This was no gauche boy who'd never undressed a woman, never seen one naked. He had done this before, with some other girl, maybe with many more than one. There was no one special, he said, but he had taken his pleasures somewhere. And there were, after all, plenty of places for a young man to take his pleasures in London, plenty of willing orange girls and pretty whores who could be had for a few pennies. Plenty of maids who'd give themselves willingly, for free, to an ambitious and clever young apothecary with warm, bright eyes, who, it was plain to see, was on the rise.

I wanted to turn round and look at him, to see if this new realization made him appear any different to me. I didn't feel jealous of these unknown girls at all, but the thought of James as a man, with a man's needs and urges, did make me feel strange. In the way that noises become louder in the dark when you cannot see, I was acutely aware of every movement of his fingers at my back, every slight change in pressure. I let my dress fall to the ground and felt him loosening the laces of my corset. I peeled it off, turned round and, in just my chemise, I stepped out of the watery-blue circle of silk.

I wondered then if I'd been entirely wrong about his past experiences. For he stood transfixed, like a boy who'd never seen a woman's body before, except in his most secret dreams, as if he couldn't tear his eyes away from me. And I, who'd been a wife and borne two children and tasted another man's ardent kisses and caresses, was acting as shy and chaste as a virgin on her wedding night.

There was no need. I was not wedded anymore. I was no virgin either. I was free and ready to love another man. I did love another man. And it was not this man. My chemise slid off my shoulder. Quick as lightning, James came out of his trance and reached behind me for the shirt, held it out to me. "I'll wait outside while you put it on."

When the door had softly closed behind him, I took off my undergarments. Alone and naked, I slid my arms into the arms of James's shirt. The linen had worn very soft. It was so strange to think of my small shoulders and elbows where James's elbows and shoulders had so often been, and it was almost as if the impression left by him, the ghost of him as a boy, was still there, slipping his arms along the entire length of mine, holding me, wrapping me in a gentle embrace.

Not a lover's embrace, but the enfolding, secure and protective embrace of a brother, a twin, a part of myself. The shirt was a little too big for me, and yet it felt as if it fit as well as a hand in a glove, as well as my own skin. It still carried the faintest trace of him, the scent of herbs and fresh air that was so familiar to me. It was as if he were still in the room, standing right behind me, as if he would always be with me, no matter what.

I stepped into his breeches, smiling to myself now at the thought of which parts of his body had been in this particular garment before. I tugged the belt tight around my waist and pulled on his boots, which he'd padded with straw to make them fit. I looked down at myself and laughed out loud at the picture I made, like a she-soldier from a ballad.

"It is safe to come in now," I called.

He grinned when he saw me. "A lad with ringlets. Well, I never."

"Oops! I forgot." I scooped up my hair and knotted it at the back of my head, squashed the cap on top. "I was bound to get something wrong, since I've never been a lad before."

James came up to me and lifted my chin, smoothed a strand of hair away and arranged the collar of my shirt. "Hmm. You'll just about pass as my butterfly boy. A fitting name, since you're such an uncommonly pretty little fellow. We just have to hope they're all too busy with botany to pay too much attention to a dainty little lad with fair skin and golden lovelocks and the widest blue eyes. But then they may guess our ruse. Cross-dressing is all the rage at court, I understand."

"Would it really be so bad for you if we were found out?"

"As bad as can be," he said lightly. "They'd never forgive me for deceiving them. I'd likely be barred."

I pulled the cap lower, fiddled with my cuffs. "I can't let you take such a risk for me. I won't go."

"You can and you shall." He handed me a box of butterflies. "And since you are my assistant, you'd better make yourself useful and carry one of these."

"I'll take them both."

James picked up the other one. "You may be got up like a boy, but I'll not forget you're a little lady underneath. I'll not burden you with too heavy a load when we've such a long way to go."

IT DID NOT SEEM a long way at all. It took us well over an hour, but it was so easy and such a novelty to walk without the encumbrance of a long skirt that I practically skipped along in James's boots to the coffeehouse, wishing I could wear breeches and boots all the time. How lucky men were to be so unhindered. We talked as we walked. He told me how such establishments as we were about to enter were multiplying in London, how they had even attained some degree of political importance from the volume of talk which they caused. Each camp, sect or group of fashion had built a meeting place around the little bean, and he made them sound such lively, stimulating places that I couldn't wait to get there.

But I owed it to James to be as well prepared as it was possible to be.

"Tell me what it'll be like," I said eagerly as we made our way past the mansions and beneath the swinging wooden signs of rose garlands and cross keys. "Tell me what to expect. How should I behave? What should I do?"

He glanced at me as I gamboled along in his breeches beside him. "No point telling you just to be yourself, now, is there? But it really doesn't matter how or who you are. A coffeehouse is a place for levelers, a medley of society where each man ranks and files himself as he pleases. A silly fop can converse with a worshipful justice and a reverend nonconformist with a canting mountebank. A person shows himself to be witty or eloquent and, before he knows it, he has the whole assembly abandoning their tables and flocking to his." He patted the top of my head. "Since you're both as witty and eloquent as any man, you could cause a sensation."

"I most certainly could if they guess from the lightness of my voice that I'm not a man at all. No," I decided. "I shall hold my tongue and not say a word. It'll be much safer. I shall be quite content just to watch and listen."

"I do not believe you'd be capable of that."

I grinned. "What do they talk about?"

"Oh, there's all manner of tattle and carping."

We passed onto the great thoroughfare of Fleet Street, past the waxwork exhibition and the church of St. Dunstan's-in-the-West, where the Great Fire had stopped short. I held on to my cap as a sudden gust of wind funneled down the street and threatened to expose my curls. We passed lawyers and countless taverns and then moved on to the goldsmiths and Temple Bar.

I almost lost my nerve when it came to going inside until James slipped his arm around my shoulders, as he might have done with any apprehensive young lad in his employ. I took a deep breath to calm myself and did just as he had told me, paid my penny and made my way with him, past the benches and tables, to the far corner of the clubroom.

The air was hot and thick with a fug of pipe smoke and the strong, bitter smell of coffee. Before I knew it I was sitting on a bench, pressed up against James with a steaming dish in my hand. A tall, richly dressed gentleman with a long, straight nose and glossy wig was holding forth with great verve to an attentive group on his belief, which stood opposed to most popular and much expert opinion, that fossils were actual remains of prehistoric life. He spoke in a mild Irish accent and had a very confident set to his shoulders for one so young. Most of those listening must have been twice as old as he was, but that didn't seem to perturb him in the slightest.

I leaned in toward James's ear, shielded my mouth with my hand. "Who ever is that?"

"Hans Sloane," he told me. "Not yet twenty, training to be a physician. He's the most ambitious young man you're ever likely to meet. Has his sights set on becoming president of the Royal Society, no less. The older man to his right is the excellent John Ray. It's to him that both Hans and I owe our love of natural history. He is too thin and eats far too little, but has the energy and enthusiasm of a man a third his age. You'd like him. He's compiling an important global history of flora, from the specimens and descriptions Hans and I have collected for him."

Between puffs on his clay pipe, John Ray was warning Hans Sloane not to leap to conclusions about fossils. "To be incautious is to plunge into mere speculation and enter the borderland between science and superstition," he said patiently. Mr. Ray had a strong face, grave and inquiring, but with a touch of humor about his mouth. "We must be ruthless in our demand for accuracy of observation and in the testing of every new discovery. New knowledge is in its infancy and we must reserve judgment until the proof is compelling."

James glanced at me and smiled. "A man after your own heart, in more ways than you know. He's a minister by profession, barred from the pulpit for dissent. He cannot preach, but believes he pursues his calling by studying the works of the Lord."

For a moment I saw my father sitting in John Ray's place.

"A brilliant young naturalist friend of mine was questioning me about metamorphosis the other day," James suddenly said to his friend John Ray. "I found I could not convince her that it is irrefutable."

"Her?" Hans Sloane gave his friend a delighted, interested smile. I dipped my face to hide my hot cheeks.

"We have not yet sufficiently studied the subject and cannot venture on any rash pronouncement," John Ray replied in more measured tones. "I do not wish to disappoint your intriguing friend, whoever she is, but you must tell her that the time for a full answer is not yet arrived. It might take generations of patient investigations before we reach a satisfactory conclusion. But for what it is worth, I myself do believe in butterfly metamorphosis. We see it happen in a different way with frogs, after all."

"What is the use of butterflies, anyway?" a man called Nehemiah Grew asked.

"To delight our eyes and brighten the countryside like so many jewels," John Ray replied. "To contemplate their exquisite beauty and variety is to experience the truest pleasure and to witness the art of God."

I found I was smiling at Mr. Ray and he at me. I wished for all the world that I could shake off my disguise and talk openly to this wise old man.

"Tell me, young James," John Ray inquired. "What has been occupying you lately?"

"I have been observing the characteristic marks that distinguish day-fliers from night-fliers," James contributed, with his typical ease and unassuming friendliness. "I believe you are right, John. It seems to be clubbed antennae and whether or not wings are held erect or open when at rest."

"And whether they are seen by moon or sun, of course," Hans Sloane concluded.

"Ah, but some night-fliers are seen by day," James added, to much general interest. It was clear he was liked as much as he was respected amongst them all, be they young or old, sophisticate or novice. It made me feel very privileged to be with him, to call him my friend.

The talk abruptly shifted to apple pips, a handful of which Hans

Sloane had produced from his pocket. Then Mr. Ray talked about how his friend Willoughby had kept a tame flea on their travels in Venice. I did not catch all of what he was saying as I was distracted by other conversations going on around me. The general level of noise in the coffeehouse was extraordinary, but it didn't take me long to tune my ear to the conversations of various sects, hotly debating contents of recent pamphlets and the news in the gazettes.

James wagged his elbow at me. "Drink up before it's cold," he whispered aside to me, indicating my full dish. "It's good for you, cleanses the brain and fortifies the body."

"I can believe it. These people are most certainly fortified with something."

He laughed.

"Well now, Petiver," Hans Sloane boomed. "Share your hilarity with the rest of us. And aren't you going to introduce us to that little fellow beside you?"

If I could have slid into obscurity beneath the table, I would have done it. James cleared his throat. "My assistant, Isaac. He helps me with my butterflies."

"Does he indeed? And were you talking about butterflies just now?"

"He's not been in a coffeehouse before. He was giving me his impressions."

Mr. Sloane turned his full attention on me, as if I was the most interesting person he'd ever met. "Well, lad, what do you make of it all?"

I felt my cheeks flame, but was thankful at least that hardly anyone else seemed to be listening.

"Come, come now, let the boy speak," Mr. Sloane said in a raised voice. "It is, after all, the custom of the house to let every man begin his story and propose to answer another, as he thinks fit. 'Speak that I may see you,' does not the philosopher say? So let us see who we have here."

My throat dried, as I felt all eyes turn to me. But then I felt James's hand beneath the table slide across my knee, find my own hand and give it an encouraging squeeze.

"I believed I was coming to a coffeehouse but it seems I've stepped into a high court of justice," I said. "It seems that here anyone in a camlet cloak can take it upon himself to reorder the affairs of church and state."

Mr. Sloane hooted merrily and John Ray's eyes twinkled at me kindly. "Your little assistant is both very erudite and observant," he said. "I'm sure he's a great asset and help to you in the observation of butterflies."

"He is." James still had a hold of my hand under the table, and he pressed it a little tighter. "I could not do without him."

🦋 "YOU WERE VERY CONVINCING," James said, after the session had ended with the customary prayers and we walked back out onto Fleet Street. It was dusk and still warm. "They were all taken in by you. Hans will probably try to poach you from me, he took you for such a bright little spark."

"The sharpest wit would count for nothing if they knew what was, or rather was not, hidden inside my breeches."

"Slow down," James protested. "Why are you walking so fast?"

"Because I'm angry. And my legs are buzzing like a beehive. My head too, for that matter."

James chuckled. "Coffee does that to you, if you're not used to it. Don't be despondent, Eleanor. You did it. You outfoxed them all."

I swung round to him with my hands on my hips. "And what exactly was the good of that? What happens to me now?"

"You keep on with your work."

"It will count for nothing. None will care to know what I do. Just because my name is Eleanor, not Edward or some such. Because I am a woman."

"That's not true," James said emphatically. "You are an outstanding naturalist and you should be recognized as such."

"Oh, James . . ."

"I mean it. Already because of you I've learned there are butterflies living only on the marshes that disappear when that marshland is destroyed. That's a valuable lesson. It shows us the importance of butterflies in telling us about the world we live in. They are like little barometers, foretelling change. If a butterfly disappears, we should take note. It could be of vital importance one day."

We started walking again. "Do you honestly think so?"

"Any one of those gentlemen in that coffeehouse would think so. Any of the great scientists of the Royal Society itself would think so. Scientists living hundreds of years from now will think so. Rarities can never be conserved unless people like you discover as much as you can about them." We carried on in silence for a while.

When he resumed talking, James told me, "Hans has a vision of building a great institution, bigger than Tradescant's Ark, like a giant curio cabinet, housed in its own building, where thousands of artifacts and specimens can be displayed for all to see and study. He's always telling me that he envisions my collections forming the bedrock of the insect cabinets. Think what it would be like to contribute to that great and lasting collection—the greatest natural history collection in Britain. There's no reason why yours could not be a part of it, too."

"That would be an amazing honor," I conceded. "But I honestly didn't start collecting butterflies with any mind to fame or immortality or even to science. I read that Christopher Wren and Isaac Newton were inspired to be involved in science and mathematics by the sight of a comet. For me it was the beauty and color of a golden butterfly."

"There's nothing wrong with being first drawn to something because you think it very beautiful," James said quietly. "So long as you take the time to find out and appreciate its other virtues."

"You forget the tulip fanciers who ransomed their fortunes and ruined themselves, all for the transitory beauty of a rare flower," I said.

"Perhaps it was worth it," James said. "The ancients went so far as to worship butterflies for their beauty. They believed that the fire goddess followed young warriors onto the battlefield and made love to them, holding a butterfly between her lips."

Coming from any other man, it would have sounded like an overt flirtation, but James always seemed to be above that, his thoughts moving on the permanently higher plane of science and ideas. Our discussions had ranged over such arcane and wonderful topics in the past that we could speak of almost anything with complete ease. But when we had reached the door of the Burgeses' house, I could not help but feel relieved that our conversation had reached a natural end.

"Would you like a cup of milk before you set off back?" I didn't wait for James to answer but went straight to the jug on the table. I could hear Mary soothing one of the little ones who'd woken up, and John was no doubt in his closet, saying his prayers. I took off my hat and let down my hair, thinking how it would give my kind hosts the fright of their lives if they found a strange boy in their kitchen. Not that they would be unshocked to see me with my hair cascading over a waistcoat, all the way down to a pair of brown breeches! I was about to pour the milk when I saw a letter, propped against the jug and addressed to me.

"The writing's much tidier than mine," James said, peeping over my shoulder.

It was indeed precise, spare and bold. William Merrick's writing. I unfolded it and read. It was a short letter, but it took a disproportionately long time for me to take in the contents.

"Is everything all right, Eleanor?" James touched my arm.

I looked up at him. "I have to return to Tickenham immediately. There's been a flood, an early flood. The rivers have burst their banks. They didn't get the cows off the moor in time and many have drowned. A boy from the village was washed away and lost his life trying to save them . . . trying to save his family's livelihood."

James looked down at the letter, as if he would read much more than was contained within it. "Tell me about your home, about the moor. I have traveled so little, I don't even know exactly where it is."

I refolded the letter, tossed my hair over my shoulder and finished pouring the milk. I handed him the cup and leaned back with my hands against the table. "It lies to the north of the Mendip hills, near to the coast and the Bristol Channel. In summer the land is so fertile it produces the best cattle in all of England. But in winter it is wet and marshy. We call it the moor but it's really a low-lying expanse of peat, threaded with rivers. We are used to a regular onset of great autumn and winter floods that sweep in during October or November and remain until January, sometimes returning throughout February and March and early spring. You'd think it a strange spectacle to see people striding on stilts through the water, or a congregation forced to come to church in boats and carry their dead across the water to bury them. But that is life for us, has been life for us for generations." I smiled. "I'm sorry. I'm sure you didn't want to know all that."

"You speak about it as if you love it very much."

"In summer there is nowhere I would rather be, and even the floods bring their own mystery and magic."

He drank some of the milk and waited for me to go on.

"The people of Somersetshire have waged a war against water for centuries," I said. "I grew up hearing stories of the disastrous flood of the year sixteen hundred and seven, when a high tide met with land floods so violent that they overwhelmed everything built to withstand their force. Walls and banks were eaten through and the moor was inundated to a depth of twelve feet. The floodwaters were littered with pieces of bobbing timber and the floating corpses of dead cattle and goats. Whole villages were sunk right up to the tops of the trees, so it appeared as if they'd been built at the bottom of the sea."

James was listening with rapt attention, as if I was weaving a fantastical story.

"So you see, we are used to floods," I said. "But nobody expects them in September. Nobody is ready for them."

"Isn't it too late now? What can you do? Why must you go back?"

"I am their squire now. I do not know if I shall make a very good one, but I am all they have. These people are my family, James. The women kept me company when I was having my first baby. They will look to me."

"But what can you do?"

I threw up my hands with a small shrug. "Have the kitchen cook up a vat of broth. Send out laborers and carts to mend any breach in the seawall. Take a bucket and start bailing. I shall not know where I am most needed until I am there."

"Tickenham is blessed to have you." He plopped my hat back on top of my curls. "You will make a most able little squire, I think."

"I hope so. I shall do my very best."

He handed the cup of milk to me, brought out his flask and poured a dash of whiskey into it. "If you are going to go, I shall have to give you your gift now."

"My gift?"

He smiled. "I do know how you like gifts. I was saving it for New Year, but you must take it home with you now." He hunted around in the pot cupboard. "Mary has been keeping it safe for me. Now, where might she have hidden it?" He moved onto the settle, opened up the seat and peered inside. "Ah, here it is."

I'd been expecting more butterfly wings, but instead he produced a large and intriguing wooden box. "James, whatever is it?"

He placed it in front of me on the table and stood back. "Open it and see."

I took off the lid and brought it out, recognizing immediately what it was from the pictures I'd gazed at in the book my father had burned, fearing it might carry the plague to us. I lifted it out and set it on the table, a heavy instrument with polished brass knobs and glass lenses and dials. "A microscope." I looked at James, but I couldn't see him all that well, since my eyes were blurred with tears. "I've wanted one for years."

He looked so happy, as if it was he who'd been given the most wonderful gift, not me. "It's from Christopher Cock's workshop in Long Acre," he said. "One of the best instrument makers. By royal appointment."

I put my eye against the eyepiece.

"You really need a lamp globe to help illuminate specimens properly. I was planning to bring mine over here for you to try, but you'll work out how to get a satisfactory image using sunlight."

"I don't know what to say. How to thank you." I looked at him, suddenly distraught. "But James, I don't have anything to give you in return."

"Yes you do," he said. "You can give me a promise never again to say your work has no merit." He took my hand in his, as if binding me to a pledge. "Promise me that you will never, ever give up your love of butterflies, and that is all the thanks I shall ever need."

I saw the earnestness behind his smile. It was as if he was asking me to remain faithful to our friendship, since butterflies had always been the link between us.

"I swear it."

"I will teach you how to use the microscope properly," he said, "just as soon as you return to London."

. . .

🐝 I DIDN'T GO UP to bed when James left. I placed a candle as near to the microscope as I dared. It had been sold with some prepared glass slides and I slipped one under the lens, peered down the eyepiece at it, but saw nothing at all. I needed James to show me how to use it. I needed him to help me see with clarity. Maybe I would come back to London soon, but for now the summer was over. Despite repeated adjustments to the knobs and dials, all I could see before me was darkness.

Part Three

Autumn

1684

FOUR YEARS LATER

orest and little Mary were playing with a litter of kittens by the stone fireplace in the great hall when I told them we were expecting a guest.

Mary jumped up and clapped her hands. "Who?" she asked eagerly.

I couldn't answer her. It was too strange, as if time had reeled backward. Sitting beside my daughter, I saw a ghost child in a starched white cap and dark wool dress. I heard my father tell me we were expecting guests. I saw myself jump up and clap my hands and ask who it was, just as little Mary had done.

"William Merrick," I said, like an echo from that other time.

I saw little Mary's excitement drain out of her as she turned her attention back to the kittens. She didn't particularly like Mr. Merrick, just as I had not liked him.

Still, I had anticipated his visit so eagerly that day years ago, because I was curious to meet the gentleman who was to come with him. A gentleman from Suffolk. I had looked forward to meeting him, not knowing that he was to be my husband, the father of my children, the friend of the man I had loved beyond any other.

For all that had happened to me in between, England, and especially the West Country, had not changed so very much. It was not even a safer, more secure place for my children than it had been for me as a child. We had beheaded one king then, and now here we were, a good few years on, and there had been several attempts and rumors of attempts to assassinate the new restored one. It seemed that lessons were not so easily learned, that mistakes were made only to be repeated.

The country was rife with rumors of uprisings and plots to seize London and conspiracies to destroy the monarchy. The King's dashing illegitimate son, the Duke of Monmouth, claimed to be the rightful heir to the throne and had attempted to displace his named successor, James, King Charles's brother. The Duke had proved his popular following with a progress through our own county, through Ilchester and Bath, where the children and I had gone for the waters and been caught up amongst the thousands who were there to greet him and strew his way with herbs and flowers. The handbills and broadsheets now claimed he was at the head of the plot to kill his father and had fled to Holland, with a five-hundred-pound price on his head, but everyone knew it was only a matter of time before he would return to the West Country and amass an army of supporters.

At least my son was too young to join them, I thought with relief, though he would leap at any excuse for a fight and harried me at every turn. Right now he was mercilessly pulling a kitten's tail. She had, with good reason, turned on him with a little hiss and bared her tiny pointed teeth.

"Oh, don't tease her, Forest," I said. "You are so cruel sometimes."

He stuck his lip out sullenly. "You kill butterflies."

"So that I can study them." That subtle difference was no doubt entirely lost on a seven-year-old. He was, in all honesty, probably learning something about nature by pulling a kitten's tail and watching to see how it responded. "Don't be impertinent," I ended half-heartedly, with too much on my mind to start another battle with him.

"Don't be angry with Forest," Mary said sweetly, defending her brother, automatically siding with him against me, as was the way with brothers and sisters. She never saw bad in anyone, was as placid and good as she had looked from the moment she was born.

In that respect at least, this situation was very different from that other day so many years ago. I had no need to echo my father and tell my own daughter to tidy her hair and clean her hands before our guests arrived, so that she looked like a little lady, not a vagabond. She was only four years old, but bless her, she always looked and behaved like a perfect little lady, and was well loved for it by everyone.

She stuffed her hand in the pocket fastened around her waist and produced a sugared almond, which she immediately offered to her brother.

"Where did you get that?" I smiled at her. "As if I couldn't guess."

"From Cook."

Mistress Keene was forever slipping her tidbits and treats from the kitchen. "She spoils you." All the servants did. They adored Mary. Would do anything for her. Not that I could blame them at all. I had thought we would be the same, she and I, but we were not. She resembled Edmund physically, with her red hair and freckles, but also in her personality. She was her father in every way, a girl who would be perfectly content with marriage to a man just like him, would look for nothing more than a quiet life of domesticity. In one part of me I was intensely glad for her, but I could not help feeling a little sorry too. Mary would be spared the pain, but she would miss out on the passion.

"Can we go outside?" Forest challenged, in a tone I recognized as far more like my own.

"You may go once you have greeted our visitor, so long as you promise to stay in the garden."

"You never let us do what we want," Forest exploded, scowling at me and stamping his feet in a fit of childish rage.

Swift and direct as an archer's arrow, he had found my most vulnerable point. He knew very well that the one thing I wanted for my children was for them to be as unconstrained and free as it was possible to be. "That is not true, Forest, and well you know it."

Further argument between us was prevented by a knock at the door. "That must be Mr. Merrick." Or William, as he insisted I now call him.

Mary stood demurely to receive our visitor, but as soon as Bess had admitted him into the great hall and he had bowed and kissed my hand, Forest slunk straight for the door, head down in a sulk.

William was not impressed and caught him by his shoulders, but Forest threw him off so roughly that if he'd been a year or two older and stronger, he'd have run the risk of unseating our guest's expensive new periwig. The thought of which made me smile to myself. Was it any wonder my son was such a little insurgent?

"I told him he could go, William," I said, irritated at the interference. "Rather now through the door, than out of a window at dead of night."

William's square jaw had slackened into jowls with age, but he was as loud and bombastic as ever. "You are far too lenient with the little jackanapes. He'll become completely ungovernable."

"He is only seven. And I like his spirit."

"No good will come of spoiling that child, I tell you."

I managed to hold my tongue. No good would come of me reminding William Merrick that he wasn't my guardian anymore, had no jurisdiction anymore over how I chose to run my household and my family. Nobody had any jurisdiction over me now. I had discovered that there was some small consolation to being a widow. To have a husband and see him die, to sleep alone and unloved in a cold bed every night for the rest of her life, was one way for a woman to be completely free. The only way for a woman to be completely free. I had nobody to hold me, nobody to kiss me and caress me, nobody to share my life with, but I was at last masterless. None in the world could call me to account, and I liked that very much.

I told Mary she might go back to the kittens once she had asked Bess to bring us some coffee.

"You've a biddable little girl there," William conceded. "But young Forest needs a man in his life to restore some discipline."

"If there was a man in his life to discipline him, I'd have to be obedient to that man too." I smiled wryly. "No, thank you."

"You've had no more offers?"

"I'm a wealthy widow. Naturally I have had offers."

"From Richard Glanville again?"

Just to hear his name caused an ache of loss and of emptiness in my heart. "From him."

There had been other suitors besides Richard, fortune hunters one and all. I barely even recalled their names, and if I had not seen them off by subtly refusing every one of their oft-repeated invitations, they soon abandoned their quest when I told them in no uncertain terms that I had no wish to wed ever again. Only Richard had not given up. He had tried to see me more than a half-dozen times since Edmund's death. Once every six months or so he rode to Tickenham unannounced, as he had that Valentine's morning. But each time I had told Bess to send him away. I refused to speak to him. I turned him away from my door, when he'd ridden for days to see me, without even offering him the common courtesy I'd show to a beggar. I didn't trust myself to let him in, even to offer him some bread and cheese and ale to refresh him after the long ride before I sent him on his way again.

"I thought as much," William said with some mirth. "I ran into him again last week, drowning his sorrows in a bottle of rum at a dock-side inn."

I felt the prick of tears behind my eyes. I did not want to know. And yet I did. Oh, I did. "You spoke to him?"

"He spoke to me. Begged me to tell him when last I had seen you. If you were well, if there were any other gentlemen paying you any attention. I tell you, I pitied the poor, lovesick lad. But you've got to give him credit, he's mightily tenacious. I guarantee he'll be back."

I did not doubt it. But it would make no difference how many times he came. I would not see him. No matter how much my body burned for him and my heart pined just to hear his voice, to see his face, to touch him. This was my punishment, my penance. And it was the price I paid for my freedom. If you could call it freedom, when I was bound by the spiraling costs of this waterlogged land and with main-taining this ancient, crumbling house, bound by obligation to tenants and servants, by the constant nagging fear that my children might fall ill or drown.

"He'd not make such a bad husband, you know," William said. "Richard Glanville. Nor such a bad lord for Tickenham."

I found myself wondering then if my former guardian had helped Richard to drown his sorrows in that Bristol inn, and just what the two of them had found to talk about besides me. As if I could not guess. "With his dying breath, my father warned me to be on my guard against unscrupulous Cavaliers," I said viciously.

"But your father, my dear, could sometimes be a terrible bigot."

"I will not hear him spoken of that way, sir. Do you hear me?"

"You disagree with me?"

"I do not wish to discuss my father. And I especially do not wish to discuss Richard Glanville. Not now. Not ever."

He gave a noncommittal shrug. "As you wish."

"All Forest needs is to be able to go outside to play and tire himself," I said, changing the subject back. "All he wants to do is fly kites and climb trees and kick his ball about on the moor. And soon it will be safe for him to do all that, won't it? Soon no more boys will lose their lives trying to save drowning cows. Soon there will be no more floods. That is, after all, why you are here."

"Indeed."

"I trust you have more to report this time than the last."

"I am pleased to inform you that the necessary permissions have at long last been granted, an engineer has almost been appointed, and two hundred pounds allotted to commence work. I have every confidence that a date will soon be set for the summer. My, how long we'll have waited for such a day!"

To me it felt like a lifetime. I could not help but remember how I had been cajoled into agreeing to this scheme, so that Edmund might solicit my hand, and now, before the first sod had even been dug, I was a widow of four years' standing.

I WOKE IN THE DARKNESS to the unmistakable and haunting call of a wedge of swans arriving to spend winter on the wetlands. As well as their eerie honking, I swore I could hear the beating of many great white wings.

I waited until dawn and then went to rouse Forest and Mary from their beds.

"The swans are here," I whispered into their intricate little ears. "Come and see them."

Together we stood by the window in my chamber, a child on either side of me, my arms draped around their shoulders, as we gazed out over the dawn-lit flooded moor, empty yesterday save for the mallards and a few geese, but now miraculously thronged with hundreds, almost thousands it seemed, of our serene white winter visitors.

I was not too absorbed by the magic and mystery of their appearance to miss the exchange of glances 'twixt my son and daughter, which resulted in Mary's putting forth a request. "Could we take the boat out to see them up close?" she asked tentatively.

"All right." I acquiesced, thinking how there might be few chances left. "So long as you both wrap up warm."

They scampered off gleefully and Mary came back minutes later, carrying cloak, bonnet and muff. Forest had put on his thick riding coat and boots. Mary took hold of my hand and Forest's and we walked linked together.

Forest wanted to row the boat and I watched him proudly as he pulled on the oars with enough might to propel our little vessel between the majestic gliding birds.

"Beautiful, aren't they?" I said, wrapping my cloak tighter around me.

Forest's face was a picture of indifference, no sign of wonder or love for this land etched there at all, despite my best and continued efforts to instill such feelings in him.

"Have you ever wondered where the swans go in summer?" I asked both children.

Disappointingly, my question was met with the shaking of two heads, one dark, one copper. Mary was too young, I consoled myself, and Forest too obstinate. If he did wonder, he would never admit it to me. Yet I so wanted him to love this land that would one day be his, wanted it to mean as much to him as it did to me.

"When I was a little girl, I used to wonder," I told them. "I used to imagine that perhaps they came with the winter and flew away again in spring, because they were white and were snow birds who took the cold away with them. It is the same ones who come back every year, though I have no idea how they find their way. I did sometimes wish I could fly away with them, wherever it was that they went, or rather that I could do the opposite of what they do, and leave Tickenham in winter and return in spring when the floods have gone. But soon the floods will be gone for good, Forest," I said to him, wondering where the swans would go then. "The drainage work will begin. By the time you are a grown man, it will be complete."

This at least appeared to have spiked his interest, though for entirely the wrong reasons. "And I shall be as rich as William Merrick?" he asked with a keenness that made me uneasy, young as he was.

As he had grown, the greedy side of Forest's nature had increasingly tended toward an unpleasant avariciousness that I did not like at all, did my utmost to discourage. "You will only be as rich as Mr. Merrick if you are as devious and ruthless as he is," I said severely. "Which I sincerely hope you will not be."

"What are we to have for dinner?" he asked then. "I'm hungry."

"So am I," Mary agreed.

"I hope it is not pike again," Forest grumbled.

"I hope it's not, either," Mary echoed supportively.

Forest stuck out his tongue, pretending to gag. "If we eat any more pike, we'll look like one." He sucked in his cheeks and pouted his mouth, fishlike, making Mary giggle behind her hand.

"What would you like to eat, then?" I asked.

"Venison," he said. "Like Mr. Merrick always has."

"Hmmm. Well, when you are squire you can eat venison every day if you like, but for now I suggest we send to the inn for a barrel of oysters. As a treat, we shall all three of us eat them by the fire."

Forest scowled at me until I screwed up my face and scowled back comically, managing at last to make him grin.

Spring

1685

There were several occurrences in the course of the spring that proved the people of Tickenham were as resistant to drainage as ever.

First the ale barrels in the buttery were prized apart, allowing the contents to swill all over the floor. Days later, the chickens were all found dead in their coop, their necks wrung, and the fresh eggs broken in a mess of yolk and white and shell. Then two of the pigs were butchered in the sty, their throats slit wide, splattering so much bright red blood that it resembled a slaughterhouse.

I was more angered by the needless waste than by the destruction of my property, but at least anger served to hold fear at bay, for a time. Unsurprisingly, all around me had suddenly been struck mute, deaf and blind. Nobody had seen or heard anything, it seemed. When the constable questioned them, tenants and commoners and servants all denied having even the glimmer of a suspicion about who might have committed these vengeful crimes. Even Bess remained guiltily tight-lipped, her loyalties clearly torn in a way that disturbed me more than anything, made me more certain than ever that her brother was behind it all. She refused to meet my eye, even when Forest told me, in her hearing, that Thomas had asked him, some while ago, if he knew what a Fen tiger was.

"And do you?" I asked Forest cautiously, wondering if that was why he had taken to following me around and standing quietly at my side.

"Thomas told me they are not really tigers at all," he said. "But angry men."

We were in the great hall. I sat down on the settle, and for the first time in I don't know how long, Forest let me take him onto my lap. I wrapped my arms around his strong little body and held him tight. "Did Thomas say anything else, Forest?"

"He said the tigers were being bred in Somersetshire now. Right here, in Tickenham, and that Somersetshire tigers are angrier even than their Fen cousins. He said they would take revenge on us for robbing the commoners of their way of life." He twisted round to look at me. "It's them who killed the pigs and the hens, isn't it?"

He did not deserve a lie. I stroked his hair. "I think it must be."

"They are not done yet, are they?" he said with a heartrending perception way beyond his years.

WHEN WILLIAM MERRICK CAME to inspect the carnage in the pigsty he told me to show forbearance, but even he seemed to have lost much of his old brash self-assurance. He appeared almost cowed.

"I had hoped it would be different this time," I said, as we watched two silent laborers, their pails brimming with red water, scrubbing the blood off the walls. "I hoped the memory of that poor boy's death in the last serious floods would make a difference. What, in God's name, does it take to convince them?"

"Evidently much more than it takes to convince the investors to withdraw their funding," William said morosely. "Unfortunately they have heard of these recent disturbances and it has undermined their confidence in the whole project." I had never seen my former guardian so disconsolate. "They will back out if there is even a whiff of more trouble. The fear is that once the work commences, the vandals will turn their attention from destroying your property to sabotaging the new sluices and walls and rhynes. Such setbacks in the Fens cost the investors dear, almost brought about their ruin. My partners had not anticipated such disastrous disturbances here." He looked at me scathingly. As if it was my fault that I had not carried the people with me, as if to say that all would have been very different if Edmund, or indeed any other man, were here to calm, coerce and inspire solid confidence. I did not think it would have been different at all, but I would have given much to hear Edmund's unshakable assurances that what we were doing was right, that even the commoners would come to see that eventually. Without him, doubts assailed me again. It was my decision now, not my father's, not my guardian's, not my husband's. But having no one to tell me what to do meant there was no one to share the responsibility. My decision. And by it I should stand or fall.

"William, do you honestly believe they have no justification for what they do?"

His eyes almost popped out of their sockets. "Justification?"

"I know there is no excuse for violence, but they see their rights being stripped away from them and what else can they do?"

"Are you actually questioning if certain circumstances make it acceptable to break the laws of this land?"

"It is not as simple as that."

"No," he said drily. "Nothing is ever simple where you are concerned. You'd find a dozen different sides to examine on a triangle."

I laughed, glad at least that he would joke with me now. My father had liked him. I should like to find a way to like him too, and perhaps, now that we were on a more equal footing, it would be possible.

We had turned and walked back inside the house. The children had gone to their beds not ten minutes before, but I heard Mary scream with terror as she sometimes did when awoken from a bad dream in the middle of the night. The scream was followed by the pounding of her bare feet on the stairs as she came running to find me in her nightshift, her thick plait of red hair flying. I caught her up in my arms and hugged her, her little arms clinging tight around my neck and her legs wrapped round my waist like a monkey. "Whatever's the matter, sweetheart?"

"An eel," she sobbed. "An eel in my bed."

"In your bed? Are you sure?"

She nodded vigorously, her tawny eyelashes wet with tears.

"Let's go up together and see, shall we?"

In the nursery I pulled back the blankets, and there it was, its slippery, glistening body dark against the white linen bedding of my daughter's cot, like an evil black serpent.

For Mary's sake, I made light of it, did not let her see my anger flare almost beyond control, destroying any lingering sympathy I might have had for the commoners. Damn whoever did this, I thought. Damn them all to Hell. She's just a little girl. "It is just an eel," I said. "It can't hurt you."

She hid her face, had always been squeamish in a way I had never been. "Is it . . . dead, Mama?"

It wasn't. Quite. I reached out and took hold of its slithery, twitching body, and with a calmness I did not feel, I took it to the window and threw it out.

For once I was grateful that Mary did not ask the questions I would have asked at her age. She did not even ask how the eel could have got into her bed. Like her father, she did not dwell on things, would not dwell on who might have crept secretly into the house and up to the nursery and pushed it between her sheets. I knew better than to even think for a moment that this might be a prank of Forest's. He doted on Mary, would never have done anything that might frighten or upset her.

"We'll get the chambermaid to change the sheets in the morning," I said, hugging her close. "You shall sleep with me tonight."

WILLIAM HAD LEFT. I did not close the curtains around the bed and I kept the candle lit. I closed my eyes, but every muscle in my body remained tense, my ears alert for any sound. All I had wanted was to make our home, our little world, a better, safer place, and it seemed I had done just the opposite. And Heaven knows, there was danger and unrest enough in this county without creating more.

Everyone said the Duke of Monmouth would sail from the continent and bring war again to the West Country any day now. His father, King Charles, had died in February and Charles's brother James had been crowned in his place, an avowed Catholic, in a country that still despised Catholicism, was still utterly opposed to a Papist on the throne. The dashing duke was Protestant, and because of that at least half the country favored him as king. Monmouth would move soon to take the crown of England by force. The rivers of this land would run red with blood again, as men I had known all my life rose up to fight for the grand old cause, for the battles my father had already fought and ultimately lost. I could do nothing at all to prevent that. But I had hoped to rid Tickenham of its lethal floods.

I sat up, pushed my hand under the pillow and reached for my notebook, knowing it was the only chance I had of finding some peace. Mary sat up too and snuggled into my side as she did when we were reading a storybook together. "Is that your book about flufflies?" my enchanting daughter lisped, with her own endearing pronunciation that I could not bear to correct, dreading the day when she called butterflies by their proper name.

I put my arm around her, pulled the blankets up around her. "It is, my little love."

"Why do you write about them?"

"Because I like to." But it was more than that, so much more. Because I have to, I could have said. Because I believe it is what I am meant to do. Because it is the only thing I can do. Because it is the only thing that really makes me happy. Because it stops me from thinking. Because I began to study butterflies and to write about them as a cure for longing and I am still longing, and it is still the only cure for it that I have.

I had the time and freedom now to spend on my own observations and catalogues and had amassed a collection of specimens and records of which even I was proud. With Ned Tucker's help, I was cultivating a butterfly garden near the orchard, stocked with all the plants that seemed to attract them. But I did not write to James anymore; thought it was simpler, fairer. I had sensed his deepening affection for me and knew I could never love him that way. There was only one man I loved. Since the day I had first seen Richard, he was all I had wanted. Even if I never saw him again, it seemed likely that my last thoughts this side of the grave would be of him.

I slipped a letter from inside the back cover of my observation book. Richard had kept on writing to me, just as he kept on trying to see me. I had consigned all his letters to the fire, except for this one. In a moment of weakness I had opened it, read it, and once I had, I could never have destroyed it. It was a lovely letter.

My eyes drifted to the closing paragraph.

What I once took for poverty, I now see as the greatest riches. I think I would be content now just to be able to look at you, to talk to you, to hold

*your hand, to be your friend, if only you would let me. But in a way it
makes no difference that you refuse to see me. Know that when you are
dancing, when the fields and the rivers are lit by moonlight, when the
floodwaters freeze thick enough to skate upon, I am there with you, waiting for you. I shall always be there, Nell. I shall always be waiting.*

A window shattered below stairs. I sat bolt upright. I did not drop
the letter, but rather my fingers tightened upon it, as if I would cling
to it on a journey through the jaws of Hell.

It was silent now. It had been raining, but the rain had stopped and
there was only the occasional drip from the wooden guttering. Otherwise, perfect stillness and silence. Except for the violent hammering of my own heart.

Another window smashed and Mary sprang awake. "What was
that, Mama? I heard a noise."

I clutched her tight. "Shush," I told her, as reassuringly as I could.

"We know you are there," a voice shouted from outside. "Show
yourself."

"Who's that?" Mary squeaked.

A different voice: "You can't hide from us."

There were two of them, then. "Just village lads who've been drinking," I said to my daughter. "That's all." I put my hand over her ear
and pressed her red head against me, gathered her to me more closely,
as if I could shield her from all harm with my own body.

"Come out now, if you know what's good for you."

I recognized that voice, recognized the spite and the malice in it.
Thomas Knight. Three of them, then.

"Come out now or we'll burn down this house."

I leapt out of bed as if it was already in flames. "Stay right there,"
I said to Mary as I threw a loose gown over my shift.

"Don't leave me," she squealed, her face filled with terror.

"Go and get into bed with Forest. But do not come below stairs, do you understand?"

"They are going to set us on fire!"

I took her shoulders, looked intently into her face. "They will do no such thing, Mary. They will not."

If at least three, then maybe more. Maybe a whole rabble, come to protest and besiege the house just like the angry mobs that had gathered when they'd tried to drain the Fens. But there was no doubt in my mind that Thomas Knight was the instigator, and Bess would talk sense into him. I must hold them off long enough for someone to fetch her from the cottage where she lived with Ned and Sam.

I ran to the door of the room Susan Walker, the dairymaid, shared with her sister, who worked in the bakehouse. "Susan. Wake up."

Silence.

I lifted the latch and flung open the door. The room was empty. I flew down the dark passage to the next room, where Mistress Keene slept. She wasn't there either. Everyone had gone.

My legs were shaking so much I could hardly stand. I was all alone in the house with two small children and a gang of angry men outside, threatening to burn us alive.

Another window shattered.

I ran down the stairs and grabbed my father's flintlock musket and bayonet off the wall, found the cartridge box in the buffet and ripped the twisted paper tail off the cartridge with my teeth as my father had shown me. With trembling fingers, I half cocked the trigger, poured some of the black powder into the pan to prime it, turned the gun and emptied the rest of the charge and the lead ball down the muzzle. Then I whipped out the ramrod and rammed it down the barrel hard to force the powder and ball into place.

The gun was heavy and nearly as tall as me but as I slung it over my shoulder and headed for the door, I took courage from remembering that women during the civil wars had defended their houses against besieging enemy armies, against neighbors and friends and people with whom they had once shared their meals and whom they had counted as family. If they could do it, then so could I.

The mob that I faced was more than two dozen strong. Thomas Knight was there, Jane Jennings's husband, Matthew. There was John Hort, the eeler. Ned too, as were the Bennett boys and their father, plus two other tenant farmers' lads. Two dozen against one. There might just as well have been fifty. They were all armed with pitchforks, axes, pikes and scythes—those cruel and murdering weapons with their long poles and curved blades. Thomas Knight and two of the others were waving flaming torches while swigging something from a small flagon that they handed between them.

Thomas Knight was staring at the musket. "What's she going to do with that, d'you think?"

"I do not want to do anything with it." I tried to keep my voice from shaking and looked directly at Ned. "For God's sake, go home. All of you. Go back to your wives and your children and your mothers."

"We don't want any trouble," Ned said nonsensically.

"Then what are you doing here?"

"You've left us no option," he half apologized. "If we're to go on being able to afford to put bread on our tables, to feed our families . . ."

"The moor is ours," one of the farmers' boys yelled ferociously. "You've no right to take it from us."

They all started shouting at once, each as vociferous as the next, so I could not make out a word. They'd inched forward as one body, drawn more tightly around me. They were gesticulating angrily, pointing at me menacingly with their assorted weapons, stabbing the air between us with their pikes and pitchforks. The sound was deafening, like a crowd at a bearbaiting.

"Get back," I shouted. "All of you." I leveled the musket, pressed it against my shoulder, aimed the long barrel into the middle of the crowd. "I swear I'll use it if I have to."

They quieted, one or two even backed off.

"Come on, don't be cowards," Mark Walker sniggered. "She's just a lass, and a small one at that. She won't know how to use it."

I waved the gun at them, narrowed my eyes. "Do not wager on that, Mark."

At the edge of my vision I glimpsed someone else, the caped silhouette of a lone rider, some distance off to the right under the trees by Monk's Pool, but I had no time to wonder who he was or why he was not joining in.

"She might fire at us." Thomas Knight stepped forward, his sharp jaw clenched, his eyes black as bile, black as pitch. "I wouldn't put her to the test. She's never been quite right in the head after all, never been like other girls. And she's been without a man so long, she's forgotten what it is to be a woman." He came up closer to me. "That's why she's involving herself in men's business—business she doesn't understand."

"She needs reminding of her place in the world," John Hort sneered.

"You're the man for it, Tom," John Bennett piped up. "You've been itching to know what it'd be like to lie in the squire's bed. Now's your chance."

I could smell the spirits on Thomas Knight's breath, just like I'd done in the copse on May Day when I'd had a butterfly in my hands, instead of a musket. I felt no safer for the exchange.

"Go on, Tom," Matthew Jennings said. "I bet she has a different taste from other girls, with her fair skin and her clean hair and her full set of teeth. You can tell she needs it. She's probably not had a man since her husband, and he died years ago."

The threat in Thomas's eyes was not remotely sexual but rather covetous, as if it was not my virtue he wanted from me, such virtue as I had, but something else entirely.

I tensed my shoulders. Strands of hair had fallen loose from my night-plait and I tossed my head to flick them away from my face. He was so close that if I swung the bayonet at him it would cut his cheek, scar him for life or take out his eye. I'd never fired a musket but I couldn't fail to hit him. I did not want to shoot him or stab him. He was Bess's brother and his father's favorite. It would destroy Mr. Knight if anything happened to his son. Also, I saw then that Thomas bore an almost uncanny and disturbing resemblance to my own son. With his black hair and deep-set, belligerent black eyes, he had such a look of Forest that it made the idea of harming him suddenly even more abhorrent.

"We could strike a bargain," he said. "Like the one you made with those men from Bristol who are coming to take our commonland."

"What is it that you want?" I said. "Tell me what you want and I'll do my best to get it for you."

"Aye, tell her, Thomas," someone leered. "Tell her that if she lets you bed her now, between clean linen sheets in the squire's own chamber, we'll do her no harm."

"Leave her alone, or I'll kill every damned one of you."

It was a well-loved voice, a voice from my dreams, but the rider who came galloping across from Monk's Pool in a thunder of hooves was very real. He wore a long dark cloak and a scarlet plume in his hat, and his right arm was raised, sword unsheathed.

Richard.

His beautiful face alight with courage, he rode his black Barbary stallion directly into the heart of the mob, wielding one sword amongst a lethal forest of pikes and pitchforks and scythes and flaming torches. John Hort turned on him, brandishing his pitchfork. The spikes glanced off the horse's flank, making it rear up, high enough to unseat even an experienced rider. But not this one. Grappling the reins in one hand, he lunged with the other. Even from the saddle of a rearing stallion, his aim was true. John Hort screamed, dropped his pitchfork, stared in shock at his assailant and then staggered off toward the church, clutching his arm. Richard sliced the sword through the air above their heads. "Who is to be next?" The ferocity in his eyes and in his voice was enough to make them scatter in all directions. Some dropped their weapons in their hurry to be away and some clung to them, but within seconds all of them were gone.

Richard slid his sword back in its scabbard, not looking at me. A light rain had started to fall again and I felt droplets on my cheeks, like tears. His cloak was studded with raindrops as if with tiny diamonds. The horse sidled, tossed its head and snorted, lifted first one hoof and then the other as if it were prancing on burning coals. Richard leaned forward and stroked its neck, making soft, soothing noises to calm it. All the while, he steadfastly kept his eyes averted from mine, even though he must have felt me watching him.

I'd thought every line and curve of his perfect profile was etched indelibly onto my soul. The curl of his long lashes as they lay against his cheeks, the little indentations at the corners of his kissable, childish mouth, the dark curls that fell over his smooth brow and coiled softly into his neck. But it was a ghost that I had been holding on to, a lovely but faded ghost, and here, before me now, in the moonlit rain, his beauty was almost too much for me. And yet I wanted to gaze at nothing else but the exquisite lines of his face. I could look for a lifetime at him and never have enough of looking. He was the brightest star, shining in the darkness. He was everything to me.

I should have been angry with him for what he had just done, for being so rash and hotheaded. I had not invited him here, was not ready for this, should send him away as I had done all the times before. But I could not find it in my heart to be angry with him, did not want to send him away. I had missed him. So much. I was so glad just to see him.

His face averted, still soothing his horse, he said, "Aren't you going to thank me for getting rid of them for you?" It was spoken with an attempt at nonchalance, at the charming confidence at which I knew him to be so proficient, but he did not quite manage to pitch it right this time.

"Thank you?" I asked halfheartedly. "You wounded a man."

"A warning, that's all."

"You think they won't be back? More of them next time, and better armed."

Now at last he turned to me, with those lovely deep blue eyes that had never lost their strange and powerful hold on my heart. "I will stay and protect you."

It was said with a touching and ardent chivalry, but at that precise moment he did not look capable of protecting anyone, looked in far more need of protection himself. He looked so tired, his eyelids almost too heavy for him to hold open, and any resolve I had left in me to resist him suddenly vanished.

He must have seen it, since his lips came up at one side in a sweetly lopsided smile, and he was suddenly surer of himself again. He reached down and snatched the musket from my hand. "Is it primed and loaded?"

"It is."

He looked impressed. "What man would care about dying if it was at the hands of such a pretty little musketeer?" He tossed the gun in the air and caught it. "You were not intending to fire it, though?"

I smiled at him. "I had been hoping to find a more peaceable way to reach an agreement."

He aimed the musket into the sky, pulled the trigger and discharged it with a thunderous crack, turned to me in the drifting smoke from the exploding cartridge. "Aye, so I saw. A whore's way."

"You are not jealous? Of Thomas Knight?"

He slid from the saddle, propped the musket against a feeding trough. He took off his hat and hooked it over the muzzle. "How can I not be driven half mad by jealousy, when you have kept me away from you for nearly five years?" I heard an ache of loneliness in his voice, but he seemed reluctant to step any closer to me. Did not try to touch me. Then I saw he was looking beyond me into the dark hall. "Did all the commotion wake you, lad?" he said gently.

I spun round to see Forest, standing there in his long white nightshirt, his eyes wide with wonder. "You stabbed him, sir," he said, with awe in his voice. "Did you see him, Mama? I watched from the window and saw it all. The horse up on its hind legs, kicking at the air, the flash of the sword and that man running away with blood spurting out of his arm."

I heard Richard give a soft chuckle as I went to my son. "Come now, Forest," I said. "You were far too far away to see blood, and it wasn't exactly spurting."

"It was like a real battle."

It was a real battle. "Well, it's over now, so you can go back to bed. Bid good night to Mr. Glanville."

"Good night, sir."

Richard smiled at him. "Good night, young fellow."

When still he made no move, I took Forest's shoulders and spun him round, gave him a nudge in the direction of the stairs. "Bed, Forest. Now." I watched him go reluctantly, dragging his small bare feet, glancing back longingly into the hall where Richard had come, uninvited, to stand close behind me. "Would you like some spiced wine?" I asked Richard. "There's nobody here to serve you, but I'll gladly warm some for you myself."

He smiled. "I'm sure it would taste all the better."

"You can have your usual bed too, if you'd like."

"I'll curl up by the fire with the dogs. I'd rather. It won't matter where I am. I shall not sleep."

I do not know if he moved closer to me or I to him, but whichever way it happened, there was hardly any space between us anymore.

"I do not want wine or a bed," he said quietly. "I just want you." His arms were down by his sides. He made a small uncertain move to hold out his hand. I did the same. The backs of them brushed against each other. Our fingers caught, turned, entwined. I leaned my head toward his and for a moment we stood holding hands, our foreheads resting against each other. I put my arms around him and felt him shudder against me.

"If only you knew," he murmured. "How I have wanted to be with you."

"I know." I lifted my hand onto the back of his head, stroked his soft curly hair. "I know."

My mouth found his, clung to it, as if his kiss was the very breath of life to me. And it was. All the time I had been away from him had been as one long night, a little death, and now, beneath the touch of his mouth and hands, I felt every part of me waking, softening, opening, coming back to life—a sweet, agonizing fullness in my groin that was like a ripening, a bursting open. I wrapped my arms around him and clasped him to my heart, cradled his head against my shoulder, and I wondered only how I had borne to be without him for so long.

He swept me up into his arms and up the twisting stone stairs, my long plait falling around us both like a gilded rope that bound us together. He lay down beside me on the bed, slipped warm hands inside my shift, stroked from my breasts to my belly, moved down between my legs, and I lay quivering beneath his touch until I could stand it no longer and pulled his face down to mine to kiss him again.

Then he was kissing my eyelids, my cheeks, my chin, my throat, my ears, my breasts, my stomach. He whispered my name, over and over, the name that only he had ever called me. The sweetest name, the sweetest word I had ever heard. "Nell."

He lifted my shift off over my head and I helped him with his shirt. I undid the laces of his breeches and slid my hand inside, and as I caressed him there, his whole body gave a spasm that filled me with a sense of power, of fulfillment. It was as if my body had been made for this and only this, had been shaped and created for the giving and receiving of this pleasure, had been made to love him and for him to love.

He unfastened my plait so that my hair spilled all over him like a golden waterfall, and he let it run through his fingers. The only light in the chamber came from the hearth, and our bodies were bathed in a dim, red-gold glow. I sat back for a moment to look at him, naked on the high-canopied bed. I ran my fingers over the taut muscles of his belly and his erect penis, made him moan soft and low in the back of his throat. He reached out with both of his hands to stroke my hips, my buttocks, the insides of my thighs, the triangle of pale hair.

I slid out from his grasp, bent to scatter hungry kisses across his chest, biting, licking, brushing my lips against the soft little hairs that formed a denser line that led down from his navel to his groin. I kissed and licked and sucked at his nipples as if I was a kitten. I moved down that line of dark hair and kissed his hard, flat belly, and the hardness of his sex. He grasped my head in both of his hands and gave an agonized groan, pulled me closer. I could feel his heart beating so fast against mine. Then he rolled me over as a wave will roll a pebble on the shore, so he was above me once more, lying between my legs, straining against me but holding back, so that I almost cried out for him to come inside me.

But all at once he froze. He hurled himself away from me and off the bed, dragging a rug around him to cover himself. He clutched the carved bedpost and stared down at me, lying on my back, panting for breath, naked save for a pale, gossamer veil of hair. But I knew it was not me he saw anymore. There was a haunted expression in his eyes, a look almost of horror, and I remembered how he had clutched that same bedpost for support as he had stared down at Edmund's lifeless body.

It was so very long ago. I had spent a thousand lonely nights in this bed since then. But for the first time it occurred to me that it could be a curse rather than a blessing to be so tied to a place, to be expected to live out an entire life in one house, to be born, to be bedded and to die in the same damned great ancestral bed. It shocked me to see him seemingly so troubled now, for having loved his friend's wife, when it did not seem to have affected him so much when Edmund was still living. I was a wife no longer but a widow now. I had spent too many nights alone.

I scrambled from the bed, quickly gathered up a pile of pillows and rugs, took them over to the fireplace. I felt him watching me as I deposited the bedding by the hearth, quickly arranged it into a little nest. I stood beside it in the warm orange glow of the flickering flames and I held out my hand to him, but still he did not move. The shadows had gone from his eyes, were replaced by something else entirely.

"God, Nell, you are so beautiful."

"Come to me, then," I said softly.

He shook his head, almost imperceptibly. "I cannot," he said. "I need . . . I need . . ."

"What do you need, love?"

"More than this. Don't you understand? I need more than a romp with you every five years. I need to know that you are mine forever. All mine. Only mine."

I waited for him to say it, to ask me. He did not. But he did come to me. "Hold me," he said. "I need you to hold me."

I lay down on the rugs and he lay beside me and I held him and stroked his hair until he went to sleep, his arms wound tight around me and his beloved dark, curly head resting between my breasts.

IN THE MORNING I awoke stiff and cold and alone on the floor by a fire that was no more than a few embers.

I dressed myself and, not even pausing to fasten back my tumbled hair or put on stockings, ran downstairs. Bess was going about her daily duties as if nothing had happened. I had no time for her, for any of them. All I cared about was one person. His was the only face I wanted to see. But he was not there.

I ran out into the yard to see if his horse was in the barn, but it too had gone.

"He left about twenty minutes ago, Ma'am. You'll probably catch him if you ride hard." Ned carried on forking fresh straw in the stable, ashamed to look me in the face, looking instead at my bare ankles poking out from beneath my long skirts, which I was still holding up from running.

Ned was a good man. I couldn't believe he'd really meant any harm last night. He was just concerned for the future, like the rest of them. All he wanted to do was care for Bess and raise their son and have enough food to feed them all. He'd been saving for years for enough to pay for a tenancy and thought I was threatening that future. He was doing his best to make amends.

"Which way did he go, Ned, do you know?"

"Clevedon. Ladye Bay."

Without waiting to be asked, he led my mare from the stable, but before he'd exchanged the halter for a bridle and saddled her, I led her to the mounting block, hitched up my skirts and grabbed a handful of her mane, mounted her bareback and astride like a boy. I touched my heels to her flanks and urged her into a gallop, my hair flying out behind me. I let the mare have her head, as she charged full pelt toward the rutted trackway over the ridge that led all the way from Tickenham to the coast, a distance of some four miles or so. It was a mild morning that carried a promise of summer on the faint sea breeze. It was a lovely walk on a fine day, and a short ride, but it wasn't short enough for me then, when all that mattered to me was getting there fast enough to find Richard.

Ladye Bay was a rocky cove, very secluded and cut deep into craggy cliffs, with a shingle beach that was scattered with boulders. I'd spent hours there, with my father, alone, and then with my own children, scrambling over the rocks and upturning stones, hunting for sea anemones and ferns. I didn't take Richard for a geologist or a botanist, I just hoped little Ladye Bay had enough to occupy him for as long as it took for me to get there.

I smelled the sea, and then my heart danced when I saw his horse at the top of the cliffs, tethered to a rock and contentedly nibbling grass. I left my mare there too and clambered down the steep winding path that led to the shore, slipping and sliding on the stones, sending them tumbling before me in my haste.

At high tide the waves crashed against the rocks with an explosion of white froth and foam, but the tide was low now and the sea was as calm as the water that lay over the moor in winter.

The small, secluded beach was deserted. I was about to turn back, assuming that for some strange reason he must have dismounted and carried on along the coastal path on foot. Then I saw something, far out in the middle of the bay, just above the surface of the gray ocean, sleek and secretive as an otter. But it was no otter, it was the head of a man, a swimmer, heading out toward the headland and the wide, open sea.

I stood with the waves lapping at my slippers and the hem of my gown, my hair whipped by the sea breeze, and I watched him grow smaller. I was gripped with fear, could barely blink my eyes lest I open them again and didn't see him anymore, and yet a part of me was thrilled and awed to see a man so at one with the ocean, that wildest and most untamed aspect of the whole of creation, exerting such power over lowland dwellers like me.

He had turned round and begun swimming back toward the shore with surprising speed.

When he was about ten feet away from me, he stopped swimming and stood up, waist deep, with water streaming off his shoulders, his naked chest and his black hair. I smiled to myself with a sudden certainty that he had intended it to happen just this way. He knew I would come to look for him, and had gone swimming to impress me, to demonstrate his prowess for my appreciation. He was aware, undoubtedly, of how extraordinarily beautiful he looked, striding through the breaking waves in his wet, skintight breeches. He walked toward me out of the water, like the most vivid early dreams I'd had of him, waking dreams that I'd had before I'd ever met him. He came to stand in front of me, his bare feet shining wet in the sand, grains of it stuck to his toes. The fine covering of dark hairs on his chest glistened with droplets of seawater.

"Will you teach me how to swim?"

He ran his fingers through his hair to shake some of the moisture from it. "You'd faint from the cold."

I turned my face up to his, which was framed by wet black curls, his long eyelashes spiked with saltwater. "Remember how quickly I learned to skate? I surprised you then, did I not?"

He smiled, touched my hair. "Skating. Dancing. Swimming. Is it my role to bring excitement and danger into your quiet little life?"

"It is certainly quieter when you are not here. Safer too. But I never did want a quiet life. Or a safe one."

"Didn't you?"

I gave a small shake of my head. "No. I wanted my life to be like . . ." I cast about for a way to describe what I was trying to say. "A firework. I wanted to live in an explosion of color and light."

He smiled. "And why are you so eager to swim?"

"I want to know what it's like. How it is done." I had such a desire just to touch him again, to bend my head to his chest and lick the droplets of salt water from his skin, to feel the tautness of the muscles in his arms, muscles that had the strength to propel him through waves. "I've lived all my life in a world of sky and water. I'd like to know what it is like to fly like a bird or a butterfly, but since that's impossible, the next best thing is to learn to swim like a fish."

"Did no one ever tell you it was dangerous to be too inquiring, little Pandora?"

"They did, many times. But I chose not to listen."

He smiled. "You'd make a better bird than fish, I think. You are most definitely of air and angels."

I recognized the line from John Donne. "I did not know you were a poet."

"There is so much you do not know about me, Nell. Though you must surely know that for just one of your impish smiles, I'd do anything you asked of me." He made a slow scan of the sea, as if considering how it was best done. The waves made a hushing sound, sucked at my feet, impatient to drag me in.

"Is it really so cold?"

"No woman I've ever met would last more than one minute in it."

"One minute, you say?"

He grinned, held up a finger. "Aye, one minute."

It was all the encouragement I needed. In an instant I was out of my dress, laughing and running headlong into the waves in my cambric chemise. The first shock of the water snatched my breath away, made every muscle in my body go rigid, made me pull myself up straight and suck in my belly. I held my arms out of the water, bent like wings, and plunged on in until I was up to my waist, bracing myself as each wave slammed into my body, almost knocking me over. I let one pass and then carried on, waited for the next onslaught, pushed through it. Already, I felt a little less cold. The salt water was soft as silk against my legs.

"That's far enough," called Richard, raising his voice above the tumult of the pounding breakers, striding through them to stand in front of me. "Wherever are you going? I did not think we were walking to Wales."

"So what do I do?"

He cleared his throat, as if he was unsure how to begin, held his arms out in front of him. "Push out, then round and back," he said as he demonstrated. "Kick with your legs at the same time."

"Like a frog."

"Yes, I suppose. Like a frog."

I tried to copy him. Obviously failed.

"No. Not like that, like this."

He took a tight hold of both my wrists and drew my arms toward him, then pushed them out firmly to the side in an arc, more gently folded them back to the center again, in an attitude almost of prayer. I might no longer have time for God but old habits are not so easy to abandon and I whispered a silent prayer or two right then. Don't let me make a fool of myself in front of him. Do not let me drown, or be washed out to sea either.

"Let's try," he said. "Shall we?"

I stretched out on the surface of the sea, my arms spread wide. I felt his hands go underneath me, palms upward, and lifted my feet off the seabed, felt the pressure and warmth of his fingers against my belly and my chest, holding me up so that I was floating.

I tried to do as he'd shown me.

"Wider and slower," he said. "Keep your fingers together. Now, kick. Hard as you can."

I tried to keep my body horizontal in the water and made a sudden lurch forward, carried in part by a wave. He took one hand away, so he was just supporting me under my belly. Then he let go completely and instantly my head sank beneath the water, my knees scraped the rocky seabed, and my mouth filled with salt water. The undertow of the wave was dragging at me. I breathed in and choked, scrambled for a footing, came up spluttering.

"You let go of me too soon," I gasped, wiping the hair from my face.

"It takes practice." He clearly found it all quite entertaining. "Are you all right?"

"I am trying very hard to be dignified, even though my teeth are chattering."

"You look as lovely as a mermaid."

"I shall swim like a mermaid, too, before this day is done. Let's try again."

"You are a determined little doxy, aren't you?"

I smiled, took his hand and pressed it palm-flat against my stomach. "This time, please keep it there until I say otherwise."

He bobbed his head, his eyes glittering. "I am at your service, my lady. Now. Spread your legs."

I giggled. "For you, sir, anytime." I sank down into the water, to assume a swimming posture again.

"And this time, for pity's sake, if you are about to go under, hold your breath," he instructed.

I took my time and cleared my head before I lifted my feet off the seabed again and kicked out, once, twice. This time he let go of me one finger at a time. When I felt his hand fall away completely I took a gulp of air just before I sank. There was a rushing in my ears, then an eerie silence. I did not panic but kept on scrabbling at the water. One stroke, two. I was floating just beneath the surface, freed from the pull of the earth. I opened my eyes onto a murky blue world.

My lungs were bursting and as I tried to push up my feet went down. I broke through a wave and was back in the world again. I turned round elatedly to find Richard. "I did it!"

"You did."

"I can swim!"

"Almost."

"I did not sink!"

"You did not. The sea has declared you a little witch, for sure."

I frowned to see how close he was. "I thought I had gone further though."

"I came after you," he said. "In case you needed me to fish you out."

He pushed through the water and stood in front of me, gently wiped the wet hair off my face and coiled a dripping strand of it around his hand. "You shouldn't stay in too long or the cold will make your muscles stiffen and I'll have to carry you out."

My legs felt perfectly supple. "I think they're stiff already."

He did not pick me up.

"Last night, would you have bedded that knave to save your house from burning?"

"No!" Then: "What a time to ask."

"It would not have been a loathsome sacrifice? He is desirable to you?"

"He most certainly is not!"

"You have known him a long time."

"Yes, but in any case, I do not think he had any wish to bed me."

"That I do not believe," he said softly. "There is not a man on this earth who would not wish it."

"You are not exactly impartial."

"No. I am not." Then after a moment he said seriously, "You need to beware of Thomas Knight, Nell. The man's trouble, a firebrand."

"I know. I just wish I knew why. Please can we go now? I'm frozen."

He scooped me into his arms as he had last night, my long, wet hair trailing like gold seaweed. "Swimming is not so good as skating?" he asked.

"Actually, this particular part is far better." I rested my head against his shoulder, twined my arms up around his neck, and felt myself complete again.

When we reached the shore he retrieved his cloak from behind a rock, flung it round his shoulders, opened it like great black bat wings and enfolded me in it. It smelled faintly of horses and male sweat, of smoke and cologne, of him. I tucked my fingers into his armpits to warm them and gazed into his lovely eyes.

"You are very brave," he said.

"You make me feel brave," I told him softly. "And terrified, all at the same time. You make me feel strong, stronger than I have ever felt before, and yet never have I felt weaker. When I am with you I want to laugh and to weep, all at the same time."

He was smiling at me in recognition, as if at a sudden revelation that made him very happy. "So you do love me, then?"

"Yes," I said. "I love you."

I WAS SITTING by the fire, drying my hair and warming my bare toes. Richard sat in the chair at the other side of the hearth, his long legs stretched out in front of him, tall shiny boots up on the fender. There was no sound but the crackle and hiss of the apple-scented logs.

My eyes were drawn to his mouth, the slightly open pout of his kissable lips. I wanted to rise from my chair and go to him, sit at his feet and put my head in his lap, or for him to come to me so that I could stroke the black curls off his brow and bury my face in them. But I spied Forest peering round the door, seemingly almost as fascinated by this man and as desperate to be with him as I was. I sent Forest off to ask Bess to warm some wine for us. I felt very selfish, wanted Richard all to myself, even if all he was going to do was sit there, withdrawn, and stare morosely into the fire, in a way that kept me firmly in my chair and him in his.

"What's the matter?" I asked him.

He looked up from the flames, the light of them still reflected in his eyes, but said nothing.

"What is it?" I repeated, unnerved. "What's wrong?"

His right arm was resting on his thigh and I saw him flex his fingers, clench them. "Five years," he said ominously. "You have tortured me for five years. You say you love me, and yet you let me be miserable for five whole years."

I felt a terrible pang of remorse and I did not know what to reply. I had not expected such recrimination and yet I saw that it was inevitable, that it was a conversation we had to have at some time. "I have been miserable too," I told him.

"Then it was all of your own making. You have none to blame but yourself."

"I did not think I deserved to be happy."

His eyes flared, blazed darkly, and it was no longer the firelight that made them do so. "Nor I?"

I gave a small shake of my head.

He turned away from me, so that I could not see his face.

"We did a bad thing, Richard. We deceived Edmund. We betrayed his trust. He did not deserve that."

He was on his feet and in two strides he was standing before me. "You think I don't know that? Of course he didn't deserve it. He did not deserve to die either. But all I did was to love you . . . more than I have ever loved anyone else. It was utterly beyond my control. Did that warrant your unkindness to me? The cruel treatment you have shown me? You were cruel, Nell, make no mistake. Did you want me to suffer to make yourself feel better? Is that it? Every time you sent me away, every time you spurned me and humiliated me, did it make you feel that little bit more righteous? Damn it! Who are you to set yourself above God, to mete out penalties and punishment?"

I stood, squaring myself up to him as best I could. "I was punishing myself."

"Oh, aye. You Puritans are all for that, aren't you? Make life a bloody misery so your rewards in Heaven will be all the greater." He ran his fingers through his black curls. "So, you have decided that our penance is done now, have you, Eleanor? That I am to be your hair shirt no longer? You've decided, after all, not to wait for Heaven to claim your reward?"

I let my breath steady. "I am Eleanor to you again, am I?" I said quietly. "Not Nell anymore?"

That seemed to penetrate his anger, dispel it. He lowered his eyes, bent his head. After a moment he let me take hold of his hand. I brought it to my lips, held it there to kiss his fingers.

"I am so sorry," I said.

He turned his face up to mine. "All the letters I sent to you. What did you do with them?"

"I . . . I burned them."

He made to take his hand away but I held on to it.

"Before you read them? Or afterward?" he asked.

"Before," I admitted, ashamedly. "All but one," I added quickly. "One of them I opened. And read, and once I had done, then I had to keep it. I have slept with it under my pillow ever since. Every single night."

He gave me a little smile. "Have you?"

I stroked his face. "Please, don't let us argue anymore. What's done is done. We have both suffered enough."

He gave me an odd look. "Tell me this. Have you ever thought it would have been more just if I had died instead of Edmund?"

"You can't ask me . . ."

"Because I have thought it. Time and again I have thought it."

"Stop it."

"Edmund should be here now, instead of me. He should be here with you and his children, shouldn't he? Would you rather that? Would you rather . . ."

"No!" Then more quietly: "No."

He calmed a little, as if my words vindicated him somehow. "Shall I tell you why I did not abandon my pursuit of you years ago, the first time you refused to see me?"

"Tell me."

"Edmund said to me once that he could see why you loved butterflies so much. Because they are proof that there is real beauty in this world. Well, you are my butterfly, Nell. Despite everything, you are the best and most beautiful thing that has ever happened to me."

I kissed him, very gently, on his lips, then I led him back to his chair and I sat on the floor at his feet, offered him my hand to hold again. For a long while we were silent, but it was a companionable silence this time rather than a tense one.

I caught Forest peeping round the door once more, though he

scurried away when he knew himself discovered. "You seem to have won a devoted admirer in my son." I smiled at Richard. "As it should be. You are his sponsor, after all."

"It's not a child's admiration I seek, Nell."

"You won mine before I even met you," I confessed. "When I first heard you could swim. How did you learn? Who taught you?" Despite all that he had already shared with me, I realized that there was still much I did not know about him and I wanted to know it all, everything, all at once. I wanted to know every tiny detail of his life, what were his hopes, his opinions, his fears. I hardly knew where to begin. "Where did you learn to quote poetry? And where did you learn to handle a sword so expertly? Were you ever in the militia?"

He smiled his lovely smile and I was so glad to see it again. It was like sunshine after rain. "So many questions. Which shall I answer first? I was educated at St. John's College, Cambridge, where I developed a love of music and literature, but regrettably left without gaining a degree. No, I am no militiaman. I fear I am far too undisciplined ever to be a very good soldier or scholar. But amongst those in exile were fine horsemen and swordsmen, with time on their hands, who were willing to act as riding and fencing masters to me. I was put into the saddle before I was two, was handed a sword and pistol almost before I had learned the words to ask for them. When the King lost his head and my father lost everything he had, except for me, he determined that I would never lose anything ever again, that I should learn to ride and hunt and shoot and swim too, so that when I grew to be a man I would be the best at everything, have the best of everything."

"That sounds exhausting." I thought how it was also a route to disillusionment and disappointment.

"It was certainly no boon to be thrown into a lake," he said. "Told to swim or drown. My first lesson in life."

I sensed from the tone in his voice and the look in his eyes that he'd been a boy who had had no particular stomach for daredevilry, who had developed a taste for it but at some personal cost, learning through those hard years of exile to constantly hold his fears in check.

"That is a cruel lesson," I said, "one no little boy should have to learn."

"Aren't all lessons that children have to learn rather cruel?"

"They do not have to be."

"What d'you teach your son?"

Bess came in then with two conical glasses and the earthenware decanter of wine. She barely faltered when she saw whom the extra glass was for, but by her reaction it was clear she knew him to be the same man who had unleashed his sword on the rabble last night. I found that I could not bear for her to think unkindly of Richard. It was alarming how one person could have come to mean so much to me, how my own happiness and peace of mind were so entirely bound to his, and I knew that there was nothing I would not do for him, nothing I would not do to make him happy.

"My son knows I would do anything to keep him safe," I said, for Bess's benefit.

I don't think Richard even heard me. "How is the man who was injured?" he asked Bess directly.

She nearly spilled the wine all over him. "I believe he is recovering, sir."

"Was he badly hurt?"

She flicked a suspicious glance at him, but read his concern as entirely genuine and softened. "It is just a surface wound. It will mend."

"I am glad. Who is he? What is his name?"

"John Hort.

"And what does he do for a living?"

Bess was as surprised as was I at this depth of interest. "He's an eeler, sir."

Richard put his hand in the pocket of his breeches. "Here." He held out a little pile of gold coins. "Take this to him, with my good wishes. There's enough to see he gets proper treatment and to compensate him for loss of earnings until he is fit again. Take a sovereign yourself for your trouble."

Bess took the money willingly, as if she could not believe her good fortune. "Thank you, sir." She bobbed the prettiest little curtsy. "That's very kind of you, sir."

"That was very charitable," I said when she'd gone. "I've never heard Bess call anyone 'sir' so many times in such a short conversation. You've certainly won her over and no doubt will win over the entire Hort clan. Maybe even the whole village."

"It is far better to be revered than reviled. That is another lesson I learned from my years in exile. To live too long without friendship and love is not to live at all."

I saw that there'd been no scheme behind what he'd just done beyond a simple and deep need to be loved and respected. "You do not live here," I pointed out quietly.

His eyes met mine. "I shall do if you agree to marry me."

He took my hands and stood, raising me to my feet with him.

"I have money enough to bribe a chaplain." He slid his open fingers into my hair, lifted the long strands of it that were still damp at the ends, but which the seawater had made curlier than ever. He arranged it very carefully, so it fell around my face and over my breasts. "We could go to a Bristol church and have it done immediately. You could be my wife tonight. In a few hours we would be together."

I caught his hand and trapped it against my cheek, turned my face into it and kissed his palm. "You could take me and make me your wife right now," I suggested softly. "Once our promise is made we are as good as wedded. It is permitted and proper for us to lie with one another."

He snatched his hand away as if I had bitten him.

"We do not need to do it in that bed," I said, misunderstanding. "There are . . . other places."

"I will not lie with you, in a bed or otherwise, until you are properly mine," he said. "I cannot lie with Edmund's widow, with Eleanor Ashfield. I need you to be Eleanor Glanville."

I smiled, surprised by his intensity but thinking it a quaint sentiment. "I want to be Eleanor Glanville," I said. "I want it more than anything. But surely you are not serious about Bristol?"

"Either you leave with me now, or I leave alone."

"I am being held to ransom, for a kiss?"

"If that is how you choose to see it."

I opened my mouth to say yes, I would go with him. I would go wherever he wanted me to go, do whatever he wanted me to do. But I stopped. Other words came out. I was no serving maid who could marry as I pleased without care or consideration. I was first and foremost a landowner, guardian of an estate. "It took months to arrange my first marriage," I said. "There were contracts to be drawn up and to be signed, all kinds of negotiations."

"I don't want there to be any negotiating between us, Nell. I want us to be married like commoners and to live like kings."

"You mean, in debauchery?"

"I mean in some luxury," he said, ignoring my weak attempt at humor. "That is what you've always yearned for, I think? Twenty gowns and footmen in livery and a velvet-upholstered coach drawn by four horses? As my wife, I would make sure you had all that. I would make sure you had all you ever wanted, and more besides."

"I cannot do it like this. For my children's sake, I cannot."

He picked up his glass and downed the contents in one gulp, his eyes flaring with mercurial light. "First Edmund stood between us and now it is his children. I thought there were just the two of us now, but seemingly already there are four."

He must know as well as I did that children of a previous marriage always suffered if a widowed mother married again. "Tickenham Court is Forest's rightful inheritance," I said. "The estate's wealth is my daughter's marriage portion. But if I marry you tonight and we should have children, those children would take precedence over Edmund's son and daughter. My little Ashfield children would be the ones to lose out. I love you, so much, and I want to be your wife. I want you in my bed, this night and every night, for the rest of my life. I want your face to be my first sight when I awake and the last before I sleep. I want you to get a dozen children on me. I am ready right now to give up my freedom, to give you my body and my soul and my heart, but I am not prepared to hand you my children's home, their security, their future."

He was already walking toward the door.

"Wait! Please wait!"

He did.

"There has to be a way."

He looked doubtful, but he was listening.

"Let me find one. I will find one."

"You sound very certain of it."

"You said yourself, I am a determined little doxy. I would not marry you tonight, in any case," I said, finding a smile for him. "I do not want to sneak off by ourselves to a church and then to a tavern. I do not want to do it quietly, not this time. You also said to me once that if I became your wife, you'd want to celebrate before everyone, with a feast that went on for twelve days."

I instantly regretted referring to the conversation we had had that dark Valentine's Day morning, for conjuring Edmund's ghost to stand between us again. But oddly, Richard seemed not to be troubled by the memory of our illicit kiss, as he was evidently still so troubled by Edmund's death. I did not want to dwell on why that might be. "Twelve days of feasting." He smiled. "I did say that, didn't I?"

RICHARD SLEPT in the chamber he had stayed in when Edmund was alive, and this time I woke before he did. I rode back toward Clevedon to visit George Digby. I would ask him if he knew how I might make provision for my children should I take another husband. As he was a member of Parliament, I trusted that he had some understanding of such legal matters.

Impressively attired in sumptuous tawny silk, the Earl was playing an effortless game of tennis on the Clevedon Court lawn with his tall, gangly son, but he readily broke off to entertain me. Elegantly mopping his brow with scented linen, he declared he was glad of an excuse to catch his breath while he was two games ahead. "I did at least gain one useful skill during my years in exile," he said. "Enforced idleness and lack of funds meant that I spent days and days playing tennis. Much cheaper than hunting, you see. And even now that I can afford to hunt all day long if I so please, I've never lost my love of the racket."

I smiled to myself, struck by a memory I thought long forgotten.

"I do count myself a great wit," he said pleasantly. "But I had not thought to be one at the present. Yet it seems I have inadvertently amused you."

"My father once told me how Cavaliers enjoyed tennis so much they'd brawl and duel over the results," I explained. "It seems he was right about that, as about much else."

"To be precise, the duel was over a bet of seven sovereigns on who would win the game. It was a measure of the depth of irritability and frustration we all suffered from, the tensions of exile. So tell me," he asked jovially as we walked past the knot garden toward the terrace. "What else did your good father have to say about us? Besides a penchant for dueling and tennis, did he allot us any other vices?"

I hesitated.

"Come now," Digby encouraged. "I am intrigued. And I promise you, I shall not be offended at all."

I smiled. "Other vices? Well, let me see now. Debauchery. Drunkenness. Adultery. Fornication. Lust." I ticked the list off on my fingers. "General excess and moral corruption."

"Is that why you constantly refuse that lad?" the Earl asked, with a wickedly impudent gleam in his eyes. "Is it that you fear him to be debauched and morally corrupt?" He grinned at my astonished face. "Oh, Richard petitioned me not a month ago to appeal to you on his behalf. I was waiting for the right opportunity to present itself."

"It is because of him that I am here, sir."

"Ah."

Seated in a gold-and-green-paneled room on plump chairs covered in striped silk, and sipping sweetened tea served in a delicate gilded china tea set, I started to explain my predicament.

"So I have no need to petition you," the Earl interrupted. "Young Richard has succeeded in his pursuit of you at last, and without any help. Good for him. I am glad for him—for you both."

"I have not agreed to wed him yet," I said quietly.

He peered at me over the rim of his cup, arched one eyebrow. "And you will not agree if I cannot provide you with the information you need?"

"It must be a common problem," I persisted. "There must be a solution."

He laughed. "What a wonderfully optimistic approach to life you have, my dear lady." He set down the cup with a tinkle. "You are right, of course, that many landed gentlemen leave behind pretty widows who are still of childbearing age, but you are wrong to think that many of those ladies are as intent on defending the position of their first-born as are you. Or else, if they are, I imagine they take the standard precautions to ensure that there is no issue from their second marriage. A matter of timing, I understand, either of the moon or else of a man's rod at the pinnacle of pleasure?"

I laughed, did not blush at such base talk as I would once have done, but I was rather shocked to hear it from the lips of so lofty a person as the Earl. Even if he had spent years in exile with a young king in waiting who presided over the most dissolute and debauched court. "I would not deny Richard the joy of a child," I said seriously.

"But you would deny him the joy of seeing that child inherit your estate? I do believe you would deny yourself the joy of marriage, if it came to it." His lips curled in a knowing smile. "It is a cool head you have on your pretty little shoulders," he said contemplatively. "When I watched the two of you dancing here together, some years ago, I saw only the charge of passion between you. But it seems that your passion for Tickenham Court is the stronger, hmm?"

"I do this for my children," I said. "Not for Tickenham Court. Not for myself."

"But a marriage settlement will also benefit you considerably."

"A marriage settlement?"

He grinned. "An excellent invention and one commonly enough used now amongst the gentry. Quite simply, it is a signed agreement that preserves a wife's property rights and allows her to avoid giving up her liberty, estate and all authority to her husband. In real terms, with such a settlement in place, Tickenham Court would remain yours after you marry, whosoever you marry. It even remains yours to dispose of upon your death."

I set down my own cup, felt a stirring of happiness which I held in abeyance. For now. "And gentlemen willingly agree to a settlement that so diminishes their position?"

The Earl shrugged. "It depends on the gentleman in question, of course. On how amenable he is. But most are quite content with the arrangement." He studied me, saw I was still unconvinced. "Oho. I do detect Major Goodricke's influence and unfavorable opinions of us lingering in your generous and loving heart. Much as you love young Richard, you cannot help thinking of his passion for Spanish stallions and silk suits and sack, and you deduce, therefore, that he'll not be satisfied with any less than all of the coins in your coffers. Am I right? Much as you are drawn to him, you cannot help assuming that, being a Cavalier, he is therefore inclined to luxury and ease, and entirely profligate?"

"Of course not."

But the Earl smiled almost delightedly, as if he did not mind at all my harboring such dark opinions of all Royalists, himself included.

"It is my guess that you find profligacy not so unattractive, after a life of frugal living with your papa and Edmund Ashfield. And who would ever blame you for that, little lady? Now, I do not know your Richard nearly well enough to know if he is a wastrel or not, but I do know that life as an exile can be the most wretched existence. I know that in all likelihood, he'd have spent his most tender years in paralyzing unhappiness, endless uncertainty and much personal distress, as well as in precarious and constant need of money and a home. So I imagine he'd be more than content with regular payments from your estate, only too glad to be granted the security of an independent income. And when and if your estate reaps the rewards of drainage, his percentage will be all the more attractive. Although I imagine he might willingly forgo those extra riches to retain the goodwill of his neighbors. During those years as a fugitive, he'll have witnessed enough faction fighting and personal feuds to last him a lifetime, given that he strikes me as a rather overly sensitive boy, not very robust in his emotions. You are just what he needs, I think." He raised his teacup as if in a toast. "I vouch the lad will not refuse your terms, whatever they may be."

WHEN I ARRIVED BACK at Tickenham Court, I found Richard entertaining William Merrick in the parlor. They seemed to be on good terms but broke off their conversation and stood as I entered.

"William," I said, letting my former guardian kiss me. "I was not expecting you."

"My partners were not expecting to hear that a mob had tried to burn down this house," he said gruffly. "As I have already told Richard, I fear we will never win them round now."

"I don't think we should even try," I said carefully, with a glance at Richard. "I think we should let them take their money away for good and use it where it will be better appreciated. We leave the common to the commoners. And to the swans and the Swallowtails."

"What?"

"It seems I am to spend my entire adult life sifting through my father's principles and beliefs and sorting the pearls from the pebbles," I said. "But I think in this he was right. It seems to me there is enough land for all to have a share. And yes, it might be better for some who live on the wetlands, the people at least, if the land was dry all year, but until a way is found for us to have dry land and everyone to have enough of it to grow their own vegetables and cut their turfs and graze their cattle, I think it is better that we let well alone."

William's eyes flew in appeal to Richard, who looked away.

"I have said all I have to say," I finished firmly. "Let that be an end to it. And now I would be grateful if you would leave us, William. There are matters Richard and I need to discuss, matters of far more importance than this."

William stormed out of the room, head down like a charging bull, nearly crashing into Bess, who was entering with a tray of wine and sweetmeats.

"Did I do wrong?" I asked Richard, slipping my hand into his when we were alone.

He gave a slow shake of his head. "It is a pity you cannot join George Digby in Parliament. What a little champion you would be for the poor and the hungry and the dispossessed." He grinned. "Not to mention the birds and the butterflies. I cannot imagine what Merrick made of that."

"He can make of it what he will. It is no matter." I took Richard's other hand, held both of them. "I found a way," I said quietly. "I said I would find a way for us to marry, and I have."

We moved to the chairs by the fire, where Bess had set out the drinks and food on a little table.

Of necessity, a betrothal involving a landowning family was always preceded by such negotiations as I had to have with Richard, but that did not mean I found the conversation easy. No more, seemingly, did he. He sat opposite me, very still and unsmiling, screwing his heavy ring around his finger as he listened while I explained, as tactfully as I possibly could, how the Earl of Bristol, at my behest, would have his solicitor draw up a marriage settlement that would secure Forest's position as heir to Tickenham Court, leave it in my sole charge, whilst awarding Richard an independent and regular income from the estate once he became my husband. I thought the pair of us no different from a couple of coldhearted traders discussing a shipment of sugar, except that the glasses of spiced wine and plate of sweetmeats remained totally untouched before us on the low table.

"Is this really what you want?" Richard asked me dully when he had heard me out.

"We could not hope to find a better solution," I said steadily.

"No. I am sure that you could not."

I saw that he did not like it, not at all. Why not? I felt a flicker of misgiving, turned my head away from him for a moment and then chided myself. It was his complicated combination of pride and insecurity which was standing in the way, that was all, wasn't it?

"Is it the money?" I challenged, my tone brittle. "Is it not enough?"

His laugh sounded more like a cough, and there was no humor in it at all.

"George Digby suggested a sum he believed to be very generous, that would make good provision for you." Only after I had spoken did I realize how condescending I had sounded. Oh, why was he making this so difficult? "I am sorry. I did not mean to . . ."

"It is not the money, Nell."

"It is that you want control of the estate, then. Is that it? Because you can have it, with my blessing, if it matters so much to you." I tried to summon a smile, tried not to think why it should matter to him. "Believe me, I shall not stand in your way if you want to mediate in endless squabbles about boundaries and rights of pasturing, if you want to harangue the tenants for their rents."

"You would defend the rights of Tickenham tenants," he said evenly. "And the damned swans. And yet you pay scant regard to the rights of your intended husband."

"Rights?"

"You married Edmund without a settlement," he said abruptly. "You gave him everything."

"And you therefore assumed it would be the same this time? Is that why you want me?"

He looked at me as if my question was beneath contempt, beneath even warranting a reply.

"I did not even know there was such a thing as a marriage settlement when I married Edmund," I said shakily. "I did not have children to consider then. Surely you can see that this situation is entirely different."

"Yes," he said curtly. "I do see that, all too plainly."

His attention was diverted by something at the door. I knew who it was before I even looked. Forest was peering round again, wide-eyed with guilt for being caught in the act of spying.

"Darling, you shouldn't be listening," I said a little impatiently, wondering how long he had been there and how much he had overheard and understood. "Go and find your shuttlecock and battledores and I will come and play with you in a while."

He ignored me, bolted round the door and across the floor. I assumed he was running to me but instead he ran straight to Richard's side. Standing at his shoulder, making it utterly clear where his allegiance lay, he turned to me accusingly. "Mr. Glanville is not going to come and live with us now? He is not going to be my father?"

I looked to Richard, with the same question in my eyes and a lump in my throat. I was not the only person who loved him. Forest clearly did too. But I was doing this *for* Forest. And I could not bear for my little boy to be as distressed as I would be if Richard's answer was no.

"I want to play battledores with you, sir," Forest implored, laying his hand appealingly on Richard's silk-clad arm. "Mama is no good at it at all. I don't want to play with her."

That made Richard chuckle, and when he looked at me the laughter was still in his eyes. He knew I considered myself particularly good at the game, which was not unlike catching butterflies with a trap net.

He seemed genuinely heartened by Forest's rush of affection, as if it changed everything for him. Astonishingly, he brought Forest gently round to face him, so they were on a level. He looked into my son's solemn black eyes, as if whatever he saw there would help him to reach his decision.

I sent out a silent plea: Please realize I am doing what I am doing only for this little boy and his sister. Please agree to it for their sake. Richard was Forest's sponsor after all. Let that count for something.

"I will come and live here, rapscallion," Richard said gently to Forest. "I will be glad to be your father. I will play battledores with you until you are so good at it you can never be beaten." An aside to me. "I will sign the settlement, Nell. I will sign whatever damned paper you want me to sign."

Bess came to ask Forest if he would like to play leapfrog with her Sam, and he ran off, battledores forgotten for now.

"Tell me you are not angry with me, Richard," I said.

"I am not angry with you."

"I am sorry for what I said."

"I can see that you are."

"You do still want me?"

For a moment that felt like a lifetime, he did not answer. "Nell, I would want you if you were but a beggar, the daughter of beggars. If you were dressed in rags and had nothing to give me but your heart."

I realized with a tinge of regret that I was not idealistic enough anymore to believe him wholly, but it was the prettiest sentiment nonetheless, expressed in the manner of the poets he said he admired, and I felt joy bubble up inside me like the springs that bubbled up all over Tickenham land.

He pushed up abruptly from his chair, as if shaking a great weight from his shoulders; as if he had a sudden, urgent need for action, to obliterate something. He came round to my side of the table, grabbed my hand and pulled me to my feet. "I propose that we ride at once into Bristol and hire a coach to take us to Cheapside to buy your ring," he said with an impulsiveness that made me giggle. "We can go to the New Exchange too, for material for a wedding gown, and anything else we might fancy."

WE SAT TOGETHER in the rocking coach as we left the gold-smith's and headed for the New Exchange on the Strand, Mecca for followers of the new fashion for shopping as an entertainment, a place that was filled with all that was rich and new and rare—a place that all the religious instruction I had ever received had taught me to regard as evil and corrupt as Sodom.

I could hardly wait to see it.

Even now, when we were promised to each other, Richard stood by his strange but rather touching resolution not to bed me while I still bore Edmund's name, while I was Eleanor Ashfield not Eleanor Glanville. But that did not prevent us from spending the entire journey to London touching and stroking and kissing and murmuring little words to each other, until we were both driven half to distraction. We cooled our ardor only by concentrating on discussing preparations for the wedding, planning who should come to the celebration and what amusements we would have, what fresh-killed livestock we'd need for the serving of meats; roast, baked or boiled.

I wrote it all down in the notebook I had once carried with me when I was observing butterflies, in what already seemed like a different life. I had no need of butterflies anymore. I had what I had longed for. I had him right here beside me.

I had the top of the pencil in my mouth, was sucking it as I was thinking about puddings. I felt Richard watching me.

"We should make an application to the Episcopal authorities for a license to marry at St. Mary's Redcliffe in Bristol," he declared softly. "Queen Elizabeth herself called it the goodliest, fairest and most famous parish church in all of England. You should be a bride in no less a place."

"But we can return to Tickenham for the feasting? And have dancing on the grass?"

"Surely. We can do whatever you want, my little Nell. We can have new silver plate for the top table, and gloves and bridal ribbons for every guest."

"Oh, yes." My second marriage would begin in color and brightness and joy, and so in color and brightness and joy it would continue. "I have longed for a merry wedding since I was a child," I said, tossing notebook and pencil aside.

He kissed me, laid his cool cheek against mine, whispered into my hair. "Did you have such sweet dimples then? What were you like?"

I let my hand wander over his thigh, slip round to the inside of it. "I was forever getting into trouble and doing things I shouldn't." My hand drifted up slowly to his crotch. "I was very curious, you see," I whispered. "I still am. I like to experiment."

He closed his eyes, dropped his head onto my shoulder, shifted nearer to me as I rubbed him, felt his desire rising at my touch. When he rested back against the velvet upholstered seat, I watched the little lines between his brows pucker now with pleasure and I leaned over and put my lips against them, kissed also the grooved crescents at either side of his mouth.

"Nell," he moaned. "What are you trying to do to me?"

"I want to love you," I whispered. "I love you so much."

"Do you?"

"Surely you know that I do?"

But he did not look sure at all.

Too soon the coach came to an abrupt halt and we were there, on the paved street in front of the arcaded façade with its expanses of plate glass, behind which were the most beautiful displays of fans and feathers and lace.

We followed the other elegantly dressed shoppers who sauntered inside into one of the sheltered long galleries. It was lined with merchants' booths, with counters and glass fronts and awnings, and shelf upon shelf of all that I had been taught to see as foreign and decadent and Popish.

Richard slipped his hand almost possessively round my waist and I felt my pulse quicken again, did not know, though, if it was with desire for him or desire for all the unimaginable and once forbidden luxury arrayed before me. I felt like a child before a table laden with cakes and sweetmeats.

"If I lived in London I should come here every day," I said.

"Would you?" He gave me an interested smile. "Perhaps we should live in London, then."

"Oh, I could never leave Tickenham. But we must visit often."

I was as delighted by the liberty of the women I saw as I was by the goods, the way they seemed free to parade publicly with their friends, to drink coffee and gossip and shop as they chose. After my experience of the closed world of scientific societies and coffeehouse clubs, this was a revelation.

"Are we going to just stand here gawping all day, Nell?" Richard smiled. "Or are we going to shop?"

I carried on gawping. "I don't know where to start. I've completely forgotten what we need."

"It is not all about what you need, my love," he said to me, softly suggestive. "It is about what you want."

"You know very well what it is that I want."

"Besides that," he said, his eyes crinkling. "Besides what you already have on order for your wedding night."

I giggled. "You are scandalous, sir, to talk so in a public place."

But we were not alone in our flirting. It seemed the desires of shopping were linked very closely to the desires of the flesh. Perhaps the sermon writers had a point when they associated shopping with encouraging illicit sex, even going so far as to accuse the women in this place of being little better than harlots.

The mercer's servant certainly had a tongue far freer than any I had ever heard. "Oh, there's nothing like the feel of fine linen on your skin," she said in seductive tones, as she caressed a bale of sheets and fluttered her eyelashes at Richard. "Do have a feel, sir. Go on, do. 'Tis not often you get offered such a pleasure for no charge."

"Nor from the lips of such a pretty face." Richard returned her smile, as he walked his elegant fingers over the sheet she offered him.

"Have you touched anything finer or smoother?" she cooed.

"Only a young girl's skin." He flirted back, clearly enjoying the repartee and obviously not unpracticed in it.

"Can you imagine having anything better close to your naked skin?" she went on. "Can you imagine anything better to lie upon or beneath?"

"Only a young girl's skin," Richard repeated, with a chuckle.

I twined my arm very firmly around his and dragged him off up the broad avenue.

"But we need new sheets," he protested laughingly.

"Not from the likes of her, we don't. One more second and she'd have been over the counter and ripping off your shirt, fine linen or no."

He laughed. "Now who is jealous?" But as if it pleased him.

I slid my hand around his waist, let it rest lightly on his hip, just above the hilt of his sword. He shepherded me past a booth named Pomegranate and another shop called The Flying Horse. We bought luxurious gold silk from Naples for my gown, a bolt of burgundy wrought velvet for Richard's suit, gold lace to trim cloaks. We bought coffee, chocolate, tea, sugar and spices, and then went to a stall selling gems. "Show me the biggest Oriental pearls you have," Richard said. "The brightest and the roundest."

He bargained with assurance and skill, drove down the price by a half and then bought them, with a small lacquered cabinet for keeping them in.

I had never seen him so at ease. "I'd never have guessed you'd be so interested in browsing the wares of drapers and haberdashers and perfumers and silk mercers," I said, tucking my hand back inside his belt. "You like it here as much as I do."

He kissed my hair. "I like buying things for you."

"You must have something too. What will it be?"

He chose a jewel-encrusted scabbard and silver dagger and I was sure that must be the last purchase, but he had moved on to another silver merchant. We had already bought trenchers and a sugar box, new mustard pots and saltcellars and wine pots, but he picked up an escalloped fruit dish, the kind that would be displayed on the buffet, and I felt a shadow pass over me, transitory as the shadow of the wings of a swan in flight but enough to ruin my enjoyment, because I knew, as everyone did, that plate was displayed as a symbol of status and of wealth. I understood how much it must matter to Richard, because he had seen what it did to his father to have it all plundered and stripped away. I understood it, but it troubled me.

He saw that I was troubled, mistook the reason. "Regard it as an investment," he said. "If we are ever in need of ready money, we can have it melted down."

"We will have to do it immediately, if we spend any more."

"No we won't," he said easily. "The world runs on credit now. Dealers in luxuries are particularly glad to extend credit to landed gentlemen and ladies. Enjoy it now, pay for it later."

"Why does that sound more like a warning than an opportunity?"

I tried to put George Digby's comment about profligacy from my head. Failed.

Richard was looking at me strangely and I slid my eyes away from him to the floor. "What is it?" he said very low.

I raised my face to his. "I think a beggar girl might not do for you after all," I tried to tease, but his eyes flared, the blue of them suddenly glacial.

I thought how I would have to grow accustomed to this unnerving changeability of his. I would learn to notice the warning signs and triggers and find ways to avoid them and divert him, I told myself, as I had learned to divert Forest from the tantrums that erupted whenever he did not get what he wanted. Sometimes.

WHEN JOHN SMYTHE RODE over from Ashton Court to see him, Richard was with Forest in the great hall, where they had both been for most of the morning. Richard had removed his small ornamental sword from his hip and was demonstrating with great patience just how to hold the hilt and draw it from the jeweled scabbard to make a lunge.

Our neighbor was a trim-bearded and very aristocratic young man who behaved as if he was twice as old as his years. He had already adopted the irascibility and pomposity of his father, Sir Hugh, who had died several years ago. In his role as deputy lord lieutenant, John Smythe had come to tell us that the militia was being put on readiness for an invasion by the Duke of Monmouth.

It should not have come as any great surprise. Talk of rebellion had been brewing since before the second King Charles died and the new King James took the throne. But why did it have to happen now, just days before my wedding?

"You will join us, of course, sir?" John Smythe said to Richard. "Colonel Portman has sent out a call for young and able gentleman to lead our troops."

My eyes flew to him as my heart turned over. With a hiss of metal that reminded me poignantly of skates on ice, Richard dropped the sword into its sheath, handed the encrusted hilt back to Forest.

The boy took it in a trance, watching him as intently as was I. "Will you go and fight, Mr. Glanville?" my son asked eagerly.

The civil war was not even a distant memory for him, no more than a thrilling adventure from the ballads that made no mention of Somersetshire being turned into a blood-soaked battlefield, of people being starved out of their houses and those houses pillaged and burned, of children being raped and murdered before their mothers' eyes, of the inhabitants of this country being reduced to a state close to destitution from which many were only just recovering. I had been born into that aftermath and it was still very real and raw for me. My blood felt chilled to think such hardship might return. Richard showed no outward fear, except that his lovely face had gone ashen and the tension was evident in every line of his body. I sank down into a chair, suddenly lacking the energy or the will to stand.

"Will you go, sir?" I had not noticed Bess come into the room, carrying an armful of my new gowns.

I glanced at her and her eyes told me everything. Ned and Thomas would be going to join the rebels. Their fathers were club men in the civil war. They would see it as their duty to defend the grand old cause, the Protestant cause, just as my father would have defended it to his dying breath. He would turn in his grave to see John Smythe in his house, asking my intended husband to help lead the militia in support of a Catholic king against a Protestant pretender.

The differences between us had seemed of no account before, but never had I felt them so keenly as now, when Ned and Thomas and the other Tickenham men were probably already collecting pitch-forks and scythes and rounding up their friends to rally to the cause of the Duke. The war had never been over for my father, and it seemed it was never really over for England, least of all the West Country. If Richard joined the militia, our family would be split in two. Bess and I would be on opposing sides, our men at war with one another. We would be enemies under the same roof.

Richard came over to me and sat himself down quietly on the arm of my chair. I slid my hand over to rest on his thigh, not sure if it was to comfort him or myself.

"I am to be married in a few days," he said, finally answering the question only I had not dared to ask. "Nothing will disrupt that, not war, nor flood nor famine. After it is done, if the militia still needs me, I will decide what to do."

"Very well, sir. Thank you." With an abrupt click of his heels, John Smythe bowed and left.

Forest whipped out the little sword, sliced the air with it. "How old d'you have to be to fight?"

"Old enough to know what you are fighting for," Richard said.

"What are the rebels fighting for?" my son asked.

"To rid the country of kings and Papists," Richard said sardoni-cally. "Same as it ever was."

I had never quite shaken off my conviction that Edmund had died of Papist poison. I could not help fearing what it would mean to have a Catholic on the throne, could not help thinking it might be better if the rebels won—except that Richard would be fighting against them. If they won, he would have lost, just like his father, and I did not know how he would cope with that.

Forest came over to Richard and handed back the little sword with obvious reluctance.

"Keep it," Richard said.

Forest's eyes were wide as trenchers. "Really, sir? Can I?"

"It is too dangerous, Richard," I said, ignoring my son's scowl. "He is too young."

"I was only four when my father gave me my first sword," Richard said easily, reminding me, as if I needed reminding, of that pressure his father had put on him from such an early age, to win, always to win.

I could not be so cruel as to remind him that his father had also thrown him into a lake, to drown or swim. I could not be so cruel as to remind him that he was not the father of my son. Though looking at them both, with their two heads of black hair, Forest looked to be more Richard's child than mine.

I glanced from my husband, the son of a Cavalier, to my son, the grandson of a Roundhead major, and felt truly thankful that my father was no longer here to see them together.

"Who will win?" Forest asked, practicing a parry with the sheathed sword. "The rebels or the King?"

"Ah, now, that is always the question," Richard said. "Tell me, who would you stake your money on? A king with trained infantry and mighty guns, or a disorderly rabble with scythes and pitchforks? Whose side would you rather be on?"

The words came to my tongue of their own volition, were out of my mouth before I could bite them back. "You should not be so confident," I said. "You, of all people, should not need reminding that the first King Charles did not win. For all his battalions."

His expression changed, darkened. "You speak as if you would see our King and all his armies defeated too."

"I no longer care," I said slowly, "whether a person be Puritan, Protestant or Papist. Just as I do not care if they be kin to Roundhead or to Cavalier."

"Are you quite sure of that, Nell?"

Summer

1685

My second wedding day could not have been more different from the first.

The predicted invasion had not happened, and I refused to let the threat of it spoil the day.

It began with much eating and drinking, so even before we made it to church half our party, Bess and Ned, John Hort and the Walkers and Mother Wall, were all headed for mild intoxication, everyone very loud and merry.

Richard and I traveled to Bristol in a coach with glass windows and liveried pages, the sun shining brightly all the way. I had a golden dress to match my golden curls, and a necklace of sapphires and diamonds that Richard had given to me as a wedding gift.

The soaring church of St. Mary Redcliffe was festooned inside with violets and roses. Precious little of the medieval stained glass had survived destruction during the Reformation and by Cromwell's army, but the very highest windows were still intact and were enough to illuminate the spacious interior with a myriad of colors. The sunlight filtered through them and made colored patterns on the floor. It gleamed on the golden basin in which the guests were to cast their brightly wrapped gifts.

"Look," I said to Richard, as we walked to the aisle over a pool of red and yellow and purple light. "We have found the foot of a rainbow."

He stroked back a wisp of hair that had drifted over my cheek. "And see, here is the gold."

But for all the radiance around us, he appeared today as if haunted by his own private shadow. He seemed more than usually preoccupied and troubled, and I imagined it must be the promise he had made to John Smythe that was distressing him. He'd said he would join the militia, if need be, as soon as our wedding was over. I took his hand in mine, leaned into him and kissed him, to be rewarded with a gentle, transforming smile. There was a mischievous sparkle in his eyes again as he whispered to me of the wedding vow that Protestants had foresworn as pagan idolatry. "I shall worship you with my body, Nell, forever, so long as you will always worship me with yours."

"Oh, I will. I will."

It was enough to irk even the mild Puritan in William Merrick, who muttered that the whole event was a shameful display of pomp. And that was before he found out what was planned for later.

The bridesmaids showered us with flowers and sprinkled us with wheat as we proceeded from the church, and my smiles turned to an amazed stare when I saw what was waiting to greet us for our return to Tickenham. A hundred riders on horseback had come to escort us back to the house, and all the grand families—the Smythes from Ashton Court, the Digbys from Clevedon Court and the Gorgeses of Wraxall—had turned out in their finest coaches.

"It is only fitting," Richard said. "How else should a lady and new lord be welcomed back after their wedding?"

I turned to him. "You knew they were planning this?"

I saw by his quiet smile that he had had more than a hand in that planning, had obviously taken it upon himself to visit all the local gentry whom my father, and even Edmund, had failed to count as friends. But clearly they were all Richard's friends now, had all succumbed to his gentle, winning charm. How could they not?

The commoners and tenants were no different, seemingly. The Bennett boys came up alongside the carriage and threw flowers in at the windows, and Alice Walker rode up with her father and handed me a bouquet of marigolds. Everyone was carrying flowers and wearing flowers and throwing garlands and posies at us all along the way.

"They were all very happy when I said that, instead of draining the land, we were planning a great feast and dole for them all," Richard explained.

"I am sure they were."

I insisted we stop the coach so we could get out and ride on top with the coachman for the rest of the journey, so as to have the best view of the cavalcade of drums and bagpipes and fiddlers and dancers that accompanied us, and I smiled at all the well-wishers, reached down to touch their hands.

A girl threw a rosebud and Richard reached out and snatched it from the air. He held it to his lips and looked at me over it with the most roguish, twinkling smile. "Soon your rose will be all mine," he whispered. "The secret rose you keep between your legs, with petals as pink as these. I shall be like a bee, or one of your butterflies, and put my tongue into those petals."

"Hush," I said, flushing as hotly as a greensick girl. Just imagining him doing what he described made me almost delirious. I was glad we were in the open air, that there was a breeze to cool my skin. I was glad I had the procession to watch to distract me. It danced us back to the house and through the flower-filled rooms to the great hall and the wedding table decorated with floral rose cake.

More than a hundred guests sat down for the first sitting, to scoff breads and meats and puddings and cheeses. Fulfilling his duty as groom, Richard served me with beef and mustard, and John Foskett raised a glass and joined in, offering blessings and drinking healths. The merriment was naturally restrained while the clergyman was present and I was impatient for him to go. I was not interested in edification. I wanted mirth and fun, bawdy jests and devilish ditties. I wanted to make a May game of this wedding. I delighted in seeing cakes and ale relished, and every lusty lad with a wench at his side, all pulling at laces and loosening each other's clothes.

"There is so much kissing and flirting, I doubt many will still be maids by evening," Richard whispered into my ear.

"It's like a wedding from the old days," Mistress Knight came up especially to say to him, her wrinkled old face alight as if she was just a girl again. "I never thought we'd see the likes of it again, now that the gentry folk are so anxious to save their shillings."

Richard handed her a posy from the table decoration, gave her his most adorable smile. "What is the good of having shillings if they are not spent and scattered amongst friends?"

She beamed back at him and almost danced away with the little bouquet, as if her gnarled old legs pained her no more.

"Damn me," I said, slipping my hand into his. "But is there nobody my husband has not utterly charmed?"

There was one person, I realized, but I imagined that was because Richard had not even tried. Mistress Knight was seated at a bench with her husband, Arthur, and Bess and Ned, but I noted that Thomas was not with them. How he must hate me, to deny himself a feast rather than be here celebrating my wedding day, and for a moment I felt a little chill. What had I done to make him hate me so much? I shrugged. Well, it was his loss that he was missing out on today.

We had been showered with presents from everyone else. To the

ones we had received in church were added more money and silverware and all manner of food or drink: swans, capons, a brace of duck,
hares and fish and puddings and spices.

I took a moment to take note of every detail, so I should remember
it always. This great hall that had seen such austerity was utterly transformed with sprigs and bouquets on every table, the feasting guests
decked out in their silver buttons and scarlet stockings and with scarlet and blue bridal ribbons round their wrists and hands and hats. My
children, giddy from too much sun and cider, were hiding under tables
with Bess's Sam and scores of other village children. I did not want the
day ever to end. But when it did, I consoled myself that there would
be eleven more to follow just like it.

Richard had been softly caressing the inside of my wrist with little
circular movements of his thumb, and now his tongue was in my ear.
It tickled deliciously and I wriggled away. His arm tightened around
my waist, but I came back willingly for more. He kissed me and his
mouth tasted of wine. His hand strayed now under the table, found
its way up under my skirts, his fingers moving up slowly between my
legs, stroking me, touching the secret parts of me.

"I want you, Nell," he whispered urgently. "I cannot wait any
longer."

The guests must have worried that if we were not soon sent to our
bed we would take our marriage joys right there on the wedding table,
unable to hold back from doing the act before them all. The bride
cake and the posset were speedily brought forth, and then everyone
followed us upstairs for the public disrobing, crowding round to catch
the ribbons and laces that held our clothes together. I did not even
see who caught the most admired trophy, my garter. I had eyes only
for Richard, for my husband. And he was looking only at me, smiling
at me, that beautiful angel's smile, and there was nothing else in the
world for me but him.

They all took their leave of us eventually and we tore off the rest of each other's clothes, getting in a tangle in our haste and tumbling each other naked to the bed.

Richard raised himself above me and I parted my legs for him, but for a while he seemed to want to do no more than hold himself against me as I stroked him and he gazed intently into my face. The hardness of his cock was pressing into me, stirring me, and when he began to move, very slowly, my need for him became so unbearable that my body took charge and responded to him of its own accord. I pressed back, began thrusting softly against him. I did not stop, could not stop, wanted more and more of him, just to touch and be touched, to give myself to him, to give myself up to feeling. It was a letting-go. Like dancing and letting the music take hold of my body, like skating on ice and not caring if I could not stop, like the wonderful weightlessness of swimming. It was beauty and bliss unbound. The sensation of his skin against mine, such soft skin, on a body that was hard and lean, took me to a world beyond any world I had ever known, a world of fire and of ice, of the deepest darkness and the brightest light. Curls as black as night and eyes as bright as a summer sky . . .

"Love me," I whispered. "Make me yours." And he did love me, as I had never been loved before. It was a love to be completely lost in, consumed by. It was like being split open and it was like being made whole, like receiving a blessing, like coming home.

I wept against his shoulder and cried out and clutched his hair, and when he stroked me with his warm hands it was as if the music that had played all day played on in my head, a glorious cacophony of sound. Entangled, grappling, our limbs entwined, we were warmed as if by the hottest, brightest midsummer sun, even as dusk was falling. A bead of sweat trickled down the small cleft between my breasts, and his thighs glistened as if he had just walked out of the sea.

It was all that life could be, all that it was meant to be, a sensuous explosion of touch and taste, of sight and sound and smell. The taste of his mouth, his skin. The smell of his warm perfumed curls, his sex. The sound of his moans of ecstasy. His naked body was beautiful to behold and the hardness of his cock a delight.

His hands were all over me, caressing every part of me, making my skin tingle until it was as if it was fused with his, so I could not tell where he ended and I began.

"I can't hold on any longer," he whispered. "I want to be inside you." And the feel of him penetrating me at last made me cry out with the joy of being able to give myself to him completely, to give to him finally all that I had to give.

I wrapped my limbs tight around him and arched my back to draw him deeper, wanting to be closer to him still, closer, understanding only now what it meant for two bodies to become one. When I cried out for him to finish it and he finally found his relief, it was as if the sun had burst inside me, the music rising in a great crescendo and all the church bells ringing, ringing, for Christmas.

WE WERE LYING in each other's arms and I was drifting in the pleasant transitory state just beyond wakefulness when Richard suddenly cried out in his sleep, words that were unintelligible but full of distress. He pushed me roughly away from him, thrashed his legs, kicking out at me as if he was fighting me off, as if in his dream I was something to be feared and meant him harm. His eyes were tightly closed, his brow furrowed, as if in pain or anguish.

I reached out to him and took hold of his shoulder, gave it a gentle shake. "Richard."

He turned his face into the pillow, twisted his head back again violently, as if he was trying to escape from something.

I shook him a little harder. "Richard. Wake up."

His eyes flew open, stared at me, unseeing but filled with terror, so that I knew he was not properly awake but still trapped in a nightmare world.

I stroked his hair off his face and felt that it was damp with sweat. "I'm here," I said. "It's me."

I slid my arm up under his and around his back and found that his body was running with sweat, and yet he was trembling. I held him tighter, felt the ferocious pounding of his heart through my bones.

"You had a dream," I said. "Do you remember what it was?"

He shook his head, his eyes suddenly guarded, so that I wondered if he did remember quite clearly but was either too ashamed or too afraid to talk about it.

"It's all right," I murmured, kissing his brow, my mouth wet with his sweat. "It's all right."

Gradually his heart steadied, but he held on to me as if the fear had not left him.

WHEN I WOKE, the morning of Friday the twelfth of June, it was to a greeting of more drums and fiddles and bawdy laughter. I dressed and went below stairs to find the tables laid with food and my husband happily breaking his fast with the new guests, who were arriving from the more far-flung villages to bring their congratulations.

Goodwill and joy rang through the hall until Thomas Knight burst through the doors in a state of great agitation. He climbed up onto one of the tables, trampling the flowers beneath his boots, and seized a musket from the wall. Silence fell instantly and completely, as if everyone had been turned to stone.

"This is no time for feasting," he declared before anyone had had a chance to react. He clutched the weapon to his chest, excitement gleaming in his eyes. "Every able man must take up his arms and make ready. I have it from a messenger. The Duke of Monmouth's fleet landed at Lyme at sunset yesterday. Hundreds are rallying to his support."

I threw back my chair and ran outside to the orchard. Richard tried to grab my hand to stop me, but I would not be stopped. I needed air, sky, space.

Not now. It could not happen now.

The sun was still shining. The sky was a perfect summery blue and the birds were twittering. I was still newly married. But the wedding feast would not go on for twelve days. Instead of music and laughter, the air would reverberate again with the sound of cannon fire. Instead of sharing hospitality and good cheer, neighbor would turn once again against neighbor. Blood was to be spilled once more over Somerset-shire's black peat. I had wanted this marriage to begin favorably, in a blaze of color and in joy. Instead it was to begin in darkness and in battle.

RICHARD HAD HIS FEET UP on the wedding table, amidst the crushed flowers and debris of the abandoned feast. He was quaffing a cup of canary wine from a leftover flagon, his eyes strangely bright and glittering. I rested my hand on his shoulder, dropped a kiss on the top of his curly head. "I am so sorry that marriage to me has landed you in the West Country now," I said softly. "If you had stayed away from me, far away from me, you might not have been embroiled in this rebellion."

He reached back and laid his hand upon mine. Swinging his feet to the floor, he pulled me gently down into his lap. "I could not stay away from you, Nell," he said, almost ominously. "I had to have you, even if it meant my damnation."

They were words he might have intended as flattery, no more than that. They meant nothing. No. They meant something, though I did not know what. Did not in truth want to know, even to contemplate.

He tipped the cup to my lips for me to drink, but I pushed it away. "Will you go now? Will you go and help try to put down the rebellion?"

"You mean, will I fight for our crowned and anointed King?" With the backs of his fingers he traced the low, lace-edged neckline of my gown and he smiled that lovely inquiring smile of his. "I had a healthy regard for our second King Charles and his passion for wenching and wine," he said. "But I can't say I care as much for his brother. So maybe I should join the rebels instead, support the heroic Protestant duke? Would you like that, little daughter of a Roundhead, my little Puritan maid? Would you like me to turn renegade for love of you?"

I flung my arms around his neck. "All I want is for you to stay with me," I blurted, close to tears. "I do not want you to support anyone."

"Then perhaps I won't."

But I did not for a moment believe this studied indifference. He was blessedly unfettered by dogma, prayed like a perfect Anglican, but this rebellion was not just about religion, not for him. He had an unshakable alliance to the monarchy, and the monarchy was once again under threat.

I pushed back so I could see his face. "Thomas Knight and Ned and John Hort have already gone," I said.

"Good for them."

"They see it as their duty to fight for the cause their fathers fought for," I added carefully.

"Hah! It is more that they are ready to fight for any cause, especially one led by a colorful popular hero such as the Duke of Monmouth. Albeit that he is King Charles's bastard son, he is a very courageous and charming bastard. It's not so very hard for the political agitators to rouse a band of young hot-blooded men, ready for action and glory.

They'd ride into any battle so long as it gave them a chance to wield a musket or a pike and be a hero. You have a little boy. You know the games boys like to play."

"Thomas and Ned are both older than you," I said. I knew he was just toying with me, knew he would go and lead the militia, would be lured, like the rest of them, by the promise of action and adventure and glory. More than that, even if he would not admit it even to himself, he would surely also be lured by what he could not fail to see as a chance, finally, to avenge the death of his brother and the ruin of his family fortunes.

I linked my arms around his neck, threaded my fingers into the silken black curls and kissed him, frantic little kisses, all over his face. "I will not let you go," I said. His eyes were so deep and so blue that I felt almost as if I could dive into them. How I wished I could. "If you do join the militia, then I am coming with you. I shall be like a camp follower in the war, the women who went to be with their husbands, to face whatever perils they faced. I will cook for you and make sure you fight on a full stomach. I will be there to tend to you if you are wounded. I will lay down my life and die on the battlefield with you, if it should come to that."

"I would not have you put in danger," he said. "Not for my sake."

"But *you* will be in danger," I cried.

He gazed at me as if he wanted to fix an image of me in his mind, and I saw in his eyes a fatalistic acceptance of the hand that might be dealt him.

"Are you afraid, love?" I asked him.

"Of scythe men and musketeers?" He shook his head. "No."

"Of what, then?"

"I am afraid of losing you."

"You will not lose me. Why would you lose me?"

He did not reply.

"You are frightening me, Richard. Don't look at me that way."

"What way?"

"As if you might never see me again."

He stroked the stray tendrils of hair from my cheek. "I waited so long for you, my little Nell, so long. But maybe you were right. Maybe we should not be together. Maybe we do not deserve happiness, even now. Maybe I do not deserve it."

I took his lovely face between my hands, forced him to look at me. "You do deserve it, Richard," I said adamantly. "You do. And you shall have it. I shall make you happy."

He kissed me, almost savagely, as if to defy a fate, or a God, that might break us apart, and then he left me. He swung himself up into the saddle and rode away from me and into battle.

BESS AND I WAITED together for news, even though the men we loved were fighting on opposing sides, even though good news for one of us must mean bad news for the other. We waited in the same empty rooms for the same empty, eternal days, when even the long hours of warm summer sunshine could not dispel the darkness that had fallen over Tickenham Court once again. As I tossed corn to the clucking hens, collected eggs, weeded the soggy vegetable patch, helped Sam do his father's work and feed and groom the horses, waiting for them to be requisitioned for who could say which side, I did not feel like a new wife fresh from the marriage bed. I felt like a widow still, a widow who had lost not one young husband but two.

I was helping Mary with her Latin and Bess was sweeping the floor when Florence Smythe, John's tall and elegant eldest sister, rode over with news, finally, but news that brought no relief to either of us, that made the waiting even more unbearable.

"Monmouth's army is on the move," she said. "It is now three thousand strong. The Devon militia to the west and the Somersetshire militia to the east are converging on Axminster to prevent their advance."

I dropped my face into little Mary's curly red hair. If it were not for her and her brother, I would have left for Axminster right then. I was sure this waiting was far worse than being at the vanguard of any fighting, no matter how brutal. But still we must wait, knowing now that a confrontation between the two armies was imminent. Still we must wait, dreading the worst.

Florence had promised she would come back as soon as she had further news, but when nearly a week had crawled by, I felt so certain something must have happened, I could wait no longer. I set out to ride to Ashton Court. A pale sun was struggling to break through the mist and as I rode through the deer park, a stag with enormous antlers appeared from out of nowhere and crossed the path in front of me, like a strange, majestic spirit.

I did not reach the mansion, but met Florence riding toward me, her cloak draped elegantly over her horse's hindquarters. As she reined in and we faced each other on our mounts, I saw that her eyes were brimming with tears.

"How did you know?" she said. "I was on my way to tell you."

I clutched the pommel of the saddle to stop myself from slipping off.

"Oh Eleanor, dear, do not be alarmed." With a jingle of the bridle Florence leaned across to rest her hand on mine. "It is with relief that I cry, and more than a little trepidation, but not for sorrow."

The herd of red deer over toward the ancient oak woods stopped watching us and resumed their grazing. "It is over, so quickly? Monmouth is defeated?"

"No," she said, tightening the reins to hold her horse steady. "He is not. But it is over for our men. We have just had it from the messenger. Monmouth's rebels sent cannon and musketeers to line the routes of entry into Axminster, and in the face of such determination the militia were forced to retreat. The army marched on to Chard. The militia met them again there but were routed, abandoning their weapons and uniforms by the roadside." She laughed even as she cried. "It was a shamefully disorderly and humiliating defeat, and my brother will be so displeased. It means the way is left open to Taunton and then for Monmouth to try for a tilt at Bristol, but at least our men can come home to us and leave it to the royal dragoons."

I could not share her relief. "But Florence, where are the dragoons?"

"They are on their way. The King's commander in chief also, to inspect the city defenses."

I turned to the left, where the mist was clearing now, revealing spectacular views across the city. "And if they do not hold? If Bristol should be taken?"

Bristol was too close. Much too close.

I DID NOT HEAR the hooves of Richard's horse clatter into the yard, though I had been listening out for the sound all day, so quietly did he come back to me. He walked into the great hall as the light was failing, his riding boots caked in mud, his cloak splattered with it. Even the glinting sword buckled at his side was tarnished. There were several days' growth of dark stubble on his face, his skin was gray with weariness and his eyes looked bruised. The instant I saw him, I checked myself from running to greet him and throwing myself into his arms, from giving him the welcome I could see he did not want, did not believe he deserved. I went and took his hand and kissed it. "My love, thank God that you are safe."

"They have proclaimed the Duke of Monmouth king," he said emptily, as if it mattered to him very much. "He received a rapturous welcome in Taunton and the declaration was made in the presence of a corporation brought by sword point."

"Surely they cannot do that?"

"They just did. They have hailed him the new King James."

I saw that he found defeat almost impossible to accept. He had wanted to return to me with tales of valor, to come out on the winning side this time. And though he would never have admitted it, I knew he was afraid of what might happen if he did not.

"The rebel infantry are only five miles from Bristol," he said. "The Duke of Beaufort has said he would see the city burned, would burn it himself rather than let it fall to traitors. A vessel in the quay, a merchantman, has already taken fire. There is nothing we can do to stop them."

"The King's forces will stop them. They will." I led him to the settle, pressed him to sit. Seeing that his boots were wet, I knelt by his feet and pulled them off. I went to the buffet and poured a cup of wine for him, brought the flagon over and set it on the table by the fire. He took the cup in shaking hands and drank it dry.

I knelt by him again, rested my arm on his leg and reached up to stroke his hair. "Richard, please don't take this so hard. You did your best. You had charge of a band of ill-trained and inexperienced part-time troops, not a proper fighting unit at all." I did not add that matters were made so much worse because they were led by gentlemen officers with no military experience. "There is much sympathy for the rebels. It is no wonder there were desertions."

He picked up the flagon and tried to pour it, spilled wine on himself and the floor. I put my hand over his to steady it, poured for him.

"Tell me this, Nell," he said. "Can you honestly say that in your heart you were not hoping for this, that some of your loyalty at least does not lie with the rebels? That, at the last, your Puritan blood does not run thicker than your love for me?"

"How can you ask . . . ?"

"Your loyalty to Tickenham's men, then? To Bess's Ned and Thomas."

"I cannot help hoping they will come home safe, for her sake," I said after a moment. "Is that so very wrong of me?"

BESS HAD GIVEN UP on her reading and writing lessons and forgotten most of what I had taught her, but not before she had passed on the rudiments to Ned, and to Thomas, apparently. Bess said her brother had picked it up quicker than she could teach him, worked most of it out for himself. She came to me now with a letter from Ned, which he had sent with a carrier, and which she wanted me to read for her.

I hesitated. "Are you sure?"

"Just because Mr. Glanville was with the militia does not make you one of them, now does it? You are your father's daughter, and you know as well as I do that he would have been marching at Monmouth's shoulder."

I gave her a look, unfolded the letter and read aloud the message from her husband. "We have met with the King's Life Guards, bonny Bess, a hundred of them, at Keynsham. There have been injuries but do not fear, Tom and I have not taken even a scratch, such able cavalrymen we have become, but the troops of the rebel horse are scattered and Monmouth has been forced to give up his designs on Bristol. I cannot say where we are to march to now but it will not be in your direction, praise God. I pray that we are not overtaken by the King's troops and I pray that we have good weather.

"We are all so ill-shod and exhausted from toiling through deep mud under heavy rain, not that I am not well used to mud and to rain, nor mind the toil. Tom sends his wishes and I send you all my love and kisses, bonny Bessie. I hope Sam is tending the horses well for me. Keep him safe. Pray for us all."

Richard had come silently into the hall; he wore the expression of a man who has caught his wife in the act of cuckolding him. I refused to let him make me feel guilty for having read Ned's letter to Bess. I refolded it, unhurried, and handed it back to her.

Richard turned and walked away toward the parlor.

"It is people I care about, not causes," I said, going after him and reaching for his arm. "Can you not understand that?"

He poured himself some wine. "It is which people you care about the most that I don't quite understand."

"I care about you," I said almost despairingly. Why could he not believe that? Why was he so unsure of my love for him? Why, when I loved him so very much, was it not enough? What did he need from me that he did not already have?

Damn this rebellion, I thought. Damn Monmouth. Damn the King.

I removed the wineglass from his hand, moved closer to him, so our bodies were touching. I slid my hand down between them, felt his desire.

"You want me?" I asked him.

"I always want you."

"Come with me, then," I said softly. "And let me show you just how much I care about you."

It was enough to bring a smile back to his beautiful mouth. "There is an offer I'll not refuse."

WE LEARNED FROM JOHN SMYTHE that Monmouth's musketeers and scythe men had finally met with a full frontal attack by the royal army of four thousand men in the hilly country just outside

Philipsnorton. It was a fierce bombardment that lasted for six hours and in which over a hundred perished. Fatal injuries had included skulls being cleaved in half, scattering blood and brain, guts torn out with bayonets, and cannon fire ripping clean through a man's body from front to back.

But Ned had written to Bess again from Bridgewater to assure her that he and Thomas were unharmed. They had spent a miserable night on the wet moors en route from Wells, where they'd quartered in the cathedral and taken lead from the roof to make bullets while they awaited a promised horde of thousands of club men, armed with flails and bludgeons. These reinforcements had, in the end, numbered less than two hundred.

"It does not look good for them now, does it?" Bess said, clutching Ned's letter to her.

It looked far worse when John Smythe came to report that the reprisals had already begun, that royal dragoons and horse guards had been ransacking rebel properties and had begun hanging prisoners at Pensford. When we learned that the royal army had set up an encampment outside Westonzoyland on Sedgemoor, with all roads and bridges secured, I sent Bess home to wait with Sam and her mother.

RICHARD RODE INTO BRISTOL FOR NEWS. The first account to be had of the battle was fragmentary and scant. But because the end came on Sedgemoor, a land so like Tickenham land, because the strategic points were rhynes and bridges and flat, muddy, mist-shrouded water meadows, I could picture it all too clearly.

Monmouth had moved his troops out of Bridgewater late in the evening of the fifth of July. The plan had been for the rebel infantry to launch a surprise attack at night, destroying the King's forces. In the summer fog they had marched in a silent column round Chedzoy, to form in line and advance across the deep Bussex Rhyne toward the red tents of the royal encampment. But the King's forces were alerted by a stray musket shot and set up a volley of cannon fire that went on across the rhyne all through the night.

The rebels didn't stand a chance. The horse guards came over the Lower Plungeon River with their sabers and attacked Monmouth's men to the right, and the Oxford Blues came over the Upper Plungeon on Monmouth's left flank. By dawn the rebel army was beginning to crumble. They were pursued across the moor and cut down by horsemen on all sides, slaughtered in cornfields and ditches. It was more massacre than battle. Over a thousand were dead and three hundred taken prisoner. Monmouth himself was found asleep in a drain, dressed in the clothes of a peasant. Only the star of the Order of the Garter gave away his identity.

There was no way of knowing yet if Ned and Thomas were amongst those wounded or captured, no way of knowing even whether they were alive or dead. We just had to wait until they and the other Tickenham men came home.

Or until they did not.

Bess did not sleep for waiting. She kept a rushlight burning at the window of her little cottage all night to guide Ned and Thomas if they should be making their weary way home, and for much of the time she sat beside the light, keeping watch for them. It was almost a superstition, I think. If she kept the light burning they could not have perished. If she let the light go out, if she turned her back on the window, she was abandoning them, abandoning hope.

She kept up her vigil even when we heard that five hundred rebels, many of them wounded, had been rounded up on Sedgemoor and herded into the parish church at Westonzoyland. She waited even when we knew that many had been hanged outside the church in chains, and when more still were hanged without trial in Bridgewater and Taunton.

She carried on waiting for Ned and Thomas to return even when the local constables were ordered to report on all those who had been absent from home during the time of the rebellion, when she knew that mancatchers were offered five shillings for every rebel they handed over. When neighbor was pitched against neighbor in a way that even we who had been born into civil war would hardly have imagined possible.

Richard found me standing at the chamber window, looking out over the empty moonlit causeway, thinking of Bess doing the same. "If you care about her and this family at all," he said, coming to stand beside me, "the best you can hope for is that Ned and Thomas Knight, John Hort and the rest of them all died a hero's death in battle and never return."

"How can you say that?" I rounded on him. "How can you be so heartless?"

I saw him struggle to control himself. "If they come back here they will endanger the lives of their families, or whoever harbors them under their roof or so much as offers them a crust of bread. You should not need to be reminded that jails all across the West Country are crammed with those suspected of sympathizing with the rebellion, as well as with the men who were known to have been in the infantry. You know as well as I that hundreds are being exhorted to confess, under pretense of pardon, and then being condemned to death without trial."

"I have known these men all my life. Ned has a son, a wife. Don't you care . . ."

He took me by my shoulders and pulled me round to face him. "I am not heartless, Nell. Do not say that I am heartless. Just tell me this. What does Bess plan to do if her prayers and best hopes are fulfilled and Ned and Thomas do come home? How does she plan to hide them and keep them from the constables and the mancatchers?"

"I have not asked her."

He looked deep into my eyes. "Give me your word that if she tries to bring them here, you will not take them in."

When I did not reply, his grip tightened on my shoulders until it hurt, until I could feel his nails digging into my flesh. "Bailiffs are seizing the property of sympathizers as forfeiture to the crown. I thought you loved this house, this land. Do you want to have it taken from you? Destroyed?"

"Of course not."

"I do not want to see you reduced to living in want and in fear," he said quietly. "I do not want to see you hungry and cold and sick and unhappy. I do not want you to die of a broken heart in a filthy charity hospital."

I took hold of both his hands, held them tight. His face was so careworn that it tore at my heart. "That is not going to happen," I said. "Do you hear me?"

He looked at me in silence, as if he had not heard me at all. "Your word, Nell. Give it to me."

I gave one small, imperceptible nod, doubting that I should ever be put to the test. With each day that passed, it seemed less likely that we would be faced with the problem of what to do with Tickenham's rebels if they should come home.

Autumn

1685

It was nearly five weeks after the battle on Sedgemoor when I was woken in the middle of the night by Bess, standing at the side of the bed with a candle, oblivious to the hot wax that was about to spill all over her hand. "It's Thomas," she cried, with quiet urgency. "You have to help me."

Richard stirred, rolled over onto his stomach. He put out his arm as if to try to find me and his eyelids fluttered, but he did not wake. With a guilty glance at his peaceful sleeping face, I slipped quickly from the warmth of our bed, letting the hangings ripple shut behind me. I grabbed Bess's arm and pulled her with me out of the chamber, closing the door softly after us.

She was shaking, her face blotched from crying. "He is badly wounded." She was struggling, in her distress, to keep her voice to a whisper. "He was shot in his side and I think his arm is broken. Ned is . . ." She broke down and sobbed.

I put my arms around her heaving shoulders. "Bess, are you sure?"

"Tom was with him," she rasped. "He saw the bayonet go right through . . . Ned's chest. He still has the blood all over his shirt." She made an effort to calm herself. "Tom will die too, if we don't help him."

"Where is he?"

"Below stairs. The hall. My father said we should bring Tom here. He said you would know what to do, how to treat the wounds. I've told my father to wait outside. To keep a lookout."

"Good," I said, with a glance back at the chamber door, wishing a sentry could be posted there too, in case Richard should wake, to keep him from knowing how I was deceiving him.

Bess had propped her brother on the settle, but he was so weak and sick that he had slumped over, his eyes closed and his breathing fitful. His clothes were ragged and filthy. He had grown a thick beard and mustache, and the rest of his face was so ingrained with dirt as to render him almost unrecognizable.

Bess ran to him, crouched down on the floor beside him and stroked his mud-caked hair. She held the candle for me while I moved him as gently as I could to examine the injury.

"Someone has removed the missile and debris and tried to bandage him," I said. "They must have been too afraid to let him stay."

The cloths needed changing; they were bloody and stinking and had stuck to his skin. He barely winced as I eased them away, though the pain must have been great. The wound underneath showed no sign of healing, was suppurating, still gaping and ragged and oozing fresh blood and yellow pus. I turned away and covered my mouth, trying not to retch. The pale bone of his rib was almost visible through the mess. He was so thin that the rest of his ribs were scarcely better covered.

"It needs stitching," I said. "Warm some water and fetch some lint and vinegar, my strongest silk thread and needle, and a large measure of Bristol milk . . . make that three. I'll light the fire and mix up an ointment."

"He needs a surgeon," Bess said.

I shook my head. "We cannot risk it. Besides, I have more faith in my mother's remedy book than ever I have had in surgeons."

I tipped Thomas's head back and made him drink the sherry, threw a hefty dose down my own throat, handed the glass to Bess. "Drink," I ordered. "You're going to need it." I gave Thomas a cloth to bite on, so he would not make a noise when he cried out. With Bess still holding the candle, angling it to give the best possible light, I took a deep breath and tried to stop my hands from trembling as I drew together the jagged edges of the skin as well as I could. The feeling of needle going through flesh was horrible, and never before had I wished I was more skilled at needlework. But I sewed as neatly as I could, suturing the wound and leaving an orifice for it to drain before rebandaging.

I turned my attention to Thomas's left arm next. It was hanging limp and was badly misshapen just above the elbow. With a glance at his half-conscious face, I put my hands either side of the fracture and did my best to jerk it straight. There was a ghastly sensation of crunching, but if there was any sound it was masked by Thomas's scream. Bess clamped her hand over his mouth until his eyes ceased rolling in their sockets. I bound the arm to a splint of kindling wood.

"What do we do now?" Bess asked, her eyes darting toward me as we changed Thomas into one of Richard's clean shirts that she had fetched from the laundry and she trickled water between her brother's parched lips. "Where can he go? My cottage is the first place they will look and there is nowhere for him to hide in my father's, either. Someone will see him. He will be found immediately."

"I know what you are asking of me, Bess, and I cannot do it."

"If you won't do it for Thomas, then do it for me, for my father and mother."

"I am a mother too," I reminded her. "I am a mother of two children who need me. For their sake, I cannot risk a traitor's death." I did not mention Richard, who had expressly forbidden me to have any contact with the rebels, and who would surely see what I was doing now as traitorous to him and to our marriage.

"The constable will not come knocking at this door," Bess said.

"I cannot guarantee that. And even if he does not, there's plenty who'd betray us for a bounty of five shillings."

"Your father would have been the first to join the Duke of Monmouth," Bess pleaded desperately. "He'd have gone into battle with Thomas and Ned, you know it. He might have met his death on Sedgemoor, or he might have survived and needed somewhere to hide, someone to take a risk and save him from the gallows. He would not have turned Tom away, in the most dire need, when he had been fighting for the cause. Your father would have been prepared to sacrifice his own life for that cause."

"He did sacrifice his own life for it," I said a little harshly. "And so left me all alone. I would not sacrifice my life so readily when there are two children depending on me."

"Then I'll tell you why you should help Thomas." We looked up and saw Arthur Knight standing by the doorway. "Mistress Glanville," he said to me quietly, "if you turn Thomas out this night and do not help him, you are abandoning your own flesh and blood."

"What do you mean?"

"Thomas is your half brother."

"That is a low trick, Arthur."

"I swear it is no trick."

"I'll not believe it. My father would be the last person to . . ."

"Tom is not your father's son. He is your mother's."

"No." I shook my head. "No." But it was an instinctive response, and even as I gave it, I knew that what Arthur Knight had said must be true. The disparaging comments his wife had made about my mother, my father's dying words about the base desires and carnality of women.

"It was when she was engaged to be married to your father," Arthur Knight began clumsily. "She had always had a . . . a fondness for me. She preferred the company of ordinary folk, had a great love for the people of this estate. She had no time for fine, false gentlemen, she said, or for parties and balls. She liked to be out on the moor, chattering to me while I cut the sedges and taught her to recognize the plants and birds. We never spoke of love. We did not need to. But of course, it could not be. And then . . . Thomas. It was kept very quiet. She went away for a while, to your father's relatives in Ribston, where he set out to redeem her. He would not let her keep the baby. But my wife loved me enough to love my son, even if he was the child of another woman. Pride made her refuse any payment, though your father did offer it."

If I wanted to know why my father was so zealous, here was one answer. He'd feared that my mother's sins proved her unworthy, that she was not one of the Puritan elect, was not destined for salvation but was condemned. And I too, since I was of the female line.

After a silence it was Bess who asked: "Does Tom know?"

"Yes," I answered, on Arthur Knight's behalf. "Thomas has always known. That's why he has always despised me. That is why he told me once that I had stolen from him. Why he looks at me so covetously. He is my mother's only son. If he was not base born, Tickenham Court would be all his."

"We didn't intend to tell him," Arthur said hurriedly. "But he was ill with a fever. Your mother came to the cottage then, insisted on nursing him herself day and night. It seemed certain he would die and she asked if she might tell him the truth. I think he would have half guessed it anyway, from the way she was with him. Your mother loved Tom," Arthur Knight insisted. "She saved his life with her care. She would want you to save it now, with yours."

I could not take it in. Did not have time to take it in now. All those years I'd thought I had nobody, I had a brother, living not half a mile away. A brother who hated me, who had threatened me, led a riot to my door to torch my house. Because to his mind, but for an accident of birth, it should have been his. What was mine should all have belonged to him. But I did not have time to dwell on such thoughts. I had to act, to make a decision. "All right," I said hastily. "He can stay. Just until he is stronger. Help me move him."

His father sat beside him and hooked one of Thomas's arms around my shoulders, stood and hauled him up between us.

"Where to?" he asked.

"This way. Quickly, before anyone wakes."

I supported Thomas's other arm, wedging my shoulder beneath his armpit. Bess took his feet and together we half lifted, half dragged him over to the great fireplace.

"Put him down here," I said.

"Here?"

"Just do as I say."

They did.

I lifted up the candle, ran my fingers over the wall at the side of the fireplace, dug my fingers into the crack in the wainscoting and heaved. The oak panel swung open like the small door it was, to reveal a niche cut deep into the side of the massive chimney breast, just large enough to hide one man, possibly two. "It is not very comfortable," I said. "But it is warm and dry and, except for me and now the two of you, nobody who lives here even knows it exists."

Bess peered inside doubtfully.

"It was constructed for just such a purpose," I told her.

"It's a priest hole," Arthur Knight said with wonder. "Where they hid Catholics during the Reformation."

"Ironic, really." I smiled. "Given that Thomas is here because he tried to get rid of a Catholic king."

"How did you know it was here?" Bess asked.

"My mother told Mary Burges and she told me to look for it,

which I did, a long time ago." I shone the candle into a low recess in the thick wall. As I crouched down and crawled in, my chest tightened with the primal fear of confinement.

We eased Thomas in and I made him as comfortable as I could, with a straw pallet and blankets and pillows to support his head.

"Do you think you could bear to stay with him, in case he wakes?" I said to Bess, knowing I was asking her to do something I was not at all sure I'd have been able to do myself. "If he cries out he will endanger us all."

Bess nodded fearfully. She squeezed herself up against the wall, took her brother's hand. Her half brother, I reminded myself. My half brother. It was so odd to think that Thomas was as much my kin as he was Bess's. We were both his sisters, which made it feel almost as if she and I were related, were sisters too, as I had always felt that we were.

I brought a jug of ale, a plate of bread and cheese, and some custard tarts, as well as a chamber pot, a small stool and a spare candle. "That should see you through until I can come back again tomorrow night," I said. "Is there anything else you want me to fetch?"

Bess shook her head, then grabbed my arm as I turned to crawl back out and leave them. "Thank you," she said. "I know what a risk you are taking for us."

"We are all taking the most terrible risk, Bess. By sheltering a man who, in the eyes of the law, is guilty of treason, we are committing treason too. If we should be caught we will burn, or hang, or be beheaded as enemies of the crown. You do realize that?"

"What else could we do?"

I fitted the paneling back in place and had rested my back against it, glanced up into the dark stairwell to where Richard must still have been sleeping, oblivious of what I had done. Arthur Knight touched my arm, as if he was too overcome with gratitude to speak. "It is nearly dawn," I said to him. "Go home, before anyone sees you here."

I walked weakly up the stairs. Only when I sat on the edge of the bed did I realize my legs were trembling uncontrollably. I felt sick, sick to my stomach and sick to my heart. I made myself take long, deep breaths, like I did when I was ill whilst carrying Forest. I realized then I had been feeling sick on and off for days, that my monthly was late. How late? I saw that my nightgown was stained with Thomas's blood and with sudden horror tore it off, bundled it up and pushed it under the bed. I climbed naked under the sheets and nestled up close to Richard, resting my cold cheek against the smooth dark hairs on his warm chest. He stirred, gathered me into his arms and turned onto his side. I felt his cock probing my belly, stiff as a cudgel. He found my hand, guided it down and I wrapped my fingers around him.

He sucked his breath in with a hiss. "Hell's teeth, where have you been, Nell? Your fingers are icy. It's all right," he added quickly, with a smile in his voice, grabbing me as I went to withdraw my hand. "I don't mind if you warm them on me."

He mounted me, looked down into my eyes with love and desire and I felt so deceitful, was so sure that he would read my deception, was so afraid of having him read it, that I averted my face.

He froze.

I turned back to him, saw his hurt. "Richard, I need to tell you something," I said. But he tensed, as if he suspected what it might be, and the words lodged in my throat.

At my sudden silence, he pushed up on his arms, pinning me beneath him, his hipbones jutting painfully into my belly. "I am listening," he said.

I felt totally trapped. How could I keep such a dangerous secret from him? How could I tell him the truth when I had already broken my word to him? I could not tell him Thomas was my half brother when I could scarce comprehend it myself.

"I feel sick," I said feebly but truthfully. "Let me up."

He released me, sat with me as I gulped deep breaths, waiting until I looked to be recovered before he pressed me again. "What is it that you need to tell me, Nell?"

I rested my hand on my belly. "Nothing," I said. "It was nothing." I could not even tell him that I thought I might be carrying his child.

"I heard at the inn last night that Monmouth has been executed at Tower Hill," he said quietly. "It is over now. Thank God, it is all over."

But I knew, by the way he hurled back the covers, that he had seen, rightly, that I could not share his relief, not at all, and that he believed, wrongly, that it was because I wished the outcome had been different.

I ASSUMED THAT Richard had gone for a swim. It was not the first time that he had been driven out of the warmth of our bed to the coldness of the sea, as if by unnamed demons he could only seem to banish with an early morning dunking in the waves. I had tried not to dwell on what it was that he seemed to need to wash away after he had lain with me, what he needed to cool, to exorcise, but this time I knew all too well, and this time it did not seem to have worked. Previously he had always returned before I was even dressed, but now it was mid-morning and still he was not back.

I took Mary to fly her kite on the moor, anything to be out of that house, where my eyes constantly drifted to the panel by the fireplace in the great hall.

"Higher," Mary kept begging. "Higher." And I reeled the kite out further, shielding my eyes to watch it soar into the infinite blue as still it tugged and tugged against its tether to be free. Then the wind suddenly dropped and it plummeted to the ground, landed with a crash that I felt in my very bones.

Mary ran with it and threw it into the sky, but it was not quite windy enough to get it properly airborne again. I suggested to the children that we ride out to Ladye Bay, but I did not find Richard there as once I had done. I sat on the cliff top and watched Mary and Forest down on the beach, skimming flat pebbles across the waves. Gulls screamed, the sound harsh and desolate, and I felt a first prickle of fear. What if, in his anger, Richard had swum out too far, had not been as alert as he should have been to the currents and the undertow? I tried not to think of how he could have been dragged out to sea, his body hurled against the rocks.

I tried not to think of the treason trials that were already under way, but now that I myself was amongst the guilty, all that I had read in the gazettes over the past weeks seemed suddenly very vivid.

The trials had begun in earnest at Dorchester, where three hundred and forty were brought to court accused of rebellion. They were pipe makers and yeomen, tailors and butchers and merchants, ordinary men who'd had no real craving for another revolution. To serve as the most awful warning to all would-be rebels, many of the condemned were to be taken down from the gallows before they were quite dead, to have their entrails drawn out of them and their bodies butchered. And so that none would miss out on the spectacle, these most gruesome of executions were taking place at crossroads and marketplaces and village greens all across the West Country. Heads and limbs were being boiled in salt and tarred for preservation and public display. The streets of Somersetshire were running with blood again, and it seemed to me that even here the very air reeked of decomposing corpses.

The danger of discovery seemed greater now that the Assizes had come closer, to Wells. Of the five hundred and forty arraigned, five hundred and eighteen were accused of levying war against the King. The fortunate ones were sentenced to transportation to the plantations of Barbados and Jamaica. A hundred were to be hanged, as widely as possible, in Wells and in Bath. And at Bristol.

My eye was caught by a tawny and black butterfly, and my mind latched on to it, my time-honored salvation from sorrow and distress. The wing patterns were subtly but crucially different from those on the Marsh Fritillaries that frequented the moor and a Straw May Fritillary that James had once drawn for me. They were redder. This one was more orange and had unusual white-and-black-spotted tips to the forewings. There was another, just the same, just as different from all the Fritillaries I had seen before, on the wing or even on paper. I swiped at it almost angrily and felled it, stowed it away in the pocket I wore fastened round my waist, called down to the children that we were going home.

I was sitting on the window seat, watching the mist curling off the river, when Richard finally stumbled in, none too steady on his feet.

"Where have you been?" I asked him.

"Bristol," he offered too readily, his voice slightly slurred. He unbuckled his sword, threw it down with a clatter on the table. "The talk there is all of the treason trials. People are calling them the Bloody Assizes."

"Please, Richard. Not now."

He came to stand over me. "Where are they, Nell?" he said very low.

"Who?"

"You know damn well who. Ned Tucker and Thomas Knight. Do you take me for a fool? That is what you almost told me this morning, isn't it? You know where they are, don't you?"

"No." The lie had come to my lips of its own volition.

He said no more, nor did he move. He seemed to be waiting for me to reconsider, for me to say something else. When I did not, he flung the latest copy of the gazette at me, called for Bess to bring him a bath in front of the chamber fire.

My eyes strayed to the print. Tentatively, I reached out my hand and picked up the newssheet. What I read made me tremble so much I had to rest it out on my lap to finish it.

Chief Justice Jeffreys and his judges are determined to show no mercy to the harborers of fugitives. Lady Alice Lisle, widow of a man who had sat on the High Court of Justice, was accused of sheltering an escaped rebel, a dissenting minister, who had not even been tried himself. At any sign of sympathy Judge Jeffreys swore and cursed in a language no well-bred man would use at a cockfight, and he decreed that Widow Lisle should receive the only sentence possible for a woman condemned for high treason, that she was to be burned alive. Ladies of high rank tried to intercede and a plea for mercy was made by no less than the Duke of Clarendon, the King's own brother. On account of the widow's age, the sentence was commuted from burning to beheading and Lady Lisle was put to death on the scaffold in the marketplace at Winchester. She suffered her fate with serenity and courage.

After a while, I don't know how long, I made myself go up to Richard. He had undressed and climbed into the steaming, scented water. He was resting against the linen-draped back of the tub, arms extended along the sides, his eyes shut, dark lashes casting little shadows over his cheeks in the firelight. His black curls framed his pale face, lovely as a seraph's. I knelt at the side of the tub, leaned over and kissed his closed lids, felt the lashes brush my lips.

He opened his eyes languorously, looked at me questioningly, sadly, and I was so near to confiding in him, so longed to confide in him. And the reason I did not quite dare was not that I did not love him enough, but that I loved him too much and the thought of losing him, of having him be angry with me and disappointed in me, was utterly intolerable.

In silence I ladled water over his head, soaped his back for him. I rubbed the tension from his shoulders with my fingers. I dried his hair with fresh linen. I acted the part of a dutiful and devoted wife, when I had so betrayed my husband that I had put both our lives in jeopardy.

LIKE THE CONSPIRATOR I was, I waited for darkness, waited until Richard was safely sleeping, and then I slid from the warmth of his arms and of our bed, creeping down the drafty stone stairwell to mix up an ointment of egg yolk, oil of roses and turpentine. I pulled back the oak panel, ducked through into the cramped little cell and tried not to gag at the smell that had tainted the confined air.

Bess was sitting on the little stool beside her brother, my brother. "How is he?"

"Awake, at least. He has taken a little bread and some cheese."

Thomas's narrow eyes flared feral and dark in the gloom, like a wounded, cornered animal. My mother's son. I did not think I should ever be able to think of him in those terms.

"Hello, Thomas." I knelt down beside him, carefully lifted his shirt to examine him.

His skin glistened with sweat.

"He has a fever," Bess said.

"It is poison from the wound."

"Shouldn't he be bled?"

I shook my head. "From the look of him, he has already lost enough blood."

I started to remove the bandages, but he grabbed hold of my wrist with startling strength.

I looked at him. "I'm sorry if I hurt you."

"Why are you helping me?" He looked at me with the black eyes of my son: Forest's eyes, proud and antagonistic and hungry. I knew now it was no coincidence that they looked so alike. This man was my son's uncle.

"I am helping you for Bess's sake. And because of what your father told me," I said matter-of-factly. "But don't worry." I smiled wryly. "I'll not expect you to suddenly start showering me with brotherly affection." I twisted my arm free and carried on with my task. "Now, I have to change your bandages, and I would advise you to hold still or it will hurt even more."

FOR THE FIRST TIME in years I had an urge to write to James Petiver. Though he was the very last person to boast of his abilities, I knew he was as skilled as any surgeon and as many a physician. I craved his advice and reassurance, needed to know that I was treating Thomas's wound properly, doing all I could possibly do to speed his recovery and hasten the day when he was fit enough to leave Ticken-ham for a safer refuge.

I was at my writing table, composing the letter. There was no way of knowing if it might be intercepted and I could not risk implicating James in any way, so I was searching for a way to ask him indirectly about the treatment of deep wounds when Richard surprised me. "Who is James?" he asked coldly, catching the salutation.

Guiltily, I whipped my arm across the letter to shield its contents from him, for all the world as if it had been a secret love letter.

"Who is he, Nell?"

I must have seemed to be behaving so oddly these past days that I did not blame him at all for being suspicious. "James is a butterfly collector," I said. "I have corresponded with him for years. About butterflies," I added unnecessarily.

"The constable is here," he said darkly. "Along with two lackeys armed with muskets."

I felt as if I had been wounded, so mortally that the blood was draining very quickly from my head and from my legs. At a loss as to what else to do with it, I folded the letter very small and pushed it down the tight-boned bodice of my dress. Then I walked to the door and greeted the constable, trying to appear as if I had nothing to hide, nothing at all to fear.

I knew John Piggott, a stocky, florid, self-important little man who strode about the village sticking his purple-veined nose where it was not wanted. He was clearly enjoying the even more elevated position of power he had with two armed men to accompany him.

"How can we help you, Mr. Piggott?" I had not quite stilled the tremor in my voice.

"Routine inspection," he said self-righteously, stepping past me, out of the steadily falling rain and into the hall, his hands clasped behind his back. He pulled himself up straight and glanced around as if to show he meant business. "We're on the hunt for that scoundrel Thomas Knight. He's not shown up as yet in the prisons or on the death roll." He pushed his face up closer to mine. "Not seen him by any chance, have you, Ma'am?"

I shook my head, my mouth dry as ash. A cold bead of sweat trickled down my back. I glanced at Richard. His jaw was clenched and a muscle in his cheek began to twitch. He had not taken his eyes off me, was watching me even more closely than was the constable.

"This would be the last place Thomas Knight would come," I managed. "As you know, it was not so long ago that he led a mob up here and threatened to set fire to the house, while my children were asleep in their beds."

"His sister's still your maid though, isn't she? Wouldn't mind having a word with her, if she's about?"

"She's in the dairy. But she'll not be able to tell you any more than I have. Her brother is not here, nor has he ever been."

"Forgive me if I don't take your word for it, Madam. I'll have a look around the place, if I may."

I stood back as they swarmed all over the house, searching every room. They threw open the doors of the court cupboard and turned over tables, pulled the tapestries off the walls and dragged drapes down from the windows. I heard their boots stamping about upstairs and sounds that indicated they were throwing up the lid of every chest, opening every garderobe, jabbing their muskets under every bed. Next they turned their attention to the new stables and the hayloft and the pigsty and the chicken shed, kicking at hay bales, upending feeding troughs.

All the time Richard watched not the constable and his men but me, as if the wanton destruction of our property was nothing compared with what I had so wantonly destroyed.

Little Mary ran to me and tried to hide herself in my skirts. "Why is the constable here, Mama?"

I stroked her hair and did not let myself think of what would happen to her if they found something now, or later, that gave me away. I did not let myself think what would happen to my children if their mother and stepfather died as traitors.

John Piggott came back to the hall, breathless and frustrated. "Your maid broke down at mention of her brother's name. Either she is grief-stricken or guilt-stricken, but I can get no sense out of her at all. Maybe we'll pay a call on the old Knight woman and her husband again."

"Leave them be," I said. "They know nothing. Have given their son up for dead."

"Right they are." Mr. Piggott snorted. "He won't be able to hide forever. If he's not dead already, he'll be swinging by his neck soon enough."

They left us amidst the upheaval. I stroked Mary's head and told her it was all over now, even though I knew it was not.

"I never knew you had such a talent for lying," Richard said darkly. "You were very convincing. Except that I can read your face like a page in a book. You did not convince me at all."

Mary clung so close to me that she trod on the hem of my skirt and I could not move. Richard thrust his hand roughly down the front of my bodice, his nails scratching me, and retrieved my half-written letter to James. I tried to grab it off him but he turned his back on me, fluttered it high out of my reach as he read. When he had done, he screwed the letter into a tight ball, opened his fist and dropped it to the floor. "Show me where you keep him."

Holding Mary gently away from me, I turned and walked very calmly to the fireplace. I was almost relieved to have it done with now, for the secret to be out, but my heart was hammering so hard I was sure it would burst through my rib cage. I glanced at Richard as I dug my fingers into the wainscoting and pulled back the entrance to the priest hole, standing aside to let him enter, just as Bess came running into the great hall.

Richard made no sound at all, stared down at Thomas, who lay on the soiled pallet, shielding his eyes from the sudden burst of light. As if he had seen more than enough and was suffocating, Richard staggered back out of the enclosure.

He went to the window, raised his arm and leaned against the lintel to steady himself. He balled his hand into a fist and smashed it into the rough stone above his head with a ferocity that made me flinch. "I always knew there was something between you and that sprat," he growled, turning to me. "I'll bet he's enjoyed having you sneaking down to his grubby little lair to minister to him in the middle of the night. I'll bet you've both enjoyed it. Well, I shall see to it that you enjoy it no more. Or rather, John Piggott will see to it. By making sure Knight swings. If you do not want to join him, I suggest you turn him out now, so that he is far enough away from here by the time he is caught."

I did not dare to dismiss it as an idle threat. I had never seen Richard so angry. I knew that he was hurt, desperately hurt, and was not a person to manage such emotions easily. He was liable to lash out, to do something rash that he might later regret.

He was already at the door, had banged it closed behind him.

I came to my senses, leapt to my feet, hurled the door open again. "You are right," I called after him. "There *is* something between me and Thomas."

He halted, spun round to face me.

It was still raining, a cold, gray rain that was fast turning the ground outside the house into a sea of mud. His hair was already wet and he did not have coat or cloak. I walked toward him, oblivious of the deepening puddles, soaking the hem of my silk gown.

"There always has been something between me and Thomas," I said, having to raise my voice above the hammering of the rain. "Only I never knew it until a few nights ago, when his father told me, in order to persuade me to give him shelter rather than turn him out as I had fully intended to do. Richard, Thomas is my half brother. My mother's illegitimate son."

He looked at me as if he didn't believe me.

"It is perfectly true, sir," Bess said from behind me.

"I beg you, Richard, let him go. You have no cause to be jealous of Thomas. He was born first, and born a boy, but I have Tickenham

Court while he has nothing. Because of that he hates me, has always hated me."

"But still you would beg me to spare his life?"

"He is my brother," I said, giving weight to the word. "He is Bess's brother."

The rain fell like a shroud between us. The anger had gone from Richard's face, and had been replaced by . . . nothing. There was an emptiness in his eyes, a deadness, as if my deception had killed something in him.

He turned from me, toward the stables and his horse.

"IT IS NOT SAFE for Thomas to stay here," I told Bess. "Not for any of us."

"Mr. Glanville will not betray us?"

"No," I said, my voice faltering. "He will not. He had a brother once. He knows what it is to lose one. He will not bring about the death of yours and mine. But the constable will not give up."

"Tom is not strong enough to ride."

"I know he is not. You must take the cart for him to lie in. But you must leave, Bess. As soon as it is dark."

Like smugglers with an illegal cargo, we bundled Thomas into the cart under cover of night. We laid down straw to muffle the sound of wheels on the cobbles and wrapped rags around the horses' hooves. We used more straw and blankets to cushion the cart and make Thomas as warm and comfortable as possible.

I packed up a basket of bread and cheese, cold meat and fruit, and gave Bess all the coins I had in my pocketbook.

"Where will you go?" I asked her, as she climbed onto the seat of the cart and took up the reins.

"The same place you run to whenever you are in trouble," she said bravely. "To Mary and John Burges in Hackney. Nobody will ever find us there, or think to look for us, even. Mary and John will help us."

They would, even though they were Catholic and Thomas had been wounded for his hatred of them. They would help him because they were good people, who offered love and respect to every person, no matter their creed or character. "You take care, Bess," I said with a glance at Thomas. I hoped he survived long enough for me to have at least some time in which to adjust to our new-discovered relationship.

Once the cart had trundled out of the yard, I wasted no time in dragging the soiled pallet out of the priest hole and into the stable. I rolled up my sleeves and brought a bucket of water and a cloth. I bunched my silk skirts beneath my knees on the dirty floor and I scrubbed and scrubbed at that incommodious little hole, as if I could scrub away all that had happened. It was almost daybreak when I was satisfied that all evidence of Thomas's presence there was obliterated. Almost daybreak, and still Richard had not come back. I was sure he must have gone to the inn at Bristol, taken a room there for the night. There was only one thing to do, I decided. If he was not coming home to me, I would go to him. I would beg his forgiveness, fetch him back. It was my fault and I would put it right.

The children ran out into the yard as I mounted my horse, and Forest asked me where I was going.

"To Bristol, darling. I will not be long."

"Are you going to see the hangings?" he asked with a hint of glee that was, I knew, prompted by his devotion to Richard, whose enemies the hanged men had been. "I heard the servants talking," he qualified. "It is to be today."

"I am not going to see the hangings, Forest." I gave a jerk on my mare's reins, then spun back. "You didn't happen to hear where in Bristol, exactly?"

He shook his head.

I knew well before I reached the city walls that I had come the wrong way. A pall of death hung over the wide new streets. Bristol was the richest port of trade in Britain, with the exception of London, but the usual bustle and color of it were sadly diminished. People walked by with faces downcast and gloomy. The sledges drawing the heavy goods and the merchants in their fine coaches did not seem to be going about their business with the same zest. I rode up toward the Redcliffe Gate, toward the church where Richard and I were married. I had paid no attention then to the oddly truncated tower that had famously been struck by lightning over a hundred years ago and never rebuilt, but now it seemed ill-omened. As ill-omened as the crack in the tablet of commandments in the church where I'd married Edmund, or as Monmouth's rebellion beginning during the celebrations for my second wedding.

The ghastly structure of the gallows cast its shadow over Redcliffe Hill. Six executions had taken place, only six, a small fraction of the number being put to death all across the west. But they made a grisly display, hanging from the noose, with their tongues dark and lolling, their breeches stained with the final voiding of their bowels and bladders, their faces contorted into fixed, grotesque grimaces. A punishment as horrible as any you could find in Hell. All the more terrible because I knew it could have been me swinging from that crossbeam, could still be the punishment that awaited me for what I had done.

I rode across the bridge over the Avon, saw the docks spiked with masts of the ships that had blown into port from the Caribbean and the tropics, the scent of adventure still in their sails, and a part of me wished that I could just sail away with them. I rode on toward the elegant new houses on King Street that had been built for the merchants in the tamed marsh area by the quayside. Past the Merchant Venturers' Hall and opposite the almshouses was a row of half-timbered buildings with overhanging eaves and projecting gables.

The last building in the row was the Llandoger Trow, the inn I knew Richard had frequented on the many past occasions when he had tried to see me and I had turned him away.

With its low blackened ceiling and sawdust-strewn floor, it was a rough sort of a place behind its grand façade, a dark place where it was not difficult to imagine dark deeds being done. Mr. Merrick had told me its position so close to the docks made it the haunt of slave traders and smugglers and pirates and it was easy to believe, judging by the gang of low characters sharing tankards of ale with my husband. He did not look particularly at ease amongst them, nor did he look particularly at ease with the buxom, brassy blonde who had her arm draped provocatively around his neck, but he was letting her keep it there.

I was torn between a desire to rush at her and scratch her eyes out and the need to turn away, to pretend I had not seen them together. For a moment I just watched them, unwilling and totally unable to go any closer, my mind in an agony of paralyzed confusion. She was expensively but gaudily dressed in a low-cut crimson gown, her face painted and patched. For all that, she looked like me, I realized, albeit a bigger and brasher version of me. She was not gentry, but clearly prosperous, the widow or daughter, wife even, of a merchant or a lawyer or a goldsmith. One of the new moneyed class who were gaining dominance and power in England, who understood the getting and the making of money and whose collective wealth already surpassed that of the impoverished nobility. A natural choice for a man who liked to be on the winning side, I thought bitterly. Merchants and lawyers were not ruined by bad harvests and unpaid rents. They were building new mansions instead of borrowing to repair crumbling ones.

There were enough women occupying the inn's benches to make my arrival relatively inconspicuous. Nobody paid me much attention, beyond pinching me as I made my way over. Richard saw me but did not acknowledge me, though the girl did. She sized me up, as if measuring me against her expectations and finding me even more negligible than she had imagined. She moved away, casting me a supercilious look. "You know where to find me if you want me," she said seductively to Richard, trailing her fingers along his chest.

"Do you want her, Richard?" I found myself asking, forcing the question through the tightness in my throat. "Or have you already satisfied your wanting?"

He called the landlady over to refill his pot. "Sarah is just a friend. As you say that butterfly collector is yours. Surely you can have no objection to that?"

"James and I became friends and have remained so because we share a common interest. What interest do you share with that trollop, I wonder?"

"Gaming," he said. "Sarah has a great liking for cards and dicing."

She was watching me with hatred, because I had him and she did not. He was a man to inspire the fiercest jealousy and I was afraid of the jealousy I saw in that woman's eyes. If Richard did not want her, I knew beyond a shadow of a doubt that she wanted him, very much, and with the inexplicable intuition that women have for the characters of other women, I sensed she had made it, or intended to make it, nigh on impossible for him to resist her. Given half a chance she would dig her claws into him and rip us apart. She was opportunistic, scheming, not at all kind. There was a hardness, an almost chilling coldness about her, which made me desperate to get us both far, far away from her. "She is not your friend, Richard," I said to him softly. "These people are not your friends."

He stared into his pot, swilled the ale, drank. "It seems I have no others."

"Oh, that is not true." I reached out to touch the back of his hand, thinking I had never known anyone to feel things so deeply, to take everything so personally. "I am your friend. I shall always, always be your friend. I would have told you about Thomas," I said. "I so wanted to tell you. I did not want to keep it from you. If only you had not become so embittered toward the rebels."

"If only you had not risked your life and mine to save one of them."

"You said you did not want to lose me," I said quietly, seeking his eyes. "Do not let this battle become our battle."

"It is you who have allowed that. It is you who harbored a traitor under our roof without telling me. Ah, but I forget. It is *your* roof, isn't it?"

I was stunned that he should bring that up now, and I shrank back a little from him. "Does that still rankle with you so much?"

"It rankles that I have a wife who cares so little for my wishes and feelings."

"If that is true, why am I here?"

"I don't know. Why are you?"

I knew that the best thing I could do was to say no more, to turn my back on him and walk away, and that is just what I did. With tears streaming down my face and my heart breaking, I mounted my horse and rode back down Redcliffe Hill, past the bodies of the executed rebels, swinging from the gibbet.

So much damage had been done to this county, I feared it would never recover. So much damage had been done to my marriage, I feared it would never recover either. I still had not told Richard I was carrying his child.

As I rode out past St. Mary Redcliffe Church, the low autumn sun appeared from behind a cloud. A butterfly fluttered beside me, the kind that James and I had named Tortoiseshells, with bright red-and-blue shining wings. This one, though, was faded and ragged, like most of its kind at the end of the summer. But it flitted along beside me for a while, playing on the breeze that blew in from the estuary.

For all its faded wings, it was a symbol of hope, and I always was very willing to let hope enter my heart. The butterfly reminded me that there was still brightness and beauty in the world. It reminded me how happy I had been on my wedding day, such a short time ago.

Judge Jeffreys was returning to London. The Bloody Assizes were over. These had been dark days for all who lived in Somersetshire, but maybe they were at an end. Maybe that battle of Sedgemoor would be the last we would see fought on England's soil for a while. Maybe Richard would find a way to lay past battles to rest, and I would find a way to win back his trust.

Anything was possible. Even that my husband would come galloping after me not long after I had passed through the city gates and turned onto the open road.

I heard the distant thud of a horse's hooves behind me, but I hardly dared to turn round and risk disappointment. I counted to ten, closed my eyes and made a quick wish, then glanced quickly over my shoulder and laughed with delight to see him, some way off still, his cloak flying behind him, the hooves of his stallion kicking up a small cloud of dust. I had just enough time to wipe away my tears and arrange the heavy skirts of my gown and cape so they draped most appealingly around me before he reined in alongside, the tumult causing my mount to sidle. I glanced at him out of the corner of my eye.

"Why did you not slow down, Nell?" he demanded, but good-humoredly. His dark mood had dispersed as completely as mist burned away by sunshine and he was all gentle, devastating charm again. It was very unnerving and exhilarating at the same time, like skating on melting ice. I had once lived such a dull and quiet life, but never would it be dull with him.

I gave him a sidelong smile. "I did not slow, but you will note that nor did I urge my horse into a gallop to try and outrace you. Not that I would now," I said meaningfully, resting a hand on my belly. "I must ride with care these next eight months."

There was a silence. "How long have you known?"

"Not long."

"Is that why you came to fetch me back? Because you are with child?"

I cocked my head, glanced at him sideways. "Well, it is true I would not rob another of my babies of the chance to know the man who had sired him," I said. "Nor would I wish to rob Forest of another father, after he has already lost one."

"I see."

I reached out, waited for him to do the same, felt his fingers catch mine and hold on.

"More pressing than that, love," I said, "is the fact that I cannot be another night without you."

He gave me his most raffish smile, and after a while he said, "Do you know what we should do?"

"What's that?"

"Some more shopping, I think. If you want to make absolutely sure I come home to you every night, we must see to it that your home is as inviting and pleasing as your own little person. And at present it is still as austere as a nun's cell."

Spring

1686

It troubled me that for some reason the news that I was carrying his child did not seem to make Richard nearly as happy as I had assumed it would. Where Edmund had anticipated the arrival of our children with real excitement, had been almost overly solicitous toward me and quietly so very proud, Richard did his utmost to ignore my pregnancy, even as my expanding belly made that increasingly difficult.

I remembered how longingly he had looked at me at Forest's baptism, how he had spoken with such yearning of the children it seemed then that we would never have. I remembered what a good father he had been to Edmund's son, and could make no sense of it at all. I wondered if deep down he was still upset with me, for the way I had shunned him after Edmund's death, for deceiving him by giving shelter to Thomas Knight. Or was it something else?

He had made no further mention of shopping, and I kept quiet about it. Even in the mid-stages of pregnancy, the last thing I needed was to be jolted in a coach all the way to London and back. I soon found out, though, that my husband had never intended for us to do our shopping as we had before, with an expedition to the New Exchange. His aborted foray with the militia had not been entirely unfruitful. It seemed that he'd spent most of the journey to Axminster talking to John Smythe about the new craze for bestowing money and labor on beautifying mansions and gardens.

"John's sister Florence has an eye for furnishing rooms with all that is being called modern," Richard told me as I hunted in a trunk for Forest's whipping top and little drum to pass down to the new baby. "But she does not waste time traipsing round to different merchants. She just sends a list of what she wants to an agent in London, a cousin who has room at the Inns of Court. He does all the buying for her and ships everything up here."

"How convenient." I stood and stretched, with my hands supporting the small of my aching back.

Richard caught me lovingly around my middle, but when he felt its growing girth, which had necessitated the loosening of the laces of my stomacher again, he let go of me just as swiftly, as if he did not want to be reminded. "I spoke to Florence some time ago and she kindly added some items for us to her list," he said. "She is sending them over later today."

"That's good." I watched his face. "Richard, you are glad we are going to have a baby?"

"Of course I am, sweetheart." But his eyes, sliding away from me, seemed to tell a different story.

DURING THE FOLLOWING WEEKS dozens of consignments of boxes arrived on wagons from Ashton Court, with Florence Smythe trotting over on her pretty mare to escort them, after which Richard escorted her round the house, his hand courteously upon her elbow as she pointed with her elegant, painted-leather gloved fingers to one wall or corner or another, suggesting where the new looking glass might hang or where the clock and French glassware and Chinese porcelain might stand.

As I watched them together I was surprised to feel a stirring of jealousy. I knew it had to do with the fact that something was not right between Richard and me, and that I did not know what it was or how to make it better. I found myself wondering about that woman in Bristol. Sarah. What was she to him? What had she been to him? All those years, when I had kept him from my bed and he had gone to find solace at that Bristol inn, had he comforted himself with more than just a bottle of rum? He must have done sometimes, if not with her, then with someone else. And why should he not? But had he continued to see her since we were married? Had he seen her again since I had discovered them together? No. I was quite sure the answer to those questions was no. I did not listen to the voice in my head that said: *How can you trust him? His morals are not your morals. He was raised amongst Cavaliers.*

I was at least sure that Florence Smythe was no threat whatsoever. She didn't consider it even worth flirting with anyone who was not of the highest rank, much as Richard clearly sought her regard, as, of course, he had always sought everyone's, male and female, yeoman and gentleman, simply because he needed so badly to be loved.

He looked over at me now, from where he stood beside the new japanned table at the far corner of the room. Florence was chattering away to him, but I could tell he was only half listening and his smile was for me alone. I smiled back. Rationalist that I was, doubter of magic, I'd have sworn there was magic in that smile of his. Just one smile and instantly all my worries were laid to rest. Just one smile, and all was well with the world once more.

I ran my hands over a pretty toilet set, comprising a mirror and basket and candlesticks set in silver with scenes of chinoiserie. I had always wanted to see these rooms filled with bright and pretty things.

It was worth mortgaging some of our land to have silk quilts and striped muslin curtains, worth being indebted to the Gorgeses of Wraxall as well as to William Merrick for a house filled with silk damask arm-chairs and stools with tapestry cushions. I tried not to worry too much about the growing tangle of credit and mortgages within which Rich-ard was enmeshing us. We could afford them, he said we could. As long as the rents kept rolling in and the harvests were good and the fisheries prospered. After the recent upheavals, nobody had the stom-ach even to mention drainage.

Florence stayed for tea served from the new silver tea service.

"John said you were considering remodeling the house and garden," she said to my husband, sipping politely from her cup. "You could turn your great hall into a stylish entrance lobby, and your land is positively crying out for vistas and terraces and avenues and a fountain."

"What need have we for a fountain when for half the year we have a whole lake to look at?" I asked, a bit alarmed at the prospect of such expensive and grandiose schemes.

She shrugged and stood to leave. "Well, be sure to let me know what else you want."

Richard assured her that he would.

"We should have asked for more mirrors," I said to him when she had gone. I loved the way that, even propped against the wall, waiting to be hung, they filled the rooms with light and made them look as if they went on and on. I studied my own silvery reflection, framed by gilded carving, then turned sideways and stroked the luminous folds of my saffron gown where it fell over my rounded stomach. "I could fill the whole house with mirrors," I added. "If only it did not mean I should be confronted with my great belly at every turn."

Richard came to stand behind me, slipped his arms over mine and linked our fingers. I pressed back against him, relishing the intimacy, relishing even more the fact that we were both cradling our unborn child. He looked into my reflected eyes. "Your belly is beautiful to me, Nell," he said.

"Is it?"

He swept my hair aside, kissed the nape of my neck. "You are so beautiful, my Nell, it is only right that you should have beautiful things all around you."

"These are fitting surroundings, then, in which to raise your child?"

His body tensed against me. "My firstborn," he said, "who will be born into a house we have made beautiful, a house to which he or she will have no claim."

Now I thought I understood the problem at last. And I had already considered this. Very carefully. "Our son or daughter will have Elmsett Manor," I reminded him, twisting round in his arms to look at him properly. "A Glanville child will inherit the Glanville estate, which is as it should be. You must take us to see Elmsett, just as soon as the baby is born."

"There is nothing worth seeing," he said, letting go of me. "Nothing but a small moated manor left to rot during the Commonwealth."

"Then we shall restore it, or have a new house built on the land."

"I would have liked the very best for my children," he said, a peculiar lifelessness in his eyes. "But even my firstborn must take second place."

Summer

1687

The birth of Richard's first child, my third, was so swift and easy compared with the previous two that I found it quite exhilarating, would almost go so far as to say I enjoyed it. Perhaps it was because the baby was smaller than either of Edmund's babies had been. It was a boy, and I suggested he be named after his father, hoping it would encourage Richard to take an interest in him. Though Dickon, as he was known to avoid confusion, did not resemble his father in any way.

He looked exactly like me, flaxen-haired and blue-eyed, with skin that turned honey-colored at the first touch of the sun and was prone to a faint dusting of freckles. From the moment he was born it was clear he had my inquisitiveness too, but a gentler, more patient, altogether sweeter version of it.

It was a joy to me to encourage his interest in the world, to take him down to the moor to see the dragonflies and the otters and show him all the things I had so enjoyed being shown as a child. He was far too young as yet to comprehend how the black dots in the gelatinous spheres of frogspawn were growing tails and then legs, but I told him anyway, and it renewed my own passion for transformation. Dickon seemed to like the hatchlings best of all, the fluffy flotillas of cygnets and ducklings that glided up and down the rhynes.

My own little flock was growing rapidly. I had quickly fallen pregnant again, as half the country rejoiced in expectation of a first child being born to King James, while the other half dreaded the securing of a Catholic succession.

"The country may not be entirely united with the King in hoping for a boy but I must certainly hope you and I have another one." Richard smiled at me as he kicked off his riding boots and pulled his shirt over his head.

I was eating a bowl of cherries, lounging on the bolsters in my bodice and petticoat, with one hand resting on the mound of my belly. "I am surprised you even have a preference," I said, unable to help sounding critical. "You barely notice poor little Dickon. I am sure he knows, young as he is, that Forest is your favorite. Why d'you want another son?"

I had not meant to sound so sharp and I tensed in readiness for one of Richard's tempers. Instead, he threw himself down next to me on the bed, naked save for his breeches, and held another cherry to my lips for me to bite.

"You gave Edmund a son and then a daughter," he said with a facetiousness that was almost worse than anger, which I did not like in him at all. "I have followed him into your bed but I do not want to follow in every one of his rather shambling footsteps. I should like you to give me two sons."

I flicked his hand away crossly. "For God's sake, Richard, why must you turn everything into a contest?" I stared up at the tester, rolled my head toward him and dared myself to say it: "You know, sometimes when you say such things, I cannot help but wonder if you only wanted me in the first place to prove that you could take me from Edmund."

That silenced him, though he did not appear particularly surprised or shocked by my accusation. Nor did he deny it. We simply looked at each other, as if we had reached some kind of an impasse. Then he slipped his hand down inside my bodice, began to tease my nipple with his thumb. He said: "Not much of a contest, was it?"

I gave a gasp, jerked away from him. "What's wrong with you? That's a horrible thing to say." I had never seen him like this before, never heard him sound so cynical.

He tried to pull me nearer to him again but I would not let him. "Why are you angry with me all the time, Richard? Is it still because of those years when I would not see you?"

"No."

"Thomas Knight?"

"No."

"What, then?"

His eyes dwelt upon my face and he seemed to want to say something, struggled with himself for a moment, as if unsure of whether to speak or not, or else unsure of how to frame the words.

"Talk to me, Richard," I said more gently. "Whatever it is, you can tell me."

But he couldn't, clearly. I saw him give up, almost despairingly. "Forget what I said about Edmund, Nell. I'm sorry. Please forget it, can't you?"

"I wish you'd say what is making you unhappy." I faced another possibility, then asked quietly, "Is it her? Do you want to be with her?"

"Who? What are you talking about?"

"That woman in Bristol." I made myself say her name. "Sarah."

"Hell, no." He smiled, almost with relief, it seemed, as if for a brief moment my jealousy made him feel much better. He touched my lips. "It's you I want, Nell. And I am not unhappy. So long as I have you, then I am quite contented."

I smiled and frowned at the same time, because it was said with honesty and earnestness, and yet for all that he said he was content, he looked so burdened.

"You are the most puzzling person I have ever met."

"Am I?"

"You are."

I let him run his fingers enticingly up my petticoat. His eyes were concentrating on my face, watching to see me slowly relax under his touch, as if he was determined to turn every skill he had to making me give myself up to him, as if that might make everything all right. And who was I to deny it? Maybe it could, for a while at least. My eyes slid closed and my lips parted as he worked his fingers to pleasure me, until I was lost, whimpering and writhing on a knife edge of ecstasy and agony. He somehow knew the exact moment when I was certain I could bear no more but was also equally desperate for it never to end, and then abruptly he stopped what he was doing, began instead to torment me with his tongue until he brought me back to the summit again. It was the most exquisite kind of torture.

"Is there anything wrong with wanting to have the best and to be the best?" he whispered sweetly, seductively, as he entered me.

"You are the best, love," I sighed. "The very best."

He released himself inside me, as if that was all he needed to hear.

Autumn

1687

Too tired and heavy to walk down to the moor, I went instead to wander in the orchard. With my pregnant belly gliding before me, I was as stately as a swan. The sunlight was ripe and golden as the apples that hung heavy on the boughs, waiting to be loaded into the wagons. After a night of heavy wind, windfalls lay scattered on the grass around the twisted, lichen-encrusted trees. There was the scent of overripe fruit that was starting to decay and ferment, an oversweet, cloying, poignant fragrance that stirred something within me. I stood resting my hands on one of the crooked boughs and inhaled deeply, drinking in the mysterious tranquil stillness and peace of the ancient orchard.

Too soon I would be cooped up inside a dark and stuffy birthing room again. It would have been unbearable to me if it wasn't for the prospect of holding another newborn baby in my arms, Richard's second, which was more than enough recompense. I hoped this one would please him more.

I watched dreamily as two Red Admiral butterflies came sailing into the orchard and settled on one of the fallen fruits, their vivid orange-banded wings fanning slowly. I thought of James Petiver, wondered what he was doing now and if he still thought of me. I decided I'd bring little Dickon to the orchard and sit him down on the grass by the fallen fruit so he could have a close view of the butterflies. It was not too early to start teaching him all that James had taught me.

Still in a dream I watched as Alice Walker, the new little cookmaid, came in through the wooden gate with a basket on her arm and started bending to collect the fallen apples at her feet. I watched her place two in her basket and then stoop to pick up a third.

"Don't," I said, more harshly than I had intended. "Leave them be."

"Leave the apples on the ground, Ma'am?" She looked at me with a frown. "But Cook needs them for baking. Mr. Glanville said there would be half a dozen extra for supper."

It was the first I had heard of it, but Richard was forever inviting people to dine without informing me, either the most illustrious of the local gentry or a hard-drinking, hard-gambling set of young men from Bristol whose company he seemed to prefer to mine nowadays.

"Take the apples from the trees," I said to Alice. As if to demonstrate, I plucked one from the branch and took a large bite into its juicy flesh.

I had thrown the girl into a complete quandary. "What is the matter now, Alice?"

"Cook specifically told me to collect the windfalls, Ma'am. She hates to see waste. It seems a shame to let the apples just rot."

"Then take the best ones from the trees before they fall," I said, mildly despairing of this mismanagement. "The rotten ones will not be wasted. There are some little creatures that like rotten fruit all the better. If the fruit is all gone they will not come."

She bobbed a quick curtsy. "As you wish, Ma'am." She put down her basket and started pulling apples indiscriminately off the tree nearest to where she stood, as if she wanted to be away before I made another alarming request. Her basket only half filled, she scurried away as if she couldn't be gone from me quick enough.

I sighed, imagining what tall tale Alice would rush to take to Cook about the strange notions of their mistress. I took another bite of my apple, rested back against a tree and hoped they would put it down to my current condition.

THE MAID EVIDENTLY WHISPERED to more people than just Cook. We had a footman now, Jane Jennings's son, Will. Resplendent in his new livery of blue and gold braid, he gave me a peculiar look when he served me at dinner, almost sympathetic, as if he felt sorry for me, as if I was ill. Yet his look was wary too, as if he was one of those who regarded insects as sinister creatures and an interest in them as somehow distasteful, if not dangerous. Richard hardly acknowledged me either, though I assumed that was at least in part due to the fact that he was so preoccupied with trying to impress our eminent guests, if they were not impressed enough already by the livery and by the great seven-branched candelabras that flickered above the sparkling silver plates and knives and spoons and the jugs of rich claret.

As well as George Digby and John Smythe, we were joined by Ferdinando Gorges of Wraxall.

At first the talk was all of William of Orange and an open letter that had been written by him to the people of England.

"There is no question that it is a subtle bid for kingship," George Digby pronounced. "The man has been attempting to influence English politics for the whole of this past year. I'd not be at all surprised if he was massing an invasion force already."

My hand went defensively to my womb. "Please tell me we are not about to be invaded again?"

"So long as Orange chooses not to march through Somerset-shire in Monmouth's trail." John Smythe guffawed. "I have no stomach for getting embroiled in another affray. Bet you haven't either, Glanville?"

As Richard reached for a hefty swig of his wine, I noted the tension in his jaw at this mention of the militia's crushing defeat at the start of the Monmouth rebellion. "It would be different this time," he said steadily.

"No doubt about that," the Earl snorted. "If William of Orange does come to try to conquer the throne, he will bring a fleet to rival the Armada."

The conversation turned to less serious matters, then to pure frivolity that I found very wearisome.

I nibbled at the rich feast of partridge and stuffed goose and puddings, not bothering to concentrate as the candles burned lower and the conversation became more rowdy and drunken. When Richard accidentally knocked over a bottle of fine wine and it spilled all over the gleaming new parquet floor we had barely paid for, he suggested everyone go through to the withdrawing room for cards, and I rose from the table with the excuse that I needed to rest.

"I can't interest you in a game of whist?" George Digby asked blithely and with such immense charm that I was almost tempted.

"Save your breath, George," my husband said meanly. "Eleanor does not care for card games. It is such a regular pursuit for a lady, and my wife is anything but regular."

"You lucky devil." Ferdinando Gorges guffawed.

But I knew Richard had not meant to pay me a compliment. I

knew that the servants had run to him with their tales and that they had irritated him. If he had been more at ease with me, did not have this perplexing need to keep picking fights with me, I knew it would not have mattered to him at all. There was a time when he would have instantly defended me. He would have dismissed it with a shrug, or applauded it even, seeing it as part of the wildness and individuality he said he had first so loved in me. But because something had soured between us, he had not taken it that way. Had taken against me instead.

NEXT MORNING, as I was rising just after sunup, Richard swayed into the room. He sat down heavily on the edge of the bed, groaning and holding his head.

I was not very sympathetic. "You should have learned by now that too much of a good thing makes you sick."

He dragged the drapes closed around the bed to shut out the pale morning light and he climbed under the covers without even taking off his clothes, pulling the heavy blankets up tightly around him. His face was ashen and his eyes bloodshot.

I scrambled back up onto the bed, gripped by fear, knowing in that instant that no matter our differences, he was dearer and more precious to me than ever. "What's wrong, love? Are you not well?" I laid my hand on his forehead, terrified of what I would find, but his skin was quite cool.

He had closed his eyes and thrown one arm across them, as if the light still hurt him, dim as it was beneath the tester. "When I do die, it will be in a debtors' jail."

I looked at him, lying beneath the richly brocaded tester, under rich damask blankets that I had wanted almost as much as he had. "It can't be that bad."

"Nell, we have mortgages and debts owing to every wealthy merchant and gentleman who was supping here yesterday. I borrow from one to pay t'other and then hope to win some of it back off 'em at cards."

"Did you win last night?" I asked in a small voice.

"No, sweetheart," he said, deeply despondent, but in a way that made me realize he had totally forgotten our disagreement yesterday, or else considered it of no consequence now. "I lost. It seems that despite my best efforts, I always lose."

Was it just anxiety over money that had been making him so irritable with me? If it was, then it was understandable. I was just glad he was sharing it with me now and strangely relieved to think that might be the extent of our problems, that it was not something else, something worse. Such as what? I did not want to think.

"We can sell the plate," I suggested.

"That would barely pay for the repair of the guttering, let alone the crack that has appeared in the west wall of the hall and all the holes in the roof."

"Sell my jewels, then. I don't need them all."

"And have everyone pity you for having a wastrel for a husband?"

"I don't care what they think."

"I am well aware of it."

I did not rise to that. "We could drain the land," I said. "William Merrick has always said it would bring a great fortune."

He blinked open his eyes and stared at me hard. "You tried that before, remember? When you antagonized all the tenants and yeomen for miles around and they came to smoke you out."

"So? We could try again."

I had never seen him look so afraid. "And what if we failed, Nell? Like they did at first in the Fens? What if this land cannot be reclaimed? We waste a fortune instead of making one. Lose all respect and goodwill. We lose everything." He clung to the damask cover as if he feared it was about to be dragged off him. "What does any of it matter anyway? You heard what Digby said last night. The country is on the brink of revolution again. If the King does not abdicate the throne, then William of Orange may demand his head. There could be another civil war. We could lose this house to the victors if not the creditors, just as my father lost his."

I crept back under the covers and took him in my arms. He smelt of sweat and stale wine but I stroked back his thick black curls and pressed my mouth against his forehead. "You have me," I said. "Come revolution or ruin, whatever happens, whatever else we lose, we shall have each other. That is all that matters."

He settled himself against me and eventually he went to sleep. I drew the blanket over him as if he was a little boy and stayed with him until he woke. It was almost dusk when I went to fetch him a thick slice of bacon and some bread, and a glass of fresh milk to soothe his stomach.

"I am not an invalid," he snapped ungratefully, pushing the tray away and throwing back the covers. "Nor am I quite a peasant yet. I don't want to sup on bread and bacon like some poor farmer. I want canary wine and a supper of at least four dishes."

I understood that where once he had been willing to let me witness his vulnerability and his fear, he resented me now for having seen it, almost as if our current predicament was somehow my fault.

I TRIED TO FORGET all about debts and mortgages, cosseted from the real world by the preparations for my lying-in. The gossips assembled round my candlelit bed with their chatter and their needlework and their comfits and it was just as companionable as the first time I had given birth. There was Mistress Knight, Mistress Keene, Florence Smythe and Mistress Gorges, Jane Jennings, Mistress Walker from the mill, John Hort's wife, Lucy, with her new baby son in her arms. These women, many of whom I had known all my life, were still my friends. They had seen two of my three babies born and they wished me well with my fourth. They were still at ease in my company. Until my pains grew so bad and I cried out so loud that Florence Smythe, newly delivered of a daughter herself, reached for the King James Bible that I had left beside my bed.

It fell open at a particular page and two pressed golden butterfly wings came fluttering out. Jane Jennings gave a little squeal and threw back her arms as if she had seen dried toads.

"Calm yourself, woman," Mistress Keene scolded. "They're dead 'uns. She used to collect 'em as a child."

"I heard tell of a witch that had a butterfly as her familiar instead of a cat," Jane Jennings whispered. "It flew beside her shoulder."

"Well, them's not flying anywhere," Mistress Keene said baldly.

But Jane was not done. "Instead of feeding off flowers, the insect servant supped from a Devil's teat on the witch's palm."

I felt a dozen eyes scrutinize my own hands and my bloated abdomen for sign of such a diabolical mark. I felt a chill in my bones, and then I was lost to a surge of gripping pain that told me my baby was about to enter the world. I put my hands between my legs and felt the dome of a slippery head and I bore down and gave one final mighty push. There was heat and wetness and a tearing agony, and then there was a silence. It was shattered by the unmistakable, miraculous wail of a newborn infant.

Mother Wall told me that I had not given Richard a second son as he had wished. The pattern had been repeated. We had a daughter.

"Her name is Eleanor," I said, suddenly wanting some unbreakable link with this house, with the past, for all I had avoided it with Forest. "She is to be named for my mother. We shall call her Ellie."

Jane Jennings peered at her suspiciously to see if she was properly formed, but already I knew that she was perfect.

Autumn

1688

or once the sound of the steady falling autumn rain did not dispirit me. I did not dread the coming of winter. My baby girl had mild blue eyes as soft as the mist, and her gummy smile was a little ray of sunshine that made me forget the rising floods entirely. The pitter-patter of the rain against the window was a soothing sound that only served to make the nursery seem all the more snug and warm.

The infinite nature of love astounded me. I loved my husband and my three children with my whole heart. But then along came another baby, and the amount of love I had to give expanded. I did not love any of them less for the fact that they had to share me with one more little person.

Ellie drew Richard and me closer together again too. Now that he had met her, he did not seem to mind at all that she was a girl. On the contrary, he seemed glad, was utterly enchanted by his tiny daughter. He had taken to going to sleep with her curled up on his chest, and to propping her up on plump cushions so he could play the lute and sing to her, which was the most adorable thing to see. And to hear. Richard had a lovely singing voice, deeper than his spoken voice, very gentle. When he declared that he'd far prefer a houseful of daughters to more sons, would like me to breed a whole gaggle of girls as sweet as Ellie, I told him it would be my greatest pleasure to oblige.

"I swear that little lass grows prettier by the day." He smiled when he strolled into the parlor and saw me cradling Ellie by a blazing fire. Raindrops jeweled his dark cloak, and his breath, when he leaned over to kiss us both in turn, smelled exotically of rum. He had been hunting deer at Ashton Court, drinking with the Smythes and Digbys, and it had put him in a particularly bright mood. "She is as lovely as her mother," he said, kissing me again on my lips. "Pretty as a princess, in fact. A duchess at least."

"She is."

He swung his cloak off his shoulders, unbuckled his sword and sprawled before the hearth at my feet. "I have the most beautiful wife and the most beautiful baby daughter. Any man would envy me, I think."

"Even with insurmountable debts?" I could not help but ask.

"What of them?" He gave one of the logs a kick with his boot and made the sparks fly. "We have a loan from the Earl of Bristol, no less."

Winter

1688

It was the Earl himself who rode over to share the news that William of Orange had landed at Torbay in Devon. On the very anniversary of the Gunpowder Plot, he had marched onto English soil beneath a banner that proclaimed, *The Liberties of England and the Protestant Religion, I will maintain.*

William's fleet did more than rival the Armada, it was four times the size of it. Sixty thousand men and five thousand horses had sailed into the English Channel in a square formation twenty-five ships deep, so vast that it saluted Dover Castle and Calais simultaneously to demonstrate its strength. But, as George Digby returned to report, William's men did not forage or plunder or do anything to antagonize the English people, who in turn had neither rallied behind the King nor declared for William. War-weary, we all merely waited to see what turn events would take.

The first royal blood was shed in a skirmish in Somersetshire, at Wincanton, but bar that and a few anti-Catholic riots, it turned out to be a blessedly bloodless revolution that was soon ended. By the close of December, King James had fled to France, paving the way for William and Mary to be offered the throne as joint rulers.

"The real ruler now is Parliament, of course," George Digby said with an incorrigibly merry smile as Richard poured him yet another measure of celebratory claret. "The passing of the Bill of Rights means that never again will a king or queen of England hold absolute power. Furthermore, it takes away forever the possibility of a Catholic monarchy." He turned his arresting gaze from Richard to me. "Your good father can rest in peace at last," he said. "Catholicism is dead forever in England." He quaffed more wine and raised his glass in a blithe and generous toast to the neighbor who had loathed him. "A glorious revolution indeed. So here's to Major Goodricke. His battle is now over. He got what he wanted in the end."

"Save that his daughter is clad in the most un-Puritanical silk and sapphires and ribbons." Richard smiled, twining one of my gold ringlets around his finger.

Over the rim of my wine goblet, in the flickering golden light of the best wax candles, I returned the mildly drunken but fond gazes of my glamorous husband and his equally glamorous friend, who were both now openly admiring me in my pearls and cerulean gown of silk brocade. I had all that I wanted too. I had all that I had ever desired, and yet it felt that something vital was still missing from my life. It lacked some purpose. It lacked that sense of adventure and discovery that had always been so necessary to me.

Stop being greedy, Eleanor. Do not ask for too much, or you might lose all that you already have.

Part Four

Spring

1695

I looked down into my younger son's cupped hands as we stalked through the knee-high summer growth of rushes and sedges on the moor. "What have you found this time, Dickon?"

He stopped. I crouched down in front of him as he opened his fingers like a clamshell and I met the beady yellow eyes and pulsating throat of a small green toad. With one finger Dickon caressed its knobbly back. "He was so far away from the river I was worried he would dry out in the heat. I am going to keep him for a while and then set him free again by Monk's Pool."

"He will be in very good company in the nursery, what with the grass snake and the runt of the piglets and the blind hound." I smiled fondly. "Not to mention Snowflake."

Dickon looked at me with his infinitely trusting pale blue eyes. "You said she would fly away with the others when they left in the spring but she did not seem to want to go, did she, Mama?"

"No, she did not." I stroked his sun-streaked yellow hair. "You have obviously made her far too comfortable to want to go anywhere."

The swan had a damaged wing, and Dickon had reared her from a cygnet, feeding her from his hand. He had a talent for caring for animals that were wounded or in need of nurturing, people too, including his baby sister, Ellen.

I could see Ellie now, with Mary, at the bottom of the water meadow. In ringlets and ribbons and matching lemon gowns over white frilled petticoats, they were a beguiling sight, my two daughters, capering amidst the sunlit daisies and buttercups. Ellen was picking flowers while dancing. She danced wherever she went.

I knew that Mary was missing Forest. He had left a week ago on a ship bound for the Low Countries, where William Merrick had acquaintances. Forest was eighteen now, and Flanders was said to be so like Somersetshire that I hoped he would not feel too homesick. Their agricultural techniques were far in advance of ours, and it was my hope that this adventure would give Forest the perfect opportunity to learn how to manage the land he would one day inherit.

The plans to drain had never materialized, nor would they now, at least not in my lifetime. If I'd not put paid to those plans before Sedgemoor, I would have done it in the aftermath. It would take a long time for the West Country to recover from Monmouth's uprising and I had no desire to bring more distress to the people of Tickenham, any more than did Richard, who had taken great pains, with doles and feasts, to help them forget their losses, forget he had ever sided with the militia. It would be Forest's decision now, to drain or not to drain, and I meant him to be better informed than I or my father had ever been.

I saw Bess crossing the arched stone bridge on her way back from taking a bowl of broth to her mother, old now and ill for some time.

"How is she?" Dickon inquired of Bess before I had a chance.

"Not much better, I am afraid." She regarded him warmly, her gap-toothed smile even more pronounced as she had aged and grown stouter. "But thank you for asking, Dickon."

"We could take her some pottage and apple pie tomorrow," Dickon said. "And some salves for the sores on her back."

"That is very thoughtful. She'd appreciate that," Bess said.

"Is there anything else she needs?" I asked.

"She keeps asking for Tom."

I took a deep breath. "Then you must send for him, Bess. Tell him to come right away."

"I did," she admitted awkwardly. "He is already here." Then: "Do you mind?"

"It is right that he should come back to Tickenham," I said. "It is his home, after all."

Since Richard had insisted we keep pace with the grandest households and hire a housekeeper and a steward, Bess had been given the official title of waiting woman to me, but neither of us had spoken about Thomas for a long time, beyond Bess mentioning that he had found employment in the Billingsgate fish market. He had remained in London even after the official pardon had been issued. The rest of the men, John Hort's son and the one surviving Bennett boy, had come out of hiding, but Thomas had not returned to Tickenham and I could not pretend that I had not been relieved. Now that the reason for his hostility toward me had been brought out into the open, I feared it would be harder to face him somehow. I knew that I would never feel so at ease when I brought the children down for walks on the moor if I knew he might be there, resentful that it was not his moor we walked upon.

Bess walked with Dickon and me to the butterfly garden that her Ned had helped me plant so long ago. It was an abundant, kingly garden now, all cloaked in royal purple and gold, with thistles and purple loosestrife and the violet of the marjoram contrasting with the yellow of the marsh marigolds.

There was always a profusion of butterflies there, but this morning the combination of bright sunshine and still air had brought out a whole host of them that quite took my breath away. I halted my step. There were dozens, Large Whites, Large Coppers, Tortoiseshells, Brimstones, Fritillaries, Red Admirals, so many they were almost alarming in their great multitude. It was as if they had convened for some special purpose and we had intruded.

"A plague of butterflies," Bess whispered with wonder.

As I took a few half-wary steps into the bright blizzard, a great swarm of them rose up in unison, an angelic ambush. I ducked and raised my hand to shield my face from the disquieting flicker and quiver of so many little wings.

The throng descended, like a handful of winged flowers, living petals thrown at a fairy bride on her wedding day, and I realized that Dickon still had not moved, was standing enraptured at the arched stone entrance to the garden. It was with a strange sweet longing for my childhood that I watched my son as he watched the butterflies that continued to flit around like animated jewels, spangling the warm, clear air and dancing from flower to flower.

The summer had been late in coming and recently they seemed to be getting shorter with every year, so short that the harvests were failing, bread was in poor supply, and people were going hungry. Since the start of the new decade the winters had been colder and longer, with weeks of ice and snow and frost. So the butterflies were a particularly welcome sight. And so many, almost as if they had been biding their time, waiting for this rare warmth and sunshine, determined to make the best of it while it lasted.

"Don't you want to catch one of them?" Bess asked Dickon.

He shook his head very definitely.

"Your mother used to."

I'd thought that I had no real interest in butterflies anymore, that the enchantment had left me for good, but now I was not so sure. Standing amongst this lovely cornucopia, I had a stirring of desire for them, like a tingle in my fingertips.

Bess was watching me. "Are you wishing you had your net, even now?"

I sat down on a stone bench in an arbor. "Look at me." I flicked my skirt with my ribboned slipper and made it swish. I was wearing emerald silk and there were rubies around my throat and in my ears. "I have a closetful of silk dresses and a casketful of gems. I have a house filled with liveried footmen and japanned looking-glasses and French glassware and Chinese porcelain. What need have I to go chasing after tiny fragments of color anymore?"

If I did not exactly encourage Richard's increasing extravagance, I did not discourage it either. I had loved to hear him talk once of the elegantly proportioned Dutch merchants' houses fronting the canals in Amsterdam, the likes of which were being replicated in Bath now that we had a Dutch king. If we could not have the colonnades and domes that so impressed Richard as a destitute child, we could at least have rich interiors and replicate the grand state rooms of the Bath houses. Now we had striped muslin curtains, silk damask armchairs and a glass-windowed coach in a new coach house. But they had become like bright disguises to lay over the cracks that had opened up in our marriage, like the Oriental carpets we had bought to lay over the cold stone flags and the hand-painted silk paper we used to cover the fissures in the crumbling walls.

I had not found possessing such things nearly as fulfilling as I had once thought it would be, but the more Richard had, the more he seemed to want. Nothing seemed to be enough for him, as if there was a need in him that could never be met, a void that could never be filled, not even by me, least of all by me.

Dickon came to stand in front of me. "The toad needs shade."

"You take him on up to the house then, darling. I'll come in a while."

He delayed, unwilling to go. "Is my father home?"

"No. He has gone to Wraxall."

His bony little shoulders relaxed and he set off up the path.

"I do wish the two of them could get along better," I sighed.

"Mr. Glanville always made such an effort with Forest that I can forgive him much," Bess said, leaping to Richard's defense in a way that made me smile. "It was a wonder to see, how he was with Mr. Edmund's fatherless little boy, and how Forest was with him. They still have a rare bond, don't they? It would be unusual enough for father and son to be so close, but for stepson and stepfather . . . well, you have to admit it is extraordinary."

"It is."

I remembered what Richard had said: *I would have liked the best for my children. But even my firstborn son must take second place.* A reference to the marriage settlement. Always that. But a tiny part of me also feared it held the key to the preferential treatment Richard always showed Forest. He was the lord in waiting, the heir, when no son of Richard's ever could be.

"I agree it is a pity he does not have the same bond with his own little boy," Bess said.

"Dickon is such a timid, sensitive child," I said. "And I think Richard probably was once too, but was never allowed to be, and now he finds it difficult to accept his own son, which only makes Dickon all the more nervous around him."

"Well," Bess said. "I'll go and keep the lad company, see if he wants a glass of cider. You stay here and enjoy the sunshine. And the butterflies."

THAT NIGHT I HAD the strangest dream. A swarm of yellow butterflies, far greater than had gathered in the garden, had invaded my darkened chamber and found their way inside the bed curtains that, in my dream, were closed despite the airless summer night. In my sleep I was tormented and almost suffocated by the luminous, insistent wings. They gently battered and brushed my face, swirled before my eyes and filled my head, as if to rouse me to action.

My father, like all Puritans, had set much store by dreams and what they revealed about a person's character and destiny. I did not understand what this dream meant, but even when I woke it did not entirely leave me, remained with me throughout the morning.

When Richard came to find me, I had returned to the butterfly garden. He sat down on the sunny stone bench beside me, waved his hand in front of my face. "Where are you, Nell?" he asked, with a touch of impatience. "You seem very far away."

I could often have said the same about him. Somehow, though I still loved him, knew he loved me, we had grown very far away from each other. How had that happened? Why?

I took his hand, brought it to my lips and kissed it. "See? I am right here."

The bright sunlight highlighted the slight streaks of silver in his black curls, around his temples and his ears. There was doubtless gray in my own hair too, but it did not show up so clearly against the gold. There was the faintest web of lines around his eyes too, but only when he smiled, and the blue of them had not faded. If anything the years had made him more attractive, rather than less, had added a character and dignity to his face that made it all the more compelling to me. He was still beautiful, still by turns devastatingly charming and charmingly vulnerable. He still suffered from nightmares he would never talk about, was more prone than ever to being withdrawn, more troubled than ever he had been before we were married. And nothing I did seemed to help him at all, so that I had practically abandoned any attempt to do so.

He was wearing ink-blue breeches and a long waistcoat but had no jacket on. I rested my cheek against the soft linen gathers of his shirtsleeves, smoothed them down lest I be smothered by the fullness of them.

"George Digby has invited me on a deer hunt," he said. "D'you think Dickon would like to come?"

I straightened. "Oh, Richard, love, I don't. He would hate it."

"You've turned the boy into a milksop," he said harshly. "I don't know how to talk to him."

"Yes you do. Talk to him as you talk to me. As you talk to the girls."

"But he is not a girl, damn it!"

"My father treated me as if I was a boy, and I'd not have had it any other way. I was different from other girls, and Dickon is different from other boys. He does not like hunting and swordplay, any more than I liked crewelwork and embroidery. You have to respect that."

I sensed he was on the brink of arguing with me, but held himself back as if he did not have the stomach for another quarrel. No more than did I. "So what shall you do today," he asked, "if you are not to be kept busy with a needle?"

"Oh, I expect I shall find something."

When he had kissed me good-bye, I realized that what I wanted to do was some hunting of my own. Butterfly hunting.

With mounting excitement, I went to the oak chest in the corner of our bedchamber and dug deep down, through layers of silk gowns and velvet capes, to the very bottom, to my books and boxes of specimens. I carefully took them out and laid them on the bed, going back for my observation book and all the letters from James I had kept.

I looked back over my notes and studied each butterfly, reacquainting myself with long-lost and dearly beloved friends. I reread the book James had made for me and every one of his letters, the ink faded now to a pale ocher. I devoured it all, the way I used to devour my first meal after a long fast. Then I dusted down my butterfly equipment, picked up my silk skirts and ran down onto the moor.

Dickon had carried his swan to the river and was standing at a bend, upstream from John Hort and the other fishermen and eelers, trying without success to encourage the great white bird to go for a swim. He had his stockings off and was ankle deep in the sparkling water, but the bird was paddling about in the reedy shallows, its webbed feet firmly rooted to the muddy riverbed.

"Pitiful." I grinned. "Even I could do better."

"You can swim, Mama?" Dickon exclaimed with surprise.

"Your father showed me how to do it a long time ago. I think, by now, that I am probably an even better swimmer than he is, but for Heaven's sake, don't ever tell him I said that."

Dickon regarded the clap net and pins and pine collecting box with cautious interest. "You don't swim with those?"

"No." I laughed, holding out my hand to him. "Come with me and you'll see what these are for."

He left his swan to splash about and scrambled out of the river, under the scornful stare of one of the fishermen. I realized with a shock that it was Thomas Knight. So he had turned to fishing now. My half brother. The years had not been kind to him at all and his bitterness showed in a harshening of the lines of his long face, which looked wolfish. It was almost as if his lips and his eyes had narrowed permanently for lack of joy in his life. His hair was cropped, thinning and receding. He was leaner than ever, as if resentment was eating away at his insides. He carried his damaged arm crookedly, dragging on his shoulder so that he stood slightly stooped and twisted, like a hunchback.

"Good day to you, Thomas," I called across to him. "Welcome back."

He stared at me as if I was not even worthy of acknowledgment.

I walked away and Dickon ambled after me. We had gone less than a yard when a little Blue Wing obligingly fluttered past our noses, and with a leap and a reflex swipe of the net, I had it instantly pinioned, my fingers pressing on its thorax.

Dickon was aghast. "Why do you have to kill them?"

"To catalogue them and map the different variations and species."

"But it is God's commandment that we must not kill."

"We kill cattle and geese, Dickon. God would not want us to starve."

"We do not eat butterflies," he pointed out.

"But we do need to learn about them."

He did not argue, and I could see him mulling on that as we carried on.

I threw my arm to stop him in his tracks when I sighted an unusually wide-banded Marsh Fritillary, feeding on the pale domed flower of a devil's-bit scabious. I put my fingers to my lips to signal that he keep quiet and stealthily started to creep toward it. I was about to whip out my net again, but this time it was Dickon who held me back, with a restraining hand on my arm. "Don't, Mama, please."

He sat on his heels and watched as the little butterfly eagerly unwound its proboscis into the flower and waved its distinctive orange-tipped antennae as it outspread its red-brown and yellow wings.

"See?" he whispered. "It is far more interesting alive than dead."

I let it go on feeding then flit away, just for the pleasure of seeing my son's sweet, victorious smile.

I stroked his gold hair. "I've never shown you my collection, have I? Butterflies that are set well are just as beautiful as those basking in the sunshine. With their wings outspread, they look as if they could fly away at any moment. You'll see what I mean. And you'll see that there is a purpose to killing them, I promise."

But Dickon was not interested in the dead butterflies, was in fact quite perturbed by them. What interested him instead was why there was one book amongst the butterfly paraphernalia which seemed to have no connection with it whatsoever, though it had perhaps more importance to it than any other. The King James Bible. I told Dickon what his grandfather had told me, so long ago now, about butterflies being a token, a promise, and in the telling of that story I felt the stirring of excitement that I had experienced when first I heard it. A wellspring of hope.

When Dickon had gone to bed, I sat down beside the Bible, wary almost to touch it, to open its pages after so many years. Eventually I put the candle on the stand and reached out my hand, lifted the great book into my lap. I felt the weight of it, ran my fingers over the worn leather and tooled gold lettering. I turned it on its side and let it fall open where it would. The Gospel of John, chapter eight, verse twelve. The page where I had pressed the first golden butterfly. The light of the candle caught a very faint indentation in the page, the finest sparkling of bright dust.

I let my eyes rest on the words, words that had once been as familiar to me as my own name but which I had let fall silent.

I read them now out loud.

"Then spake Jesus again unto them, saying, 'I am the light of the world: he that followeth me shall not walk in darkness but have the light of life.'"

I felt a strange peace descend on me, such as I had not felt for a very long time. I heard my father's voice, so clear he could almost have been sitting right beside me. *The only light you need is the light of the Lord.*

I went to Dickon's chamber. Cadbury, the blind hound which he had found wandering, abandoned on Cadbury Camp, was curled up at the foot of the bed and she gave a low growl as she heard me enter.

I crouched down next to her, let her sniff my hand and fondled her ears until her tail started to thump against the floor. "Well done, girl. You guard him well."

I lowered myself onto the edge of the bed, reached over and stroked Dickon's golden cheek. "You shall be my example," I whispered to him. "I shall study living butterflies from now on, do you hear me, my little darling? I am going to rear them, instead of killing them."

I was going to witness the transformation, from worm, to coffin, to butterfly. From birth, to death, to resurrection.

I WOKE as I had woken as a child, eager and full of plans for the day. At sunrise I slid out of Richard's arms and out of bed, pulled on a simple morning gown, unfastened my hair from its plait and tied it in a knot at the back of my head. I went down to the kitchen for a widemouthed glass jar and was out on the moor before even the eelers were about to check their wicker traps. Only the marsh birds were awake, twittering and singing away as if they shared my anticipation, a perfect accompaniment to a glorious morning, heralding what would be another hot day. For now, it was neither too hot nor too cool, though the ground was still damp with dew, as I discovered when I got down on my hands and knees and started crawling around in the undergrowth. I paid no heed to the dark wet patches that stained my skirt, nor to the nettles which stung and scratched my hands nor the twigs that caught in my hair. I carried on regardless, even when Thomas Knight, John Hort and the fishermen did come to take up their positions, even when I felt them watching me censoriously. What did it matter if they disapproved? What could they do?

The first worm I found had a brownish-olive body, covered with long white hairs. Hiding under the scabious, I discovered two tiny pale yellow larvae. My search of the nettles revealed a larger worm, greenish ocher in color, with a black head. Satisfied for now, I stood and smoothed my hand over my head and tucked a stray strand of hair behind my ears, smiling to see the scandalized stares of the fishermen, with their early morning catch still twitching on the riverbank beside them. "I bid you good morning, gentlemen," I said, as if greeting the Earl of Bristol in the parlor, but bending instead to pluck another few nettle leaves to add to my supply. I giggled to myself at the picture I made. Chin held high, swishing serenely through the grass in my damp-stained gown, with my jar of wriggling worms held carefully in both hands like a goblet of finest wine.

I went directly to the dovecote, a lime-coated corner which I had decided to appropriate for my butterfly birthing room. It was sheltered and warm and, with the rows of separate openings for the birds, always well ventilated.

Over the course of the next day and night, I tended my quadruplet worms as devotedly as I had tended my four babies. It was a similar toil and done with similar willingness. I brought them fresh leaves, cleaned out their droppings, fretted over whether they were too cold or too warm, were sleeping too much or not enough, were having enough to eat. I kept a record of it all, but I had to record that, one by one, all the worms died.

I threw them out and swilled the jar clean in the horse trough. A good proportion must perish in the wild. I just needed a greater quantity to guarantee success.

Ellen and Dickon were keen to help me, and Dickon also recruited Annie Sherburne, one of the tenant farmers' daughters, who sometimes went to feed the ducks with him. She was a tall girl with flyaway soft brown hair and the doleful eyes of a puppy. She wore a woolen dress that was thin with age and several inches too short, but which still hung off her skinny frame.

Annie proved herself a diligent little helper, young and naive enough in the ways of the world not to be too perturbed when I took her out into the fields and beat at bushes with a long stick, when I gave her a linen sheet and instructed her and Dickon to hold it spread out beneath the bushes to collect the worms dislodged from the branches by my thrashing.

"Will you sell them at market?" she asked, as I crouched down to scoop a score of them into a jar.

I managed to keep my face straight at this natural question from a farmer's girl, for whom every crop had a market value. Why would caterpillars be any different from apples or eggs or pike, gathered in to be sold for profit? "No, Annie," I told her kindly. "Nobody would want them."

"Why d'you want 'em, then?"

I stood up, the jar and its squirming contents in my hand. "To me they are valuable because of what I can learn from them."

"How valuable, exactly?" She leaned on the beating stick, her little face very serious. "I told my brother Tim what I do for you, and he has been collecting worms too," she explained. "How much would you give him for 'em?"

"Well now, how about twopence a dozen?" I suggested. "Would he accept that as a fair price, do you think?"

She nodded vigorously.

"Good. You tell him to bring me however many he can find."

"We need every penny we can get," Annie said, "with the bad harvests we've had these past two years and bread so costly. Ma says we'll soon have to choose whether to eat or have a roof over our heads, especially with two extra mouths to feed now." She clamped her little hand over her own mouth as if to push back the words.

"What extra mouths, Annie?"

She shook her head, much afraid.

"You can tell me. I promise I shall not be angry."

"My cousin and her baby," she murmured. "She was thrown out of her parish when they found out she was with child. I know it is forbidden, but she had nowhere to go so we took her in."

"I should hope you did. And did she have a little boy or a girl?"

"Boy." She smiled. "He is called Harry."

"It must be very cramped in your cottage," I said. "With all your sisters and brothers and grandmother."

"There's ten of us now, Ma'am. It'll be a squeeze come winter, when it floods downstairs and we all have to live in the one room up top."

"Tell your mother not to worry about the rent," I said. "She can pay half, or whatever she can afford. And tell your cousin that she can have the cottage along the lane from yours, for a penny. It has been empty for I don't know how long."

Annie's eyes were round with surprise and wonder. "They'll never believe me." She looked like she didn't believe her luck either.

"And how would you like to be my apprentice, Annie?"

"Oh, but my father can't pay you for an apprenticeship."

"Why should he pay, when it is you who is doing me the service? No, it is I who will pay you, Annie. A good wage. Here." I put my hand in my pocket, took out a coin for her. I had spent too long squandering money on things that I was now coming to realize mattered not at all. "You tell your brother to bring those worms. I might even give him sixpence if they are good ones."

RICHARD HAD RIDDEN OUT to the village, collecting rents with the steward, and as usual they had ended up in the inn, but when he waylaid me on my way back from the pantry, where I had gone for a fresh collecting jar, I saw that it had not put him in a very good humor. He caught me in his arms in a gentle enough embrace that nevertheless held me fast. "What are you doing, Nell?" he asked probingly.

"Something that I love," I said. "I had forgotten how much. Please do not try to stop me."

"Could I stop you?" he challenged. "If I asked you to give it up, would you do it?"

I reached back and put my hands over each of his, slowly but deliberately pushing them down and away from me. "Would you be asking, or would you be ordering?"

"Would it make a difference?"

I shook my head. "In this instance, I think not."

"I am your husband. You vowed to obey me. You are commanded by God to obey my orders."

I stiffened. "So, are you ordering me, Richard?"

"God knows I should do," he said. "For the sake of local harmony, if nothing else. You need to know that Jack and Margaret Sherburne are none too comfortable about their Annie spending so much time with you, even if you do pay her for it. Her father is swayed by the wages and your rash offer of reduced rent, but Annie's mother does not want her here, not even with those extraordinary carrots dangled before her. I take it you have a plan as to how we meet our debts, by the way, if you reduce rents to a peppercorn on a whim? Perhaps in future you'd at least do me the courtesy of informing me of your decisions, even if you see no need to discuss them."

"I'm sorry. I should have talked to you."

"Why should you?" he said acerbically. "It is your right to do as you wish. After all, it is your estate."

"God in Heaven, Richard, just for once can we not come back to that? I wonder that you ever agreed to marry me, when you knew you could not have Tickenham Court as well, or were you counting on the fact that I loved you enough for the settlement to make little difference? I have never denied you money, never denied you anything, have I? So why can you never let it rest?"

He was staring at me very oddly and I feared I had gone too far, but I could not seem to stop. "Is that why you favor Forest over your own son? Because he is my heir?"

I saw the warning flash in his blue eyes, like lightning in a summer sky, swift and searing, a charge of angry power that suddenly made me almost afraid of him.

"Forgive me. I should not have said that."

"By all means." His tone was very cold. "It makes no difference whether you say it or not. If it is what you think."

"I don't think. I wasn't thinking. I am just angry. Why do the Sherburnes not want Annie to work with me, for God's sake?"

"They are not the only ones who think the girl should not be doing what you've had her doing," he said flatly.

"Collecting caterpillars and assisting with their care? What the devil is so wrong with that?"

"Have you even paused to wonder why Mistress Keene has lost her help in the kitchen and since yesterday there is no longer anyone to work in the brew house?"

Admittedly I had been rather preoccupied of late, but the issue with the kitchenmaid I did know about. "Alice Walker was needed at the mill, wasn't she?"

"Only because her brothers didn't want her near this house. They have heard tales," Richard said. "They have all heard tales."

"What kind of tales?"

"That you seek out caterpillars and keep their coffins, waiting for the worms to grow wings. They say only a witch would be concerned with such things. They say it is evil."

I felt my spine tingle at the use of those words. "I had hoped it was godly."

"Shape-shifting, Nell? Use the brain God gave you! They see it as unholy, akin to attempting to breed a werewolf."

That was not quite so preposterous as it might sound, since metamorphosis had been put forward as proof that werewolves could exist, just as it had been used to argue that alchemy was a possibility. "This is tavern talk," I said angrily. "Vicious tattle. Malicious gossip. It is Thomas Knight's doing. He's not been back a month and already he's causing trouble for me. It is he who has been stirring them all up, isn't it?"

"Whipping them up, more like, but then you have made it so damnably easy for him."

"Why can't he leave me alone?" I exploded. "Why can't they all leave me alone? I harm no one."

"Except for yourself. Except for your reputation. And mine."

"You did tell them it is all nonsense?" I studied his face. "You didn't, did you? You did not speak up in defense of me at all. For pity's sake, Richard. Why not?"

"I saw nothing to be gained from having them think that both of us are cracked."

Tears pricked my eyes. I could bear being talked about, gossiped about, so long as I had his support. If he even half believed them, sided with them against me, I did not know what I would do. "I am cracked?" I raged. "Is that really what you think of me?"

"What I think," he stormed. "What I think is that you have been writing to him again, haven't you? That is what has got you started on all this again, isn't it? You have been writing to that damned quack apothecary."

"His name is James. And he is no quack. I have not written to him for years, but rest assured, I shall," I shouted vengefully. "Oh, I shall. Just as soon as I have something to tell him."

Richard snatched the glass jar out of my hand and hurled it against the wall, where it shattered into shards like splinters of ice.

We stood, eyes flashing, chests heaving. Out of habit, I smoothed the loose tendrils of hair off my face, and at that familiar gesture of mine I saw the anger in his eyes change into passion of a different kind. I knew that this argument would end the way most arguments between us usually did, with lovemaking, and I wanted that as much as I knew Richard did. Having him inside me was the only way I ever felt close to him anymore, though even then it never seemed close enough.

He stepped nearer to me, pushed me back against the wall, his body pressing against mine. I matched his hard, angry kisses with hard and angry kisses of my own, kisses that had in them more despair than desire. I hooked one leg up around his thigh, my arm around his shoulder and my hand in his hair, to bring him nearer. His fingers were working at the fastenings of my gown, but it was taking too long, for both of us.

I put my lips to his ear. "Rip it," I whispered. "I want you to rip it."

I turned round to face the wall, flattened myself against the stone and swept up my hair with my arm, so he could get more easily at the row of tiny buttons down my back. I felt him give a sharp, swift tug which sent them scattering like hailstones.

He stripped the gown off me and slammed into me, took me quickly and passionately up against the wall, but though the pleasure was intense, I could tell he was left as strangely dissatisfied as I.

It was no better when we did it again in bed, more slowly and lingeringly. There was something missing, always something in the way, standing between us and keeping us apart. What?

As I lay in his arms afterward, my thoughts returned to the local unrest, then ran off, as they were wont to do, on a tangent. The window was open and a faint breeze blew in, scented with river water and new-scythed grass. I drew little circles with my finger in the hairs on Richard's chest.

"Do you remember when we celebrated William and Mary coming to the throne, and George Digby said the Bill of Rights would change England forever?"

"Aye, I remember," Richard said. He turned over on his side so he could see my face. He was accustomed by now to the no doubt puzzling paths my mind sometimes chose to wander and stroked strands of sweaty hair off my face with the flat of his hand, waiting for me to go on.

I propped my head up on my elbow, looked at him. "By removing any chance of having a Papist take the throne, it has dispelled much of the hatred of Catholics, making England a safer place for them, and others too of differing faiths. In that respect England has changed indeed. Yet some things have not changed at all."

"Where is this leading us, Nell?" Richard asked wearily.

"We may have a queen ruling jointly with her king, but nothing has changed for women like me, has it? Why should I be viewed with suspicion just because I take an interest in the world? Just because I want to do something other than household accounts?"

"I don't know, Nell." The light suddenly went out of his eyes. "But you are right that hatred of Catholics is not the only prejudice. There are others," he added. "There are plenty of others, and they can be just as malign, just as dangerous." He rolled away from me, onto his back, threw his arm up over his eyes, almost as if he needed to blot out the sight of my face. I had not the faintest idea what he was talking about, or what I had done now to upset him.

BESS USHERED my apprentice's scrawny little brother into the parlor. He was carrying a dented but perfectly polished copper pan and he stood on the threshold, wary of coming any closer, as if he took me for a witch.

"You have some worms for me?" I said gently, aware that this was not a question to put him much at ease.

He nodded, gulping down his terror.

"May I see them, Tim?"

He shuffled two steps closer and held out the pan with dirty hands that stuck out from frayed shirtsleeves he had long outgrown.

I looked into the pan, where a few miserable-looking maggots were squirming. The wrong kind of worms entirely, but an easy enough mistake to have made.

"Where did you find them?" I asked.

He swallowed hard again, tossed his head to flick the limp brown hair out of his eyes. "In a cowpat, Ma'am."

I smiled. Only a small boy would go digging in cowpats. "What a good idea," I said enthusiastically. "I'd never have thought to look there."

He thrust the pan at me. "Are you going to take 'em?"

"Thank you, Tim. They will do very well." I emptied the unpleasant contents of the pan into a pot and handed him his sixpence.

He snatched it off me and bolted for the door, almost forgetting to reclaim the pan and hardly daring to come back for it. That was something I marked well. If a small boy was so eager to be away from me that he would forsake the only means by which his mother could cook his dinner, I must be fearsome indeed.

EACH MORNING when I went to the dovecote, there were more curled corpses to remove from the jars, until there was just a spotted one left, barely moving. When I came back next day, I expected it to have gone the way of the rest, thought at first that it had somehow just vanished. But when I looked more closely I saw something hanging from the muslin I had fastened over the top of the jar to prevent any escape.

Dickon was rubbing Cadbury's belly when I ran to fetch him. The hound sat up and Dickon looped his arm around her neck. She turned her head and licked his face with her great pink tongue, nearly knocking him over.

"Come with me, Dickon," I said to him. "There's something I want to show you."

We looked together at the small, dark, elongated shape, slightly curved, like a tiny ripening fruit, that had anchored itself to the cloth lid with a minute button of silk.

"What is it, Mama?"

"It is a little butterfly coffin. It has to be!"

I sat down at my desk and wrote to James. I asked if he had his own apothecary shop yet, and was he still corresponding with butterfly collectors across the globe. I apologized for breaking off our correspondence, telling him I had married again, had been busy with babies, but that I had collected more butterflies since last I saw him and had cultivated a butterfly garden. And now I had reared a pupa, and it was like a small kernel of hope.

Devoted as a mourner, I took to visiting the little coffin and sitting beside it for long stretches at a time, as the pigeons and doves flapped and cooed around me. I did not know how long it took for a butterfly to emerge but I would not risk missing it. I came half dressed at dusk, and at sunrise, and in the afternoon. I watched and I waited until my limbs grew stiff from sitting so still. Over a matter of days the coffin changed, almost imperceptibly, grew paler, nearly translucent, so that I almost believed I saw the ghost of wings beneath its gossamer casing.

But then, when Annie and Dickon and I went to check on it together, we saw it changed again, blackened, shriveled to an empty shell, one from which the life had not been expelled but had been entirely extinguished. There was to be no newborn butterfly.

"Damn it," I said quietly.

"Why is it so important to you, Mistress Glanville?" Annie asked.

I looked from Dickon's nervous eyes into Annie's hungry ones, looked at her bony little body, tried to explain. "The preachers have been telling us all this century that the end of the world is nigh," I said. "They have been preaching that the Horsemen of the Apocalypse are nearly upon us. In my short lifetime I have lived through war and plague and fire, and now it seems that if the harvests continue to fail, we are on the brink of a famine."

Annie nodded gravely. I was telling her nothing she had not already heard from the pulpit a score of times.

"They say the comets that were seen crossing the skies before the war foretold these calamities that have befallen our age."

She nodded again.

"Well, all I wanted, all I was hoping for, I suppose, was to see a more promising sign for once, something to hold on to in this dark time we live in."

"A sign?" Annie said. "From a worm, Ma'am?"

"I hoped I would see it become more than a worm." I smiled weakly.

"That it is, Mama," Dickon exclaimed. "Look!"

I stepped back in revulsion. The shriveled pupa was disintegrating before our eyes. Something was emerging from it after all. Instead of a butterfly there was a small swarm of tiny nasty pesky flies, like the ones that fed on carrion, as if to prove to me once and for all that nothing glorious ever arose from any coffin, that a tomb was a place only where rotting flesh was devoured and turned to dust.

Old habits die hard. It was still a struggle for me to discount signs and portents as nothing but superstition, hard to believe that what I had just seen meant nothing. That was why, despite instantly recognizing the untidy handwriting on the package which Richard held out to me, had indeed come down to the dovecote especially to give to me, I took it from him with some foreboding, not wanting to open it right away. That it should arrive at just that moment!

"What is it?" Richard asked me suspiciously.

Our recent differences had been set aside, if not exactly resolved, which was the best I could ever hope for. Sometimes I knew why my husband was angry or withdrawn or had fallen into a dark mood, but usually I had no notion. I did know that there was no point in asking him, since he would never talk about it, but that it would pass. All I could do was try not to aggravate the situation by retaliating, try to be patient with him, which was not always easy.

I was glad to see now that he was in good spirits, and did not want to risk spoiling it by having him find out that the parcel was from James Petiver.

"I think it must be a book," I said, wondering what it was that James had enclosed with his reply to my letter. Well, whatever it was, it could wait.

I set the package aside, took Richard's arm and walked with him out onto the sunlit moor. The sky arced above us, a heavenly blue, tufted with wispy clouds that were driven along by the silkiest breeze, rustling in the willows and the long grass.

"Did you ever lie on your back and look for shapes in the clouds?" he asked me.

I smiled. "Doesn't everyone?"

"I don't know. Do they?"

"I am sure that everyone who lives under a Somerset sky, or a Fenland one, must."

We had been walking over an area of grass and sedge, grazed short by the cattle, but he drew me off to the side, into a patch where the grass was still thigh high, and took off his coat and spread it out. He pulled me gently down with him, lay out on his back with his arms behind his head and his legs crossed at the ankles.

I lay next to him and he unfolded one arm for me to pillow my head upon, bent it down and around my shoulder so his hand rested lightly over my breast. We were completely hidden and it was surprisingly comfortable. The ground was soft and spongy, and the air was filled with the scent of crushed grass.

"What do you see, then?" I asked him.

"In truth, not much." He laughed.

I watched as two white butterflies played in the air above us like living snowflakes.

"Do you know, Cabbage White butterflies have the most extraordinary and elaborate mating ritual," I told him very softly. "They are the most erotic little creatures on earth."

He idly stroked my breast with his elegant fingers. "I think *you* are the most erotic little creature on earth."

I smiled, nestled closer to him and tilted my head closer so it rested against the side of his. "I have watched them often," I said. "They chase after each other and flirt for ages, until they alight on the same flower and join their bodies. But the amazing thing is that they stay together like that and carry each other upward into the sky. Sometimes they remain locked together for hours after their coupling, and sometimes they cannot separate at all and they die still joined. They literally die of love."

Richard lifted himself above me, looked down into my face and gave me a gentle kiss that had in it much of sorrow and regret. Or maybe that is just how I remember it, because of what happened afterward. A kiss of farewell.

It was a glorious pleasure to me to make love outside, to feel fresh air on my thighs, on my breasts, to feel the prickle of the sedges and grass beneath me and the sun on my face as our bodies moved and rocked together, the murmurs and sighs and little moans of lovemaking mingling with the calling of the marsh birds and the distant croak of a frog.

He stayed inside me awhile after he was spent, and then moved over so we lay side by side, still wrapped in each other's arms.

"There is much to be said for being a white butterfly," he said, his mouth in my hair and a smile in his voice.

"If I died now," I told him, "I should die quite happy."

I stroked his tumbled curls and saw that more clouds had come into the sky, not fluffy white ones for lying and gazing up at, but massing, gray, windblown clouds that scudded much too fast ever to see shapes in. A chill had crept into the air that was almost wintry. The summer was over when it had only just begun. The world was turning back into darkness once more. But when I looked back to that time, afterward, I had a notion that if only I had closed my eyes, the storm clouds would have rushed on over us and eventually have passed us by, and that I could have kept Richard safe in my arms forever. That we could have been like the white butterflies, two souls joined, drifting together on the warm currents of the air for all eternity.

I TOOK JAMES'S PARCEL to the willow tree in the bend in the river, where I had read countless other letters from him. Inky rain clouds had gathered now on the horizon, were advancing toward the moor. With the sun still shining behind and around them, they cast a heavy golden-blue light.

I doubted I would finish the letter before the rain began, given that it was such a very long one, many pages long in fact, as if James had been saving up things to tell me all these years. It was indeed a book he had enclosed with the letter, small and slim-bound, but I set it aside without so much as a glance at the title, suddenly eager only to read what James had written. He began by answering my questions. Yes, he said, he had his own shop, at the sign of the white cross on Aldersgate Street, and it was prospering. His customers included sea captains and ship's surgeons who still collected specimens for him from all over the world. His friend the botanist John Ray had recently recommended him for Fellowship of the Royal Society, and he had been elected for membership a month ago.

That gave me pause. I knew how much it would mean to James to be welcomed into Fellowship of the foremost scientific society of Europe. He had described for me the great laboratories of Gresham College, where crucibles and furnaces were used to investigate the properties of rocks and minerals and curiosities from distant lands. He described the activities of the Royal Society so well that by the time I reached the last page of his letter, I almost felt I'd met its president, Samuel Pepys, and Isaac Newton and Edmund Halley, had listened with my own ears to the hot debates on classification, as well as to experiments in the more marginal sciences of astronomy, mathematics and physics. I felt almost as if I had witnessed for myself the dawn of science, of a new world. But I had not. When James spoke of a general feeling that England was at the center of a worldwide scientific enterprise of lasting importance, what he really meant was London. Not Somersetshire.

And the little book he had enclosed? He said he had wanted to send it to me years ago, when first it was published, but had not done so because it would have seemed a strange thing to send to me out of the blue. It had been translated from French, he said. The author was Robert Talbor, the feverologist, who, it transpired, had sold the formula for his cure for ague to King Louis of France, on condition it not be made public until after Talbor's death. James said he remembered the interest I had once shown in Jesuits' Powder and thought I would be interested, therefore, to learn that it was indeed the secret ingredient in Talbor's mysterious miracle cure. A strong infusion of it, mixed with six drams of rose leaves and two ounces of lemon juice.

I frowned, no more than puzzled at first. If Jesuits' Powder was a miracle cure rather than a deadly Papist poison, why had Edmund died?

My brain seemed to be working very slowly and the obvious, natural explanation eluded me, hovering somewhere just out of reach, too grotesquely ugly to face. As realization dawned, the rushing of the river faded away. The sound of the wind in the trees dimmed. In absolute silence, the book slid from my fingers. It seemed to take the longest time to fall, and when it tumbled at last into the grass, the sound of it was like a falling tree, like a breaking heart.

I sank back against the trunk of the willow, slid down it to the ground. Realization was like a wave crashing over my head, dragging me down. I felt ice cold, as if I had been washed away. I felt something twist and tear irrevocably inside me.

If Jesuits' Powder was a cure and not a poison, then it could not have been Jesuits' Powder that I had given to Edmund. It could not have been Jesuits' Powder that Richard had brought back from London and given to me for him.

My heart had turned to lead. It felt too heavy to go on beating. The first raindrop fell on Robert Talbor's book, then on my hands, my face. The downpour came on quickly, heavily, but I could no more stand up than take flight. I did not think I would ever be able to stand up or walk again. I watched the ink on James's letter start to blur, the words begin to run. I drew up my legs away from the book, as if it was tainted. I wrapped my arms around my knees, watching the rain pimple the cover. The river began to rush, but there was no break in the clouds. In what seemed like no time at all, dusk had fallen, deepened by the rain that came down now in a slanting torrent and had soaked me to my skin. I did not feel it, did not feel anything, was totally numb, wanted only to stay that way for as long as I could. I dreaded the numbness receding, as it must, giving way to a horror that would be intolerable. I rested my head against my knees, closed my eyes, wished I could sleep, sleep forever and never wake.

I did not even hear the soft thud of a horse's hooves on the damp earth. I let Richard pick me up in his arms and put me carefully into the saddle. I watched him pick up the pulpy little book and letter and put them in his pocket. I let him hold me gently all the way back over the moor to the house. He carried me into the great hall and up the stairs to the bedchamber. Bess rushed in and started fussing around me, but it was Richard who unfastened my sodden gown, pulled my wet chemise off over my head as if I was a small child. It was Richard who loosened my hair and gently dried it. I let him wipe my face, rub my arms. I let him wrap a warm blanket over me and I knew that soon, when feeling returned, I should not be able to bear for him to touch me ever again.

"Nell, in Jesus' name, what is the matter?" he said, sitting down beside me.

I turned my eyes on him dumbly, unable to reply. I wanted only to scream: What have you done? Oh God, Richard. What have you done? Did you kill Edmund? Did you have me murder Edmund?

"It is just a turn, I'm sure," Bess said. "She's had too much sun to her head. We're not used to it, after all the cold."

Richard looked cold now, and frightened, very frightened. But he would do, wouldn't he, harboring a guilt such as that for years? No wonder that haunted, guarded look so often came into his eyes. No wonder the black moods, the nightmares, the sleeplessness. No wonder the distance between us.

I watched in a trance as he took off his shirt and untied the laces of his breeches. My eyes were drawn to the thin scar on his left thigh, remnant of an injury he told me he had sustained when, aged eight, he had engaged in swordplay with a particularly vicious Parisian boy two years older than he. He had damaged his shoulder that time he had tried to jump his horse over the River Yeo, and by the end of each day it tended to stiffen, though I knew just where to rub it to make the ache go away. I had kissed that little scar so often, stroked it with my fingers. I knew his body as intimately as I knew my own. It seemed there was not a part of it I did not know, had not caressed and kissed, but had I ever known the soul that resided in that beautiful body at all?

When he climbed into the bed he reached out to take me into his arms. I flinched from his touch and straightaway scrambled out of the other side. There was a flash in his eyes then, like the slash of a sword, and it was as if a mask had been cut away. He stared at me, angry and aggrieved. He said nothing, did not ask me now what was wrong. He looked as if he knew that I finally understood exactly what he had done. As if there was no further need for pretense. There was no mistaking it, he stared at me with guilt. And with hatred.

I TOOK A TORCH and walked down to the moor again, found myself wandering over the river and across the Tickenham Road, up the stony track to Folly Farm, an isolated low little farmhouse, nestled in trees at the foot of Cadbury Camp. It had not been tenanted for years because it had fallen into disrepair, and the funds that might have been used to repair it had been spent instead on the new coach house. The door hung on its hinges and the kitchen was empty except for a rickety table and stools. It was dirty and dark and cold. There was a hole in the crooked lath ceiling and a corresponding one in the thatched roof in the room above, so that it was possible to look up and see right through to chinks of starry sky. But at least, being built where the ground started to rise, it was quite dry. It was a sin that it had been left empty so long. I would see it put to rights and turned into a good home for someone.

There was half a bushel in the grate, enough to get a small fire going, and I curled up on the bare floor beside it with my cloak as a blanket. My face and my hands were warm enough, but the fire did not even air the room or do much to compensate for the broken roof. I slept with an icy chill at my back.

In the morning I went out to the well at the back of the farmhouse and washed in a bucket of cold water before I went back to the house to find Bess.

She waited for me to finish sneezing before she handed me the cup of hot cider. "Well, if you will stay out in a rainstorm, what do you expect, if you don't mind me saying?"

"Where is Richard?" I asked, wrapping my fingers around the warmth of the cup to stop them trembling.

"I take it the two of you had another falling-out? Why else would you go for a midnight wander and he ride off as if the hounds of Hell were on his tail?"

They are, I wanted to tell her. Bess, they are. They have been for years.

But I could not voice my fears. If I did, it made them real.

"I need to go to bed," I said to her. But I did not know where to go. Not to the chamber I shared with Richard, nor the one he had always used when he came here as Edmund's guest. I wanted to sleep somewhere where he would not think to look for me. "I shall go to your room," I said to Bess.

She looked aghast. "In the attic, Ma'am?"

"Yes."

I lay down on the little pallet, but I could not sleep. Thoughts flew at me haphazardly, like an ambush of arrows all fired from different angles. No judge would ever find him guilty. Even if it was Richard who had come back from London with poison, it was I who had administered it, I who put it into the claret and held it to Edmund's lips for him to drink. So easy it would have been for Richard to do it. So easy to visit an apothecary and purchase a poison instead of a cure. But why? Was it out of desperation? Out of love for me? That competitive spirit of his? Because he could not stand for Edmund to have me? Or was it the pursuit of wealth that had motivated him? Why else would he have been so against a marriage settlement? Why else ...

What was I thinking? I loved him, had lived with him and shared his bed every night for ten years. Richard was not capable of murder ... was he? The vulnerability and impulsiveness that had so enchanted me now seemed sure indications of a character that was dangerously unstable. I needed to see him. If I could only see him, only look into his eyes again, I'd know that I'd been mistaken, horribly mistaken. I'd know it could not be true.

I heard my father's voice then, so loud he might have come to sit right beside me. *These are men who would break any trust or dare any act of treachery to satisfy their passions and appetites, who are uncontrolled by any fear of God or man. . . . You will be prey to every unscrupulous Cavalier.*

"You have a visitor, Ma'am," Bess came to tell me later, much later, when the sun was sinking in the sky again. "Shall I tell him you are ill, or shall I help you to dress?"

"Who is it?"

"Gentleman by the name of Joseph Barnes. Asked to see the lady who collects butterflies."

"I'll see him," I decided, thinking that anything was preferable to lying here, with suspicion battering my head until it throbbed.

Bess helped me into my gown of moss-green silk and fastened up my hair, but as soon as she was gone I shook it loose since my head was hurting so much.

Joseph Barnes was a foppish young gentleman traveler who explained effusively that he was on the way to sample the excellent waters in Bath. "I decided to stop at the inn in Tickenham for the night and couldn't help hearing the locals talking over their ale about the lady of the manor who is paying anyone who brings her worms. I went to the trouble of finding some, just for the privilege of seeing you for myself."

"Did you?" If I'd not had so much on my mind, it would probably have unnerved me to know I was being talked about in such a way, that I was attracting such interest, but now it only added to the strange air of unreality. "I did not realize I was a local curiosity, sir," I said, sneezing again. "You'd find the caves of Cheddar Gorge far more interesting, or the cove at Ladye Bay. Even the rhynes and moors, I can assure you. They attract dragonflies and butterflies that even the Royal Society finds of interest. I am afraid I must be a great disappointment."

He made a little bow. "On the contrary. You are uncommonly pretty and erudite. I had imagined an old hag."

I laughed and it sounded very odd to my ears, as if I should never laugh again. "So where are these worms?" He did not appear to have come with any vessel at all.

He produced a highly ornamented snuffbox and opened it. Two striking little creatures wriggled most obligingly, black speckled with yellow. Despite everything, because of everything, my interest was spiked.

"I stung myself on the nettles, getting them for you," he complained.

"Did you bring any with you?"

"Nettles, you mean?" He frowned. "I am afraid not."

"These are good specimens," I said, giving one a tiny prod with my finger. "But they will need a plentiful supply of the right food plant. Can you show me exactly where you found them?"

He seemed glad of the chance to walk with me, and set off as frisky as a young pup, bounding haphazardly from one new and thrilling scent to another.

The light was failing, the dusky blue of the vast sky streaked with palest lemon. The air was busy with gnats, and in the distance, a plover was calling. We walked over Cut Bush Field toward the Yeo, and just before the mill, my fashionable companion indicated a patch of common nettles by the trackside.

"You are sure that is the plant?"

"I am quite certain."

I thanked him, paid him sixpence and sent him on his way, then bent to pick some of the stalks. I chose the healthiest shoots and took a whole handful, tearing off the muslin trim on my gown to bind them and protect my hands from the serrated leaves. I walked back alone across the twilit moor.

Richard was standing beneath the oriel, staring not at my hair that hung down to my hips, nor at my ripped gown, but at the Gothic prickly posy I carried through the dusk. He stared as if it was of great significance, as if within its spiky leaves lay a hidden truth, an answer, as if I had come to scatter our marriage bed with stinging nettles, where once it had been scattered with bright summer flowers.

As I came closer I saw that there was something very wrong with him. He had been drinking, and his eyes were dark, so dark against the unnatural pallor of his face, as cold and as hard as winter stars. I came on, and if I had hoped to see a man incapable of murder, I saw the opposite. I saw rage and a naked, glittering, unadulterated hatred that made me falter and drop the nettles, afraid to go any closer. He was breathing deeply and there were beads of sweat on his brow.

He stepped up to me, raised his hand and slapped me across my cheek, so hard that my head whipped to the side and it felt as if my neck would snap. My skin stung; there was a sharp pain in my lip and the metallic taste of blood in my mouth. Before I had a chance to recover, he grabbed my arm with such force it felt as if it would be wrenched from its socket, and dragged me, stumbling behind him, into the hall and up the narrow stone stairs. The clothes chest was thrown open, and my boxes and observation books and an untidy pile of James's letters were heaped beside it, opened. Richard took up one of the letters, held it in front of my face and slowly ripped it in half. With one swift fluid movement he put the two halves together and tore again, let the pieces scatter to the floorboards.

He took hold of another, and started to tear.

"No!" Fury erupted inside me—uncontrolled, desperate, searing fury. I grabbed the collecting box and hit him with it. He tore the box from me, smashed it down over my hands, cutting them and driving splinters into my skin. He snatched a specimen box and did the same with that, and with a single violent swipe of his arm he knocked the rest off the bed, sending them crashing to the floor in a flutter of broken wings and little broken furry bodies. I collapsed beside them in a flurry of silk and lace and petticoats, and he brought the spurred heel of his boot down on the little wings and crushed them as if he would crush and trample my heart.

"I should have seen it before," he said, in a guttural voice I hardly recognized as his. "As soon as you started with this absurd fixation. Beating at trees and crawling under bushes, rambling around half dressed, like a gypsy. Talking gibberish about miracles and worms. Now you carry a gruesome bouquet of weeds, as if they were the sweetest roses. You grieve for dead maggots and pay people a small fortune to bring you live ones. You stir a pile of cow manure like a cook with the broth."

I shook my head, shaped my mouth to deny that, but no sound came.

"Do not try to gainsay it," he spat. "Your word stands for naught. All that they say about you is true. It has taken me long enough to see it, but I see it now. You are not in your right mind. You must be . . . completely insane."

NEXT TO ACCUSING ME of witchcraft, lunacy was the most dangerous charge he could have made. The mad were creatures to inspire terror. They were bewitched, visited by Satan, possessed by demons, souls who were preyed upon by the armies of the night. Lunacy was a charge which carried with it the threat of chains and confinement, of asylums, of the loss of all rights and liberties.

It was the only charge he could have made that would enable him to overturn the marriage settlement and seize control of my estate. I did not know how easy it would be for him to accomplish, I could not even be sure that was what he planned to do, but I did know that there were plenty of people who would support such claims.

I would fight him, fight them all with everything that I had, but my first thought was to get the children away to safety. As soon as Richard had fallen into a rum-induced sleep in a chair in the parlor, I packed a trunk and went to wake the girls and Dickon.

"Hurry and put on your clothes," I urged Ellen, setting a candle on the table and depositing a heap of gowns and stockings and breeches on the bed.

"Where are we going?" she mumbled, clutching the linen sheet over her body.

"To London," I said, trying to make an adventure of it.

"But it's dark outside," she complained. "Can't we wait until morning?"

"No, sweetheart." I pulled a petticoat over Ellen's head. "I'm afraid

we cannot. Here." I put my hand into my pocket. "I have brought you
a treat."

"Marchpane! In the middle of the night?"

"Why not?"

The bribe worked and I helped Ellen into her stockings, made sure
Mary had her cloak. I saw the three of them out to the waiting coach,
carrying Ellen in my arms, still wrapped tight in her rich colored blanket, with Dickon clinging anxiously to my skirts, as if he thought I
might leave him behind or that someone might try to snatch him from
me. The coachman folded down the iron steps and handed the girls
in. The lanterns were already lit, the lights from them hazy in the mist.

Dickon suddenly turned and sprinted back to the house. I ran after
him to the nursery, where he began collecting up all the animals cur-
rently residing there, namely two chickens, a piglet, a toad, a pike and
the swan. Together we carried them outside and set them free in a
wild flurry of wings and feathers. I took the bucket and tipped the
toad and the pike into Monk's Pool and Dickon came back with
Cadbury at his heels.

I helped him heft her into the coach.

"You know I cannot come with you while my mother is still ill,"
Bess told me as I lifted my skirts and put my foot on the first step.

"I understand."

"Where shall I tell him that you have gone?"

"Say that you do not know."

"He is sure to guess."

"No matter, so long as I am not here." Here, I might have added,
where thanks to our brother few were likely to question my husband
too closely if he said I was not fit to manage my affairs, that I must
be locked up.

The coach lurched into motion. So afraid was I of Richard waking
to find us gone and coming in pursuit of us that I shouted up to the

coachman to go faster. For the first few miles he drove the horses on through the night with a flailing whip. But after we had, of necessity, slowed to a steadier roll, Dickon gave me a little tug to tell me that he wanted to say something to me privately. He had not spoken one word to me since I had woken him and bundled him into the coach, but I had caught him glancing worriedly at my cut lip. He sensed my fear in a way the girls had not, knew this was no adventure. I lowered my head so he could whisper.

"Mama, are we running away from my father?"

It sounded such a despairing thing to do, I would not admit to it. And somehow it did not feel true. It did not feel as if we were running from anything, but toward it.

I turned to look down at the little head of his sleeping sister, curled in my other arm, and over to Mary, who was gazing out of the window at the blue dawn-lit fields. "No, darling," I said to my youngest son. "We are not running away. Look. See where the sky is turning pink. That is where we are going. We are traveling east. We are following the sun."

"We will come back?"

"Oh, yes," I said. "We will come back. As soon as I have worked out what to do."

I heard my father's voice once again. . . . *Never forget that you carry the stain of Eve's sins upon your soul. . . . Never forget that Eden was lost to her because of that sin.*

Tickenham was my home, it was mine and my children's, and I would never let Richard or anyone else take it from me.

I HAD NOT EXPECTED Aldersgate Street to be so grand. It was very long and spacious, lined with innumerable inns and taverns, interspersed amongst mansions fit for dukes and marquesses.

I had left all three children at Mary Burges's table, eating pottage and pudding, and I was glad that I had at least taken the time to change into a gown of rose silk and creamy lace, and had tidied my hair and dabbed rose water on my wrists and throat.

A bell tinkled in the shop as I opened the door on a room like none I had ever seen before, a strange, eccentric, wonderful room. There was a grand carved fireplace and oak floor and oak wainscot paneling. The far wall was lined with tiny drawers and shelves full of beautiful glazed apothecary jars and pill slabs. There was a dish filled with dried vipers, and a crocodile skin hung from the ceiling. Even the air was different, heavy with the exotic, pungent scent of herbs.

James was serving a customer from behind a wide oak counter, his corn-blond hair tied back, sleeves rolled up and a pestle and mortar at his elbow. He did not see me when I entered, too busy measuring powder on brass scales. "Angelica can be used to treat any epidemic diseases, though pray you have no use for it on your voyage, Robert," he said as he handed over a sachet in exchange for coins. He made notes in a ledger. Then he looked up, saw me, and his quill stopped in midair. For a moment he looked at me so oddly that I half thought he did not know who I was. Until he smiled.

I smiled back, gestured with my hand. "Please, do not neglect your customer on my behalf."

James tore his eyes away, back to the man at the counter, as if he feared I might disappear while he was otherwise engaged. "Robert, this is Eleanor Glanville," he said. "She will be as interested as I am in the specimens you send back from the Americas. Mistress Glanville," he said to me, "meet Robert Rutherford, ship's surgeon."

Mr. Rutherford bowed.

"That is everything, I think, Robert," James said. "Except for something to help rid you of the tetters, which I can see is still troubling you."

The surgeon touched the back of his hand where the skin was red and flaky. "Oh, I'm resigned to living with the itch now," he said.

"Well, you shouldn't have to be. Try some bryony. Its leaves are good for cleansing all sores and the powder of the dried root cleanses the skin." James handed over another sachet. "Take both, with my compliments."

Mr. Rutherford added them to his chest. "You are a generous man, Mr. Petiver. I am much obliged to you, much obliged indeed."

"As I am to you." James opened a drawer behind the counter, handed over a thermometer and some quires of brown paper. "For the plants. And here's a fresh collecting book. You have a net and bottles?"

"I do, and the printed instructions for preserving specimens which you gave to me the last time. Don't worry, sir, I know what to do now." Rutherford grinned. "I will be sure on this voyage to look in the stomachs of sharks for strange animals as I was unable to do last time. It'll be as if you've been to South Carolina and Massachusetts Bay yourself when you see all that I'll bring back for you."

"I wish you a very speedy return, then," James said, as the surgeon headed for the door. "But above all a safe one."

"Aye, I heard how your collectors keep dying off, done in by natives and mysterious diseases or lost at sea. Don't worry, I'll not fail you. I will be back."

"When do you sail?"

"Next Thursday with the tide, wind permitting. Good day to you, Mr. Petiver." He gave a nod to me as he passed me on his way out. "Good day to you too, Mistress Glanville."

James came around to the other side of the counter and took my hands. "You have come back at last. Why has it taken you so long?"

"I honestly don't know."

I looked for changes in him, but found none to speak of. Not even a hint of gray in his fair hair. He was just the same, lithesome and slight, with eyes that radiated warmth and boundless enthusiasm and intelligence, and were flecked with all of nature's colors. I could not even see any lines around them.

"I had not imagined your shop would be quite so extraordinary and grand," I said. "Even though I know you are a member of the Royal Society and a respected man of medicine now."

He stood back to look at me. "You are grand and extraordinary enough yourself." He smiled generously. "I still do not even pretend to follow fashion, but I know enough to recognize a very fine gown and cloak when I see one." He touched my arm, seeing that my eyes were not half as bright as my clothes, even after a little flattery. "We cannot talk properly here," he said. "I'll close the shop and we'll go to the tavern and you can tell me how everything is with you."

We walked up Aldersgate Street toward St. Botolph's Church and the city gate. We passed numerous taverns on the way but James led me to the Bell Inn, a respectable establishment with wagons drawn up outside. Within it was full of gentlemen travelers, smoking clay pipes and eating oysters, beneath the low sloping ceiling. We took our pots of ale and found a quiet corner where a mongrel was curled by the fire.

"You have achieved all you set out to achieve," I said, after he'd drawn up a stool opposite mine.

"Oh, there is always more to do, more to discover. I will never have the time to finish even a fraction of all I want to do, if I live to be seventy."

He could well live to such a great age. He looked so full of life and vigor still.

"What has made you come back to London now, Eleanor? After all this time?"

I looked down at my hands, lightly folded in my lap, and I did not know where to begin.

He touched the cut on my lip, almost healed after four days' traveling, but still visible. "He has hurt you?"

"He did," I admitted. "But only once. And not badly. It is his right, after all," I added bitterly. "As my husband he has every authority, over my body and my conduct. If he wished to beat me, no law in the country would come to my defense. But I could bear a beating. It is not that. He says that I am mad."

Silence fell briefly. "It is not the first time you've had that accusation made against you, is it?" James said at length. "I have suffered it too, as has anyone who collects butterflies. Just last week I had a letter from a sea captain who was collecting for me in Spain when he was set upon by locals. They accused him of sorcery and of necromancy, of chasing butterflies in an attempt to commune with the spirits of the dead."

I was shocked. "Surely, nobody really believed he was a necromancer?"

"I am afraid that the Age of Reason has not reached some parts of Spain."

"Just as it has not reached some parts of England." I clutched my pot of ale. "I came to London because I am afraid of what Richard will try to do. I am afraid that he means to have me locked up so he can take possession of my estate. As my wedded husband, he could do that, couldn't he? He could lock me up and seize everything. That is what they do to the insane, isn't it?"

"It happens," James said bluntly, and I was so grateful to him for not trying to belittle my fears. "But he would have to bring lunacy proceedings against you before he would be allowed to keep you under any restraint. He would have to petition the Lord Chancellor and convince a jury that you were incapable of managing yourself or your estate."

"There are enough people who would support his claim." I put down my pot and fingered the cascades of lace at the sleeves of my gown. "James, you must have been to see the lunatics in the new Bedlam?" I whispered the question with a morbid fascination. "Is it as terrible as they say? Are they filthy and naked and ranting, left to rattle their shackles and starve in cells that are stinking and damp and always dark?"

"Nobody is going to send you to Bedlam," he said quietly. "Nor anywhere like it. The asylums are for the poor." He gave a half-smile. "Those who are wealthy and insane are committed to the care of a physician, and if they are confined, it is in a warm and comfortable room in their own country mansion. But Eleanor, you are not mad," he reassured me. "You are exuberant and enthusiastic. You are passionate and you are obsessive. To many that may look very like madness, but you are probably the sanest person I have ever met."

"You do not subscribe, then, to the notion that there are demons which prey on obsession and passion?"

"I believe that is a most convenient deterrent, put about to discourage obsession and passion, which I think is a very great pity and makes the world a far poorer place."

I smiled at that. "You are a wonderful person."

"Coming from you, that is the highest praise."

"You do not believe that all women are creatures of weak reason either?"

He let his hands fall from mine. "I cannot speak for all women. I have known too few of them, and those whom I have known I have known too vaguely. I have always been too busy."

"That sounds a lame excuse."

"Does it? Perhaps it is. I admit I have little faith in the state of matrimony. It does not seem to bring many people contentment. You yourself have tried it twice and it seems to me that both have led to great sorrow and pain, of one sort or another."

"If I had not married, I would not have my children," I said. "If I had not married Richard, I would not have little Ellen, who is as exquisite as a doll, and Dickon, who is so clever and kind it humbles me." I smiled. "Oh, James, you should see how he turned the house into an ark with all the wounded creatures he takes in. He has a talent for healing them. But I worry for him. He is so sensitive. He has never really got along with his father. I shall have to go back to Tickenham, to face Richard's accusations, but I do not want Dickon there with me."

"How old is he?"

"Nine."

"Is he tall? Would he pass for a couple of years older?"

"In manner, most definitely."

"Then bring him to me and I will take him as my apprentice."

Instantly I saw that it was a perfect solution. Since the Glanville family seat at Elmsett was ruined and there were no funds to repair it, Dickon would have to make his own way in the world. He would need a profession, and medicine would suit him more than most. I could not wish for a better master to tutor him.

"Don't worry." James smiled. "I will not make him bed down under the counter, like the usual sort of apprentice. He will have his own dormitory and eat his meals at my table." His eyes held mine with rare tenderness. "I promise to care for him as if he was my own son."

"Thank you, James."

"It is you who is doing me the greater service," he said with his usual generosity. "I need help with my work, and I know any son of yours will be honest and quick to learn and very charming company with it."

I felt a little pang of shameful envy that I tried very hard to quash, but could not quite. All I could think was that I should like very much to be bound as James Petiver's apprentice. I should like nothing better than to know that I would be learning from him, working side by side with him, every day for the next seven years.

ENVY MADE ME a little impatient with Dickon as I helped him sort his own possessions from the trunk and put them into a small portmanteau we had borrowed from John Burges. Dickon was as dejected as Cadbury, who trailed at his heels with her tail between her legs.

"I'll take care of her for you, I promise," I tried to assure him.

He turned to me then, his bottom lip trembling. "I want to stay with you," he said, plaintively. "Mama, why do I have to go?"

Faced with his doleful eyes, I felt my heart completely melt. I went to him and wrapped him in my arms, a knot in my own throat. I clasped his head to my chest and pressed my lips into his hair. "This is a great opportunity, Dickon," I told him gently. "You could not have a better master than James Petiver. He is a good man, a clever man, my dearest friend. You will learn so much from him. Will you try to be brave, Dickon, for me?"

He nodded.

James welcomed him with an arm about his shoulders and took him off on a tour of the premises. The back of the shop was even more bizarre and amazing than the front, like a sorcerer's laboratory, with cauldrons bubbling and steaming and liquids distilling in bottles and tubes. Outside was something equally amazing and sublime. James had established his own idyllic little physic garden.

I felt like Cadbury as I trailed behind them, up the straight grassed avenues and neat rows of herbs and medicinal plants, trying to quell the pangs of regret that only magnified with each friendly, enthusiastic word James spoke to my young son and made me wish, now more than ever, that I had been born a boy.

"You will accompany me on my rounds and become familiar with patients and diseases in a way that medical students in Oxford and Cambridge, who are restricted to academic learning, never have the chance to do," James said. "There will be a few menial tasks, I'm afraid, but not too many. Most of the time you'll be learning about the mystery and craft of compounding drugs and simples, and how to recognize medicinal plants and where they grow in woods and meadows. Several times each year we shall take the Apothecary Society's state barge up the river with the other masters and apprentices and roam around the meadows of Gravesend and Tickenham, collecting plants to bring back here or take to the Company Hall for discussion." James flicked a humorous sideways glance at me. "Your mother was always very interested to hear about those days and the riotous suppers which usually end them."

I glanced away, in case the envy had so magnified it had turned my blue eyes to green.

When we had completed a full circuit and were back in the shop, I knew I could delay no longer. "I will be on my way, then," I said, going to Dickon to kiss him good-bye. His lip was trembling again. "Don't," I commanded softly. "Or I will start too."

"Mama, I will miss you."

I stroked his cheek. "I will miss you too, my little love."

"Ach, stop it, the pair of you," James said. "You will neither of you have the chance to miss each other. Dickon, your mother is welcome here anytime, she should know that. She can come to the shop every day to see you, if she wants to." He was addressing my son, but his words were very definitely directed at me. Then he turned to me and I knew that it was a waste of time trying to conceal anything from him. My face was an open book to him. James, like Richard, read it as easily as my father used to read the Bible. He smiled, as if at some private joke shared between us. "She can be as an apprentice herself, if that is what she would like to be."

. . .

I MADE MYSELF GIVE Dickon a day or two to settle in on his own. When I went back to the shop, I was impressed anew by its extraordinary atmosphere, part scientific, part magical. For many, the study of herbs was still allied to magic, for all that apothecaries worked side by side with physicians. Camphor vied for shelf space with brimstone, artists' dyes with substances used in alchemy. And in the midst of it all was James, standing betwixt the old world and the new.

He looked up from grinding some dried leaves and salt in the mortar and smiled to see me. "He's in the laboratory," he said. "Go and see."

Dickon was seated at a bench, wearing an apron and measuring out a jar of juice into a bowl of oil. "It is self-heal and oil of roses," he said. "If you anoint the temples and forehead, it is very effectual in removing headache."

"Always good to know."

"And if you mix it with honey of roses, it heals ulcers in the mouth."

"I'll try to remember," I said.

"I cannot stop, or it will spoil," he told me.

"I'll not interrupt you, then." I wandered back out to the shop, feeling superfluous. "You keep my son too busy to talk to me," I complained teasingly to James.

He put down his pestle and gave me his full attention. "He's a capable boy. He takes notes of everything I tell him and knows the properties of the contents of a good proportion of the jars already." I smiled with the pleasure of any mother at hearing her child praised. "If he carries on at this rate, I'll be able to leave him in charge in a couple of months and concentrate on cataloguing my specimens." He saw my eyes brighten for a different reason. "I have so many sent to me now, from all over the world, that I can't keep up. I am afraid they are in the most terrible muddle. But I fear your son will be no help to me in that respect. I tried to show him some lizard specimens but he became almost distressed. Couldn't get away from them and scuttle back to the laboratory fast enough, in fact."

I smiled. "He does not approve of killing so much as a fly."

"It is no matter. My collection is not to everyone's liking."

"You know it would be very much to mine."

He looked almost abashed. "If I am to show it to you, it would mean going up to my rooms."

"It may be improper, but I am a most improper person." I smiled, linking my arm through his. "Ask anyone in Tickenham."

James left Dickon listening out for callers and led the way up a flight of steep, narrow stairs that ran up the outside of the shop and led to a little parlor. It smelled clean and fresh, with a hint of lavender and pencil shavings, but it was an utter mess. Clothes and books were heaped on chairs and the table, as were piles and piles of papers and letters. There were bottles of frogs, lizards, grasshoppers, and all varieties of small creatures—spiders, wasps, flies, lobsters, urchins—drowned in rum. Boxes of shells and cases of beetles were stacked on the floor or against the walls. There was an anaconda and a rattle-snake that still looked capable of slithering across the floor. It was like being in a dreamland, being given a tantalizing glimpse of a new world rich in color, utterly different from any I had ever known or even dreamed of.

But I turned to James and pulled a face.

He read my dismay and shrugged. "I did warn you."

"You did." I laughed. "But still, I was not quite prepared. Good Lord, James, I have never seen such a jumble."

But it was a treasure trove of a jumble, filled with promise. I raised my skirts as I would in the wet, and picked my way over to the table, where I lifted a box of beetles and was met with a glimpse of a stunning butterfly beneath. It had black-and-white-striped wings, in the sickle shape of a Swallowtail, and came from South Carolina, according to the note pinned beneath it.

"There are plenty rarer and far more beautiful even than that," James said. He gestured helplessly around the room, scratched the back of his head. "If only one knew where to look."

I itched to see more, but was reluctant to relegate the precious South Carolina butterfly back to its precarious pile in order to free up my hands. I might be consigning it to oblivion forever. I looked round for a more suitable place but there was none, not one clear surface.

James strode over a tower of collecting books and came to stand beside me. "I have tried to make some inroads."

"You have?"

He removed the American butterfly from my grasp and set it down, turned to a cabinet behind him and opened a long shallow drawer like a tray, releasing a lovely scent of cedarwood. Contained within it was a box of butterflies, their silvery-white wings marked with brown and orange borders and striking black eyespots. "White Peacocks, from the West Indies," he told me.

I ran my fingers over the glass, and it felt like trying to reach the sky or touch the stars.

"There are butterflies in this room from all over the world," James said tantalizingly. "Antigua. Barbados. New York. St. Christopher's Island."

"The sea captains and ship's surgeons send them to you, just like you said they would?"

"Aye, and in greater quantities than ever I had hoped."

I let my eyes linger on the captivating White Peacocks for a little longer. They were not perfect, missing a leg here or an antenna there, were ragged around the edges, but it did not seem to matter. It was heartening to know James no longer sought perfection. That he would not discard a pretty creature just for a broken wing.

"I have promised my friend John Ray that I will catalogue them, so he can include them in his great history of insects. But I lack the time."

"What you need, then"—I smiled—"is a person with some experience of cataloguing. A person who has plenty of time and is badly in need of some distracting occupation."

"And would you happen to know of such a person, by any chance?"

"Oh, I most certainly would."

Summer

1695

There was no formal arrangement as such, but I fell into a habit of going to the sign of the white cross at least every other day, and for most of those days, while James and Dickon were about their apothecary business, I climbed the narrow stairs to James's rooms above the shop and tidied and organized and was happy as a bee in clover. I spent the mornings with beetles and lizards and shells; the afternoons were devoted to butterflies, which I ordered according to color and then subdivided by size, until they were neatly graded in their cases like jewels strung on a necklace. In this room, if in no other part of my life, I had complete control. It was cathartic, putting things to rights, restoring order, squandering hours just marveling at the glorious little beings.

If I kept myself well occupied, I managed not to think of Richard, of what he was doing all alone at Tickenham. But at night, it was not so easy. It was so long since I had slept without him, and I missed the comforting sound of his breathing, missed lying in his arms, missed talking to him, missed making love to him, no matter how much I told myself that that was where I had gone wrong. Had my father not warned me that the heart is seldom wise and that a woman's body is driven by base desires?

It unnerved me that Richard had made no effort to contact me in all those weeks. If I am honest, it hurt me too, and in my hurt I took his silence as proof, if ever I needed it, that all he had ever wanted was Tickenham Court and that though he might be willing to let me go, he would not relinquish my estate without a fight. I knew that I must go back and fight him for it. But I could not face it, not yet. The girls were so happy being schooled by Mary; Dickon was happy with his books of herbals and anatomy. I did not know if Forest was happy. I had written to him twice in Flanders. Mary had written to him, but there had been no reply, and I did not doubt that he had had word from his stepfather and had taken his side, as he always had.

Sometimes, when the shop was quiet, or when I was so absorbed that I worked late into the evening, James came up with two pots of warm ale to join me, or brought up a plate of cheese and bread and fruit for us to share, and I showed him particular marvels I had just unearthed.

"Look," I said, "this has to be my absolute favorite."

"It is very lovely." James smiled at my delight and looked closer at the exquisite butterfly from Surinam, with iridescent wings of green and gold and a splash of deepest crimson.

I was so proud of it that it was almost as if I had discovered it in its natural habitat, rather than in the turmoil of a little London parlor. Almost, but not quite.

"Imagine how dazzling it would be on the wing," I said. "How I would like to see such a sight."

"You'll have to travel to Surinam, then," James said pragmatically.

"Wouldn't you like to?"

By way of an answer, he opened a collecting book he had brought up with him, and I gasped at the enormous Jamaican Swallowtail within. The wingspan was awesome, nearly half a foot at least, banded with luminous yellow and black. "In his covering letter, Allen Broderick described how because of its great size, it must hover before flowers while it feeds," James explained. "Of course I should like to see that for myself, but I am happy enough just to know it exists. I lack the funds to travel and I cannot neglect the shop and my trade for months on end. Besides, I am not nearly adventurous enough. I far prefer to let others better suited to it do the traveling for me." He closed the book on the Swallowtail, handed me another specimen to file. "I have promised Edmund Bouhn this will be called Bouhn's Yellow Spotted Carolina butterfly."

I laughed. "A very accurate description, since it has yellow spots, was found in Carolina and by a man named Bouhn."

It was a strategic description too. I had learned that James was very wily. Promising his collectors the kudos of having specimens named after them, and seeing their names in print, was one way he spurred them on to bring back more. I had found the catalogues he printed in which he listed finds and named donors.

"I would like to have a butterfly named after me," I said wistfully. "I would like to be connected for all time with the most beautiful of all creatures. I would feel then that my life had some significance. That would be immortality, of a kind."

"Of all the people in all the world to have a butterfly named after them, it should be you," James said. "You love them more than anyone I have ever met. You even look like one, as graceful and pretty and joyful as a little brimstone."

"But I have no wings." I smiled. "I can never travel, either." I spoke with a tug of longing that surprised me with its strength. After days spent amongst these exotic dead creatures and meeting in the shop some of the surgeons and captains bound for distant lands, I realized for the first time just how much I had always yearned to see more of the world, ever since I'd studied the names of foreign lands on my father's globe. "I am a woman of some means, but I am just as hampered as you, since ladies do not travel alone to far-off continents. And what are the chances of me discovering a new species in England? All the butterflies I see have been seen before by one of your friends. Although I did once see a Fritillary, on the cliffs, that I could have sworn had different markings from all the others."

"But there are dozens of undiscovered butterflies still flying in English skies," James said, in his usual tone of optimism and subtle encouragement. "You could be the person to find one of them." He looked around the now almost tidy parlor. "After all, it can be no more taxing than trying to find anything in this room, and yet you have found just about everything."

"I'm not quite finished yet." I indicated the piles of letters still stacked against the wall. "They should really be filed."

He seemed to sense my reluctance to pry into his correspondence. "You are welcome to read them, Eleanor," he said. "I keep no secrets from you."

1695

 ow that I had unearthed the table, James said he
had put it to use and had invited Hans Sloane to
dine. "I want Hans to meet you, and you him," he
said with a grin. "Properly, I mean, rather than in
disguise."

"What about John Ray too?" I asked. "Don't you want to let him
have the collections for his book now?"

"Regrettably John is too old and ill to come to London anymore.
His legs pain him so much, he cannot even walk in his own orchard."

"Oh." I could not hide my disappointment, had such fond memories of the kindly, wise old man. "I was looking forward to showing
him what I've done. I should enjoy being able to talk to him, without
worrying whether my voice sounds too high for me to pass as a boy."

This time it was Hans Sloane who looked as if he had come in
costume. I would never have recognized him if James's manservant,
George, had not announced him, so regal had he become. He had
served as physician to the Duke of Albemarle, governor of Jamaica,
and was now secretary to the Royal Society, physician to King William and Queen Mary, but he looked like a duke or a king himself, as

opulently dressed and stately, with a lustrous periwig and heavily embroidered coat, a widening girth, broad chest and genial, booming
voice.

James introduced us.

"Ah." Hans Sloane gave me an ebullient smile and swept a gracious
bow. "Petiver's Lady of the Butterflies. James has told me so much
about you, I feel as if we have met already."

I restrained a giggle, did not dare look at James. "Likewise, sir."

I heard James choke back his own mirth.

We were joined for dinner by James's friend Samuel Doody, who
was as obsessive about moss and ferns as James was about insects, and
by James's new lodger, Dr. David Krieg, a Saxon physician and artist,
who had come to London in the service of various noblemen and
who was soon to sail again for America. Also present was Edmund
Bouhn, he of Bouhn's Yellow Spotted Carolina butterfly.

"I'm too sunburned and wind-beaten now for you to see," Mr.
Bouhn said jocularly. "But beneath this tan, I'm still jaundiced from
a bout of yellow fever. I was practically the same color as my butterfly.
Though fortunately, I was spared the pox, so I'm not spotted as well
as yellow."

Mr. Bouhn seemed never to tire of talking about America, and Mr.
Sloane never tired of talking of Jamaica and his collection of bright
hummingbirds. I was sure I could have listened to their travelers' tales
all day. As they talked, the carriage wheels and the constant clop of
hooves on the cobbles outside the parlor window faded away, so that
I was transported to a new and shining land.

"You could explore the Americas all your life and never know half
of it," Mr. Bouhn said, sipping his wine. "It is so wild and so vast and
so empty, so full of promise and possibilities. There are wild horses
and thousand-acre forests full of bears, rivers teeming with fish. The

soil is so fertile that the flowers grow waist high, and there are crabs almost as big as turtles. I envy you, Dr. Krieg. I would return there tomorrow."

I envied David Krieg too, as I envied all the sea captains and ship's surgeons who every day staggered into the shop on their sea legs, who made my mouth water for the taste of pineapple and pomegranates, who spoke of giant spotted cats and fish that flew and butterflies with great wings of flashing metallic blue. I could have listened to their travelers' tales all day.

"I am very fortunate," David Krieg said. "But I have Mr. Petiver to thank for the fact I do not have to return to Germany and can travel, safe in the knowledge that my family will want for nothing while I am away."

Everyone around the table cast warm appreciative glances at James, and I had the sense that everyone here apart from myself knew exactly what Dr. Krieg meant, but I had no chance to discern more, because the discussion rapidly moved on.

Hans Sloane cut a piece of the lamb. As he carved, he told us he had just spent a vast sum on the purchase of a new selection of butterflies. "I don't suppose you're any more inclined to sell yours to me, James?"

"No, Hans," James replied, amiable but firm. "Not for a good while yet, at any rate."

"But how am I to found the British Museum if my dearest friend will not even contribute?"

James poured some more wine. "Is there no end to your quest for legacy?"

Hans eyed James with a grin. "You should have a mind to your own legacy, my friend. Especially since you show no sign of fathering a dynasty of little Petivers. Or are you content to go down in history as the father of British entomology, the man who made natural science popular?" He drummed his fingers on the table. "Then again, I suppose that is not such a bad epitaph." He gave an even heavier sigh. "We will all of us be buried with our own dead butterflies, like the ancients were buried with their gold."

"I think I'd rather have living ones fluttering in my tomb," I said.

"Hmmm. That's a very pretty image, my dear," Hans mused. "Almost mystical. Like a fable."

"I fear it is a fable that butterflies are birthed from their own little tombs," I said. "I reared a pupa, and all I got for my efforts were flies. But I imagine even flies deserve a place in the British Museum, sir."

"Indeed so," Hans enthused. "Well said, my dear. Well said."

"Why not go the whole way and call your collection the Hans Sloane Museum?" James asked.

"Too parochial." Hans stretched back in his chair, patted his tight paunch. "The British Museum would always be the biggest and the best, unsurpassed."

James laughed. "You are an arrogant swine, Hans."

Hans Sloane had the grace to laugh too. "The cocoa importers called me arrogant when I said their therapeutic drink was not palatable to the Europeans when mixed with honey and pepper, like they take it in the West Indies. But when I suggested they drink it with milk, I was hailed as a veritable genius. Now drinking chocolate is a delicacy as fashionable as coffee."

"And you have made your fortune from the commercial production of it in ingenious blocks," James put in.

"I made a greater fortune from importing Jesuits' Powder as a remedy for tertian ague."

"What does it look like?" I asked abruptly, urgently. "Jesuits' Powder, what color is it?"

"Dark rust red," Hans said. "Like cinnamon. It is flaky. Very bitter to taste."

I gripped my hands, twisted them. "Is there any other substance that resembles it?"

"Undoubtedly."

"Something poisonous?"

Hans glanced at James. James glanced at Hans. It was James who spoke. "Jesuits' Powder is highly poisonous, Eleanor," he said carefully. "Given in high enough doses, it is lethal. Anything above eight drams is dangerous. The Protestants were right to fear it, in a way, though I do not believe for a moment the Catholics ever intended to use it to harm them."

"How many drams are there in two spoonfuls?"

James frowned. "A dozen, maybe more."

"What are the symptoms of poisoning?"

James deferred to Hans. "Ringing in the ears, stomach cramps and vomiting, chaotic pulse, skin rash, blindness, headache."

"Death?"

"In some instances, yes. Not thinking of poisoning anyone, are you, Mistress Glanville?" Hans's tone was teasing, until he saw my face. "My dear lady. Are you unwell?"

I put my hand to my cheek, almost as if to remind myself of the way Richard had hit me, the violence with which he had accused me of insanity, the look of absolute and unmistakable guilt that I had seen so clearly in his eyes. It made no difference that he had given me the right medicine but the wrong dosage, did it? It changed nothing.

"HANS WAS MUCH TAKEN with you," James said when everyone had gone. "It is no small thing to count as your friend and patron one of the most powerful and esteemed scientists of our day."

It was the right thing to say, as he always did find the right thing. He sensed I wanted to talk no more of Jesuits' Powder now, had always understood me implicitly, had always known what I most needed, even before I knew it myself, and now he made a suggestion. "Would you like to try to birth a butterfly again? I'll gladly help you."

"Oh, James, there is nothing I would like more."

He smiled. "We can start just as soon as you finish sorting those letters."

"And I was worried that when they were done, I would have no more reason to be here."

"You do not need a reason," he said warmly. "You should know that. But now I have given you one anyway."

There was no sign of George coming to clear the table, so I gave up waiting and went to sit on a stool with my back against the wall. I picked the top letter off the largest stack, then the next, checked date and signature, started two new piles.

James had very many devoted friends. That was very plain from the sheer volume of letters he had amassed. What struck me most was the loyalty and dedication of his correspondents, the warmth with which they addressed him and the considerable efforts and often even more considerable dangers to which they had gone, time after time, to collect specimens for him.

As I read, I had found a recurring theme. Payment had been made to the English wife of ship's surgeon Robert Rutherford, and to the wife of Patrick Rattray, shipmaster in Virginia, to whom James had also given free medical advice about the pox. I remembered Dr. Krieg's comment over dinner, which hinted that he was only free to travel because he was certain his family would want for nothing.

There was only one explanation. With sublime generosity James had undertaken to offer succor and support to the needy relations his many correspondents and specimen gatherers were forced to leave behind, while they sailed the seas. It made no difference whether the men were in the pay of the British navy or of merchants, James had still made their dependents his responsibility. No wonder he said he could not afford to leave the shop, to go traveling himself.

It was my own personal experience that James was good and kind, but I had not realized the great extent of his goodness and his kindness, had not realized that I was by no means the primary recipient of it, that others received it in equal or even greater measure. It made me wonder now if I had been wrong, all those years ago, when I had worried that he wanted there to be something more between us. It seemed that I was the very poorest judge of character.

I did not find my own letters to James amongst the piles, and wondered where they were, what had happened to them.

When the door opened at last, it startled me. It was only George, but he had not come to clear the table. "Mr. Petiver asks you to join him in the shop immediately," he said. "He has something he wants to show you."

THE SOMETHING James had to show me was a batch of hairy green caterpillars in a chip box.

"You're not the only one who has been busy this afternoon." He beamed. "I took George with me to Primrose Hill and we have scoured every bed of stinging nettles."

"And brought half of them back with you, by the look of it." I nodded toward the bucket of spiky green plants by his feet. He had collected not just the leaves, as I had done, but dug up entire plants by their roots. While I had been discovering the depth of his kindness, he had been out all afternoon doing the kindest of things for me.

"I'm sure the key to rearing butterflies must be to re-create an environment that mimics conditions in the wild as closely as possible," he enthused, holding out his hand to me. "Come and see what I've done."

I let him lead me out through the garden, to a small stone herbarium at the end of the grass path, which housed a collection of dried plants, some mounted and classified and labeled, and, inevitably, a great many that were not. But because the building was reserved for plants alone, there was an order to it, a certain serenity. There was tree bark stacked like driftwood in one corner, and little dishes of seeds. The plants, like orchids, that could not be pressed without losing their form were suspended in jars of liquid on a shelf that ran all around the room and gave the little building a strangely exotic and dreamlike quality.

On a table just inside the door James had set up a large breeding cage, inside which was a large earthenware pot filled with soil. Beside it were a brass barometer and a thermometer. On the ground by the table was a charcoal brazier already glowing with coals.

"To regulate the temperature, now that it is autumn," he explained. "Pretend it is summer for as long as possible."

"It all looks very scientific."

"So it should. We are conducting an experiment after all."

"It will work," I said, my confidence soaring. "I know it."

James handed me a trowel. "I thought you'd like to help with the planting and with introducing the little creatures to their new home."

I pushed up my sleeves and worked beside him as he took each plant and bedded the roots into the crumbly soil. I watched the firm but gentle pressure of his hands against the soft, dark earth, the hands of a gardener and of a scientist, of an artist and a doctor.

He sprinkled water from a can and then let me release the worms onto the leaves, while he checked the instruments. "Did you ever master how to use a microscope?" he asked conversationally, as he made a note of the readings.

I angled my hand to encourage the last worm to wriggle off onto the nettle and shook my head. "You were going to teach me, weren't you? It is my fault you never had the chance. I never came back to London."

"You are here now."

I smiled. "And I have distracted you from your work all afternoon. Shouldn't you get back to the shop?"

"Probably."

"Later, then," I said.

"Later," he echoed, catching hold of my dirty hand as if it was the fragrant, gloved hand of a duchess.

WHEN I WENT BACK to Hackney, I generally broke in on scenes of such domestic harmony it made me feel superfluous. My daughter, Mary, was either busy with her crayons or with her needle, or reading texts that Mary Burges had set her to learn, while Ellen was regularly to be found balancing a hefty Bible on her lap in a way that would have done her grandfather proud.

This time, though, Mary was playing the flute and Ellen was dancing around the floor, in wider and wider twirls. When she saw me, she stopped dancing and rushed into my arms, hugging me and crying, "Mama, Mama," and showering me with kisses.

I kissed her back and then turned to Mary, saw the despondent look in her eyes. "Still no word from your brother?"

Mary shook her head. "He used to write to me so regularly," she said. "What if something has happened to him?"

"We would have heard," I reassured her, but I utterly failed to reassure myself.

DICKON WAS in the laboratory, crushing dry leaves with a pestle and mortar. His forearms had grown sinewy and strong from this

regular work and his fair curls flopped over his forehead, in just the
way that his father's dark ones did. He looked up, gave me a confident
yet very gentle, very lovely, very charming smile. So help me God, his
father's smile.

I sat down on the bench beside him, tucking my skirts out of
his way. "Are you enjoying your work, Dickon? Do you like it here,
after all?"

He paused from his compounding and set his pestle down on the
table. "I like it best when Mr. Petiver takes me with him to visit patients and I help him with letting blood and drawing teeth and ad-
ministering enemas and blisters."

I wrinkled my nose. "Strange boy."

He grinned. "I like it when we go to the surgeons' hall to watch a
dissection too."

"Ugh. This is the person who once flinched from a dead butterfly?"

"You told me there was nothing wrong with looking at dead things,
so long as you can learn from them. I want to learn all about anatomy.
I want to be more than a shopkeeper and compounder of herbs,"
he said very earnestly. "I have decided that I am going to be a doctor.
One who attends the needs of the sick poor, who cannot afford a
physician."

My heart swelled with pride, but at the same time I was fearful
for him.

"Then you will be at the forefront of open warfare," I said lightly.
"A bitter conflict that goes back to before even the civil war, when the
apothecaries declared for Parliament and the physicians were for the
King." I did not want to discourage him, but neither could I bear to
think of him disillusioned, his ambitions frustrated. I knew a little of
what that felt like. "You know that apothecaries who prescribe medicines independently of a physician or give separate advice or treatment still risk prosecution?"

"Of course I know that, Mama," he said, as patient and kindly condescending as if our roles were reversed and I was the child and he the parent. "I know very well that the Society of Physicians have the right to march into this shop anytime they like and destroy any substances of which they do not approve."

I nodded. "Fair enough. What does James say? Mr. Petiver, I mean. Have you talked to him about this?"

"He says I am like you, because I am determined to go my own way."

I laughed. "Well, I hope you are more successful at it than I have been."

"Mr. Petiver says that you are very respected. Mr. Petiver says," he began again, "that the physicians' monopoly on medical practice cannot last forever. He says that the physicians are only too happy for us to attend emergencies at night when they don't want to be disturbed, just as they all fled and left the apothecaries to treat the victims of the plague. Mr. Petiver says the poor already regard us as their doctors, they respect our seven years of training. It is only right that we should be allowed to attend them."

"I cannot argue with you." I smiled. "Or with Mr. Petiver."

"I met two young physicians at the coffeehouse yesterday," Dickon went on eagerly. "John Radcliffe and Richard Mead. Dr. Mead has a plan to start a practice of coffeehouse consultations that could set us up as general medical practitioners and pave the way for us to be given a legal right to practice. It could change medical practice in this country forever."

I looked at his soft blue eyes, so alight with hope, with ambition and plans, and I knew then that I had done right in bringing him here. James's kindness and enthusiasm were evident in every word Dickon spoke.

I could picture Dickon returning to Somersetshire after his training, a learned professional, surrounded by dogs and cats and several swans and ducks, respected in his village as a general medical practitioner, an alternative to quacks and surgeons like Dr. Duckett, the first person to whom ordinary families turned when they were sick and in need.

"You were right, Mama. James Petiver is a good man. I can see why you care for him so much."

I don't know which of our faces flushed the brightest. "Listen to me, Dickon," I said. "James and I have been friends for a very long time. I love him as I would love a brother. I may not be with your father now, but you must understand that I am still his wife. I love him more than I have ever loved any man. I have never been faithless or untrue to him."

Dickon's boyish jaw had stiffened. "James Petiver is more a father to me than Richard Glanville will ever be," he said, his voice breaking with emotion. "He is kind and good and he guides and teaches like a father should. It is him I want to emulate. My father is a cruel man. I know he hit you. I despise him." Dickon looked suddenly shy. "Mama, James Petiver is like a father to me. And anyone could see that he loves you and cares for you like a husband should love and care for you, like you deserve to be loved and cared for."

I was taken aback. "I don't know about that."

"Well, I do."

I HAD STUDIED NATURE all my life, but the sheer ingenuity of creation never failed to surprise and amaze me. I had never been more surprised or amazed than I was when I visited the nettle pot in the herbarium with James and found that the worms had turned architects and builders and constructed a neat little tent out of leaves at the base of the plant. They had bound the leaves tidily together with silk and were inside it, happily wriggling and munching away.

"Well, that certainly didn't happen last time," I said.

"Different species," James concluded. "Butterflies are creatures of great diversity, as we know."

The tent structure grew, as the worms grew and shed their skins. They cut through stems and pulled the whole shoot over to extend their home. And then half a dozen of them spun themselves little coffins, which hung suspended on small hooks and pads of silk, inside the shelter. We had to peer inside very carefully, so as not to disturb them. The coffins, too, were quite different from the ones I had seen before, grayish and shot with shimmering gold.

"I feel I've witnessed a small miracle already," I said. "Even if they do not turn into butterflies."

"They will," James replied. "I am sure of it."

I was convinced by his quiet assurance, wanted it to happen more for his sake now than for mine. "We should keep a vigil," I said. "I'll keep watch and then you take a turn, so we do not miss it."

"That sounds a rather lonely way to go about it." He smiled. "D'you think we could perhaps time it so that our watches overlapped now and again?"

JAMES ASKED ME if I would like to go with him to visit John Ray and I said that nothing would please me more. I helped him fill a saddlebag with as many carefully wrapped specimen trays as would safely fit. Then, wrapped in cloaks against the autumnal breeze, we set off on horseback for the hamlet of Black Notley, near Braintree in Essex, where John Ray had grown up, the son of a blacksmith, and where he still lived in a small Tudor timber-framed house called Dewlands. It stood on a knoll and had dormer windows that looked out over a stream, the smithy and a small cluster of cottages.

We were welcomed by John Ray's wife, Margaret, twenty years his junior and a former governess to his friend's family, who showed us into a parlor that was built around a great chimney and crowded with books, collections and four small, noisy little girls with lace caps on their heads. Margaret went to fetch her husband from his study over the brew house, and John Ray greeted James with a hug of great affection before turning to me with interest. "Ah, Isaac, my boy," he said with a gentle humor. "I must say you are suited much better to petticoats than you are to breeches."

I let out a ripple of laughter.

"How long have you known?" James exclaimed.

"Since you never mentioned your butterfly boy again, but spoke instead, constantly, of your Lady of the Butterflies."

"Ah." James busied himself opening up the portmanteau and handed the trays to John Ray while his girls crowded round to watch.

Seeing how poor Mr. Ray was obviously racked with pain from the sores on his legs, I helped him shift books off the comfortable but threadbare chairs, so they could all sit down by the crackling fire. All the books were marked with soot from the chimney and ink stains from the children, but their father made no apology for that fact.

"You have Eleanor to thank for the cataloguing," James said, as John Ray's eyes lingered on a tray of blues. "It is all her work."

"Excellent work it is too." He asked his eldest daughter to take the trays to his study and bring back his manuscript.

"Insects are so numerous and the observation of all kinds of them so difficult, I think I must give the task over to more able and younger persons. But the chapter on Papilos I will endeavor to continue, if I manage to live through the winter." He handed the sheets over to James. "Please pardon my scribbling. Some days I can scarce manage a pen."

Even so, the writing was elegant and flowing, and it pleased me to see that the lists of butterflies were catalogued after the fashion I had adopted, but had descriptions not just of the imagos but of their caterpillars and pupae too. James's name appeared many times, and I felt a surge of pride to see it, as much as if it was my own name. *Butterfly blue. Mr. Petiver found in garden near Enfield. Mr. Petiver thinks it a different sex rather than species.*

Margaret Ray brought wine, and despite his pain, her husband demonstrated his phenomenal memory as he talked about his completed books: on fishes, birds, plants, flowers, the wisdom of God. He spoke fondly of a recent visit by Dr. David Krieg, who had stayed two days and made several exceedingly good drawings. He spoke most lovingly of how, now that his legs had failed him, his four young daughters went out with their nets at dusk, to collect nocturnals to bring to him.

When it was almost time to go, James presented John with the parcels of sugar and tobacco and a bottle of canary wine we had brought for him. "With my very best wishes," James said.

"You are too generous, James. Thank you. But you do not need to bring gifts. You should know that your company and your collections are ample enough."

"I'll take these to Margaret, then," James said amiably. "She has the common sense to be appreciative."

James went off to the kitchen, two of the girls skipping after him.

"I have a dread of loneliness," John said to me candidly, scooping one of his daughters up onto his lap, trying not to grimace at the pain it clearly caused him. "I find it hard to understand why any man would choose to live alone. But I gave up urging James to find himself a wife long ago. I knew there was some secret lady who was preventing him from forming any other attachment."

I stared at him.

"Come, you must know, surely?"

"Sir, are you saying that James . . . ?"

"That he loves you, my dear, always has, for as long as I've had the pleasure of his acquaintance, and I suspect always will."

"He has never really given me any indication."

"That is not his way, is it? He seeks to make others happy, rather than be happy himself. He is the most selfless man I've ever met, doles out friendship and love, and all he asks in return is . . . well, butterflies and beetles." A wry grin. "You are from Somersetshire, aren't you? I had the privilege of making a tour of that spectacular county, in the year after the Great Fire, and of hunting out the little white pointed leaves of the water parsnip. I do so regret no longer being able to go out in the field to collect flora and fauna. But James told me in his last letter that you are as interested in breeding butterflies as in collecting them. Tell me, did the hints I passed on prove successful? Have you hatched a pupa yet?"

"Not quite yet. But it looks promising. Forgive me. I did not know you had a hand in it."

"Well, well. I am glad to see that James isn't always quite so self-effacing. That just once in a while, he is capable of a little ruse, in order to impress a lass."

Did he want to impress me? Did he really?

"You have bred butterflies too, then?" I asked.

"My chief concern has always been to reinterpret the Christian faith in the light of a sound knowledge of nature. Understanding transformation is a matter of the greatest importance. To study just the imago is to study but half a life. Now, did you come up against the disturbing problem of false metamorphosis, when you hatched a fly instead of a butterfly?"

"Yes!" I exclaimed. "The first time. That is exactly what happened."

"Ah," he said, turning grave. "It has blighted the hopes of all us breeders at one point or another, but we are still not much closer to knowing quite how, or why. I truly believe we are on the brink of discounting the theory of spontaneous generation, but that is the final prop, still taken by some as proof enough that lice can be created by dirty hair and an old shawl be the originator of a moth, which in my personal opinion is bunkum, used to erroneously diminish God's power and undermine our faith in Him."

"It never undermined your faith, sir?"

"Have you ever dissected a pupa?"

"I could never bear to waste one."

"It is no waste. The intermediate state between caterpillar and butterfly is a formless broth. Only a divine creator could organize that broth into a new creature. Only a divine creator, and one with an artistic flair, I might add, could design wings of such perfect symmetry and diversity and beauty. We'll debunk spontaneous generation one of these days. We'll prove that life comes from God, not matter, if only we have enough young naturalists, like you and James, with a love of insects."

Margaret Ray sent us back to London with fresh bread and homemade cheese, in a parcel twice as large as the ones we had given to her.

"You see," James said to me, when we dismounted under an old oak tree to eat our picnic amidst a carpet of gold and crimson leaves. "There is a gentleman who is proof, if ever you or anyone else needed it, that devotion to natural history is a sign of learning and piety, rather than of insanity."

"Oh, but our circumstances are so very different, James." I fingered a piece of bread. "John Ray has published books that more than compensate for the strangeness of what he does. They have brought him respect. I am not respected in Tickenham. Here, in London, when I am with you, with John Ray or Hans Sloane, I am an entomologist, a natural philosopher, an experimenter. But in Somersetshire, I am no different from your collector in Spain, alone with my net and my love of shape-changing insects that are commonly believed to represent the souls of the dead. I am a witch, a madwoman, a sorceress. A nec-romancer."

James held my eyes, as a sudden squall of wind shook the tree and sent a flurry of golden leaves floating down on our heads. "So leave Somersetshire for good," he said simply.

I half expected him to finish by suggesting I stay in London, with him, but he did not.

JAMES HAD BROUGHT BREAD to toast on a fork in the brazier in the herbarium and had skewered the first slice. There was a nip in the dusky air and we had both huddled close to the heat, our toes touching. He leaned forward to put his bread in the fire and I leaned forward too, my elbows on my knees and my chin propped in my hands, to watch the bread slowly browning and crisping. He turned to me in the flickering firelight and our lips were so close we could have kissed, but he made no attempt to kiss me.

He handed me my toast and I crunched a corner. "How long do we carry on?" It had gone on for days, one week that had stretched into two, now nearly to three.

"You have had enough already?"

I would never have enough. I did not want this time to end, but I knew James would never be the one to suggest we give up and one of us had to, sooner or later. "That is their mausoleum, I think?" I gestured at the leaf tent, willing him to contradict me. "These worms not only build their own gilded coffins but they build a whole crypt for themselves too."

James was shaking his head very slowly, with a leisurely smile animating his face. "You did not look closely enough," he said. "There is a change."

"Oh, I did look closely," I said. "This is exactly what happened before. Days passed without movement and then the pupae distended and darkened and shriveled to nothing at all. They have all died, I am sure of it."

"I don't believe so." I hadn't even dented his confidence. "Well, we will know by morning, I should think. If it is going to happen, it will be soon. When the sun comes up would be the most likely time. I have brought blankets. So we may stay all night."

I had not noticed the blankets, folded neatly in a basket behind the table. I recognized them as the ones that had covered his bed. He fetched one and draped it around my shoulders. My eyes already felt gritty with tiredness, and I stifled a yawn as I clutched the blanket around me and snuggled down into it. It was not richly brocaded like the ones on the bed at Tickenham, but simple woven wool, fragranced with the heady scent of herbs and lavender and just a touch of brimstone, the same aromas that clung to James's hair and hands and clothes. I breathed them in like balm. He brought his stool around, so he was next to me, very close. I leaned my head on his shoulder and, after a moment, he put his arm around me.

"Sleep now," he said and the vibration of his voice traveled into my own body and made it hum. "I promise you that I will not. I will wake you the moment anything starts to happen."

I closed my eyes, my cheek against the slightly prickly cloth of his coat, his arm enfolding me. I had never felt so safe, so at peace. His body was smaller and less muscular than the bodies of the two men I had married, was more like my own. It fit around me perfectly. We were a perfect match. I felt each rhythmic rise and fall of his chest as he breathed, until my own breathing seemed to balance with his.

"Go to sleep," he urged again.

"I am trying."

"You do trust me?"

"James, I have always trusted you."

I could feel the thud of his heart, beating strongly, purposefully. I nestled up closer and was overcome with a sense of profound and sweet tranquillity. I slept. I slept so deeply and so soundly that when he bent his head to my ear and whispered for me to wake up, it was impossible to believe it was dawn.

"One of the pupae is opening," he said, as I twisted round to look into his tired but happy face.

I was fully awake and on my feet in an instant.

With one finger I carefully lifted the leaves at the front of the tent and saw that one of the little shells was indeed moving, quivering slightly. I looked at James. I rubbed my sleep-blurred eyes and looked back at the coffin. I hardly dared to breathe, lest it upset the transformation process. The pupa shook more vigorously and then it split, like an egg about to hatch. An abdomen thrust forward, threadlike legs scrabbled through the opening. It was happening with such raw, astonishing speed that I was afraid to blink, in case I missed it. There was a trickle of fluid the color of blood and then a glistening rush as the butterfly burst forth, its coffin instantly reduced to nothing now but a fragile husk, empty and abandoned.

"It is true," I whispered in awe.

I could feel the warmth of James's smile on my face, even though I could not tear my eyes away from the butterfly to look at him. I was as entranced as I was at the birth of my own children.

"Who claimed the age of miracles is past?" he said.

The new butterfly crept out of the leaf tent and climbed tentatively up onto the stems of the plant. It rested, very still. But then it stirred. The familiar wings unfolded like fans. Dark wings, with a band of vivid orange and splashes of scarlet and the purest snowy white.

"A Red Admiral," I whispered with wonder. It seemed extraordinary that the first butterfly we had seen being born was one we had named together, as we would have named a child.

We watched it, pumping its wings, as another butterfly emerged.

"They will be hungry," James said, and from somewhere he produced a honeycomb. "Let's see if they will take some from you." He took my finger and dipped it into one of the waxy cells, then made me turn it upward and hold it out toward the butterflies, one of which fluttered up and then down onto my wrist, turned and walked with its wings closed, down toward the honey. One of its little feet made contact with the stickiness and it paused, did a strange stepping dance.

"It's as if it tastes with its toes," I whispered.

It uncurled its proboscis and started to feed. Its glorious wings opened. There, perched on my finger, the butterfly that I had witnessed being born. As soon as she had had her fill she flittered off up to the rafters.

I turned to James and I kissed him, on his lips. "Thank you," I said, but it did not seem enough, not nearly enough. He had given me so much, now and over the years, he had always been there, a friend to turn to, whenever I was in trouble or unhappy, always ready to enthuse and inspire, just like my father had always been, and like John Ray said, he had never demanded anything in return, except that I did not let go of my dreams. And now, I wanted to give him something back.

In the stillness of the dawn, as the rising sun tinged the sky with peach and the air turned a pearly blue, I spread out the blanket on the earthen floor and took his hand, led him to it. We knelt upon it together, slowly undressing each other, as the butterflies drifted down and flickered around us on their silent, velvet wings, like tiny luminous bats. James plucked at the laces of my corset and I felt the air brush my breasts, as if for the first time. We lay down, naked, and traced every line and curve of each other's bodies, until two of the Red Admirals came gliding down from the shadowy roof and landed on my belly, where James had touched me and left a trace of sweet honey. It was an awesome, exquisite sensation, to feel them walking so lightly over my skin, where it had just been caressed. James kissed me, my mouth opened for him, and I felt as if all the burdens of this life were pouring out of me. Weightless, I had been lifted up on golden wings.

He ran his fingers over my back and down the insides of my arms, his touch as soft and warm as the silken touch of the morning sun, as soothing as a benediction, and I knew that, though he had never given me any hint of it, he had made love to me in his dreams a thousand times over. I stroked him and his muscles quivered like the gilded coffin before it had burst open. The beat of him within me was the firm and powerful rhythm of a Swallowtail in flight over the moors, the pulsing of the newborn Red Admiral as it slowly beat its scarlet and black wings, until they were fully open and shining and perfect. His final release was as mystical as the transformed life that had burst forth from its shell. I closed my eyes, and when I opened them, I saw that the final Red Admiral had been born and had risen from its coffin into the light.

JAMES TOOK ME by the hand and led me through to the laboratory.

"What are we doing now?"

He pressed me down onto the bench before the microscope. "Oh," I said. "I see."

"That is just it," he said with a smile. "You don't see. Not properly. Not yet."

I felt a tingle of excitement.

He scanned the cauldrons and vials and tubes in the laboratory, but seemed to find nothing suitable. "Wait there," he said. "I know exactly what you should look at."

I heard him going up the wooden stairs to his rooms, two steps at a time, and then down them again, just as fast. He had a casket in his hand. Inside were all the letters I had ever sent to him, and beneath them, wings of broken butterflies, but not just any butterflies. I was puzzled at first. One wing was tiger-striped, another vivid green, another small and blue. Stupidly, I took them for the ones James had sent to me over the years and I wondered how on earth they came to be here, when I had left them safely hidden in my Bible. Then it dawned on me that, of course, these were not my wings, but the opposite wings of the same butterflies. Where I had a right wing, James had a left. He had broken the butterflies in two and sent me one of the wings, keeping the other for himself, as others would bite into a coin and keep half each, as a token, a love token.

"Which should it be, do you think? The exotic Brazilian or the pretty little English blue?"

"You choose," I said.

He selected the blue and I watched his fingers at work, as he skillfully fixed it onto a pin, slid it under the lens. He sat directly behind me on the bench, so that I was perched between his legs, with his arms around me. I rested my hands on his thighs, as he brought his head down over my shoulder, his face cheek-to-cheek with mine. He made more adjustments to the various screws, moving the butterfly up and down and from side to side.

He covered my left eye with his hand. "Look now," he instructed.

I bent toward the lens, and my eyes widened with wonder. The image was incredibly, breathtakingly clear, and yet I could not believe I was looking at a butterfly. There were ridges of tiny plated mirrors, like the scales on a fish, like a suit of the most delicate polished armor, of an impossibly bright lapis blue.

When I eventually moved back, the rows of shining mirrors still danced before my eyes.

"Tell me exactly what you see." I felt the breath of his words in my hair, like a soft summer breeze. "Describe it to me, as if you were my eyes and I couldn't see it for myself."

"I see . . ." I broke off and thought. "I see the blue of the brightest silk and satin, of the most lustrous taffeta. Of the sky in summer and of the sea. I see the blue of ribbons and of sapphires. I see that all the riches I ever needed are right there."

Except, said the voice in my head, for the deepest, most beautiful blue of one man's eyes.

❦ I FED THE BUTTERFLIES in the herbarium every day, and they soon learned that there was always honey or the juice of an over-ripe plum on my fingers, so that all I had to do was open the door of the little herbarium for all three of them to come sailing down to perch on my hand, my shoulder, my head, sometimes getting tangled in my long hair. I marveled at it each time. It was the simplest, purest pleasure. They made me feel blessed, as if I had been granted a special privilege.

I heard, or sensed, James come in softly through the door at the side, stand watching for a while.

"Don't take this wrongly, now," he whispered. "I am not accusing you of communing with the dead. But it is almost as if you commune with those butterflies. Almost as if you are one of them."

I smiled up at James through my lashes. "I am surprised you are not a great distraction to them," I said. He had been to the Master's Day celebrations at the Apothecaries' Company Hall in Blackfriars, and he looked very fine and handsome in his ceremonial livery of dark blue with gold braid. "Shut in here all their lives, the poor little things have never seen anything half so bright."

"They have seen you." James smiled.

The butterflies flew off and I watched them go dancing upward, not toward an open sky but a dark entrapping roof. "I know I cannot keep them forever," I said sadly, as protective and possessive as a new mother. "They are a week old now, already. We should set them free, shouldn't we? It is not fair to keep them here."

James did not answer, and I was sure he felt as I did, that when the butterflies were gone, everything would come to an end. Their serenity, their carefree joy and simple beauty were symbols of the brief idyll of the past few weeks, an interlude which could not last forever. In a few days it would be November. The summer had ended long ago. I had been in London for weeks, too many weeks.

"You believe Richard Glanville is responsible for your first husband's death, don't you?" he said quietly. "You believe he poisoned him with Jesuits' Powder."

"How did you . . . ?"

"You fear him. More than you would fear a person whose only crime was to accuse you of insanity. Edmund suffered from ague, the cure for which is the powder, and yet you asked Hans how much could kill a person."

"I sent Richard to London for it," I said steadily. "I gave it to Edmund and he died, a horrible, painful death. For a long time I believed that the worst I had heard about Papist poison must be true. Then you sent me Robert Talbor's book, and I knew it was a cure, after all, and so I was sure it was something else Richard had given to me. Now I know he just told me to give Edmund a dose that was too high, fatally high."

"Eleanor, the physicians still do not know how much of the powder is most effective. Maybe it was just a mistake. And maybe it was not even his mistake. Maybe it was the mistake of the apothecary who sold it to him."

"You do not really believe that?"

"I do not know what to believe. And neither do you, I think. You have not confronted him with this, have you?"

I shook my head. "He would only deny it."

"With words, perhaps. But unless he is a monster, you will know if he is telling the truth or not."

"That is just it. I already know, James. I saw his guilt, as clear as day."

He regarded me almost sadly. "It is just that your heart will not accept it, will it? Because you loved him, because you love him still. And so you cannot accept the evidence of your eyes, or of your head. Nor should you. Listen to me, Eleanor. There are times for weighing evidence and making reasoned deductions and times when you should set all that aside, when you should listen to what your heart tells you, though your eyes cannot see it and your mind cannot understand. 'If a man will begin with certainties, he shall end in doubts; but if he will be content to begin with doubts, he shall end in certainties.'"

"Francis Bacon?"

"But Sir Francis's admirable philosophy cannot be applied to love. With love it is just the opposite. There must only be certainties. Beginning with doubts is no good, no good at all."

"But I have always doubted Richard," I admitted. "I could not help but love him, desire him, but I have always had my doubts about him, and now I know that I was right to doubt."

One of the butterflies was fluttering round my head again and I raised my hand to let it settle. I walked past James with it still on my palm and I pushed open the door. The sun was shining, a dying autumn sun, very soft and rich. I stood and let the butterfly feel the air on its wings, before I gently tossed up my arm. I watched it flutter off, over the herb garden and away. One by one the other butterflies went soaring after the first, until all three of them were gone, over the rooftops and the trees, into the sky, which suddenly looked very small compared with Tickenham's skies.

"I have to go home, James," I said.

"I know that you do. Whether he is guilty or not, whether you love him or not, the law of the land says that you married him and therefore belong to him."

"Oh, a pox on the law."

James laughed. "You are a glorious, lawless little person, Eleanor Glanville, and you should belong to no one. You were born to be as free as the Red Admirals. It is a tragedy that you are not."

"But I shall not be locked up," I said. "If Richard still claims that I am mad, I know I have friends, powerful friends, who will refute those claims. I have you, and I have Hans Sloane and John Ray, three of the most respected natural philosophers in the country. I can depend on you, can't I?"

"Always." James put his arm around my shoulder. "And you must keep on writing to me regularly now," he said, half serious. "For if you do not, I shall fear something is amiss and I shall be haring up to Somersetshire to rescue you."

"I shall hold on to that." I put my hand over his. "I swear I shall never break off our correspondence again," I said. "Not for anything."

"When will you leave?"

"After I've seen Dickon go off with you on the herbalizing expedition tomorrow. He wanted to show me the state barge."

A LARGE AND NOISY GROUP of apprentices and their masters boarded the grand apothecaries' barge that was drawn up by the steep river steps at Blackfriars, ready to take them on a last collecting trip before winter. A picnic had already been loaded onto the boat, baskets of bread and cheese and meats and a barrel of ale, and all the apprentices, dressed in their blue uniforms, carried an assortment of glass bottles and pencils and collecting books. Bright pennants and banners cracked in the stiff breeze beneath a leaden sky.

I had told Dickon that as soon as I had watched him depart, I would be leaving London to return to Tickenham, and he was so happy in his work now, and with James, that he did not mind at all. "You have a good day," I said, hugging him tight, before he climbed down to the boat. "I hope it is a successful one."

"I'd rather be spending my time with patients, instead of plants," he said artlessly.

"Well, keep your eyes open and who knows, you might find something that'll help your patients. A plant nobody's ever found before, one that can cure cankers, or start a heart again when it has stopped."

He looked dubious. "I am going to Tickenham, Mama, not off to the New World."

I laughed. "Even so."

"I'm happy to leave all the exploration and experimentation and the making of new discoveries to the likes of you and Mr. Petiver. I've no ambition to have an herb named after me, or have my name in the annals of the Royal Society. I'd rather just take all the knowledge that others have collected and put it to good use."

I touched his soft cheek with the back of my hand. "You are a good boy, Dickon. You will be such a wonderful doctor."

"Do you think so?"

"I know so. I am so proud of you."

He looked down at his polished shoes, embarrassed, as if he did not believe me. "So long as I do not have to go and fight in a war," he said. "You would not be so proud of me then. I am not like your father. I am not like my father, or my brother. I would not be able to face a musket, or wield a sword."

I had not realized Richard's criticisms of him had cut so deep.

"Listen to me." I put my hand under his chin and lifted his face to mine. "To my mind, there is something wrong with a world that rewards women only for being modest and pretty, and men for their courage on the battlefield. I once met a fine physician, who had led the cavalry, but decided he would rather save lives than take them. You tell me which is the more heroic."

"Thank you, Mama." He kissed my cheek, smiled. "I have the worst of fathers, but the very best of mothers."

And yet his father, the man he called the worst of fathers, had just such a smile, gentle and charming and utterly adorable, and I missed seeing it, I missed having him smile that smile at me, even though I feared he was a murderer.

I grabbed Dickon and hugged him tight again, so that he would not see that I was crying, and he went off, happy and excited, down the river steps, to join James and the others on the barge. He sat toward the back of the boat, behind the raised, crimson damask–covered chair that was reserved for the master of the company, and he turned and lifted his hand in farewell to me, as the drum started to beat a rhythm that sounded to my ears very somber and ominous. The rows of watermen took up their oars and started to pull out onto the swirling gray water. They were sailing with an incoming tide and the barge moved swiftly upstream and away. I stood and watched, long after Dickon had stopped waving, long after his face was just a pale shape against the gray of the river. I gripped the railing at the jetty and strained my eyes, dreading the moment when he would disappear entirely. I watched the barge grow smaller, until it was as tiny as a toy boat and the expanse of water between us seemed wider than the widest ocean.

I had the strangest superstition that I had said good-bye to Dickon forever. That I would never see my son again.

. . .

IT HAD TURNED COLD, and as the coach rocked through the village of Nailsea and into the mire of the Tickenham Road, ragged curtains of thick fog whipped passed the windows. It was so thick as to almost obscure the other travelers on the road, the ubiquitous fishermen, a woman with a brace of duck and a boy on a scraggy skewbald nag. I could not really see their faces, and so I was not particularly perturbed that they did not trouble to smile or wave or doff their caps when the coach swayed by and they caught a glimpse of my face at the window, half hidden in the dark hood of my cloak.

Down on the moor, at the edge of the floodwater, they were finishing building the Gunpowder Treason Night bonfires and I could hardly believe the fires would be lit in a few hours, that it was November already. In London, with James and the butterflies, winter had seemed so very far away.

The ghostly figures, moving to and fro in the mist, looked almost sinister as they carried branches and armfuls of brushwood and fagots to add to the shadowy skeleton of sticks.

Maybe it was time we stopped celebrating the Gunpowder Plot. It happened nearly a century ago, after all. Though I had loved the festivities once, when it was the only celebration Oliver Cromwell did not ban. He forbade Christmas and the May Revels, but he had encouraged this dark festival that bred hatred against Catholicism. It was a gruesome celebration though, when one thought about it, centered as it was around the burning of an effigy.

I had left my daughters in the care of Catholics, the kindest-hearted people I had ever known.

I saw the church tower dimly in the mist. To the right was the lane that led to Folly Farm, at the foot of Cadbury Camp. We were almost there now, and as if she guessed my anxiety, I felt Dickon's hound trembling against my legs. At Hackney, Cadbury had sensed my imminent departure and had attached herself firmly to my skirts. In Dickon's absence she seemed to have transferred all her slobbering and unconditional devotion to me and I was glad that I had brought her with me, was glad of her company now. I reached down to stroke her floppy ears and let her lick my fingers. "There, girl." I patted her side. "I promised Dickon I would care for you, and I shall. There's no need to be afraid," I said, thinking how her blindness was a fate almost worse than death, confining her to the terror of perpetual darkness.

The coach lumbered into the cobbled yard but nobody came out to greet me; not even the groom was there to attend to the horses. Smoke was rising from the chimneys, but otherwise the house had a strange, abandoned air about it. I was surprised that everyone had been given leave to attend the bonfire before the festivities were properly under way, and it was with a sense of foreboding that I walked up to the heavy door leading into the great hall and opened it.

Will Jennings, the footman, was coming out of the cross passage, with a salver of steaming roast pike.

"Where is everyone, Will?" I asked. "Where is my husband?"

He hesitated, looked right through me. He carried on through to the parlor, as if he had not heard me, as if I were a ghost. I stared after him, dumbfounded, followed him into the parlor, with Cadbury trailing at my heels, and when I saw that there was nobody there, I turned and ran up the spiral stone stairs to my chamber. The clothes chest had been removed, I noticed, and the washstand had been shifted to the opposite corner of the room. A man's shirt was tossed on the bed, not one of Richard's.

"If you're looking for him, you'll not find him here." I spun round to see Forest, leaning lazily, with his arm braced against the door frame, his stockinged ankles casually crossed. "Richard has left me in charge," Forest said, using his stepfather's given name, as if they were equals, as if the two of them were accomplices. My husband, whose claim that I was mad could enable him to wrest control of my estate, and my son, heir to that estate, who would inherit it all once I was gone.

Forest was head and shoulders taller than me now, and he had grown a soft black beard and mustache. In a new tailored coat and fawn breeches, tight over his muscular thighs, he was no longer a boy. It did not seem so long ago that he was a babe in arms and I was sitting with him under the apple tree and whispering to him how I wanted him to grow to be a good, kind man, who made me proud.

"Why are you not still in Flanders, Forest?"

"I asked Richard to pay my passage home and he did."

"You saw no reason to tell me that you were back?"

"You should not have left him," Forest said with startling passion. "It is not right. You are his wife. You are supposed to love him. But you don't care about him at all, do you?"

I could not help but be moved by such ardent loyalty, even while it unnerved me. I knew Forest had always been almost slavishly devoted to Richard, but until that moment, I don't think I understood just quite how much he loved him. I could not blame him for taking his side now, when he had not been here to witness what had passed between us.

"Forest, please understand that I had no choice but to go. Your stepfather made . . . allegations against me, allegations that made it impossible for me to stay."

"He said you were mad," Forest said flatly. "I know. And I agree with him."

It felt as if my legs would give way beneath me, and I put my hand out to the bedpost to support myself. "How can you say that?"

"I speak only as I find."

I turned my back on him, went to the window, pressed my hands down against the ledge and took a deep breath. "Your real father was such a good man, Forest. I wish you could have known him."

"Well, he is dead," Forest spat. "And you are as dead to me as he is. I no longer have a mother. And in future I will thank you not to come into my chamber uninvited."

I spun back to face him, felt the blood surge up into my head, pounding behind my eyes, so that I could almost see it, a haze of red. "I am very much alive, Forest. So help me God, you do have a mother. This is my chamber, my house, and it will remain mine until I do die, and unless you are willing to murder me, there is nothing at all that you, or your stepfather, can do about it."

"Oh, isn't there?" He pushed himself into an upright position and his face was hardened in a cunning and steely resolve.

"I could ride to Bristol right now and draw up a will to disinherit you."

"You could." His tone indicated I would be wasting my time. He smirked, unperturbed, as if he knew something that I did not, as if nothing I did could make any difference, as if nothing I did could stop them.

"Where is he, Forest? Where is Richard?"

His smile was full of malice. "You will know soon enough where he is."

THE KITCHEN WAS a hive of activity, everyone busy in preparation for the great bonfire feast. Pots bubbled over the fire, above which hung rabbits, ducks, geese and fish, waiting to go in them. The vast room was warm with aromatic steam. On the long table there were puddings and pies, bowls of sugar and spices and great slabs of butter. Trenchers were already set out with roast pike and trout and baked eels. The maids chattered gaily as they chopped piles of apples and rolled pastry, scurrying to and fro from oven to table, while Mistress Keene shouted instructions above the din.

They all stopped when they saw me, frozen in motion like a tableau.

"I'd like a plate of bread and cheese," I ordered. "And some warmed ale."

For a moment nobody moved, and then they resumed their tasks and their chatter, as if I had not spoken. Nobody even acknowledged my demand. Only Mistress Keene looked at me, still standing there. She wiped her liver-spotted hands on her apron, grabbed a loaf of bread and came bustling round the table. She thrust the bread at me, as if I was a beggar.

"You should go," she mumbled aside. "While you still can."

She had turned away, but I grabbed her arm. "What do you mean?"

"I didn't do it," she said, looking back at me with pity. "I might not approve of some of your ways, but I'd not betray myself, for one thing." She glanced furtively round the kitchen, as if to check who was listening to what she was saying to me. They all were, but were trying to pretend they were not, eyes down, ears open. "Only a fool would sign something, when they could not read what had been written. How do I know if it is even close to what I said? They could have writ down any answer and asked me to sign it as gospel truth and I would not know any different."

"What are you talking about?"

She shook her head, took up her wooden spoon and went back to her post.

I snatched a quarter round of cheese and a flagon of cider, like a thief in my own kitchen, and I ate and drank as I walked down to where the flat-bottomed boat was tethered by the humpbacked bridge. Cadbury seemed determined to come with me, so I guided her aboard, and as I rowed between the drowned trees and reed beds, she sat upright in the bow, her nose high and sniffing the air and her ears flicking back and forth to the noisy honking of the swans and the geese and the eerie cries of the marsh birds.

Bess was stirring a pot over the fire in her cottage, wading about in half an inch of silt and water that had seeped in under the door, as the floods had risen. She was thinner; her once lustrous hair hung lank and her apron was grimy. I had always relied on her to be sharp and direct but she would not look at me now.

She laid three wooden bowls and spoons on the table. One for herself and one for her son, Sam. The other was for Thomas, I presumed. There was no fourth bowl for her mother.

"She died a month ago," Bess volunteered.

"I did not know."

"How could you? You were not here." There was recrimination in her voice, as if she thought I had stayed away too long. It seemed that I had, but I was beginning to wish I had not come back at all.

"She will be much missed."

Bess went back to her stirring. The broth was thin and pale and did not smell good. "Thomas and Sam are both out at the bonfire, but they'll be back soon and in need of something to warm them," she said.

"Bess, tell me what is going on."

She seemed reluctant. "Mr. Glanville left Forest in charge and, as you no doubt have already seen for yourself, he's acting like he's already the squire and having a high time of it."

"And Richard?" I asked. "Where is he? Do you know?"

She glanced up at me from her stirring. "No. But I do know this. He's not been moping for you. He's had someone to warm his bed for him at night."

I felt my stomach clench. "Who? What do you mean?"

"Sarah Gideon. Floozy from Bristol, near as damn it moved herself into the big house, as soon as you were gone."

It was as if an icicle had been driven like a spear into my heart, dripping cold ice into my blood. Sarah. The woman in the red dress, from the Llandoger Trow. From so many years ago. In how many ways had he betrayed me? Had our marriage been a complete sham?

I was sure I did not want Richard anymore, that he was a villain, a murderer. But if I no longer wanted him, why did the images that rushed into my head cause me such agony? Why did the thought of that woman in bed with him make me want to be sick? Why did the thought of him touching her, of her touching him, make me want to weep, to scream, to kill them both? Why did the thought of him kissing her, of her kissing him, make me feel as if my heart was being ripped out of me? Why did the image of him making love to her make me feel that the world was an ugly, ugly place and that life was hardly worth living anymore? Above all, why did the thought that he might actually care for her fill me with the most terrible emptiness and loneliness and despair?

"Is she with him now?"

Bess shrugged. "She left for Elmsett. About two days ago. Good riddance to her, I say. Don't like her much. Nobody does." She flashed me one of her bold looks, her face red and moist from the steam coming off the pot. "They'd not oblige the likes of her. They'd not even do it for Mr. Glanville, much as they liked him, before all this turned him sour. They do it for Thomas."

I frowned. "Do what for Thomas?"

"She's been visiting us all, with a man who makes us swear an oath. They have a sheet of vellum with a list of questions on it. She goes through the questions one by one, writes down the answers that people give her, writes and writes and writes, every single word we say. Then she has us put a name to it."

"What are the questions about?"

"You."

"Me?"

"Yes, lamb," Bess said. "You."

"Richard's mistress is collecting sworn affidavits against me?"

"If that's what they are called, then yes."

"But why?" I was sure Sarah Gideon hated me, but what did she hope to achieve by gathering testimonies against me? It seemed a lot of trouble to go to just for spite.

Bess stirred more vigorously. "God's blood, don't tell me I need to spell it out for you."

"It seems that you do, Bess."

"Your husband and his harpy want to prove you are of unsound mind and take charge of your estate. Thomas helps them and in return he gets the share he's always felt he was owed."

My head was hurting, felt dulled, as if I had suffered a blow to it, or drunk too much wine. "Why do they need him to . . . help them?"

"Some oblige because it makes 'em feel important, or because they have some ax of their own to grind with you. But a lot are afraid of putting their name to what they cannot understand. But they do it for Thomas. They trust Thomas. They will do as he asks them."

"And what exactly does Thomas ask them to do?"

"Answer the questions just how she wants 'em answered. Give her what she wants to hear."

"What does she want to hear?"

The stirring slowed, until it had almost stopped and she rested the handle of the spoon against the side of the pot. "She wants to know all about your butterflies. About how you chase after them and what you do with them."

"What do people tell her? Let me guess now. Communing with the dead? Witchcraft? Shape-shifting?"

Bess looked scornfully at the dog trailing at my heels. "They say you care more for butterflies and even for a blind bitch than for your own children. They say only a madwoman would prize butterflies as if they were jewels, would take more interest in the hunting of butterflies than fish or fowl to fill the larder shelves. They say that you'd rather pay servants to lay sheets beneath bushes on the moor rather than on beds, and that you pay more for worms than most would pay for a round of cheddar."

"What did you tell her, Bess?"

"I refused to talk to her. Got the sharp end of Thomas's tongue for it."

"Thank you."

She shrugged. "Makes no difference what I say or what I don't say. Add a few whispers together and they're as loud as a shout. And there always were plenty of whispers about you."

IT WAS ALMOST DARK. Down on the moor people were gathering round the great beast that was already turning slowly on the spit over the flames. Soon they would be lighting the bonfires. I found my feet taking me down toward the crowd, toward these people who had been my friends, but who had now spoken out against me.

I stopped short when the stuffed effigy of the Pope began to be slow-marched to its pyre across the dark, flat wasteland, to the menacing beat of a drum. I pulled my hood up and walked the rest of the way to the edge of the crowd, as all eyes watched the effigy hoisted atop the bonfire. The fire itself was being set alight with flaming torches. The flames caught and flared and leapt triumphantly higher. Dark figures moved around it like specters, their faces phantasmagorical in the flames. I looked to find my half brother amongst them, but I could not see him.

As I moved through the midst of the crowd, I felt hostility like a knife in my back. Mistress Keene, Mistress Jennings, Mistress Bennett and Mistress Hort: these women had known me since I was a child, had been with me in the birthing chamber when my own children were born. They and their families had served at the house and worked the land for generations. They were my family, and yet they treated me now as an outcast.

They had always been mildly disapproving of me, mistrusted and misunderstood me, because I did not conform to their image of what a lady should be, but now Sarah Gideon and Thomas had taken that mistrust and bent it to their own ends, and in doing so, had legitimized it, magnified it, given it full rein. And Richard, had he helped to turn them against me, where once he had rescued me?

There was the same tension in the air as there had been when the mob had come to the house and threatened to burn it. Every member of this crowd now treated me with the same enmity that Thomas had always shown. A contempt that had spread like a canker had infected them all like a plague. They were glancing toward me, hissing and whispering. As I passed through them, they moved back, gave me ground. Alice Walker hurled an apple, someone else threw an onion. It was surprising how much it hurt, when I was hit between my shoulders, on my arm. I ignored it. I did not bow my head in shame. I did not lower my eyes. I kept on walking. I ignored the catcalling boys and cursing drunkards. I ignored the fingers clawing my cloak, pulling my hair.

Then a great cheer went up and all attention was diverted back to the fire. The flames had reached the effigy of the Pope and caught the stuffed feet. I watched them lick up the straw legs, catch a hand and devour an arm.

I looked around for Forest, but I caught the eye of little Annie Sherburne. She gave me a timid smile that meant more than I'd probably ever be able to tell her. She was holding her little brother's hand and in her other arm she cradled a baby, and when I smiled back at her, she came over to me.

"Is this Harry, your cousin's child?" I asked her.

She nodded. "He is almost walking now."

The heat of the fire was so searing, it made my eyes water. Annie turned her head toward the back of the crowd, to her mother and a girl I took for the mother of the infant. I had weak smiles from both women.

"I'm glad to see not everyone hates me, Annie."

"Oh, but we could never hate you, Mistress Glanville," the girl said earnestly. "Not when you have been so kind to us." She lowered her eyes as her father came to stand at her side.

"Good day to you, Mistress Glanville," he said with gruff courtesy.

"Good day to you too, Jack."

"I'd have you know that I did not want to talk to that woman," he said. "But I was left with no choice." Jack Sherburne was a large man with a rugged, weathered face, but his eyes were honest and kind, though he kept them averted from me, looked directly ahead as he spoke, to make it look like he was not really speaking to me at all. His face was strained. "Your son said the rent would be tripled if we did not cooperate."

"She made me talk too," Annie said, and I felt her grave young eyes entreating me to forgive her. "All I said was that I helped you collect worms and helped you feed them and care for them. There's no harm in that, is there?"

"No, Annie," I said. "There is no harm in it at all."

I noticed there was a man weaving through the crowd. Dressed in wool coat and cap, he appeared to be looking for someone, with some urgency.

"I told her how good-humored and well pleased you always were when we were working with the butterflies," Annie said enthusiastically. "And how I liked collecting the worms and how you paid me very well for it."

Her father spoke again. "I made a point of saying how generous you have been to us. How you gave a home to my niece and her little one when she had nowhere else to go. That must count for something."

I did not doubt that it would only count against me: that I paid good money for butterflies and worms, but failed to collect proper rents, but I thanked them both, all the same. "Do you know what others have said?"

Jack Sherburne was a good Anglican. He would not want to repeat slander.

The man who was searching the crowd had stopped to speak to someone, someone who was pointing in my direction. "Please, Jack. I have to hear it."

"They all agree that you do not live according to your station," he continued gravely. "That you wander around on the moor half dressed. That you are so busy with your worms, you do not keep enough food in the house and have to send out to the public brew house, instead of brewing yourself as a gentlewoman should. They say you beat your maid with a holly stick when the worms died, which we all know is the foulest lie. But you know how it is?" he said apologetically. "Once this kind of thing gets a hold, it runs rife and twisted as bindweed."

With some cultivation, most certainly. I saw Thomas now, standing by the spit roast, surveying the scene almost proprietorially. Someone who was integrated in this community, someone who had lived amongst the commoners all his life, so that he was accepted amongst them, someone who had led a near riot and carried everyone with him before; someone who still nursed his own vendetta against me, his own grievance. Thomas Knight, who had put words into these people's mouths and incited them to speak against me. Thomas Knight, whose life I had saved, at risk of my own. Whose life I had begged Richard to spare.

Annie's little brother turned his face into his sister's wool skirt. "Can we go now, Annie, please. I don't like this part."

I saw that Thomas was bending low, trying to tie the top of a writhing hessian sack. I knew, from years of attending these occasions, that the sack contained a litter of kittens.

I listened to the crackle and hiss of the fire. I watched the flames reflected on the floodwater like a river of molten gold. Little sparks and embers shot up into the black sky and looked, briefly, so like golden butterflies that I wondered if I really was losing my grip on sanity. Thomas raised his arm high, the pathetic wriggling burlap sack clenched in his fist. As the effigy of the Pope toppled from his fiery throne, Thomas swung his arm and hurled the sack with all his might onto the flames, just so that the drama of the occasion could be enhanced by the terrible, desperate screaming of the kittens as they were burned alive. I had seen this standard but most gruesome Gunpowder Night ceremony performed many times before, but never had it repulsed me as much as it did now.

The man in the cap had seen me and was hurrying over. Only when he swept off his hat did I see that it was James's manservant, George. My heart lifted for a moment, so pleased was I just to see a friendly face, one associated with happier times. His eyes were red-rimmed with tiredness, the lines of his face ingrained with dust as if he had ridden hard all day. "Whatever are you doing here, George?"

"Looking for you, Ma'am. I have been looking for you all over." He held out a letter. "Mr. Petiver said I was to give it to nobody but you and that I was to stay with you until you had read it."

The seriousness of his tone alarmed me. "Has something happened?"

"Please." He nodded toward the letter.

I broke the seal and unfolded the paper with trembling fingers. It was quite different from the letters James had sent me in the past, only a few short, hastily scribbled lines, which I could just make out in the lantern Annie held up for me.

I turned to George. "You were there?" My voice was very quiet. "You saw what took place?"

A short nod. "A gentleman came to the shop," he said carefully. "Dark hair, blue eyes, drunk as a sailor. He demanded to see you, and when I swore you'd gone, it was young Mr. Glanville he wanted. When my master told him your son was not available either, he vaulted over the counter and took hold of Mr. Petiver by the throat, accused him of . . . well, I won't repeat the exact words . . . taking liberties with you. I tell you, I thought my master was done for. But your son heard the scuffle and came out of the laboratory. When he saw who it was that had come looking for him, he turned as white as a winding-sheet, but he was very brave. He bade the man leave go of Mr. Petiver and that he did, though his hand stayed on the hilt of his sword. Your boy did not try to make a run for it," George said finally, "but I cannot tell you he went willingly."

James's letter was almost screwed up in my hand, I was gripping it so tightly. "What does he want?"

"That I do not know."

"He must have said something. What did he say? What does he want with my son?" Dickon was Richard's son too, I reminded myself, trying to take heart from it. It was Forest who was the heir to my estate. There was nothing to be gained by harming Dickon. "He could not hurt him," I said, more a question than a statement of fact. "He would not hurt his own son."

There was a silence. "Is there anything at all that I can do for you?" George asked.

I shook my head. "Only go directly back to London and tell James that I am grateful of his offer to come to me but that he must not. It would only make matters worse. Tell him to stay where he is, in case Dickon comes back or is still in London and needs his help. And, George, tell him . . . tell him to be careful."

He hesitated. "What will you do, Ma'am?"

"I shall find them. I shall find my son."

I RAN ALL THE WAY back over the marshy moor, my cloak flying back from my shoulders, my lungs bursting and the muscles in the backs of my calves as hot as irons by the time I reached the stables. There was no sign of the coachman, and I doubted he'd do my bidding now, even if I could find him.

I took a dagger from the armory to defend myself from vagabonds and highwaymen, filled a pouch with some of my jewels so that I could sell them and, stowing both hurriedly in my pocket, ran down to the stable, to my mare Kestrel's stall. I slipped the bridle over her head, threw on the saddle, tightened the girth, then led her out to the mounting block and swung myself up onto her back. I clicked to her to walk and felt the strong muscles roll beneath me as we clattered out of the yard.

It would have been wise to wait until morning, to set out on my journey in the light rather than in the dark, but I could not wait. I did not know the way to Suffolk except that it lay east, and that first I must therefore pass through Bristol and on into Gloucestershire. I had a dwindling purse of money, which I had brought back with me from London. Together with the jewels, I reckoned it would be enough. It would have to be enough. The mist thinned as I rode out of Tickenham, but the smoke of countless bonfires made it look as if drifting patches of it still lingered. The air was heavy with the pungent smell of burning. There were great bonfires still flaring bright as beacons on village greens and at street corners, and rows of much smaller fires outside the doors of little hovels and cottages. The sporadic explosion of fireworks sounded like the rumble of distant cannon fire, as if all England was at war again, except that everywhere there was revelry and merrymaking. The festivities meant that people were abroad late into the night, drinking and carousing and throwing crackers and squibs, so that the dark roads at least were far from deserted.

I rode on. It grew quieter as I traveled through Bristol and out onto the Tetbury Road toward Cirencester. But the mired, rutted lanes and byways of Somersetshire had given way to firmer, drier ground, which made the going easier and quicker, and I could not think of stopping. I could not rest my head not knowing where Dickon was resting his.

The horse plodded through the night and its steady gait made me drowsy, even though I tried to stay alert to the many dangers of the night road, especially for a woman traveling alone. I could not get out of my mind the last time I had seen Dickon, when he had told me that he had the best of mothers and the worst of fathers and then waved good-bye. He had always been afraid of his father, but I hoped he trusted me enough to know that I would be coming to get him.

I rode on. Dawn broke cold and windy. I was so tired I fell half asleep in the saddle and woke only when I almost slipped off it. I stopped to breakfast at an inn on the outskirts of Tetbury, hoping the wheaten bread and butter would revive me a little, before continuing on to the Roman town of Cirencester, now a flourishing wool town with a large and bustling market square that drew people in for many miles around. I was sure that there must be somebody there who could tell me the way to Suffolk. I asked two stallholders, but in the end it was a cloth merchant who said that I should head toward Oxford and thence to the large village of Aylesbury. He knew the way well, since it was a center for lace-making and he had traded there.

"You should reach Oxford by nightfall with the wind behind you," he said.

I rode, saddle-sore and exhausted, through the rolling Cotswolds. Through the riverside village of Bibury and up the steep, narrow track through Burford, each secluded village made desolate and almost apocalyptical by the smoldering heaps of cinders that marked the places where the bonfires had been. There was a keen wind. It blew the gray ash into the air, like a storm of dirty snowflakes.

I rode on. Oxford was a very pleasant place, with its twilit towers and spires and noble high street that was surprisingly clean, well paved, and of great length. I rested again, slept a little, and next came to the village green at Aylesbury. I stopped to eat at a humble inn, where a woman served me mutton stew that had been stewing for much too long, but was at least piping hot. She insisted on talking to me, but I was so fatigued I could barely make my lips move. She told me proudly that her husband and son were both craftsmen. I told her, just as proudly, that my son was an apothecary, but was going to be a doctor to the poor.

"Send him this way," she said with a chuckle, and I did not tell her that he had probably already passed through Aylesbury.

I came to Cambridge. Cromwell's country. Where Richard had gone to college and developed a love of music and literature. Where once fluttered Fritillaries and Large Coppers and Swallowtails. It reminded me of home, surrounded as it was by willows. It lay in a valley, with marsh and bog and fen all around it. The buildings were indifferent and the streets narrow, badly paved and dirty, but I felt more comfortable there than in almost any other place I had stayed on this interminable journey. When I asked the innkeeper for directions to Suffolk, he agreed to let his son guide me partway, in the morning, for a shilling.

The boy did not say much as he trotted alongside me on a little mule, except to caution me that Sudbury was a grim town on the River Stour, very populous and very poor. But I was still ill prepared for the strange hinterland I found myself traveling through, a place of ramshackle dwellings and narrow, filthy lanes. Great gangs of urchin children ran around barefoot, their pinched faces pockmarked and their feet red-raw in the November frost. A little beggar boy ran up to us, with running sores on his hands and around his mouth, and I tossed him a coin when he told me his sister and his mother were both dead of the bloody flux.

"How far to Elmsett?" I asked, desperate to be away from these harrowing sights that filled me with nothing but apprehension.

He frowned. "Don't know it. But Ipswich is only about ten miles away."

My guide and I parted company and I rode on to Ipswich alone. It was as different from Sudbury as could be, a large seaport on the banks of the River Orwell, with prosperous houses and streets that were clean and broad and paved with small stones and led down to the waterfront. More houses huddled alongside the extensive docks that were crowded with tall-masted ships being loaded and off-loaded with timber and iron, corn and wool. Masters, mates, boat-swains and carpenters milled about. I stopped half a dozen of them, but they were either arriving from Newcastle or Scandinavia, or em-barking for the Low Countries. They had never heard of Elmsett either.

I rode up into the town center with its abundance of medieval churches and an inn called the White Horse, right at its heart.

There was an old gray-bearded man behind the bar, who looked more like a sea captain than any man at the harbor. "Can you tell me how to get to Elmsett, sir?" I felt like a person from a ballad or myth, doomed to keep on traveling, repeating this one question, searching for somewhere that did not exist, that I would never find.

"Eight miles northwest of here," he said. "Look out for the elm trees and the ancient church above the valley."

I SAW the small flint church, a stark outline against the colorless November sky. It stood on a hill above valley sides that were cloaked with a forest of autumnal elm trees. I rode past a farm and a mill and came to a small village green, with a large tree where the smithy had his forge. A farmer was waiting to have his horse shod and the blacksmith was at work with his anvil and hammer on a glowing horseshoe. I asked the farmer the way to Elmsett Manor, for what I hoped was the last time.

He shielded his eyes to look up at me in the saddle, my gown and riding cloak clearly of good quality but dusty and disheveled.

"I take it you've come to see young Mr. Glanville." He winked aside to the blacksmith, as if to hint that I was just one in a line of loose but well-bred young women who had come looking for Richard Glanville in the wilds of Suffolk. "You're too late, I'm afraid. He was here, but he left about a day or so ago."

My spirits plummeted. "Are you sure?"

He nodded. "Just his father there now, old Mr. Glanville."

I had not even known that Richard's father was still living.

The blacksmith said that Elmsett Manor lay not a quarter of a mile away, at the edge of the forest, and I continued on with a heavy heart, but with a little flicker of curiosity to meet this man about whom I had heard so much, and none of it very favorable.

I passed through fields and meadows left uncultivated and badly run to seed. Withered leaves drifted down from the eponymous elms as I rode through them, ducking to avoid low branches, the horse's hooves muffled by the dead foliage on the ground. I thought how this would be a strange and melancholy place, even in summer, when these most funereal of trees were in full leaf.

I came upon Elmsett Manor unexpectedly, a small gabled manor built of silver-gray flint, set amidst meadows left uncultivated and run badly to seed. The house was set well back in the trees, half hidden by them and encircled by a little moat, silvery also under the white sky. One wing of the house was crumbled away, roofless, entirely derelict, and the rest looked to be in very poor repair, but that only added to the romantic air, made it even more like a place in a story, a place where a fairy princess, rather than a young apprentice boy, might have been held captive, a place for a sleeping beauty to wait for her one true love to find her and wake her with a kiss.

An elderly man was sitting on a stone bench beside the moat, a worn blanket over his knees. He was holding a fishing net. The drawbridge was down and I crossed over it, the horse's hooves making a hollow clop on the damp and rotten planks that sagged alarmingly as we passed over.

The man looked up. He did not acknowledge me, but lifted the blanket, folded it, rose and came toward me. He had thick hair which would once have been very dark, but was now as silvery as the water in the moat. His eyes had the shape of Richard's, but were brown, not blue. He must have been in his early sixties, but was tall and still slender, very striking.

I slid down from the saddle and hooked the bridle over a gatepost. "Mr. Glanville?"

"That is me," the man replied.

"I am Eleanor Glanville, Richard's wife."

"I have been expecting you."

"Where is my son Dickon, sir? Have you seen him?"

"Yes, I have seen him."

"Is he well? Is he safe?"

"I believe so. Please." He held out his hand to me. "You look very tired. Won't you come inside and share some supper with me?"

There was a time when it would have delighted me to be in a place so connected with Richard's past, and to meet his father. I could not equate him at all with the embittered, uncaring man who had so mercilessly pushed his son to succeed, had thrown him in the lake, to drown or swim. Either Richard had lied to me, as seemed entirely likely, or else time had mellowed him.

I was shown through to a dilapidated parlor. Despite the dark and heavy decayed furnishings, the faded tapestries that failed to cover the evidence of peeling, badly damp-stained walls, Elmsett Manor was not quite how I had imagined it either, not totally ruined. Only two or three rooms seemed to be habitable, but with sufficient funds to lavish on its restoration, it could be beautiful again.

We sat at a small worn table and were served with baked trout that Richard's father ate in the old way, with a spoon, a knife and his fingers.

"Do you know where they have gone?" I asked him.

"They headed up the coast. A place called Whitby, in the North Riding of Yorkshire."

"Yorkshire? So far away? Why?"

Richard's father rested his spoon on the edge of the plate. "None of this is Richard's doing," he said. "You must believe that."

"I am afraid I find that rather hard."

"It was jealousy that drove him to take the boy."

"Jealousy?"

There was a stiffening of the lines of his face, a flicker of anger in his eyes that was strangely familiar to me. "You bound your boy, my son's boy, as apprentice to your lover."

I lowered my eyes, suffered a stab of remorse. It seemed pointless to argue that James and I had become lovers only after Dickon's apprenticeship had begun.

"They knew this was the first place you'd come looking for them," Richard's father said. "Your boy is refusing to cooperate. They took him to Yorkshire to give them more time to convince him."

"Convince him of what? What do they want from him?"

"Sarah Gideon is the widow of an attorney," Mr. Glanville explained. "She has a devious, grasping nature and a good knowledge of the law, a formidable mix. They are putting pressure on your son to sign affidavits against you, testifying to your unsuitable way of life, your state of mind, your unhealthy interest in butterflies."

"Don't they have enough against me already?"

"The boy's testimony will count for much. He acted as your assistant, I understand." He picked up his spoon again, put it in his mouth. "I believe they have taken a lodging near the harbor, above an inn."

"Why would you tell me that?" I asked, instantly suspicious. "Why help me to find them, when you and I are strangers to one another?"

"I do not condone this," he said quietly. "And your son is my grandson."

"Then why did you let him go?" I burst out. "Why did you not find a way to help him?"

He looked at me as if to say that I knew the answer already. A man in his sixties was no match for the unstable, hostile man my husband had become. "I helped your boy every day, in the only way I could. I tried to get pen and ink to him. He wrote a letter to you but Richard discovered it and it seemed to cause him some distress. I am afraid he destroyed it."

"Do you know what it said?"

"Your son said only that you could trust him, and that he trusted you and that he did not believe the many wounding things his father said about you." He looked down at his plate. "I secretly took him food, even though that woman vowed to have me thrown out of my own home if she discovered one morsel of bread had passed the boy's lips."

I pushed my own plate away in horror. "She means to starve him?"

"Oh, she threatens much."

"What has she threatened?"

"She has told your lad that if he does not sign the documents, he will starve to death. Or else he will be sold as a slave to plantation owners in the New World. Threats as ludicrous and empty as they are vicious."

"But Dickon does not know that," I shouted. "He will believe her."

"Richard would not see harm done . . ."

"Then why does he not stop her? Why is he doing this? Does he hate me so very much?"

Mr. Glanville lowered his eyes, did not answer that. "He is not himself," he said. "He is drinking too much, not sleeping enough." His father ran his hand over his face. "He has always been rather highly strung. I am afraid I was a very poor father to him. He was a child who desperately needed warmth, affection, a confidant, to be hugged and held. Above all else he needed approval, but I was able to give him none. I had nothing left to give." His eyes were full of regretful tears. "If ever there was a boy needed a mother's love," he said, "it was that little lad."

I held up my hand to silence him, stood, walked quickly, distractedly, to the other side of the room. There was a mottled mirror hanging on the wall, and for a moment it was not my face I saw, but Richard's, as he had looked when I had first fallen in love with him. Youthful, beautiful, troubled. Memories rushed at me. His angelic smile, gentle and uncertain when I held him in my arms, after he fell from his horse, the need and the loneliness I had sensed in him when he had danced with me. The passion and the intensity of that first kiss. I wanted to weep. I felt a dragging in my heart that was like compassion, like love, and a need to protect and comfort that somehow transcended all that was happening now, made it seem completely unreal, almost irrelevant. I suffered a moment of deceptive lucidity, during which I was quite certain that Richard had not murdered Edmund, that somehow I had brought all this upon myself. But the moment passed and reality came back like a blow to my heart.

I blinked, and his image in the mirror was replaced by my own and I thought how the dilapidated surroundings suited me very well. With violet smudges under my eyes, dirt on my cheeks, my dress filthy and torn and straggles of hair hanging loose and uncombed about my shoulders, I no longer looked like a lady who would live in a fine mansion. I looked like a vagabond, a gypsy who wandered from place to place, who had no belongings and no fixed abode, and I found that I would not mind that at all.

"I believe Richard has convinced himself this is all for my benefit," his father was saying. "We were estranged, you see, for so many years. I did not even know he had married, or that I had two grandchildren. And I think he feels guilty for that now, wants to make some kind of recompense. He saw how distraught I was to see this house in ruins when we returned from exile. He knew how important it is to me, to this family, and I think he hoped to find a way to enable me to see it restored before I die."

My heart hardened. "He has it in mind to abandon Tickenham Court," I said. "Doesn't he? He plans to sell it off to the drainage speculators and use the profit to rebuild Elmsett?"

It would not matter to Richard if the commoners were bent on destruction and vandalism, would not matter if he was loathed and spurned in Tickenham, if he no longer lived there, if he had already taken the money and fled.

I was not a gypsy. There *was* somewhere that I belonged. I belonged at Tickenham Court. I was Eleanor Glanville of Tickenham Court. I had sworn to my father that I would protect it from unscrupulous Cavaliers and so far I had made a very sorry job of it, but I would do my best to put it right, just as soon as I had found my son.

WHITBY WAS many, many miles away from Elmsett, too many miles, but the route was straightforward at least. All I had to do was go north toward the Fens and the great estuary of The Wash, and then follow the east coastline all the rest of the way.

I rode first toward Stowmarket and had to cross a tributary of the River Gipping to the south of the town. It was deep and fast-flowing, and Kestrel shied and sidled when I tried to urge her to walk into the water. She would not be persuaded and I had to dismount and lead her in. When the water was up to my waist I climbed back into the saddle and leaned forward, my arms wrapped around her neck as her hooves slipped on the smooth rounded stones on the riverbed and she bucked and stumbled.

We made it through with no mishap but my skirts were still dripping wet and I was shivering when we reached the market town of Bury St. Edmunds, a place famed for its beautiful situation and wholesome air, with a ruined abbey haunting the town center. The monks had long gone, replaced by gentry and people of fashion, who thronged the fair to buy toys and trinkets. There was a time when I would have loved nothing better than to stop and join them, to browse and to shop. But I had nothing in common with such people anymore. I felt very distant from them now, and I could not have made polite conversation if my life depended upon it.

Just as dusk was falling, I arrived in Thetford, another market town with another ruined priory and buildings of flint stone. I stopped at

the Bell Inn and was served a supper of sprats and given a bed with
sheets grimy and infested with lice. I spent the night itching and
scratching and continued itching as I rode on again to King's Lynn,
the port on the east bank of the Great Ouse, the vast-mouthed river
that carried the outfall of all the waterways which drained the Fens.

King's Lynn had a guildhall with a medieval flint-checkered
façade, fine medieval merchants' houses on cobbled lanes, and a new
customs house overlooking the medieval harbor and quay, where grain
and butter, hides and wool were loaded onto ships bound for the
Netherlands. But for all its ancient grandeur, it felt like a town on the
margin, a final outpost of civility at the edge of the flat lowland of
the Fens and the vast three-sided bay that was The Wash.

I fed Kestrel a bag of oats and rode out into the wilderness. A
bleaker, more inhospitable place I had never seen or dared to imagine.
The wildness and vast desolation of The Wash made the marshland
of Tickenham seem tame in comparison. It was raining, a cold, windswept rain that poured down from banks of leaden clouds and was
carried over the expanses of salt marshes and shifting sandbanks.

The tide was far out, exposing the ridges of sand and mud and
sheets of shallow water cut with deep channels as far as the eye could
see. There were dense flocks of wetland birds, oystercatchers and terns,
geese and ducks and waders, and their forlorn cries added to the utter
desolation and strangeness. A few souls braved the treacherous wastes,
hunting for shrimps and cockles, but their presence did not make the
place seem any less lonely. So caked were they in mud from head to
toe that they scarcely resembled human beings at all.

The flat lowland was such a quagmire that Kestrel sank up to her
shanks, so I had to dismount to urge her on, slipping and sliding from
one clump of higher ground to another. Time after time, I went into
bog up to my knees. I was accustomed to Somersetshire bog and
marsh, but this was different, a sucking, viscous, frightening mud. I

hauled myself clear with difficulty. My boots were so heavy and caked that it felt as if I had rocks tied to my feet. I had mud up to the tops of my legs, over my hands and splattered on my face. My skirt and cloak were slick with it and wet from the rain, and my hair was plastered to my head. I grunted with effort and frustration and despair. But not once did I consider turning back.

I rode on, the rain stinging my face like biting insects, trying not to think that Dickon had been made to travel through this godforsaken place, without a good dinner in his belly to warm him. I could not think that mud might be the least of the dangers facing him.

I rode on to the rickety bridge across the River Nene, thence to the River Welland, which was shallow enough for me to wash myself. I rode on to the River Witham, and into Lincolnshire.

I had run out of money, but I parted with a pearl necklace for a straw pallet to sleep on and a bowl of burned porridge, and cold water to wash in. I felt as if I had been traveling forever, and yet I was only halfway there, with over a hundred miles left to go. I woke feeling feverish. My head throbbed and every bone and muscle in my body ached. I hardly knew where I was, or even who I was anymore.

I held on grimly to the reins with my chapped hands and clung to the image of the boy I was pursuing. I had chased butterflies over fields and ditches and I would follow my son to the ends of the earth, if need be. He would always be my baby, no matter how big he grew. Since the day he was born, every small hurt or minor distress he ever suffered had been as a thorn upon my soul. I would suffer any danger or discomfort, any accusation and slur, any number of locks and chains to know that he was safe. I would willingly trade my life for his, if it came to it.

The roads and days merged, each new town, each new inn very much like all the rest. All I could do was keep going, one step at a time, one mile at a time, counting down the landmarks. The medieval city of Lincoln, with the castle atop the steep hill, the half-timbered Tudor houses and Gothic bridge and the magnificent cathedral, with its central tower like a finger of stone pointing to Heaven. My way lay in a different direction entirely, north, to Driffield in the Wolds, where there were trout streams to cross, further north still, along a straight Roman road to the fortified town of Malton, with a shallow ford over the Derwent.

I passed the alum works and saw the Gothic pillars and arches of Whitby Abbey, standing high on the headland, high above the German Ocean with the black North York Moors behind it, and I could not believe I had journeyed so far to come to such a place. A little fishing port with white houses, closely and irregularly built on narrow cobbled streets. A cold, wet, windswept place of slanting sunbeams.

There were two inns on the harbor side, only one with lodgings above it, more a tavern really, that looked like a smuggler's den.

The landlady was a wrinkled old woman who smelled of fish. What teeth she had left were blackened stumps and she spoke in a North Country accent that was almost incomprehensible. Yet she looked at me most disapprovingly, warily even, as if it was I who was to be mistrusted. She kept me outside the door of her apartment, only opened the door partway and peered round it, as she informed me that a man and boy and woman who fit the description I gave her of Dickon and Richard and Sarah Gideon had lodged with her but had left on Monday.

"What day is it now?" I had lost all track of days and of time.

"Tuesday."

I had come all this way and again I had missed him by just one day. I collapsed at the top of the dingy stairwell and wept with fatigue and despair.

The woman took pity on me when I sobbed and told her Dickon was my son. She helped me down to the tavern, where she sat me in a corner and had them serve me smoked herrings in cream.

"They were your boy's favorite," she encouraged. "He could gobble up two whole platefuls in one sitting. Surely you can manage a few bites."

"He was having enough to eat?" I asked. "He was not too thin?"

She looked at me as if my concerns were quite pathetic. "Like I say, he was never full up, like all young lads, but he certainly wasn't starving to death. It's you who's too thin, madam, if you don't mind my saying."

I took a bite. The fish melted in my mouth, was delicious. I had not realized how hungry I was.

"Did he seem unhappy or frightened in any way?"

"Cheerful more like."

"Cheerful?"

"For sure. Especially the last night they were here and he stayed up drinking brandy and talking with his father until past midnight."

"Did you hear what they talked about?"

"Some of it." She helped herself to a swig of ale from my pot. "Doctoring mostly. His father was promising to set him up with his own examination rooms."

I should have been relieved that Dickon was not in distress. But it disturbed me to think that he was so easily won over, with what were surely false bribes and promises. I despised myself for being disappointed to hear that he seemed at ease now in his father's company, that they were companionable, were making plans together. Then it occurred to me that Richard, or Sarah Gideon, or both of them were entirely capable of bribing this woman to feed me this story.

"Was there no animosity at all between the two of them?" I tested.

"Only over the papers."

"What papers?"

"Some papers Mr. Glanville seemed keen for the boy to sign. Couldn't help but notice." She apologized for her nosiness. "His father pushed them at him that night, before the talk about medicine. The lad pushed them back. Mr. Glanville refolded them and put them back in his pocket, said that they would keep for another day."

I should not have doubted him. Dickon was just playing along, still refusing to sign anything, stalling until I came to rescue him, as he knew I would.

"Do you have any idea where they might be now?" I asked, hoping to God her inquisitiveness extended that far.

She tapped the side of her nose with her forefinger. "I could make a guess that they are on their way to Newington Green."

"Near London." She might as well have said Mexico, for the great distance it seemed to me then. "What makes you think they have gone there?"

"Mistress Gideon asked me to post a letter for her. Then lo and behold a letter comes back and the next day they set off. My bet is she was writing to a relative of hers to ask if they could pay a visit. I think I can just about remember the address."

I would always be a few miles, a few hours behind them. They had not covered their trail very well but they did not need to. So long as they kept on moving from place to place, I would never catch them. But I would die before I ceased trying.

I PARTED with my last necklace in Lincoln and bought a brown wool dress from a secondhand clothes seller. It was too big for me and it undoubtedly had lice living in the seams, but I had lice aplenty already and at least it was thick and warm and not in rags and tatters like my own gown.

I stayed at the same inn in King's Lynn that I had stayed at before, but the landlord did not recognize me. Instead of giving me the best room that was reserved for quality folk, I was allotted a pallet under the eaves.

It took me two weeks to reach Newington Green, to find the small cottage owned by a shady character whose name was Street. He denied all knowledge of Sarah Gideon or of Richard Glanville until I gave him every last penny I had, and he told me that they had gone to Mitcham.

"Mitcham?"

"It is the Montpellier of England, don't you know, surrounded by fields of lavender and chamomile and peppermint for the London perfumers."

"But why have Sarah Gideon and Richard Glanville gone there?"

"There are many fine, fine houses. John Donne lived there, and Sir Walter Raleigh."

"Please, sir. I have no more money to give you."

"Sarah had an appointment with a French tailor, to be measured for her wedding gown." He closed the door in my face.

I FILCHED A PIE from a market stall and spent the night beneath a tree, shivering myself to sleep, with my fingers wrapped ever more tightly around the dagger. I was in fear for my life now. I was searching for Richard and yet I was in terror of him finding me first, of him finding me and taking his sword to my throat. Of Sarah Gideon doing the job for him.

She was no longer content to be his mistress. She wanted to be his wife and Richard was evidently prepared to overlook entirely the fact that he already had a wife. It was no longer enough just to prove I was mad and to lock me away. They were not prepared to wait until eventually nobody even remembered I existed. Sarah had gone to Mitcham to have her wedding gown made. They wanted me out of the way immediately, altogether, forever.

James had written to me of Mitcham, so long ago it seemed like a dream, a dream of swaths of violet flowers that exuded the most soothing fragrance and attracted clouds of white butterflies. There was no lavender now. The fields were brown instead of purple. There were no white butterflies. It seemed there was no beauty left in the world, no hope.

I rode over the common to the manor of Mitcham Cannons. If Mitcham was anything like Tickenham, whoever resided there would be aware of any visitors to the village. The benevolent gentleman who opened the door took me for a beggar woman and invited me in for bread and cheese and to warm myself by the fire. He never even had the chance to tell me his name. My own name caused too much of a stir.

"I am Eleanor Glanville of Tickenham Court in Somersetshire," I said, my voice croaking with disuse. "I am looking for my son. He is traveling with my husband, Richard Glanville, and a woman. I was told they were in Mitcham."

The man stared at me aghast and I thought I knew why. I was still clutching the dagger beneath my tattered riding cloak, beneath which I was wearing an old dress that hung off my shoulders and trailed past my feet. My boots had holes in them and my hair hung in snarls around my dirty face. I had been traveling so long that I had quite forgotten how to be still and I paced back and forth, as I chewed on bread that I held in fingers cracked and bleeding from the cold. I must look like a madwoman for sure. I felt like one.

"He told you I was mad, sir?"

He shook his head very slowly. "No, madam. He did not tell me you were mad. He told me that you were dead."

My feet stopped pacing. "Dead?"

"It was my understanding that Richard Glanville's wife died of ague some months ago."

How cruel. It was the cruelest mockery, to claim I had died of the disease that had killed the rest of my family, the disease that I had feared all of my life.

"Dead?" I repeated, walking again. I took five paces forward, came up against the wall and turned, took five paces back. "Dead of ague?"

"They obviously feared it might be called into question. While she was having her wedding gown fitted, Mr. Glanville had an appointment with a solicitor, to have an affidavit drawn up to present to the clergyman who was to conduct their wedding, to prove that he was free to marry, to prove that his first wife was no longer living and that he was a widower."

Five steps forward, turn, five steps back. "Who signed it? Who signed the affidavit?"

"They planned for the boy to sign, Mr. Glanville's son."

"Did he do it?"

"Apparently he came down with some affliction and was unable."

"He is my son too," I said. "And he is a good boy. He will not commit perjury to enable his father to commit bigamy. He would not swear before God that I am dead, when he knows it for a lie."

"Then you should take great care, madam," the gentleman said. "Maybe your boy will leave them no option but to turn the lie into truth."

"Where are they now?"

"They were on their way to Somersetshire."

THE LIVERIED FOOTMAN who opened the door of William Merrick's grand square-fronted residence on King Street in Bristol took one look at me and would have shut the door on me immediately, had I not anticipated his reaction and stuck my foot in the way.

"Please tell him Eleanor Glanville is here to see him," I said, and obviously managed to convey enough dignity in my voice to make him reconsider.

I was eventually taken through to the silk-papered drawing room and I sat and waited on an overstuffed silk chair. The normality and luxury of it was such a contrast to my recent surroundings that it was almost offensive.

Mr. Merrick strode in, checked when he saw me, bowed and raised my hand to his lips but did not kiss it, as if he feared to contract a disease. "Eleanor. It has been some time. I heard from Forest that you were . . . traveling."

I had no time to waste on pleasantries. "You know why?"

He took the time to sit down properly, waited for me to do the same. "I know that after you ran out on your husband, he looked to find consolation in drink and found it also in the arms of another woman, and that other woman happens to be a conniving little minx named Sarah Gideon, widow of an attorney, who no doubt is using your husband's drunkenness and misery to her own ends."

"He met her at the Llandoger Trow, didn't he? I saw her with him, a long time ago."

"She and her now dead husband both frequented that particular tavern, yes. I do believe she always had a fondness for your husband, as most women seem to."

"She and Richard, with the help of Thomas Knight, have collected affidavits against me, to prove I am mad, so that they could take control of my estate, but now it seems that is no longer enough and they are bent on passing me off as dead, or else seeing to it that I really am, for all I know."

William shook his head from side to side in weary dismay. "Your father believed I would advise you wisely and I trust that I have always done so when you have allowed me. But I am afraid that I am at a loss as to how to advise you in your current predicament. This is outside any moral code that I can understand. I am an enterprising businessman. Richard Glanville, it would appear, is naught but an oversexed adventurer, as ruthless and corrupt as a buccaneer. And now he is unstable and a drunkard with it, and under the influence of a manipulative harlot."

"I did not come here for your advice, William," I said. "I wish to write a new will, to supersede the existing one that was drawn up for me by George Digby's attorney, along with the marriage settlement." I did not explain that the Earl of Bristol was so similar to Richard in his affiliations and background that I had not wanted to go back to him or to his attorney. "I wish to have you witness it, William, and ensure it is given into the hands of your solicitor."

He looked vaguely uncomfortable.

"You can do that for me?"

He gave a brief nod, showed me to a rosewood writing desk by the window, handed me a sheet of vellum and a quill.

My hands were shaking as I sat, dipped the pen in the ink and began to write. The scratching of the nib on the paper was the only sound in the room. I wrote three lines and then I signed my name. "There. It is done."

"So quickly?"

I vacated the chair, dipped the nib again, handed Mr. Merrick the pen for him to sign as witness.

He did not take it, but bent his head over the paper as he read what I had written. He stiffened, straightened slightly and looked at me askance, as if he doubted I knew what I was doing. He was clearly reluctant to put his name to the document.

"It is my right, is it not, under the terms of a marriage settlement, to have my estate and possessions disposed of exactly as I see fit?"

"Indeed so, but . . ."

"It is my wish to leave everything to my uncle, Henry Goodricke, fourth baronet of Ribston, my late great-aunt Elizabeth's son. He was taught to love Tickenham by my mother. So it is fitting that I entrust her estate into his care. Everything but a few pounds, which I bequeath to each of my children and to Mary and John Burges."

"You would disinherit your own son?"

"I have no choice," I said. "Forest is in collusion with his stepfather, and as it stands he has everything to gain by my death. But it is not only that I must do this in order to safeguard my life, it is that I want to safeguard the future of Tickenham Court, as I swore to do. And if I leave it to Forest, I am as good as leaving it to Richard, to his mistress, and if I am to face my father in Heaven, I cannot have that on my conscience." I pushed the pen at William. "Please. Sign it."

He vacillated. He took the pen gingerly, but still he did not put it to the paper. He had the look of a person upon whom it had suddenly dawned that he was in the company of someone not wholly sane.

I gripped the back of the chair. "You do not think I am capable of making a will? You do not think I am of sound mind?"

His laugh was almost nervous. "Now that you mention it, I confess I am in some agreement with your commoners. As you know, I have long thought that nobody wholly in possession of their wits would go in pursuit of butterflies."

My hand went for the dagger I still kept in my pocket, and I pulled it out. With my other hand I grabbed William Merrick's wrist. "Sign. God, damn it."

He looked so terrified that I laughed, which only frightened him more, as if he feared I was hysterical, a cackling loon. But whatever he thought of me, he did not dare refuse me. I stood over him as he wrote his name and then I made him fetch the footman to be second witness, and since the boy did not know how to write, he signed with a thick, dark cross.

"What is your name?" I asked the boy.

"Richard," he said.

It almost winded me. "Well, Richard," I said gently, folding the new paper and handing it to him. "You take this for me, now, to your master's solicitor."

He nodded, and with a glance at my former guardian, who, funnily enough, did not contradict my instruction, he turned and ran out of the room.

THE SUN DISAPPEARED behind dense clouds and a fine rain spat in my face. Then the rain eased and mist rolled in, low and thick as a gray sea. When I breathed, it looked as if mist came out of my mouth, as if it had finally penetrated me, body and soul.

I waited to feel Kestrel's hooves sink beneath me into the mud. My mind reeled back, so that I could have sworn I was on the east coast again, and that soon I would see the great tidal mudflats and hear the lonely cries of wading birds. But the mist cleared and it was the flooded moors of Tickenham which spread out all around me, shimmering in a winter sunset. There must have been prolonged and torrential rain while I had been away, for the water had come up high, high enough to inundate most of Cut Bush Field, deep enough to drown the causeway completely, and was gushing and lapping now at the road as if to wash me away.

I saw a man, standing alone further down the road, at the point where the track veered off to the left up to Tickenham Court and the rectory. My heart gave a jolt. It was not Richard. Nor was it Dickon.

But it was someone I knew instantly, even from a distance, from his profile, from the angle of his shoulders and the way he stood, keen and watchful, perfectly at peace amidst the swans and the geese.

James.

I was sure it was not really him, that he was not really here, that I was as stark raving mad as they said I was, but he turned toward the road, as if he had been watching out for me, waiting for me. He started to walk toward me, and suddenly I knew that I wasn't imagining it at all, and it did not matter that I was dirty and worn-out with tiredness, that my hands shook and that the servants he had met had inevitably warned him that I was completely insane. All that mattered was that he was here.

I rode toward him, tumbled from my horse and splashed on unsteady legs across the flooded road, into his arms. If he was shocked at my appearance, he did not show it at all. All that showed in his eyes was the deepest sympathy and concern.

"I am too late," I said. "Dickon is not here, is he? I cannot find him, James." My breath was a sob, and if he had not been holding me up I would have fallen in the mud at his feet. "I have searched all over the country and I cannot find him."

He smoothed my windswept hair away from my pale, dirt-streaked cheeks. "He is here," he said quietly. "He is quite safe. But you cannot go to him."

"I must." I tried to break away from his embrace but he held me fast. "James, I must see him."

"It was Thomas Knight who sent for me," James explained steadily. "It seems he had an attack of conscience, on account of the fact that he owes his life to you. He wrote to me, to warn me, to warn you, not to go back to the house, not to stay here. Thomas is convinced that they mean to have you declared insane so that it will appear as if you have taken your own life. He says they will shut you away where you can never be found. He says Sarah Gideon is determined to be Sarah Glanville before the month is out."

"Is she here? Is she in my house? With my sons, my husband?"

He took a breath, reluctant to confirm it. "She is."

I tethered Kestrel safely to a tree, turned from him and waded ankle deep through the floodwater, scaring a pair of mallards into hasty, clattering flight, as I retrieved the rowing boat James had brought with him. When he saw there was no arguing with me or stopping me, he climbed aboard too. We each took up an oar.

The flooded expanse of the moor offered no place at all to hide, no opportunity to reach the house with any degree of secrecy. She'd have been able to see us approaching from far away, and she was there, waiting for us in the great hall, alone.

She looked almost no different from how she had before, only even more showy and extravagantly dressed, in vermillion silk and dripping garnets as red as her painted lips.

She took in my dirty face and hands, my ragged hair and clothes in tatters, and she looked well pleased, offered me the most self-satisfied smirk and then said condescendingly, and with astonishing gall, "I bid you welcome to Tickenham Court."

I stared at her smug, overpainted face, and it was as if all the distress I'd kept bottled up over the ordeals of the past days was suddenly channeled, had to find a way out. Unthinking, I did to her what Richard had done to me. I slapped her. Hard. Across her face. "That was for Dickon," I said in a voice so calm and yet so wrathful that it did not sound like my own.

It had not wiped the smile off her face, though, only widened it, sharpened it, and I realized that my appearance and my actions only served to confirm the accusations of insanity. I was proving them all right, playing into her hands. I was my own worst enemy. But I did not care anymore. I did not care. In fact it was almost liberating to be considered mad. I could do whatever I liked. "Where is he? Where is Dickon?"

She removed her hand from her cheek, which I was pleased to see was now much redder than the other one, despite the ridiculous amount of rouge she was wearing. I was quite prepared to pull out the dagger that had so alarmed William Merrick if I did not get a satisfactory answer from her. "D'you hear me, you bitch. I want my son."

"Well, you cannot have him, I am afraid," she said, a touch flustered now. "He is out."

I did not believe her. "Out?"

"He's gone to one of the tenants' cottages. A child is running a fever. He insisted on taking some medicine, on staying with the boy until the fever has broken."

That was so like Dickon that I did not doubt now that she was telling the truth, but I was suspicious, and also disheartened.

"You let him go?" I asked. "You broke him then, in the end? He has done . . . what you wanted him to do?"

I saw, instantly, that it was not so. "His brother has gone with him," she said. "To mind him, bring him back."

Tears sprang into my eyes. *Well done, Dickon. And you said you were not brave.*

"Where is my husband?"

"He is sleeping."

For some inexplicable reason, that threw me. There was an intimacy in those three words, a familiarity. *He is sleeping.* They put an image in my head, an image I did not want. I knew, so well, how Richard looked when he was asleep. So many times I had watched over his sleep after he suffered a nightmare. In the early days of our marriage, it was the greatest pleasure to me to just lie beside him and watch him. I knew the way his hair curled on the pillow, and his eyelashes fluttered when he was dreaming. I knew how his lips slightly parted. I knew that he preferred to sleep on his stomach, with his arm thrown up over his head, or on his right side, and that sometimes he would curl up his legs and his arms like a little boy. I knew the sound his breath made.

What did it matter to me? I never wanted to sleep beside him ever again.

"Wake him," I commanded.

She did not move.

"Wake him," I said, "or I shall."

She backed herself against the door, palms against the wood, barring my way, as if for some reason she wanted to keep us apart, was determined to prevent me from going to him. "I cannot."

"Why not?"

"He's drunk."

I looked at the floor, at the ceiling, back at her. "So. He is a drunkard, a debtor, a would-be bigamist and a murderer. The pair of you are very well suited."

She frowned. "Murder?" She shook her head, gave a short laugh. "Who said anything about murder? You think he means to kill you? Oh, no. Far better for us just to lock you away and throw away the key than run the risk of being had for murder. He did say that for you, though, death would be far kinder than confinement."

I was sorely tempted to tell her how Richard had already murdered his own friend, but I did not want to drag poor Edmund into this, did not want to involve him in any way in the sordid mess that my life had become. Besides, there seemed a strong chance she would commend such behavior in any case.

"You were always so set on having my husband, weren't you? Why? Why him? Why would you go to all this trouble?"

In the moment's pause before she answered, as my eyes met hers, I knew that it was not that she loved him, or that even if she thought she did, then it was a self-seeking kind of love, that looked only for what was to be gained, and I told myself that they were indeed well suited, were well deserving of one another, for Richard had loved me no better, had he?

Considering the way she had systematically set about turning my friends and neighbors against me and destroying my life, I'd assumed she must hate me. But I realized also that just as she was incapable of real love, so she must be incapable of hate. She did not hate me, but was altogether indifferent to my feelings, as I imagined she was indifferent to the feelings of everyone but herself. Which made her the most dangerous kind of person. She was driven not by love or by hatred, but by self-interest, and maybe Richard was just the same. Maybe they had been planning this for years.

"Why do I want him?" she repeated with a snigger. "Are you blind? He is a beautiful man. A gentleman." She fingered one of her jeweled rings. "He and I share an appreciation of beautiful things."

"Then it is a wonder what he sees in you."

Behind me, I heard James give a quietly congratulatory chuckle.

She narrowed her eyes. "He said you had a sharp tongue at times. 'Tis a pity your mind's not so sharp."

I did not want to hear what Richard had said to her about me.

"I expect it must be difficult for you," she went on, "seeing me here, in your house. Knowing it is I now who share your handsome husband's bed at night." She stroked her stomach. "Knowing I am to bear his child."

I stared at her.

"That's right," she said. "I am carrying Richard Glanville's baby."

"That is a lie," I said, very quietly, but how could I be certain?

How could Richard? If it was true that she was with child, it might not be his. Even if it was, why did it matter to me now? I had said it myself: Richard Glanville was a drunkard and a debtor, a bigamist and a murderer. I did not want him anymore. I never wanted to see him again, in fact. The pair of them were in this together, were equally to blame. My husband had colluded and conspired with this woman to abduct his own son, to blackmail him, to accuse me of unspeakable things.

"May you rot in Hell," I said.

"Oh, I don't doubt that I shall. But I think Hell would be a much more interesting place to spend eternity than Heaven, don't you?"

Her total remorselessness was utterly chilling. And it served somehow to confirm my worst suspicions of Richard, to suddenly take away all the pain of losing him. The man I had thought him would find no comfort in this woman's arms, would want nothing to do with her kind. A man who had murdered his friend and sought to swindle his wife and child out of their inheritance, however . . .

"You could not win him back, you know," she said, "no matter how hard you tried. You never did know how to satisfy him, did you, how to give him what he needed? I pity him, wedded to a lunatic for so long, shackled to such an unsuitable wife. If he is a drunk and a debtor and a bigamist, then have you ever considered that it is you who have made him so?"

I didn't understand what she meant, nor why that stung me, but it did. James saw that it did and he grabbed hold of my arm. "She is not worth it, Eleanor."

There was a noise, footsteps in the cross passage, voices. It was Will Jennings together with John Hort, both carrying muskets taken from my father's armory. "Everything all right, Ma'am?" Will asked.

I experienced a moment's relief at seeing them, was about to reassure him that all was under control, until I realized he was not addressing me, but her.

"I suggest you leave now," she said icily, "while you still can."

James gave an insistent tug on my arm, but I stood rooted. I stared her down, was glad to see that for the first time she looked almost afraid, despite the armed men waiting to do her bidding. I hoped in that moment that I looked truly and totally insane. I hoped that I looked like a madwoman, like a witch, a sorceress, like a necromancer. I hoped my eyes blazed with a wild and terrifying vengeful light that would haunt her for the rest of her days.

For added effect, I gathered a gob of spit in my mouth and hurled it at her face, and as I let James lead me quietly out of the great hall, I looked back at her over my shoulder, kept on staring at her as I watched her dab it off with a lace-edged cloth.

Then the great oak door closed between us with a resounding clang. I was standing in the familiar muddy, misty yard, outside my own door, on my own land, and I felt utterly lost.

James was looking at me, with what appeared to be unequivocal approval. God bless him. What other man would approve of my behavior just now? "I told you I should have been born a boy," I said, not sure now whether I wanted to laugh or cry. "Ladies do not curse and spit, do they? I hadn't been planning a barroom brawl, I assure you."

"You gave her no more than she deserved," James said. "And you got what you came for too, didn't you?" he added gently. "You did not see Dickon but I think that is probably just as well. It would only distress him. You know he is well, and happy enough. He is being allowed to do what he loves. And when you are no longer a threat to their plans they will no longer be a threat to his. Even if that harpy has a child, now, or at some point in the future, and is determined to have it inherit your husband's estate instead of Dickon, as she surely will be, they will be doing Dickon a great service. He is not destined to be a squire, but a country doctor. Squiring an estate would only get in the way of doctoring, and that's all the boy wants to do."

I nodded. "But what do I do now, James?"

"Walk with me," he said, as if it would solve everything, and I almost believed it could. "Show me that little cove where you saw the unusual Fritillary."

As we rowed away, I looked back toward the house rearing starkly against the apricot and saffron sky. The last rays of the low winter sun lit the traceried windows of the hall, but instead of making it look welcoming, it looked blank, foreboding.

James handed me his flask of whiskey, and when I had thrown a warming slug of it down my throat, he produced two hard-boiled eggs from his pocket, staple diet for all expeditions.

"Whiskey and eggs," I said, my lips cracking, as they tried to form the unfamiliar shape of a smile. "I feel better already."

James looked appreciatively around him at the swans and wild geese and the submerged trees, the arc of the sky.

"Living beneath such a sky," he said. "It is no wonder you have such a love for all that's in it, for creatures with wings."

"My father always did tell me my mind should never be on earthly things."

"How could it be, in such a place as this? You said it was magical at this time of year, but it is more wild and beautiful even than I had imagined."

All I wanted for now was just to walk away from it, with James, to the coast. And when we came at last to the edge of the water we mounted Kestrel and started toward the ancient ridge that led to Clevedon.

He made me talk of other things. Of the Royal Society, Hans Sloane and John Ray.

"How is John?"

"No better, sadly. David Krieg went to stay with him recently and prescribed some new physic for his legs. You do remember David Krieg, the Saxon physician?" James asked with an odd significance I did not even try to understand.

"Of course I remember him."

"He is sailing from Bristol for Virginia in a few days," James said, as if this news should be of the greatest importance to me.

"Is he?" I said, not much interested.

"He is in a fever of excitement to be there and take up his paint-brush. He has promised to bring back for me some more of the black and white sickle wings, and the yellow-spotted wings. You remember those, too?"

"I do." The memory of magnificent butterflies rose and flickered in my mind, sparks of beauty and promise, where for so long there had only been despair.

"America is a new world," James said, as a skein of wild geese called overhead and he lifted his eyes to watch them. "It is there wait-ing, for those who are not daunted by wide rivers and endless skies, those who are brave enough to walk their own path across wild open plains."

I must have had an inkling then, of where he was leading me, but I was so weary I could not think, could not resist. I was flotsam, car-ried along on a tide. I'd have let him take me anywhere, could have ridden with him beneath Somersetshire's vast sky forever. But too soon the track came to an end and there we were, with Ladye Bay below us, and a sea crested with white. We dismounted and James took me to him and we stood in a gentle embrace atop the rugged, windy cliff. We watched the winter sun sink lower in the sky and lay a shining path over the sea that led all the way to the far horizon.

"Remember the Red Admirals," James said, so quiet I was not sure whether he had spoken at all and it was only a whisper on the wind.

"Remember how you wanted so much to keep them. But you knew that if they were kept shut up in the dark, they might as well never have been born."

Instinctively, my arms tightened around his back. "Do not say any more."

"I don't need to say it. You know it yourself. You know what you have to do, what you are meant to do. A husband does not need the law of coverture to take from his wife all that she has, all that she is. He does not need to lock her in an asylum to rob her of her freedom, her very essence. We live in a society which expects a wife to be a helpmeet, prepared to suppress any interests or passions of her own, in order to devote every waking hour to tending her man's needs and wishes, to find complete contentment in ordering his household. And that is not you."

I drew away a little, so I could see his face. "But have you never wanted someone to do that for you, James?"

"What I want, what I have always wanted, is to see you become all that you can be. It is because I love you that I let you go. You were not made to be confined, Eleanor, not in any way. When you were sitting at the table in my parlor, which you tidied so diligently, when you were reading the travelers' tales from sea captains and ship's surgeons, when you listened to them talk over the shop counter of their voyages and listened to David Krieg talk of America at dinner, when you saw the wonderful creatures they brought back with them from distant lands and distant seas, can you tell me you did not wish yourself far, far away from London and from my little shop?"

"No! Yes! Sometimes."

The golden path across the sea widened as the sun dipped lower to the rim of the world. It was so solid and so bright, it seemed you could step out onto it.

"I am no explorer, as you know," James said. "Nonetheless, I have been doing some exploring today. There's a little cave in this cliff, with a ledge inside it, always dry. A girl could go into that cave and it would be like a cocoon. She could shed her gown, and if she found something waiting for her on that ledge, she could come out again as a butterfly boy, as Isaac, and if her discarded gown was found by the seashore, all would believe she had gone from this world and she would be free forever."

The golden track across the sea shimmered enticingly, as I stared. "Come with me."

"Who would there be to receive all those specimens and letters?"

"They are only letters."

"But I have made them my life's task. And you should not belittle their importance. You and I have said a hundred times more words to each other in letters than we have ever spoken face-to-face. And it will be no different, wherever you are. I shall go on hearing your voice in the words that you write to me, as though you are right there beside me. Your letters sustained me through all the years I have loved you. I hear your smile, when you write something amusing. I touch the page your hand has touched as it formed those words, and I feel as if you are as close to me as you are now."

"Your letters sustained me too," I admitted. "They were always my escape and my sanctuary."

He reached into his coat and took out his observation book and a pencil, handed them both to me. "Now you must write to someone else. Now you must escape for good and find a new sanctuary."

Eventually I took the book and the pencil, found a blank page, scratched out a few shaky lines. For Dickon. But for his father's eyes. I tore out the page and folded it, gave the book and the pencil back to James. "I don't want her to get her hands on it."

"I will go back to the house and send him to you." James did not put the observation book in his pocket again immediately. "It is a pity it is not summer," he added. "This is where you saw your mysterious little Fritillary, isn't it? We could have looked for one."

"I have one already," I said. "Pressed in my Bible, in my chamber. Take it."

"If it turns out to be a new species, it will be named for you, and you will be remembered in butterfly books for all time."

"It is you who should be remembered."

"I am content to catalogue the finds of others, and for them to form the bedrock of a great museum to the natural world."

"If I am remembered, I think it is more likely to be as the lady whose relations tried to prove she was mad, on the grounds that nobody in their right mind would go in pursuit of butterflies."

He smiled. "No matter. Nobody reading about you in years to come will think it at all strange to love butterflies and to want to learn more about them."

"You taught me all I needed to know," I said. "About butterflies and about so much more. Always know that those weeks with the Red Admirals were the most peaceful days and nights of my life."

"Like the Red Admirals themselves. Beautiful and short-lived, and all the more lovely for it." He reached inside his coat to put his book away and drew out something else, a pistol. He placed it in my hand. "I have spoken to Richard Glanville," he said. "He is not like her at all. I do not think for one moment that he would do you harm, but just in case I am wrong . . ."

I curled my fingers round the cold, dead weight of the gun and I felt a knot in my throat. "I can't say good-bye to you."

He kissed me, a warm, open, loving kiss. "Does that feel like good-bye?"

It did not.

"Will you think about what I have said?"

"I will." But I could not watch him ride away.

. . .

IF JAMES HAD LOOKED back as he left me, he would have seen me standing alone on the edge of the cliff, staring out to sea with the wind blowing my skirts back against my legs, whipping my tangled mane of pale hair back from my face.

I closed my eyes and prayed for deliverance.

The faces of all my four children came in turn into my mind. Mary, kissing a pink rose. Ellen with her rosary. Dickon trying to teach his pet swan to swim. Forest rowing a boat out on the floodwater. I lingered on each one and practiced saying farewell. Then I saw my first family, my father and mother and my little sister, their faces so clear again they could have been standing right there before me, beckoning me to join them.

I thought then of Edmund, of Richard and of James. My father told me that the three stages of the life cycle of a butterfly symbolized the three states of being. Life and death and resurrection. And yet I felt I had gone through three stages already. Three men I had loved, three so very different men. My life with Edmund an uncomplicated and pleasant routine of day-to-day living, of eating, sleeping, raising a family, which for the most part had made me content, might have continued to content me, had not Richard stirred up in me a maelstrom of wild emotion and dark intensity, like the miraculous transforming soup inside a pupa, potent and intoxicating and giving of life. And then James had loved me. His love had given me wings at last and would set me truly free, if I could only let it.

A pair of gulls glided beneath me. If I held out my arms and jumped, I was sure I would not fall but fly.

When Richard found me, I had been standing on the cliff-top so long I felt as if I was a statue, a carved masthead on a galleon, proud and strong and forward-facing. I sensed his presence behind me and slowly turned to him. I still did not know if I was going to leave this life behind, leave Tickenham forever, but just the possibility made me feel unfettered, strangely powerful.

In the gathering twilight, I saw that the past weeks had taken a far worse toll on him even than they had on me. He looked ill, was unkempt, unshaven. He wore no cloak, no coat even, just a shirt that was badly crumpled, the lace coming unstitched. His eyes looked bruised. And yet those beautiful eyes, like his whole being, still blazed with raw emotion. They never left my face.

"How could you, Richard?"

He seemed unable to answer, to utter a single word. He just went on staring fixedly at me, as if he would climb inside my skull. He wore both dagger and sword at his hip and I held the pistol down at my side, but my fingers instinctively tightened around the trigger. He saw me do it. He saw everything.

"How could you?" I repeated.

At last he found his voice, but only to echo what I had asked. "How could you?"

"What did I do?"

There was the longest silence. "You did not . . . trust me."

This answer was so utterly unexpected, that for a moment it stunned me, so that I did not move when he stepped up to me, did not register what was happening until I saw that he had raised his hand, as if he would strike me again or push me over the cliff. But he did not hit me, he did not push me, he touched my cheek, as if he needed confirmation that I was actually there. "You did not trust me," he whispered again. "Why did you not trust me, Nell? 'Love always trusts.' Is that not what Paul said to the Corinthians? But you did not trust. You have always been so ready to think the very worst of me."

I wanted to deny it. Could not.

"You never could hide your thoughts from me and it was always there, on your face and in your eyes. Mistrust. I pretended not to see it, learned to ignore it, hoping it would go away. But every time I saw it, every time you turned away from me, it was like a dagger piercing my side, twisting. When I saw the horror and fear in your face after I carried you in from the rain, and when I read that book Petiver had sent to you about Jesuits' Powder, I knew that you believed I had willingly brought about Edmund's death, that I was capable of murder. You believed me wicked enough to have killed my friend. They said you were mad and I wanted to believe them. I *had* to believe them, do you see? I accused you of madness, I wanted to hear everyone accuse you of madness in the most powerful terms. I wanted them all to sign their name to declarations against you. I needed to convince myself that you knew not what you did, that you had lost your wits. How else could I bear it?"

He spoke very quietly, very calmly. His words carried neither reproach nor recrimination, but were all the harder to hear for that and there was in his voice and his eyes a mesmerizing quality which meant I could not look away, could barely blink. Could only stare at him with mounting horror.

"From what James Petiver has told me, I take it you now know that it *was* Jesuits' Powder I brought back from London. But you still suspected me, didn't you? You thought I purposefully gave you the wrong information about how to administer it? I did not. Nor was I negligent or careless with the instructions, Nell. I never had any. You forget that there was so much fear surrounding the powder then. I was served by an apprentice who wanted to rush me out of the shop faster than you could say Hail Mary. He did not trouble to mention dosage, and when you asked me, I did not have the heart to tell you that I had no idea. I could not bear to disappoint you. I so wanted to prove myself worthy of the trust you had placed in me, that I had seen blazing in your eyes when I left for London, that I had seen so very seldom. And never saw again."

Tears stung my eyes. I could not shape a single thought, nor shape my mouth to speak. I was aware only of sensations of the most agonizing pain.

"I rode without rest," he said. "I was so tired, it was as if I was drunk, and I spoke without thinking, did not believe it mattered so much anyway. Prescriptions are usually so arbitrary, aren't they? One physician tells you one dose and another tells you quite different. I made the most terrible, terrible mistake and it is that which has haunted me ever since, that which has given me nightmares. You did see guilt in my eyes, oh yes, every time I lay with you and felt a moment's happiness in your arms. I suffered the most insufferable guilt, but I loved you so much I'd rather have suffered it a million times over than be without you. You chose to believe I was guilty of murder, not of a mistake. You say you loved me, but that is not love, is it? You loved only despite your better judgment. You never for a moment loved me unreservedly. And I needed that, Nell. It was all I ever wanted."

"Richard, I . . ."

But he was not ready to let me speak. "Every time we argued about the marriage settlement, I saw doubt and mistrust in your eyes. Every time. That is why I kept raising it. I hoped your reaction would change, but even after a decade of being married to me, you still half took me for a fortune hunter. That should not have mattered to me so much, when so many marriages are founded on fortune hunting, but it did matter to me. Why did it not occur to you that I resisted that settlement from the start, that it always hurt me, only because I needed some proof, something to hold on to, something to show me that you loved me above all else. I know you did it for Edmund's children, but I could not help but think that you loved the land and that house more than you loved me. That you loved Edmund more than you loved me. It seemed to me that you gave everything to him so readily, your estate, all of your trust. I wanted you to give to me what you had given to him. There is nothing I would not have done for you, nothing I would not have given to you. I would have died for you, Nell. That is how you know if you love a person, I think. If you would give your life for them. I would have given my life for you. But you gave me so little.

"The only time I laid a hand on you, you thought I had finally revealed myself as the ruthless villain you had always half suspected me to be. But I had read your treasured letters from James Petiver, and I saw, even if you did not, that he loved you, that for years he had loved you. He shared a passion for butterflies with you, the mainstay of your life, and it was as if you spoke to each other a different language, a language I could not understand; you entered a world with him in which I had no place. If you had trusted me and loved me as I wanted you to, that would not have mattered. But you did not trust me and so I could not trust you. I doubted your love for me and so his presence in your life, your affection for him and his for you, was a torture to me. I hated James Petiver, I hated him, because he loved you and because it was he who sent you that book, the book that damned me in your eyes."

I watched, appalled, as a single tear slid down his face. He wiped it away impatiently with his sleeve like a child and went on. "I thought that in some way I could atone for what I had done to Edmund, by being a good father to his son. That is why I worked so hard at winning Forest's trust. Because I wanted to be a father to him, since he had no other. But even that disturbed you, didn't it? You distrusted my motives."

"Why did you not say something?" I cried. "Why did you keep all this to yourself?"

"What could I say? What would it have changed?" His face was wet with tears now and he let them fall, unchecked. "Half of the time I did not even know how I felt. It is astonishing, the capacity we have for denial, to practice deception upon ourselves, to block out a truth that is too painful to bear."

I moved closer to him and he did not move away. He let me put my arms around him and his own arms went around my back, his fingers clutching at me. He turned his face into my neck and I felt the wetness of his tears and the scratch of stubble against my skin.

I stroked his tangled windblown curls and he made a sound, half moan, half whimper, and his shoulders shuddered.

"Hush," I said, holding him tighter, kissing him and sobbing into his hair. "Hush."

I did not need a court to judge me. This felt like my own day of judgment. I had thought myself so enlightened. And it was as if only now had a mirror been held up to my own face, and I saw that I had been as blind as Dickon's hound, as blind as Edmund when he died.

It was not only Edmund who had been poisoned, it was me, and it was a far more dangerous, invidious poison I had taken than Jesuits' Powder.

Oh, yes, I had been so bent on questioning my father's every belief: in eternal life, in metamorphosis, resistance to land reclamation, hatred of Papists; but I had clung in the pit of my being to his most ardent contempt for the men who had been his enemies in the civil wars, the men he believed to be untrustworthy, depraved and dissolute, morally corrupt. The things he hated and feared most, because my mother had broken her most sacred vows to him and committed adultery with a sedge-cutter. So deep had mistrust been rooted within me that I never had entirely overcome it. *Reserve judgment until the truth is compelling*, wasn't that what John Ray had once said? Yet that is not what I had done.

There was a certain justice in my current predicament, I realized. Thomas Knight had used as his weapon against me the prejudice against women who did not behave as was expected of them. But I was guilty of a far worse prejudice against my own husband. I had been reared on hatred and I had allowed the vestiges of that hatred to taint my judgment of the man I loved, who had so loved me.

He drew away. "When you left me I went to get drunk in Bristol," he said. "I have no recollection of it. I do not know how long I was there, or how much I drank, or how I ended up in her bed."

"You don't need to explain any more."

"She told me she wanted to be my wife, to have my baby. She wants our baby to inherit Elmsett, as if I had never had another wife, as if you had never been. And I wanted that too, Nell, I wanted it. I wanted to obliterate you. I did not care what she did," he finished. "I was beyond caring, about anything."

"And you hated me," I said softly. "You wanted vengeance, you wanted to hurt me, as I had hurt you. You wanted to betray me, as I had betrayed you."

He did not answer, did not need to. That is the danger of loving too deeply. The capacity to hate just as deeply is always there. The light and the dark.

"Can you ever forgive me?"

"I love you," he said simply, starkly. "I can forgive you anything."

"I love you too," I sobbed, stroking his face. "I never stopped loving you. You need to know that. Even when I feared what you had done, what you would do to me, even when I saw that you hated me. I still loved you."

He gave me a little smile and it lacerated me. "Can you forgive me, Nell? I need you to forgive me."

"What is there to forgive?" He had taken a manipulative, scheming Jezebel into his bed, but only after I had turned him out of mine.

He had taken our son, but only after I had already taken him from his father and placed him in the care of a man who was my lover. He had accused me of madness, and what was it but a kind of madness not to trust the man who had given me so much love? What was it but madness to accuse of the worst possible crime the man whose smile had always lit up my heart with its gentle charm and beauty? "There is nothing to forgive," I said. "Nothing."

But how could we ever even begin to find our way back from here, how ever could we find a way forward? There was too much against us. I did not see how it was possible. And yet how could I go, how could I begin anew, as James had suggested, without the person I loved most in all the world? How could I ever leave him now? How could I go on living without ever seeing that lovely smile, without ever looking into his beautiful eyes? How could I kiss him good-bye and know it was the last kiss?

How could I stay?

I let go of him. I turned my back and walked away down the narrow rocky path to the bay. I carried on down the beach, and at the water's edge I waited for him. The tide was coming in, crashing against the headland, as low gray clouds scudded above us. The encroaching waves hissed on the shingle, like the whispers of conspirators.

He wrapped his arms around himself, his hands tucked under his armpits.

"On his deathbed my father warned me to protect Tickenham Court against unscrupulous Cavaliers," I said. "And it was those words which stayed with me, which shaped the way I saw you, saw every-thing. And because of that I don't want Tickenham Court, not any of it. The very thought of it sickens me. I cannot be Eleanor Glanville of Tickenham Court anymore. But there is only one way for me to be free, truly free." Only now did I hold out the letter.

When he reached out and took it, I saw that his hand was trembling.

"If I had known what you have just told me, I might not have written it," I said. "But I think, in a way, it is as well that I did. I've told Dickon to sign the affidavits that say I am mad. Or that he may sign the one that says I am dead. I told him he could not be accused of perjury, whatever he says about me. If he swears that I am dead he will be committing no sin. I shall be dead, dead to this world and gone to a new and better one." I let my cloak slip to the ground and shrugged off my secondhand woolen dress. I bundled them both up and handed them to Richard. "Put them on the rocks for me. Where they will easily be found, when they come to search for me. It will be all the proof they need. They think I am mad, and this is what the mad do."

"But Nell, you can swim," he said desperately. "I taught you how to swim."

"You did." I smiled. "You taught me well. And Dickon knows it. James too. Nobody else. I am asking you to guard my secret for me, Richard. You wanted me to trust you and I am putting all of my trust in you now." I put the clothes on the pebbles by his feet. "Will you do this for me? Will you do as I ask?"

"Do not ask it of me!" He lurched for me and grabbed my hands and somehow we both collapsed on our knees in the lapping water, were pulled down with each other. I sank beside him in the wet sand and took him in my arms, held him tight and we clutched at each other, rocking together to the rocking of the waves.

"Please, Nell, I beg you. Don't go. Stay with me."

He stroked my face, kissed it as I kissed his, both wet with tears.

"I have to go," I wept. "I have to."

"Where?"

"I don't know yet. I shall only know it when I find it."

"I will come to you," he said. "Let me come. Wherever it is."

"You need a home," I said gently. "You cannot go back to wandering. Whereas I . . . I think I need to wander."

"Then so do I. All the years I was in exile, I dreamed of coming home. I thought that home was a manor house, surrounded by water meadows and filled with beautiful things that I would never have to lose or leave. But Elmsett is not home. Tickenham Court is not home. You are home for me, Nell. Only you. Wherever you are is where I want to be. I told you once I'd love you if you had nothing to give me but your heart. I swear I will ask nothing from you but that. There would be no secrets between us now, nothing that we cannot share. Believe me, trust me, as you have never trusted me before. Send for me and I will come. Wherever it is that you are going."

I did not tell him that it could not be. I gifted him hope. I gifted it to myself. For is not hope the most precious gift there is?

Virginia: Summer

1700

FIVE YEARS LATER

o, James, we go on with our letters, just as we began. This is a new beginning for me, in a new world. It has taken me many months and much hardship and subterfuge to reach it, but now I am here. In God's own country.

My clothes were found on the rocks where Richard left them, and he and Dickon and you are the only ones who knew I exchanged them for the shirt and breeches you had left for me, with your uncanny foresight, even before I came back to Tickenham. With the moonlight making a silver path on the black sea just like the gold path the sun had made earlier, I walked as a lad to Bristol and found David Krieg and, with him, later boarded the ship bound for America.

It was such a typically thoughtful suggestion of yours that the little orange and black butterfly be named the Glanville Fritillary. I like to think that Richard's name will live on too, that he and I are bound together for all time, that we shall soar forever together on those lovely bright wings.

It is only love that prevails in the end, and there are so many different kinds of love, aren't there? And one of the most precious of all must be a mother's love, of which Richard was deprived, a love that is unconditional and eternally forgiving.

I can forgive Forest entirely for what he has done. Of course I forgive him. There is surely nothing a child could do to a mother that she could not find it in her heart to utterly forgive.

I always knew that my will would never stand and that he would use my alleged madness to try to have it overthrown. I knew that the girls would take direction from their older brother, would be swayed by him, as they always were. I wanted them all to be free, as I am now free, but they were, of course, perfectly free to choose differently. And if Forest had accepted my last wishes, there would not have been the grand spectacle of the court case. How I should have liked to be there to see that for myself!

All those affidavits presented against me, signed by the people of Tickenham, accusing me of committing the very great sin of beating bushes with sticks for worms, wandering the moors at dawn with my clothing in disarray, and surely the greatest crime of all, having to send out to the inn for ale, because I did not brew my own as a gentlewoman should!

I am glad I was so vilified. Had I not been, then the great Hans Sloane and John Ray would not have been subpoenaed to come to the Assizes in Exeter, to defend me, to testify that entomology is a sane and sober science, and that I was a great entomologist. It does not matter that even their testimony was not enough to prove my sanity, to prove that it is a valid occupation to observe butterflies. It was enough for me. I was so astonished and so touched to know those gentlemen regarded me so highly. It is just a pity that recognition so often comes only after death.

I am glad that I saved Thomas Knight's life, for he has given me mine.

If I had not been so maligned, I should not be here.

Awake thou that sleepest and arise from the dead, and Christ shall give thee light.

James, I have awoken and I am bathed in light. I find I am in the most wondrous place. There are bright, fragrant flowers of unspeakable beauty, and lush green grass and mighty forests and ravines and in the distance a range of mountains that look almost blue. The people of this land are adorned with beads and with the bright feathers of wild birds. The air is scented with honeysuckle and it is alive with butterflies, so many butterflies, with iridescent wings as wide as my hand.

Instead of white swans, there are pink birds living on this land's swamps. Imagine that! There are crimson birds and birds with brilliant green wings and blue heads. And they are always singing. Here, the sun is always shining, even in the autumn, when the leaves burn with scarlet and gold of such vividness it is a sight to behold. And I hope that, through my eyes, you too can see this magnificent new world you say you are not brave enough to see for yourself.

The old one is dead to me, as I am dead to it. Eleanor Glanville is dead. Water claimed me in the end, as seems fitting. I have no burial place. My coffin was the dark and stinking hold of that ship, my shroud a pair of boy's nankeen breeches and a shirt, the clothes of Isaac, the butterfly boy, bound for America to help the good Dr. Krieg, to devote every waking moment to collecting specimens, for you. Sleeping belowdecks every night, swaddled in a hammock, my mind turned, naturally, to caterpillars awaiting metamorphosis.

I left the gray English waters behind and sailed to an ocean that glowed with phosphorescence, that was alive with schools of jellyfish, where dolphins swam beside the ship and great whales broke through the waves. The water claimed me, but only so that I could be liberated, baptized, so that I could throw off suffering and pain and enter a bright new world. Like a butterfly, I once gorged on material things; I was entombed; and then I took flight and am transformed.

Now I am free to watch butterflies every day, to do what I was put upon this earth to do. My life is very simple. I live off the land and what you pay me for the specimens I send to you, which will form the bedrock of that great museum, as beautiful a shrine to our friendship as ever there could be.

I am reborn, just as my father always told me I would be. I know now that all that he taught me, on that count, was good and true. And secure in that knowledge, we have nothing at all to fear.

Because if I have learned anything at all, it is this: There is always, always hope, even when it seems that all hope is lost.

So please tell Dickon that he may let his father know that my name now is Hannah. It is a good Puritan name, but I did not choose it for that. I chose it for my own reason. It means the grace of God.

Historical Notes

Lady of the Butterflies is based on fact. The Glanville Fritillary is named after Eleanor Glanville, who is now recognized as a distinguished pioneer entomologist. According to her biographer, she "gained happiness from natural history in the midst of great fear and sorrow." When her relatives, led by her son Forest, brought lunacy proceedings to set aside her will on the grounds that "no one who was not deprived of their senses would go in pursuit of butterflies," it became a cause célèbre.

Eleanor's escape to America is my own flight of fancy, but her true final resting place remains a mystery, as does that of Richard Glanville. Among James Petiver's many correspondents there was an unknown girl from Virginia, named Hannah.

James Petiver (1663–1718) was the first person to give butterflies English names, many of which—Brimstone, Admiral, Argus, Tortoiseshell—are still used to this day. It is with his catalogues and preserved specimens that the documented history of butterflies begins. After his death, his collections were purchased by Sir Hans Sloane and formed the foundations of the British Museum, later the Natural History Museum, where some of his correspondence with Eleanor and the folios in which he pasted specimens are preserved. It is recorded fact that Eleanor's son Richard was James Petiver's apprentice and that he was abducted from Aldersgate Street by his father, though I have brought the period of his apprenticeship and abduction forward a few years for the sake of narrative drive.

After overturning Eleanor's will, Forest sold the Manor and Lordship of Tickenham. He apparently lived on at various houses in the parish. He died unmarried at the age of forty-four and left no will. None of those who left testimonies had anything good to say about him. Richard Glanville, Jr. (Dickon), married and settled near the Somerset village of Wedmore and was one of the first general practitioners. I understand that his descendants still live in Wedmore. Eleanor's daughters seemed wary of marriage after their mother's experience of it. Mary Ashfield died a spinster in 1730, and of Eleanor Glanville II (Ellen) it is known only that she was living unmarried in Rome in 1733. Counter to accusations presented against Eleanor at the Assizes, her son Richard went on lasting record as saying that he had "the best of mothers and the worst of fathers."

The disease commonly known in the seventeenth century as ague, which claimed so many lives in the Fens and Somerset Levels, was eventually identified as malaria. Peruvian bark, the so-called Jesuits' Powder, is the source of quinine.

The Tickenham, Nailsea and Kenn moors were not properly drained until the last years of the eighteenth century, but fenland was one of the earliest habitats lost to butterflies. The progressive draining that was begun in the seventeenth century left less than three percent of fenland remaining by the 1900s. This destruction resulted in the first known butterfly extinction, that of the Large Copper, which was last seen in 1851. The Swallowtail survives only in the Norfolk Broads. Seventy-one percent of Britain's butterflies are now declining and forty-five percent of species are threatened, mainly because of loss of habitat. The Glanville Fritillary is classified as rare, but is still to be found on the Isle of Wight. I am reliably informed that English Nature has plans to reintroduce it to Sandy Bay at Weston-Super-Mare, a few miles from Eleanor's ancestral home.

During the course of my writing this novel, Britain was hit by repeated and devastating floods, caused in part, according to leading environmentalists, by the loss of wetland floodplains. In 2007, the study of butterflies was formally accepted by the government as an important environmental barometer.

Acknowledgments

I referred to many books while researching the various aspects of this novel.

For details of Eleanor's life and for suggesting the title of this book, I am indebted to *The Making of a Manor: The Story of Tickenham Court* by Denys Forrest (Moonraker, 1975). Further biographical material on Eleanor is from "Elizabeth Glanville, an Early Entomologist" by Ronald Sterne Wilkinson (*Entomologist's Gazette*, vol. 17); "The Life of a Distinguished Woman Naturalist, Eleanor Glanville" by W. S. Bristowe (*Entomologist's Gazette*, vol. 18); and "Mrs Glanville and Her Fritillary" by P. B. M. Allan (*Entomologist's Record and Journal of Variation*, vol. 63).

Details of James Petiver's life and career are taken from "James Petiver: Promoter of Natural Science" by Raymond Phineas Stearns (*Proceedings of the American Antiquarian Society*, October 1952). Michael A. Salmon's *The Aurelian Legacy: British Butterflies and Their Collectors* (Harley Books, 2000) contains invaluable advice on early butterfly collecting and collectors, while more timeless information about butterflies is to be found in *Butterflies* by Dick Vane-Wright (Natural History Museum, 2003), *The Millennium Atlas of Butterflies in Britain and Ireland* (Oxford University Press, 2001), and *Breeding Butterflies and Moths: A Practical Handbook for British and European Species* by Ekkehard Friedrich (Harley Books, 1986). *The Spirit of Butterflies: Myth, Magic, and Art* by Maraleen Manos-Jones (Harry

N. Abrams, 2000), *The Pursuit of Butterflies and Moths: An Anthology* by Patrick Matthews (Chatto and Windus, 1957), and *Butterfly Cooing Like a Dove* by Miriam Rothschild (Doubleday, 1991) go a long way to capturing the magic of butterflies.

For details of life in seventeenth-century England, I relied very heavily on David Cressy's *Birth, Marriage & Death: Ritual, Religion, and the Life-Cycle in Tudor and Stuart England* (Oxford University Press, 1997), *The Weaker Vessel: Woman's Lot in Seventeenth-Century England* by Antonia Fraser (Phoenix, 2002), and *Ingenious Pursuits: Building the Scientific Revolution* by Lisa Jardine (Little, Brown, 1999). Also of great assistance were *The World of the Country House in Seventeenth-Century England* by J. T. Cliffe (Yale University Press, 1999), Liza Picard's *Restoration London: Everyday Life in the 1660s* (Phoenix, 1997), *Bonfires and Bells* by David Cressy (Weidenfeld & Nicolson, 1989), *Women and Property in Early Modern England* by Amy Louise Erickson (Routledge, 1993), *Mind-Forg'd Manacles: A History of Madness in England from the Restoration to the Regency* by Roy Porter (Athlone, 1987), and *The Cavaliers in Exile, 1640–1660* by Geoffrey Smith (Palgrave Macmillan, 2003). For the history of malaria, I referred to *The Miraculous Fever-Tree: Malaria and the Quest for a Cure That Changed the World* by Fiammetta Rocco (HarperCollins, 2004).

Her Own Life: Autobiographical Writings by Seventeenth-Century Englishwomen (Routledge, 1992) helped me find Eleanor's voice and some of her vocabulary, while *The Somerset Levels* by Robin Williams and Romey Williams (Ex Libris, 1996) and *The Natural History of the Somerset Levels* by Bernard Storer (Dovecote, 1972) helped me describe her home. Michael Williams's *The Draining of the Somerset Levels* (Cambridge University Press, 1970) and Robert Dunning's *The Monmouth Rebellion: A Guide to the Rebellion and Bloody Assizes* (Dovecote, 1984) were also invaluable resources.

I had almost finished writing *Lady of the Butterflies* when I discovered two books, one old and one newly published, that provided me with fresh inspiration and information on the quest to understand metamorphosis: *John Ray, Naturalist: His Life and Works* by Charles E. Raven (Cambridge University Press, 1950) and the wonderful *Chrysalis: Maria Sibylla Merian and the Secrets of Metamorphosis* by Kim Todd (I. B. Tauris, 2007), the latter the fascinating biography of a seventeenth-century butterfly collector and artist who was obsessed with butterfly life cycles and traveled on an expedition to the New World to study them.

My great thanks go to Stewart Plant, who gave me access to Eleanor's lovely home and the now well-drained moors, as well as providing insight into what it is like to grow up and live at Tickenham Court. Thanks also to Dave Goodyear of the Natural History Museum and the researchers at the Guildhall Museum.

For endless encouragement and patience, my thanks as always to Tim, and to Daniel, James, Gabriel and Kezia (who was born at the same time as the idea for this book). Also to Jane Gridley. A big thank you to Broo Doherty for her belief and support, and to Rosie de Courcy and all at Preface. Last to David, for being my inspiration.